Lusty Lee: The Entire Logs
From Prequel to Confronting

by Jason Pinaster

Jason Pinaster has published numerous other stories, most notably the Christopher Carter Series and the Pro Dom series. For a full list of his stories, please see his Amazon author profile or the notes at the back of this volume.

Cover credits: The lady in the colorful bikini is Maganda of DropTopGal Mang 25 on Flickr and her images were used either pursuant to a Creative Commons licence or by direct, not to mention generous, permission. All photoshoping was done by me.

Acknowledgement: Many thanks for the suggestions from and proofreading by Sallyann Cole. All errors remain mine.

Author's note: All characters depicted in this work of fiction are 18 years of age or older.

Table of Contents

Prequel   Lusty Lee's Log Minus-One

I was in the kitchen fixing dinner. And as usual when I was engaged in my second-most favorite activity, I was fantasizing about my favorite activity — sex.

Dinner was going to be a small roasted chicken with broccoli florets, bok choi, and a low carb squash nestled around it. All the carbs — carbohydrates — were going to be in the desert: Black Forest Cake. I inserted a meat thermometer into the chicken. One can never be too careful in the kitchen. It read 180 degrees Fahrenheit. I added the vegetables around the bird. They would be overcooked, but that's how Pete liked them. In half an hour, bites of chicken, vegetables and chicken juice would be masticating inside our mouths!

Pete was Peter. Peter Peter Pumpkin-eater. Actually Peter Henge. Pete was my partner in everything that mattered: sex, work, and love. Not always in that order, but tonight definitely in that order.

Tonight the sex would be celebrating my success with the latest variant on the lo-carb/high protein diet which had seen me rapidly drop my weight eighty pounds down to an almost scrawny 110 pounds. If not scrawny, a hundred and ten pounds on a five-foot-five-inch frame was certainly skinny!

Work would be dispatched over dinner. Peter and I ran a small private investigation agency. That's how I had met him. He had run a background check on my friend's fiancé, saving her from all manner of grief. I'd helped a bit and he'd been impressed. Three months later he had taken me on as a partner. Six months after that, a larger apartment opened up in my building and I had scooped it up and persuaded Pete to move in with me.

We had been together for two years now. Good fun, good sex, good food. We were hardly ever apart, except for this past week. Peter had been working on something mysterious, dodging my calls, so when I had finally persuaded him to come home for dinner, I'd decided it should be something special.

My plan was to decompress Pete over dinner, let him talk out the hassles of the day. Over dessert, I'd tell him about how I'd tracked down Georgina Crawford, the absconding debtor who'd been evading us for weeks. He'd be *sooo* happy with me!

I looked at myself in the mirror. As always, my long, ever so subtly curly, brown hair framed my face in a flattering way. But now that I'd lost weight, my cheekbones formed a counterpoint to my sparkling blue eyes instead of merely surrounding them. And my cheeks no longer pressed my eyes half shut. I smiled and watched my face actually change shape. Spectacular!

Puffed up around my neck, I was wearing a heavy frock and over that, a cooking apron, both extending down almost down to my knees. Decidedly unsexy. But this was all that Peter would see until I brought out the Black Forest Cake. I'd serve him the first piece, let him get the first bite into his mouth. Then I would step out of my outer clothes wearing nothing but a skimpy blue bikini. Peter would want to skip dessert, but I'd make him eat every bite!

Peter was nothing special to look at and he liked it that way. Said being able to blend in made surveillance easier. But if you looked at him carefully, he was hard to forget. Black hair, always cut an inch high. Which made him six-foot-two in total. Brown eyes, soft if he wanted, but penetrating when the situation called for penetrating. Like when he wanted my body! Dressed up, he was an ordinary dude. But underneath, he was all muscle, hard, wiry, well-defined muscle. Manly masterly muscle. He had a scar on his left chest, above his nipple that he'd tried to cover up with a tattoo of a Roman soldier pulling his sword from his scabbard. The scar was right beneath the sword and depending how Peter turned or flexed his muscles, it looked like an oversized cock. His actual cock wasn't quite the size of a sword, but it was more than ample! It was almost a crime when he covered his body up with a suit and tie.

But today, he would not be wearing a suit. Today he was working. When Peter was on an investigation, he liked to wear a black leather jacket. Usually he wore deodorant and dress casual underneath, but today he was undercover, posing as deliveryman for the restaurant trade. Today he'd have only T-shirt and jeans under his jacket. Tonight he'd come home smelling only of himself, with an undercurrent of fancy food, beer and wine wrapped up in leather. I took a deep breath through my nose, imagining what he'd smell like. Heavenly!

He would come in the door and we'd kiss passionately. He'd be wound up tight, like he always was after a day on the job, his muscles in tight knots. I'd rub up against the rough fabric of his jeans, feeling him all the way through the thin fabric of my bikini. Feeling him against my breasts, against my nipples, feeling him against my pussy. Feeling him lift me right off the floor and twirl me around in a tight spiral!

The leather of his jacket would be soft, sensual, arousing to my touch. I'd peel it back an inch and be hit with his intoxicating aromas, his manly musk. I'd hold onto his jacket with all my might because the heat between my hips would drain all the strength from my knees.

I would want him then and there. He'd want me then and there. And if I wasn't careful, he'd *take* me, then and there!

But the fragrance of roast chicken and vegetables would beckon us with even more force and we'd sit down to eat, each morsel, each syllable swirling around other even more physical desires.

I was in love with Peter, his strength, his tenderness. I'd first realized I was in love with him when he'd told me how good the steak had tasted. I'd burned it badly and it was tougher than the leather in his jacket. But he chewed each bite. He'd smiled as he'd chewed. Here was a man who would be blind to all my sins. A man who would laugh at all my mistakes, as if they were some cosmic joke meant for our amusement. A man who would ignore my faults. No that wasn't right. A man who would *love* all my faults, every last one.

After the main course had been finished, we would lean back and smile silently at each other. Then he'd begin to slowly stir.

"Ready for dessert," I'd ask.

He'd nod and lean back in his chair.

I'd stand and remove my cooking apron. This would provoke only the slightest of slight interest because the frock underneath was frumpy to say the least, and even more chaste.

"Whatever happens, you have to stay in your chair," I'd tell him.

"'Whatever' is too broad. Shouldn't there be exceptions?"

I'd shake my head, a mixture of stern and eight-year old. "Promise."

"But—"

"Promise."

He'd sigh and nod his head.

"Promise! Say it!"

He'd sigh again. "Promise."

I would grab the frock by my hips, then raise it up to my knee, then slowly each inch, watching his eyes go wider and wider, wondering when there might be another piece of clothing under the frock. I'd stop just short of my bikini bottom and move the frock back and forth, teasing. I'd lift it half and inch too high and he'd catch a glimpse of the bright blue swimsuit.

Then I'd drop the frock back down. I'd like to say that I would be able to keep this tease going on forever, but by this point I'd be so hot under my bikini bottom that I'd lift the frock up and over my head in one smooth motion. I'd slowly fold the frock up and place it on a chair, turning just enough that he'd think he was going to catch a glimpse of my butt, but not turning so much that he'd actually succeed.

I'd bend down so that he'd see my full round breasts. "Guess what's for dessert?" I'd ask, moving closer so that he'd be able to reach up and grab me. But dancing away when he tried.

"Ice cream," he'd guess.

I'd shake my head, rotating my hips 'round 'n 'round.

"Cheese cake?"

I'd shake my head again, thrusting my hips forward suggestively, feeling the bikini's fabric rubbing against me.

"Angel food cake?"

I'd shake my head and stand completely still. "Do I look like an angel to you?"

"Devil's food cake?"

I'd grab a breast in each hand and gently squeeze. It would feel so good. Then I'd pretend to remember him and shake my head. "Close, but no. Guess again."

"Crème brulé?"

I'd shake my head, hands on my hips, rocking my pelvis back and forth. "Devils food cake was closer."

"Rice pudding?"

"No!" At this point I would know that he knew that it was Black Forest cake and that he was just playing. I had never served him rice pudding, or even seen him choose it at the buffet. I would turn my butt towards him and slap it in disdain.

If he didn't guess again, I would turn back towards him, hands on my hips, but standing still.

"Is it..." he would begin and I'd let my right hand slide down the front of my bikini. "Is it...," he'd start again and I'd press a finger against the front of my bikini. "Is it..." and I'd rub my finger up and down feeling a tingling inside, wanting more, but not giving in. "Is it black..." I'd pause, but if he didn't continue, I would pull by bikini into the crack between my vulva folds.

"There's only one black dessert." I'd hold the bikini tight, then slowly start to let it slide down, looser.

"Black Forest cake!"

I'd nod, flash my tits out from under my bikini, slowly adjust them back into place, watch him start to lift himself up from his chair, then scamper back into the kitchen.

Cake in its box, plates, knife and forks all on the table. Peter would reach to cut the cake, but I'd motion his hand away. The knife would slide through layers of black and white, pausing as it encountered cherries. Peter would dig into the dessert, his mind momentarily distracted from sex. Hopefully only *momentarily!*

Instead of starting to cut a piece for myself, I would fish out two half cherries and work them down under my bikini top, on top of my nipples. They'd be cold and wet and sexy and my nipples would harden underneath the cherries, making the cherries even more prominent. Peter would look at my boobs, torn between the cake in front of him and the two cherries on the other side of the table. I'd fish the cherries out and make a show of eating them. Peter would watch, his eyes transfixed on the two wet points at the center of my bikini top.

I'd eat my piece of cake, satisfied that there was a bulge growing inside Peter's pants.

Peter would finish first. I'd rush to catch up, but he'd have had a head start and I would have cut myself too large a piece. He would swallow his last bite. I would still have two more bites to go. He would smile an evil smile. I would swallow and cut my last piece in half. He'd be behind me as soon as I'd be able to get it in my mouth. I would be trying to swallow but two strong hands would be gently grabbing my breasts, gently squeezing and releasing. I would try to eat, but his hands on my breasts would feel so wonderful, especially where my bikini was still wet from the cherries.

My fork would return to my plate and I'd shut my eyes.

Then Peter would lift my hands up and pull me towards the living room. He'd try to lead me to the sofa, but I'd turn tables on him at the last minute and land on top of him. Leather balling up in my hands, the sight of his stubble, the taste of chocolate and whipped cream still in my mouth, the sound of my body rubbing against him and the couch creaking beneath us. But most of all, the intoxicating smells of his sweat and arousal would almost make me come then and there!

His lips would suck me into him, then his tongue would press inside my mouth. My pussy would press against him as hard as she could, wishing *she* was the one being invaded, instead of just my mouth.

I shut my eyes and saw it as if it had already happened.

I was all his now, tricking him beneath me on the sofa had been the last act of will I'd be capable of tonight. His hands grasped my buttocks and mashed me cruelly against him. If I hadn't still been wearing my bikini bottom he would have drawn blood. As it was, it sent shivers of delight up my spine.

He lifted me up and pressed me against the wall. He pushed my bikini top up as if it wasn't there and took each of my nipples between thumb and forefinger.

"Peter," I gasped.

"What do you want?" His lips were next to my ears, his voice deep and rumbling.

"You."

"And what do you want of me?" I could feel his voice inside my chest, it's syllables caressing my heart.

"I want you to make love to me."

He twisted my nipples, not enough to hurt, but enough that I could feel it. "That's not what you want, is it?"

When I didn't respond immediately, he twisted some more, stopping only when I gasped, "No."

Then he did a cruel thing. He let go and stepped back. "What do you want?" he demanded in the same whisper. But he was a foot away and his voice had lost its power over me.

I wanted him touching me, to be under his power. "Peter," I pleaded.

"Tell me what you want. Say it!"

"Peter..."

"Say it!"

"I want you," I started out at normal speaking voice,

but faded to a whisper, "to fuck me."

"Louder!"

He would know that I'd want him to make me say it, he'd know that I'd be quivering inside.

"Say it." His voice was soft, so soft as to be almost inaudible, it's softness exerting his power over me.

"Fuck me!" I screamed.

He stepped forward and pulled my bikini top from my body, then watched my chest heave, watched my breasts heave. My whole body cried out to be near him but I was powerless to move.

Then he stepped into me, his right leg between my legs, pressing up and down and I could feel him all the way inside. He stripped off his jacket. More heavenly smells, his leg up and down melting me. Then he ripped his Tshirt up and over his head. All the other smells were gone and it was just Peter flooding up into my nostrils.

He stepped back and I saw the tattoo on his chest, the Roman soldier's sword glowing purple. A moment later Peter's jeans and underwear were on the floor and there was something else in the room glowing purple. Glowing and throbbing!

Then he was against me again. He kissed me, drawing my entire being inside him as he inhaled, filling me, overpowering me with himself as he exhaled. His hands were on my hips, pushing me down, in the process spreading my knees. If he hadn't been pressing me firmly against the wall I would have fallen. His hands released my hips, one moving to my breast, the other sliding down the front of my bikini.

A finger touched the top of my pubic hair. Peter liked a full untamed bush. But I'd trimmed it slightly as I was losing weight. I hoped he liked — the finger tugged upwards and I felt my entire sex pulled up, pussy lips caressing each other, clit being rubbed. Then the finger started making circles and my clitoris was rotated turning my knees to jelly.

He dipped his fingers lower lightly, ever so lightly, brushing against my clit. Then lower still, brushing lightly against the edges of my pussy lips. His fingers pressed deeper with every stroke, engorging my pussy lips with uncontrolled arousal. Then the fingers dipped inside. I was so wet I felt a drop dribble outside. I was so wet I couldn't tell how many fingers he'd inserted. Then another finger slipped inside. There had to be at least three!

He was stroking in and out, upwards against the roof of my vagina, searching for my g-spot. As soon as he would touch it, I'd come. I didn't want him to find it, I wanted this moment to last forever. Me in his control, floating in bliss, every fiber of my body being taken to every higher and higher heights of pleasure.

Then he found it! I exploded inside. Two jolts into my buttocks! A lightning strike burning up my spine. Waves of heat down my wobbly legs. And pulsing swirling fire inside my sex. Everything contracted inside my cunt. Then it burst outward. When the burst subsided, Peter resumed his finger swirls, ready to inflict its glorious fury on me all over again.

"No, Peter, stop—"

But he didn't stop and electricity gathered itself into a ball at the bottom of my spine, pulling pleasure up into my brain, then sending it down to my toes, as if it was playing with a yo-yo.

"Peter, I can't ta—"

This time the furies gathered just beneath my clit and, instead of going up and down, wound themselves so tight that every muscle in my body was pulled completely taut in their direction. Then they snapped loose and I gushed all over Peter's fingers, drenching my bikini.

He pulled his fingers out and I was able to breathe. But he intended the respite to be only momentary. He pressed his fingers against the front of my bikini, pressing it into me. An inch. Two inches. Three inches inside. I breathed deeply. He was drying me out before penetrating me with his cock. Otherwise he'd just slide right back out. Four inches inside my cum-drenched pussy. Five inches.

He withdrew his fingers, leaving my bikini inside.

What was he — then he slowly withdrew my bikini, making me feel each fold of the cloth as he withdrew it! The bastard! I wanted to beat my fists against his chest, but I didn't have the energy. At last he had my swimsuit out, and I readied for his cock, but instead, he caressed my swimsuit all over my pussy and it was sexy. Especially when he brushed across my clit. Really sexy!

I was about to come again, but he dropped my bikini to the floor. The he spread my legs, put his hands under my buttocks and lifted me up. This was the payoff for losing so much weight. I was going to get Peter's special rag-doll treatment — all the choreography we'd mastered on the dance floor, twirling and spinning, plus, plus *plus*!

Soon I was pressed against his belly. Being lowered down. My vagina spread wide open and the tip of his penis inched inside. Teasing me. Teasing himself. I wanted him all the way inside. He wanted to be inside. But we were savoring the moment, savoring the moment before. Then I was being lowered, impaled on his cock, sliding into pubic bones each pressing against each other.

We were rubbing together, but only lightly. I wanted to scream out, 'harder! harder!' but I knew that that would only make him tease me more mercilessly. He moved us away from the wall, walking towards the kitchen with me skewered on his cock. The rocking motion of each step tickled my clit up and down her entire length. If only we had a larger apartment!

In the kitchen, he put the back two inches of my butt on the counter and opened the fridge. This pulled him out, but only half way.

Peter handed me a can of caffeine soda. "Here, drink this."

"But I'll never get to sleep."

"After tonight, you'll never sleep again."

"What if I have to pee?"

"That's what sweat glands are for."

And he was right, I suddenly realized that we were

both drenched in sweat. I guzzled down as much of the drink as I could and he finished the rest.

Peter slammed the empty can on the counter to signal I was about to get my rag doll fuck in earnest. He picked me up and leaned back slightly, my clit rubbing softy against his pelvic bone. Then he started to bounce me up and down, using both his hips and his arms to lift me almost off his cock and then to immediately slide me back down, sending his cock all the way back inside my cunt.

There was nothing soft about this bouncing fuck! Each quick pull up almost sucked my insides out after his cock. Each plunge down shoved my cunt half way to my lungs. My clit, pressed tight, was raked back and forth across his rough pubic hair. And his fingers dug into my butt.

My breasts jumped up and down against his chest, inflaming my nipples with pain and passion as they scraped against his hard chest muscles. My nipples sought his nipples in their own separate love dance.

This was my reward for losing so much weight. His strong hands and muscles and legs throwing me around as if I was a feather made all the denial of the past months worth it! All my consciousness concentrated on maximizing the friction of cock in cunt, pubic bone against pubic bone, nipples against nipples, clit against pubis.

He lifted me up, but this time only part way. My eyes opened. He was about to do something different. His bouncing accelerated, short strokes, but really, really fast. I couldn't hold any longer! The contractions — I was about to —

Then he slowed and began to rotate, twirling us like a merry-go-round, he in the middle, me on the outside, little strokes, like a horsey going up and down as it moved along its circular track in the amusement park. I started to hear merry-go-round music as he whirled, he in the center, me on the outer ring, his cock hitting new areas as our bodies shifted.

Peter was spinning faster and faster and his cock was going deeper and deeper and faster and faster as he mastered the new rhythm. The contractions started again, right where they had just left off. They swirled around his fingers where they were digging into my butt, then they concentrated in my cunt, teasing me with the power they were soon to unleash. I hung on to Peter for dear life. The first wave kicked my feet up and out and now it was Peter hanging on for dear life. The second wave twisted up my spine, wringing out so much pleasure that I screamed right next to his ears, suddenly aware that I had been holding my breath forever. I sucked in precious oxygen, pressing our chests together, mashing my breasts against his rock-hard chest, wriggling my nipples with delight. Little tingles of joy fluttered all over my body as the orgasm dissipated.

He was stopping the merry-go-round, lengthening his thrusts. Then he was twirling, but in the opposite direction.

"No! Peter! I can't take—"

But he paid me no mind and soon we were spinning at half speed with different areas of my sex being caressed with the new directionality. Around and around, in and out, up and down. He was swiftly at full tilt—fast with long full thrusts. And I was back into orgasm, not intense this time, but warm throughout my entire body, waves of pleasure emanating from my sex up to my head, down to my toes.

Peter stopped spinning and stood completely still. I melted into his arms, my flesh all jelly, no bones, no muscle. He lifted me up higher this time and my cunt was empty. He lowered me down, the tip of his cock touching my labia, just barely in the opening of my vagina. We kissed. Long, languid kisses. Time stood still. I was in his chest, he was in mine. Our breathing slowed as we shared all the oxygen in the universe.

Then I was suddenly lifted up, my bottom against his belly, his hands holding my hips tightly against him. I barely had time to register how sore my butt was where he'd been digging his fingers into it. I was floundering around, truly a rag doll now, my legs thrashing in space, all control abandoned to my lover.

Then my hands touched the couch and I grabbed on for

dear life! Peter let me go and if I hadn't been clutching the couch, I would have fallen flat on my face. My toes touched the floor and I relaxed. Peter's hands behind me adjusted my hips. His cock slammed into my cunt. No warning — just a sword stabbing up and into me. His thumbs dug into the back of my hips, his fingers gripped the front. He pulled back out, almost sucking my insides out with him.

And he lifted my feet up off the floor. My thighs and calves and feet were flailing about as he slammed himself back inside. I could barely hold onto the couch, but if I let go, the force of his thrusts centered around his hands on my hips would snap me in half. Peter was taking his rag doll right to her limits! In and out and legs slapped and wrenched, in and out and legs flailing against the couch, in and out and my legs smacking against his.

He slowed and I could feel him concentrating on his cock. I managed to tighten my thigh muscles and pull my knees towards my chest, finally gaining some control over them.

He pulled himself out, let go of my hips and let me fall face-first into the couch. I took deep breath after deep breath. I stretched my hands out, feeling circulation return to my fingers.

Letting go of the couch so soon had been a mistake. Peter's strong hands grabbed my shoulders and turned me around to him, his cock right at my lips. He placed his fingers on the back of my head and encouraged me forward. I took a deep breath and suddenly his cock was in my mouth. I inhaled through my nose and sucked his cock down my throat. I grabbed his balls in my right hand and held onto his butt with my left.

Now he was in *my* control! No longer was I his rag doll. He was mine to play with. His man-parts were *my* toys. I gave his balls a caressing squeeze as I moved my lips up and down his cock, increasing my suction as I reached just below his tip, then breathing out as I slid my lips back down. He moved gently in sync with me, his legs soft, his torso waving like grass in the wind.

Then suddenly he stopped floating. His legs were sturdy tree trunks. His torso thrust forward, urging me to accelerate my head jumping up and down his shaft. Then his whole body became one tight statue. Except the muscles behind his balls. These pumped uncontrollably and I felt, then tasted his sticky hot cum inside my mouth.

I had won! I'd been fucked like a rag doll but it had been Peter who'd spurted, Peter who'd submitted —

But he was bending down, grabbing me around my waist, pulling me back from the couch, turning me upside down. He let me down, first my hands, then my shoulders on the floor, his eyes gleaming evilly down at me. He walked his hands down my legs — *up* my legs since I was upside down? Up my things, up my calves. Then his fingers gripped me firmly around my ankles and he lifted me up, starting to spin. My hair brushed against the couch. Around and around, blood flooding into my brain! Then letting go and flopping me hard against the couch.

He picked me up again. His darling, his little rag doll. He kissed me firm and hard, then pulled me up by my waist, sucking each of my nipples in turn into his mouth. My toes left the floor as he lifted me higher, hands on bum to kiss my belly button. He lifted me until my head touched the ceiling, his mouth hungering to devour my pussy. I bent down around his head, but this just pulled my pussy away from his tongue.

Peter twirled me around like a cheerleader's baton, my face against his chest, my bum brushing the ceiling, then he slowly lowered me. His penis was flaccid. He held me firmly, his shoulders around my torso. His lips kissed my pubic hair. He lowered me slightly and his tongue circled my clit. Hot wet flicks sending tingles down to my nipples. I let my knees rest against his shoulders, my head against his thighs. He rocked me back and forth, his tongue tracing lazy paths down my sex and dreamy meanderings back up.

His tongue's little point, hot and wet, circled my clit,

then weaved back and forth along, under and on top of my pussy lips, then back up again. My clit was a hard little knob, poking as high as it could to call out to its dance partner, to beg him to stay and tango with only her.

But Peter's circuit 'round and 'round my sex was only teasing my clit and every time his tongue touched the bottom of my sex, he'd venture lower. I lapped away at the cum on his penis and was pleasantly surprised to see it salute my efforts by gradually growing in size. Peter's tongue had dipped lower and touched the top of my anus. He wouldn't *dare*! He knew that the other end was where he should be focusing!

His cock was now erect and I sucked the first few inches inside my mouth. Above, his tongue was slithering down my pussy lips. But it didn't stop. It went right into my ass! I gasped and his cock went all the way down my throat. A tickle went directly down my spine. Then his tongue raced back up my sex and he sucked my clit into his mouth. I sucked his cock, begging him to suck my clit. He got the message. I sucked hard, he sucked soft.

The tingles started in my toes, then up my calves, into my thighs, building in intensity as they went. By the time they got to my clit they were pulsing electricity. Pulsing up and down my clit. Each time he delicately sucked up my shaft, the tingles went further inside. Each time he sucked down, the tingles intensified. I sucked his cock, then exhaled through my mouth and this exploded my tingling cunt. I felt my cum dribble down to my face as his tongue begin to lap up as much of the the liquid gushing out of my sex as he could.

I sucked harder, wanting his spurts inside my mouth, but he whirled me around and tossed me onto the couch.

He looked down at me, his defenseless prey. "Spread your legs."

I hooked one ankle up over the back of the couch and put my other foot flat onto the floor. I arched my pelvis towards him, one last act of defiance. He knelt between my legs, his cock throbbing.

He reached under me, arching my pussy even higher towards him. "Shut your eyes."

I shut my eyes. One last act of surrender. I could feel his heat through the blackness. He was there. The moment stretched into an eternity. Then he smashed inside, hot rigid power. Three thrusts, hot liquid and he collapsed on top of me.

The oven's timer chime dragged me back towards the present and I almost stumbled as I pulled the oven door open. The chicken smelled heavenly. Not as heavenly as Peter would smell, but heavenly nonetheless.

Dinner didn't quite proceed as I'd planned. Peter came in all tight and uptight, kissing me on the cheek. If you can call a dry peck a kiss. He caught a whiff of the chicken and relaxed just a notch. He sat down at the table without removing his jacket, which wasn't polite, but since it'd give the aromas underneath more time to percolate, it was fine by me. I asked him how he was feeling, but that provoked only a grunt. Nonetheless there was the beginnings of a smile on his lips as I set the chicken in front of him and his smile widened as he started carving the bird.

One bite of chicken, two bites of broccoli, a third bite of a bit of everything and he was ready to tell me about his day, "You know the bookkeeper we think might be skimming?"

I nodded, thankful that all the prodding he needed could be provided by head movements and monosyllables. The chicken fat—it's so wonderful that the low-carb diets encourage the consumption of fat, so no guilt there—has been perfectly basted into the chicken and it squirted out into the vegetables with every bite. And the bouquet of smells from the pot rose perfectly over these tastes.

"She's not skimming herself, but she's letting the manager skim."

"Why?"

"He's giving her a kickback."

I chewed, looking at him uncomprehendingly, and Peter got the hint, "It's the perfect setup. She hides his skimming, he has to deflect suspicion away from her. His skimming insulates her. If anything starts to go wrong, she can suddenly 'discover' that he's stealing and blow the whistle on him. His guilt will be obvious so they won't believe him about her. Why would she blow the whistle if she's involved?"

"Hmm Hmm." The bok choi slid smoothly over my tongue until I maneuvered it under my teeth.

"I made an oral report to the manager. He's setting up a fake buy and delivery for tomorrow so that we can catch them, bookkeeper and manager both."

He was satisfied with himself and pushed a large combination of chicken and vegetables into his mouth.

I swallowed, feeling the heat from the food trickle all the way down to my bikini. "I found our recalcitrant debtor."

I'd expected high-fives or at the very least, 'Congrats! That's great!'. But all I got was a vague grunt. I waited until he finished chewing. Maybe he wanted to ask a question before being convinced that I'd closed the case. I waited for him to speak.

"Lee, this isn't working."

"What isn't working?" I had no idea what he was talking about, so I wasn't even concerned.

He panned his hand around the apartment. "This. Us. Everything."

"What do you mean?" This didn't sound good, but everything was great between us.

"I need to move out."

"Peter?"

"I need to move out."

"I heard you. I just don't understand. We get along. The sex is good. No, the sex is *great*. And the business is growing."

He reached over and put his hand on mine. "Lee, you're right, but it's just not where I need to be at this point in my life."

"There's another *woman*?!?" I jerked my hand back, out

and under from his.

He shook his head. "No." He looked down at the table, then up into my eyes. "Not yet. But I need more."

"More what?" I tried to dial back the acid in my voice, but we had a perfectly good apartment. We weren't exactly raking in the dough, but we were comfortable. Just what did he expect?!?

"I've got a place. I'll take my things. You can have everything else."

The SOB was serious! He reached for my hand again. I was tempted to stab it with the carving knife, but there were laws against such things. I contented myself with making a show of not letting him touch me.

I stared at him in shock, anger and disbelief. He looked back sorrowfully. This went on for an eternity. The chicken cooled, no longer smelling good.

"I don't think we can continue in the business together." He was talking again, but I hadn't heard him.

"What?" I was pleased that I'd still had enough energy to be able to spit the word into his face.

"I don't think we can continue in the business together. It'll be too uncomfortable."

He quickly scooped up his toiletries as I stared at the wall. A wall which I, now unemployed, would now be unable to afford. And the rent was due next week!

Keys were placed on the table in front of me. I stared down at them as there was a soft click at the door. He was gone. Peter was gone! I cried a feeble cry in the emptiness inside my chest.

An hour later, I was devouring my third slice of Black Forest cake. I had stripped down to my bikini, the better to shadow-box Peter to a pulp. I looked into the mirror. Puffy red eyes. Tomorrow, I'd be back on my diet, wondering whether it was easier to gain weight or to lose it. At least my yo-yo dieting was great for undercover work. No one ever connected the skinny me with the Rubenesque me. I stabbed my fork into the cake. Up-down weight might be good for undercover work. But I didn't have any work, let alone any *undercover* work!

The Case, Lusty Lee Log #1

I had spent the morning in my office alternating between freaking out that I had no income and jotting down wayward, and mostly impractical, ideas as to how to drum up business. I couldn't afford rent for a real office so my "office" was really a small storage room with a chair and my laptop perched precariously on an old typewriter stand. The storage room was in my apartment which I couldn't really afford either.

Now I was in the bedroom frantically deciding what to wear. I had just got a call to come down to our biggest client, a large downtown Toronto law firm. My go-to outfit—a professional looking navy pantsuit—was on the bed: Navy pants, navy jacket, pastel-blue shirt. It was go-to because it brought out the blue in my eyes and didn't contrast too obviously with my curly brown hair. The rest of my wardrobe was, item-by-item being ripped out of the closet, thrown on and subjected to harsh scrutiny. I rejected the red miniskirt as no longer being appropriate for a twenty-nine year-old. The green dress hugged my still-svelte 120-pound frame perfectly—the ten pounds I'd put onto my five-foot-five frame last week having made all the difference. But it made me look too busty for a business meeting. The pink skirt with multi-colored top played havoc with my blue eyes and made me look like a teenybopper.

So it was the tried and true, if somewhat boring, navy-blue suit. I compensated with underwear woven of a mesh so fine that it was almost transparent. My nipples perked up at the thought and pressed hard against the thin fabric as it rubbed against them. No one would see this, but *I* would know. I glanced in the mirror and smiled back at my physically-fit and professionally-clad body. My face was slightly round, but pleasant, just short of pretty, the right mix to attract a male subject, but not so attractive as to make a female subject defensive. And my smile made them all to ready to answer my questions.

I had no idea what the meeting was about. The assistant had said only that it was a new case and muttered something about 'all hands on deck'. But the 'all hands on deck' might have just been an excuse for the short notice.

The assistant, a perky twenty-something, ushered me into the boardroom. I had timed my arrival to be exactly punctual. Not desperately early or disrespectfully late. But maybe I should have been a bit early; everyone else was already there. The two largest private investigation firms in the city had each sent a pair — one from the office, the other an operative from the field. Also present were Martinson & Macdougal, the family firm who were our perennial competition.

The lawyer standing at the front, Michael Everett Rayburn, turned to me as the door opened, "And you all know Lee Brandt". It was at that moment, just as the lights were being turned down that I noticed Peter sitting in the far corner. Peter, my former partner. Peter my former boyfriend.

The lights went out. I could either stand or try to fumble around in the darkness to the only vacant seat, the one next to Peter. I decided to remain standing. Michael Rayburn, introduced the junior lawyer on the case, Cathy something, then began his PowerPoint presentation.

It seemed that some unknown culprit had posted embarrassing images onto the internet. One of these images had upset one of the firm's clients, in Rayburn's words, "a very *very* important client." The firm's client hadn't wanted to come forward for fear of deepening the profile of the offending posting, but when the culprit posted images of someone else, the firm's client had offered to fund "all available countermeasures".

Michael Rayburn continued on with his presentation, showing the culprit's past postings, emphasizing that he, as the lawyer in charge, would have to approve all actions taken by the investigator chosen by the firm. The firm's client was not to be involved in the investigation or implicated in any way.

Flecks of grey in his light brown hair pegged Rayburn as a few years older than Peter. And maybe an inch shorter. Many pounds lighter, less muscular. But masculine and handsome, even more so than Peter. And his blue over Peter's brown eyes were a definite improvement. What would it be like to have a man who could actually fit between my thighs? And his wide mouth, full lips, clear and precise pronunciation meant he'd be a good kisser.

Rayburn pointed to a slide listing the services he required, "You will note that undercover work will feature prominently."

Suddenly the presentation screen was blank and the lights came back on. Peter was looking straight at me but his thoughts were hidden behind his well-practiced poker face.

The representatives of the two large private firms looked at each other and shook their heads. The first suit turned to Rayburn, "Michael, I don't think that this case falls within our areas of expertise. But if you need to consult with any of our IT experts, we would be pleased to help."

The second suit nodded his agreement, "We'd be in the same boat, Michael."

Rayburn shook their hands and the two pairs left. 'Not within our area of expertise' was code for not wanting the case because it was too risky and a failure might imperil other, more lucrative, business. Me, I had no other business and *needed* this case if I was to have any chance of paying the rent.

Rayburn then turned to Martinson who had been chatting with Macdougal, his son-in-law. "Mr. Martinson?"

"What sort of investigation did you have in mind?" He looked uncomfortable and was clearly playing for time. This was out of his comfort zone of tracking down deadbeats, serving absconding debtors and checking for gaps in police investigations.

I watched Peter, mentally ticking off the seconds of silence. As soon as Peter started to take a breath, I jumped in, "The undercover work will require an experienced *female* operative."

Rayburn had kept his eyes on Martinson. "Mr. Martinson?"

Martinson nodded, looking relieved. "I think she's right, Mr. Rayburn. Regrettably we do not at present employ any experienced female operatives." From Martinson's point of view, the case obviously had difficulty and uncertainty written all over it.

Rayburn thanked them for coming. Cathy saw them to the door and excused herself from the meeting noting that she needed to discuss another case with Martinson.

Rayburn looked back and forth between Peter and I. He could tell that something wasn't quite right, but he had no idea what it was. "I guess it's up to your firm to track this cyber asshole down."

Rayburn still thought our firm was together. My mind flashed back to last week, when Peter Henge and I still lived together. When I'd prepared his favorite meal to celebrate my dieting down to 110 pounds. When he'd thrown me around in a mad and ecstatic session of ragdoll sex. Driving me to orgasms standing, lying and hanging upside down. Last week when he'd told me that 'this isn't working' and moved out of our apartment leaving me solely on the hook for the rent. Last week when he'd informed me that we couldn't continue in the business together. Last week when I'd devoured an entire Black Forest Cake in one sitting.

Peter looked at the floor, cleared his throat and was about to look up when I beat him to the punch again, "Mr. Rayburn, I'm sorry, but Mr. Henge and I are no longer partners."

Rayburn was dumbfounded, "But I..."

"It was a recent development," I told him.

Rayburn looked at Peter who nodded, confirming my news. The lawyer skipped a beat as he digested the information. Then he sat at the table, waving me to take a seat. I thought about moving forward to sit closer to him, but I wanted to be able to see Peter, to counter any moves he might make. I sat down opposite Peter and the three of us made a rather large triangle around the huge boardroom table.

Rayburn looked at Peter who'd always been our senior partner, "Mr. Henge, what are your thoughts?"

"I would be pleased to be of assistance." That was Peter-speak for he'd like the job, but didn't want to commit to anything specific. And it usually worked, most clients didn't want to know how we obtained our results.

But this wasn't the usual case, and Rayburn wanted at least some detail. "Do you agree that the case will require undercover work?"

Peter nodded. "Probably." He relaxed his chest and smiled reassuringly. I was itching to jump in, but I had to keep my silence.

"With a female operative?"

Peter nodded.

"And who do you have?"

Peter's right hand and his eyes moved in my direction. The movements were barely perceptible, but Rayburn, trained in interpreting the micro-expressions of dissembling witnesses, caught them and turned to me. And in that moment, I got the case.

The last photo posted by the Cyber Culprit had been taken at a bar in Montreal, so after I'd deposited the cheque Michael Rayburn had given me into my bank account, paid my rent for this month and last and filled my wallet with five one-hundred dollar bills, I hopped onto the train to Canada's second-largest but by far it's most interesting city: Montréal.

All the way to Montréal, *More Ray Al* as the locals called it, I kept pulling out my wallet to slide the new plastic bills apart. I'd never had so much money in my wallet before! I could have taken the plane, after all Rayburn's firm was paying *all* the expenses, but when you factor in the taxi ride to the airport in Toronto, the long lines at the airport and the taxi ride into downtown Montréal, flying wasn't really that much faster.

Besides the train trip would give me a chance to study the file. Cyber Culprit had been posting images of men and women onto various web platforms for several months now. Most of the images had been freely available elsewhere either as porn teasers or on public websites such as Flickr. Most of the time he—I thought of him as a 'he' even though we had no actual evidence one way or the other because most criminals of this type are male. Most of the time he posted to other photo-sharing sites. But sometimes he hacked into other people's webpages and deposited the photos into these random locations. There hadn't seemed to be any rhyme or reason to his postings until he'd followed up his posting of our client—a senior bank executive—with the posting of a well-known sports commentator. Both with their mistresses.

The sports commentator had been photographed picking up a woman not his wife in a bar in Montreal. Photographs taken over a four-hour span had wound up on the internet. The commentator's marriage had taken a hit, but he'd kept his job. And I was on my way to the bar in question. Thankfully the bar was in an Anglo area of Montreal and I wouldn't have to strain my high-school French.

The bar was large and only half full. Still, not bad for a Wednesday night. And everyone seemed to be enjoying themselves. I spread some of Rayburn's money around to the barkeepers, but none remembered the philandering sportscaster. A big black man asked me to dance—black men are fine, usually *more* than fine, but tonight I refused. I didn't need the sight of a black man dancing with a white woman distracting those I wanted to talk to. Instead I bought drinks for anyone who seemed to be attending the bar for the purpose of watching other patrons. But I struck out again there too.

Work done, it was time for fun. I stopped looking for people who were watching other people. I started long for men who were watching women. Or more accurately, I started looking for men who were watching women's body parts. Men who wanted anonymous sex. I didn't want talk or backstory or flirting. Tonight I wanted fucking. A zipless fuck to be exact.

Tonight I'd worn jeans and a Tshirt. Body hugging to be sure, but not a miniskirt which I could slide up my thigh to the bottom of my buttocks. The man I wanted likely wouldn't be looking at me. He'd be looking at women with skirts that teased a view of their panties or with tits half hanging out.

And there he was, at the corner of the bar where he could surreptitiously glance in any direction he chose. And he was doing more than glancing! Any woman with cleavage showing was being devoured by his eyes. And any round bums which strolled by were being followed for as long as he could.

He was short and stocky. His head barely came to my chin, but he could probably carry two of me for a mile without breaking a sweat. His hands were either pale white or covered with black spots—the hands of a man who worked with automobile engines all day but had spent an hour trying to clean the oil and grease off his hands. The hard work explained the muscles, the efforts to clean the hard work off his hands indicated a man who might be an attentive lover. Like me, he was wearing jeans and a tight Tshirt.

His head was round. There were no black spots on his face. A man who was careful and meticulous—better yet! In my mind, I named him 'Charlie'. It seemed better than 'Zipless'.

I slipped next to Charlie at the bar, careful to position myself so that the round curves of my breasts would occupy as much of his visual field as possible. "Hi," I said to remove any doubt that I'd specifically chosen that stool to be close to him.

As he sat straight to look me up and down, I turned towards him and pulled my shoulders back to stretch my Tshirt tight across my breasts. "Would you like to fuck?" I asked.

There it was, the essence of the zipless fuck. No names, no information, just an offer, bare as bare can be.

He looked me up and down and started to smile. "Would you like a drink?"

"No."

"But you want to fuck?"

"Yes."

"Where?"

"My hotel room." I dangled the key.

In my hotel room, I locked the door, but didn't draw the security bar. Charlie would make short work of anyone stupid enough to try to break in and it'd fun to watch.

As I turned, Charlie was opening his mouth, "Do we —
"

My lips sucking the air out of his lungs told him that tonight was not to be a night for talking.

But I came up for air before he was out of breath. "I don't know anything about you," he gasped.

"I want you to fuck me."

"I don't even know your name." His mother had obviously raised Charlie with good manners, but manners were not what the night called for.

"I want you to fuck me."

"I'm —"

I kissed him again, even harder. Still he was trying to speak. If I could ever get him into bed, he'd have the endurance of a stallion! I gasped air into my lungs. "I don't want your name, I don't want to know anything about you. I want your cock. I want you to fuck me. I *need* you to fuck me." I took a deep breath. "Please."

He looked at me quizzically, then nodded.

"No words."

He nodded again.

I leaned forward to kiss him, but he whirled me against the wall. I reached down to unzip his jeans, but he grabbed my wrists and held them against the wall until I stopped trying to resist.

He gently caressed my breasts. I wanted him to grope and squeeze and mash, but without words, I had no way to urge him to ferocity. He rubbed up and down the front of my jeans. I wanted him to force his hand under my jeans, under my panties, to attack my most sensitive parts, to thrust his round stubby fingers inside my roiling cauldron!

But Charlie was proceeding slowly, methodically, forcing me to adapt myself to his pace, like when a rollercoaster slowly ratchets its intended victims chain-link by chain-link up the ever-increasing incline. He slowly unzipped my jeans and slid his hand down the back of my buttocks, hard raw flesh against my soft bottom. He squeezed gently. It was all I could do to restrain myself from yelling at him to rip every last thread from my body. But each link Charlie was ratcheting me up promised ever-increasing intensity for when our rollercoaster would plummet back down to earth.

He squeezed each buttock with one of his stubby strong hands. He squeezed again, this time with both hands, and I realized that my hands were free. I groped for his zipper and pulled it down. He let go of my bottom, grabbed my loosened jeans by my hips and propelled me sitting onto the bed. I pulled his pants down below his hips and his cock sprang free. Knobby and gnarly like the rest of him. A thing of true beauty. I reached forward to swallow him down my throat.

But Charlie had other ideas. He pushed back on my shoulders—gently, mind you—and, grasping my jeans once more, pulled them off my feet. My panties got stuck halfway down my thighs. As he carefully removed them, I made another try for his cock but he turned his hip to block the attempt. I had, however, managed to get my feet back onto the floor.

He turned me around and pushed forward. I had to put my hands out against the mattress to prevent myself from falling forward. His feet against my feet spread my legs. It was happening, we were starting up the incline. The zipless fuck in all its glory and he wouldn't even be able to see my eyes!

But it wasn't his cock. It was his finger. One measly finger! And not even this single finger was thrusting inside. It was softly maneuvering between my pussy lips, making sure that I was lubricated, and then tenderly stroking in and out. I waited until his finger had pulled almost all the way out, then thrust my hips back, plunging his finger as far as it would go and smacking his knuckles against my tender pussy parts. I lifted myself on tiptoes to rub his knuckles against me as hard as I could.

At last Charlie started to get the idea and there were two of his fingers inside me, rubbing the top of my vaginal canal. Presumably he was searching for my g-spot, but I just wanted to be fucked silly. I thrust myself back and forth doing my best to rub against him, to move the night's festivities forward. He strained to hold me in place. But at last I'd frustrated him and he shoved me forward onto the bed.

I scooted away from him, then spread my legs as wide as they'd go. "Fuck me, you bastard!"

He pushed his jeans and underwear to the floor, then pulled his Tshirt over his head. He was round and muscular, swarthy, a chest-full of hair, not an ounce of fat. His cock stood out from his body, not long, but wide of girth like his master.

"Fuck me," I repeated. "Fuck me hard!"

"You have a dirty mouth."

"There's only one way to shut me up." I glanced down at his cock, then looked into his eyes with hard desire.

He slowly climbed between my legs, pressing his knees between my inner thighs. He lowered himself on top of my belly. I couldn't move, but he wasn't smothering me either. He levered himself forward so that the tip of his cock was pressed against my pussy opening.

I put my hands against his chest and moved them forward until my fingers were covered in his hair. I pulled him towards me. "F—"

But he'd dropped his entire weight on top of me and thrust himself inside all in one fluid motion. I couldn't breathe. He was rocking his hips, his cock sliding in and out. My pussy lips were in joyful caress. I couldn't breathe. Pulses of pleasure were coursing up and down my love canal. I couldn't breathe!

With my last ounce of breath, I let out a plaintive gasp.

Attentive lover that he was, Charlie felt the sign and lifted himself up off me. "No more dirty words?"

I flopped my head from side to side as I gulped air into my screaming lungs. Charlie held his stomach lightly against mine and slowly increased the pace of his thrusts. I shut my eyes and caressed the luxurious mat of hair on his chest. Each thrust of his cock pumped pleasure into my cunt, expanding the potential of the climax building inside me, climbing me further up the hill.

Then I was on the plateau. Floating where there was nothing but bliss. Floating where there was nothing by Charlie's buttocks plunging his cock into me. Floating where there was nothing but pelvises rubbing together. Floating where Charlie's manly scents wafted deep into my brain. Floating towards the edge, knowing the edge was there in some vague future sense, but not being affected by the knowledge.

And then the edge was there, all-consuming, riveting my entire attention to it. I was approaching the edge, too close to back away without a colossal exercise of will. And Charlie was even closer. His breaths were mere shallow gasps. His thrusts were a series of quick little jerks, while he gathered his strength, followed by deep hard thrusts.

I opened my eyes. Charlie was no longer attending to me. His eyes were shut, all the lines in his face smoothed into blessed harmony. All his attention was focused down into his glorious cock. The glorious cock that was slamming into me with ever-increasing force!

If I wanted to keep up with Charlie, to meet together at the edge, I'd have to become as single-minded as he was. I shut my eyes and dove down into my pussy. His cock was teasing little frissons of pleasure through my pussy lips. I shut my legs and was immediately rewarded by a ten-fold increase in the pleasure. I angled my pelvis and his cock stroked the spot which had eluded his fingers. I rotated my hips and, at the outer edges of each rotation, jolts of electricity shot through my clit.

Charlie's thrusts shuddered to a sudden halt. He'd reached the edge but was momentarily paralyzed from advancing further. I ground our pubic bones together and felt an initial teasing contraction. I pressed up, as hard as I could go and this time the contraction was deeper, unmistakable. I pulled out.

I was about to rise, rock my hips and rotate all at the same time when Charlie's climax slammed me against the bed. His cock was on fire. He roared from deep inside his chest. Spurting cream tickled inside.

Charlie's orgasm had dislodged me from my own climax and I was immediately worried that he might be one of those guys whose thrusts taper into nothing after he comes, but not my Charlie! He pumped and ground himself into me as if on a crusade to stuff his orgasm into me forever.

And I was back teetering on the edge, half of me on firm land, half of me in mid-air, evenly balanced. I would explode if I let myself over the edge, even a millimeter. I struggled to maintain control, my mind pulling my cunt back from misadventure, my fingers digging deep into Charlie's butt to keep me here, on the plateau, safe.

A drop of Charlie's sweat landed between my breasts. It was so light, almost imperceptible, but that was all it took to almost send me over the edge. I could feel my cunt clamp onto Charlie's cock, my whole insides rotating into a tight vortex. I crawled back to balance.

But Charlie would have none of that. He thrust deep inside, ground his pubic bone into mine, then wrenched sharply up and around. I plunged off the edge into the abyss. And I was falling and contracting. Lightning was shooting through my body, then exploding within the center of my cunt frying my brain, curling my toes.

Only when I went limp did Charlie stop fucking me. He collapsed beside me. Our sweat mixed. He fell asleep, but only seconds before I started to join him in well-deserved oblivion. I was aware that I hadn't ejaculated—something I usually did only when I felt completely comfortable with a lover—but still my orgasm had been stupendous.

The next night I returned to the bar. It was Thursday. Three quarters full and somewhat louder. But at least there were fewer people tapping away on their laptops. I spread good cheer wherever I thought it would do any good. But no one remembered the sportscaster. Same thing Friday night.

Saturday I'd dressed up for date night: a tight white cotton shirt, buttons down the middle. Black lace bra to be visible under the shirt. And a short denim miniskirt that could easily be slid up or down my thighs. But my luck in chasing down the Cyber Culprit wasn't any better and I was about to leave when Zipless Charlie came into the bar with friend in tow. Charlie spotted me and waved me over to a table which was just coming free. We gestured towards the bar until the barkeeper understood that we wanted a pitcher, no make that *two* pitchers, of beer.

Charlie—turns out his name really *was* Charlie— pointed to his friend, "This is Luc." Then he pointed to me, "This is the girl I told you about." He turned back to me and pointed to where he thought my cellphone was. "Show him the picture."

I reached into my other pocket, flipped to the photo of the sportscaster and showed it to Luc. "Did you see him here?" I asked.

Luc nodded but we were interrupted by the arrival of the beer and me paying and Charlie pouring and everyone taking a large pull from their glass. Luc was almost a foot taller than Charlie, but about the same weight. His face was long, not handsome, not ugly: nondescript. His skin was dark, like someone who worked outside. The way he carried himself, his muscles would be wiry, but strong. He was wearing a tight button-down shirt and blue pants: dress casual. Charlie was still wearing jeans and a Tshirt. At least *someone* was interested in impressing me!

When I saw Luc put his glass down, I showed him the photo of the sportscaster that had been posted by the Cyber Culprit, "Did you see him?"

Luc nodded, "It was here. A month ago. They were dancing and kissing. How you say, 'lovee-dovee'?"

I nodded, glad that Luc's English was better than my French. "Did you see anything else?"

Luc shrugged. "There were lots of people here, having a good time. Everyone drinking." At the mention of drinking Luc remembered his beer and finished off his glass. Charlie immediately filled it. One pitcher down.

"Did you see anything else?" One more try before suggesting what I wanted to hear.

Luc smiled. "Charlie said you'd show me a good time."

I waved at Luc to drink his beer and moved around the table so that our thighs were almost touching. When he had another half-glass in his belly, I leaned over to my left, undid two buttons and angled my chest for Luc's maximum viewing pleasure. "Charlie's right. I will show you a good time. But business first. That way we'll be free spirits celebrating. That way I'll have only one thing on my mind."

I lifted my left leg over Luc's and put his hand on my knee. He looked around to make sure no one, or at least no one besides Charlie, was looking then slowly slipped his hand towards my crotch. His hand was hard. A workingman's hand. Just like Charlie's. Not rough, just hard. He would be fun to get into the sack. So it took all my willpower to quickly pull my leg away and put my foot back onto the floor.

"Business first," I remonstrated.

Luc swallowed, and not beer. "I saw him. His hands were all over the woman. But she seemed to be enjoying it."

I sighed. I hated asking leading questions. People

would want to be helpful, tell you what you wanted to hear. But all they'd be doing is sending you on a wild goose chase. "Was anybody watching them?"

Luc nodded, smiling at being able to give me useful information, "Everybody was watching them."

"Anybody in particular?"

Luc shook his head.

"Was anybody taking photographs?"

"Lots. Lots of people were taking pictures."

I swore inside. Our Cyber Culprit would have been hiding in plain sight. If I'd been there the night after the sportscaster, I might have been able to get security footage — yes, I'd checked, they erase and record over every week — and might have been able to use the footage to get images of everyone who'd been snapping cellphone pics. But now the trail was too cold.

But Luc was *not* too cold and a promise was a promise! "Ready for some fun?" I asked.

Luc nodded. "Charlie says we can not talk."

I smiled. "That was for Charlie. *You* can talk as much as you like."

He smiled back at me but didn't say anything further.

On the way back to my hotel, Luc reached out and took my hand as we strolled down the street. "Charlie say you like it rough."

"I like sex, Luc. What do you like?"

"I like sex too." Not exactly helpful. But then I hadn't been any more specific.

I squeezed his hand. "What *kind* of sex do you like?"

"I like touching."

"I like being touched." With that he spun me around and gave me a light kiss. It was nice not to have to bend down. He was smiling, no longer nondescript but exceedingly attractive.

In the hotel room, I let Luc unbutton my shirt and slide it off my shoulders which he tenderly kissed. He unbuttoned my skirt and let it drop to the floor. He ran his fingers over every inch of my body, holding me at arms-length so that he could admire my curves as he went. His devotion stimulated the first stirrings of desire in my belly.

He touched my bra so softly I could barely feel anything on my breasts, but I smiled knowing that he would come back to favor my nipples with the same gentle touch. He touched my panties the same way, but my skin was more sensitive there and his probings tingled all over my pussy. I spread my legs and he stroked lower forcing me to hold onto his arms.

"So beautiful you are," he murmured.

I smiled at him. He could talk as much as he wanted to, but I had no intention of saying anything.

He turned me around and his fingers were little circles of warmth where they touched my skin. My bra was unclasped and I shook it to the floor. He kissed down the center of my back, his fingers on the outside of my curves. When his fingers encountered my panties, he pulled them gently to the floor as he kissed down my legs, tickling the back of my knees. He kissed each and every one of my toes.

"Magnifique!" he proclaimed.

Luc lay on the floor looking up at my legs into the center of my body. I was tempted to lower myself onto his lips, but his expression was worshipful, not lustful. Instead, I stepped off and pulled him to his feet. He tried to touch me again, but I pushed his hands away and quickly unbuttoned and removed his shirt. I caressed his nipples; they were almost as responsive as mine. He reached forward and I let him touch my nipples, but only for a moment (a heavenly moment!).

"Nice little boutons," he gasped

I sat on the bed, pulling him with me by the top of his pants. I undid his belt, unbuttoned his pants and pulled down on the zipper. The zipper was sticky because something was pressing up against it. I pulled down on the zipper, anticipating the treat pressing up against it. His underwear was ordinary Canadian Stanfield briefs. But white as the driven snow. I lifted them up and over, and there was my treat!

His penis was longer and thinner than Charlie's, almost exactly in tune with their other physical differences. The skin under Luc's briefs was almost a white as had been the briefs themselves. Little testicles dangled below. I ran my fingers along his shaft, as softly as he'd touched my panties. His cock quivered. I let go and caressed his testicles. His cock quivered again.

He groaned, halfway to speechless. This was going to be fun!

I grabbed Luc's cock in one hand, holding it still for my lips. As soon as I kissed it, there was a salty drop of pre-cum. I readied to take him deeper into my mouth, but Luc's strong hands pulled me up.

Luc shook his head. "I want us to do everything together." He was smiling ear to ear.

I smiled back. Fine by me. I walked backward on all fours until I was lying flat on the bed. Luc crawled on top of me and lay down. His hips were just slightly wider then mine. I spread my legs further and felt his cock pressed against me. He steadily increased the pressure and bit by bit, inch by inch, he slid in, gradually filling me with the promise of joyful conjugal union. His belly touched mine. In and in he went. Our pubic bones touched. And then he was all the way inside.

He kissed me, at first tenderly, then with more suction. He tongue traced around my lips, then darted inside. I tried to touch my tongue to his, but he danced away. Below he was making short rocking motions, just enough to keep himself erect and me lubricated, but nothing more. I dodged his tongue and was inside his mouth. His tongue had no choice but to do the full tango with mine.

Then he was pumping, not vigorously, but most of the way out before gliding back in. I bucked against him, urging him to more forceful thrusts. His response was to roll me over on top of him. Boy was he strong!

"I like to touch," he reminded me.

And he lay still as he caressed my breasts every way possible: lightly all over but avoiding nipples, a gentle squeeze, running his palms over my breasts, this time rubbing against my nipples, pinching my nipples then softly soothing them, twisting my nipples, then firmly squeezing my whole breasts, letting them go to repeat a gentle caress all over, then grabbing them firmly and giving them a gentle twist.

Luc may have liked to touch, but my desires were more visceral. And on top, *I* was in full control. I rocked my hips, pulling his shaft almost out, then sliding quickly back down its length. I crossed my legs and clenched him tight. My attention was as focused on my genitals as his was distracted by his fingers and I had him on the brink of orgasm before he realized it.

Luc's eyes locked on mine, rebuking me for the trick I'd played on him. But he was too far gone to pull back. I smiled in triumph knowing —

But he rolled me back onto my back as easily as if I'd been a feather. Now it was his turn to smile. He pulled himself out, then plunged his entire shaft back inside me. He pulled himself out, half-sucking my genitals with him. In and out and in and out, the friction making both of us hot between our legs.

Now he had me on the brink and he knew it. "Say my name, Lee. Say it!"

"Luc."

"With *passion*."

"Luc!" Not ownership, but deep friendship.

"Say it like I own you. Say it!"

"Luc!" And he did own me, shuddering and contracting up and down my body. "Luc! *Luc*!"

"Lee!" Our spurting juices mixed together making him suddenly slippery and I had to concentrate on keeping him inside me.

"Luc."

"Lee."

He rolled me over on top of him again and that's where I fell asleep.

Three nights ago, fucking Charlie had been to erase Peter from my muscle memory. Making love to Luc made me human again.

Next morning Luc was just shutting the door behind him when my phone rang. It was Michael Rayburn, the lawyer. "Did you find anything?" Even *I* had treated Charlie to more foreplay than this.

"I found the trail, but it's gone cold. There were too many people snapping pics of the victim for us to be able to ID the culprit who posted them on the internet." I quickly filled him in on the details.

"There's been another posting. Nobody famous. The victims were at a local swingers club."

"Montreal?" A day of R & R here instead of rattling back to TO on the rails sounded like a good idea.

"Toronto. The club's dark until Thursday, but I've arranged for you to meet the owner and his staff tomorrow evening. They're freaked out, worried that no one will come to their club if pictures of their members end up on the internet. So at least for the time being, they're maximally motivated to be helpful."

'Maximally'. A fifty-dollar yuppie word if I ever heard one. But the bottom line was that I'd have to hop on the first train out of Montréal in the morning. So much for sleeping in.

Next day on the train, I sprang, or rather Rayburn's client sprang, for the Wifi car in the train. In between an online shoot-em-up game, winning sixty-bucks at a poker site and Skyping with Luc, I received an email from Rayburn. He included a URL to the culprit's posting which he urged me to access immediately as it was in the process of being taken down.

I downloaded the video to my hard drive. It showed a middle-aged couple in the throes of healthy sweaty consensual and mutually enjoyable sex. They were somewhat identifiable. It's not the loving couple who should be ashamed; it's the people who wanted them to be ashamed who should be ashamed. Ashamed or worse. But the world was the world and I wasn't going to change it overnight.

The rest of Michael's — should I call him Michael or Rayburn or Mr. Rayburn? I decided that it was safer to call him 'Mister Rayburn' out loud. But inside my own head, I'd call him whatever I pleased. The rest of Michael's email described the typical night at the club: couples starting to arrive around ten, dancing starting at eleven, some flirting on the dance floor, some at the bar. Some were swingers, some not. Later on there was sex at the back, sometimes in dark corners, sometimes in the center of the room for all to see, for all to cheer. It was during one of these hyper-public displays that the offending video had been recorded. The club had a strict no-photography rule.

Swinging, Lusty Lee Log #2

Montreal had been nice, but it was still good to be back home. I spent the morning, or what was left of the morning after I'd brought the amount of caffeine in my bloodstream back to baseline levels, filling in the details in my log book: The Cyber Culprit had photographed the sports commentator in the bar we had identified. The background clearly matched the shots of the victim and his mistress which had been posted on the internet. But there was no way to identify who'd taken the photos. Score one for the Cyber Culprit. While the commentator had been easy to identify, we had no identity for the two swingers whose photos has been the subject of the Culprit's latest posting.

Mid-day I'd finally been able to reach the owners of the local swingers' club. Michael Rayburn, my ostensible client, had arranged for me to meet them that night, but I begged off, postponing the interview until Sunday evening. After all, they, or one of their staff, could have been involved in posting the photos of the orgy at their club to the internet. I wanted to visit the club incognito first before revealing my identity to the owners or their staff. The owners were disappointed at not meeting me that night, but readily agreed to the change in schedule. Michael had been right, they were 'maximally motivated to be helpful'.

Instead of interviewing the swing club owners, I met with the sports broadcaster whose images from the Montreal bar with his mistress had been posted earlier. Tom LeBlanc was in TO covering a Canadian Football League match between the Alouettes and the Argonauts.

LeBlanc rose from his table at the patio café we'd agreed to meet at. "Ms. ...," he began but then his phone rang and he immediately answered it, without even an attempt at apology. He waved me to a seat. Our interview was constantly interrupted by his phone which he always answered on the first ring. If he wasn't talking, he was texting. I have eliminated the interruptions from my logbook.

I showed him the posting of himself and his mistress on the internet. He nodded, "Yes, that's us."

"Do you know who was photographing you or why?"

LeBlanc shrugged. "I'm famous? Handsome?"

I studied the posting. He was somewhat handsome. "Did you receive a ransom demand?"

"Ransom? No one was kidnapped."

"No request for money or other blackmail?"

He shook his head.

"Did you make a complaint or ask that the posting be removed?"

"No point, just adds fuel to the fire."

I gave him my card and he agreed to call if anyone contacted him or he thought of anything else.

The next night I was in my bedroom trying to decide what to wear to the swingers club. I'd be going as a single female, a 'unicorn' in swinger lingo. For Friday I'd decided to go conservative, or at least conservative within the parameters of a swingers club. So I chose a simple one-piece black dress with black satin lingerie to match. Tomorrow I'd go risqué to the max.

Friday nights the club allows single males to attend so I was constantly being hit upon by them. Couples looking for a threesome seemed primarily interested in the single men. I stayed just off the bar where I could see everyone coming in and watch the goings-on on the dance floor. The men who struck out with me hooked up with the couples who seemed to be trolling for the third point on their triangle. One or two couples had cellphones, but they only took them out for seconds at a time. Still, the club's 'no camera' rule seemed to be being honored in the breach.

Shortly after midnight, I gave up on our mystery couple showing up and took a stroll around the club. Behind the dance floor, there was a large open area with raised foam platforms covered in black vinyl. I casually looked around for cameras, but didn't see anything obvious. No cords or antennas. I located the vantage point from which our mystery couple had been photographed, but there was nothing indicating that a camera had ever been placed there.

Back at the bar, our mystery couple had yet to appear and it seemed highly unlikely that they'd be showing up that night. So when a skinny Asian man asked me to dance, I nodded assent. Experience had taught me that Asian men who have a thing for white women are wonderfully attentive lovers. At first there was no one else on the dance floor, the music being some sort of a techno-house hybrid patterned after a waltz. However, my partner seemed quite at home with the music and he whirled me around rather expertly.

When the music slowed and the dance floor filled up, I stepped into him with his right leg between my legs and my hard and soft parts pleasantly rubbing against his body. I felt something alter its shape against my pelvis. Game on! The song changed and the crowd shifted, giving us slightly more room. I stepped back and began to rub the long sausage which had taken shape under the front of his pants. His pants were a silk wool blend — seriously sensuous. His hand reached under my dress and I felt a long thin finger rub back and forth between my pussy lips. We both gasped and held on to each other.

"Chin," he said.

"Lee," I breathed back.

The secret to making a man come standing up on the dance floor was long soft strokes from the balls to the tip of the penis. Each stroke had to be different than the one before. He had to be floating. Too firm a hand and he'd come back down to earth. I calculated I'd be able to make him come right on the dance floor — he was certainly well on the way to making *me* come. But I needed to ask him a question, not have him run away to clean up the mess I'd created.

So I pulled him off the dance floor and into the back room where I kicked off my shoes, lay down on top of the largest of the soft-foam platforms and scooted to its far corner. Chin had no option but to follow me into the corner. He lay beside me and bent to kiss me but was stopped by my cellphone in his face.

"Do you recognize these people?" I asked.

"You a cop?"

"No, I'm not a cop. I'm a friend of the owners. You don't want any trouble, do you?" The club catered primarily to couples and was strict about single males behaving themselves. On the other hand, unicorns like myself could do no wrong.

He looked carefully at the images of the mystery couple on my cellphone, then shook his head. "Sorry. No."

He stayed back, unsure whether he should try to touch my body. Which was fine by me because I'd decided what I wanted from him — more of his long, soft, dexterous fingers. But first he needed a blowjob to remove his other options.

I slid my hands down his torso, pausing at his crotch to unbutton his pants and pull his zipper half down. He was wearing red cotton briefs. Not original, but attractive enough. I hadn't even touched him yet and he was already half erect, the best compliment that can be paid a woman. I pulled him to the edge of the bed so that only his bum remained firmly on the mattress.

A flick of the wrist and Chin's cock was free of his briefs. I blew on it and it engorged noticeably. Pants and briefs on the floor, I kissed his cock and gently cupped his large balls which were hanging loosely. That's all it took to bring Chin fully erect. He tasted vaguely of soy sauce. I sucked him into my mouth. It wasn't soy sauce, it was a wondrous blend of every Asian spice I'd ever tasted.

Instead of my usual technique of vigorous up/down in/out hard sucking, I kept my strokes long and slow, concentrating on alternating my sucking from full vacuum to almost no vacuum at all. I wanted him to come, sure, but not to be fully beat up. I wanted him engaged whilst he was exploring me with his fingers.

Chin's balls pulled themselves tight against his crotch. Stage one. His cock was rock hard and hot inside my mouth. I accelerated my sucking and releasing into quick little cycles. Three quick. Three long and slow. I slid my hands up his chest and lightly pinched his nipples. Three quick suctions. Three long and slow. I lightly scratched his tiny little balls. Above me, there was a sharp intake of breath and he flopped back onto the mattress. Stage two.

I let his cock out of my mouth and licked up its entire length. Coming back down, I looped my tongue around his balls. Chin's cock was throbbing. I played my fingers in circular motions up and down his cock. His breathing was erratic. Stage three—he was ready to come. I pulled his cock into my mouth and pressed my thumb just beneath his balls. I plunged his cock down my throat, then sucked hard as I drew my head back up. My hands massaged in a circular motion beneath his balls and I sucked my way back down his cock. Halfway into the upward stroke, Chin came inside my mouth. I kept my mouth over the tip of his cock and swallowed the spurts my hand were milking from him. I didn't want any mess to delay the second act.

Chin's breathing slowed. And his eyes had closed. We couldn't have that. I leaned over him and took his right nipple between my teeth and gave it a sharp nip. That opened his eyes, but my nip provoked no further reaction. I scratched my fingernails down his torso, provoking a sharp intake of breath. I dug my nails into his hips and he sat up. Now that I had an audience, I pulled my dress over my head, and threw it beside him. I unclasped my bra and threw it at his face, but he dodged the projectile. Then I stepped into him and started to scratch upwards, but he grabbed my wrists and tried to pull me towards him. Instead, I grabbed his wrists and pulled him standing.

I moved one of his hands to my left breast and the other to my crotch. "Touch me, Chin," I breathed.

And that was all I needed to say.

His fingers danced across my breasts, like chopsticks, stirring around my nipples, gathering them to full erection, then pulling them up to his lips. His lips caressed my little knobs, then he sucked them inside his mouth where he twirled his tongue around them. Then Chin used all ten of his digits to pull my breasts up and forward, like he was gathering noodles out of a boiling pot, gently twisting them to the point of maximum pleasure, stopping just before pain, then gently releasing them.

Breasts suitably caressed, Chin put his right hand between my legs, leaving his left to meander over the entirety of my skin. His right index finger pressed far forward, almost to my ass, then stroked forward against my satin panty. At the bottom of my sex, I could feel the sensation of the fabric change as it encountered dampness. Chin must have felt it too, because he began to waggle his finger back and forth as he brought it ever so slowly — tortuously slowly — up my pussy lips. He reduced the pressure of his touch as he reached my clit, circling my pleasure spot until if fairly shouted its demand for a more forceful touch.

But Chin had no intentions of giving into immature demands. Instead he turned me around to face the wall. He spread my legs while gently pushing my breasts and tummy flat against the wall. He pressed his finger firmly into the center of my ass and rotated it. He was the master and would press where and how he chose. I was glad I had the wall to hold onto.

Then his fingers pressed forward, his index finger lightly teasing my clit, the digits to the side rocking and caressing my pussy lips. His own lips brushed against my neck. I don't like my neck being played with. It's ticklish, not sexy. But tonight was different. Instead of jolts of electricity jabbing down my spine, the electricity was flowing in the opposite direction, from my cunt *up* my spine. Like a thousand little orgasms but without me coming. Wall or no, I was about to melt into jelly.

Mercifully, Chin pulled my panties to the floor and let me step out of them. He turned me facing him and at the same time pressed my butt firmly against the wall. He locked his eyes into mine and inserted his left index finger into his mouth, thoroughly coating it with his saliva. His eyes told me exactly where he was going to put it and I shuddered with a mixture of dread and desire.

Chin pulled me forward with his right hand, then spread my buttocks with his left. His moistened index finger pressed against my ass and I knew I was to be violated. His finger pressed inside. His eyes stopped my breathing, heightening my violation. His finger pressed slowly all the way inside and I was his slave.

His right hand on my pubic bone pressed me back against the wall. His fingers teased lower. I was hot and uncontrollably wet. He fingers slipped and slid over, between and around my clit and pussy lips. I could feel my toes try to curl in a vain attempt to counteract the contortions inside my pussy.

Then he had two fingers inside my cunt. They felt completely different, what with something already pressing in through the back door. A small orgasm immediately sparked up my spine.

Then he found my spot! His finger up my ass had oriented it for maximum exposure, maximum contact with the fingers in my cunt. And he was stroking it! I contracted all my muscles to resist. But that just oriented my g-spot to allow more surface area for his fingers to stroke. I couldn't breathe. I couldn't move. 'Stop it!' I pleaded, but no sound came out my lips.

But he didn't stop, he stroked mercilessly until I surrendered, releasing all my muscles to him. I gulped air into my lungs. My muscles were being contracted again, but not though my will but in spite of it. He stroked forward and my legs were solid poles anchored to the center of the earth. He stroked back and my spine sparked with electricity. He massaged in a circle and my cunt became a cauldron. He tapped upwards three times and all my consciousness was sucked to the points of his fingers. I had no choice but to shut my eyes. He pressed against the sides of my spot and my breath was sucked into my cunt.

Then he began to fuck my ass. All my muscles were released. I tried to struggle, but his hands held me in place. His finger moved in and out, mixing discomfort and surrender and delight depending where he touched.

"You bastard!" I cried. But all he did was laugh. I tried to beat my fists against his chest but we were standing too close. He smiled.

He was fucking my ass with long quick strokes. It was starting to burn. But I was so aroused sexually that the burn was pleasure, not pain. Then the fucking stopped. His two fingers inside my cunt were making circular motions around the surface of my spot and I suddenly realized that he had me teetering on the precipice of a monster orgasm, that he was toying with me, that he could either leave me completely frustrated or propel me into glorious rapture.

I took a deep breath. "Please!" I whispered, holding as much breath inside as I could.

His fingers continued to circle lightly, holding me on the cusp. The entire universe was black. All I could see was the dot behind my eyes. I struggled not to exhale. My lungs cried out for more oxygen.

Air started to leak out of my mouth. Then his fingers pressed firmly, stroked back and forth.

"Fuck!" and all the air in my lungs escaped. "Fuck!" "Fuck!" I sucked air back into my screaming lungs as all the muscles in my cunt vibrated, then contracted and released in spasmodic ecstasy. Partway through, Chin laid me onto the bed, keeping up gentle stroking inside my cunt. I shut my eyes and floated away.

Saturday night, I decided to do the full fantasy-costume unicorn thing, white fishnet stockings held up by white garters, white lace panties and a white lace bra. The only things which would be dark would be my nipples and the remaining tuft of my pubic hair. I looked at myself in the mirror; the extra weight I'd put on since I'd broken up with Peter filled out the outfit perfectly. And the white would be accentuated by the club's ultraviolet lighting. A fantastical unicorn I'd be!

Over this lingerie, I'd wear a white diaphanous gown. To and from the club, I'd wear a loose (and very opaque) white dress which I'd put in one of the club's lockers upon arrival.

When I arrived at the club, shortly after it had opened at nine, I adopted the same position that I'd occupied the night before, just off the bar. I was almost alone in the club, so I played with one of several video terminals which had been set up and loaded with the clubs private dating app. None of the blurry photos looked like our mystery couple.

Saturday was couples-only, hence I didn't have to fight off any single men, but there were several couples looking for a third participant, so I was still fending off suitors. Had wearing day-glo white under the UV lighting really been such a great idea? I took short breaks to survey for stray cameras, but didn't find any. The DJ's computer's camera faced only him.

Our missing middle-aged couple, the ostensible victims in the wrongful internet post portraying them in the throes of healthy sweaty consensual and mutually enjoyable sex, were nowhere to be seen. A middle-aged couple came in. Could they be the ones? I glanced down at my cellphone — nope, not them. The couple in the internet posting was only somewhat identifiable, but anyone knowing them, or seeing them, would be able to make the connection.

The larger number of couples had started to arrive around ten and now, at eleven, there were several dancing in the middle of the room. Every time the music paused, some of the couples flirted unabashedly with the other couples. It seemed to be the women taking the lead in the mating rituals, both at the bar and on the dance floor. Given the number rebuffs to these flirtations, not all the couples present were open to swinging. The flirters took their rebuffs with good cheer. By eleven thirty, there was more groping on the dance floor and two swinger's sandwiches had been formed, women dancing in the middle, men changing spots at their bums.

I kept getting polite offers to engage in a threesome, but so far I'd fended them off in the hopes that our mystery couple would arrive.

When I toured the back room at midnight, there were several couples engaging in sexual congress, two in dark corners, one in the center of the room. There was a small, but boisterous, audience around the couple in the middle. The audience was enjoying the performance which alternated between coitus and 'sixty-nine' oral sex. The couple was enjoying the performance *and* the attention. There was no indication of cellphones or other photographic equipment.

Back in the main room, I took a spot facing the dance floor. A couple in black pleather looked over at me. She was an inch taller than me, five-foot-six, he was just over six feet tall. He was skinny, she was close to double his weight, but hard and powerful. They were both wearing pleather — fake leather — tight on their bodies, he pants and a tank-top, she a tank-top and miniskirt. They started to put on a show for me, moving and twirling and smiling. When they saw that they had my attention, she caressed his chest. Seeing that I'd liked that, he caressed her chest. She had no bra but her breasts were firm, her nipples responsive. He dropped his hands down her torso, thighs. Since they now had my rapt attention, she moved to his side and slid her hands to his crotch, fondling his cock to full attention under the thin tight fabric. She made sure I was watching. We smiled at each other.

I took a step towards the dance floor but then I spotted a new couple coming into the club. It was them! I cast a wistful glance in the direction of the pleather couple and tried to smile in their direction as best I could. All three of us were disappointed that all we'd be sharing were smiles.

I moved back beside the bar scouting our victim couple to decide the best manner of approach. I needn't have bothered, they walked right up to me and she said, "Hi, I'm Judy."

"Lee," I said and we shook hands.

She kissed me lightly on the cheek and indicated her partner, "This is Don."

I gave Don a light hug and he hugged me back, pressing me against the length of his body.

I was about to show them themselves on the internet, but I changed my mind. I was fully worked up after my titillation with the pleather couple. Besides, what better way to establish trust than through sex!

They were both in their early forties. He was barely taller than me, she was much shorter than me. Don had a small paunch, but manageable. Judy took better care of herself. He was wearing a dress shirt and slacks, both dark blue. She was wearing a mini-skirt and tank top, both pink.

Judy held out her hand, "Would you like to dance?" True to swinger form, she, not Don, was making the first moves.

I smiled and soon we were on the dance floor. The first song had a fast beat so we danced apart. I had about ninety seconds to decide how far I was prepared to go with Judy. She wouldn't be the first woman I'd ever had sex with, but you could count the others on the fingers of my hands—and you wouldn't need to decide whether thumbs counted as fingers. Some of these encounters had been fun, I'd even come once or twice, but I had a definite preference for the male of our species. If all went well, this would be my first threesome. But was I ready?

The song changed to slow and the soft way in which Judy pulled me into her decided me. Besides, Don would be involved, so it would be bisexual, not lesbian. She slid her hand under my semi-transparent gown, and played with my garter straps where they fastened to my stockings. This molded her breasts below mine and allowed her nose to come to the top of my breasts. Her miniskirt was synthetic, but very thin and very soft. I gave her buttocks a gentle squeeze and she tightened them in response.

Judy slid her hand around to the back of my panties and I used her motion to insert my right leg between her legs, rubbing our vulvas slowly up and down each other's legs. In for a penny, in for a pound. She reached her hands up and slowly caressed my breasts. As the song ended, we looked over to see Don watching us intently. Judy looked up at me. I nodded. She smiled and waved her husband over.

The next song was a little faster so we danced apart in a little triangle. Don twirled Judy around, then stopped and twirled me around. For an overweight man, his movements were confident and coordinated. The next song was slower and Don pulled me into him. His pants were made of a supremely thin material and his cock rubbed up and down against me. Behind, Judy pressed us even closer. Their fingers played up and down my body, concentrating on my non-erogenous areas. I concentrated on teasing Don's nipples. It was wonderful having two people caressing me — no worries, all I had to do was to relax into the sensations.

Halfway through the song, Don gently turned me around and I was facing Judy. Her hands caressed my breasts through the thin lace of my bra. My nipples strained hard to be as close to her as possible. Then her right hand moved below to gently caress the lace between my legs. I could feel myself hot and moist. Don's cock rubbed up and down my butt crack. I was having difficulty keeping enough air in my lungs.

I slipped my right hand between Judy's legs. All she had there was a thin little thong. She rocked her hips and my fingers slid into her feminine opening. She was as turned on as I was. I reached behind for Don with my other hand and he moved to one side, letting me grasp his engorged cock.

The song changed, another slow number, and Don turned me towards him. I rubbed both my hands up and down the front of his pants, feeling him big and hard underneath. He slipped a hand underneath my panties and softly caressed my pubic hair. Then he pulled up, sending jolts into my sex and distracting my knees from holding me up.

I couldn't wait to have him inside me. "Should we go to the back?" I suggested. He nodded and led the way.

In the back room, we quickly stuffed our excess clothes into a locker. I kept by bra and panties on, Judy her tiny thong, but Don went buck-naked. We were all barefoot. Don and Judy avoided the center bed where they'd previously been photographed but instead directed me into a corner.

I squatted down and began to give Don a blowjob. He smelt of barbeque smoke, but I couldn't detect any taste. He was big and long and I could feel myself dilate between my legs in anticipation. Hands, presumably Judy's unclasped my bra, then slid forward to gently pinch my nipples. Cock in mouth, fingers on nipples — what could be better?

As if to answer my silent question, the hands behind me moved lower and began to stroke the outside of my panties. I had to adjust my feet to maintain my balance. Then a finger slipped up inside the side of my panties and began to stroke up and down my pussy lips. Spread as I was, it was easy for the fingers to push inside me and I was immediately warm and soft. I lost my balance and Judy had to steady me and pull me to my feet.

Don pulled me onto the bed, flat on my back, my feet flat at the edge. This angled my sex upwards and Judy immediately began to kiss and nuzzle it. She licked everywhere there was hair. Her head adjusted position and then started to jerk softly forward. I started to hear the gentle slapping of skin on skin. Don must be taking her from the rear.

Judy angled her tongue lower and I began to feel gentle forward strokes against my clit each time Don slapped his cock into her. The masculine energy being imparted into Judy's tongue and against my clit was an improvement on my previous girl-girl encounters. Still, it impeded Judy from more delicate and targeted stimulation.

Then she made a downward 'V' with her fingers, planting each divided set on my outer vulva mounds. Every time Don pushed her forward, she spread her fingers; every time he pulled back she brought her fingers together. This coordinated caress was stupendous, much better than could have been possible without the male oomphs being transmitted through her tongue.

Her fingers vanished and Judy pulled back, lapping her tongue up and down my inner lips. Her tongue was deliciously rough, especially when she poked it inside. And her continued synchronization with Don's thrusts heightened the sensation. Then her tongue was back on my clit. She caressed my lower sex with her fingers, but this time instead of a 'V', she inserted three fingers into my vagina and timed her thrusts with Don's, but with a much longer stroke than her tongue was applying to my clit. Without my willing it, contractions clamped around her fingers, but she pressed harder, maintaining her strokes. I gasped air and the gentle waves of a small orgasm coursed up my spine.

Judy took my mini-climax as her signal to withdraw her fingers and stand up. I lifted myself up on my elbows to see what would happen next. Judy pulled herself up onto the bed next to me and adopted the same position I was in. Apparently I was to stand on the floor and give her oral sex. Don applied a condom to his cock. Ever the gentleman.

I jumped down to the floor but, given our differences in

height, I was too tall to give Judy oral sex in this position. We perched her up on a couple of pillows and were good to go. Her hoo-ha was completely shaved and smelled faintly of oysters. There was a tattoo of a butterfly atop her pubic mound. Her inner lips were larger than mine and wrinkly. I kissed her softly all over, adjusting to the differences in hardness, softness and texture in her sex. I kept my teeth well clear, waiting for Don to insert himself into the equation.

And insert he did! He pushed forcefully up my vagina, filling me entirely and half-lifting my feet off the floor. When he pulled back out, I had to hold onto Judy's hips to prevent myself following him. The next thrust was easier to accommodate, but I still kept my lips only gently on Judy so that I was not pushed too forcefully into her. The smell of oysters was stronger, but less pungent.

Don's next thrust only moved my head slightly and I began to lick at Judy's clit, resolving to follow her pattern of stimulation. Presumably she was the more experienced one. Her clit hardened nicely as I flicked my tongue up and around, each stroke being accelerated when Don pushed in or pulled out. I licked down her pussy lips which were now engorged and hardening. Her aromas were intoxicating, especially with each of Don's thrusts swirling them around inside my head!

Two fingers inside Judy's cunt united the three of us completely together into one line of sexual stimulation. I felt Don's cock inside my fingers as I stroked the top of Judy's vagina searching for her g-spot. I felt his heat slap through my thighs, up my spine, out my tongue and into Judy's clit. The heat from Judy's twat trickled back down my spine, priming my cunt's increasingly insistent responses to Don's frantic pumping behind me.

And then we were all there together, quavering at the point were we no longer controlled our bodies but they controlled us. Judy went first, screaming blue bloody murder and clutching my fingers so tightly I couldn't move them. I lifted my head as Don slammed spasms up my spine and an incoherent grunt out my throat. Then he paused momentarily before thrusting so hard my head ended up on Judy's belly where he mashed us together over and over before collapsing onto both of us!

Afterwards, at an iconic Canadian fast-food chain—the damn things never close—I sat across from our mystery-no-more couple. Don's face now looked pasty-white. Judy's wrinkles were more pronounced. I showed them the internet posting of their previous raunchiness. "Is this you?"

They nodded in unison.

"Were you aware of the posting?

More synchronized nodding.

"What did you do?"

Don shrugged. "We didn't think that there was anything we could do?"

Judy reached for my hand. "Can you do something?"

"You could sue. But that's expensive. And it may draw more attention to the posting. Did anyone recognize you?"

"From the club, a couple of people," said Don.

"And Andrew and Marsha," chimed in Judy.

"The club owners?" I asked.

More harmonious nodding.

"No one else?"

They shook their heads in unison.

I tapped my phone. "Were they reposted elsewhere?"

They pulled out their phones and showed me repostings to two obscure websites.

"We decided," said Don, effecting firmness, "to just tell people that it wasn't us, that someone had photoshopped our faces in in."

Judy nodded. "So far it hasn't come up." She made a show of crossing her fingers.

After a few hours of sleep, I was back at the self-same table across from Andrew and Marsha, the club owners. They were a bit wilted, having come straight from closing down the club for the night. Wilted but very concerned.

"What can we do?" asked Andrew, taking the lead.

"You can put in surveillance cameras," I told him.

"That will make matters worse. Our patrons are exhibitionists, but they don't like being spied upon." He arched his eyebrows, acknowledging the inconsistency.

"You can absolutely prohibit cellphones."

"It may come to that, but for now, people are just too connected to their tech."

We tossed ideas back and forth, but came to no resolution. They agreed to maintain absolute vigilance and to call me if they encountered anything out of the ordinary or if they became aware of other postings.

The next morning my phone rang at the ungodly hour of eleven am. It was lawyer Michael Rayburn. If anyone should have realized I'd been working until all hours the night before, it should have been Rayburn.

"Did you find anything?" he wanted to know.

"I located the victims and spoke to the owners. Neither had any useful information."

"Time is ticking away. Are you sure you're up to this?"

"Of course I'm up to this. We just have to be methodical."

"Keep me in the loop." And then he rang off.

'We just have to be methodical.' What did that even mean?!? Anyways, my bullshit had baffled his brains. For now. And for now all I could do was to go back to sleep.

Monday morning's mail brought a cheque from Rayburn—his law firm had paid my fees in full. And every last expense I'd submitted. I remembered his question, 'Are you sure you're up to this?' I'd bloody well better be. The alternative was being evicted from my apartment and losing the case to my bastard of an ex-boyfriend.

But if I wanted to keep this case, I'd need help. I pulled out the two unsolicited job applications we'd received before Peter had terminated our partnership. One was a hunk. I called him first. But he'd already obtained employment at another firm.

The other applicant, Eric Craigie, was 26 years old, skinny, tall, red hair, green eyes. He was into yoga, mixed martial arts, and running. He was a bit of a nerd to say the least. I called and arranged an interview for later in the week.

My phone beeped. It was an email from Rayburn: they'd discovered two more postings by the Cyber Culprit. One was old. It had resulted in a three-month suspension of a popular teacher. I vaguely recalled it being in the news.

The other posting had just gone up yesterday. It was a photo of a group of middle-aged women at Rodney's, a male strip club. Michael had circled one of them. Apparently her husband had worked himself into an early grave and now she was a wealthy philanthropist.

I googled Rodney's but I got Rodney's LeFoxx in Kentucky. I narrowed the search to Toronto, and there it was. Big hunks with rods pressed against the front of their pants. Someone had posted a video of a bachelorette party. The bride to be was on the stage, dancing between two strippers. Somebody handed her up a shot and judging by the way she was weaving, it wasn't the first to have gone down her throat that night. The strippers were wearing only thongs and their thingies were fully erect and barely restrained by the spandex. There were shouts of, "Go Girl!" in the background. One stripper pulled her shirt off over her head, the other pulled her jeans down the floor and off her feet. Then the two men mashed her between them, rubbing up and down.

I smiled to myself—this was going to be *fun*!

Strip Club, Lusty Lee Log #3

The day began with a meeting at Michael Rayburn's law firm. Apparently he thought that I hadn't read his briefing notes, so now he was going over everything in excruciating detail. Or maybe he just wanted to get close to me. I liked that theory better, and besides he'd booked a small boardroom for us to be alone in.

We were seated across a glass table. I was tempted to kick

my shoe off and massage his crotch with my foot. I'd be able to see, and feel, the bulge grow in his pants. But I thought better of it.

Michael had a projector set up and was showing me the photo of a middle-aged woman at a male strip club. Her name was Amanda Thorkelstein. When her husband had died, he'd left her a ton of cash, and she was spreading it among all manner of worthy charities. The photograph had been posted by the Cyber Culprit and had derailed her efforts to assist more than one needy group. Michael had set up a lunch meeting for Amanda and I.

Michael closed the photo of Amanda and activated the bachelorette video from the same strip club which I'd already seen the day before. The bridesmaids had pushed the bride-to-be up on the stage between one white hunk dressed as a fireman and a big— and I do mean *big*—black man dressed as a cop. Velcro straps were ripped off and soon the two men were down to thongs which barely covered their manhood.

My thoughts drifted to the possibility of the black stripper's manhood fulfilling the needs which were twitching between my legs. *Fill* was the operative word. He was certainly bigger than Peter, my former partner, but would he be as imaginative? Or was what you saw all you'd get? A pretty face used to letting others do the work?

And what kind of lover would Michael Rayburn be? Certainly not as big or powerful as the stripper. But he was in a thinking profession, so he'd be creative. And he had the right equipment: height, blue eyes. More importantly, his wide mouth and full lips, well-exercised by the regular requirements for clear and precise pronunciation, meant he'd good at kissing my lips and other body parts. I shut my eyes at the mid-point of the video and imagined Michael's tongue teasing mine, flicking my nipples to arousal, kissing down my tummy, swirling around my clit and lapping up and down my pussy lips.

I adjusted myself in my seat as the video came to an end. What was I thinking?!? Michael Rayburn was way, way out of my league. He was a *lawyer* for god sakes!

Rayburn finished the meeting off by reminding me that we still had no firm leads as to the identity of the Cyber Culprit and that he continued to be a menace to society as we knew it.

My lunch with Amanda Thorkelstein had been set up at a small East Indian restaurant. The type of place Amanda had never been to before and would never go to again. Anonymity. I ordered beef Vindaloo and a plate of roti. She ordered the same, likely to save herself the trouble of trying to understand Indian cuisine.

Just as the waiter left, Amanda's phone buzzed. She looked at it, then back up at me.

I made a show of taking my phone out. "Maybe we should turn these off?"

I turned mine off. She nodded and did the same. But I could tell that she was extremely reluctant to do so.

"So tell me about the night you were at Rodney's?" I began.

"Just an ordinary outing."

"We're you with friends?"

"Friend. But her face wasn't posted. This doesn't involve her."

"Would it be possible to interview her?"

"No." The emphatic tone in Amanda's voice told me that this was a dead end and that pursuing it would alienate her.

"Not a special occasion?"

"No." I was sure it was a special occasion, but again, no point in antagonizing her.

"Had you ever been to a strip club before?"

"No." I was right—it had been something special.

"Or since?"

"No!"

"Tell me what happened."

But just then, our food arrived. I tore off a piece of the flatbread and used it to scoop up a morsel of beef and a generous helping of the curry sauce it had been cooked in. Amanda used her knife and fork—even on the bread which she cut into tiny squares to dip into the sauce. I scooped another succulent morsel into my mouth. What good were money and manners if they meant that you had to give up on enjoying life?

As she finished, I repeated my last question, "What happened that night?"

"We arrived, got good seats. The female owner came out, said sex was forbidden and that we were not allowed to touch the 'performers'. There were murmurs of 'yeah, right!' from the audience and the announcer smiled. So we immediately understood that there'd be audience participation. Then the announcer said 'no cameras allowed'. But everyone had a cellphone, so she didn't seem real serious about that either.

"When the performance started, everyone had their cellphones out, taking pictures of the strippers. There was fondling throughout, especially by the audience, but sometimes by the strippers as well. You've seen the photographs."

The most revealing photograph had shown the black stripper lying across Amanda's lap, her hand on his buttocks. The hand of the woman beside Amanda, whose face was blocked by the stripper, was up his crotch. The stripper's right hand was squeezing Amanda's right breast. The hand was squeezing through her blouse, but still. And Amanda's smile was ear to ear.

"Were you aware of anyone watching you at the time?"
She shook her head.
"How has the posting affected you?"
"A lot of people don't want to talk to me. It's devastating."
"Do you have any idea who could have posted the photo?"
"One of the women present, presumably." Amanda, the purpose of an interview is to tell me something I *don't* know.
"Is there anyone who would want to harm you?"
She shook her head.

Amanda begged off desert, but I had *gulab jamun* and made a show of enjoying the milk-flour balls dipped in sugar and rosewater. After she left, I made a note: 'Could the cyber culprit be female? Most hackers are male… But still.'

That night, I got dressed to go out to the club where Amanda had been photographed. I decided to wear a pair of grey yoga pants. They would show off my round bum, but not allow easy penetration. Up top, I wore a grey bra and a long white shirt. The shirt had buttons, so I could reveal as little or as much as the situation called for. And the shirt was long enough that it could cover below my waist if I wanted. I inspected myself in the mirror—I'd put on weight, now up to 140 pounds, but so far my tummy had only grown a small amount and the new pounds had mostly enhanced my breasts and butt. At five-feet and five inches, maybe this was my ideal weight!

My plan had been to arrive early, to scope out the place. I had my cellphone in my purse; maybe I'd be able to take a few pictures. But even though I'd arrived before eight, the party was already in full swing and almost every seat was full. A dancer was just leaving the stage to raucous applause. He was okay, but nothing special. Hopefully there would be some muscle-bound hunks before the night was out.

There seemed to be two bachelorette parties, one composed of twenty-year olds, the other of women in their late forties. The twenty-somethings were on the right side of the stage, the older women on the left. The seats Amanda and her friend had sat in were occupied by a couple—he the only male in the audience—and a woman presumably his wife. I stood in the back, waiting for them to leave. I needed to sit in Amanda's seat to scope out where the photographer's camera had been when it captured the image of her with her hand on the stripper's butt.

The next dancer was Ernesto, a short Latino. He was wearing a small red sombrero, a white shirt with the sleeves ripped off and green spandex pants. He had big bulging muscles and a bulge between his legs as well. As he took the stage, he was strumming a spirited Latin dance number on his guitar, alternating the position of the guitar to reveal or to conceal his crotch. He finished the song with gusto and was rewarded with spirited applause.

As Ernesto handed his guitar off to a backstage assistant, the bachelorette parties began to make piles of money on either side of the stage. Ernesto alternated back and forth between the piles of money. If a pile had grown marginally, he rotated his hips before turning away, if there was significant growth, he turned his bum towards the audience and gyrated rudely. If there was substantial growth, he stroked up and down the front of his tight spandex pants and a certain part of his anatomy made its appreciation quite, *quite* clear.

Ultimately, the older crowd amassed the larger fortune and Ernesto hopped down from the stage to dance in their midst. Actually 'dancing' was being generous. All he was doing was shaking his pelvis to the music and occasionally rotating his hips. But the squeals of female delight indicated that this was more than sufficient. There was the sound of velcro ripping and Ernesto's torso was immediately bare. But bare for only an instant. Then female hands all but covered his body.

And their hands didn't stop at his waist. They were caressing up and down his legs. Only his hands steadfastly guarding his crotch prevented Ernesto's privates from being mauled! Ernesto spotted the bride, gave her a kiss, planted his red hat on her head, and danced back onto the stage. He pranced around for a while, whipping the crowd into a frenzy. Then he squatted in front of the older bride. The crowd hushed. As he gradually stood up, he lifted his tight green pants up and against his protruding manhood. The older women went wild and tried to rush the stage. But he held his hand up and signaled that only the bride should approach. The song was soft, sensuous.

He slipped out of his pants, revealing a thong in the colors of the Mexican flag: red, green and white diagonals.

Her friends made room for the bride and Ernesto snatched the sombrero from her head and placed it on his. He was on his knees, his legs spread wide to give her a good view as she stood next to the stage. They kissed. Her friends let out a collective "oooh". They broke off the kiss and there was a collective "aaah". They kissed again and she slid her hands down his chest. More "ooohs", louder this time. The music had changed to a techno beat.

Ernesto started to caress her breasts and her friends broke out into cheers of "Jenny, Jenny! *Jenny*!" She strained forward to touch his genitals but they were just out of her reach. She wanted to break off the kiss to let her hand get closer to its goal, but put his hands on her ears to hold her close. "Jenny, Jenny! *Jenny*!" He let her go so that they both could breathe. She lunged forward and managed a brief touch before he danced away. Her friends stamped their feet on the floor, drowning out even the loud techno beat. As the stomping died down, their cheer came back, "Jenny, Jenny! *Jenny*!"

So much for the weaker sex being better-behaved. When men go to a strip club, they know they're there to watch and that touching is strictly forbidden.

Ernesto was followed by a big black man dressed as a cop. This time there was no stopping the younger crowd and their pile of cash was quickly ten times the size of the older party's. He danced at the edge of the stage, but had to keep retreating back to avoid being mobbed by the young bachelorettes. However every time he moved to the center of the stage, he'd remove a piece of his whiter-than-white latex uniform, cuffs, baton, belt. His top ripped off to sounds of metal snaps releasing. His undershirt was so thin as to be transparent giving us all a good view of his pectorals and puckering nipples.

'Sir'—at least that was his stage name according to the announcer—jumped quickly among the twenty-something bachelorettes. Quick as he was, they'd torn off his pants before he could squirm his way back to the stage. And they'd grabbed a hold of his undershirt compelling him to shrug it off to make good his escape. Now clad only in a skimpy white thong, Sir strutted up and down the front of both sides of the stage, skipping out of the reach of any of the young women's hands trying to touch his thong.

Then he stopped and pointed down, directly at the far-too-young-to-be-a-bride. She was a skinny blonde, wearing jeans and a T-shirt. Her friends made room around her. He crooked his finger towards her, indicating she should join him on stage. She held back, suddenly shy. Her friends converged on her and propelled her forward and up beside the stripper. She stood awkwardly on the stage as the big black man, fully a head taller than she and twice her weight, circled her.

The music paused between songs and he bent down to her ears. The entire room heard his question, "Want to have some fun?" The whole room saw her nod, shyly yes, but unmistakably nonetheless. "Abby! Abby! Abby!" her friends chanted.

As music changed to a 'fifties jive he took her hand and twirled her around him as she pirouetted around his hand held above her head. As soon as she'd completed one rotation around him, he bent down grabbed her under her knees and swung her up and over his head. His other hand under her armpit, he swung her around and around, her hair flying sideways from her head.

Then the music turned slow, and he let her down the front of his body, kissing her torso, lifting his head around her breasts, then kissing her gently on her cheeks. He was about to release her back to her friends when Abby's shyness suddenly vanished. She kissed him full on the lips and grabbed his cock which had pressed forward against his latex thong sufficiently for her to get a good grip. Sir gasped at the suddenness of it. Then he recovered, pried her hand loose, bent to her ear and whispered something while pointing to a door at the far end of the stage. The letters 'VIP' were displayed prominently above the door.

The next dancer was a stocky Scottish bloke, kilt and all. 'Malcolm' according to the announcer. The man sitting next to Amber's seat slapped a one-hundred dollar bill onto the stage in front of his wife. The bachelorette parties seemed to have run out of cash and his was the only bid. He stood and motioned to Malcolm to bend down so that he could whisper something to him. He made arm gestures between his wife's dress and Malcolm's kilt.

Malcolm stepped back and began to dance only for the lady in Amber's seat. She hiked her skirt up and pulled her shirt up and over her breasts. She was wearing neither bra nor panties. Husband slipped one hand between her legs, bent over to kiss the nipple closest to him and caressed her other breast with his other hand. One of her hands caressed the hair on his head, the other rested on the hand between her legs. Her eyes were transfixed on Malcolm.

Malcolm's clothes were swiftly off. Apparently the husband's hundred dollars had nothing to do with the 'tease' part of striptease. Malcolm began to stroke his hands up and down the shaft of his cock. There was a stirring among the security guards behind me. Apparently Malcolm's performance went beyond what was normally permitted on stage. Malcolm's cock, like him, was stocky: not particularly long, but wide of girth. He kept time with the wife's hand on top of her husband's. His eyes were locked on hers. Her eyes were locked onto his cock.

Then she gasped and shut her eyes. She moved her hands to her breasts and squeezed hard. Her hips bucked up against her husband's hand and he had to hug her waist with his other hand to hold on. She thrashed. Her face turned red. She jerked her eyes open, fighting the forces which had been unleashed in her body. Once more her eyes were fixated upon Malcolm's cock. She lifted her husband's hand off her sex and up to her breast, then began to furiously rub up and down the length of her sex.

The husband nodded at Malcolm. The Scotsman jumped off the stage and stood over the wife. Now she looked into his eyes. Even though no parts of their bodies were touching, the feverish connection between them was undeniable. No one spoke a word. At some point the music had been turned off. Up and down his shaft went his hand. She grabbed her clit and mashed it back and forth against her hand and her surrounding sex. Each took a sharp intake of breath. Husband let go of her breasts and sat back.

She clamped her eyes shut; Malcolm devoured her with his. He ejaculated all over her, her legs, the hand caressing her sex, her dress, her arms, her belly, her breasts. What reached her lips, she hungrily licked into her mouth. The hand between her legs continued to rub furiously up and down her sex. Malcolm leaned back against the stage. Her hand slowed, then stopped.

The stopping of her hand seemed to break the spell. The women erupted in raucous cheer. Two security guards, scooped

Malcolm and his clothes off the stage and hustled him out the door from which he'd entered. Two more security guards rushed to husband and wife with towels. But the husband stopped them and instead gave his wife his jacket. There was a brief tussle as the security guards tried to clean Malcolm's come off the wife, but they relented. One hustled husband and wife out of the door. The other guard cleaned their seats with his towel.

As soon as the security guard left with his towel, I slipped into the seat that the wife had just vacated. I could still feel her heat, even through my clothes. I quickly lined up the line of sight would have been necessary for the photo of Amanda with her hand on the stripper's bum. Surprise, surprise. It could not have been taken by an audience member. To get the angle in the photo, the camera would have had to have been much higher than anyone in the audience. The only way someone in the audience could have taken the photo would have been to stand on a chair and hold the camera high above her head. Never presume, always verify.

The next dancer came onto the stage and the two bachelorette parties recommenced their bidding war. I slid out behind the younger bachelorettes and looked up to the ceiling. The ceiling had been painted black to save the cost of a drop ceiling; all the wiring and plumbing were exposed. Plenty of places to attach something to. There were two wires hanging down and they were holding up the bracket for the latest go-everywhere action camera. The one which was advertising how it was so easy to control it remotely.

I went to the door marked 'VIP' and pushed it open. There was a security guard there and behind them several doors opening into small rooms.

I handed the guard a twenty. "Can I get Sir, the black cop?"

He nodded and fished a cellphone from his pocket.

"And a bottle of vodka, on ice?"

"No booze allowed in the VIP area."

I fished out a hundred and showed it to him.

He shrugged, "I'll see what I can do."

He reached for the hundred, but I pulled it back. "When everything arrives," I told him.

He left and I selected the second room to the right. There was a bed on the left side. To the right of the bed were two chairs, close together, each bolted to the floor. On the wall between the chairs was a CD player.

Ten minutes later the security guard ushered Sir, dressed in his white latex cop uniform, into the room I'd selected. The guard deposited a bottle of vodka sitting in an ice bucket onto one of the chairs. I gave him the hundred and shut the door behind him.

Sir's uniform was so tight it could have been painted on him. Every ripple and curve of his pectoral muscles was clearly outlined. I could even see his nipples. The top lacked sleeves so his bulging arm muscles were directly available to be drooled over. He'd be able to lift me up with as little effort as he'd required to hoist the young bachelorette over his head.

His pants were of the same material, just as tight, and extended almost to his ankles. I could see the outline of his thong and the large cock and balls beneath. Black metal snaps down the from of his shirt and along each thigh begged to be ripped open. I stepped close to him and unsnapped his top button. My hands drifted to his hips and fondled his baton and handcuffs.

"I want you to fuck me," I told him.

He shook his head. "Only the dance is included." He reached for the CD player.

I opened my purse and showed him my billfold. "I want you to fuck me," I repeated.

I peeled off a hundred. He shook his head. I peeled off two more. He shook his head again, but less emphatically. I peeled off another, slowly, then another and pulled them off the billfold. I shut my purse and held the money out to him. He nodded and the bills disappeared so fast I had now idea where they went.

"How do you want it?" he asked.

"However you want to give it to me." I popped open the rest of the buttons on his shirt and reached for his crotch.

He grabbed my hand and held it motionless just out of reach of his crotch. "You're a crazy white bitch."

With my left hand, I popped a few of the snaps by his hip. "And how do you like fucking crazy white bitches?"

He spun me around, rubbed his crotch against my bum and whispered in my ear, "Take off my pants and you'll find out." He pushed me away.

I reached up under my shirt and slid my tights and panties to the floor. I moved to his right thigh and pulled his pants apart, unsnapping all the buttons on that side. He stood motionless. I unsnapped all the buttons on his left thigh, one by one, sliding my breasts down his hard tree trunk as I went, and his pants fell to the floor.

I felt his hands on my head. He tugged on my hair and pulled me upright. "Bitch."

"Fuck me," I breathed.

He flipped his thong to one side. His big black cock—wide and long—immediately sprang out. He lifted me up by my haunches and propelled me down onto his cock. It hurt! But then the burn turned to heat, then warmth, as he slammed me up and down his shaft. I was in the middle of the room, no support on my back. Just his washboard abs in front of me and his thigh-sized biceps pumping me up and down. I held onto the back of his neck which flexed as he lifted me up, then relaxed as he let me back down.

We were beginning to sweat. No man had ever smelled so strong before. It overpowered both my nose and my cunt. Our sweat let me slide faster up and especially down the wide and long shaft on which I was being impaled. The acceleration began to force little contractions and releases inside my cunt—a mini orgasm every time I went up and down. My little lips and my outer lips licked him each time he went in and out.

His hands were slippery against the sweat on my thighs, but he grabbed harder and I arched my hips into him. Neither of us was willing to concede that he'd have to let me down. My clit rubbed against his pubis with every stroke, sending jolts of joy swirling around my sex and up my spine. He owned me and it was glorious! His neck was too slick for me to hold onto it, so I interlaced my fingers behind him. But try as he might, he was beginning to lose his grip on my thighs and his thrusts were shorter, less rhythmic.

He slammed me against the wall. Rough plaster scraped my skin where it was exposed, but the only effect was to make me more alive. His chest and abs were covered in sweat, but my clothes provided some friction. Once again, he plunged his cock fully into me and sucked it back out. I gasped for air, but I could hardly breathe with him pressed against me. I tried to push him off, but my arms were impotent against his strength. An orgasm rocketed up my spine, mocking my inability to breathe.

My body went limp, preserving oxygen and this caused him to lose his grip. I almost fell to the floor, but instead he flung me onto the bed. He stood over me, heaving oxygen into his lungs. I quickly removed every last stitch of clothing from my body. He pushed his thong to the floor.

Sir climbed on top of me and positioned the tip of his penis at the opening of my vagina. "Beg for it!" he commanded.

"Fuck you."

He pushed forward but barely perceptibly. "Beg for it, bitch!"

"Fuck—"

His cock blasted the rest of my thought out the top of my skull. He rocked back and forth on his hip, little thrusts, but maximum stimulation up and down my clit. Then a series of long hard thrusts followed by more rocking of his hips. I was floating then crashing into explosive orgasms, my consciousness having to collect itself after every climax, but unable to find solid ground, being forced to float where he had captured me. His pumping cock had wound my cunt hard around him and my cunt had wound my entire being around her. His sweat oozed into my every pore; even his sweat was fucking me!

Sir pulled himself out of me and flipped me onto my stomach. He pushed my legs apart, put his knees between mine and pulled my hips up towards him. His movements were practiced and true. Then his cock was once again inside my cunt, thrusting in and out. He was a master; I had not felt a single jerk to my head or neck. His thrusts were now slower, still long and powerful, but slower. I relaxed to the gentle slap of his legs against the back of my thighs, resting to regain my strength. His thrusts were pleasant, but no longer sending me into uncontrolled orgasms. I resolved to let him wear himself out. If it was possible to wear this magnificent stallion out!

But he did slow and I scooted forward to let him flop out of me. I directed him to one of the chairs, and gently pushed him into seated position. I lifted my right leg and slid myself down onto him. I sat there for a moment, using my kegel muscles to massage the massive cock pressing up and into my stomach.

I pulled myself up, using the back of the chair and what strength I could still muster from my legs, and let myself slide back down his cock. I had just been fucked more thoroughly than I'd ever been fucked before. And Sir was exhausted too. His cock was still rock hard, but he lacked the ability to move. His eyes were shut. Peter had been good, but never *this* good. It had been pure animal intensity, his power making ingenuity unnecessary. I lifted myself, but only got halfway up Sir's shaft before I had to let myself back down. Michael would certainly exercise more imagination. But now I was luxuriating in the exhaustion of being all fucked out.

I tried to pull myself up again, but I couldn't. I reached over to Sir's handcuffs and quickly snapped them tightly onto his left wrist. His eyes flashed open and I barely had time to escape before he grabbed me with his right hand. He tried to stand, but as soon as the handcuffs put pressure on his arm, he collapsed back down into the chair.

"Bitch!"

"Tell me about the camera."

He quickly scanned the room, then brought his eyes back to me. "There is no camera, you crazy—"

"Not here. By the stage."

"I don't know nothin' 'bout no camera. Now let me go, you crazy bitch!"

His chest heaved as I stared into his eyes. He was telling the truth.

"Where's the panic button?" I asked.

He angled his head towards the door hinges. I saw the little black button. I pressed it, then quickly dressed. In a moment there was rustling outside, a key unlocked the door and the security guard burst in.

I picked up Sir's baton and waved it back and forth between the two men. "Get me your head of security," I told the guard.

The security guard looked at Sir who nodded. In a few moments Sir and the security guard had left the room and I was talking to a thin, but very tall, dude in a black suit.

I opened the photo of Amanda which had been posted to the internet on my cellphone and held it up to his face. "What can you tell me about this?"

"And *this* is?" He was still thinking about tossing me out on my butt.

"It's a photo of one of your patrons, at your club, and it's been posted to the internet."

He looked at it closely. "It does appear to have been taken at the club." He had calmed down and now seemed genuinely concerned. "But it's the first I've seen of it."

I took Black Suit Dude back to the performance area. The music was East Indian sitar and a thin South Asian man was performing yoga contortions. The ladies were studying him with rapt attention, trying to figure out how he'd managed to place his body in such awkward poses.

I pointed to the go-everywhere action camera bracket in the ceiling. "How did that get there," I asked.

He shook his head and shrugged. "Lots of people come in. Guys, women. All types. He pulled a chair over, stood on it and unhooked the bracket. "This would be easy to throw up, even without a ladder."

"Why didn't the guy who threw it up take it back down?"

He motioned to the chair and stood back up. "Easy to throw up without being seen, not so easy to remove it without being seen."

I took a picture of the camera bracket with my cellphone and left.

If Michael Rayburn was right about one thing, it was that we still had no firm leads as to the identity of the Cyber Culprit. And while I was certainly fleshing out the background details of the incidents he'd photographed and posted on the web, my skill-set in the cyber realm was only ordinary. As well, the amount of information Rayburn was gathering from freely-available sources was starting to become overwhelming.

So I'd been reviewing résumés and conducting interviews. Actually only two interviews, but still enough to be plural. The first guy, an ex-cop, had spent an hour telling me how to run my business. Thanks, but no thanks! It was *my* business. The second prospect was happily married and absolutely refused to have sex undercover. If I'd learned anything about this case so far, an open mind in the sex department was going to be an essential element in catching the Cyber Culprit.

Which is why I was interviewing Eric Craigie. Craigie's résumé was a bit vague, but he seemed to be a bit of a nerd, so maybe he'd be of some help with computers and the internet and such. He was into yoga and mixed martial arts, which was bit of a contradiction—bliss and peace but liked to kick people's heads in.

In the flesh, Craigie was younger, taller and, on average, lighter than me: 26, six-foot three and 165 pounds. That and red hair with green eyes made him a sight to be seen. I immediately tried to figure out how to disguise him and was pleased to note that a change of hair color and tinted contact lenses would change his appearance noticeably.

"What makes you want to be a private investigator?" I started out.

"Excitement and mental stimulation."

"How would you handle stakeouts?"

"Keep my mind busy with other things while keeping my eyes open." Not bad. Total bullshit, but not bad.

"What if I tell you to break into someone's house?"

"That's against the law, so there'd have to be a pretty good reason." Excellent: Cautious but realizes that sometimes legalities need to be pushed.

"My current case involves someone who's catching people in sexually-compromising situations and then posting pictures of them in these situations to the internet. What are your attitudes towards free speech and privacy?"

"Both are good."

"You'll have to do better than that."

"Free speech is necessary for democracy. But that doesn't require the exposure of the private moments of citizens. Unless of course a public figure is saying one thing in public but doing something totally different in private."

"So if somebody says that family values and monogamy and fidelity are important and professes to follow those dictates but is really whoring around town, he's fair game. But not otherwise?"

Craigie nodded, "But not otherwise."

"Are you willing to work undercover?"

"Yes, of course. Aren't all PIs?" No, they aren't, but no need to disabuse a new recruit.

I nodded. "Is there anything you'd refuse to do undercover?"

"I don't do drugs."

"Alcohol?"

He shook his head.

"Why not?"

"They aren't healthy." Oh, joy. A religious fanatic.

"Okay, we'll give you a medical condition. What about sex?"

"Sex is fine."

"Any boundaries?" No booze, but sex is okay? What kind of a wacko religion is this?

"I'm bisexual, so as long as no one's being hurt, I'm good." Bisexual?!?

"What's your religious background?"

"Nothing specific. Eclectic, I guess."

"So you do whatever you want?"

"I do what I think is right."

I reached my hand out and we shook on it. Working with Eric Craigie promised to be very, *very* interesting.

Just at that moment, my phone rang. I was about to turn it off when I saw that it was from Michael Rayburn. "Our boss," I told Eric before putting him on speaker. "Hello, Mr. Rayburn. I have my new partner, Eric Craigie, here with me."

Eric smiled. He'd just been promoted.

Michael's voice boomed over the phone, "Good there's been a new posting. Check your email and get back to me." He sounded harassed, so I excused his terseness.

"Will do."

"Thanks." And then the line was dead.

I opened up my email and Eric crowded over my shoulder. The Cyber Culprit's latest posting was a video of a member of Toronto's upper crust negotiating sexual favors with a prostitute, complete with sound.

The video was a bit grainy, but I recognized the rotund guy in the pinstriped suit from the business pages. The hooker was small and skinny, dressed in a red spandex top that hugged her breasts and almost allowed her nipples to poke through. Below she was wearing a shiny silver miniskirt which barely covered her crotch.

The rotund guy removed a billfold from his pocket. "What can I get for a thousand?" he asked.

The Escort, Lusty Lee Log #4

Working with a lawyer from a big downtown law firm had definite advantages. Michael Rayburn had had little difficulty in setting up a meeting for me with John Littlefield [name changed to protect the guilty]. Littlefield was the prominent owner/Chief Executive Officer of an international conglomerate headquartered in Toronto. But I wasn't visiting this member of Toronto's upper crust to discuss his business. I was in his office to discuss the video the Cyber Culprit had taken of him as he had negotiated sexual favors with a prostitute.

I began the meeting by playing the video, complete with sound. Littlefield had welcomed me into his office, had me sign the non-disclosure agreement proffered by his assistant, then dismissed his assistant, telling her to shut the door behind her. The video showed Littlefield, in a pinstriped suit flirting with short and skinny blonde woman wearing a tight red spandex top and a silver miniskirt that extended below her hips, but only just barely. The video ended with Littlefield removing a billfold from his pocket and asking, "What can I get for a thousand?"

Today Littlefield's suit wasn't pinstriped, but it was custom-tailored to hide as much of his rotund body as possible. His office was a corner suite, high above the city. His large desk separated us. The walls behind me and to my left side were covered with video screens, some playing domestic and foreign news programs, some showing stock-market feeds while others streamed data in a form I couldn't recognize. There were three landlines on his desk and five cellphones, all arranged in a row on the left side. On the right side was a keyboard and two monitor screens. The screen closest to me was angled so that I could see his triple-booked schedule.

I tapped my phone where I'd paused the video at the point at which he was showing his billfold to the hooker. "How did you meet this woman?"

"Through an agency. I pay them a set fee. They arrange a meeting. Sex is not included in their fee. Whatever I arrange with the woman is strictly between the two of us."

"What's the name of the agency?"

He pulled a blank sheet of paper from a drawer in his desk, wrote out a phone number and slid the paper across to me.

"What did you get for your thousand dollars?"

"Is that pertinent to your investigation?"

I nodded.

He sighed. "She did this yoga pose where she stands on her head and let me pour champagne into her cooch, then suck it out."

"That's it?"

He shot me a dirty look. "Then we poured champagne all over each other and had sex."

"Do you know how to contact her?"

He shook his head and pointed to the paper he had slid over to me, "Only through that number."

"Is the video still up on the 'net?"

"No."

"How did you get it removed?"

"I have an Information Technology department."

"Did you have to pay a ransom?"

He shook his head. "There was no demand."

I showed him the number he had written on the paper. "Have you been back?"

He slowly shook his head. There was a look of ruefulness on his face. "IT and Publicity say it would be a bad idea." It was now the *company* owing *him*, not the other way around. I folded up the paper and thanked him for his time.

That afternoon, I introduced my new associate, Eric Craigie, to Michael Rayburn. After all, if Rayburn's law firm was going to be paying a thousand dollars so that Eric could have under-the-covers undercover fun, Michael should be able to put a face to the expense-account charge.

I needn't have worried; Michael immediately assumed the role of uncle to Eric, who was ten years his junior, and started to give him a full briefing on our pursuit of the Cyber Culprit. I should have been vaguely insulted at Michael's assumption that I hadn't given Eric a full report, but what-the-hell, the client calls the shots and besides Eric and I were both on the clock.

"Our target's victims have included a sports broadcaster filmed with his mistress, a philanthropist at a strip club, two swingers at an orgy and now a well-known businessman with a prostitute."

Eric nodded, but kept quiet. I was proud of how my new associate was going with the flow and not showing off his encyclopedic knowledge of the case.

"Our target," Michael summarized, "has been putting random images and videos of a variety of persons, most of them prominent in their own way, onto the internet. But he has not contacted any of them directly or made any sort of demands."

"So we have no knowledge of his or her motive?"

Michael shook his head. "The postings have come at random times, on random sites." Michael started to detail his efforts to determine the IP addresses used by the Cyber Culprit, and Eric's questions became more technical. I tuned out the nerd talk to watch the two men and their body language.

Eric's red hair contrasted sharply with Michael's brown with flecks of grey. Michael was several inches shorter than Eric, but noticeably heavier, and not all of the excess was muscle. Then again, almost anyone would be heavier than Eric's skin-to-the-bone thinness. Michael was better looking than Eric, especially in his tailored suit and tie.

Eric might be more fun in the sack than Michael. He was technically my employee, so clearly off-limits, but a little fantasy was harmless. His green eyes would be mesmerizing, make me melt powerless to do whatever he wanted me to. And his long limbs, trained in jujitsu and yoga, wrapped around me, or holding me in new and novel positions, would surely bring me off in ways I'd never been brought off before. He'd start missionary, he on top, to establish who's boss, then roll over so I'd be on top, then he'd lift me up and off, twirl me around and slide me back down so I'd ride him reverse cowgirl. Then up and over, pushing me forward into doggie style. From there, he'd transition into me onto my side, he on my back, arms and legs wrapped around me rubbing himself directly on my g-spot all the way to heaven!

Michael was more conventionally masculine than Eric, especially in his power-role as lawyer. His blue eyes weren't mesmerizing, but they were seductive, and perhaps that was better. His wide lips and full mouth would kiss me almost to orgasm. And the way words twirled off his tongue, sometimes short and staccato, at others long and melodic, promised equal delights down lower. He wasn't as skinny as Eric, but still, he'd fit between my hips. Yes, missionary, man-on-top, was where I'd like to be with Michael. Not like Peter who overwhelmed around and over my hips—

Shit! Why was I even thinking about Peter, especially when Michael was here in the flesh to stoke my fantasies? Peter Henge—bastard-in-chief—had broken up with me and now I had the case which should have been ours and that should be that!

Later that evening, back in my apartment, I watched as Eric dialed the number which our erstwhile CEO had given me over lunch. We had the phone on speaker so that I could listen in.

"Elegant Escorts," a pleasant woman's voice answered.

"Hi." Eric had obviously never done this before.

"Yes, sir. How may I help you?" Thankfully it wasn't our receptionist's first time.

"I'd like to meet a girl."

"Any particular girl?"

"Do you have a webpage where I could look…?"

"I'm sorry, sir. We do not put our ladies' images on the internet."

"I don't know. A girl." I fought to keep my eyes from rolling over in their grave.

"We have a mixer every evening at seven-thirty. Would you like to come?"

"Sure."

Thankfully Eric was better at taking down addresses than describing his carnal desires. I counted off twenty one-hundred dollar bills and watched him roll them up and stuff them into his pocket. The new plastic bills tended to unroll more easily than the classic paper ones had, but Eric seemed to have mastered the new technology.

"Make sure you keep your cellphone on," I told him, then watched as he turned his iPhone towards me. I turned my Samsung phone towards him. It may be a knockoff to Apple's flagship, but I had found it more dependable. "I'll be here if you need anything."

At the door, I held his arm. "Eyes peeled, ears open." He was dress-casual, handsome. Any bar in the city, he could have any woman for free. "Be safe, have fun."

"Yes, mother." He bent over and kissed the top of my head.

I gave him a playful jab to his mid-section. "And I want a *full* report."

He nodded. Then he was gone and I was alone in my apartment.

My evening boiled down to a choice between masturbating to the prostitution scenes in *Diary of a Nymphomaniac* or watching the similar scenes in art-house comedy *Never on a Sunday*. I decided on both, resolving to come on the alleyway scene in *Nymphomaniac* where she backs him against the iron fence and fucks his brains out. I popped *Never* into my DVD player and settled back for a good laugh.

At three a.m. I felt a vibration in my crotch. I glanced up at the TV. It was the menu screen for *Never on a Sunday*. I reached down to my crotch. Time to put *Nymphomaniac* on screen and put my vibrator to proper use. But when I reached down, it was my phone that had vibrated me awake. Slipping it into the top of my panties had obviously been a good idea. I glanced at the screen. It was Eric Craigie.

What kind of trouble had Eric got himself into?!? But it was just an email alert. He had filed his report. I quickly opened it on my phone and scrolled to the end. He was safe and sound, signing off and going to bed. I looked into the mirror. My eyes were bleary, but it'd be at least another hour before enough adrenaline had drained from my system to allow me to go back to sleep.

I popped a bag of popcorn into the microwave, poured myself a root beer—no caffeine—and downloaded the report of Eric's assignations into my laptop. As I waited for the corn to pop, I inspected myself in the mirror.

I was now up to a full one hundred and fifty pounds — forty more than when Peter had dumped me. Mostly it was good — enhanced bust, rounder bottom. But a little extra had accumulated around my tummy. I'd have to hit the gym tomorrow if I didn't want any more weight to accumulate on my five-foot five frame.

I glanced back and forth between my laptop and the microwave. Eric's report was one long narrative. I'd have to show him how to format his reports in the future. As it was, I'd have to read it word for word. The microwave beeped. I tore open the bag and inhaled the heavenly fragrance. I munched my first handful as I began to read:

The mixer was in a room off the reception. The guy behind the bar was even skinnier than me. I asked for a Perrier. There were three other men in the room and seven ladies. The woman who had met with CEO Littlefield was not present. One of the men left with a woman and two more women came in. Both were small and skinny, one blonde, the other African-American. One of the newcomers, the blonde, *was* the woman who had met with Littlefield and I moved towards her.

But before I could even get close, one of the other men had called her over. I waited for a moment, hoping that she would become available, but before I even got within ten feet, the other man had ushered her out the door. I turned back to the woman who had come in with our target — was she her friend, or had it been a coincidence they'd come in together?

I was immediately captivated. She was a little black cutie. Five-foot four, taller on the stiletto heels she was wearing. Black leather leggings accentuated her slim figure. A deep green, but bright, satin blouse gripped tight around her figure, and accentuated the roundness of her breasts. But this was not the cause of my captivation. I was captivated because there were two circular stains on her blouse, right over the center of each breast.

And more, I was captivated by the thought that she might still be lactating. I immediately moved over and introduced myself, "Hi, I'm Eric."

She looked up at me contemplating whether Eric was my real name or not and what name she should use. "Lisa."

"How long have you worked here?" An innocent question now, much too intrusive if saved for later.

"A few years. I'm just coming back now."

"How do you like working here?"

"It's okay."

"Are the other girls friendly?"

She nodded and smiled. "Very. What brings you here?"

Damn! I wanted to talk about you, and especially about your friend. I recovered and smiled. "I wanted to meet someone."

"Someone like me?"

I nodded.

"Or someone like my friend, the one I came in with?"

"Someone like you." Professionally a lie, personally true.

"I have to be home by midnight. Is that okay?"

I shrugged. "Why midnight?"

"And that's the other thing. I'm breast-feeding. Will that be a problem?"

She waited for me to respond. I shook my head. Making love to a mother who was nursing had been one of my strongest fantasies since puberty. I'd made the mistake of telling my third girlfriend about how wonderful it'd be if mother's milk was spraying over me during sex. She'd called me a 'Perve' and broken our relationship off then and there. I'd gone in for therapy. The first session was a disaster. I'd got a hard-on describing making love to a big-breasted woman dressed in a T-shirt and watching her milk stain ever-widening circles. The hard-on remained through the entire session. After that, we'd stuck to generalities. Ten sessions and a thousand dollars later, the shrink had told me that I got turned on by the thought of lactating mothers. I had marched out, resolving to keep my thoughts to myself.

"Lactation turns you on."

I nodded, resolving to practice my poker face before my next undercover assignment.

"So I'm a kink for you?"

"You're a very beautiful woman, a wonderful human being, a devoted mother. Yes, all of these things turn me on."

She looked deep into my eyes. Then her eyelids flickered. She'd make up her mind. "Licking is okay, but absolutely no sucking. What leaks out is fair game, but you can't try to express any more."

I nodded. "What comes next?"

"You pay five hundred dollars at the front desk as we go out. You take me to your hotel room and we talk." 'Your hotel room' meant I'd be paying for it.

"Talk?"

She looked at me as if I was a moron, then slowly ran her hand across her bosom.

Half an hour later, we were in a mid-sized hotel room. One queen-sized bed so that we'd have space to move around. I turned to latch the chain-lock across the door.

"Don't," she said. "Not until we've decided."

"Decided?"

"What we're going to do."

"I'd like to have sex with you."

"Straight sex?"

I nodded and pointed to her breasts, making a vague circular motion.

"With milk?"

I swallowed and nodded again.

"You have to use a condom."

I nodded and took one out of my pocket. She smiled and I turned back to latch the door.

"Five hundred dollars."

I turned back to her. "I paid back at the office."

"That was for them. This is for me."

I shrugged. It wasn't my money. I counted out five more bills, hiding the remainder so that she couldn't see how much more I had. I turned again to lock the door and this time I was able to slide the chain into place without another protest from her. I could feel my cock half hard already. As I turned around from locking the door, she was undoing the top button of her blouse.

"Don't," I told her.

She looked at me quizzically, "Eric?"

"I thought we were going to talk."

"'Talk' is a metaphor. You've been thinking about this for a long time. If we talk now, it's all you'll be thinking about. You won't be talking to *me*, as a person."

She looked at me, daring me to contradict her. I nodded. She unbuttoned the top button.

"Don't," I told her. "Let me."

"It's another hundred if you want to soil my clothes."

I did want. More than anything. The money was soon transferred. It didn't matter, she was going to get that and more as a tip.

Lisa motioned up and down my body. "Take your clothes off."

Pants and shirt were quickly removed.

She pointed to my briefs. I had worn grey briefs, cotton/spandex, the latest thing. And matching socks. "Every last stitch." She pointed to my left foot, then my right.

When she was satisfied that the only thing standing between us was my rock hard cock, she pushed me against the wall and began to rub her chest up and down my belly. Her blouse was satin and smooth. It felt cool against my flushed belly. Then I could feel something hard and rough underneath and slightly damp. The roughness became lubricated and she was sliding freely once more. This beautiful woman was rubbing her milk-slicked mammaries up and down my chest. I almost came, then and there!

I gently pushed her back to the edge of the bed and unbuttoned her blouse. The front was drenched with her milk. It would be such a shame to send it in for cleaning. I laid it carefully on the night table. She helped me peel down her leggings. She wouldn't let me touch her shoes. Apparently I was not allowed to have both a foot fetish and a lactation fetish. At least not on the same night. And quicker than I could complete the thought, she had her shoes off.

Her lingerie was purple, lace bra and thin-as-thin-can-be panties. The panties had no edge and had not been visible under her pleather tights, notwithstanding how tight they'd been. I reached down to touch her panties and she spread her legs. She was hot and damp. She reached around to hug me close and I could feel her two milk-wet hot little buttons on my tummy. It's heat only increased as she dug her fingernails into my back.

I took half a step backward and touched her bra, being careful to avoid her nipples. Still my fingers were wet. She was rubbing herself against my cock and I felt ready to come. I knew that if I even touched her nipples, I would spurt my semen all over her.

I reached down to remove her panties, but she brushed my hand away. "Just let me touch you the first time. The second time, you can come inside."

"But what if there isn't a second?" I protested.

"There will be," she assured me. "He's almost ready to come now." I looked down. She was right.

She led me to one of the chairs in the room and pushed me sitting. She straddled my left leg and bent down so that she could rub her crotch back and forth along its length. I reached up and gently caressed her bra. It was wet and sticky and wonderful! Her breasts fit perfectly inside her bra. At five hundred dollars a pop, she could afford custom-fitted. I estimated her cup size to be somewhere a C and a D.

Even my gentle caresses were making milk come out. She wasn't using her hands on my cock, rather she was lightly scratching and pinching up my torso. But that along with her leg rubbing against my balls, and occasionally against my cock was enough to have me poised to lurch over the edge.

And I didn't want to go over the edge. I wanted this to last forever.

Her milk, nectar of the gods, was covering my entire palms. It sent warmth up my arms. And I could smell it, the smell of sweet soft ice cream. I moved my hands to the side of her bra, bent forward to lick her milk. She bent forward to let me. Such a wonderful sharing mother! She tasted fine cappuccino. Forever, I cried for this to last *forever*.

To last forever along with my memories of all the nursing mothers I'd ever lusted after. The mother furtively nursing her baby on the bus. The redhead, nude to the waist, defiantly nursing twins at the beach. The Latina standing next to me on the subway — weaving to within inches of my chest as the train swayed back and forth — whose T-shirt started with one, then two, little circular wet spots, then larger and larger with me doing multiplication tables in my head to stop my crotch bursting through my jeans. The time I'd bought baby formula, mixed it, and put it inside a condom to masturbate with. Our Asian neighbor nursing next door when she didn't think anyone was looking.

I licked for another taste for all eternity. But her hands were on my cock, rubbing up and down.

"No!" I cried as I spurted on her belly. "No!" I cried as I dribbled between her fingers.

She looked at me strangely. "Are you okay?"

"I wanted it to last forever."

Lisa kissed me on the lips, lightly, but on the lips. "Go clean up." She pointed to the bathroom.

In the bathroom, I cleaned myself off with a wet facecloth. My cock was barely tender, not how it usually is after sex, even if it had just been me jerking off. But by the time I'd returned to the room, I had plunged into depression. Here I was with the most gorgeous woman in the world and my cock was as flaccid as porridge.

"Eric?" She had seen the look on my face.

"It's over."

"Only for a little while. Do you want to talk?"

I should be jumping in with all sorts of questions, but all I could do was nod.

"When you came to the mixer tonight, what did you expect to find? You certainly didn't know that I'd be there to fulfill your fantasy."

The carpet on the floor had a repeating abstract pattern. "You'll hate me."

"Eric. Look at me." She was still in her thoroughly soiled bra. There were spots of my semen on top of her panties. Her hair was mussed, her lipstick smeared. Her eyes were tired from years of accumulating wisdom. She was the most attractive woman in the world. "Hate is not in my nature."

I sighed. "I came to find your friend, the blonde."

"Sally?!"

"If that's her name, yes, Sally."

"To have sex?"

"No, to talk."

"Like this?" She smiled, enjoying the tease.

"No, she was photographed with someone. I need to know if she knew she was being photographed and by who."

"I'll give you her number." She took a writing pad and pen from the night table drawer and wrote out a phone number. She put the pad on top of my pants.

"Thanks."

"You're still sad."

I looked down between my legs. My cock was still as soft as warm butter.

"Shut your eyes." The room went black. "Now, remember what we did after you took your socks off."

I remembered her blouse stroking up and down my chest, soft and smooth, then rough, then liquid. I remembered her milk leaking through her bra and gushing onto my hands. I remembered its sweet smell and even sweeter taste. I remembered her hands on my cock milking —

There was a rustling. I opened my eyes. Lisa was on the bed, scooting towards its center. And she was completely

nude. Her black body, splayed on the white sheets, was
exotic. Her toenails and fingernails were bright purple. Her
legs were smooth, almost glistening. Hips wide and maternal
added a sensuous curve between legs and tummy rising to a
jet black brambly forest in the center. Her torso was flat—not
with defined abs, but with taut muscles underneath from
exercising while pregnant and more strenuously afterwards.
Her breasts, round and full and swollen, perched like majestic
peaks on her chest. Her nipples were deep ebony and there
was a drop of white on each protruding promontory. Her
eyes sparkled, her smile invited. I wanted to stand and
admire her until the end of time. I stared at her breasts
yearning to see the drops of white expand and dribble down
the black mountains.

But Lisa's long thin arm was holding a condom up to
me. I glanced down between my legs. My cock was once
again a sturdy flagpole. I ripped the package open and
unfurled the latex down my entire shaft, holding it so that she
could see me give the bottom a gentle tug to introduce a touch
of slack and see me set the bottom ring firmly against my
pubis.

I climbed atop this fertile goddess and flicked my
tongue out so that it just touched the top of the first drop of
her milk. The milk adhered to my tongue and I carefully
brought my tongue back inside my mouth and swallowed. I
would never be hungry again. Ever. I realized I hadn't been
breathing and I sucked air into my lungs. The smell of her
sweat, my sweat and her white manna floated me into eternal
bliss.

I flicked my tongue to the globule of milk on her other
nipple, but there was a spurt and milk squirted up the entire
length of my tongue! It's taste flooded, overwhelmed behind
my nose, shot down my spine and throbbed inside my cock.
This time I didn't swallow, but spread the warm nectar
around my entire mouth, savoring the tastes of honey,
jasmine, salt, cream and lactose.

I held my mouth over her other nipple, not touching,

but close enough that I could feel her heat on my lips. With one hand, I caressed around her breast. It was hard and firm, unlike any other breast I'd ever felt. Another droplet of milk began to form. Then I felt Lisa's hand on my cock, pulling me into her. I bent my back forward, grateful for the flexibility yoga had given me, and just managed to scoop the droplet onto my tongue before she arched her tummy up to suck my cock deep inside her.

Her breasts were warm, her milk warmer, but her cunny was hot, even through the latex condom. She pumped and squeezed, obviously enjoying her work, and I gasped at the mastery she'd obtained over her sex muscles. But now I had to press both my hands on the mattress to maintain my own position. And I was unable to bend my head all the way down to her nipples.

I gave her a full body hug and slid my hands under her buttocks. Their feel was slightly coarse, with little pokes of hair. But her pumping *glutei*, not the change in texture was what I felt. And boy were they pumping! Ordinarily I'd've come long ago, but the previous hand-job and the condom were allowing me to last. I shifted her weight and pulled her on top of me.

My shift in position failed to alter the rhythm of her pumping, but she pushed off the mattress with her hands to improve her leverage. And her breasts were there, swaying only slightly above me. I reached up to caress them and milk spurted all over my chest. I pulled her down atop me and our chests slipped and slid against each other, heating up her mammary lubrication.

She propped herself up and I lightly ran my fingers around the dark circles surrounding her nipples. Lisa groaned and her pumping *glutes* slowed. Now I ran my fingers around the outside of the shafts of her nipples. They puckered even harder and two drops of milk appeared. She stopped her pumping altogether so I pushed up lightly, just enough to maintain our arousal, but not enough to push it forward.

"Fuck me," she pleaded.

But I had captured control and I had no intention of relinquishing it. I stroked up and down and around her nipples, angling them towards my mouth.

She tried to rock her hips but the effect was minimal. "Fuck me."

I squeezed lightly on her breasts, now completely full with their primary function. A small spurt hit my nose. I altered the angle of my mouth towards the points of her nipples and returned to stroking them up, down, around. One nipple spurted directly into my mouth, then the other! I couldn't help but swallow. I was floating, all my muscles slack as I luxuriated in the sensations of her milk sliding down my throat, into my stomach and radiating into each and every part of my body.

That moment of inattention was all she needed to push herself up and off me. She kneeled, looking down at me.

"Are you going to fuck me, or what?" she demanded. I reached for her breasts but she gently brushed my hands away. "Are you?" she repeated.

I had no answer.

She sighed. "Have you ever made love to a pregnant woman?"

I shook my head.

"You have to do it doggy style. But since everything's pressed so tightly, it's the most intense."

I looked at her breasts. They were what I wanted.

"Please," she pleaded, her eyes doleful. "If you penetrate all the way, your hands will be able to reach my breasts."

She was right, they would. I nodded and she turned around, arching her butt towards me. Her buttocks were dark brown, but her pubic area, hair and cunny lips were completely black. In the center of blackest Africa gleamed a slit of bright bright pink.

I lifted myself up to kneel behind her, pressing my cock against her pink slit in wonderment as it slowly expanded. I made sure my condom was on properly and slid myself half way — she gabbed my balls, arched her butt and I was suddenly all the way in. Her grip on my balls was gentle, but ever so firm. It was clear she wouldn't let go until she'd got what she wanted.

"Fuck me." She was no longer pleading.

I began to move gently in and out.

"Fuck me," she demanded. The firm squeeze on my balls made it clear that gentle was not what she wanted.

I grabbed her hips and pushed myself in as far as I could go. She loosened her grip on my balls and I began to slam my cock in and out of her cunny. She groaned and let loose of my balls altogether, propping herself up on her elbows. I reached down to caress her breasts but this obviously took my attention from where it belonged because her fingers were once again kneading my balls.

After a few tries and errors, I had my thrusts down so that I was hitting all the parts Lisa felt needed hitting. Every fifth thrust, I could free one hand to caress her breasts while inserting my other fingers along her vulva to squeeze it, and her clit hard against my cock. Every time I touched her breasts, milk dribbled out and I had to bite my lip to stop from coming.

Then Lisa started rocking her hips like a bucking bronco and I had to hold fast onto both her hips to stop myself from slipping out of her cunny. She was hot against my cock, hot against my hands. As far as I could tell, she'd stopped breathing.

"S H I T!" A blood-curdling scream below me. "Shit! Fuck! *Shit!*"

Her body had gone totally slack, except for the contractions against my cock. I held on tight to her hips, slapping our thighs together as I plunged myself in and out. She stopped moving altogether so I pulled myself out, pushed her to the bed and onto her back.

She lay before me spent, powerless. I caressed each of her breasts. Milk spurted out. She couldn't move, couldn't protest, couldn't reach up to my cock. I mounted her and entered my full length inside her. I moved back and forth gently while caressing her breasts and massaging her milk all around her nipples. My cock began to pulse and I held myself motionless to savor its contractions pumping my semen inside her as I stared at the milk dribbling down her breasts.

As we dressed, I glanced at the phone number Lisa had written on the hotel's pad. It was the agency's main number, not the blonde's who'd been with Littlefield. I caught Lisa's attention and pointed to the pad. "What about a threesome with your friend the blonde? I think you said her name was Sally?"

She laughed and pointed at my crotch. "You really think you're up for a threesome?"

I glanced down to where she was pointing. Not only was he softer than soft, he'd shrunk to almost nothing. I looked back at her. "Coffee?"

She smiled, nodded and reached for her cellphone. I looked down at my cock. He was still soft and small. Not even the vision of dribbling milk into dark coffee had stirred him.

An hour later, Lisa, Sally and I were in an all-night coffee bar. It was a pleasant and rollicking conversation, dopamine still flooding our brain cells, but Sally didn't know any more about Littlefield beyond what was in the video. And she'd had no idea anyone was videotaping, nor how they'd accomplished the taping. But she was pissed that she'd been posted with one of her clients — alone was okay, advertising was good for business, but not if it outed a client.

*****

Eric Craigie's report was good, but I'd have to edit out some of the explicit sex before submitting it to Michael Rayburn and his bevy of lawyers. *All* of the personal reflections would have to go. But my operative had shown good tradecraft by following his instinct to make friends with

Sally's associate in order to get close to her. The fact that Sally had no useful information was beside the point. Sherlock Holmes had repeatedly driven home the point that it's important to establish what isn't there.

I was halfway through revising Eric's report when my phone buzzed again.

It was an email from Michael Rayburn about new postings by the Cyber Culprit: five photos and a video. They were all from a BDSM — bondage domination sado-masochism — event held at the city's premiere leather club. The photos showed a variety of activities ranging from nude butts being flogged, collared pets being led around and nude bodies, male and female, bound spread-eagled on St. Andrew's Crosses.

The video showed a buxom woman dressed in a black leather string bikini with two men binding her wrists to a bar above her head. They then took a bar almost three feet long and attached it to each of her ankles, forcing her to spread her legs. One of the men started to lightly whip her back with a cat-o-nine-tails until she broke out in a sweat and began to breathe heavily. He then paused, untied her bikini and in a moment she was nude. She smiled defiantly at her tormentor as he lowered the bar above her head a foot to give her a small degree of freedom of movement. He stroked her nipples with his whip, then between her legs. Then he started to flog her butt, harder this time. She tried, but failed to move out of the way of his blows. Then she stuck her butt out to give him a clear target. The second man placed a buzzing vibrator between her legs. She bit her lip and began to swoon as his blows continued to rain down on her butt.

I went on the internet. The leather club's next event was this coming Saturday.

Leather, Lusty Lee Log #5

With the lights turned on, the leather club looked less

foreboding than it had on the internet video. But I could clearly see the flogging posts, benches and St. Andrew's crosses. The metal binding rings gleamed in the light. It turned out that most of the people who had attended the club were regulars who were known to the owner and he was able to gather several for me to interview. They were somewhat pissed at having had their pictures posted to the internet without their permission but, on the other hand, they were reveling in their moment of fame.

The first regular was a skinny guy I recognized from a photo of him having his butt whacked. I showed him the photo we'd downloaded from the 'net. "Is this you?"

He nodded and promptly pulled down his pants, turning to show me a series of red streaks on his buttocks. When he turned back to me, his smile was ear-to-ear.

"Did you know you were being photographed?"

He shook his head as he pulled his pants back up. "Cameras are forbidden."

I recognized the next pair as being master and pet. He wasn't wearing a collar and she wasn't holding him by a leash, but his body language clearly showed his devotion the same way her eyes established her dominance. Today they were dressed in office attire, but that night she had been wearing a red leather corset and mini-skirt and he'd been nude except for a diminutive leather thong.

I showed them the photo that had been posted by the Cyber Culprit. She scowled in the direction of her pet. "He pissed his pants." Her pet hung his head. "I had to potty-train him all over again." They smiled at each other; potty training had obviously had significant elements of mutual enjoyment.

"At the time, were you aware that this photograph was being taken?"

They both shook their heads.

The last woman had had a video posted of her being stripped nude, bound spread-eagled and whipped with a cat-o-nine-tails until her body was covered with sweat. Today she was dressed more demurely and watched the video with rapt attention. The video had ended with her swooning as a vibrator was placed between her legs. When the screen went black, she looked up at me expectantly.

"Were you aware you were being filmed?"

"No."

"How did you find out about the video?"

"Benny told me." Benny was the club owner.

"Is anybody else you know aware of the video?"

"No—" Her phone buzzed and she took it out of her pocket. "Sorry, I have to take this."

After her call was over, I gathered everyone around for a final spiel, "Thank you all for coming. We will do our best to take all copies of these images down from the 'net. I will be attending your club undercover later this week. Please don't show that you recognize me."

They all nodded.

Later that day, I dropped into Northbound Leather, Toronto's premier fetish emporium, to purchase suitable attire for going undercover at the leather club. The first outfit was a miniskirt, a pair of garters, panties, bra, choker and bracelets—all black, all leather. The second outfit was a white leather corset and a pair of white leggings, half spandex, half leather. And then there were accessories: two riding crops, a small whip and a set of tit clamps. Shopping on an expense account was *fun*!

That night I was alone in Michael Rayburn's office. Not in one of the law firm's boardrooms, but in his *personal* office. It was slightly more than fifteen feet wide by twenty feet deep with a window at the back, solid oak desk, his chair behind, two client chairs in front. There was a bookshelf to the side with the usual collection of intimidating legal books. In far back corner was a small couch—a love seat really—with a small coffee table in front.

Michael was making notes on a pad of paper as I modeled the white corset outfit I'd purchased that afternoon. His eyes went suitably wide as I bent over his desk to let him look down my cleavage and admire my butt when I turned around to touch my toes. What would happen if I cozied up to him, let him touch the leather I was wearing? What would happen if I kissed his cheek, let him know that he turned me on? There was no one here to see us, no one to hear. What would happen if I unloosened his tie, unbuttoned his shirt? What would—

"You said you bought two outfits," he reminded me.

I pranced out and in a few moments returned dressed in black: miniskirt, bra, garters, and fishnet stockings.

I did a pirouette and readied to move into a risqué dance routine, but he tapped the photos on his desk. "The postings show people being bound with ropes and whipped. Is that what really goes on at a leather club?"

I nodded. What did he think went on?

"Is there sex?" he continued.

"Sometimes."

"Are you sure you're up to this?"

"It's part of the job you hired me for."

"Will you be safe?"

I smiled and nodded.

He narrowed his eyes, then decided on another approach, "Have you ever done this before?"

I nodded. "I was in college and the group I was running with was into pushing each other to expand our boundaries, confront our fears. Back then I had this fear of injury, of pain. Couldn't take pain. So they decided to spank me. Donna, the most adventurous sexually, lifted my skirt and gave me three sharp swats." I lifted my skirt slightly and swayed my bum back and forth. Michael's wide eyes were a clear indication that he was starting to get turned on. But I couldn't figure out whether the idea of spanking or being spanked was what was turning him on. "Couldn't sit down for two weeks."

"Sounds cruel."

"It seemed cruel at the time. But it has given me the strength to deal with my fears."

Michael turned over the page he had been writing on to expose a fresh page on his pad. "What exactly happened? Where were you?" He wrote out his questions as he went, leaving space for my answers. "Were you standing or sitting? What did they spank you with?"

"We were in the college's photography studio that Chris, one of my friends had booked. He had his cameras and lights and everything set up. The whole group was there. They made me slowly remove each piece of my clothing while they all stared. They were all dressed in leather, black make-up, like vampires. Then Kelly rubbed almond oil over every part of my body, and I mean *every* part. That made me horny, less worried about pain. They made me kneel on the floor. I wasn't tied or anything. I was free to back out but then I wouldn't be in the group. Anyway, I kneeled down, my ass high in the air.

"Donna, the kinkiest," I continued, "was dressed in leather garters, panties, and she was wearing a leather bra, choker and bracelets." I moved my hands over my outfit, emphasizing how similar it was to what Donna had worn. "The leather had chrome studs on it. For a feminine touch she had lace stockings. Leather gloves. All black. And a small leather-covered paddle. Anyway, she removed her choker and bracelets and put them on me. She leaned down and whispered in my ear that I was to do everything she told me to."

Michael looked up from his pad. "How did this make you feel?" He swallowed nervously.

I smiled. He *was* being turned on. "Afraid and horny and empowered."

"What happened next?"

"Donna stood back by my ass and told me to wiggle it. I wiggled and she swatted. Hard. I stopped wiggling but she told me to wiggle again. I did and there was another swat. Wiggle, swat, wiggle, swat until my butt was burning! Then she pulled me up by my hair. Slowly, every so slowly, she removed her panties, then pressed my face into her crotch." I stuck out my tongue and flicked it back and forth.

"You licked…?" This time he *really* swallowed.

I stifled my smile and nodded, "Then everyone took turns spanking my poor bottom."

"Was that the end of it?"

"No. Next Donna led me to the wall where she attached the bracelets to two hooks in the wall. She said that each of them was now going to hurt me and that if I cried out, she would spank me again. Kelly twisted both of my nipples, stopping just when I was about to scream."

Michael was writing furiously to hide his embarrassment.

"Mark fucked me hard pushing my tender rump against the wall. He came quick, the bastard. Chris, the photographer, gave me hickies up the inside of my legs. Donna put on a dildo and she pushed it inside, the studs on her bra scratching my tits with each thrust. She at least had the good grace not to stop until I'd had the most powerful orgasm of my life."

Michael scribbled madly. "Would you do it again?"

"You can never do the first time a second time."

"Are you still afraid?"

I nodded. "Just not of the same things."

"Why do people put themselves through unnecessary pain?"

"Pain releases endorphins, powerful and extremely pleasurable neural hormones. And then there's the idea of submitting yourself to someone else's power which can also be extremely sexual."

"Isn't that dangerous?"

"No more than other things."

"What about visiting the club tomorrow? By yourself. In a room of strangers?"

He wants to come with me! It was totally hot and totally impossible. He'd blow my cover in two seconds flat. I thought about bending him over his desk and spanking him. I thought about bending over my chair for him to spank me.

There was a familiar stirring in my loins. If only he'd push me onto his little couch and fuck my brains out!

I wanted to put my heels on his desk and let him look all the way up my legs. Instead I asked, "Should I go as a dom or as a sub?"

"What's a dom?"

"A dom is a dominant, the one in charge. A sub is a submissive, the person surrendering to the dom's will. Or I could go as a switch."

"Switch?"

"Someone who exchanges power, sometimes dominating, sometimes submitting."

"Which is the safest?"

"A switch has the most flexibility — from an investigatory point of view, it'd be better to go as a switch."

"Which is the safest?"

"Subs are the safest. Doms often get into pissing matches. But everyone protects the submissives."

"Then you should go as a submissive."

I shook my head. "Dominants love to make submissives stand in one place. All evening. I won't be able to find out a thing."

"Do you even know how to be a dominant?"

At that moment, I wanted one thing in the whole universe. I wanted to show Michael Rayburn that I did know how to be a dominant. I wanted to spank him with one hand while stroking his gonads with my other. I wanted him quivering at my knees. I wanted — Instead I nodded, gathered up my stuff and left his office, horny and frustrated. Frustrated with a capital 'F'!

Last night, when I'd gotten home, I had wanted to make a beeline to my chest of vibrators. I was so hot and bothered that two minutes of buzzing would have been enough to climax me. But I'd had a cold shower instead.

And it had worked. I was horny, *horny* to the max.

I was wearing the black leather miniskirt, bra and garters outfit. The garters held up black fishnet stockings.

The white corset ensemble was visually more appealing, but the black set would give me more flexibility during the night's festivities. Every step I took, the leather panties rubbed seductively against my sex.

At the front of the club, the receptionist, a thin dom, took my outer robe and handed it to a pudgy submissive who stamped my left inner wrist with the check number. The receptionist ran her eyes up and down my body, her obvious interest making me even hotter, as she ran through the club's safety protocol, "If a sub says 'Green' that means that everything is okay and you can push his limits further. If she says 'Yellow', that means that she's reached her limit and you shouldn't press further. If someone says, 'Red', then all play must immediately stop and the sub must be checked out to make sure he or she is okay." Her cellphone rang and she answered, forgetting me entirely. The call seemed to last an eternity of boring small talk. Then the receptionist pointed to a tall-muscle-bound hunk in the corner, "The Dungeon Master will be patrolling the play area, you must obey his commands at all times."

I smiled at the Dungeon Master. He was wearing tight leather pants. Otherwise he was nude except for a chain-link harness on his upper chest. He ignored my smile.

The atmosphere in the play area was definitely kinkier with the lights turned down. There was a flogging post at either end, two benches against the far wall. The walls to the left and right of the entrance featured St. Andrew's crosses, each in the shape of an 'X' with metal rings at each extremity to facilitate bondage. In fact there were metal rings everywhere, including on the floor and suspended from the ceiling. By the entrance was a wall full of tool hooks, each hook holding a variety of whips, riding crops, leather bindings, handcuffs, clamps or other implements of torture. The smell of leather was intoxicating, almost overwhelming.

The room was only partially full. Half of those attending were couples, mostly heterosexual, but about thirty-percent gay. The rest were single men and women, mostly men. Of the singles, I couldn't tell who was gay and who was straight or who might swing both ways. Their body types ran the gamut from skinny to fat, tall to short, black to white, muscular to flabby, hairy to shaved, and everything in between. Almost all were wearing black leather of some sort: dresses, pants, harnesses, bikinis, or just thongs. The club owner had said that about half would be regulars with the rest attending for their first or second time.

I waved over to one of the males who was milling about. He was a bit taller than me, about my age, fit but not buff. He was wearing leather shorts — barely larger than a bikini — and a leather T-shirt. He ignored me. Was he gay? Was I ugly? Was I not being forceful enough?

As I looked back and forth between him and the wall of whips next to the entrance, contemplating my next move, my questions were answered. A large man dressed in leather pants and a white cotton dress shirt came over to my target, took him by the ear and moved him over to a flogging post where he willingly submitted to being strapped in.

The next man I set eyes on was wearing a red latex tank top, barely thicker than a condom and I could see that one of his nipples was pierced. Below, he was wearing black leather shorts with laces pulled the leather tight in front. I made eye contact and jiggled my breasts, belly-dancer style. He smiled back. Actually it was more like a leer. First base: definitely hetero. And his leer meant that I was going to have some fun teaching him proper manners.

I walked over and pinched him above and below the nipple which had been pierced. "Lick my boots." The latex was soft and shiny; on my fingers it gave a wonderfully firm grip.

My boots were high-heeled lace-up numbers which extended six inches above my ankles. Three-inch heels struck the right balance between walkability and jutting my butt out. I let go of my new-found slave's nipple and he dropped to the floor where he enthusiastically licked up and down my boots.

I had no idea whether his boot-licking was turning my

slave on, but it was doing absolutely nothing for me. I grabbed his hair and lifted him back to standing. With my high-heels, he was barely taller than me. His blonde hair was curly and cut short, barely enough to grab onto. He had no flab, but was only average-muscled. The bones of his face emerged at right angles, as if trying to escape his skin. His eyes were grey-green and sparkled with anticipation. His smile was still a leer, but we both knew it was part of the game.

"What is your name, slave?"

He hesitated and in that moment of willfulness I realized how turned on I was at the thought of dominating this man. My legs were unsteady and between them was hot and moist.

I grabbed both his nipples and pinched, not hard, but hard enough. "What is your name, *slave*?" I enunciated every syllable and emphasized the last word. I could feel eyes watching us.

"Steven."

"Are you willing to be my slave, *Steve*?"

Again he hesitated.

I twisted the pierced nipple. "Are you willing to be my slave, *Steve*?"

"Yes."

"Yes, *what*?" I twisted just a little further to emphasize my point.

"Yes, Mistress."

I let go of the pierced nipple and glanced down at his shorts. They were tighter due to a burgeoning bulge at the front. I pointed to the wall by the entrance. Someone had just chosen a crop and was showing it to her husband. "Choose."

He stood still.

Again he was challenging me. I had no intention of feeding his desire to be manhandled every time I wanted something to be done. I let go of his other nipple. "If you want to be my slave, you will choose."

Once more he hesitated. I wanted to grab the front of

his shorts, to rip them open, to suck him into my mouth, to guide him into me, to — but none of that would happen without his conceding my mastery. I rocked back and forth on my boots, my leather panties caressing me under my miniskirt. If only I could put my finger…

Steve took a step towards the whips and handcuffs. "Faster!"

His last two steps *were* faster. Time to rock and roll!

At the wall, he lifted a soft leather riding crop. I held out my hand and he placed the handle right in my palm. The leather was soft, but the construction was firm. The shaft was rubberized but the small square tip at the end was leather. A rather excellent choice.

Steve was standing still again, but I decided not to make an issue of it. I pointed to two wrist cuffs and several strands of leather. "Put the wrist cuffs on, bring the straps and follow me."

I turned to walk to the center of the floor, not glancing back at Steve. This would be the final test of his submission to my will. It was risky to walk so far away from him, but necessary.

I stood in the center of the room under two of the rings suspended from the ceiling and turned slowly back towards Steve. Several people were watching us, mostly hetero couples. Steve was wearing the wrist cuffs and holding the strands of leather. But he was walking slowly. I slapped the riding crop against my boots. "Hurry!"

Steve hurried and in a moment, I had one of the strands of leather tied to the ring on his right wrist cuff. I looped the other end of the strand through one of the rings in the ceiling and pulled it tight, forcing Steve to step forward, our bodies now gently touching. "I own you, Steven. You are my slave."

"Yes, Mistress."

"I will do with you what I will." I rubbed my leg back and forth against his crotch.

"Yes, Mistress."

"And you will obey my every command."

He hesitated half a heartbeat, but conceded, "Yes, Mistress."

I grabbed his crotch and squeezed, not hard, but not gently either. "Immediately and without hesitation."

"Yes, Mistress," he gasped.

I rubbed his crotch, more gently this time. I could feel his cock through the leather. It was long and strong—just right!

I gave him a swat on his bottom, leather on leather. "Green light?"

"Green."

I swatted him harder. He made no reaction. I swatted twice as hard and readied to raise the crop again.

"Yellow," he conceded.

I swatted his bare legs and back, establishing his limits in the same way. Then it was time to get down to work. I struck every inch of his leather-clad buttocks, sometimes a bit softer, but never above his limit. When I moved to his back, I was more gentle, but he flinched nonetheless. I moderated the force of my blows and he began to sway in sync with my rhythm. I was so hot that I knew if I reached even one finger to press against my panties, I'd come then and there!

I moved my blows to between his legs, starting below his knees and striking back and forth as I moved up to his crotch. Several gasps escaped his throat, but they were gasps of pleasure, not pain. When I reached his crotch, I struck gently upwards against his balls.

"Green light?" I asked.

"Green."

I struck upwards again, this time with more force. "If it's green, say it. Every time."

I struck again.

"Green."

Twice as hard I struck. "Green," he gasped.

Once more, harder. He was silent but refused to concede yellow.

I dropped the crop between his legs and moved around

beside him. I hiked my skirt up above my hips and began to rub my panties against his left leg. The leather rubbing against his leg made me wet and the leather began to rub directly against my pussy lips, even teasing my clit. I almost stumbled and had to hold tight onto him.

When I recovered my balance, I began to rub against the front of his shorts. His cock was pressed tight against the soft leather. I knew I could make him come inside his shorts, but I wanted everyone to see how completely I'd mastered him. Every time I stroked up and down, I pulled at the laces holding the front of his shorts together, gradually loosening them.

Then I had his shorts loose enough to slip one hand inside. As I pulled the top of his shorts open, the scents of sweat and male musk and leather shot up my nostrils and into my cunt. It's a good thing I hadn't grabbed ahold of his cock, because I stumbled forward then back, only saving myself from falling because I still had a hold of his shorts. But the shorts pulled hard against his cock.

"Yellow! Yellow!" he yelped.

"Sorry," I whispered. But louder, I told him, "Don't be such a baby."

I grabbed his cock. His girth filled my hand. He was rock hard, only the thin outer skin of his cock had any softness. His cock was throbbing, both from the punishment I'd inflicted, but more and more from pure sexual excitement. I slid my hand gently up and down his shaft.

"Are you ready?" I whispered.

He nodded, not daring to speak and then I was ready too. I tried to mash my breasts into him, wishing I had had time to shed my bra. I gripped his cock firmly with my right hand and moved up and down his shaft in time with my grindings against his leg.

He spurted hot on top of my hand. But my pussy was even hotter inside her leather panties and she began her contractions just as Steve's last semen dribbled down between my fingers. The spasms started as slow tinglings up and down my pussy lips, then gathered inside my clit, almost hiding themselves. Then they burst over and under my cunt, wrenching my pelvis forward to allow easy access to my spine. The contractions weakened as they climbed upwards, but spread warmth, then heat upwards, upwards to heaven.

As I recovered from my orgasm, I felt two strong hands undoing Steve's wrists. It's *extremely* bad form to interfere with another Dom's slave, but I was too weak to protest.

"Are you ready to switch?" asked the deep booming voice attached to the monstrous biceps untying Steve.

His chest was hairy; the only thing he was wearing above his leather pants was a harness composed of strips of leather held together with iron rings. He had muscles on muscles. His eyes were hard and grey. I couldn't tell if they were teasing me. But his lips, now forming into a smile, were friendly and gentle.

"Yes, Master." It was the only thing to say.

Master undid the wrist cuffs I'd put on Steve and put them on my wrists. He looped one of the leather lacings through the ring on my left wrist and pulled me forward towards one of the St. Andrew's crosses. He had the riding crop I'd used on Steve in his other hand. When Steve didn't follow, Master turned to him. "Slave! I own her and *all* her possessions. Follow one step behind her."

"Yes, Master," I heard Steve say. And without hesitation!

At the St. Andrew's cross, Master released me and turned to Steve. "Remove her clothes."

Steve's had his shorts back on and he leered evilly up and down my body. He started with my leather bra. His hand caressed my breast. A jolt went down my spine when his hard palm brushed my nipple.

Thump! Master had hit Steve hard on the back of his shorts. "Just the clothes," he told our slave. "I'll tell you when you can touch her."

Steve removed the rest of my clothes in swift silence, but couldn't resist an extra touch of my feet as he removed my boots, or a gentle, and very delicious, tug on my panties before letting them fall to the floor.

Master turned me towards the St. Andrew's cross and began to attach my wrists to its upper arms. In the bondage/domination scene, St. Andrew's was really a fancy way of saying 'X'. My wrists were now attached to the two upper arms of the X and I could feel cuffs being attached to my ankles and secured to the two bottom legs. The cross to which I being attached was bulkier than the one on the opposite wall and had several levers and latches as well as a circular contraption in the middle. I suspected that this meant that the cross could be rotated in some fashion.

I felt a whirling flailing start on my back. The whip had fine strands. This would be horsehair, warming my skin for stronger floggings. Master stopped when my entire backside was warm, just short of hot, like when I'd been sun-tanning and just before my skin was about to start to burn.

Stronger leather strands replaced the horsehair. Master started the cat-o-nine tails on the top of my shoulders. The blows smarted, but certainly not more than I could bear. I was in the hands of an experienced dominant, one who did not need to ask green/yellow, one who instinctively knew what I could bear, what I needed. He softened his blows as he moved down my back.

Then *thwack!*

My right buttock stung *red-hot*.

Thwack!

My left buttock now *stung* as well. He began a steady series of blows on my buttocks, not as hard as the first two. Where the cat's leather strands hit the same places as the first two blows, exquisitely painful shocks lit my butt on fire. Where they struck a new band of skin, there was a wonderfully soft counterpoint.

Master began to alternate his flogging to my legs, but always came back up to my bottom. Once in a while he went back to my shoulders. But Master was definitely an ass man and concentrated on my butt. I shut my eyes to concentrate on the sensations from every blow.

The entire surface of my skin started to feel flushed, even on the front of my body where Master's whip had not even touched. These were the endorphins, pleasure hormones, released everywhere, engorging my nipples, teasing my pussy lips, making my cunt gush, turning me into one huge clit, ready to climax no matter where or how it was touched. And every time he hit my buttocks, more and more endorphins flooded into my epidermis!

I started to float a little closer back to earth and opened my eyes. I was no longer being flogged. Instead Master and Steve were fiddling with the latches behind the St. Andrew's cross. In a moment, they had it figured out and I was rotated out to the left, then forward, then they slid me right and I was locked back into place, facing the center of the room.

Master began to run his rough hands back and forth across my breasts. Ordinarily such harsh skin against my tender nipples would be painful but after his preparation of my skin for coarse caresses, I was in heaven. The sensations weren't leaving my breasts, rather they were making my whole chest churn with lust and passion. And then he rubbed his own chest against mine. I shut my eyes to drink in the sensations. Leather and sweat swirled inside my nostrils. His thick hairy bristles were harsher than his hands but even so I wanted to give myself entirely over to him. And the leather of his harness scraped delightfully against my nipples.

Rough hands on my bum gasped my eyes open. Every place his whip had touched seared with pain! Even before I realized that my body had tensed with resistance, his hands were gone from my butt. He was even more in touch with me than I was with myself.

Our chests continued to make out and then there was something between my legs. A rough finger moving up and down my pussy lips. Just the right amount of friction for maximum pleasure. Then it dipped inside, sparking little jerks of joy at every nerve it touched. I shut my eyes to float in the ecstasy.

And then he was gone. I was all alone. I opened my eyes.

Master had moved to my left side, his lips next to my ear. His lips should be on my lips, kissing me, drawing out my passion, lighting —

"You're a raging slut, aren't you?"

"Yes, Master."

"Say it."

"I'm a raging slut."

He squeezed my breast. Hard! "Louder!" he demanded.

"I'm a raging slut!"

There was a round of applause and I realized that everyone was watching us.

"I need to be punished," he whispered.

"I need to be punished!" I shouted.

"By my slave."

"By my slave!"

"By my *slave*," he emphasized.

"By my *slave*!"

Steve was by my right side, squeezing my other breast and dipping two fingers into my pussy. His technique was sloppy compared to Master's, but since it was at Master's command, Steve fingers stimulated me the same way Master's had.

Then no one was touching me. Anywhere! They were fiddling with the latches behind the cross. Leave the fasteners alone, you bastards! I need —

I was spinning, not figuratively, not in my head, but my entire body. Slowly at first to a forty-five degree angle, then ninety degrees, my body parallel to the floor. I could see a bulge inside Master's pants, the only reward a devoted slave needs.

More spinning and I was upside down. The men latched me in place, their movements blowing cool breezes around my pussy lips.

"Lick her," Master commanded.

Steve's tongue lapped upwards from my belly, then into my pubic hair. This relieved the physical tension in my genitals while at the same time heightening the sexual tension building within. I had never before had sex upside down and I concentrated on remembering every sensation.

Steve's leather shorts pressed against me as his tongue made a circle outside the perimeter of my pussy lips. First he went slow, then faster and faster and I couldn't think. All I could do was feel his tongue circling, drawing me up and into its lascivious gyrations.

He dipped his tongue into my roiling pussy, lapping up my juices, the way a cat laps milk. A spasm of pleasure shuddered up and down my body. He brought the smooth backside of his tongue against my clit, flicking it in and out. It was pleasant and soft, not enough to bring me to orgasm, but enough to keep me floating forever.

Then the tongue circled, alternating soft-smooth with rough-hard. Over and over soft-smooth rough-hard, soft-smooth rough-hard, soft-smooth rough-hard. Now I had to fight for control or I'd go over the edge and it would all be over. He was *my* slave. *I* would take what pleasure *I* wanted.

"Now," Master's voice boomed.

Steve moved his mouth upwards sucking all my juices into his mouth, all my pussy lips. And his own bottom lip massaged up and down my thrice-engorged clit. Over the edge I plunged, an orspasm jerking my body taut against my wrist restraints, then released, my body trembling, then taut again, then loose and trembling, then taut again and I swooned into glorious nothingness.

Steve's licking and sucking had brought all my available blood up into my cunt, but now as my orgasm faded, it drained down to my head. The men rotated me upright. Every one in the room was standing completely still as Master pressed a large vibrator against my sex while rubbing his hirsute chest against my tender nipples. I could feel another orgasm beginning to build.

But one man in the audience wasn't standing still. He

was moving about. His clothes were all black leather, pants and a shirt with large black snaps. His pants had a chrome snap at the waist. I had seen those movements before. Where...? Master's vibrator had me halfway to heaven. It was at a wedding. The photographer had been trying to get the perfect angle to record the couple cutting their wedding cake.

"Stop him," I yelled, jerking my head towards the photographer.

The photographer made the mistake of attempting to run and two strong pairs of hands held him tight. The Dungeon Master moved his muscle-bound frame towards them.

Delivering my report to Michael in the small law office boardroom was almost as much fun as being at the leather club the previous night had been. My tall and skinny assistant Eric Craigie was with us. Michael's assistant, a pretty girl, barely twenty was there taking notes. Every time I revealed a particularly salacious detail, Michael changed position to accommodate the bulge in his pants, while fighting to keep his expression neutral. The table was small. I could touch his hands. I could put my foot between his legs. One gentle caress and he'd cream his pants. One gentle foot-rub and he'd surrender all his power to me.

"Regrettably," I concluded, "I was unable to determine how the Cyber Culprit took the photos or recorded the video he posted to the internet."

"What about the photographer you captured?" the lawyer wanted to know.

I shook my head. "His equipment was extremely limited. Only capable of low quality low resolution images. Clearly not a match for the Cyber Culprit's postings."

"What happened to him?" Eric wanted to know. He was watching Michael's assistant, who was writing madly and trying to keep her head as close to her writing pad as possible.

I was tempted to play with the assistant's embarrassment, but instead told the truth, "I didn't stay to find out."

Michael smiled at me. "Thank you, Lee." At this point, he'd usually stand, but today he kept his seat. "In the interim, we've had another posting. This time from Jamaica."

He slid a series of photographs over to me. I recognized one as an aerial shot of Hedonism II, the notorious Caribbean sex resort. Others showed various people on the dance floor groping and fondling each other. As I finished with each, I passed it onto Eric. Several shots showed people taking selfies of each other on the beach or on a boat. The last one showed a nude and muscular man half lying, half sitting on a massage table. A woman was sucking his cock into her mouth. There was a line-up of women behind her, each watching intently what the woman in front of the massage table was doing."

Michael pointed to the last photograph, "There's a video of that as well."

"And they each…?" I asked.

Michael nodded.

"Can we see the video?"

Michael's assistant's face turned beet-red.

Michael shook his head, "Maybe later." His assistant looked relieved.

I tapped the photos. "Looks like Eric and I will be heading to Jamaica."

Michael nodded. "I hope your passports are up to date."

I glanced at Eric who nodded. "Both," I confirmed.

"Where are we at with the investigation?" Eric wanted to know.

What the fuck! Who cared where the investigation was?!? Just so long as it kept going. Just so long as my wardrobe, not to mention my bank account, was expanding. Just so long as I got to go to Jamaica. If we'd been alone, I'd have kicked Eric—yes there—and in other places as well.

But we weren't alone, so I smiled at Michael. "We have established that our quarry frequents a variety of venues including a bar, a swinger's club, an escort agency, a BDSM joint, a male strip club, and now a Caribbean resort. All of these have a sexual component. Investigations like these require dogged persistence. The Cyber Culprit will sooner, or later, make a mistake, and then we'll catch him."

I pointed to the photos on the table. "He's already becoming careless, taking photos of more and more people, at different times and places. Sooner or later, someone will have realized that they were being photographed and will be able to furnish us with a description of the criminal mastermind behind these attacks."

Michael nodded, apparently satisfied with my summary. I would deal with Eric later. Most weeks Hedo had its own leather night and I had a new riding crop that needed to be broken in.

Hedonism, Lusty Lee Log #6

Arriving at Hedonism II was like being swept into an alternate universe. The first hint was being separated from our suitcases by smiling Jamaican porters at the front. The second was the long marble check-in desk with blue art deco polka-dots on the wall behind. The third was being invited to enjoy the buffet even before we were properly registered. But the kicker was the buffet itself. Hot food, cold food, breads, cheeses and fruits. Chicken ranging from fried to stew to jerk, the latter being Jamaica's own invention. The odd couple was nude and few were wearing nothing more than skimpy bikinis. Nevertheless, no one took notice of how overdressed Eric and I were.

As soon as we stepped into to our room, both pairs of our eyes shot upward to check out the stories we'd heard about the mirrors in the ceilings above the beds. It was even larger than I'd imagined. Without a word, I stripped nude and flopped onto the bed. The firm mattress was cool against my round bottom as I stared up at the curly brown hair framing my slightly round face. I smiled as I batted my eyebrows to verify that my blue eyes still had sparkle and sizzle. Eric was only a moment behind me and jiggled my full breasts as he hit the bed. There we were, me a voluptuous five-foot five, he a scrawny six-foot three. With his red hair and green eyes, we were truly the oddest of odd pair. Next to Eric, it was clear I could afford to lose a few pounds. I resolved to go easy at the buffet and to burn more calories than I ingested.

I watched Eric shut his eyes. My assistant's male member wasn't huge, but it was more than adequate. Too bad it was flaccid and flopping to the right instead of being full and upright. I stared straight at his penis and by the force of my will, it started to engorge, steadily rising and moving to center. Eric was nominally my employee and so ostensibly off limits for sexual shenanigans, but we were at Hedo where we could be wicked for a week and no one need know. Eric's penis was now fully erect, his testicles tucked in tight and out of the way. I shut my eyes and imagined straddling his hips, slowly sliding myself down over him, feeling him caressing my pussy lips, feeling him fill my womanhood. As I slid down his last inch, he opened his eyes and stared up into my eyes. I leaned down to kiss him and he shut his eyes. I clenched my muscles lower down and began to rock my hips to pull him in and out. His eyes were open again and I knew that he was looking up into the mirror, watching the rhythm of my butt muscles clenching and releasing around him.

I woke up first, hornier than hell. Eric was still flaccid, still flopping right, but now he was gently snoring. Apparently he hadn't been dreaming of me the way I'd been dreaming of him. I started working on my notes of the illicit internet postings the Cyber Culprit had made from Hedonism. The photos seemed recent: groping and fondling in the disco, guests taking selfies and photos of each other on the beach, similar shots on a boat. And then there was the *pièce de résistance*: a nude and muscular man half lying, half sitting on a massage table enjoying a blow job, and a line-up of women each waiting her turn to suck his cock into her mouth. A video of the serial fellatio has also been posted and I watched it, making mental notes of each woman's technique.

My cellphone rang. It was Michael Rayburn, the lawyer who'd given me the assignment to track down the Cyber Culprit. I hesitated and the phone rang again; the assignment was extremely lucrative and fun. What Michael had given, he could take away. I picked up as the phone started to ring a third time.

As usual, Michael got straight to the point, "The Cyber Culprit is branching out: He's posted an app to allow people to protest loud commercials and amber alerts."

"How does it work?" I asked.

"You remember all the protests when the police took over radios and TVs with a loud claxon when they were trying to find missing children? There were a couple of accidents when drivers were startled by their radios suddenly blaring out the amber alarm?"

"Yes." I had almost hit the guardrail myself.

"And how commercials are almost always louder than the program being broadcast?"

"Uh, uh."

"Well, the App allows users to randomly triple or quadruple the volume on phones used by TV executives, or the executives of the companies advertising, or the CRTC, the regulatory body in charge of radio and TV, and anyone else connected with amber alerts, even the police."

My voice had stirred Eric so I put the phone on speaker. Michael brought Eric up to speed and the two men were quickly immersed in nerd talk.

I busied myself with selecting and putting on a red bikini. Over this I put on a light shirt, unbuttoned down the front and a pair of very short shorts. I selected sandals to wear and inspected myself in the mirror. I was obviously a guest of the resort but still dressed respectfully enough for my foray back to the front desk.

Finally Eric and Michael rang off.

I took a pair of sunglasses — spyglasses really — and

fitted them onto Eric's nose.

*****

Lee put the sunglasses too low on my nose, so I pushed then higher and looked at myself in the mirror. They were mega cool—horn rimmed, large framed, very retro. The monochrome black frames were perfectly matched to my red hair and green eyes. There were mirrors over each eye allowing me to see behind. I turned around and looked Lee up and down as she came forward to touch the frame next to my right ear.

"There's a camera," she indicated.

In the upper right of the inside of my glasses, the image she'd just captured of herself flashed briefly.

"You take a picture," she directed.

I aimed the glasses at her breasts, felt for the button by my ear and pressed. The shot was perfect.

"The one by your left ear takes a shot behind you."

I felt for the left button and pressed it. An image of the room flashed briefly on my left visual field. "Is this what the Cyber Culprit used?"

She shook her head. "It's too low resolution. But it will give us an idea of where he was when he took the photos he put up onto the internet."

She stepped back to admire me and I reached for my swimsuit.

Her hand on my wrist stopped me. "Most of the shots were from the nude beach. You're not allowed to wear clothes. Go see what you can find out."

I dropped my swimsuit back into my suitcase and snapped a few more pictures.

She pushed me towards the door. "Have fun with your new toy. Just make sure you get pictures from every vantage point used by the Cyber Culprit."

The beach at Hedonism was divided into two. To the south was the prude side. There swimsuits were worn and the crowd tended to be younger. The north beach was the nude beach, announced by a sign proclaiming "Nude Beach Only. No Photography." Beneath the official sign was another, hand-painted, "No clothing allowed". Here almost everyone was over thirty, some well over. There was not a stich of clothing in sight.

What there was here was wall-to-wall tits and ass and cock and pussy. Some of the women had their legs spread wide so that you could look straight up. Several couples were engaged in PDAs—public displays of affection. Lots of kissing, many hands caressing breasts, several hands caressing genitals. On the raft anchored off shore, one gentleman had his head between his wife's thighs and her moans could be heard all along the beach.

As I strolled along the beach, a man in his mid-forties waved me over to the lounge chairs he and his wife were sitting on. He had a noticeable paunch, she was voluptuous, a long thing strand of pubic hair extending down towards her genitals.

He stood and held out his hand, "Hi, I'm Jeremy." He gestured towards his wife, "This is Jennifer."

She stood too and kissed my cheek. Her breasts and belly pressed against me and I could feel her pubic hair tickle my thigh. She stepped back and they were both smiling at me.

I held my hand out to her, "Eric."

She raised her eyebrows. It was clear that she wanted more than a handshake. I swallowed, bent to kiss her cheek, muttered something about 'maybe later' and got out of there as quickly as I could. Changes between my legs made it hard to walk fast. I glanced back through the mirrors inside my sunglasses. Jeremy and Jennifer were noticeably disappointed.

All along the beach, guests were lounging, many reading, several texting. The readers were divided almost equally between those with paper books and those using a tablet or eReader of some sort. Every so often a cellphone would come out to take a selfie, usually with a mate, sometimes with a new-found friend. The picture-takers seemed to always choose an angle which ensured that no other guest would be in the background. I used my back and forward cameras to capture as many images of those taking pictures of themselves as I could.

And then I saw the massage table where the Cyber Culprit had found a line of women waiting for their chance. But today the line-up was composed of men. A few feet further up the beach and I saw what they were lined up for.

Two women were kneeling on top of the table and loosely embracing each other. Behind each woman was a man gently caressing the female bottoms interspersed with reaching around to caress their breasts. Occasionally these men would glance up and surreptitiously insert a hand between the thighs of the woman in front of him.

The women were kissing each other passionately, tongues flicking in and out. Low moans escaped their mouths, especially then hands caressed between their thighs. The woman on the right was white, but well tanned. She was skinny, even skinnier than me. Her breasts were small, but from what I could see, her nipples more than made up for her diminutive mammaries. The woman on the left was African American, but light skinned. She was amply rounded, especially her breasts which were two good handfuls for the man behind her.

A stirring between my legs reminded me that I had a job to do and I snapped a few pictures from the same vantage point the Cyper Culprit had used. The men who'd been caressing the women ceded their spots to the next pair in line and I stepped into the line, touching my left ear to snap a few shots of the spot which the Cyber Culprit would have occupied.

*****

Satisfied that Eric would be absorbed in his task for at

least the next hour, I returned to the art deco front desk. Michael Rayburn, ever the efficient lawyer, had cleared the way for me. "What can we do for you, Miss Lee?" was the only thing the woman standing behind the desk wanted to know.

I smiled back at her. "I need to know the names of all current guests who were here eight days ago." The Cyber Culprit's photos had been taken then. Most guests stay only a week, but I was hoping to get lucky.

She quickly set about obtaining the information I'd requested. I stared at the art deco polka dots as she worked, feeling a twinge of nostalgia. Three years ago, when Peter had brought me here, the entrance had consisted of an informal table with a large ceramic mural of the resort's name surrounded by large-lipped women. Pity that this hippie vibe was now deemed passé by the new owners.

The woman behind the desk handed me two guest profiles. The first profile indicated that the couple had been here three times before and that they were enthusiastic participants in the swingers' lifestyle. The other couple had visited only once before. They were both teachers, here primarily for scuba diving and definitely not part of the swinger lifestyle. They loved eroticism and the hedonistic experience, but wanted to keep it between themselves.

I tapped the profiles against the marble top and thanked the receptionist.

She smiled. Black skin, white teeth, red lips. A beauty from the Garden of Eden. "Is there anything else I can do for you?"

I nodded. "What percentage of your guests are swingers?"

She shrugged. "It varies by week. About thirty percent overall."

Back in our room, I shed my clothes and wrapped a towel around me. Down on the nude beach, I plopped the towel down on the first vacant lounge chair and instantly felt the sun warm my body all the way inside. Further up the beach, there was a line of men leading towards the massage hut. Eric's red hair was at the front of the line.

As I ambled up, the women kneeling on top of the massage table separated and stepped down. There was a collective groan from the assembled males, most loudly from Eric.

I put my arm around Eric. "Poor, baby."

The men behind were grumbling, not sure whether to stay or whether to go. An Asian woman strolled behind the massage table and I made eye contact with her. After an exchange of gestures, she understood that I was inviting her atop the massage table. She shrugged 'why not' and we both climbed on top of the table.

Eric hesitated, unsure whether to move behind me or behind the Asian woman. I angled my head to behind her as I took her hands. "I'm Lee."

"Seiko."

Her eyes were dark brown, her hair long, black and straight. I estimated her age to be well below thirty, but sometimes it was hard to tell with Japanese women. She was slim, her breasts gentle rises on her chest. I touched her nipples and the small dark buttons immediately hardened as she gasped. In return, she lightly danced her fingers across my breasts, sending frissons of joy below every time she brushed against my nipples.

Other hands were touching our breasts, larger, firmer hands. So I moved my hands lower, across her hard torso. Her belly button was so small I couldn't fit a finger in and she didn't react when I touched it so I moved lower, playing with her remaining tuft of pubic hair. Her hands had moved lower as well as I felt other hands squeezing and kneading my bottom.

She kissed me then. Her mouth was small and delicate, her lips fitting between mine. I flicked my tongue along the separation between her lips. They were closed, but she puckered so that I could run my tongue back and forth across their entire surface. Then her tongue was a little protrusion between our lips. I made my tongue a small point and our tongues met. Then she gradually opened her mouth and more and more of my tongue was touching hers.

The man behind me was doing a good job of caressing my breasts and rotating his fingers around my nipples. He released my breast and began kissing down my spine, massaging my butt and trailing his fingers up and down my legs. All and good. But *between* my legs there was only longing —

And then Seiko's delicate little fingers were there, catering to my most pressing needs. Her fingers frolicked up and down my pussy lips, rubbing, feathering, tugging in succession. Then one finger lightly tapped my clit and a full orchestra began to rouse my full passions.

I dipped my finger inside Seiko. She was small, her pussy lips so delicate as to be barely perceptible. But she was warm and hot and moist and my finger slipped easily inside. Then I felt another finger approach. Eric's?!? and I swiftly removed my hand.

At the same moment, two fingers pressed inside me and headed straight for my g-spot. Whoever it was behind me knew exactly what he was doing. He stroked and tapped my g-spot and in a moment I was on the brink. I grabbed Seiko's hips, pulled her close to me, then slid my hands lower to her butt. I hugged us close together and our pubic bones began to grind circles against each other.

She had pulled her lips back so that she could breathe through her mouth, but our tongues were still sliding and swirling around each other.

The two fingers inside my cunt tapped twice firmly and I exploded all around them. The first contraction locked my legs together. The second made my spine ramrod straight. And then my muscles were jelly and I had to hold onto Seiko to stop from falling off the table. Heat was slowly spreading out from my pelvis and upwards. Little bursts were detonating inside my cunt, around my ass, up my spine and all over my tits. Then my cunt became an inferno and wave after wave of joy and delight roared up my spine. I ejaculated all over the fingers inside me. I was floating inside whiteness. All I could see were bright lights.

*****

As Lee hugged Seiko against her, I reached around my glasses with my left hand and snapped a few pictures of the festivities. My cock was throbbing, but all that seemed to be permitted was to touch the little goddess in front of me. Her back was the stem of flower, long and exquisite. Her hair was as soft as silk. Between her legs, her pussy lips were so tiny that I could barely feel them, but the way she shuddered against my fingers, I knew that she was enjoying my touch.

I glided my hands up the outsides of her thighs then slightly to center over the subtle and graceful rise of her buttocks. Continuing upwards, her hips guided my hands gently outwards but her waist led them back towards center. She was truly full of charm and beauty, fit for an Emperor! And now, at least for this moment, I was that *Emperor!*

My cock throbbed again, demanding to be put into the heart of my latest imperial possession. Or at the very least to have my hand jerk him off. But I took a deep breath, glided my hand back over her buttocks and into the heavenly space between her legs.

Opposite Seiko, Lee was totally consumed by animal lust. As I touched the exquisite Japanese jewel in front of me, I was not only touching her, not only arousing Seiko, but arousing Lee as well. My cocked throbbed again, even more insistently.

I slid a finger inside, provoking an even stronger shudder. I slid my finger back and forth. Her breathing quickened, became shallower. I rotated my finger facing downward and was about to pull it back when her pussy clamped tight against it. I couldn't move it. I tried to pull my finger back, but she had it tight. I flexed my finger downward and there was something round and hard inside. I could only move my finger very very slightly, could only lightly massage this little button.

As I massaged Seiko's internal button, we were suddenly all together: me, Seiko, Lee, and the man behind her. I was teetering on the edge of control, Seiko was a deep river, ready to burst its banks, Lee was a raging inferno about to explode. The other man was glorying in his power, lusting for more.

Seiko gasped again. Her body went rigid. I felt contractions, rapid little waves against my finger, then softer and slower. She relaxed and I pulled my finger out, then slid it back in. She gasped again. She was elegant, even in orgasm.

Seiko and Lee were both still. Then there was shuffling and the two women separated and climbed down off the massage table. The other man and I moved away. Two other women climbed onto the table and two other men moved forward.

Back in our room, Lee and I uploaded the pictures I'd taken with my glasses into her laptop. Her mumbles as she went through them were interspersed with the occasional "good".

When she got to Jeremy and Jennifer, she turned the laptop towards me. "Who are they?" she wanted to know.

"A couple."

"Swingers?"

I nodded. "They tried to pick me up."

She turned the laptop back towards herself and continued her mumblings interspersed with one or two grunts of approval.

When Lee got to the shot of Seiko's back and the side of her head, she pressed several buttons on her laptop and announced that "I'm deleting these."

I shrugged. I still had a copy inside the glasses. "Any luck at the front desk?"

Lee nodded. "Two couples are still here." She slid over a guest profile. "George and Sally don't swing. They're teachers, mostly into scuba diving. We'll interview them this afternoon."

An hour later, after we'd both had a shower, it was time for our interviews

I was interviewing George by the chessboard, Lee was talking to Sally back up in their room. *The* chessboard is almost fifteen feet square with pieces sized to match. For example the black king, behind which I was standing, was almost three feet high. George and I were alone in the large grass-covered courtyard where the chessboard was located.

I showed him the recent internet posting which had featured them. The photos were relatively tame, just two nude people in a group of other nude people. "Were you aware of these being posted?" I asked.

George nodded, picked up the pawn in front of his Queen and lifted it one space forward. Not an outright stupid move, but it was clear he was no grandmaster. "We found out a few days ago," he said. "Sally was devastated about what her friends would think. So we decided to stay an extra week, let things calm down. I agreed to the extra week, because the way she was talking, she might never agree to come back."

I moved my King's pawn two spaces forward. "Has she calmed down?"

He nodded and pushed his Queen's Bishop two spaces forward. Now that *was* a stupid move. "Some of her friends found out. Most were sympathetic and opened up to Sally about their sexual predilections. So maybe now she'll relax, be more open, be unafraid of who she is."

I mimicked his move with my King's Bishop. I was going to have to work hard to lose the game. "Do you have any idea as to how the photos were taken?"

He shook his head and moved his Bishop again.

I picked up the pawn which had been in front of my King's Bishop and deposited it on the square two spaces forward. If this game was going to end any time soon, I needed to open paths of attack against my King. I wanted to lose the game so George would play me again if need be.

"Any idea as to why anybody would want to hurt you?"

He shook his head and moved the pawn in front of his King's Rook one space forward. I suppressed a sigh. This game was going to take a very, *very* long time.

*****

Sally's room was nicer and larger than ours. It must be one of the newly renovated ones. I estimated her to be almost forty. She was blonde, just slightly overweight, but less in need of a diet than I was at this point. Attractive. Full figure.

When she had opened the door, I'd extended my hand and introduced myself, "I'm Lee and I'm investigating the internet postings." She hadn't said anything but she had gestured for me to come in and now we were sitting on a bench by the window.

I showed her the postings. "What can you tell me about these?"

She shrugged. "Suddenly they were there. My friends were sending me emails about how they never thought *I* would be caught in a place like that. It was devastating."

"Do you have any idea as to how the photos were taken?"

She shook her head, becoming more mournful by the minute.

"Were you aware of the photos being taken?"

She shook her head.

"Is there anyone who would want to hurt you?"

She thought about that for a moment, then slowly shook her head. Her cellphone rang. She glanced at it. "Sorry, I have to take this."

For the next twenty minutes I listened to her discussing next week's grocery list with her daughter. She rang off, briefly checked for texts and then turned back to me.

"Has anyone contacted you about the photos?" I asked.

She shook her head, looking like she was about to burst into tears. "Just my friends. I never, *never* want to come back to a nudist resort!"

She burst into tears and I looked around for a tissue.

Veronica and Adam, described in their Us-Book profile as being enthusiastic participants in the swingers' lifestyle, proved to be a more difficult nut to crack. The front desk had told me that they weren't scheduled to leave for another five days, so we had time. I wanted to swing with them, both for the sheer joy of it and because, in my experience, people who've had sex with me were more likely to open up to me. Their profile showed them as Vikings participating in a live-action-role-play.

Veronica was an inch shorter than me at five-foot four and much skinnier, except for her breasts which were big and round, presumably as the result of surgical enhancement. I estimated her to be in her early thirties. Nothing jiggled as she walked, not even her breasts, so she obviously worked out. She was blonde, her hair bright — whether from being in the sun or from chemicals I couldn't tell, because she was completely shaven down below. She had a tattoo of a flying dragon — red, green and purple — on the bottom right side of her torso, its mouth opening towards her sex.

Adam was a good six-feet tall, just slightly shorter than Eric. Blonde like his wife, but like his wife, not a strand of hair other than on his head. He had the same dragon tattoo, but on his left side. His eyes sparkled blue and he smiled at everyone who looked his way. It was a swinger's smile of invitation, but he seemed to genuinely enjoy people. He was of only medium build, but fit and muscular.

Eric and I trailed them around the resort, waiting for the perfect opportunity to insinuate ourselves into their lives. But in the exercise room, Veronica and Adam immediately climbed on the treadmill, set the speed to high, ran like demons and then left abruptly before either Eric or I could sidle next to them. After lunch, they climbed onto two paddle boards. By the time Eric and I had mastered even the basic strokes without falling off into the water, they had zoomed past us and back onto shore. After an intense game of volleyball, Eric and I were too out of breath to attempt any banter. At the tennis courts, Veronica and Adam immediately hooked up with two pros. Eric and I took to the next court and hit the ball back and forth. After their lesson, Veronica and Eric left and the pros intercepted us with the offer of a lesson before we could 'just happen' to fall into step with our quarry. At least I was losing weight.

The morning of our third day of cat and mouse, Veronica and Adam had given us the slip in the spa. Eric and I retreated to the buffet to lick our wounds. Halfway through my bowl of fresh pineapple, Eric asked, "Why don't we just ask them to swing with us?"

"Because then they'll think that we had sex with them just so they'd talk to us."

"Aren't they going to figure that out as soon as we start asking questions?"

"No, because—" Because at that very moment, Veronica and Adam sat down next to us. Or rather they sat down with us, Veronica between Eric and I, Adam to my right. We were all wearing skimpy bathing suits.

I cast a triumphant smile in Eric's direction but it was wiped off my face with Veronica's first question: "How come everywhere we look, we see you two?"

Eric smiled in my direction, "Because—"

I kicked Eric under the table and shrugged. "Just coincidence I guess." I reached out to shake her hand. "I'm Lee."

She squeezed my hand at the same moment as Adam kissed my cheek. He smelled of mint and jasmine.

Veronica placed her other hand on Eric's forearm. "I'm Veronica," she told him.

"Eric."

She let go of my hand and I turned to Adam. Our noses were barely an inch apart. Would he kiss my lips, would he—

"So what kind of fun are the two of you having at Hedo?" asked Veronica.

I looked at Eric, "Swimming and snorkeling."

"Dancing at the Disco," Eric chimed in.

"And paddle-boarding," added Adam.

"Anything more adventurous?" Veronica wanted to know.

"Adventurous?" asked Eric. I was proud of the mixture of interest and ignorance he'd injected into his question.

"Swinging," murmured Adam into my ear.

I leaned into Adam making sure that both Eric and Veronica noticed.

Veronica turned into Eric, brushing her breasts against his arm. "Exploring your limits with another couple," she explained.

"Sounds like fun," I enthused, letting my left hand drop to Adam's thigh.

Veronica licked around the outer edge of Eric's ear lobe. "What about you?" she whispered.

Eric swallowed and nodded.

As newbies to the swinging scene — me ostensibly, Eric in reality — we negotiated swinging together in their room with its two queen-sized beds.

Inside their room, Adam turned to Eric, "Why don't we watch the ladies first?"

Before Eric could ask what the ladies would be doing that they'd be watching, Veronica took me into her arms and planted a wet kiss directly on my mouth. Not wanting to miss the opportunity, I swiftly loosened Veronica's top and gently squeezed her surgically enhanced boobs. They were kinda squishy but not unpleasantly so. If I didn't know what I was squeezing, I might have assumed they were real. But the tightness of the skin was a bit of a giveaway. On the plus side, her large nipples were as real as they were responsive to my touch. Veronica let her hands drift lower. In one practiced touch, she caressed my clit and slipped a finger right inside. I broke off the kiss, she stepped back and we were no longer touching. We heaved air into our lungs. Our eyes were locked on each other, were locking out the universe.

"Since they're newbies, maybe we should keep it vanilla?" Adam proposed.

Veronica, her eyes still locked on mind, nodded.

Adam gently pulled me onto the bed with him. He was already nude and in short order so was I. His cock was fully engorged—a full ten inches and bounteous girth to match. I could dimly see Eric and Veronica exploring each other's bodies on the other bed but a kiss from Adam focused my attention.

Adam pulled me onto my back. I guessed that vanilla meant missionary, male on top. But Adam's kisses were definitely of the *French* vanilla variety. He pulled his mouth back and his tongue flicked into the spots on either side of my mouth where my upper and bottom lips met. Unique and very sexy. I flicked my tongue out to his to indicate my gratitude. His cock was between my legs, touching and teasing my clit and pussy lips. Ordinarily I'd be urging him inside but tonight I wanted to learn everything Adam's previous lovers had taught him.

Then he kissed my neck. It looks great in the movies, especially as a vampire submission kink, but doesn't do anything for me. Then his mouth kissed down my belly, again, not a hot spot, and he moved quickly along. He flicked his tongue into my belly button and I tensed. He flicked twice more, then realized he was tickling, not turning me on. What a wonderfully perceptive lover!

His lips gripped my pubic hair and pulled up. I felt his nose suck my scents into him. What was he learning about me? He mashed and rotated the skin over my pubic promontory, rubbing my pussy lips against each other and up and around my clit. Now I wanted him, I really wanted him and it took all my willpower to stop me from pushing my pussy down towards his cock, his glorious cock!

And then my reward—his tongue flicked against my clit. Just the right amount of power to send a jolt up my spine, just the right amount of lubrication to protect my tender knob.

Next he quickly dragged his tongue down the outside of my right pussy lip, curling my toes, then little bites towards my right hip puckering pain into my hip. The pain subsides into a fluttering delight as he kissed up the inside my thighs.

Adam slid his body back up along mine, his touch so fine that he did not scrape, not even slightly, but he still managed to apply just enough pressure to keep sending signals into my pussy preparing her for the fireworks to come. Then he was kissing my lips and I could taste my pungent readiness mixed in with the mint and jasmine from his visit to the spa.

His cock was just inside my pussy lips which, now moistened, were licking the tip of his cock. I wiggled my bum to lick his cock some more, but he was still concentrated on my mouth. His kisses were warm and succulent, but now I wanted a more direct route to pleasure. I withdrew my tongue and half shut my mouth.

Adam got the point immediately and his cock slowly and gradually pressed itself into my pussy opening, then inched its way further and further into my love canal. Then he pulled an inch out, then quickly an inch back in, sending a frisson of pleasure up my spine. He continued these little in-and-outs until he was fully inside me. Then he returned to his optimal depth. He was half in and half out and making little jerking thrusts rubbing first up one side of my g-spot, then down the other. I could feel my inner spot swelling, sending pulses down into the soles of my feet.

Then Adam left her, thrusting himself all the way inside until our pubic bones pressed against each other. He angled his body to the right and rotated his pubic bone against mine, pulling my clit this way and that, rubbing her against him, against my vulva, against him, against my vulva in ever ascending spirals.

Just as I couldn't climb any higher without falling off, he pulled himself almost all the way out and then slammed his sword all the way into my sheath. Out, then in in furious thrusts. It wasn't as direct against my pleasure spots but his exertion, his assertion of his pleasure over mine bound us, our bodies, our genitals, closer and closer together. His frantic attack rubbed his chest against my nipples, joining all my hard little knobs into one feverish triangle. I looked up into the mirror to watch his butt pump pleasure into both of us. Squeeze in the center to plunge in, squeeze on the outside to pull back out.

He plunged in and out and I almost came. But then he stopped. I tried to rock my hips against his, but he held me tight. Then he slowly rotated gathering ever and ever hotter frissons of pleasure inside my clit. Each rotation spilled expanding pleasure into my cunt. This churning pleasure was about to burst when he held me still a second time.

We started to breathe in unison. I grabbed his chest and dug my nails into his nipples. He held himself up with one hand and squeezed one of my breasts with the other. It hurt, it was heavenly, all at the same time. I gave up first and dropped my hands. He had won. I was his. Adam would keep me imprisoned inside this pleasure palace forever.

He began a series of long slow strokes with his cock. Almost out, then sliding back all the way until our pubic bones lightly kissed. I tried to lift my head up to kiss his lips, but he kept himself high atop his arms, the twinkles in his eyes laughing down at me. He lifted himself out, then slid himself back in. But now not all the way back in, just half way. I knew what was coming, the short quick little jabs against my g-spot. And my lover didn't disappoint. Short little nudges up one side, short little tugs down the other.

Then he twitched halfway through a nudge and suddenly, without warning, the roiling pleasure which had been gathering inside my cunt *burst* throughout my body. The first contraction rocketed up my spine and erupted inside my head. Before I could recover, my cunt exploded, into my butt, down my thighs. Then everything gathered into red-hot jolts up my spine, into my tits, down my legs, frying my toes. My body was spasming uncontrollably, I couldn't tell where or how or why. The pleasure was too, *too* much to bear!

And then the spasms subsided. I couldn't move, but at least I wasn't being stimulated beyond my control. I shut my eyes and breathed relief. When I opened my eyes, I was looking directly up at his. They sparkled laughter, mocking me. But before I could plot my revenge, his cock smashed into me. Long, hard strokes and I couldn't do anything. Long hard strokes plowing into me. Long hard strokes and I couldn't feel anything. And then Adam shuddered, erupting inside me. *That* I felt.

In the afterglow, I turned on my side towards the other bed and Adam spooned against my backside. Eric was on the bottom with Veronica on top pumping hard, sweat dribbling down her back. Eric's legs were in the center, between hers and he used his long arms to squeeze her bum when her rhythms called out for them to be pressed as hard into each other as they could be. Then he traced his fingers around inside between her wide-open butt crack.

Veronica pushed herself up on her arms, her tits dangling. "Put your fingers inside," she begged. She extended her tongue, a drop of saliva perched to fall. Eric brought his right hand under her tongue and her saliva dribbled down his longest finger. Then his finger was back between her pumping glutes, tracing a circle. Seconds later his lanky flexibility paid off and his finger disappeared deep inside her ass. She circled a moment to accommodate him, then resumed her desperate pumping.

Eric moved his hand around as if attempting a series of esoteric yoga poses. Veronica's breathing was a mixture of gasps and yelps. Then she shuddered almost to a stop and Eric had to pump from below. In a moment, his mixed martial arts training paid off with a blood-curdling climax from Veronica. He transitioned her to her back and a few swift pumps later he too shuddered to a stop.

In the flush of four orgasms, I asked Veronica whether she was aware of the photos that had been posted by the Cyber Culprit.

She nodded, "We just ignore stuff like that."

"Any idea who took the photos or posted them?"

She shook her head. "Why do people do such things?"

"We were hoping you could tell us."

She shook her head. I turned to Adam. He shook his head as well.

Back in our own room, our phones were ringing madly. Eric got to his phone first and I picked up two snippets of him discussing the Cyber Culprit's Amber Alert App with Michael Rayburn before I could fish out my own phone.

I pressed to answer but I was too late and all I got was a message to call the front desk. As I listened to the outgoing dialing tones, I got the impression that the lawyer was extremely upset about the effects of the Culprit's app. The front desk picked up, "Miss Lee?"

"Yes?"

"The group leader who was here when the internet photos were taken is coming back with another group next week."

"Thanks."

Eric and I rang off at the exact same time but he spoke first. "Mr. Rayburn says all hell is breaking loose and wants us back in Toronto on the next flight."

"Is it about the App?" Eric nodded confirmation and I dialed Michael, taking a deep breath. He picked up on the first ring. "The leader of the group who had a lot of their photos posted is coming back next week," I told him before he could say anything. "I can't really help with the App. Why don't I stay here and send Eric back to Toronto?"

"Fine. Good thinking." Rayburn sounded harassed.

"Bye." But he'd already rung off.

Eric started to madly stuff his belongings into his suitcase. I relaxed on the bed looking up at myself in the mirror. Another, *all expenses paid*, week in Hedo!

Hedo II, Lusty Lee Log #7

I had Hedonism II, the notorious Jamaican sex resort, all to myself. Eric, my nerdy assistant, was back up north in Toronto, and my next interview target was not due to arrive for a few days. Paradise!

Most people who come to Hedo come as singles or as couples. But some, usually hardcore swingers, come as a group. It was the leader of one of these groups I was tasked with interviewing. He had been at Hedo when the Cyber Culprit had taken the photos now clandestinely posted to the internet. But the leader, and his group, wasn't due to arrive for two days.

So I had slept in until noon and now I had two days of freedom to gorge on the food, laze on the beach, and scope out the best-hung men before I had to get back to work. As I stripped off my nightshirt, I caught a glimpse of myself in the mirror. My belly and thighs were fat and the muscles on my arms were saggy. I slowly turned around in front of the mirror. Maybe a bit of dieting and a few workouts in the gym and in the disco were more in order than gorging and lazing. I searched for my pink sports bra.

In the gym, I climbed on one of the treadmills and began to run. For the first three minutes, I concentrated on the complex controls. Then I had the right speed set and looked up into the mirror in front of me. Ten minutes of hard running tensed my muscles, pulling in some of my belly fat. For twenty-nine years of age, I was fit enough and the arrangement of muscle and fat on my five-foot five frame meant that my bosom was ample and that my hips spread sensuously out but that my thighs narrowed back in. My face was pretty enough, a bit round, but blue eyes and curly brown hair made my head a generally attractive package. I flashed myself a smile and was pleased to see sparkle in my eyes. I smiled again when I saw that I was beginning to sweat and my now translucent Tshirt was pressing against my pink sports bra. I caught a few guys glancing at the pumping glutes under my pink spandex shorts and I smiled again.

When I was tired of looking at myself, the Jamaican gym attendant racing around the gym in his butt-cupping shorts kept me amused. He topped up our water bottles, wiped all exposed surfaces clean and replaced the free weights in their proper order. Even so, after twenty minutes, running had become boring and I cast my eyes about for a more pleasurable calorie-burning method. There were free weights, good for overall fitness, but I'd never mastered the moves. The stationary bikes were a poor excuse for the real thing—why should I pedal my heart out and get nowhere? The stationary gym equipment was too much like work and besides there were the adjustments and constant sitting down and getting up. All-in-all boring and annoying. And then there he was, just outside the window, a big black guy languidly playing pool—billiards—by himself. Tall and muscular, big belly, like a football lineman. He was exactly what I needed, someone who'd make me do all the work.

I hopped off the treadmill and strolled outside to watch him play. He sunk one shot, then two. He was wearing a green tank top that showed off his muscular arms while minimizing his belly. His long shorts were black. His head and face were clean-shaven, gleaming in the sunlight. He caught me looking at him as he lined up his third shot which would require him to nudge the ball just right. All his strength was concentrated into his face as he readied to shoot. Handsome, almost ferocious. He made the shot. His face relaxed into a smile as he watched me watching him. He muffed an easy tap in.

He handed the cue stick to me. "Bubba." His accent was American. Maybe he really *was* a lineman.

I smiled at him. "Lee." Then I pretended to concentrate on the shot. It was an easy shot; the cue ball was lined up directly in front of a ball just in front of the corner pocket. I lined the cue tip up directly in the center of the white cue ball, then moved it slightly off center. The cue ball hit the cushion, missing my 'target' ball entirely.

I handed the cue back to Bubba, but he shook his head and motioned for me to take another shot. I shrugged and wiggled my butt as I lined up a difficult shot. He shook his head and motioned for me towards an easier shot.

"But how can I?" I protested.

Bubba moved around behind me and placed his hands on mine to guide the shot. I made sure to brush my breast against his arm as he moved into position. I angled the cue stick back and forth towards the center of the cue ball. My butt was swaying too, brushing up against his shorts. Then I let the shot go and the target ball plopped into the center of the pocket.

I turned to Bubba to celebrate and his chest was right in front of my nose. I gave him a hug. There was something starting to protrude under his shorts.

I stepped back and flashed him a smile. "Double or nothing." This was vague because we weren't playing for anything, but it did invite a come-back from Bubba.

"But we aren't playing for anything," he protested.

"Next person to miss a shot takes their shirt off."

He smiled and nodded. I lined up and sunk my shot. It wasn't a difficult shot, but it was more difficult than the one I'd missed earlier. Bubba looked at me quizzically. But I missed my next shot and his smile returned—full white teeth, eyes twinkling appreciatively—as he watched me lift my Tshirt over my head. I wiggled my breasts belly-dancer style and he laughed.

He made a difficult shot, then muffed an easy one. The *game* we were playing was definitely *not* billiards.

He started to remove his Tshirt, but I laid my hands on top of his. "Let me."

He dropped his hands and I moved my right leg between his as I grabbed the bottom of his tank top and then slowly slid it up his chest. I caressed his nipples and they were immediately hard little buttons. Something pressed against my thigh. "I can't lift your shirt any higher," I apologized. My fingers continued to circle his nipples as I moved my leg back and forth against his protuberance.

Bubba moaned, then suddenly remembered that we were in public. He stepped back, pulled his shirt over his head and held it in front of his shorts. "Your shot," he reminded me.

I missed the shot. He watched with rapt devotion as I began to remove my sports bra. I stopped and shook my head. "I don't think topless is allowed here."

Hedo didn't actually enforce non-nudity, but it did express a preference that it be restricted to the nude beach. Bubba motioned to my shorts. I turned sideways and pulled them down the side to let him have a good look at my thigh and the curve of my buttock. I wondered if he'd noted the lack of panty lines.

I turned back to Bubba and pulled my shorts up tight, allowing a hint of a camel toe to form around my genitals. "If you want to collect, you'll have to come up to my room." I slapped my room key onto the top of the rail and then stepped back.

We both looked down at the cheeky slogan on the key card: "Get a room". So we did. He slowly picked up the key card. I scampered away, but not too fast. I didn't want to wear him out.

At the stairs up to my room, I paused and looked back. Judging from the look on Bubba's face, he'd been enjoying watching my rump. Pause one, pause two and when Bubba was almost next to me, I climbed the stairs, swaying my hips back and forth in an exaggeratedly seductive fashion.

At my door, I wanted to dash in and jump onto the bed, but Bubba had the key, so instead, I pressed my backside against the door. Bubba had to press close to insert the key, so I fondled the front of his shorts. Definitely my favorite something! Bubba fumbled with the key and I slid my hands up the bottom of his baggy shorts and halfway up his tree-trunk of a thigh before the door popped open. I stumbled backward and had to let go of him.

He stood in the doorway, just outside the threshold. I

reached under my sports bra, pulled it outwards, then up and over my head, jiggling my ample breasts free. Two quick strides and Bubba was on me, his hands reaching for my breasts.

But I stepped back and wagged my finger at him. "All you've won is the right to look." The door clicked shut behind him.

He pointed back and forth between my shorts and his and I nodded, smiling. In a moment, I was nude, my pubic hair matted against my skin. He was down to a bright orange thong that was barely able to contain his rising manhood.

I pointed to his thong. "Remove your thong and you can touch my breasts."

He did and his cock sprang forth, now fully erect. It was slightly blacker than the rest of him, except the tip which was slightly lighter. He had no pubic hair, in fact not a single hair anywhere on his body. His hands were warm around my breasts and his palms on my nipples made me cry for joy.

It took all my willpower to remove his hands from my breasts. "If you lie down on the bed, you can touch my breasts all you want, but nothing else. I however can do anything I want."

He looked back and forth between me, the bed and the mirror on the ceiling. "Nothing kinky," he temporized. Typical man—wants the crazy white bitch, but not the baggage.

"I won't tie you," I told him.

That seemed to satisfy Bubba and he climbed onto the king sized bed. He positioned himself at an angle so that he would fit, and spread his legs. I climbed up between his thighs. Every inch I moved forward, his penis seemed to grow an inch longer. By the time I kissed the tip of his penis, he was rock hard and throbbing. I put both hands around his shaft. I couldn't touch the tips of my fingers to my palms, so I couldn't estimate his girth. But he was almost fourteen inches long!

I took the tip of his penis into my mouth and slid a few

inches down. He was hot on my hands, even hotter inside my mouth. My fingers moved up and down the rest of his shaft. I felt his hands gently caress my hair and I pulled back off him. "No touching!" I reminded him with a light slap to his belly.

He nodded and dropped his hands back to the mattress. I swallowed his tip again, managing to get slightly more of him into my mouth before I felt myself start to gag. In a moment, I managed to coordinate my hands and mouth into a regular rhythm up and down his shaft. He tasted sweat and coconut. The first time he groaned, I let go.

I pushed his legs together and climbed on top, shuffling forward until my pussy was just above the tip of his cock. "You can touch my breasts, but nothing else," I reminded him. I started to slide down his cock and felt myself expand around him. I shut my eyes to concentrate on accommodating his girth.

When I was halfway down his shaft, I felt his hands on my breasts, at first just the tips of his fingers softly tracing patterns. Then he started to gently knead. This was a welcome distraction as I urged myself inch by inch down his shaft. I had yet to feel real pleasure; that would have to wait until I was fully relaxed around his grandeur.

I opened my eyes and waited until his hands left my breasts. "Tell me what I feel like," I directed. "Keep talking until I tell you to stop."

"You feel warm and hot. Soft above, tight below." Large hands squeezed my breasts.

I slid further and felt the tip of his cock touch up inside my tummy. I slid him in further and my tummy was uncomfortable. I took a deep breath, then another and was able to relax.

"Wet and hot sliding down. Hair tickling."

Hair tickling!?! Was I almost down? I sighed in relief as the touch of my thighs on his confirmed that I was almost there. Then I felt our pubic bones touch. He rotated his hips.

"Lovely grind you are," he encouraged.

He rotated his hips again and I felt a frisson of pleasure from my clit start to balance the discomfort inside my vagina. My lips, outer and inner, touched against his body and pleasure began to wash discomfort away.

I pulled up four inches, then down again. It wasn't pleasant, but it wasn't unpleasant. Progress. I lifted myself up and down. Five inches this time. I lifted myself six inches up. In a moment, I'd be burning calories in the best way every invented.

"Uhhgh!" he grunted.

I slapped his hands off my breasts and bent forward to twist his nipples. "That's not a description! Tell me what *I* feel like!"

"Hot and sexy and wet!"

I let go of his chest and started to pump up and down, now in a vigorous tempo. I shut my eyes and concentrated on making sure I was breathing through my nose. This wasn't sex, it was exercise and by the time I'd sweated enough, I'd be loose enough down there that all I'd be feeling was the glorious ridges of his cock sliding in and out of me.

"God you're beautiful!"

I opened my eyes. He was looking up at the mirror in the ceiling. I looked over at the mirror beside us. My breasts were bouncing, restrained only lightly by his hands. Sweat was trickling down my back. My cunt was sliding up and down his cock which glistened with my pussy juices every time I elevated myself up off him. His hands were moving in a set pattern in circles with squeezes and nipple caresses every quarter turn.

I was starting to enjoy myself, to enjoy his humongous cock sliding in and out, to enjoy the stimulation of all all my sensitive areas, lips, sheath, clit, to enjoy him rubbing the sensitive spot inside. But this was balanced by the effort I still had to make to keep myself relaxed around him. I breathed deeply and felt heartbeats pounding inside my chest.

He gasped below me and his hands squeezed chaotically. His eyes were shut and his expression was halfway between focus and release.

I slid slowly down his shaft until our pubic bones were touching and spread my hands on his chest, just above his nipples. I began to do push-ups, being careful to keep my pelvis completely still. Bubba was *not* going to come before I'd finished my workout. I caught a glimpse of my gyrating breasts in the mirror.

He opened his eyes and looked at me strangely. "What the fuck?!?"

"What does it feel like? That's *all* I want to hear."

"It feels like some crazy white woman doing push-ups on top of me."

"Good," I gasped. I calculated that I still had five more minutes left in my workout. I had to adjust my hands. We were both sweating.

He reached to touch my shoulders. "Only my breasts," I reminded him.

His grip on my breasts was firm, as if he intended to control me if things got any weirder.

And then my arms gave out and I collapsed on top of him. I slid up and down his torso, our sweat lubricating our slippery bodies, my pussy juices lubricating us down below. And now his cock had me, possessed me. There was no more exercise, no more calories, just his magnificent rod pulsing in and out of me, just his skin caressing my nipples, just—

Me beneath him. He had pushed me up, turned into me and rotated me beneath him. He plunged his cock in and out of me. His arms beside me were the size of my legs, flexing as he used his entire body to fuck me. He was a rolling wave, from his feet, up his thighs, squeezing his butt to push hard into me, his torso pushing himself all the wary into me and his arms pivoting around his pelvis to rotate his pubic bone around my clit.

I managed to slide a few inches sideways to watch him in the mirror above. His butt squeezed and I felt his cock rub against my inner spot and I exploded. He was pressed hard on top of me so the explosion couldn't escape. Rather it thundered inside, consuming, blasting my consciousness into nothingness.

The next thing I was aware was his cock, hotter even than before, sliding in and out at full speed, then something sticky between my legs. He wasn't breathing. He collapsed beside me and I stared up into his eyes, stared upward at my ivory next to his ebony. But his eyes were closed. His white teeth smile glowed.

Afterwards, stepping out of my shower, there was blessed silence. I started to take a deep breath, but my cellphone rang before I could fully inhale. At that moment, I wished that Jamaica's love-affair with telephones had been less fertile.

Eric's red hair, sparkling green eyes and gleaming smile stared up at me as I tapped the phone. "Good morning, Eric."

"Hi, Lee."

I didn't respond. While waiting for the group leader, I'd resolved to operate on vacation mode. That meant that if Eric wanted to give me his report, he'd give it, but I wasn't going to ask for it.

I looked at myself in the mirror: my breasts were still heaving and my nipples engorged thanks to the workout Bubba had given me. And my pubes were curly dark brown tufts. My belly was tighter by an inch, but more would need to be done in that regard. My diet was going to be simple, fruit and cheese for breakfast, vegetables for lunch and meat for dinner. I would do my best to avoid sauces with all their hidden calories. No my diet wasn't backed by medical advice or scientific study, but it worked for me and that's all I needed to know.

At length Eric cleared his throat and gave his report, "As you know —" I muttered to myself that if I already knew, why are you telling me? But not being telepathic, Eric continued, "The Cyber Culprit's app is a wild success. Thousands of people are using it to infect the phones of those responsible for excessively loud commercials being inserted into regular TV programming. Once uploaded, the volume on the target's phone oscillates wildly between excessively soft to painfully loud. And it's having the desired effect. At least one broadcaster is limiting the amount by which the volume of a commercial can exceed that of the underlying programming."

"What about Amber Alerts?" One of those blaring signals had startled me while I was driving and almost sent me into the guardrail. Yes, we should look for missing children, but so far the alerts had been false alarms. And there was no need to scare the bejeezus out of people unless it was for an imminent tornado.

"Same thing, but the targets are government officials and the police."

"Any reaction?"

"The police are threatening to charge people uploading the App, but so far the App's built-in re-routing algorithms are frustrating them in their efforts to identify perpetrators."

I smiled. Maybe the Cyber Culprit wasn't all-bad after all.

"And there's something more."

Vacation mode meant that he'd tell me without me asking. I moved my hands below to spread my pussy lips. Nice and pink. Ready for action.

"The Cyber Culprit has sold a zero."

Eric must be crazy. "Who would pay money for a zero?!?" I asked, trying to put as much snark in my voice as possible.

"Anyone and every one. A zero is short for 'zero day' — an undiscovered vulnerability in the target software that can be exploited before it can be fixed. It can be anything from a defect in an operating system such as Windows or as specialized as the software used by an individual bank. They're sold just like credit card numbers on the dark web."

"How much do we think he got?"

"Hard to say, anywhere between 50,000-150,000 dollars US."

"Okay. Keep me informed." I rang off wondering what the Cyber Culprit would do with his new bankroll.

The next day passed without incident: dieting, exercising, snorkeling. I allowed myself a mid-afternoon nap to work on my tan.

The next morning I watched group leader Gary Smith — obviously a pseudonym — organize his flock. They were comprised of five couples, mostly white middle-class, late thirties, early forties, reasonably fit. There were also three single females and two unattached males.

Gary himself was short — shorter than me — fat, but with big bones, big muscles and boundless energy. In the space of a minute, he went from loud to soft, calm to hassled, happy to angry, grateful to demanding. He was olive-skinned with a round head topped with long black hair. I decided he was Greek — Gary Smithopolous.

During the day, Gary got lots of attention from the ladies and I saw him sneak off with several females during the course of the night. His two unattached males were another matter. Hedo's female to male ratio typically favors the fairer sex and this week was no exception. Gary's two unattached males — I'd learned that their names were Daniel and Ryan — got no attention, let alone action, at all.

The next day, I resolved that the best way to gain Gary's trust was to be a wonton wench at the evening's upcoming toga and foam party. And to be especially wanton with Daniel and Ryan. Daniel was barely taller than me, lean and lanky. He was dark, but not handsome. However, his eyes were mischievous and constantly roving, taking everything in. I pegged him as an imaginative bookworm. Ryan was six inches taller than his mate, muscular with a hard face, his blonde hair cut short. Ryan's blue eyes darted from female to female.

Step one was at dinner when I sat my plate of grilled chicken down with Gary's two unlucky males. Ryan tried to see as much as possible of me under the toga I'd put together from my bedroom sheets. Daniel wanted to know all about my diet. Both told me that I had no need to diet. Funny how unrequited temptation brings out the charm in men. After dinner we danced toga to toga in the dining room. Both were gentlemen. Neither tried to make a move. But neither protested when I stepped forward to dance close. Ryan hugged me gently so that I could feel the controlled power of his muscles. Daniel brushed our bodies against each other and then apart with new and creative ideas.

From the week before, I'd learned a few things about the toga and foam party. First and foremost, everything gets wet. And everything that gets wet, gets heavy. So by the time I was making my way to the disco, I was wearing only a loose-fitting silk bottom and a string bikini top. Both were light blue and would become translucent in the foam. The bikini top would likely get lost in the melee (mêlée for all the teachers who'd ever tried to teach me French). Secondly, while the resort puts a mat on the floor, there would still be some slipping and sliding, so on my feet I was wearing sandals with a secure-grip tread pattern and firm Velcro ties.

When I entered the disco, the techno-beat music was already pounding, as always too loud to be healthy, or even enjoyable, but I was on a mission, receiving danger pay and so could not complain. The foam was already at my knees. I spotted Daniel and Ryan at the edge of their group. They were eyeing two redheads across the room, but the redheads had eyes only for themselves.

I waved over to my intended. They each pointed to their chests. I nodded and used both of my hands to wave them over. They both looked at each other. At that moment, Gary caught sight of our fractured sign language and gave both of them a gentle shove in my direction. Gary smiled at me as Daniel and Ryan ambled gingerly over. Daniel had fashioned a toga out of his bed sheet which would have been at home in Rome at the time of the Caesars. Ryan had settled with draping his sheet around his hips. The foam was now licking partway up my thighs.

As the two men arrived, I slipped myself between

them. I gave Ryan a kiss, full on his lips. Then when he reached to bring me close, I turned quickly to Daniel and kissed him as well, wiggling my butt against Ryan's pelvic area. I repeated this twirl several times and began to feel protruding responses under both their togas. Foam began to leak under my panties.

The music changed to reggae (finally!) and Gary's entire group came alive, dancing and rubbing their bodies against each other. I would have liked to have waded into the roiling mass that the group had become, to feel one set of hands after another caressing my body, but like I said, I was on a mission. So, for tonight, the universe would be restricted to Daniel, Ryan and me.

I stroked Ryan's large hard cock as he squeezed my breasts. Then I took one of his hands and brought it down to the center of my crotch. His touch felt heavenly through the soaked silk. I pirouetted to Daniel who unloosened the strings of my bikini top and did some sort of fractal pattern over my breasts sending jolts directly into my belly button. His cock was smaller but just as hard as the one rubbing in the center of my butt cheeks. I pulled his right hand down to my pussy and the same fractal pattern had me stamping my feet.

I turned to Ryan and was pleased to feel Daniel's fingers trace a path across my buttocks and then back between my legs. I pulled Ryan's hand against my crotch. The two men's finger's met and then jerked back as if they'd been burned by red-hot embers. My hands on their cocks pulling them close and my hands guiding theirs back to my crotch finally gave them the idea that *yes*, I wanted both of their fingers fondling me at the same time.

Their fingers were like a symphony: Ryan's firm and wide, sure of where the central themes were. Daniel's fingers were like the flutes and strings, setting up the main action, stroking the subtle parts. I swooned as they mashed me close into a tight sandwich.

Ryan's turning me around brought me back to the present. Daniel was caressing the sweetest melody out of my pussy. Ryan's finger was stroking between my butt cheeks, rotating around my ass every time he passed by. Daniel's left hand was pressing against my pussy hair, drawing her up, his thumb occasionally brushing, teasing, the top of my clit. The fingers of his left hand had my pussy lips between them and he was stroking up and down. His thumb pulsed sideways against my vulva. If I hadn't been pressed between the two of them, I would have slipped to the floor.

Ryan's finger stopped right in the middle of my ass and started to press forward. Here at least he was being gentle and tentative. But as soon as the tip of his finger was inside, the advance of his finger became relentless. Not harsh or rough, but relentless nonetheless. He slowed for my sphincter to accommodate his knuckle, then pressed all the way inside. He pulled back where his knuckle touched my sphincter, then forward with gentle thrusts, each time pulling his knuckle further into my sphincter. He popped his knuckle out beyond my sphincter, but now the tight ring was relaxed and he slid easily back inside.

Ryan's finger pressed upwards pressing the upper edge of my vagina against my g-spot. He rubbed around it in a clockwise motion. Daniel's thumb on my clit moving clockwise brought me quickly to the brink. My pussy lips were singing the symphony, my entire sex was dancing in wild frenzy, my ass was glorying in being fucked, my clit was *begging* for release. Two sharp taps from Ryan's finger granted her wish.

My ass clamped tight on the base of Ryan's finger, anchoring my orgasm against the explosion at his finger tip. A piercing contraction turned my spine to stone, then shot down my legs. I didn't feel a release, but instead another contraction sending electricity up and down at the same time. Again no release, but another contraction like a whip starting at my toes and cracking at my head. This time I felt the release and my body was hot all over. I felt myself gush down my legs and wished there was something inside my cunt to feel me ejaculating all over it. Then there was wave after wave of gentle rapture radiating outward from my sex. Gradually I recovered and became aware that I had a cock in each of my hands. I hoped that I hadn't squeezed too hard.

By this time, the foam was lapping at our necks and I could feel their togas weighing heavily. I pulled them to the exit.

In my room, we tried to have a shower together, but after a few minutes of slipping and sliding, we gave up and showered separately. Daniel was already lying on the bed when I came out of the shower. He was nude, his cock throbbing, still fully erect. I lay down beside him as Ryan entered the shower. I shut my eyes to feel Daniel trace ethereal patterns up and down my torso and around my nipples.

Daniel's hands stopped their motion and I opened my eyes. Ryan stared down at us. His cock wasn't throbbing, but it was purplish and very much erect.

I looked back and forth between the two men. "Are you ready?" I asked them.

I knew that the ladylike thing to do would have to have given them a choice, but my butt was still tender and I wanted to repay Daniel's subtle touchings with my tongue. Besides, Ryan would be better able to fill my pussy.

They nodded in unison, their cocks swaying.

I motioned Daniel to scoot himself against the bed-board, sitting up. "Spread your legs," I told him. I bent down and blew on the tip of his penis. As soon as my fingers came within an inch of his cock, it started to throb so vigorously that it reached out and touched me.

Nothing was happening behind me, so I turned to look at Ryan. He was standing uncertain. I wiggled my butt. "My pussy is ready to purr," I whispered.

I licked the tip of Daniel's cock and was pleased to feel something start to fill me from behind. Ryan was not a man who needed an engraved invitation. I flicked my tongue up and down Daniel's cock and was pleased to hear him suck air into his lungs.

Ryan's hands gripped my hips and soon his cock was pumping confidently away. At this rate, he'd be spurting inside me even before I had Daniel halfway to heaven. I picked up my right knee and slapped it against Ryan's. This threw him entirely off his rhythm and I smiled at finding his weak spot.

Daniel's cock tasted sweet in my mouth. He must have used the herbal soap I had in the shower. I slipped his shaft swiftly down my throat, then half swallowed, feeling him throb inside my throat. My fingers tickled his balls. I couldn't match his fractal patterns, but still it was enough to wiggle his cock inside me and clench his balls into little globes tight against his crotch. I sucked hard and slowly raised my head. Giving head to a small cock was so much nicer. So much more *control*!

I was suddenly aware of a growing warmth in my nether regions. Ryan had regained his rhythm and it was clear that he was climbing up the mountain in methodical fashion. I started to slip Daniel back down my throat, infusing the suction in my mouth with the sensations of Ryan's cock thrusting my insides outwards and then pulling me into him as he withdrew. I was tempted to abandon myself to his control, but I had obligations at the other end. I slapped my left knee against his and had to restrain myself from laughing as Ryan almost let go of my hips.

Now I concentrated on Daniel's cock. I grabbed his butt with my hands. I bobbed my head up and down as quickly as I could, sucking up, enveloping down. When he stopped breathing, I slowed my pace until he gasped air into his lungs. His hands were tracing fractal patterns on top of my head and I could feel them tingling my tongue.

The fingers on top of my head fluttered, stopped tracing their patterns and Daniel's hands started squeezing in time with my mouth moving up and down his cock. I could feel my mouth controlling his breathing, I could feel my power moving him closer to the point of no return. Behind me, Ryan's rhythmic pounding had resumed.

And then we were all as one — Ryan behind me pumping pleasure up my spine, my mouth funneling it into Daniel's cock, his hands on my head pulsing it back down my spine and into Ryan's cock. Gradually our consciousness gathered into me. I was sucking Daniel into my chest. I was pulling Ryan out through his cock and into my sex. Then we were all swirling together inside my navel. Everything Ryan and Dan ever were, would ever be was being drawn into me. And they would only get themselves back if they could make me come.

For a moment, I didn't want to come. I wanted to own them. I wanted their power. I wanted Daniel quivering before me for all eternity. I wanted Ryan's thighs slapping against mine pledging their undying servitude.

Then Daniel's come filled my mouth, sticky and salty spurts and the spell was broken. My thighs slapped against Ryan's and it was I who was his servant, obeying his command to milk every last drop from Daniel's cock. It was I who was obeying his command to come.

"Fuck!" I yelled in obedience to my master as his orgasm nailed my legs motionless to the bed.

"Fuck!" I yelled as my toes curled.

"Fuck!" I yelled as I swallowed Daniel's last drop.

"Fuck!" I yelled as the sheet disappeared into my fists.

"Fuck!" I cried as spasm after spasm recoiled up and down my spine.

"Fuck," I whimpered as I collapsed sideways.

"Fuck," I gasped as I tried to remember how to breathe.

The next morning, I sat down with Gary at breakfast — he had a three large pancakes stacked on his plate smothered with syrup while I had limited myself to dainty portions of cheese and fruit. God, how I wanted a piece of pancake. He smiled up at me. "Lee, thanks for showing Daniel and Ryan what Hedo's all about. I don't — "

"Gary, I'm an investigator."

He shrugged and stuffed his mouth with a three-tiered forkful of pancake. As far as Gary was concerned, I could be whatever I wanted to be. Syrup dribbled down his chin as he chewed. It took all my willpower not to lick the syrup off his face.

I brought out my phone and showed him the pictures of his last group which the Cyber Culprit had posted. "I'm investigating how these got uploaded to the internet."

He swallowed his half-chewed pancake. "I'd like to catch the bastard." He slammed his left fist onto the table. Half the room turned around to look at what had made the noise. He made a fist with his left hand, put his right fist on top of the left and twisted.

I swiped through the internet postings on my phone. "Do you have any idea as to who did this?"

Gary took out his own phone and showed me a grainy out-of-focus shot of the head and shoulders of a man. "It could have been this guy."

I stared at the photo. It wasn't much, but it *was* more than we'd had a moment ago. "How did you get this?"

"After the internet breach, I got everyone's photos. This is the only person I can't account for."

Gary emailed the photo to me and I raced back to my room to brag to Eric about the photo of the Cyber Culprit — our first significant break — but before I could dial, my phone rang. It was Michael Rayburn, the lawyer who'd given us the Cyber Culprit assignment.

"Good morning, Mr. Rayburn," I opined respectfully. After all, Michael was paying all the bills.

"Lee, there's been another posting," he blurted in his usual mile-a-minute fashion. "A wife caught cheating at a bar. Eric's up to his eyeballs with the cyber tracing. I need you on the first plane back north to run this to ground."

Michael was obviously multi-tasking. An email with a series of pictures of a woman chatting up a man in a bar started to scroll through on my cellphone screen.

So much for another day of lazing in the sun.

Log 7a Toronto: A Log by Eric Craigie

The airline lifted off the tarmac at Montego Bay's Sangster International Airport and I heaved a sigh of relief. If I'd had to stay back in Hedo with Lee, I would have had to reschedule my upcoming mixed martial arts bout. As it was, I was sure that Michael Rayburn, the lawyer who'd given us the case, would keep me hopping to track down the Cyber Culprit. I'd have just enough time to prepare for the fight.

Heidi, my girlfriend/groupie, met me at the airport and looked me up and down, accusation in her deep brown eyes. "How many times did you have sex in that den of iniquity?" She was small, barely four-foot eight, and trim. The only thing large about her was her hair—straight strands of onyx extending well below her shoulders. Heidi was a member of the Tapirapé tribe, an indigenous group from Brazil. When she was happy, she was alluring, when she was annoyed, she was fierce.

"Heidi, you know I can't discuss my cases," I told her.

"Hpmp," she exhaled, half 'hmm', half a war-cry.

"I dreamed of you every night, I can't wait—"

She slapped her palm flat against my chest. "No sex. You're in training."

I had met Heidi six months ago when she had dropped by at the gym's open house. I had greeted her briefly at the beginning of the evening and we'd smiled at each other. After that, she'd installed herself at ringside where she'd intently consumed every detail of the demonstration bouts. Half an hour before I'd been scheduled to fight, I'd sidled up next to her and asked her what she most enjoyed about mixed martial arts. "It's so real," she'd responded. I'd asked her whether she liked most: the striking, the kicking, the clinching or the grappling. "The wrestling," she had said without thinking. "Firm little butts trying to squeeze the other guy into the canvas." When I'd climbed into the ring, I was wearing skintight spandex briefs and I'd thrown my opponent to the canvas as quickly as I'd been able to.

Back in my apartment, I did a quick news search to determine what was happening as the result of the two Apps posted by the Cyber Culprit. His Amber Alert App, designed to discourage the police from taking over televisions and radios to post messages of recently kidnapped children, had resulted in many police and emergency numbers being temporarily shut down by loud claxon noises. These were the same loud claxon noises that had announced the take-over of users radios and TVs. The Loud Commercial App interfered with broadcasters' phones by intermittently increasing their volume, mimicking the increase of audio volume on televisions every time a commercial interrupted the underlying programming.

The Amber Alert protocol had been revised to remove the loud claxons and the attacks on police and emergency numbers had almost completely ceased. New users of the App were being quickly tracked down and arrested.

The Loud Commercial App was now wild. Authorities were trying to track down everyone using the App. But new hackers were now constantly posting updated versions of the App to allow its users to avoid detection.

No one was trying to chase down the Cyber Culprit, the person who had originally posted the Apps. That was apparently up to me. I set several tracking programs to start traces from a proxy server I had access to and then took a shower.

Body and mind sharpened by hot and high-velocity water jets, I returned to my computer. Several Internet Protocol locations used by the Cyber Culprit had been located by the NetstatHistory program I'd co-written with some of my college buddies. The Cyber Culprit apparently liked to hide in plain sight under the most commonly used internet ports. His usual procedure was to use a fake Internet Service Provider and hack into the main Domain Name Server, find a medium-sized enterprise with poor internet security, and use their computers to actually post to the internet. Apparently he'd used a new sub-victim's computer for each hack.

But beyond having discovering the Cyber Culprit's usual method of operation, I was no closer to discovering who he was or where he was operating from.

There were numerous addresses the CC had attempted to probe. I ran their numerical IP addresses. Several I recognized. But one popped out. It was Michael Rayburn's law firm. I immediately emailed a report to Mr. Rayburn along with a suggestion to boost his personal and firm firewalls. I also promised to make a more detailed report in a few days.

After emailing Mr. Rayburn, I went back to my proxy server and initiated ten probes in the Cyber Culprit's direction. These would gently but repeatedly probe CC's activity from all directions while I started to prepare for my mixed martial arts bout. I glanced at the clock on my computer; the fight was in three hours. I went to the kitchen to prepare my pre-fight meal.

My pre-fight countdown wasn't orthodox, or even recommended, but it worked for me. First was a hearty meal. I slowly chewed the last bite of my salad, then ate my steak as quickly as I could. Finally, there were carbs — potatoes sautéed in olive oil.

Then a brisk walk during which I slapped my face and upper torso. Passers-by tended to look at me strangely, but the fierceness of my concentration kept them at arms-length or beyond.

Next was meditation with my pre-fight mantra, 'nothing into nothingness' to melt away all my cares and stresses. With each repetition of the mantra, I became more spirit and less body. Six mantras in, all pain had vanished. Nine and my sexual urges melted away as I lost awareness below my navel. By the time I'd lost count, my mind had stilled and my awareness was reduced to my lungs sucking in universal energy and then gently exhaling the rest of the air I'd inhaled. Gradually, all awareness of my physical form vanished. I went from doing my mantra to becoming nothingness. My mantra stopped and I floated. Then bit-by-bit my body awareness returned. I began to concentrate on the upcoming bout, on my opponent, his tendencies, the fight plan my coach and I had worked out.

In the locker room, I slipped my protective cup in place. Heidi would want to make sure I'd taken all possible steps to protect my gonads. I felt my hands being taped. I knew it was my coach taping my hands only because he'd done it before. Otherwise I tried to keep centered within myself. Then gloves were slipped onto my hands. They would be light MMA gloves with only a thin layer of padding to protect my knuckles and my opponent's face. My fingers would be left free for grappling and jujitsu submitting. The gloves were velcroed tight to my wrist. Elastic supports were placed on my right wrist and left ankle. I wiggled my toes and slapped my bare feet to the concrete floor.

As I made my way to the octagon, I caught a glimpse of Heidi: a tiny jewel encased in brown skin, blessed with shiny black hair, impish face and smile, pert breasts. Her muscles stood out, as if she, not I, was the one about to enter into battle. She'd have an internal vibrator in her pussy to let her get off while she watched. Before the bout, Heidi had implored me to let the fight go deep into the third round so she'd have time for a full climax. There was a general buzz from the crowd that rose in volume as I moved towards the ring.

My opponent, Oscar Connors, was slightly shorter and slightly more muscular then I was. I was 6 foot three; he was only 6 feet tall. We had noticed from his past fights that his tendency was to bull rush into his opponents with a flurry of strikes. Connors would then pull back to avoid counter punches. If he had inflicted any damage, he would immediately rush back in with more strikes, if not he would circle and wait for another opportunity to charge back in.

Our plan was for me to constantly circle to my right and then move sharply left if Connors tried to rush in to deliver a series of blows. While moving to my left, I would either kick at his legs, counter punch to his head, or simply move out of the way. Connors' cardio was not as good as mine and we would also use his bull rush tactics to wear him out. In the early rounds I would avoid the clinch but later on I would try to move the fight to the ground where my superior flexibility and jujitsu skills would allow me to force a submission.

The fight would go three five-minute rounds. Unless one of us was stopped first. The ring commentator began to announce Connors. I glanced over at Heidi whose face was flushed with anticipation as her bum wiggled to adjust itself in the hard seat. She held up three fingers with her left hand to remind me how long she wanted the fight to last. Her right hand squeezed the vibrator's remote control.

There was a mixture of boos and cheers for Connors. The commentator began to announce me and I circled the ring, shadowboxing vigorously. There was a similar mixture of boos and cheers for me; apparently the crowd wasn't playing favorites. The ring smelled of sweat and blood and fear. The roar of the crowd was increasingly savage.

The referee motioned us towards the center of the ring and told us to touch gloves. Connors was swarthy and dark haired. My skin was white and only a few wisps of reddish hair graced my chest. I was as nervous as hell. A momentary hush. Connors' fist against my knuckles was hard and solid. We retreated to our corners — actually two sides of the octagon — and then the referee waved us back to the center with a stern "Fight!"

As predicted, Connors immediately charged at me. I dodged to my left and blocked his blows. We circled, Connors in the center of the ring, jabbing but striking only air. I moved in, looking for an opening, but at that moment Connors rushed forward and hit me square in my right cheek. I was momentarily stunned, but now I was in the fight, all nervousness gone. I circled to my left and away. I weaved around and resumed circling to my right and once again we were sparring, only rarely connecting. Then Connors tried to bull rush but I stepped to my right and kicked at his legs.

Connors stumbled and I was tempted to press my advantage but knew that Heidi would never forgive me if I ended the fight so quickly. We began to exchange blows but neither of us was doing any serious damage to the other. I broke off and circled to the right. Once more we were sparring but every so often I landed a kick to Connors' legs.

The bell rang to end the first round and the referee stepped in between us.

I moved to my 'corner'. My coach gave me a gulp of water. He and I had agreed that the customary practice of coaches shouting instructions staccato one after the other at the fighter was counterproductive. It only made the fighter confused. Instead we had agreed that I would receive only one instruction. He looked me square in the eye, "When he charges again, hit him smack dab right in the face."

Connors began the second round with another bull rush. I dodged left and hit his right cheek but he landed a solid blow against my liver and my legs stopped moving as quickly as I would have liked. He tried to hit my head but reflexes kicked in and I kicked him in the left knee sweeping his legs out from underneath him. The crowd bellowed bloodlust as my opponent toppled onto the canvas.

Immediately I jumped on top of Connors and grabbed his right arm in a Kimura, ready to force him to tap out. Just as I was about to lock the Kimura submission in place, I heard Heidi yelling at me in the center of my head, "Three rounds! Three rounds!"

I released the Kimura and hit Connors in the cheek with an elbow. He grabbed me close into full guard and I ground into him, repeatedly clenching my butt muscles as I mashed my body up and down against his. This was for Heidi's benefit—close quarters grappling to help her get her rocks off. The rest of the audience would assume I was jockeying for position. And it didn't hurt that Connors was exhausting himself trying to push me off. I let Connors transition to the top but as soon as he tried to punch down at me I swept left and once again he was on the bottom. We wrestled, me keeping Connors in a tight grip for a few minutes. The crowd grew restive and the referee stood us up.

Connors was a bit winded and took a lazy swing at me. He gulped air. I could see defeat in his eyes. I stepped inside and mashed him against the chain-links which formed the outer wall of the octagon. I alternated attempts to hit him in the stomach or legs with my right knee or to strike him in the face with my elbows. This forced Connors to defend himself, weakening his attempts to escape the clinch. I caught a glimpse of Heidi's eyes transfixed on Connors' butt.

The bell rang to end the second round.

Back in my 'corner', my coach gave me another drink of water and told me, "When he charges again, hit him smack dab right in the face." I smiled inwardly at his patience in calmly repeating an instruction that I had completely ignored.

The bell rang to start the third round and the crowd's blood lust cheer urged us to finish the fight.

Oscar Connors, predictable as always, charged straight at me. The cheers were loud and then suddenly fell silent. Connors was moving in slow motion. His right hand whizzed by my cheek as I moved to my left. He pursued, tried to strike me with his left fist. I pivoted left, standing well within the range of his fists. His hand came right at my nose, slowly as if he was under water, but I twisted to my right as I sent my right fist smack dab into the middle of his face.

Connors wobbled, then dropped like a sack of potatoes. I moved in to rain blows down on his head but the referee waved me away. I had won the fight! Heidi was staring daggers up at me… My sweat was pungent in my nostrils.

Back in my apartment, Heidi made a show of removing her vibrator's remote control from her pocket and then the vibrator itself from under her skirt. The vibrator was in the shape of a 'u', slightly larger than her hand, soft pink plastic. One end was larger than the other. She slapped them onto the kitchen table and scowled at me.

"You barely got into the third round," she accused.

She spread her legs, put her hands on her hips, and

stared up at me. Apparently there was something that I needed to do to correct matters. A red bra strap poked out from underneath her white cotton tank-top which was tight enough that I could see the outline of the rest of her bra underneath. Her black leather skirt was so snug on her hips and butt that it was almost a second skin. Muscles rippled under the smooth brown skin of her arms and thighs.

"He walked into my fist," I protested.

"You could've moved your fist out of the way."

She took a step towards me and caressed my chest making it clear exactly how she expected me to correct matters.

I took her hands and held them tenderly. "I'm tired from the fight," I protested.

She tried to move her arms but I held them tightly. "You seem to have plenty of energy," she noted.

"Heidi—"

"You still have a full round of energy, five minutes of all-out exertion. Five minutes that belong to me!"

"Heidi—"

She grabbed the front of my jeans and pulled me into the bedroom. Heidi's small dexterous fingers had my jeans at my feet almost immediately. Her removal of my briefs was aided by the fact that my penis was almost entirely flaccid, barely poking out from the russet curls surrounding it.

Heidi undid the bottom three buttons of my shirt and then flapped it upwards. "You do the rest," she commanded, kicking off her shoes.

I complied and she pulled me over to the bed then pushed me on top of it. I stared up at her as she stepped onto the bed, standing over me. Her panties matched her bra. She pulled her tank top over her head and threw it at my head. It fell softly on my face and I took a deep pull of her scent through my nose. It was feminine and ferocious.

Heidi jettisoned her skirt in the direction of my gonads and I had to reach down to protect myself. I felt a stirring in my mid-regions but probably not enough to have been visible to Heidi. She quickly slipped out of her bra, faked hurling it at my gonads then hit me with it flush in the face. It's clasp stung where Connors had hit me an hour before. But the sight of her tight breasts rippling, nipples erect, made up for it.

She began to stroke up the front of her panties, making a furrow in the center of her sex. "All you had to do was keep him standing for another two minutes!" She accused. She took off her panties, put one end around her thumb and pulled back, as if she was holding a taut rubber-band. "Another two minutes, my cunt would've been singing and the crowd yelling so loud no one would have heard me!" She let her panties fly right at my gonads.

Thankfully her panties' low mass and large surface area made the experience pleasurable instead of painful. But this just seemed to inflame her. She dropped to the bed so quickly that I didn't have time to protect my gonads. Mercifully she landed halfway down my thighs. But she made up for this mercy by forcefully grabbing my penis and balls with her panties and expertly massaging me to full arousal.

"That's better!" Heidi proclaimed.

I opened my mouth to protest but she squeezed my cock and balls to stifle what I was about to say.

"Take a deep breath," she commanded.

Given what she had ahold of, I immediately complied.

Without warning, she pirouetted and suddenly her sex was covering my nose and mouth. The taste was sharp and cut through every taste I have ever tasted. Her taste demanded that I taste her alone, no one else, nothing else. And then when I extended my tongue upwards into her slit, she tasted feral, like bait inviting you ever deeper into her forest. She quivered, and then suddenly she tasted of exotic fruits mixed with fish. I licked hungrily all around her sex, sucking as much of her intoxicating nectar into my mouth as I could. Her hair was hard and coarse, her pussy lips tiny and delicate, her vagina tight and hot, her clit hard and pulsing. My flicking licking tongue was swelling arousal into her entire sex. Heidi's hands below were having the same effect on me.

As swiftly as she had pirouetted onto my face, she pirouetted off, and I was immediately aware that my lungs needed air. As I gasped oxygen into my chest, she slithered down and pressed her sex against the tip of my cock. She slid slowly down my shaft, gradually accommodating my size into her smaller size, her whimpers declaring that the accommodating was exquisitely pleasurable.

I smiled and shut my eyes, concentrating on the textures of her pussy, concentrating on the heat of her pussy, concentrating on the slippery friction of her pussy as it slid centimeter by centimeter down the length of my shaft. When she had slid almost my entire length in, she rested herself along my torso, her heat inflaming me, the little buttons of her nipples poking into my skin. Her head was beneath mine but she angled it backwards, ready to whisper.

Pain! Searing deep pain! Poking into my skin just under and behind my armpits. Her nails. Pain!

"You're going to fuck me, Eric Craigie, she hissed, digging her fingernails deeper into my skin. "You are going to fuck me hard, Eric Craigie. You are going to *fuck* me. And it better be more than five minutes!" Her voice was firm, immovable. "It better be *a lot more* than five minutes!"

'Fuck' is such a wonderfully malleable word. It can denote anger, sex, passion, climax, anything in between, or everything all at once. It could be physical or mental or both. For Heidi, it meant that I was going to make her arouse herself into her first climax and then I was going to pummel her sex into painful submission, exhausted, depleted, fulfilled. Just the way she liked it.

I grabbed her hands and formed them into fists inside my fists to protect me from further assaults by her sharpened talons. I extended my arms outward pulling her down flat against my chest. "First, you're going to fuck *me*," I told her.

She tried to pull her hands free but I was holding them too tight. She tried to wiggle her pussy off my penis but she had neither the space nor the leverage to escape. "First, you're going to fuck me," I repeated, bucking my midsection up off the bed.

"You bastard!" she hissed. But she began to rock her hips forward and back sliding herself up off my penis and then stroking her pussy back down. I began to push myself into the bed and then up in opposition to her movements, lengthening the thrusts of my penis in and out of her pussy. A low moan escaped from her chest.

"What was it like when I had Oscar pinned against the fence?" I demanded.

"It was like he was trying to fuck you off the fence but you were looking at me, fucking me."

"And now you're going to fuck *me* just like Oscar was trying to fuck me." I brought my fists, hers still encased inside, on top of my chest and was rewarded with the sight of her breasts being clenched in time with her clenching pussy below.

"You bastard! If you think I'm going to fuck you, you're crazy!" But she squirmed her hips, doing just that.

I smiled up at her in triumph and crossed my legs up and over hers so that she couldn't escape. "If you want me to fuck you, you have to fuck me first," I told her.

And fuck me she did. Vigorously and with reckless abandon. Up and down my shaft, clenching and releasing, rotating her hips, fast little thrusts, long slow strokes, long quick climbs with dropping plunges. I wrote computer code in my head to distract me from what her pussy was doing to my penis. Then she shut her eyes and I knew she was teetering on the precipice. Her pussy shuddered, slowed, stopped. I let go of her fists and wrapped my hands around her hips and butt cheeks. I lifted her up and slammed her down my cock. Up and down, over and over again until her eyes rocketed open.

"Shit!" she yelled. "Fuck! Shit! Fuck! *Fuck!*"

Her spasms squeezed against my cock and she began frenzied strokes up and down my shaft.

"Fuck! Shit! *Fuck!*" She whipped her hair against my cheeks.

I clenched myself as hard as I could to squeeze off my own orgasm. My hands gathered sheets inside my fists.

"Fuck! Shit! Fuck!" Her spasms were subsiding, but her hips still rocked her pussy up and down my shaft. Sweat dripped off her. Her nipples were hard little points. Her ferocity stabbed up my nostrils. I shut my eyes to concentrate on the computer code.

Then she stopped. A moment later, she flopped down atop my chest, heaving air into her lungs.

I let her rest until her breathing returned to normal before rolling on top of her. "What was it like when I was on top of Oscar?" I teased.

"It was like you were fucking him, each time your butt squeezed you put your cock deeper and deeper inside his ass."

I lifted her up, spun her around and knelt behind her pumping softly in and out doggy style. I bent over to whisper into her ear, "fucking him in his ass?"

She beat her fists against the mattress. "In his ass!"

I reached around to her breasts and pinched each of her nipples between my thumbs and forefingers. "You want me to fuck *you* in *your* ass?" I twisted her nipples.

"You wouldn't *dare*!" The tone of her voice made it clear that she dearly hoped that I *would* dare.

"You want to get fucked in the ass?" I lightly brushed my fingers against her nipples.

"No," she moaned.

I leaned back, moved my right thumb to my mouth and deposited saliva onto it. I pressed my thumb lightly against her anus expanding it ever so slightly. "I won't do it unless you ask me to," I told her.

"Bastard! Yes! Fuck my *ass*."

"Just like Oscar?"

"Just like Oscar!"

I reached over, scooted a pillow underneath her midsection, and pressed her down on top of it. I thoroughly lubricated my index finger and then positioned it just behind my cock which I positioned against her anus. I pressed my cock against her anus. Then I quickly substituted my index finger for my cock and pushed it inside her ass while twisting her left nipple. She said she wanted to be fucked up her ass but I knew she wouldn't be able to accommodate my cock.

Her sphincter was tight, but once past it, my finger was inside a much looser area. I moved my finger back and forth angling downwards towards her pussy. I brought my left hand down to her sex, massaged her clit then gently stroked it up and down. I made a 'V' with my two outer fingers to pry open her outer pussy lips and stroked up and down her exposed center with my two inner fingers. She started to rock softly in sync with my strokes.

I dipped my left index finger inside her vagina then curled it. As soon as I found her g-spot, I angled my right finger to press against it from the top.

Heidi immediately went rigid. "Fuc—" but the spasms inside her cunt and ass squeezed all sound out of her throat. The contractions on my right finger felt like they were about to wrench it off at the joint.

As soon as her contractions subsided I spun her around on her back and plunged myself in and out until she screamed orgasm after orgasm. "More! More!" she begged after each climax. "Fuck me again!" Her eyes pleaded even more eloquently than her words.

I paused for a moment after each climax, then took a deep breath and resumed stroking my cock in and out of her cunt. And at each resumption she shut her eyes to concentrate below. After three rounds, I had no more computer code to write. All the code on my imaginary screen was yelling at me to come! Come!

And come I did, expending so much into her that I slipped and slithered out of her cunt. She opened her eyes beneath me, a smile slowly spreading across her face. A smile of contentment, a smile of triumph, a smile of bliss.

We cuddled together for what seemed like an eternity. Then her breathing slowed into sleep and she curled up into a little ball. I slowly detached from her, stood up and began to put my clothes back on. It was time to get back to work, but I couldn't help but stare down at her, curled and purring in the center of my bed.

At my computer console, I checked on my probes. Two had been disabled, but by hackers other than the Cyber Culprit. Six had so far come up empty. But the last one had hit paydirt! The Cyber Culprit was trying to sell a zero!

A zero, more properly a "zero day", is an undiscovered vulnerability in widely-used software that can be exploited because no one knows about it. It can be anything from a defect in an operating system such as Windows or as specialized as the software used by an individual bank. Almost as soon as a hacker uses it, day one, IT security professionals start working to fix the defect.

The zero had been up for sale on a dark website brokered by a web daemon known for his ties to the Russian mob. Grievous grief would be the only thing to be gained by probing further. Still it was interesting to note that the Cyber Culprit felt himself to be in need of money. Based on the bids prior to sale, CC had apparently netted somewhere between fifty thousand and an hundred and fifty thousand dollars. On the dark web, just because you bid doesn't mean that you pay and 'deals' are notorious for falling through.

I fixed myself a mug of coffee and glanced into the bedroom. Heidi hadn't moved since I'd left her an hour before.

I picked up my phone. It was time to check in with the other woman in my life. Lee picked up quickly enough, but she seemed supremely uncurious about the Amber Alert and Loud Commercial apps, so I moved straight to the zero. But Lee was only slightly more interested in CC's commercial activities and asked only to be kept informed. I wished I was back down in Hedo!

We rang off and I returned to my computer. Three more of my probes had been disabled. There was no trace of who had done the disabling, a clear indication that it was the Cyber Culprit. Then two more dropped out of commission,

torpedoed by unknown. I brought the entire statistical
overview of my remaining probe up on my computer screen.
It had snooped at several IP addresses which had been used
by CC, but I had established that these IP addresses had been
hijacked by CC without the owner's knowledge or permission.

Then the probe started to reverse direction, snooping
into Michael Rayburn's law firm. But his firm's firewalls
seemed to be strong enough to resist the probe and it began to
turn its attention to the proxy servers I'd used. I madly tried
to send queries back up the chain to discover who had taken
my probe over, but each query was rebuffed. In a moment,
the probe would be at my doorstep. I had no choice but to
shut it down. I heaved a sigh of relief which hurt where
Connors' fist had connected with my ribs. I stared frustrated
at my computer screen. CC was proving to be a tough, very
tough, nut to crack.

I had so little to report to Mr. Rayburn, that I wished
that I'd hadn't promised to call him by the end of the day. But
I had promised, so I got my phone out.

Actually I did have something but it wasn't actually
something that I could report. It was more of a negative. I
hadn't located the Cyber Culprit. But I knew where he wasn't.
He wasn't in Asia, Africa, or South America. But a negative
wasn't something that a layman like Mr. Rayburn would
understand as progress.

Just as I readied to dial, an email came through from
Mr. Rayburn. The Cyber Culprit had struck again, this time
posting photos and videos of a married woman hooking up
with a man at a local pick-up bar. She was a dark haired
beauty, trim and fit to boot. Maybe with Lee down south, I'd
get the chance to meet her. And given our current
investigative methods, the meeting would have come with a
wonderful set of perks.

I pressed the phone to dial Michael. "Hi, Eric," he
answered. "Have you made any progress?"

I winced, no way to dodge such a direct question. "No
sir, I can't say I have. But I'll keep working on it and some

leads are starting to open up. Have you checked your firm's internet security?"

"Rock solid."

I could tell he was about to ring off, so I spoke as quickly as I could, "I saw the most recent posting. Did you want me to look into it? Ms. Brandt won't be back —"

"I just spoke to Lee. She's coming back on the next plane. You keep working on the cyber angle."

He rang off leaving me to stare at the image of the dark haired beauty I'd never get to meet.

Cheaters, Lusty Lee Log #8

The three of us were in one of Michael Rayburn's small law-firm boardrooms. I had worn purple pants and a body-hugging blouse to show off my feminine curves. I'd gone jacket-less to display the golden tan on my bare arms. Eric, having slathered himself with sunscreen all the time we'd been in Jamaica, was pasty white. Then again red hair and green eyes on top of more than six feet of skinniness was all the color my assistant needed. Michael's only excuse for his pallor was long hours under fluorescent lighting. But still, he was handsome in his custom-tailored suit and his full lips begged to be kissed.

Eric had a small bruise on his right cheek from his recent MMA bout. But since the other guy had lost, I assumed that he looked even worse for wear.

Michael jumped right into the meeting, "Tell me what you found out?"

Eric was about to report, but I jumped in first. "We verified that the illicit internet postings were in fact taken at Hedonism II in Jamaica. We interviewed some of the people in the posting. Some were not substantially affected. One couple was significantly embarrassed. No one was aware of being photographed at the time, but one of the group leaders thinks that one of his group managed to snap a photo of the

Cyber Culprit." The 'Cyber Culprit' was the nickname we'd given the hacker who'd made several postings embarrassing to important clients of Michael Rayburn's law firm.

"Did you get a copy of the photo?" Michael, ever the lawyer, wanted to know.

I nodded and swiped a grainy out-of-focus image of the head and shoulders of a man to the top of my cellphone. Eric and Michael huddled over the small screen, intent on absorbing every detail. Behind them, my blue eyes and curly brown hair shimmered on the glass wall of the boardroom.

I sat back and watched the two men. I had already studied the photo in detail; it could be anyone. Eric, having come to the same conclusion, was the first to look up. I kept my eyes on Michael, yearning to have him focus his attention on me as completely as he was focusing it on my phone.

When Michael finally looked up, I turned to Eric and tapped the photo, "Were you able to track his Apps through cyberspace?"

Eric shook his head ruefully. "He bounced the Apps off so many servers deep inside the dark web that they were impossible to trace. And right away, people were reposting them."

The first App allowed users to inflict the extra-loud Amber Alert claxon on those inflicting it on an unwilling populace, especially the police and the regulatory body that had mandated it. The second jumped the volume of phone calls of broadcasters and advertisers who featured commercial messages at a higher volume than the regular programming they were designed to advertise.

"Are the Apps still out there?" I wanted to know.

Eric shook his head. "The authorities have suppressed them and the Cyber Culprit seems to have lost interest."

"What about the zero he sold?" Michael wanted to know.

Eric shook his head again. "The zero—the internet vulnerability—has been plugged and I was unable to trace who paid him or where the funds went."

"Or what the Cyber Culprit wanted the money for," I chimed in.

"Or what the Cyber Culprit wanted the money for," Eric confirmed.

Michael pointed a small remote controller at the ceiling and the screen on the opposite wall filled with the Cyber Culprit's latest internet upload. The posting was relatively bland by his standards: photos of an attractive woman, her hair such a deep shade of brown as to be almost black, flirting in a bar with several men, including a shot of her flashing her bra. She was carrying a bag with the logo of one of the country's best-know retailers on it.

"Note that the video clearly shows her face, but that his is almost completely obscured," the lawyer pointed out. Michael was right. Could the man be an accomplice of the Cyber Culprit?

Michael's presentation continued with a video of the dark-haired beauty ultimately leaving with one of the men she'd been flirting with, photos of the couple making their way to a hotel and a video of them making their way up to a room.

The video stopped just as she started to step into the room. "The video of the hotel is from the hotel's own surveillance system," Michael reported. "They claim that it was hacked, that they didn't give it to anyone. But they don't have any idea as to who got into their system or how."

Michael clicked the controller again and the woman's corporate profile page filled the screen. She was Sarah Grant, a retail management executive. "She's managed to keep her job," Michael reported, "but just barely."

Michael continued to press the controller and a series of images of Sarah Grant filled the screen. Ravishing was the best word to describe her. When she smiled, hearts melted. But when her lips tightened, steel would crack. I estimated Sarah to be shorter than myself, thin with wiry hard muscle. And given the internet posting, blessed with higher than average libido.

"A man in a similar executive position would have been fired," noted Eric. The two men nodded, commiserating at life's injustices.

"What about her marriage?" I asked.

"She's separated," Michael reported. "Her husband said he needed his 'space'. She's waiting to hear back from him regarding counseling."

"I'll meet her. Eric will—"

Eric's phone beeped and he looked down at it. His eyes widened. "This may be something!" He scooped up his phone and dashed out the door.

"Like I said," I continued, "Eric will continue with his cyber sleuthing."

Michael nodded. "I'll need an updated report first thing next week.

I wanted to flirt, how I wanted to stay and flirt with Michael! To watch his eyes follow my body as mine undressed his, to drop a *double entendre* and watch him try to figure out which meaning I'd intended, to dance our eyes around each other's... But I had nothing more to say and work was calling.

When Sarah Grant opened the door to her upscale condo, she was dressed only in a long white wrap buttoned at her left shoulder and waist. In person, she was more sensuous than in her photos, and her hair was even darker. She held a cellphone in her left hand.

Sarah ushered me in, her left thigh teasing from under the slit of her wrap. "I was just about to pop into the hot tub. Care to join me?"

"I'm sorry," I said shaking my head, "I didn't bring my bathing suit."

Sarah looked me up and down, her eyes showing obvious appreciation of my voluptuousness. "It's okay, I have a selection of swimwear."

She turned and took a few more steps, pausing and turning around in front of a washroom. I could see a variety of bikinis hanging inside. Ahead of us, outside a set of sliding doors was the hot tub and, in the distance, an unobstructed view of the shimmering waters of Lake Ontario. Sarah undid the clasps on her wrap and it fell to the floor. Other than her cellphone, she was completely nude.

Sarah pointed inside the washroom, "The swimsuits are inside." She looked slowly up and down my body. "Or you can go *au naturel*."

Sarah paused, waiting for me to decide. I took a deep breath and began to unbutton my blouse. I had adjusted to the idea of my interview subject being nude in front of me. Her breasts were tiny, but just right for her figure, a small handful, but certainly enough to caress and squeeze. She was clean-shaven down below, but had a tattoo of a flying dragon on her pubic bone. Her legs were strong and firm. By the time I got back to her face, her eyes were sparkling and she was adjusting her hair in an obvious preening move.

I placed my blouse on a chair and removed my bra. Sarah stared at my breasts, a smile slowly spreading on her lips. When I unzipped my pants, she turned and walked towards the hot tub. Her hips swayed suggestively, squeezing and releasing her round luscious butt with each step.

When Sarah bent over to turn the hottub jets on, her sex splayed beautifully. She must have slipped into the water when I'd turned to put my panties on the chair because when I turned to walk towards the tub, she was already in, her eyes level with my pelvis. As I arrived at the edge of the hot tub, she lifted a hand-held showerhead out of the water and sprayed me. The water was salty, slippery and hot. As I climbed in, she made a show of putting the showerhead between her legs.

The water was heavenly and I shut my eyes. In a moment I was floating in bubbles, the rest of the universe fading away.

Sarah's voice brought me back to the here and now. "You said you wanted information about the internet postings."

My eyes snapped open but she was smiling at me, I hadn't blown the interview. "Yes."

"You've seen the postings?" She leaned back and shut her eyes.

This was obviously a hint for me to ask questions. I didn't need a second invitation. "Who was the man in the video?"

"He said his name was Mark."

"Mark...?"

"Just Mark."

"Do you know anything else about him?"

She opened her eyes and turned to me. Her right breast came out of the water, its nipple engorged. She shook her head.

"Where did you meet Mark?"

"Online. At Hendricks." I had heard of the place. Upscale. Downtown. Lots of young urban professionals.

"Why Hendricks?"

"It's a hotspot for the Hook-upXplore App. You don't have to be in the bar to use Hook-upXplore, but being in the bar at least forces users to use a reasonably current photo in their profile."

"Do you know who posted the photos and videos of you?"

She shook her head again. "We only communicated via email."

Communicated?!? This was the first time the Cyber Culprit had ever communicated with any of his victims. "What did he say?" I asked.

"First he wanted money." She pushed herself up against the edge of the tub and edged closer to me. Both her nipples were engorged.

"Blackmail?"

"And I refused." She turned to me, her nipples almost touching my arm. "It wasn't the idea of giving into blackmail, but I didn't want him in my life any more than he was."

"You said that money was his first demand?"

Sarah nodded, "After that it was trash talk, how much exposing my dirty laundry in public would cost me."

"If not money, what did he want in return for keeping your tryst secret?"

"He told me that I'd have to wash him thoroughly, every nook and cranny of his body." Sarah was turning towards me and I felt the jets from the handheld showerhead on the inside of my ankle. Our toes touched.

She saw me start and knew that I had felt her energy. "What did you say?" I asked.

"There was more." The jets from the showerhead, warmer than the water in the rest of the hot tub, tickled past my knee.

"More?"

"And then I'd have to let him lick every inch of my body." Sarah had the jets directed right onto my pussy. Heat on the outside, heat on the inside. She licked her pointy little tongue around the edges of her lips. I relaxed my pelvis and spread my thighs, letting the jets from Sarah's showerhead tickle all the way inside. Who was going to lick whom, I wondered. Our heads came together, our lips touched. I closed my eyes.

All of a sudden, there was loud music. Sarah was no longer close. I opened my eyes as she reached for her phone. She touched it and the annoying ringtone stopped. "Sarah Grant here," she answered. The showerhead was thrashing about on the surface of the water. Sarah's entire focus was drawn into her phone. After a few minutes of scattered monosyllables from Sarah, it was obvious that this was going to be a long call, so I got out to get dressed.

Hendricks, the nightclub where Sarah Grant had hooked up with 'Mark' was only half full when I got there. For a Friday night, prime pick-up night, business was light. About two-thirds of the patrons were men. Most of the men had their faces buried in their phones or laptops. The women were looking at their phones, then surveying the bar, presumably trying to match profiles with the real thing.

I was wearing a short skirt and a bosom-hugging blouse. Sarah's Mark hadn't seemed the type to appreciate subtlety.

The layout was a bar jutting out from the left side of the club, almost the entire length of the room. I walked up to its far end and connected to the club's free WiFi. I had just joined Hook-upXplore and my profile described me exactly how I was: twenty-nine years old, five-foot five, medium build, physically fit, blue eyes, curly brown hair, single. I was wearing the same outfit as in my profile picture: a simple white blouse tight around my bosom and unbuttoned to reveal the top of my cleavage. Below was the same red leather skirt. At least the photo didn't show me sitting alone at a bar.

I set the App to show me who was in range and almost every man in the bar popped up. One looked startlingly like Peter Henge, my ex, who'd unceremoniously dumped me a few weeks ago. I surveyed the bar and there he was, not Peter, but close. Close enough to bring back all the hurt I'd felt when he'd dumped me, close enough to rekindle my hunger for revenge. I thought about picking him up, making him buy me an expensive dinner, then walking out. But he didn't deserve that. He wasn't Peter.

Hook-upXplore had promised to give us an upload of all activity at Hendricks. I was here to insert my activity so that Eric would be able to confirm that the upload they'd be giving us was complete. And if I got lucky, to hook up with 'Mark'.

I counted fifteen single men in the club. Were they all cheating on their significant others? Would the pain had been worse if Peter had been cheating? Or had the hurt been deeper because I just wasn't quite good enough?

Another man entered the club and immediately sat down at the other end of the bar. He was wearing a Blue Jays baseball cap, and dark sunglasses. He had short hair, dark brown. His leather jacket was loose, so I couldn't get a good read on his height or body type. His entrance hadn't popped an additional Hook-upXplore icon, so that made twelve men on the App and four off.

A few of the twelve male Hook-upXplorers were starting to make eye contact with several of the women.

At the other end of the bar, the bartender had placed a tall-necked beer bottle in front of Blue Jays Cap.

Blue Jays Cap took a long draw, then waved his bottle to take in the entire bar, "This place used to be intimate, before WiFi. Back then a guy had to actually be able to talk to a woman to get her to pay attention to him. And the women would say things, actually understand what you were saying."

The bartender nodded.

"Now, look at them, heads up their computers, inside their phones as if that's reality."

The bartender nodded, trying to back away.

But BJ Cap wasn't finished. "Government has to be sneaky to get our information, but we're freely giving it up to Google and Facebook."

The bartender watched BJ Cap take a long draw on his beer and slam it back onto to the bar, empty.

Light glinted off BJ Cap's sunglasses as he pointed to the guy in the back with his face absorbed into his laptop, "Pokemon Go has the right idea. Lure them all to their deaths. Cleanse the gene pool. But instead the police are protecting the idiots."

BJ Cap turned on his stool and stomped out of the bar.

The bartender slid down towards me and gestured towards the closing door. "No wonder he's alone, his opinions matter more than getting along." Before I could respond, one of the men not on Hook-upXplore wanted a whisky and the bartender turned to fill the order.

Actually, it was the man wanted and he slid down bar towards me. He smiled when he saw me look up from my phone. I smiled back. It took the bartender a moment to locate the target for the whisky. The man pointed at the drink and I nodded. He held two fingers to the bartender who turned around to pour another whisky.

"I'm Mark," the man said. But he wasn't the same Mark who'd picked up Sarah.

"Lee." I held out my hand for him to shake, but he kissed it instead. A good beginning.

The bartender returned with the second whisky but I ignored him and instead took a slip out of Mark's glass, looking him up and down, making the snap decision whether to blow him off or to continue the dance of romance. 'Mark' was older than me, mid-forties, his grey-flecked hair starting to go bald. He had a bit of a paunch, but not too much. His face was round, non-descript. In his favor, he was well-dressed — custom-fitted suit and shirt, silk tie just slightly loosened. But the kicker was his hands. He took the drink in his left hand, his fingers subtly caressing the amber liquid. And with his right, he took his billfold out of his pocket, maneuvered a twenty-dollar bill out from underneath the top hundred, took a five back as change, pushed the coins forward as a tip and slid the billfold back into his pocket, entirely unaware of the fascinating ballet he'd just performed. Such fingers *deserved* to touch my body. More importantly, my body *deserved* to be touched by such fingers.

I quickly pinged all twelve of the males on Hook-upXplore, swallowed the rest of the whisky in one gulp, the burn going down my throat like a dagger, and thumped the glass down on the bar. Mark began to turn towards the bartender but I shook my head.

He looked at me quizzically. "Don't you want — "

"I want you."

He looked down at his paunch. "Why would you — "

"Do you want me?"

He nodded.

I smiled. I hid the triumph, but I smiled nonetheless. "Why? What's special about me?"

"You first. What's so special about me?"

"Take out your billfold."

His eyes narrowed. "Are you a hooker?"

I shook my head and pointed to the pocket containing

his billfold. He took it out, reluctantly.

"Rearrange your money."

In a moment his smallest bills were on top, the larger ones underneath.

I pointed to five-dollar bill, now on top. "I want you to do that. To me."

He looked back and forth between his billfold, my legs, his billfold and my cleavage, his billfold and my smile. Then he smiled, stuffed his billfold back in his pocket.

"Your turn," I reminded him.

"Your curly brown locks are made for twirling my fingers in, your blue eyes sparkle delight. You smile. Smiles make a man happy. Your face is wonderfully beautiful to look at. Your breasts are full, bursting with fertility, a strong counterpoint to your delicate locks. You have hips, a woman should have curves for a man to explore. You—"

I touched my finger to his lips. "Let's go," I told him.

Inside the hotel room, the same room where another Mark had seduced Sarah a fortnight ago, I backed myself against the wall. "Touch me," I begged.

He smiled an evil little smile as he slowly removed his suit jacket and laid it on a chair. He stared at me until I whimpered. He walked slowly to me and gave me a kiss so light it was almost air.

Mark's left hand began to unbutton my blouse and his right gently squeezed my leg just below my skirt. I shut my eyes. Mark's fingers fluttered up between my thighs and brushed against the bottom of my panties. I spread my legs to give him full access.

His fingers seemed to know exactly where my feminine parts were, even without sight to guide them, or even any orientation by prior touch. They danced up and down my slit inspiring my inner lips to engorge and begin to poke out from between my *labia majora*.

Then all of his fingers were brushing their tips up my belly. Somehow they touched my breasts, under my bra. First a gentle touch all over and I had to steady myself against the wall. Next a gentle squeezing from the outside in, my nipples begging to be included. Then his fingers circled my areolae and my nipples poked up to their full height, tight and taut. At last — finally! — his fingers circled my nipples, so softly I could barely feel his touch. But the jolts up my spine to the back of my neck were unmistakable.

Fingers were replaced lips and tongue. This time, Mark's gentle suction on my nipple sent the jolts downward to my sex to meet his fingers which were tenderly plucking up on my pubic hairs, rubbing my outer lips against my inner lips and rubbing them against my clit. All my lips were wet and inside I was hot.

Then all four fingers of his right hand were pressed against my sex. His thumb rotated against my pubic bone, swiveling my clit against the surrounding skin. This aroused her ever upward and outward and his thumb dropped down to gently circle my clit directly. Somehow his fingers were touching skin-to-skin, my panties seemingly having vanished.

Two fingers slid inside my pussy, so softly, so smoothly that I was hardly aware of their advance except for the delicious pressure being exerted against my insides. I *was* fully aware of the delights on the outside, his other two fingers slipping over and under my pussy lips as they moved back and forth with their penetrating mates, his thumb circling my clit, tapping and squeezing pulses out of my pleasure knob.

He kissed me then and I melted into him. His lips on my hips, his tongue caressing my tongue, his left hand squeezing my breasts, his right hand pulling all of this pleasure downward, concentrating, contracting.

His fingers inside touched my g-spot, just the outer edge, but it was enough to buckle my knees. I would have fallen if he'd not snaked his left arm behind me, grabbed my waist and pressed his paunch against my middle.

Then the two fingers inside me circled my g-spot, teasing. All they had to do was brush against its center and I would have been gone. I might not have been unconscious, but at that moment, at that eternity, all I was aware of was the tips of the two fingers circling opposite sides of my pleasure spot. Not breathing, not standing, not falling, just two fingertips.

Then the fingers joined, pressed firmly and moved rapidly back and forth across my g-spot. My orgasm was a calm wave, a powerful wave, crashing my body against the wall, lifting it joyfully forward, pulling me towards the ceiling, releasing me back down to the floor. And then the wave was water and I gushed all over Mark's hand.

When I opened my eyes, Mark was still fully clothed. Something would have to be done about that! I gave him a gentle push towards the bed and took half a step forward. My skirt was still on, but my panties were around my left ankle. My blouse was completely unbuttoned and my breasts jiggled against my unclasped bra. How this had happened, I had no idea, except I was sure Mark's magic fingers had had something do with it!

His pants weren't wet, but the tips of his shirtsleeves were coated with my enthusiastic ejaculate. I carefully lifted his jacket up and over his shirtsleeves. His suit was a silk and wool blend, soft and almost slippery as I slid his zipper down to begin to release his erection. Mark's underwear was a pair of ordinary Stanfield briefs, but at least they were dark grey to match his suit. I lifted them up and over, and there was Mark's manhood.

Mark's manhood, sad to say was nothing to write home about. He was barely six inches long and barely thicker than a popsicle. But he was hard and waving about for my attention. I sucked him deep into my mouth and was gratified to hear a sharp gasp for breath from above.

I knew my fingers were no match for Marks, so I contented myself with holding firmly onto his soft buttocks. But my tongue and throat and suction and lips carefully covering my teeth were more than enough. I sucked hard as I pulled him out, then held just the tip of his penis in my mouth rapidly sucking as hard as I could, then releasing my pressure.

When he'd stopped breathing, I moved my mouth up and down his entire shaft as quickly as I could, alternating suction with my tongue lapping against his shaft.

Mark stumbled backward and I released him from my mouth. He fell onto the bed and I pounced on him sucking his cock once more into my mouth. A few sharp strokes up and down, timed with my fingers squeezing his balls spurted the last of Mark's strength into my mouth. He tasted of whisky. Very *salty* whisky.

The next night, I started earlier. There was a different bartender at Hendricks, a young, skinny blonde woman. The only patron present was the same guy who'd had his head in his laptop all night long. I looked at him carefully. He didn't seem to match the grainy photo of the Cyber Culprit I'd managed to score while down at Hedo.

I was wearing a similar outfit from the night before, except that my blouse was red satin and my skirt black.

The ceiling was unfinished, painted black to hide the ductwork, wiring and beams. There was tape hiding what would have been the blinking lights of the WiFi router. No tape on the smoke-detector light, presumably building code regulations forbade it. I spotted the video camera which had recorded Sarah, black like the rest of the ceiling.

I sidled over to the bar and caught the attention of the bartender. "I'm Lee," I told her.

"Sally. What can I get you?"

I pointed to the camera in the ceiling. "What's that?" I asked.

She shrugged. "It's the bar's security system. But nothing ever happens here."

"But it records?"

"I guess." She obviously wasn't the one to ask for any surveillance tapes.

"I'll have a beer," I told her. "Whatever you have on tap."

I gave her a five. Not so generous that she'd dote on me, but enough that she wouldn't remember me as a cheapskate. I carried the beer around the club, pretending to look for just the right table. But there was nothing out of place and I sat down.

Two single men came through the door. I looked around. Hendricks was nothing special. Why had the Cyber Culprit chosen it? I shrugged. Why does anybody choose anything?

Tonight my plan was to wait and see if Sarah's Mark turned up. I'd wait an hour after the time Sarah had left with him. After that, I'd be off the clock, free to pick up any male on the premises. There were three possibles: My first choice was Muscles. He was wearing jeans and a white Tshirt, his muscles bulging under and out from his shirt. Blue eyes and a full head of blonde hair completed the package. Suit-and-Tie was my second choice because I was fascinated by how the pinstripes on his suit accentuated his skinny height. Dark brown hair, brown eyes, handsome. If all else failed, there was Happy. He was rotund and short. Suit jacket, tie fully loosened, a pitcher of beer on the table and a wide smile on his lips. All three were on Hook-upXplore.

The club was almost at capacity. Unlike last night, the proportion of males to females was fairly even. I gave Eric a quick call. Nothing new on his end.

Mark—Sarah's Mark—came in just after ten. He was the quintessential bad boy—black hair slicked back on one side, hanging loose on the other, days-old stubble on his face, just long enough not to scratch, eyes radiating fun and danger and rebellion. He was wearing a black leather jacket, dark blue shirt unbuttoned half-way down to reveal a tattoo of a rose with the tip of a sword piercing up from the center of its blossom. Black dress pants completed his ensemble. Beneath were fully muscled shoulders and chest tapering down to a thin waist.

He was just what Sarah would have wished for—a challenge to try to dominate, power over her to spare if she failed.

Mark did a quick look around the nightclub, pausing a

moment at each female, but too quickly for me to flash a smile back at him. Then he strode to the bar, ordered and paid for a rum and coke, and took his drink to a table halfway up the right side of the club.

Mark took out his phone, presumably accessing the Hook-upXplore App. I followed suit, and there he was smiling back at me from my phone. His profile picture was clean-shaven with a smile, but it was clearly the same man. His profile said he worked as personal trainer and coach. Hobbies were laser tag and photography.

My phone vibrated, indicating that someone was pinging me on the App. I moved to the messaging screen but it was Happy. I pinged Mark, then sat so that he'd see my best side: strong thighs, round butt and bountiful bosom. I got another ping, this time from Muscles. Ruefully, I turned him down. Cupid finally rewarded me with a return ping from Mark. I looked up from my phone and smiled him an invitation as I tapped out a pre-arranged signal to Eric.

In the hotel, I had chosen the same room he and Sarah had been filmed entering, but Mark showed no recognition of the premises. I tried to push bad boy Mark up against the wall. But he wanted none of that. He spun me around and pushed his right leg between my legs, spreading them. The fabric on his pants was smooth. Linen?

Mark kissed me full on the mouth, his tongue shoving inside with reckless abandon. Two hands squeezed my breasts. His right leg moved up and down, stimulating self-defense lubrication inside my pussy. Sex with Mark was going to be swift, fast, vigorous and passionate!

He quickly stripped off all my clothes, then led and pushed me onto the king-sized bed. I scooted up to the headboard to watch Mark make equally quick work of removing his own clothes, his six-pack abs rippling. He picked up his pants from the floor and extracted a condom.

Mark climbed onto the bed, straddling my right leg, his knee less than an inch from my sex. He held out the condom. His cock was throbbing in front of me. It was a good twelve inches long, thick, circumcised. Its head was deep purple. I ripped open the condom packet and placed the latex sheath over the penis head. Sadly, underneath the latex, it wasn't quite a purple. But his cock was rock hard, his veins providing little ridges as I unrolled the condom. At the top of the condom, there was room for a mini-penis. I gave the condom a little tug up at the bottom and we were good to go.

But before Mark could react, I slid underneath him and licked his balls. They jiggled, then pulled tightly upwards.

Mark's hands on my head held me still as he lengthened himself down my body. I tried to shut my legs, but his hips between them held them apart.

His cock pressed against my pussy lips. "Ready?" he asked.

I nodded and took a deep breath.

Mark rocked his hips and rammed his cock all the way up inside me! The breath I'd only just taken was expelled from my lungs. I tried to breathe, but couldn't. Mark pulled himself almost out, then slammed back inside. He pulled out again, and still I couldn't breathe! It took three more savage thrusts before I could time him and gasp air into my lungs on his out-strokes.

But now I was matching his savagery. Pushing myself up when he thrust inside, rocking my hips downward when he withdrew. Sex like a hundred-yard dash, nothing held back. Sweat making our bodies slick, sweat mixing with other lubricants. He grunting, me yelping with joy!

And then we slowed, and I became aware of his subtleties—his pubic hair rasping against mine, his musk assaulting my nostrils the same way his cock had assaulted my pussy, the hard firmness of his chest, the way his tummy tightened with each thrust, the way each grunt came in the middle of each stroke. I started to float, endorphins making every cell in my body a wisp of pleasure, turning everything white behind my eyelids. But a hard squeeze on my right breast brought me back and we resumed our furious coupling.

I slipped sideways and Mark used the opening to turn

me on top of him. He caressed my breasts and ran his fingers roughly across my nipples sending jolts careening up to my throat where they emerged as plaintive keenings.

I pushed myself up into the cowgirl position so that I was kneeling atop Mark. He tried to reach for my breasts but couldn't. I was riding! I was in control! I bounced up and down, little shallow strokes to stimulate my clit.

"Harder!" he ordered, digging his fingers into the front of my butt muscles.

I shook my head, and leaned back, lifting my knees up and scooting my feet to the mattress. Mark lifted his knees and I leaned back, supporting myself with my hands on his thighs. Now I bounced higher and at a variety of angles. He helped steady me with his hands on my upper thighs, his arms against my legs providing extra support. Every time up and down was like being fucked by a different man! This version of the cowgirl—Asian—is wonderful in theory but very tiring. I fell off and lay beside Mark, heaving air into my lungs.

I may have been tired, but Mark still had stamina to burn. He rolled off the bed and pulled me down so that my butt was at the very edge of the bed. He pulled my legs up so that my calves rested on his shoulders. His hands on my thighs pressed them against his pelvis. The tip of his penis was pressed between my pussy lips. He smiled an evil smile down at me. I was totally vulnerable, too weak to resist.

And then he plunged his phallus into me. Pure animal aggression. It was too quick and I was too wet and my legs were spread too wide for me to feel anything. Except that I was being fucked. Except that I was warm all over. That I was totally helpless, that I had no choice but to surrender. That I was slave, he master.

Then Mark started to bounce up and down on his knees. The bouncing was not in sync with his thrusts so the effect was random. But every time he raised himself on tiptoes, his shaft rubbed against my clit and I started to have a second master exerting control over my cunt—an orgasm was beginning to gather!

And sometimes when he lowered himself, when he was low and just at the start of his stroke, the tip of his cock brushed against my special spot, tightening the grip of my second master each time.

My second master didn't care that I was exhausted. Her hunger dug stirrups into my hips forcing them to rock forward to direct the tip of his cock against my g-spot each time it thrust inside, each time it pulled back.

I reached for his thighs, but all I could do was scratch. "Harder!" I demanded.

My scratching felt feeble, so I slapped at the top of his hands. "Harder! *Harder!*"

And he did! Harder and faster he slammed himself into me.

"Fuck!" he yelled.

"Fuck!" I yelled back.

"Fuck!" in unison. "*Fuck!*"

He throbbed inside, his thrusts jerked spasmodically. An orgasm burst partway up my spine. Confined. Intense! I gushed outside. My cunt spasmed around his cock. We fell onto the bed, our backs to the mattress, our legs, below our knees, dangling over.

As we lay panting on the bed, Mark's penis drooping inside his condom, the door to the room creaked. Mark was unaware of what was happening until my red-headed assistant was fully into the room. Mark jumped off the bed and took a wild swing which Eric easily dodged.

"Eric! You weren't supposed to be back until tomorrow!" I screamed.

Mark took another swing at Eric but the bad boy was no match for my assistant's martial-arts skills and Eric tapped Mark on his esophagus. Mark collapsed to the bed, eyes full of fear, trying to breathe, his hands clutching his throat.

I showed Mark a photo of Sarah on my phone. "Remember her?"

Mark nodded.

I showed him the Cyber Culprit's posting of his tryst with Sarah. "Did you have anything to do with this?"

Mark shook his head.

"Were you aware of the posting?"

Mark was finally able to breathe and managed to wheeze a feeble, "No."

I turned to Eric who had his phone connected to Mark's. "Anything?" I asked.

Eric shook his head and we left to collect video surveillance from Hendricks.

Sunday morning at eleven am, Michael Rayburn's ringtone on my cell meant no rest for the wicked.

"There's been a new posting," he announced.

I put my phone on speaker and watched as the videos streamed across. I recognized the face as belonging to an actor while Michael continued, "As you can see, they are pictures of Earl Brandis, the Academy Award nominated actor." Now I recognized him. He looked completely out of place injecting a syringe into his arm. And even more out of place being pinned down by two women and a man while they each took turns kissing him all over his body, and I do mean *all* over.

Brandis made family values movies. The photos of him shooting up at an orgy would, at the very least, put a dent in his career.

After making plans to follow up with Brandis, I headed to *El Bistro*, a small café I knew Eric hung out at. I wanted to get an update of his trace of the ransom demands the Cyber Culprit had made of Sarah. Their salacious nature aside, if we could find out where they were made from, maybe we'd be able to nail the little mischief-maker's ass to the wall.

As I turned the corner, I caught a glimpse of Eric through the café's window. He was talking to someone, their heads close together. Eric smiled and laughed. Then I saw who he was talking to. It was Peter Henge. What was *Eric* doing with my ex?!?

The Actor, Lusty Lee Log #9

I shut my car door and looked back inside through the window. Just like the café window where yesterday I'd caught sight of my assistant having an intimate tête-à-tête with my ex-paramour. But confronting my assistant as to what the hell was going on would have to wait. I turned towards the rather large mansion I'd stopped in front of and began to walk up the pathway to its oversized front door.

As I rang the doorbell on the home of the Cyber Culprit's latest victim, I wondered what he'd be like in person. Earl Brandis had been nominated for several Academy Awards for his performances in several family-values movies. But the recent internet postings had exposed the actor as a sex-crazed drug addict—a photo of him injecting something into his arm and a video of him being pinned down by two women and a man while they each took turns kissing him all over his body, and I do mean *all* over. The postings would, at the very least, put a dent in his ability to attract the General Audience roles that had been his bread and butter.

Brandis opened the door thirty seconds after my first ring and looked nothing like any of my preconceptions. His eyes were clear, his voice vibrant, his diction flawless. Certainly not a drug addict. He shook my hand perfunctorily, ushered me politely into his anteroom and angled us towards opposite sides of a large table. If he'd wanted to put the make on me—and who wouldn't want to put the make on a voluptuous woman with sparkling blue eyes wearing a tight blouse and a skirt ready to be pushed up her thighs—he would have brought me deeper into his mansion and not put a table between us. But none of his neighborhood dad characters would have been at home in the linen shirt and silk pants, both black and hugging his slim frame, topped off by a white sports jacket. He was older than I'd remembered and looked vaguely like Dennis Hopper.

He didn't sit, so I began the meeting standing. "Mr. Brandis, please let me offer my sympathies for what has happened to you."

He smiled down at me. "No need to worry, Miss Lee, all publicity is good publicity." He wasn't toweringly tall, but tall enough to effortlessly project his masculinity. He motioned for us to sit down.

I adjusted my bottom into his comfortable chair, subtly shook my curly brown locks and favored him with an inviting smile.

"Actually, Lee is my first name. Lee Brandt."

"So much the better," Earl smiled back.

"I salute your optimism about all publicity being good publicity, but won't work in your area dry up as word of your proclivities spreads?"

Brandis shrugged. "If one area or type of work dries up, another area will present itself. That said, what are you doing to catch this internet infiltrator?"

"We're analyzing the posts he's made and tracking him through cyberspace. The videos of you, when were they recorded?"

He smiled. "One night of supreme debauchery."

"The injection and the orgy both?"

He nodded.

"What was in the syringe?"

"Some sort of new designer drug, legal at the time. But everyone presumed heroin."

"Do you know who filmed you?"

"No, but my publicist got ahold of the video clips and suppressed them. When they were posted to the internet, my publicist did an investigation. Turns out that her server was hacked and that someone got into her computer. They did the whole nine yards with the best IT security firm in the country, but they couldn't find out who the hacker was."

I put my hand on his jacket sleeve. "Don't worry, we'll find out who did this and make him pay."

Earl smiled and put his right hand on top of my hand. "Tracking down this internet infiltrator, that sounds like a lot of work. I wish there was something I could do to repay you."

"Mr. Brandis, meeting me, helping us, is all we could hope for."

"Still." He looked at me as if seeing me for the first time. A smile slowly spread across his lips.

I smiled back. "You could do a scene for me."

He smiled, rolling his tongue inside his mouth, savoring the thought. "Who's your favorite actor?"

"Dennis Hopper."

"Rebel Without a Cause?"

I shook my head.

He squeezed the hand I had atop his sleeve. "The Sons of Katie Elder?"

I shook my head.

He lifted the hand I'd placed atop his sleeve, kissed the back of my hand and made the sound of a Harley Davidson. "Easy Rider?"

I shook my head.

He placed his left hand on the bottom of my skirt. "Apocalypse Now?"

I shook my head.

He slid his thumb under my skirt and moved it up several inches. "Paris Trout?"

I shook my head.

He turned the hand he'd been holding over and kissed the underside of my wrist. "Speed?"

I shook my head.

Earl released my hand, placed it atop my skirt between my legs and placed his right hand beside his left. Both hands were now inching up my thighs. "Witch Hunt?"

I shook my head. He had started pushing his hands gently up my thighs towards the hand he'd laid between them. He stopped and cocked his head, a puzzled look on his face.

"Blue Velvet," I said, removing my hand from where he'd placed it atop my skirt.

Earl took a deep breath to get into character, nailed Frank's forbidding, foreboding attitude, then sneered, "Where's my bourbon?"

I nodded. "Blue Velvet." Blue Velvet was the film noir wherein Frank, the Dennis Hopper character, had kidnapped Dorothy's husband as an excuse for him to lure Dorothy into ferocious and kinky sex. The movie shows Dorothy as a victim, but I'd always conceived of her as being the one who wanted rough sex and that it was she who lured Frank into her clutches.

"That's a violent scene," Earl protested, removing his hands from my thighs. "Maybe I should just do a reading."

I shook my head. "I want to do the scene with you."

"You want to be Dorothy?"

I nodded.

He shook his head. "It's too rough."

"I like rough."

"You've seen the scene?" He replaced his hands on my thighs.

I nodded. "I like rough."

"Exactly as filmed?"

"Yes. And the parts they edited out."

He slid his hands my thighs.

I made a show of inhaling sharply. "Do you have oxygen?"

He nodded. "Sometimes we have parties." When he saw my smile, he shook his head. "Strictly low dose, too much is bad for you."

I shrugged. "I want to do the scene."

"Are you sure?"

I nodded and leaned forward, pushing his hands up to just below my panties. "Do whatever you want," I told him. Enjoy it. Fuck me. Enjoy that too. Be rough with me, because after you come, I'm going to be rough with you."

He looked at me quizzically. I was pushing his boundaries, pushing him into unchartered territory.

I smiled. "After you've finished with me, I'm going to climb on top of your face. Your tongue better be good. You better have loaded up on the oxygen. Because I'm not climbing off until I've come." I fetched a chair from the dining room.

He looked at me as if I was from another planet, shrugged and left the room. In a moment he returned, wheeling in a small oxygen canister.

I pointed to the inhalation mask atop the canister, "Can I try that?"

He shook his head. "What's your skirt made of?"

I looked down at it. It was blue, or at least blue-ish, but certainly not velvet. "Cotton." Medium weight, so it didn't need lining.

"And your blouse?"

"Satin."

"Are you ready?" he asked.

I nodded.

He smiled sheepishly and looked down at the floor. When his eyes come up, he has become Dennis Hopper. Then his face slowly transforms into Hopper's character, the violent and unpredictable Frank Booth.

I meet his gaze and Dorothy's mad lust courses through my body as I move over to the door and shut it loudly, just like in Blue Velvet. Just like in the movie. I stand by the chair. "Hello, baby."

"Shut up." His hand flies towards my face. "It's Daddy, you shithead."

"Hello, Daddy."

"Where's my bourbon!"

I look around and he gestures to a liquor cabinet. I pour him a stiff bourbon—Jim Beam 12 year old—and hand it to him. I half cast my eyes to the floor, trying to look fearful, and watch him sip his drink.

He pulls his hand back as if to hit me but instead points to the chair. "Sit!"

I sit and make a show of adjusting myself.

He studies me. "Spread your legs," he commands.

I slowly spread my legs, wishing there was someone watching, someone filming our performance.

He gestures towards my crotch, "Wider!" I smile as his pupils become as wide as my legs.

He finishes his drink and slams the glass down on a side table. He adjusts his head to one side, accommodating the alcohol.

I spread wiggle my bum and feel my skirt hike halfway up my thighs. His eyes stare hungrily up between my legs.

"Don't look at me!" he shouts.

I look sideways and smile as I feel my blouse stretch tight across my breasts.

"Wider!"

I spread my legs as far as they will go and hike my skirt up to my hips. I wonder if I should remove my panties, then remember that they're red, sheer.

He looks me up and down as if I'm meat, as if he's about to consume me. His gaze settles on my crotch and I can feel him sucking at my sex. He places the oxygen mask over his face, turns a knob at the top of the canister, and takes a deep, deep breath. "Are you ready to fuck?" he asks.

"Yes."

"Get ready to fuck!" He's talking to the room, as if commanding himself. "Daddy wants blue cotton."

I slide out of my skirt and give it to him. "Okay," I whisper.

He rubs my skirt all over his face, across his chest, down to his crotch, then back up again. I can feel myself hot under my panties, my nipples poking hard against my bra.

He bites down on my skirt and releases it from his hands.

"Don't fuckin' look at me!" He slaps me across the face, not as hard as in the movie, but hard enough to get my blood flowing!

He fondles my breasts and unbuttons my blouse. His hands are hot, hot heavenly fire!

I watch him out of the corner of my eye as he kneels between my knees and takes two hard pulls from the oxygen canister, babbling between each pull. I touch his lips with my hand and he moans.

His hands move up the sides of my legs. When his fingers touch the edge of my panties, he angles his thumbs in and down, then presses them against my sex. They're even hotter than they'd been on my breasts. He presses upwards, stoking the fires inside me. "Daddy wants red!" he demands.

I slip my panties off and hold them towards him. He rubs them on his face, then bites down on them. His eyes go wide, wild, as his fingers play across my pussy. I'm wet and hot. Two fingers push inside. Jolts ripple up my spine and down my legs.

Suddenly he stands and slaps my face. "Whore!" I look at him, my eyes full of lust and challenge. "Don't look at me!" he screams. He lifts his hand, ready to strike. I look away.

Out of the corner of my eye, I see him slide my panties down his crotch.

He pulls me roughly down to the floor and stands over me. I hold his gaze, reach behind my back and unclasp my bra.

He spits on my belly. "Whore!"

I smile up at him. "Yes, Daddy, I'm your whore. What're you going to do to me?"

I spread my legs and feel a wisp of cool air. My blouse is disheveled, totally open, my breasts half out of my bra. Below my waist, I'm totally nude.

He casts his jacket aside and reaches into his pants and pulls my panties out. He kneels and holds my panties to my nose, making me smell. His musk has overpowered my juices. He stuffs my panties into my mouth. I try to move away, but the hard floor behind my head holds me in place. Frank smiles as I shake my head to attempt to avoid his efforts.

He rubs my body roughly, moaning sickly as he does so. Has he gone too deep into Frank's character? He slaps my face. "Don't you fucking look at me!" My nipples hurt under his hand and my pussy burns as he rams three fingers inside.

He climbs on top of me, lifts my knees and angles the center of his pants so that his zipper cover is positioned along my pussy slit.

"Whores are for fucking," he tells me. He begins to slowly rub the front of his pants up and down against me.

But he's too gentle and I push up against him. "Whores are for *fucking*," I scream up at him.

He rubs me harder and there's a stab of pain. He looks down at me in triumph as he dry humps me, enjoying himself now. He moans and babbles.

I smile up at him. He pushes off and slaps me on the face. "Don't look at me!"

I turn away and hear him walking. The door opens, then shuts. "Scene!" he proclaims.

I turn. He's walking back towards me. I lift myself back up onto the chair.

I shake my head and remove my panties from my mouth. "You promised the entire scene, all the parts they left out."

"Left out?" Frank had left and there was only Earl in the room.

"Dorothy's been a bad girl. She needs to be spanked, hard. She needs to be fucked, even harder."

He shook his head. "I'm not a misogynist; I don't believe in hurting women."

"Misogyny is for feminists and psychiatrists, I just know that I enjoy the kinky savagery of the sex every time I watch the film. And now I want the real thing."

Earl looked at me uncertain. I stood up and took a step towards him. I removed my blouse and threw it aside. Then my bra. I stepped towards him again and we were only inches apart.

"I want you to hurt me," I whispered, pressing myself against him, letting him feel the heat of my nakedness.

Earl remained silent.

I rubbed myself against him. "Didn't you enjoy the scene we just did?"

He nodded in spite of himself.

I rubbed his chest with my right hand, holding him close with my left. "Wouldn't you like more?"

He was stiff, afraid, frozen. As if he'd lose control if he moved even a hair's breadth.

I dropped my right hand to his crotch and rubbed lightly. He was already half aroused. "Wouldn't you like more?" I repeated.

He grew harder and larger beneath my hand but otherwise remained motionless.

"Hurt me," I pleaded. I gave him a gentle squeeze, but he was as large as his pants would allow.

He remained rigid, motionless.

I let loose of him and stepped back. "Do you want me to hurt you?"

Not a flicker of movement.

I slapped him against his face. Not too hard, but hard enough. I raised my hand to slap him again.

He flinched, but otherwise remained motionless.

I unbuttoned his shirt and squeezed both his nipples. "Do you want *me* to hurt *you*?" I twisted his nipples until his lips quivered.

When I'd twisted harder without further reaction, I let go of his nipples and began to hit him about the head and shoulders with both my hands. I got in a particularly good slap across his right cheek and he grabbed both of my wrists and gave me a gentle shake. I smiled at him noticing my boobs jiggle.

I took a deep breath. "Hurt me," I pleaded.

"Spanking?"

"And fucking and licking," I reminded him.

"Hard?"

I nodded. "Please."

He pushes me backwards, releasing my wrists. "Put your hands behind your head."

I comply and my breasts are exposed, without my arms to protect them. I suddenly feel very naked. A frisson of fear writhes in my stomach.

Earl looks down to the floor. When he looks back up, Frank has returned, mean and raw, a sexual predator toying with his prey. He unbuttons the sleeves of his shirt and drops it to the floor. He has a layer of flab and a bit of a paunch, but there's hard muscle beneath. His pants swiftly follow. Frank's only remaining garment is a pair of black spandex briefs which barely hold his protruding cock in place.

"Put your hands on the chair," he demands.

I turn around and put my hands atop the back of the chair, standing as straight as possible, my feet together, my stomach churning.

There's a thwack by my right buttock, followed by searing pain. "Put your feet back," he rasps.

I waddle my feet back as far as I can. My breasts hang almost straight downward, ponderous.

Another thwack on exactly the same place, not as hard—had he hurt his hand? Poor baby. Delicious heat was spreading throughout my right buttock.

Thwack! He'd angled slightly and now my left buttock is aflame as well. "Spread your legs," he commands, his voice now back in control.

I hesitate, but another thwack from his hand hurries me to spread my legs as far as they will go. My pussy, ass and butt cheeks are now completely exposed.

"Has Dorothy been a bad girl?"

I try to nod but my arms are holding my head tight on either side. "Yes."

"Very bad?"

"Very *very* bad."

"And what have you done, my bad, bad whore?"

"I teased a man and he touched me all over." His fingers dance softly atop my buttocks, a soft sensation where my skin hadn't been spanked, hot where I'd felt his hand strike.

"And did you touch him?"

"I touched his chest, and his cock." I reach around and manage to grab his cock, but a loud thwack returns my hand to the top of the chair.

"Did you enjoy it when he touched you?" His fingers had now strayed from my buttocks and are lightly brushing up and down my outer pussy lips, sometimes almost touching my anus. I relax and enjoy the sensations, enjoy the slow pace he's imposing.

Two short sharp thwacks on the bottom of my buttocks shock my eyes open.

Frank has moved to my right side and spanked me with his left hand. "Did you enjoy it when he touched you?"

"Yes," I gasp, absorbing the new bands of searing heat on the bottom of my buttocks. The tops of my thighs are now warming as well.

"Tell me what it felt like."

"It felt firm and hard, pain forcing pleasure to come to its higher limits."

"And how does it feel now?"

"It—" He hit my right buttock hard, where he'd first hit me. "It feels exquisite pain, warm, wonderful. As if I'm yours completely."

"And now?" His fingers rake up and down my sex.

"And now your fingers on my vulva make her feel warm and fuzzy as if she—" He squeezes. "Yes!" I gasp Your fingers teasing up and down the tips of my pussy lips make me hot and wet inside."

"Inside?"

I wiggle my hips back and forth and his fingers slip inside where I'm hotter and wetter. I push back, lifting the front legs of the chair off the floor, pushing back against his fingers and shutting my eyes in anticipation of his fingers stroking deeper.

Instead—thwack!—there's nothing between my legs and my butt is on fire!

"Be still, Dorothy," he commands. "I decide when and how."

"Okay."

"Say my name." Two sharp thwacks.

"Frank."

"*I* decide." Another thwack.

"Yes, Frank, *you* decide."

Once more his fingers slide into my pussy. "Shut your eyes and tell me what you feel."

"You're stroking back in and out and it makes me feel hot."

"Tell me what you want."

"I want your cock plunging in—" Thwack.

"Focus on my fingers. You don't get my cock until you've finished pleasuring my fingers."

"Faster, harder!"

His strokes became hard and fast, almost violent.

I gasp a breath. "Slower."

His fingers return to a gentler pace and I relax into it. "My little whore likes this."

"She *loves* it. Your power is building inside me. I can feel your arousal through my pussy. I'm melting into your fingers, into you."

I hear him take a breath of oxygen, his fingers continuing to stroke my pussy. Then the mask is by my face and I inhale deeply.

Suddenly I'm alert, energized, and even *more* horny! He takes the mask away.

"More," I beg.

Thwack! "No, you little whore, no more oxygen. You don't know what's bad for you."

His fingers are in full control of my pussy and I abandon myself to their caresses. He has two fingers inside thrusting up and around and two fingers below teasing my inner and outer lips and pushing and prodding my sex into different orientations to add variety to his touching. His thumb is angled upward, rotating the skin around my clit, releasing a steady pattern of jolts deeper into my sex. His other hand is maintaining a steady beat of swats against my bum.

"Tell me what you're feeling," he demands.

"It's warm—"

Thwack! He hits me harder. "Not warm, *hot!*" he corrects.

"It's hot!" And it *was* hot. "My pussy is hot and wet. You're making her purr. My puss—"

Thwack! He squeezes all his fingers together and holds them motionless. "Whores don't have pussies. They have *cunts*. Say it!" He squeezes harder, and now with his thumb too.

"My *cunt*—" I gasp as his fingers resume their thrusts, faster and deeper. "My cunt is on *fire*."

His left hand is swatting steadily against my buttocks, the digits of his right hand are playing me like a fine instrument. I shut my eyes and swoon until his voice gently lifts me back. "Talk to each of my fingers."

"Your little finger is sliding up and down my pussy—cunt—lips, tickling joy up to my clit. The next finger is pulling my cunt open for the other two to thrust inside, pulling her open at different angles for each thrust. Each thrust and I'm hotter, being pushed to the edge."

I pause and he hits me harder. Not a full thwack, but enough to get my attention. "What about my thumb?"

"Your thumb is stroking my clit, jolting pleasure to the bottom of my spine and down into the depths of my cunt. My cunt is hotter, tight—"

"Enough of your cunt. What are you feeling in your heart?"

I breathe deeply. "Your animal ferocity is filling me and I too am becoming fierce—"

He grabs me tightly with his left hand and I feel his cock pressing through his brief and into my right thigh. His fingers inside me speed up and he adds a curling motion to the two inside me causing them to start rubbing intermittently over my g-spot.

Suddenly his soul is inside me, his viciousness whipping his passion into me. I was his viciousness whipping his passion into myself.

"Come, you whore, *come*!" he demands.

"Fuck!' I yell. My pussy contracts hard against his fingers.

He lets go of me with his left hand and begins to spank me hard. But I don't care how hard he's hitting me. Each blow joins with my orgasm. Thwack bouncing spasms from cunt to butt. "Fuck!" I scream.

Thwack jolting up my spine! "Fuck!"

Thwack curling my toes. "Fuck!"

Thwack reverberating my clit. "Fuck!"

Thwack exploding my cunt. "Fuck!"

Thwacking me warm all over. "Jesus!"

One last shudder and I'm still again. I feel Frank moving. He's come around to my right side. His cock is hot on my thigh, no more brief. Finally! There's something warm on my anus. What was—

"What do you feel now?"

"It's warm and wet but not inside me, on my…"

A light thwack, not even painful. "Where?"

"On my bum."

Thwack! This time his blow is harder and my eyes shock open. "This is your bum!" he reminds me. "Where is it warm and wet now?"

Another drop lands and dribbles into the opening of my anus and now there's a little pool by my back door. "On my ass," I admit.

A finger presses downwards and, with the lubrication, I'm powerless to resist.

"And what's this?" he demands.

"My asshole."

His finger is all the way in my ass. He puts other fingers into my cunt, but she's sore from the pounding he's already inflicted.

"Oxygen," I plead. My arms are dead, my back aching and my legs cramping up.

"No, you've had enough." But he's gotten the message and

the fingers inside my cunt become almost motionless.

Not so the finger up my ass. This finger strokes up and down the inner extension of my clitoris. This finger strokes my g-spot to rub against the fingers inside my cunt. This finger strokes gentle long strokes rippling sensations up and down my ass, rippling sensations into my cunt.

His cock rubs against my thigh. "Tell me what you feel."

"I feel your cock strong and hard, ready to—"

His cock disappears. "Tell me what you feel inside."

"Your finger up my ass stroking in and out, fondling my clit, rubbing my inner spot, massaging joy up and down my entire body." And I'm right—I could feel my arms again, my back is light, my legs loose.

He begins to rotate the finger he had up my ass, shortening his in and out strokes to less than an inch. I suck air into my lungs and feel it tingle every part of my sex. I'm tighter around the fingers he's gently vibrating inside my cunt.

"Are you ready?"

"No." But I am! "Yes!" It begins as a rumbling tornado around the fingers in my cunt. Then the tornado shifts to rotate around the finger up my ass, then its rotations widen to circle my entire sex, lightning flashes up my spine, swirls concentrating into my sex, lightning into my toes.

I'm still under the thrall of my climax when I feel Frank haul me off the chair and push me down to the floor. He lays me flat on my back. I lift my knees to relieve the pressure on my sore bum, but he lifts each ankle and spreads my legs as far as they'll go.

He looks down at me, his slave, his prey. I glory in his possession of me and push my pelvis up towards his throbbing cock, even though it hurts like hell beneath my butt.

He lowers himself to his knees and bends towards me. I try to tighten my cunt but he smashes himself inside despite my best efforts. He propels himself in and out with animal fury, not saying anything, not looking at me. He plunges his cock in as far as it will go, then almost out. He has me, his whore, his meat. Faster and faster he assaults my insides. I give myself to him. He doesn't care about me. His hips rock, his cock impales me with his relentless carnal assault.

And then he shudders and goes still. I rock my own hips, not caring that the floor is scraping against my tender bum. A spurt trickles down the front of my cunt. He pounds away at me. I can't move. More spurts. He collapses atop me. After a moment, when his cock softens, I manage to roll him off me.

He lies there, trying to heave oxygen into his lungs. I bring the oxygen canister over to him and offer the inhalation mask. But he shakes his head.

"Where's the washroom?" I ask.

He points.

When I come back into the room, his breathing has returned to normal. He's still lying on his back, eyes closed, cock flaccid. I fix him another bourbon, this time with ice and he opens his eyes at the clink of the ice cubes. He props himself up on one elbow.

I hand the drink to him. "How's my Frankie?"

"Frankie's fine." He takes a large gulp, consuming half the drink.

I bend down to fish one of the ice cubes out of his glass. I run the cube up and down my pussy slit and feel her contract in protest. The sore spots on my bum are more grateful. Frank's eyes are even *more* grateful. He finishes his drink and I remove the glass from his hands.

I push him down to the floor. "My turn," I tell him. I lower myself to kneel above his chest.

"But I'm—"

My cunt over his mouth silences him. Instead of licking me, he tries to breathe, so I raise myself off him and place the oxygen mask over his face. "Breathe!" I tell him.

He takes one deep breath and I motion for him to take another.

He shakes his head. "Too much is not good for you."

"Too much *oxygen*?"

"Too much of anything. Even water."

I shrug. Learn something new every day. I position my pussy over his mouth. "Ready?" I ask.

He takes a deep breath, then nods. This time when I lower myself down, he knows exactly what to do. His tongue flicks up and down the inside of my pussy lips and twirls 'round my clit like a lollypop. Little frissons burst sideways out of my pussy.

He tries to grab my buttocks, but they're too tender, so I lift his hands to my hips.

I angle my hips backwards for his mouth to suck gently on

my clit. Thankfully my love knob hadn't taken the mashing my insides had and his lips send shivers deep inside.

I lift myself up for Frank to breathe and he laps his tongue up and down my entire slit. My legs are jelly and I sit myself back down. He licks where I slide myself back and forth and licks and sucks my clit when I bring her within range.

I grab Frank's ears and look into his eyes. "Make me come if you ever want to breathe again!"

He half nods and blinks his eyes. He is *my* slave now! He sucks on my clit, confirming his devotion, sending a jolt up my spine. I steady myself on his shoulders. He angles his head and licks up my entire slit. Then back down and I'm *his* slave. He licks up and down each side of my pussy lips and I quiver in anticipation.

I mash myself into his face, rubbing my clit against his nose. I'm over the edge now, out of control. The spasms of orgasm are stalking me, laughing at my lack of defence. And Frank knows it too, because he lowers his hands and squeezes the tenderest parts of my butt.

My bum contracts to escape the pain of his squeeze. My cunt contracts to exalt the glory of my climax. My lungs scream blue bloody murder, "Shit!" My whole body collapses into the space under my clit, into the black hole. Then I burst forth light and glory! Every breath in is a wave of joy up my body. Every breath sends the waves down to my toes. Wave after wave after wave forever and ever...

I float until Earl starts to squirm beneath me. I lift myself off so that he can breathe.

The following morning, I met with Eric, my erstwhile assistant, at *El Bistro* and sat him down in the same chair he'd occupied two days ago when he'd been talking to my ex-boyfriend. Their heads had been leaning together, hush-hush secret like, Eric's red hair above Peter's black spikes.

The waitress came to take our order.

"I'll have the breakfast special," I told her. My body needed replenishing after yesterday's exertions.

"Coffee. Black," was all Eric wanted.

"How're you making out on the blackmail demand?" I leaned back so that I wouldn't have to cock my neck to look into his green eyes.

Eric launched into a technical description of his efforts, a sure sign that he'd come up with nothing. The Cyber Culprit had tried to blackmail Sarah Grant when he'd caught her cheating on her husband. If we could track down where the ransom demand had been made from, we might be able to nail the Cyber Culprit.

My breakfast arrived and I'd wolfed down the scrambled eggs before Eric paused to sip his coffee. I seized the moment, "Bottom line, you can't trace the demand."

He set his coffee down and shook his head. "No. Dead ends at every turn."

"Why were you meeting Peter?" I had decided to be blunt. After all Eric was *my* employee. Peter Henge on the other hand had been my lover, not to mention the senior partner in our private investigation firm. Until he'd abruptly left in search of some undefined "more".

Eric face reddened. "Were you following him?"

"Maybe I was following you. What were the two of you talking about?"

He took a deep breath and looked around the café, as if he'd suddenly decided he wanted a croissant. Finally his eyes returned to me. "I thought he might be able to give us some ideas."

"And why would Peter give us anything?!? We're *competitors*!"

An email on my phone from Michael Rayburn, the lawyer who'd given us the Cyber Culprit case—our only case—saved Eric from having to come up with a better answer. Eric's phone beeped too and we both swiped through the Cyber Culprit's latest posting, me between bites of breakfast, Eric between sips of coffee.

The Culprit's latest posting consisted of page after page of the customers of a well-known porn site along with their passwords. At first glance, I swiped past it, but my subconscious registered something and I swiped backwards. And there it was. Peter Henge was a customer. And the bastard had come up with LEEcious123 as his password!

I turned my phone towards Eric and tapped on Peter's name. "Is this what the two of you were discussing?"

Eric tensed, looked up from his phone, and studied the screenshot on my phone. After a moment, he relaxed, shook his head, and went back to swiping on his own phone.

My phone rang. It was Michael Rayburn. "Did you get my email?"

"Yes, Eric and I are just looking at it now." At the mention of his name, Eric looked up.

"Can Eric start tracing the source of the leak, get in touch with the website owners?"

"Mr. Rayburn wants to know if you can start tracing this." Eric nodded and went back to studying his phone. I shook my head. Sometimes men can be so obtuse. I brushed my foot against his under the table. "He wants to know if you can get working on it right away."

Eric looked up, got the point, gulped down the rest of his coffee and dashed out of the café.

"Yes, Michael. He's already working on it."

"How'd you make out with Earl Brandis?"

I sighed inwardly. "The usual. Plenty of background information, but nothing specific."

"Okay, maybe Eric will get lucky with this. Usually there's some sort of trace on a major hack such as this." He paused. "Lee, are you busy tonight?"

"No, no plans." For you, Michael, my calendar was blank until doomsday! I'd had the hots for Michael almost since the day I'd started working on this case, but until this moment, I'd figured that I had a better chance of being invited to Buckingham Palace.

"There's a new Jazz joint which has opened up near the office. Are you up for a light dinner along with some dulcet tones?"

Jazz was worse than elevator music. At least elevator music had recognizable melodies and beats. "Sure, sounds wonderful!" I told him.

That night the food was good and there was only music when the live trio was playing. Thankfully they didn't play loud and the hubbub of the restaurant softened the sound of their 'music'. Michael seemed to enjoy the music so we'd figured out how to accommodate each other on that score.

"What are you working towards," I asked him. Professionals all have goals and *love* to talk about them.

"I'm in line to make full partner next year."

"Why do you want to make partner?"

"Money, prestige, security."

"You're a shoo-in, I'm sure."

He shook his head. "There are only two spots opening up and the competition is fierce."

"How will they decide?"

"The outcome of this case, for one."

Just then dinner arrived and the trio started playing a number with a recognizable melody. I'd ordered salmon and it was succulent beyond belief. But I'd give it up in a moment for something even more succulent, the lawyer sitting opposite. Michael was tall and slim. His dark brown hair had just a hint of grey. His blue eyes sparkled as his full lips smiled up at me. His presence exuded spectacular lovemaking. If only I could have a relationship with such a man as this!

I took another bite of salmon. I'd plied Michael with enough questions; hopefully that would lead him to make reciprocal inquiries after dinner. What should I say, what would he find attractive? Should I be vague or specific? Should I be light or serious? Should—

Michael's phone went off. I'd turned mine off. After all, this was a *date*! Why couldn't he have shown the same courtesy? Why—

He looked up at me, "Lee, there's been a new posting. I've sent it to you." He looked around. "Do you have your phone?"

I took my phone out of my purse and made a show of turning it on. The new post was from a dating site and seemed to flag those who were stepping out on their partners.

I started to swipe through the pages, hoping that Eric would be able to make head or tail out of the Cyber Culprit's latest hack. Then there it was. Peter's name again. The page was dated. Peter had posted his profile while we'd still been together. I drilled down into his correspondence. He'd even been on several dates! While we were *to-get-her*!

Peter's undercover work had really been *under the covers*!

I set my teeth wondering whether this had been what Eric and Peter had really been talking about. But why the hell wouldn't Eric have told me?!?

Yearning, Lusty Lee Log #10

Eric, my assistant, and I were in my apartment reviewing the Cyber Culprit's latest internet postings. This time CC had hacked into several porn websites and a dating site. The dating website had supposedly had impenetrable security and was therefore popular with cheating spouses. I had two computers with high-speed internet connections and several large to medium sized monitor screens set up on my dining room table. Anyone looking in on us would have seen my curly brown locks motionless in front of the largest of the monitors while Eric's carrot-topped and lanky frame flitted from screen to screen.

The section of the porn site I was monitoring was focused on marital infidelity. I wondered what it would be like to cheat. But since, after having broken up with Peter, I was no longer in a relationship, I was not in a position to experiment. I waved Eric over and pointed to the screen. "Does cheating make it hotter?" I asked.

He shrugged. "I wouldn't know."

I toggled back to the porn site's home page and we watched a variety of video clip previews. There was peeing: him on her, her on him, her on her. There was a man standing with a woman on a swing; she'd swing forward, impaling herself on him, then swing back leaving his cock throbbing and swaying. A more sedate video showed a shorter motion and he maintained penetration. There was a woman being penetrated by a penis from the rear and giving head at the other end. There were two women each inserting vibrators in each other. Eric paused at a threesome involving a she-male and a heterosexual couple, penetrations in every combination. Eric stared at them intently and I let him enjoy his bisexual fantasies. Then there was a man, bound to the floor and totally encased in purple latex except for his penis which stood out erect. Two women started to bend towards his cock.

Peter Henge, my erstwhile and former lover, had been a 'member' of the porn site and his password had been one of the ones posted by the Cyber Culprit. I still didn't know whether to be more angry that he'd accessed porn while we'd still been together, that he'd chosen *LEEcious123* as his password, or that he'd met Eric at *El Bistro* to discuss the hacking of the website instead of being man enough to meet with me directly.

The next video showed an erect penis poking out of the middle of a pizza. A woman bent her mouth towards the male member. I pressed pause. "You ever do anything like that?" I asked.

Eric shook his head and cut us each a piece of banana bread from the half-eaten loaf on the other counter.

As he handed it to me, the screen moved on to a variety food-themed videos. Fruit was inserted into a variety of orifices and then eaten. Then vegetables, cucumbers being the most popular. A zucchini was inserted, fried, then eaten. Eric looked down at his slice of banana bread. "You ever do anything like that?"

I shook my head. He let out a grateful sigh and took a big bite of banana bread.

I'd wanted to ask Eric about his recent meeting with Peter, but his response to my query about cheating hadn't given me the segue I'd hoped for. Peter Henge and I had fallen in love when I'd begun working at his private investigation firm. Somewhere along the line, he had moved into my apartment, and life had been divine. Then, without even the slightest warning, Peter had moved out and severed our professional relationship. I'd gone from heaven to hell in the space of sixty seconds.

Eric and I transferred our attention to the dating/cheating site that had been hacked. As Eric rapidly scrolled down the long list of users (abusers?) I thought I saw a name I recognized, but Eric had already scrolled the name off the screen.

"Go back," I told him.

He scrolled upwards, but now the name vanished off the top of his screen.

"Down, slower," I instructed.

And as Eric scrolled down, there it was, Peter Henge. My former lover had been on this site as well. I pointed to Peter's name. "Is his profile available?"

Eric clicked on the name above Peter's, 'John Hamilton'

and his profile came up.

"Not Hamilton. Henge."

Eric sighed, made a couple of mouse clicks, and there it was, my former lover's profile. He was still using LEEcious123 as his password. And again the profile was created *before* he broke up with me.

"How was Peter's profile hacked?" I wanted to know.

Eric shrugged. "It's hard to know. There's no clear trail. It could have been a mischievous sixteen year-old. It could have been done by an irate spouse. It could have been a business competitor. It could have been a foreign state striking back at the West's loose morals."

"But we know that it was the Cyber Culprit."

"Whoever the Cyber Culprit might be," he said, nodding. "And CC may have not done the original hack, he may have been posting items already hacked by someone else."

"What were you and Peter discussing in *El Bistro*?"

Eric's face went red, not pink, red. So red that the room had suddenly got brighter. Eric was trying to stammer, but there was no sound coming out of his mouth.

Eric's phone suddenly went off. Not a call coming in, but some sort of loud alarm. I thought for a moment that it might be an amber alert, but this was different. And now it had changed to Rimsky-Korsakov's flight of the bumblebee.

"I have to go to the gym," blurted Eric. He jumped up and dashed out the door. Eric did have an upcoming fight, but his gym could have waited for him to answer my question. Why *had* he been with Peter? What had they *discussed*?!?

Eric was fighting in a mixed martial arts bout that night and had given tickets to Michael Rayburn and I. It wasn't really a date since Michael's law firm was our ostensible employer and the tickets were a goodwill gesture. But it was closer to a date than the interrupted dinner Michael and I had recently had at the local jazz joint.

Michael was waiting at the turnstiles when I arrived at

the arena. It turned out that we had great seats, ten rows from ringside, but elevated to give us an excellent line of sight through the chain link fence of the octagon. It was the first time I'd seen Michael out of a business suit. He was wearing designer blue jeans that hugged his round butt to perfection. His shirt was black—full of mystery. I wondered what it would be like to undo the buttons and find out what was underneath? The usual grey fringes to his light brown hair seemed to have been washed away by the multi-colored lights in the arena. But his blue eyes were as striking as ever.

I was sitting between Michael and Heidi, Eric's girlfriend, though the way he described their relationship, she was as much groupie as girlfriend. She was dark—native Brazilian—and radiated an intense beauty. Her long black hair was tied behind her head, pony-tail fashion.

We'd barely had time to adjust ourselves in our seats when the referee shouted, "Fight," and waved the first two opponents into the center of the ring. It was a flyweight bout and fly the fighters did, zooming around the ring so fast I couldn't tell what was going on. Both fighters were wearing tight spandex shorts and I enjoyed watching their skinny butts, but the front side was protected by a metal cup, so no joy available there.

Midway through the first round, the fighter in the red shorts landed a solid right hook and the fighter in the blue shorts fell to the canvas. Red Shorts climbed on top of Blue Shorts and rained blows down on Blue Shorts' head, some landing, some being deflected. The second round was similar and I wondered how Blue Shorts could possibly endure the blows being rained down on him. Heidi was sitting forward, mimicking Red Shorts' blows. I glanced over at Michael and was pleased to see that he looked almost as squeamish as I felt.

But the third round was different. Blue Shorts, bloody face and all, relentlessly pursued Red Shorts around the octagon, landing hard blows whenever he'd herded Red Shorts into an unfavorable position.

Michael pointed to Red Shorts. "He's punched himself out."

Michael was right. Red Shorts had expended all his energy in the first two rounds and was now in survival mode. If Blue Shorts, bloodied face, broken nose and all, could knock his opponent out, he'd win the fight. And Red Shorts was being staggered every time Blue Shorts hit him.

Blue Shorts landed a solid right hook. Red Shorts' knees buckled, but he managed to stay upright and block two more rights from Blue Shorts. But Blue Shorts' left caught him flush on the cheek and Red Shorts fell back against the fence.

The crowd roared to its feet, sensing the end of the fight, sensing victory and vindication for the beating Blue Shorts had endured. Heidi, a little ball of energy was gesturing madly towards the ring. Michael appeared calmer, but when he hugged my head close to his chest, I could feel his heart beating wildly.

Blue Shorts sucked in the crowd's energy and landed wicked hooks to Red Shorts' face. First left, then right, then left. Red Shorts seemed glued to the fence. He made lazy attempts to ward off the blows. Then his hands fell to his sides and he began to slowly slide down the fence until he was sitting on the floor. The referee stepped in between the two fighters and waved Blue Shorts off. The crowd erupted into a raucous cheer.

"What's happening?" I asked.

Heidi pointed to Blue Shorts who was prancing around the ring. "He won the fight."

In between bouts I had a chance to soak in the atmosphere. The emotion was anger and aggression. Sounds ranged from rustling and the dull rumble of idle chit-chat to snarls of hostility and thunderous demands for blood. My nostrils were tickled with a mixture of stale and fresh beer. It was impossible to get comfortable in the hard and narrow seats but Michael's arm was warm against mine. He waved one of the wandering vendors over and I was soon scarfing down peanuts and sipping beer.

Eric's bout was next. He was dressed in short orange trunks which fit tightly just above his hips but hung loosely lower down. He reached his fists above his head as he climbed into the ring, an unnecessary addition to his lanky six-foot-three frame. His hair, now cut short, matched the color of his shorts. His green eyes, usually contemplative, flashed controlled fury.

Eric's opponent, Lance Norton, was black, shorter, slightly more muscular, rough and mean. He was wearing short spandex briefs, black. The two men stared at each other with obvious malevolence. Eric had once accused Norton of cheating. I hoped that my assistant knew what he was doing.

Next to me, Heidi was fidgeting. She had something in her palm and was pressing a button. I immediately recognized it as the wireless remote controller for a popular feminine sex toy. One end of the vibrator would be sitting inside Heidi's vagina, the other would be pressed against her clitoris. I watched Heidi's small brown fingers cycle through several pulsation modes and intensity levels. She angled her hips back and forth and then seemed to be comfortable.

Inside the octagon, the referee, a diminutive Asian wearing black from head to toe, waved the fighters to the center of the ring and invited them to touch gloves. They weren't really gloves, just padding over their knuckles. Eric held his fists out. Norton grudgingly touched gloves.

The referee put his hand, flat and vertical, between the fighters, motioned them to step back and when they did, he removed his hand. "Fight!" he shouted.

Norton stepped forward to occupy the center of the ring and pursued Eric while attempting to land haymaker punches. Eric kept circling to Norton's left using his superior height and reach to flick out jabs to keep the smaller, but more powerful, fighter away. Once Eric tried to shoot in to take Norton to the canvas, but the black fighter easily parried the attempt. Norton gave up stalking Eric and instead repeatedly tried to charge into close quarters. But every time he did, Eric clipped him with a sharp jab, kicked at his legs or just slipped out of the way. Once Eric landed a solid kick to Norton's midsection. By the end of the round, both men were sweating profusely.

In between rounds, ring girls strutted around holding signs announcing the upcoming second round. I watched Michael's eyes following a scrawny blonde in a black bikini and positioned my leg close to his as he turned to follow the ring girl's wiggling bum. I was rewarded with Michael's leg brushing mine and sending shivers up my spine.

Heidi pressed the front of her jeans, then reached into her pocket. In the hush just before the referee waved the fighters forward, I could hear a light buzzing sound.

Midway through the second round, Norton landed a right cross on Eric's cheek followed immediately by an even harder left. Eric was staggered and stumbled back against the fence right in front of us. The chain links made little diamonds on Eric's ass.

Norton wailed away at Eric's head, but Eric had recovered sufficiently to fend off the blows. Norton got careless and Eric landed a solid knee into the black fighter's stomach. Norton lurched back, his hands hanging useless by his sides. Eric stepped forward to finish the black fighter off but Norton kneed him squarely in the crotch. Eric crumpled to the canvas and Norton stepped forward to punch him in the head, but the referee intervened, sending Norton back to his corner. Eric was given time to recover from the low blow. For the rest of the round, Eric kept Norton at bay with well-placed jabs and superior footwork.

The third round was a different fight altogether. Eric pursued Norton relentlessly, raining combinations of blows at his head, forcing the black fighter to cover up. But every time Norton covered up, Eric would kick away at Norton's legs, slowly but surely wearing down Norton's ability to dodge his blows. Norton tried to escape and careened into the fence directly in front of us as. Eric kicked up at the black fighter's midsection. But Norton grabbed Eric's leg and pulled, sending Eric to the canvas. Norton jumped on top and attempted to rain blows down on Eric but Eric pulled the shorter man close and they grappled chest to chest.

Beside me, Heidi was pressed as far back into her seat as she could go, her legs clamped together. Norton's leg and butt muscles were working overtime as he attempted to gain a superior position. Heidi's eyes were glued to the spandex-covered buttocks. Eric had both his legs wrapped around Norton's left leg.

Eric seized Norton's right wrist and grabbed his left forearm with his other hand. Norton's eyes bugged out in fear and he used all his strength to try to wrench his arm free. When that failed, he tried to extract his left leg from between Eric's legs. But Eric was holding him too tightly.

Michael's eyes were transfixed on Eric's hands. "He's got him in a kimura!" he shouted. I pressed myself against Michael and was rewarded by his arm around my shoulders. I glanced up at Michael, but his attention was riveted inside the ring.

Eric slowly stretched Norton's arm out. Norton grimaced with pain and his with efforts to resist the wrenching force Eric was applying to his arm and shoulder. Eric's face was contorted with the exertion he was applying but underneath was triumph.

The crowd was roaring. Half were on their feet. Heidi's body was jerking but her eyes were fixated on Eric's fists bending Norton's arm further and further back.

Norton's other hand tapped on Eric's back and the referee pried Eric's hands off Norton's arm. Heidi's eyes were shut. Michael realized that his arm was around me and discreetly withdrew it. Eric romped around the ring, savoring his victory. There were red marks all over his face but he was smiling from ear to ear.

Eric left the ring with his handlers. Heidi kissed me on the cheek and followed them.

The next bout was to be girl-on-girl. The first fighter to enter the ring was a light-skinned black woman. Her hair was tied down in cornrows. She was just a little shorter than me but thinner and more muscular. Her name was Molly. Molly's opponent, Janice, was white and almost exactly the same build. Her hair was black, cut very short. Both were wearing sports bras and short spandex shorts. Molly's were white, Janice's lime green.

I was hoping for some ring *boys* to announce the first round, but it was the same ring girls with the same signs.

Michael was sitting an inch away from me. I wondered when next we'd touch.

Molly and Janice began with a flurry of poorly-aimed punches as they stumbled about the ring in a disorganized dance. Then they ended up in a clinch against the fence, right in front of us. First Molly's butt was pressed against the chain links. White spandex and black skin was *so* sexy. Then Molly reversed and Janice's lime spandex was jiggling the chain links. Michael adjusted himself in his seat, a sure indication that he was starting to get aroused. I glanced down at his crotch, but couldn't detect any change.

The ref pried the two girls apart and they resumed their wild flailing. Janice caught Molly with an uppercut and Molly grabbed onto the white girl to prevent more punishment. Janice whirled Molly around, tripped her and the black girl ended up on her back, right in front of us. Molly held Janice close to her body.

"Full guard," Michael noted, just audible over the roar of the crowd all around us.

"Full guard?" I asked even though it was obvious what full guard was. I leaned into Michael. Again his reflex was to put his arm around me and I felt warm all over.

Janice had maneuvered Molly away from the fence and we were staring straight at their crotches grinding against each other as the women jockeyed for position. I looked down at Michael's crotch. Under denim, there was the definite outline of the shape of a sausage. The wetness in my own crotch confirmed that I'd just *love* to unzip his pants and have a taste!

After thirty seconds of neither woman being able to

gain an advantage, the ref stood them up. This time they were sufficiently tired that their efforts to hit each other were more organized.

As the round ended, I waved the hotdog vendor over. "You got any foot-long?" I asked.

He shook his head, but I could see one in with the other shorter wieners. I pointed at it. He shook his head again, "I only have the small buns."

I smiled at him. "Perfect. That's exactly want I want."

I waited until Michael had ordered another beer for each of us and a small hotdog for himself. As he was paying and looking directly at me, I sucked almost half of my foot-long into my mouth. He cocked an eyebrow. I let three inches back out and bit it off.

Before we could figure out what my hotdog play had meant, the ref was yelling "Fight!"

Round two was a bust. Michael had one hand on his hot dog, the other on his beer. I had no choice but to follow suit. Molly and Janice spent almost all of the round swing and kicking at each other, but rarely landing. Towards the end of the round, Molly tried to kick out Janice's legs, but white hands grabbed black flesh and Molly was once again on her back. But they were on the other side of the ring and we couldn't see much.

As the round ended, Michael swallowed the last bite of his hotdog and washed it down with a long swallow of beer. I looked down at my hotdog and regretted that I only had one small bite left as well.

As Michael ogled the ring girl, I sidled my breasts against his torso. "Who do you think is winning?" I asked. He felt hard and delectable against my nipples which cried out for more, *much* more. But when Michael turned to answer, I pulled straight back to preserve the innocence of my gesture.

He shrugged. "It's too close to tell. Janice has had Molly on her back twice, but she's been unable to do anything with her takedowns."

As the ring girl gave us one last swivel of her hips, I leaned over and gave Michael a virtuous kiss on his cheek. "Thanks for bringing me here tonight." My right thigh was pressed against his left.

Before he could protest the kiss or the fact that Eric had provided the tickets for free, the ref was instructing, "Fight!"

I dropped my right hand so that it was nestled between our thighs, touching both. Janice landed a lucky punch and pushed Molly against the fence right in front of us. They tried to punch each other but, as far as I could tell, without much effect. Janice's knee was between Molly's leg, pressing her butt tight against the fence.

There was something else pressing tight, and it was the same sausage shape under Michael's jeans. I clapped and shouted, "Go girl!"

When Molly reversed position and pressed Janice against the fence, I lowered my hand back to Michael's thigh, this time further up. The sausage became more prominent. I looked up at Michael, but he had eyes only for the action inside the octagon.

I took a deep breath, readying to move my hand higher, when Janice pushed Molly off her. But that was a mistake. Molly managed to land a hard elbow against the white girl's jaw. With Janice stunned, Molly lined her up for an easy uppercut and Janice collapsed to the canvass. Michael jumped to his feet along with the rest of the crowd and I had to swiftly pull my hand away.

Two hours later, I slammed the door to my apartment. Michael, ever the gentleman, had deflected my suggestions that he come up for a nightcap. I stomped over to the mirror to look at myself.

My shoes were red. Not running shoes, but not high heels either. Fun and practical. My jeans were skintight and faded, showing off my every curve, cupping my butt, framing hips ready for swaying. My shirt had buttons down the front but was ten percent lycra and therefore hugged tight around my bounteous breasts. My curly brown hair was freshly washed and gave my face a perky look, especially when I smiled, which I did at that moment. And who could misunderstand my sparkling blue eyes advertising depths within depths of sexuality!?!

How had Michael been able to resist me, let alone the package I was wrapped in?!

Michael didn't need any wrapping. Suit and tie, jeans and T, or nothing and all—it didn't matter. He was tall and strong, not physically strong, though he was certainly no weakling. He was strong inside—emotionally, spiritually. He was giving, nurturing, imaginative. He had integrity. He was established. He could provide a place of safety within which to cavort. I wanted to hug him forever, to feel his arms around me. But yes, most of all, I wanted to cavort.

I stripped down to my underwear and spun around in front of the mirror. I was wearing a red see-thru bra and panties to match. My dark brown nipples, trying to poke out through the fabric, as well as the areolae surrounding them, were clearly visible, as was the outline of my pubic hair. Too obvious? Had Michael been able to sense the raw desire lurking underneath my jeans? Maybe he just didn't want me.

Well, there was no denying I wanted Michael Rayburn. And if I couldn't have him in the flesh, I could certainly have him in my imagination!

First, I took my deep purple We Vibe, probably the same vibrator Heidi had used in her panties as she'd watched Eric submit Norton, out of its charger. I put a drop of lube on the smaller end and wiggled it under my panties inside my vagina. The larger end curled upwards towards my pubic bone and nestled just above my clit. On my phone, I used the new App to start it vibrating with a low intensity wave pattern. For now I wanted my sex only vaguely interested as I made preparations for more extensive, and more intense pleasures. The low intensity wave vibrations would make me hot and bothered with desire but would not bring me anywhere near the vicinity of full arousal, let alone climax. They would come later!

It was time to move to my king-sized bed. King for
King Peter who had abdicated. I took a deep breath, adjusted
the intensity of the vibrator in my sex up a notch and wiped
Peter Henge from my consciousness as I assembled the
equipment I'd need for the night's festivities. Second up, on
one side of the bed was my Sybian, a rounded half-tube
encased in leather, phallus poking from its top, a wire
connected to a controller box coming out its front. Beside it, I
placed a small tube of lube. In the middle of the bed, I laid out
three feathers, a ring of four-inch-square sample fabrics
together with a tube of organic aloe and olive oil cream.
Nearest to this side of the bed, I arranged tit clamps, my rabbit
vibrator, a canister of whipped cream, a carton of chocolate
custard and a bowl of strawberries. I surveyed what I had
laid out on the bed, savoring the part each item would play in
enacting my Michael fantasies.

Then I moved to the kitchen to fix myself a snack. I
paused for a moment to change the vibration mode inside my
pussy to vibrate and adjusted the intensity up a notch. I
pulled out spiced crackers, well-aged cheddar cheese and
poured myself a glass of red wine. I was instantly transported
into a high-class restaurant where Michael and I were sharing
a sumptuous feast. The crackers and cheese became a ginger
spiced carrot soup that tickled heat down my throat as I
breathed in through my nose to suck the smell of ginger deep
into my brain. The next taste was a wonderful counterpoint of
cold and piquant cheese. Michael reached across the table to
place his hand on top of mine. All sense of time and place
stopped. The vibration inside my pussy stopped. All I could
feel was the touch of Michael's fingers on top of my hand as
the warmth of being with him penetrated into every nerve in
my body. I had Michael, he had me, the universe was
complete.

I placed a cracker topped with cheese in my mouth and
pushed the cheese upwards against the top of my mouth as
my tongue absorbed the rough texture of the cracker followed
by a gentle stab of spice. The cheese was cold and smooth and

pungent. I opened my eyes to reach for my wine and discovered that I had just eaten the last of the cheese and crackers. The red wine first mixed with the cheese and crackers then washed away their taste to dominate my mouth with its own mixture of earthy currants and leather. The smell of grapes being crushed under the open sun and squeezed into oaken casks wafted up and into my nostrils.

The tempo of the restaurant's music accelerated so I adjusted my vibrator's mode to cha-cha-cha and increased its intensity a notch. Michael took me into his arms and we spun around the dance floor to the music which was now perfectly matching the rhythms inside my vagina. Michael twirled me around the dance floor and more and more the universe became our togetherness, our desire, our passion and everything else washed away. The music changed to a gentle waltz and I melted into his arms. We merged, became one. But the discordant cha-cha caressing my clitoris reminded me that I had desires that could not be satisfied on the dance floor.

I quickly stripped off my underwear and glanced at myself in the mirror. Full, even ponderous, breasts, nipples pointing forward begging to be caressed, dark brown, well-manicured hair below curled even tighter than the hair on top of my head. The sparkle of arousal in my eyes pushed their sadness aside.

I backed myself against the wall and cupped a breast in each hand squeezing firmly to imagine Michael's hands squeezing gently. I shut my eyes and his fingers brushed first up and then down across my nipples. He circled my areoles to tease my nipples fully erect then placed them between thumbs and forefingers moving his forefingers back and forth across his thumbs. Everyone else—including me—had always given my nipples a gentle twist but Michael, creative and imaginative, had found a new pathway to pleasure!

I spread my legs begging Michael to bring his fingers below and my vibrator dropped to the floor. Michael brought both his hands down to my sex and pressed his palms against the side of my vulva pulling outward to fully expose my sex. A waft of air pulled moisture off my lips and clit sending a delicious chill up my spine. Then one hand caressed up and down my pussy lips sending gentle sparks down my legs. My clit poked out as round and hard as she could begging for his touch but he teased her mercilessly with gentle strokes below and beside which engorged my pussy lips, swelling them higher and tighter than they ever been before.

At last he brushed his fingers against my clit and I felt a jolt shoot into my pussy and swirl there. Then his fingers moved down my pussy lips. On the upward stroke again they brushed against my clit and the jolt was stronger, the swirl longer. Michael kissed me then, his full lips enveloping mine, gentle quivers trained by years of precise pronunciation drawing me inside his mouth where his tongue tickled the underside of my tongue. I was his, every inch of my skin was aflame with desire for him, every inch of my skin was jealous of my clit jealous of the lightly tapping of joy he was bestowing on her.

And then Michael knew, even before I knew, that we needed something more and he led me to the bedroom. I attached the tit clamps to my nipples and screwed them tight. I bent my knees and inserted the rabbit vibrator all the way up inside my vagina and twisted it fully on. There were vibrations throughout my sex and the long shaft of the vibrator moved up and down as it rotated round and round. The little rabbit at the top tickled my engorged clit.

I sat down in the chair beside the bed and immediately Michael's body was pressed into mine, his warm musk penetrating my nostrils the same way that his penis was penetrating my pussy. In it out, round and round he thrust and my pussy became tighter and tighter as he rubbed my ass against the irregular stitching on the chair seat. Michael twisted the two tit clamps until my eyes shocked open to be mocked by the laughter inside his eyes.

Then the multidirectional thrusts he was loving into my vagina stopped. I opened my eyes to see Michael take the canister of whipped cream and spray little dollops on top of each of my nipples. This caused the tit clamps the fall off and he sucked every last molecule of whipped cream off my nipples. Then he spread chocolate all over my breasts and circled patterns in the custard with the strawberries. Every time a strawberry rubbed roughly against a nipple hot frissons jumped down into my pussy.

Michael began to lick all the custard off of my breasts and I felt my climax starting to surge inside my vagina. I pushed the contractions down and down urging them to wait until his tongue had licked every last spot of chocolate off me. But wait she would not and I thrashed on the chair rubbing chocolate custard onto Michael's chest.

Michael padded into the washroom and came back with a warm wet cloth to clean off my breasts. I almost came again as he took extra care to remove every last drop of chocolate from my nipples. He gently lifted me up and laid me lying down on top of my sheets, the force of his will, the force of his love transforming ordinary cotton into softer than soft silk.

Fingers, strong and dexterous, spread aloe olive oil cream over my entire body. In a moment the cream had raised the temperature of every inch of my skin but nowhere with more fire than on my nipples, my pussy lips and my clit. Feathers tickled up and down my body concentrating awareness first on the bottom of my feet then between my toes. Just under my knees triggered little spasms up my thigh. Up and down my pussy lips he teased the feathers and I pounded my feet up and down against the bed as if I was having a temper tantrum. But it wasn't protest, it was because the pleasure inside my pussy was too much to bear!

Silk was first to caress my nipples, soft and smooth. Then velvet, even softer and I floated in the luxury. The rough underside of leather brought me back down to earth and I opened my eyes to rebuke Michael for his cruelty but he only laughed. He made up for his unkindness by rubbing the softer side of the leather up and down the slit between my legs and once again I shut my eyes.

Momentarily, Michael's touch left me and I was about to open my eyes when I felt a pointed wetness between my pussy lips. The pointed wetness began to flutter. It was Michael's tongue! He truly was a creative linguist—no one had ever been able to flutter his tongue down there. I feel myself wet, my entire sex wet, and I could barely feel his tongue licking up and down my pussy.

Michael dried me off and quickly returned his tongue to dart up and down, sideways back and forth up one side of the pussy lip, down the other side of the pussy lip, sucking my lips together then releasing them with a burst of air, up and around my clit. Again I became too wet and again Michael dried me off. No one had ever dried my sex off. What a wonderful, wonderful lover!

Michael inserted a finger inside my pussy and his lips sucked gently up and down my clit and before I knew it, before I could struggle to prolong the pleasure, he was sucking pure ecstasy out of me. My buttocks splayed outwards, pulling my clit away from him then pressed upwards pushing it as deep into his mouth as it would go. Out and in and flicking his tongue along the bottom of my shaft like a thumbnail lighting a match. Contractions in thunderous waves wrenched screams from my lips and spurted hot liquid out of my sex and onto the sheets.

Michael was not for a moment surprised. He licked and lapped my ejaculate with sensuous abandon and reckless enjoyment. As my orgasm subsided, he lifted his head, smiled and licked the last drops off his lips. Many men would have been put off by a woman spurting on them, but not my Michael!

Now it was time for Michael to get *his* enjoyment.

I shook myself out of my stupor and climbed atop the Sybian. Its hard leather sides were like Michael's hard thighs. I was hot enough, I was wet enough that I didn't need any lubrication and slid myself easily on top of the rigid plastic phallus poking out of the Sybian. I lifted up the control box and flicked on both the rotation and vibration modes. I adjusted the speed so that it was enough to stimulate me but not so much that I wouldn't need to pull up and drop down onto Michael's cock.

And up and down Michael's cock I went. Up and down his entire shaft. Little lifts and drops. Faster, slower. He shut his eyes. Up and down. Squeeze and release. I shut my eyes and we were nothing more than cock in cunt. The whole universe was nothing except my cunt enveloping his cock. Squeezing up and down his shaft. Undulating my squeezings to milk all his cum out of him. Rocking back and forth to increase my undulations. His cock rotating and shaking inside me. I pressed down hard to mash myself into him.

I was coming again, but Michael hadn't come! I jumped up and down on top of him, clenching myself as tight as I could. "Come, Michael! Come! I want to feel your warm stickiness inside me. I *need* to feel your hard stickiness inside me." My contractions were throwing my strokes off balance. But still I jumped up and dropped myself down his shaft. "Michael!"

And then he came, spurting himself into me. Joining our life forces together. And his shaft rotating and vibrating inside me was sticky. I turned off the controls and smiled down at him as I lifted myself off his shaft.

Michael smiled up at me. I collapsed into his arms, then slid onto the sheets as euphoria surrounded us and carried us together deep into the arms of heavenly sleep. Everything was warm, everything was pure.

The universe was no more.

Later, I slowly floated up from the warm soft whiteness and began to open my eyes. I had no idea how much time had passed, for time had ceased to exist. But soon there were colors and shapes. The clutter of my bedroom brought me the rest of the way out of my bliss and I turned my cellphone back on. There was a flashing notification of an urgent email.

It was from Michael. I looked at the time stamp. Shit!

Sleeping on the job.

Michael's email stated, "I've just got an email, direct from the Cyber Culprit. I need you, and Eric, in my office right away."

I hopped into a taxi and picked Eric up at his gym. Once we were on the expressway and he couldn't escape, I pinched the red mark on his cheek. "What were you and Peter discussing at *El Bistro*? And don't tell me it was to see if he could give us some *ideas*." My sarcasm on the last word made it clear that he was not to repeat the false excuse he'd give me before.

He gently removed my hand from his face. "It was about the Cyber Culprit, I swear. Porn is a diversion. Note all the powerful people whose profiles were hacked on the dating site. Every profile the Cyber Culprit posted was for a person of some note. There were no ordinary Joes. And seeking money is just his day job. The Amber Alert App was just a pet peeve."

I reached towards his cheek again. "So he wants to take a poke at celebrities. Who doesn't? We don't know squat."

I was about to give his tender spot another pinch when he shook his head. "Actually we do know something," he said, looking at my hand about to touch his cheek. I withdrew my hand and he continued, "We know that the Cyber Culprit wasn't in Asia, Africa, or South America."

I reached for his cheek again, but we had arrived outside Michael Rayburn's building and Eric scooted out of the car.

In the boardroom, Michael, already back in suit and tie, got straight to the point, "So far we've been chasing after the fact. We need to be able to anticipate where the Cyber Culprit will attack next."

I nodded, agreeing. "Our analysis indicated that the porn website hack is a diversion. Note that all the people whose profiles were hacked on the dating site were prominent in society. There were no ordinary Joes. His efforts to extort money shows that he needs a regular income, just like the rest of us. The Apps attacking Amber Alerts and loud commercials were likewise diversions, his indulging pet peeves. He's after the rich and powerful."

Michael nodded. "I think you're right." He activated the projector in the ceiling and the email the Cyber Culprit had sent directly to Michael's firm's general account flashed on the screen. It was a long and rambling rant. But the unmistakable intent of our nemesis was embodied in his threat to 'raise the stakes'.

Michael turned his laptop computer to Eric, "Can you track this?" he asked.

Eric studied the computer at length and made several rapid keystrokes. I stared at the two most important men in my life. Both were somehow involved with Peter, Michael as his former employer, Eric as his secretive confidant. Like a day-old gooey gluey stew, somehow everything was messily interconnected. And everybody but me knew how. What the hell was going on?!?

My assistant made a few more keystrokes and then pushed Michael's laptop away. Eric ruefully shook his head.

Scandal, Lusty Lee Log #11

We were in one of Michael's law firm boardrooms attempting to track the source of the Cyber Culprit's latest posting. More of a rant than a posting. But this rant was laced with threats to 'raise the stakes'. Eric was typing frantically on Michael's laptop. Michael was the lawyer who'd retained us to track down the Cyber Culprit. Eric, my assistant, was nerd-in-chief.

Eric's typing slowed. He made a few more keystrokes and then pushed Michael's laptop away. Eric ruefully shook his head. Michael sighed, slowly lifted himself off his chair and left the room with his laptop.

Eric started to rise but I pushed him back down into his chair.

"Spill," I told him. "I want to know everything you and Peter were talking about." I had caught Eric talking to Peter, my former long-term lover. My assistant had been dodging my queries ever since.

Eric filled his lungs, began to exhale, then stopped. "He admitted to his use of porn, to the fact that he cheated on you while you were together. But mostly he was wailing like a baby about how he had been a fool to think he could ever find anyone better than you."

"Are you telling me that he wants to get back together?!?"

Eric nodded. Sheepishly.

Me and Peter? Memories of all the good times flooded into my consciousness. How safe and secure it had felt in his powerful arms. How would we reconcile? Could we reconcile? What would our relationship look like if I took him back? That sounded good, 'if *I* took him back'. But would the power dynamics really work. Would—

Michael burst back into the room, slid his laptop over to us and pointed to the screen. "This is what he meant by raising the stakes." Despite his rushed discomfiture, Michael's pinstriped suit, Armani tie and custom-tailored shirt remained exactly in place.

The Cyber Culprit's new postings were of photographs of a female politician and texts indicating that she liked to be held in bondage and ravaged by big black men. The photos showed her in skimpy bikinis, nude, and tied in knots shibari style. Her face was by turns defiant, submissive or exultant. Most exultant when covered in semen. There was a picture of her binding the balls and erect penis of one the black men to ensure that his erection would last as long as she desired.

A lesser man would have been reeling under the Cyber Culprit's latest onslaught, but Michael remained in control. Masculine, powerful. Nevertheless, his blue eyes were glimmering from the excitement bubbling within his laser-sharp mind. And his mouth was set hard. Game on! I felt a stirring between my thighs.

The Cyber Culprit's posting had included a video of the female politician provoking a large black man. She was dressed in a red silk blouse, red miniskirt, red hose and even redder stiletto high heels. Even with her high heels, the man was a head taller than she was. And he outweighed her by at least half. His only clothing was a white thong.

She slapped his face. He remained motionless, silent. Her blow had failed to move his head even a millimeter.

"Bitch," she hissed.

He remained impassive.

She pinched his nipples and twisted. "Pussy!" she almost shouted.

He ignored her.

"Black man not *man* enough fuck white cunt?"

She gave an extra twist to his nipples, then pulled her right hand back to slap him across his face.

But this time he grabbed her wrist and her body shuddered to a halt. After a heartbeat, he released her, giving her a gentle shove back. She stumbled, recovered, removed her shoes and threw them at his face. He swatted the shoes aside, shattering one against the wall.

She picked the shattered shoe up and held it to his face with her left hand. "You bastard!" She beat her right fist against his chest, repeating "You bastard! You bastard!" with each blow.

After only a few moments, she was out of breath. She stepped back and flung the shoe aside.

Then she took a step forward and grabbed his crotch fully. "You're not a man—you're a pussy." She squeezed.

He ignored her as long as he could, but finally even her small hand was able to exert enough pressure to demand relief. He tried to pry her hand loose, but she hung on tightly. He yelped with pain, let go of her hand and slapped her hard across her face, knocking her to the floor. She laid there, stunned for a moment, her long blonde hair in disarray, her legs spread wide to reveal black garters holding up her red hose, the black slit of her thong in the middle.

She stared up at him with malevolent intent, her eyes challenging him, her smile relishing what was sure to come next.

He pulled her up by her hair. "You little bitch."

"How dare you!" She struggled to slap his face, but he was holding her too far away.

He released her hair and took a step back. "You should leave now."

Instead she rushed at him swinging wildly for his face. He blocked her blows, then one landed. She dropped her hands. "*You* don't tell *me* when to leave, bitch." She reached for his crotch.

But he intercepted her hands, grabbed her breasts and shoved her back against the wall. He squeezed and twisted so hard and that two of the buttons on her blouse popped off, revealing a black bra underneath her blouse. Her nipples puckered beneath the almost transparent material. He ripped her blouse to shreds and flung it away.

"That was a thousand dollar blouse, bitch!"

He bent down, ripped off her skirt and then ripped off his thong revealing a very large and very erect cock.

For a moment, but only for a moment, she was silent. "You wouldn't dare!" she screamed. But the smile on her lips made if crystal clear that she very much hoped that he *would* dare. She spread her legs revealing the outline of her sex underneath her sheer panties.

Michael pressed the spacebar and the video stopped. I looked into the politician's eyes, into her unabashed longing for the ravishment which was about to be inflicted on her. Yesterday her life had been full of potential. Now she, Judy Bell—at last I'd finally remembered her name—was just one more woman who would never be Prime Minster.

Michael pushed the laptop towards Eric. "Can you trace this?" he asked.

Eric pulled the laptop close and began madly typing.

I took out my phone, found the video and fast-forwarded to the spot where the politician, or rather the now former politician had spread her legs. "You'll never be more than Mandingo, my slave!" she taunted, "You—"

His hand on her neck chokes off her insult. She slaps towards his cock, but he parries her blow and smacks his hand up against her crotch. She grimaces in pain, her eyes shut. She slumps to her knees and he grabs her head. When she opens her eyes, he pulls her mouth to his cock and forces her to swallow him deeply.

When he's had enough, he shoves her head back and pulls her up by her hair, forcing her to stand on tiptoes. "You're *my* slave now," he hisses.

"Never!"

He reaches down and pulls her panties up into her crotch until they're a thin strand of black between curls of blonde hair. "Submit, slave." His voice is harsh, rumbling.

She bites her lips and nods.

He pulls her to the floor, spreads her legs, pushes her panties to one side and fucks her vigorously. She screams and pounds her fists against his chest. He ignores her and plows her cunt with reckless abandon.

Then they shudder in screaming unison.

His thrusts slow and he flops down beside her. She lifts herself up and climbs on top of him. Judy Bell and her black lover smile at each other and kiss tenderly.

The video, now posted for everyone to see, would make any public career impossible to begin or immediately terminate any public career already begun.

When I looked up, Michael was reading one of his innumerable files. I sat down opposite him. After all, for the moment there was nothing we could do. I calculated that I'd have to wait another five minutes before trying to engage Michael in small talk. They used to say that food was the way to a man's heart. Wrong. It was small talk. I spent the five minutes alternating between watching Eric's green eyes, the screen of his laptop and his long thin fingers tapping away on the keyboard. His hands and fingers were anchored by long thin arms, but I knew from experience that there was power in his wiry frame.

I was in the middle of taking a breath preparatory to asking Michael how he thought the Blue Jays would fare this coming season when Eric jumped to his feet. All six-foot-three with red hair waving and fists pumping to the ceiling.

"Got 'im!" Eric yelled.

He turned the laptop towards Michael and I. The screen was filled with a familiar face.

"Jackson Harding?" Michael's voice was incredulous.

I took a closer look. Michael was right. Both Harding and the Cyber Culprit's latest victim, the rapacious female politician, were involved in an intense contest to determine who would lead the main opposition party. The photographs, not to mention the video, would torpedo her leadership run. And if it became known that Harding had posted the photos, it would knock him out of the race as well.

"Jack Harding is the Cyber Culprit?!?" I asked.

Eric nodded and cycled the screen back to a video of the politician in red harassing the big black guy. "This posting came directly from his IP address."

A quick but extensive background check on Harding revealed that he had a standing Wednesday night meeting with a hooker from the Imperial Escort Agency. It was a different hooker each time.

But it was the same hotel each week, often on the same floor. It was nice to have resources out of the reach of even the most intrepid press reporter!

Eric had had to rent Harding's likely room and the room adjoining it for several days to ensure that it would be available for the 'date' we proposed to schedule for he and I. Just as Harding was walking up to check in, Eric would phone in a cancellation for "Harding's" room. There was a doorway adjoining the rooms which could be locked from the inside of either room. Eric had drilled two holes in the door to his room and ensured that they were sufficient for the mini camcorder lens to snake through. The other hole was for a still camera. Tests on me flopping onto and off the bed and traipsing around Harding's room were satisfactory. Eric would have a clear view of both the large wingback chair and of the bed.

After he'd filmed us, the plan for the doors was for Eric to smash them into smithereens, to claim that he'd 'fallen', and to pay for the damages. That way there'd be no question about the holes he'd drilled.

Wednesday night, I dressed for my role as escort while Eric set his cameras up next door. First step was to strip nude and inspect what I would be selling. I smiled at myself in the mirror. For twenty-nine, I was still attractive. My five-foot five frame was buxom and curvaceous, especially when I sucked my belly in. I hoped that Jack Harding liked curly brown hair and blue eyes.

Down in the lobby, Eric and I sat separately trying to spot Jack's whore of the day. We had learned, with a few well-placed bribes, that Jack Harding's practice was to meet his escort in the hotel bar after he'd checked in. Our plan was to intercept the escort and pay her to leave. I'd then take her place sipping whiskey.

For the lobby, I was dressed in understated elegance. My almost transparent white blouse was hidden under a light blue vest buttoned all the way up. My mid-length skirt was of the same color with buttons up the left side. In the bar, I'd cross my legs and undo some of the buttons to change my appearance from restrained to alluring to outrageous. Underneath the skirt, I was wearing pink silk stockings, as sheer as my blouse. My makeup was a blend of light blue to match the dress and dark burgundy eye shadow to give me a mysterious air. I pressed my lips together to make sure that the darker burgundy gloss was fully covering them.

I was first to spot Jack's escort for the evening. She was a tall thin black woman dressed with understated sexuality. I waved to Eric and we moved to intercept the newcomer. My assistant was shaking hands with her as I joined them.

He stood in front of the escort and smiled. "Who are you seeing to night?"

"Who wants to know?" Her eyes were wary.

Eric removed a beige hundred-dollar bill from his pocket and held it up. "A friend."

"How good a friend?" She relaxed somewhat.

Eric stretched the bill out, holding it in the thumb and forefinger of each hand. "This good a friend."

The hooker's head started to shake but she stopped when Eric pulled out another bill. "His name is Jack," she said, pocketing the two bills. "I'm supposed to meet him at his bar." She pointed in the direction of the bar entrance.

Eric held up another beige bill, "This little portrait of Sir Robert Borden is yours if you turn around and pretend nothing happened."

This time the tall black woman shook her head vigorously. "Nothing doing. I have my principles. Our agency promises complete discretion. We—" She paused as Eric pulled out a money clip from his pocket and retrieved a pink thousand dollar bill to keep the beige one happy. "You're Jack's friend, right?" she asked.

Eric nodded solemnly. "A friend."

The escort took the money and opened her purse. Eric's hand stopped her from placing the money inside as he asked, "What are you supposed to do with him?"

The escort looked at Eric as if he was a moron. "We go up to the room. We have dinner. Do I have to draw you a picture?"

Eric ignored the sarcasm, "Anything special?"

"If you mean whips and chains, no. But if he has a hard time getting it up, I'm supposed to let him suck my pussy. Then it should be wham bam thank you ma'am."

"How does he spot you?" I asked.

"I sit in a corner. When he asks if he can buy me a drink, I tell him an Aviation."

Eric removed his hand. "Let's get you a cab."

The escort turned and stuffed the money into her purse. As Eric and the escort walked towards the front door, I unbuttoned my vest and turned towards the bar. In the bar, I found a table in the far corner, unbuttoned several buttons on my skirt and practiced turning to send the slit up my leg for when Jack would appear.

Jack arrived ten minutes later. He was dressed in a dark blue suit and a light blue paisley tie. He appeared to be a slightly pudgy upper-middle class drone. Harmless. At least until he became Prime Minister.

"What's your pleasure, sugar?" His voice was ordinary too. "Would you like a drink before dinner?"

"I'll have an Aviation."

He had a gin and tonic. He drank quickly and I matched his pace. Conversation was idle chit-chat.

Jack plunked his empty glass down. "Shall we?"

I nodded and rose, making sure he caught a glimpse of my cleavage.

The ride up in the elevator was silent. He smiled at me, I smiled back. He seemed sweet. But then I remembered what he'd done to his colleague and I hardened my resolve.

Upstairs, Jack calls room service and orders a salad with a vinaigrette dressing and a light pasta dish. He looks at me and I nod. "Make that two," he says, "And champagne on ice." The click of him hanging up the phone sounds loud in the silence.

I hear something at the door which adjoins the rooms. "What should we do while we wait for dinner?" I ask. A bit too loud? Or worse, too forward?

But Jack smiles. "Maybe we should get a better look at you."

I slowly unbutton my blouse and am gratified to see his eyes transfix on my fingers. I drop it and the vest to the floor behind me. Then I unbutton and unclasp my skirt and let it drop to the floor. I step out of my skirt and pirouette atop my red high heels.

I hear another rustle next door. Eric! I run my hands over my lingerie, "You like?" What's not to like? I'm wearing a pink bra, even more sheer than the blouse I had just unbuttoned and my nipples are visible and puckered. Below, the matching panties let the outline of my pubic hair show through. And my pink stockings are held up by a beige garter belt that almost perfectly matches the color of my skin.

Jack nods, swallows and stands to touch my lingerie. His hands look soft. Will he know how to use them? Something is bulging below his belt.

There's a knock at the hallway door.

Jack startles, then remembers. "Dinner."

I scamper to the bathroom where I hear Jack fumbling with the lock on the door. He apologizes but gets it open a moment later. He ushers the server in and pays cash. The door clicks behind the server and I see Jack sliding the key chain in place as I come out of the washroom.

"Would you care for some champagne?"

"That would be nice." As he pours the light gold liquid, I glance at the door between the rooms. I can just see Eric's holes but he's done a good job of concealing them and they'd be invisible unless you knew exactly where to look and what to look for. Jack hands me a flute of champagne. It tickles my nose.

"How about some music?" I ask.

"Sure." He gestures towards the radio, but I go for the TV and find a cable station featuring light music.

Dinner is quiet until Jack is taking his last bite. "This is your first time, isn't it?"

I almost choke, but recover just in time. I get up and pull his jacket up and off his arms, then stand behind him and begin to rub his shoulders. "Is it that obvious?" I ask.

He nods, then relaxes into the back rub. "Thank you. That feels great." He moans. "Why are you doing this?"

I continue to rub the tension from his shoulders. "Is there anything wrong in what I'm doing?"

"No. I suppose not. As long as it's what you want to do and no one's forcing you to do it."

"I like meeting new people, getting to know them."

His head lolls to the right. "Nice to meet someone who likes her work," his syllables broken up by my strokes.

"Enough about me," as I massage his scalp. "Tell me what you like."

"Excitement."

"That's what I'm here for." I'd almost said that 'excitement is my middle name'. "Anything in particular?"

"Start slow, let's learn each other's speed and then go from there."

In other words, I was going to have to do the work, including being a mind reader. I moved in front of him and made a show of adjusting my bra. "How much time do we have?"

He doesn't look at his watch. "All the time in the world."

"You're sweet, let's get comfortable." I remove his shoes and socks, making sure not to block Eric's view of his face. I smile to myself as his eyes attach themselves to my cleavage as I bend towards him.

"Stinky feet," he apologizes. His ogling of my breasts had started to get me turned on, but this spoils the mood.

"Don't worry. Just relax."

But I go to the washroom and return with an ice bucket filled with hot water. I wash his feet. He shuts his eyes, so I continue with a foot massage. He moans.

I pull the bottle of champagne from the ice bucket which room service had brought up.

He starts to get up but I push him back, "Relax, let me do the work. Just sit back."

I pour myself a flute full of champagne, but he shakes his head in the direction of the champagne and I let it slide back into the bucket.

I unbutton his pants and slowly slide his zipper down. Pulling the pants off his legs reveals a pair of white boxer shorts. He removes his own shirt. I shrug and a mouthful of champagne tingles each and every one of my taste buds. I cover each of his nipples in turn with my mouth, swirling champagne all around them. Then I suck and nip. He closes his eyes when I suck hard. Another sip of champagne allows me to send small rivulets of the amber liquid dribbling down his chest. I swallow the rest and lick his chest clean.

He pushes me to a standing position. "Now it's your turn. I want to see your luscious body in all its splendor."

I position herself so Jack will have to look right into Eric's camera. I move just slightly to the left so that my backside won't block Eric's view of Jack's face. I raise my left leg and slide my foot under Jack's thigh. My leg is at a forty-five degree angle to him so that he can see my entire profile. "How do you know that I have a luscious body?" I flirt.

"I've already seen its outline. And been teased with the top of your chest. You are beautiful and I want to see it all."

I reach my left hand down and lightly caress his crotch. He's flaccid. I wonder if Eric's still flaccid too. Time to step this up a notch if I want to make pornstar of the year!

I squeeze my breasts then clasp my hands behind my head and hold them there until he takes a gasping breath.

"Do you like what you see?"

"Very much." He grabs the handles of the chair as if to push himself up.

"No. Don't get up yet." I stand in front of him with my legs apart, my crotch inches from his and begin to swing my pelvis back and forth. This is more like it, between the rubbing of my panties against my sex and the sensation of his eyes feasting on my body for all eternity, I'm definitely beginning to get turned on.

My buttocks are contracting and relaxing. My panties are tight against my ass and beginning to move into between my butt cheeks. I smile at the thought of Eric's hard-on as he struggles to concentrate on his cameras. My next contraction pulls my panties all the way into my butt crack.

I bend down to give Eric an even better view up my ass and rub up and down the front of Jack's underwear. Definite signs of swelling! "Why don't you touch my breasts?" I ask.

He reaches up with his right hand.

"Both hands," I tell him.

His hands are soft, but instead of this being an impediment, it allows me to feel him against every inch of my breasts all at once.

"You've been such a good boy, I think its time you got to pet my pussy."

"Yes."

"Make her purr."

"Yes."

"Make her purrrrr..."

"Purr."

I step forward and take his hands in mine, pulling them to my crotch. I sway and wiggle, forcing his fingers to pleasure me. This seems to be what he wants, the newbie guiding the old pro. My wetness is starting to come out and I know he can feel it through the sheer fabric of my panties. At first he merely lets me hold his hands. When his fingers start to probe without my guidance, I let go of his hands and fondle his ears before moving to the top of his head where I run my fingers through his hair. When his fingers start to press my panties inside my pussy, I step back, pull my panties off and stuff them inside Jack's underwear. He's still flaccid, but now his penis is twice the size it was before. I step forward and he resumes his gentle, but thorough probing. I steady myself against his shoulders.

I pull back when he moans and bending towards the floor,

pulling his briefs up and over his cock as I go. Then I'm on my knees and sucking him into my mouth. He's still soft enough that I can take him all the way in without difficulty. But with a few gentle sucks while rubbing his balls he's fully erect! This is what a *pornstar* does! His cock in my mouth and hot wetness in my crotch tells me that I'm fully into movie-mode.

I stand and reach for his hands, bringing one to each side of my buttocks. I push my pubic bone towards his mouth and he begins to tongue my curlies. Gradually I raise my pelvis and his tongue slides lower. His hands press and release, his tongue probing side to side. I start to float. He licks downwards with the smooth underside of his tongue, then laps upwards with its rough side. Heat rises within me. He flicks my clit and I stumble into him.

He stands and lifts us up. "Careful now," he remonstrates.

Harding lifts me to the bed, comes to all fours, climbs on top of me and turns around, his head between my legs. Politicians may be full of hot air, but all that hot air needs a practiced tongue to guide it and Jack's tongue is certainly *practiced*. He slides his hands under my buttocks and slowly thrusts his tongue inside me. Then he grabs hard on my buttocks and slurps my juices, making gurgling sounds of gratification. Enthusiastic *and* practiced!

I can't suck his cock back into my mouth, but I caress it with my fingers as his tongue plays with my pussy. His tongue flicks up and down my pussy lips. I rub my fingers back and forth on the bottom of his balls. He gently flicks the top of my clit. I feather the tip of his cock. He moves his tongue lower and I glide my fingers down his shaft. He slides inside my pussy and wiggles around. I pinch his nipples, then squeeze his breasts. His cock flops from side to side. He laps vigorously around my sex, but is careful not to put too much pressure on my clit. Heat is gathering within.

I reach up to put my right hand on his cock and caress his balls with my left. But he puts his entire mouth over my sex. He sucks, gently but firmly, just enough to create a soft vacuum before starting to rotate his tongue around my clit. His ministrations shoot a jolt up my spine and my arms flop to the side of the bed. My pussy's *hot*, wishing he could suck her all the way inside his mouth. Harding begins to rhythmically vary the intensity of the vacuum embracing my pussy, inflaming her desire even further. Another jolt up my spine and my hands fly back up to his shaft. Then he collapses the vacuum over my entire sex and sucks lightly up and down my clit. I'm about to come when he returns his suction to my entire genitals. Climax stopped but heat and tightness increased tenfold! His cock throbs to match the faint contractions beginning inside my cunt. My pussy pleads for five more minutes of heaven. *Just five more minutes*!

But my head knows that Eric needs a shot of Jack on top. Missionary. Coitus. Fucking.

I grab his testicles in my left hand and give them a not too gentle squeeze. "Ready?"

He drops his head to the pillow. "Never readier."

I slip out from underneath, go over to my purse and fish out a condom in its plastic packet. I return to the bed, holding the packet in both of my hands, ready to open it. He's kneeling on the bed, a lewd and triumphant look on his face. His cock dangles forward, ready for its raincoat.

I remove the condom from its wrapper reach down to his crotch. The latex rolls tight over his shaft. When the bottom is near the base of his penis, I pull up and unroll it a little more. His balls are tight against his skin, having conceded prominence to his phallus, but I give them a gentle caress nonetheless.

I circle to the other side of the bed, compelling Jack to turn around. If Eric was concentrating on his camera angles, this would have let him capture Jack's penis in full profile! I lie down on the bed and spread my legs.

Jack knows when he has a willing audience and swiftly mounts me, sliding his cock all the way into my well-lubricated pussy.

"Oooh, that feels good", I croon, "press harder. I bet you'll last forever and I'll come and come!"

Jack smiles down at me but says nothing. I smile back up at him, grateful he's letting his penis do the talking. His thrusts are alright, but his cock hardly compares to his tongue.

I decide to fake an orgasm. I need to secure my pornstar status! But I'll have to keep careful watch on Jack to make sure he doesn't come too soon.

I buck my pelvis up against him. "Harder!"

Instead of harder, he goes faster.

"Yes, Jack, Yes!" I squeeze his cock as hard as I can with my pussy but it isn't much since his corpulent thighs are between my legs.

I arch my neck back and scream, "Fuck!"

He's still banging away as fast as he can. I look up at him with my best animal intensity face and try to squeeze my legs together. This time he gets the message and lifts his legs with his toes to let me slide my legs in together. He gasps as he feels the silk of my stockings against his balls.

He's still pumping hard. His face is red, grimacing with exertion, pleasure, and triumph. He's about to come.

I dig my nails into his buttocks. "Don't come yet, sugar. I want more of you than that. And if we can bring you up, then let you down, it will be better for you too."

Between heavy breaths he says "Okay." He nods and begins to move again, but slower.

I smile up at him. "Now, if you feel about to come, just stop. Then we'll start again and we'll be in heaven all night."

"Okay." His breathing is coming more easily now as he keeps up a sustainable rhythm. Ninety seconds later he shudders to a stop. He starts again, but immediately starts to tremble and I have to dig my nails into his buttocks to bring him to a stop.

"Fondle my breasts," I tell him. "And grind into me without thrusting."

He's better at grinding than he was at thrusting and I feel my orgasm start to build, first inside my clit, then deeper inside. I buck up against him, then rock my hips back. The mini-stroke on his shaft is all the encouragement Jack needs and he begins to push and pull against my rocking motions slowly then with increasing vigor. His skin is fire against me.

My orgasm explodes down into my buttocks, then drifts back up my cunt to heat my clit. The second wave shoots up my spine. But now Jack is coming too and his full weight almost smothers me as he shudders, breaking the rhythm of his thrusts.

"Fuck!" he yells.

"Fuck!" I gasp back.

I do my best to thrust my hips upwards to milk every last drop out of him. My climax is diffuse heat but I can feel his jerks inside me. He picks up the pace again and his full strength drives inside over and over. He shudders again and rolls off, breathing hard. Freed of his weight, my orgasm courses gently up my torso. I reach over to peel the condom up his shaft.

I'm careful to gather all the semen inside the condom and to tie off the end. Then I swing the condom back and forth hoping that Eric gets a close-up of my trophy.

I smile over at Jack. "That's a lot of sperm. I didn't know you were such a tiger."

He smiles back at me. "Well, it's a week's supply because we, my wife and I, didn't have sex last Saturday. We went to the opera instead. Charity function, you know."

"Yes." I reflect that I'd never been to a charity function in my life unless going to a food bank when I was twelve counted.

He lay immobile on the bed while I dressed. I wondered whether I should tell him that he'd been the best I'd ever had or whether to skip the lie and just ask for another date. But when I walked by, he was snoring. I covered him with a sheet, scooped up the room card-key and the four one-hundred dollar bills he'd left on the dresser, and left.

As I opened the door to the adjoining suite, Eric stood up and stretched. I could tell that his legs were aching from bending over all evening. The bulge in his pants must have been tormenting him with conflicting urges: ejaculate or cold shower? He slumped into the chair while I watched the live video feed from next door on his laptop. Jack's chest continued the gentle undulations of slumber.

"Did the video record properly?"

He nodded, got up gingerly, and pressed a button on his laptop. Harding and I were immediately grinding our nude bodies together in high resolution. I looked a bit chunky and resolved to take Eric up on his offer of crafting an MMA exercise routine for me.

"Did you get good stills?" I asked.

He pressed another button and a slideshow of my earlier assignations played across the screen.

"Can you send them to my phone?"

He nodded and I continued watching the photos on my phone while Eric switched his laptop back to the live video feed.

I was only halfway through the photos when Eric cleared his throat. I looked up to the video feed. Next door, Jack Harding was stirring.

"Showtime!" we announced in unison.

Jack was surprised, at first pleasantly, to see me again. But as soon as he realized I shouldn't still be there, I thrust my cellphone into his face. He watched Eric's photo slideshow of our tryst with escalating horror.

He jumped up and began to dress. "What do you want?"

I marveled at how fully in control of his voice he was. "Why did you post the photos of Judy Bell to the internet?"

"I didn't."

"Then you won't mind if we post these?" I held the phone towards him, making him look.

"Please, no! You'll destroy my family."

"Your family? What about Judy Bell's family?"

He was silent for a moment. "I'll resign. Just leave my family out of it."

I cycled the phone to the internet, to the photos he'd posted of his rival. A rival whose only crime had been to explore her sexuality.

"I had nothing to do with that!" he protested.

I slapped my fist loudly on the adjoining doors and Eric strode into the room.

I pointed to Eric. "Then you won't mind if my colleague does a full sweep of your computers and phones."

Jack shook his head.

"All of them," I added.

Jack Harding shook his head again, but more slowly this time.

Eric smashed the set of doors which faced Harding's room, paying particular attention to the areas around his drill holes.

I gathered up the camera equipment while Eric left with Harding to install tracing bugs and software on all of Harding's computers and phones while I stayed behind to settle up with the hotel for the damage done to their interior doors.

The next evening, the three of us met in Harding's office to review Eric's findings. Harding sat slumped behind his desk looking at his hands in his lap. Eric stood beside him where he could see the politician's computer screen. I stood on the opposite side of the desk, wearing the demure version of the outfit I'd worn the night before.

Eric pointed to Harding's computer, "He's right, he didn't post her photos. They were on his computer, but the actual posting was done remotely, by someone else. Harding's computer was captured as a proxy IP address."

"Who?" I asked.

"Judging by the way he covered his tracks, I'd say it was the Cyber Culprit."

I pointed to Harding and raised an eyebrow. Eric shook his head.

I pounded on the desk and when Harding looked up, he was looking into my phone and the slideshow of Judy Bell's nude photos. "How did you get these?" I demanded harshly.

"I was at my son's piano recital. They just appeared on my phone."

Thankfully at my one and only school play, cellphones had yet to be invented and my parents had actually watched my performance.

"Why didn't you delete them?" I asked.

Harding shook his head ruefully. "You never know when stuff like that might come in handy."

Harding wasn't as guilty as I'd thought. But he was guilty enough. I stared down into his eyes. "Tomorrow morning," I began, "you are going to drop out of the leadership race. You can cite family reasons. You won't run in the next election. If you ever misbehave, the photos of you we took last night will be released along with evidence that you posted your rival's photos."

"But I didn't."

"Once it's clear that you had them, no one will believe you."

Harding's head slumped back down.

"Are we clear?"

He nodded.

I called Michael Rayburn on the off chance he'd still be at the office. He was! "Would you like me to come over to give you a report?"

"Sure."

I was at his office in five minutes flat. The law firm was sublimely silent. Many of the lights were off. Michael led me to a small kitchen and fixed coffee. His tie was off and he wasn't wearing a jacket. His custom-tailored shirt hugged his chest.

"Would you like coffee?" he asked.

"Sure. Thanks." Ever *so* articulate I cursed myself.

I watched Michael's arm muscles flex and relax. The lighting in the small kitchen was far from optimal, but it set off the flecks of grey in his light brown hair to perfection. And it flickered inside his eyes.

"Success?" he asked as he set the coffee down in front of us. His full lips formed each syllable in precise pronunciation.

I held my hand out flat and rocked it back and forth to indicate some success, some failure. Half an hour later, I'd completed my report. One less old white guy prowling the corridors of power.

Michael finished his coffee and reached for my cup. But it was still half full so I was late in removing my hand. Our hands touched. We looked at each other, caught in the moment. Michael was there. Lean and handsome. He moved closer. I leaned in. His lips were puckering. I opened my mouth. His lips brushed mine. He pulled back. I leaned in, not touching, but making it clear I was available. He kissed me full on the mouth and I almost swooned inside his kiss. It was even better than I'd imagined. A perfect moment. He put his arms around me and I was safe, protected. His tongue touched just inside my lips and I moved my tongue—

Michael's phone beeped and Eric's voice, loud in the silence, filled the room. "You have to see this!"

I cursed the new App which allowed users to permit some callers to connect without the user having to press to pick up the call.

What we had to see was a press conference. Judy Bell, now dressed much more demurely than she had been in the photos posted by the Cyber Culprit, stared directly into the camera and categorically resigned.

Michael clicked his phone off and sat back in his chair. "Can you interview her tomorrow?"

I nodded.

Michael's phone beeped. "I have to take this."

He escorted me to the elevators, then turned towards his office.

Michael , Lusty Lee Log #12

Judy Bell was only slightly different in person than she was in the explicit images and videos of her that the Cyber Culprit had posted to the internet. She was still blonde and fit and attractive. Younger than her fifty years. But there was none of the animal lust I'd observed online. And the (now former) politician seemed much more relaxed. But the light in her eyes made it clear that relaxed and peaceful did not mean dead.

"You would have made a great Prime Minister," I told her.

She smiled, momentarily wistful. "Thank you, Ms. Brandt, but that's in the past now."

"What's in the future?"

"Life, law, men."

"Law?" 'Men' were more interesting, but first things first.

"Not at my old firm. A small boutique restricted to women's issues."

"It didn't seem that you lacked men."

She shook her head. "Sure, the quantity was there, and loads of excitement. But the men I met in politics never had long-term potential. They either saw me as a means to an end, a quick lay, or unattainable."

"Or as a ball-breaker?" Oops, that was uncalled for. My sternum tensed.

She smiled and nodded. My sternum relaxed.

"How did you see the men?" I asked.

"Much the same, I guess." Judy looked rueful, sad.

"No exceptions?"

"One." She held up a single finger. "Henry Cooper asked me to marry him. If I had, I'd have two adorable children and a law practice on the side. I turned him down because I thought it would have gotten in the way of my political career, now I don't even have that."

"How will the internet postings affect you?" The Cyber Culprit had posted images of Bell nude, including a shot of her smiling after having been facialized. But the kicker had been a video of her provoking a big black man to rape her. The ensuing scandal had forced her to end her leadership campaign.

She shrugged. "Some doors will open, some will close. People already know who I am."

"What about with men?"

She smiled. "The chaff will be blown away. Only men strong enough to be worthwhile will show any interest."

"Or respond to you?"

"She nodded. "And what about you, Miss Brandt? Or should I call you Lee?" I nodded. "How're you faring in the romance department?"

"Just me in my own bed at present," I told her. What was it

about this woman that I felt so comfortable sharing my intimate secrets with her? It was more than the fact that I'd already see her *in flagrante delicto* but I couldn't quite put my finger on it.

"Lee, when was the last time you got laid?"

"Oh, I get laid plenty. Just no romance." An image of Michael Rayburn popped into my head. He was definitely romance-ready *and* romance worthy. But since he was the one who'd given me my one and only money-making assignment, he was also off limits, *very* off limits.

We shared a quiet nod. We shared our mutual situation. No words, just sharing our heartbeats.

After a few moments, I pulled out the least salacious photo of Judy which had been posted by the Cyber Culprit. "Do you have any idea as to how this got onto the internet?"

She shook her head.

"Do you know where the photos came from?"

"They were hacked from my cloud account." She explained how careful she'd been when the photos were taken, about ensuring that she had the only copies. She described how she'd tagged each photo with special metadata. She showed me the promises of security that had been made by the cloud server.

"What about the video of you and the African-American man?"

She shook her head. "I have no idea. I hadn't even realized we were being videotaped."

"Is there anyone you could ask?"

She shook her head again. "I asked Jemile, he had on idea."

"Jemile?"

"The *African-American* in the video."

"Is there anyone else who might know?"

"No." A perfect politician's 'no'. I couldn't tell whether she meant that there was someone, but she wouldn't identify the person or whether there was in fact no one else.

"Could I have your cloud account password?" I asked. When she hesitated, I added, "Please, my IT guy may be able to trace who hacked your account."

She sighed and emailed me the information. I was checking her email on my phone when an urgent text came in from Michael Rayburn, the lawyer who'd hired me to track down the Cyber Culprit. He needed to see me immediately. Six o'clock on a Friday night and he needed to see me *immediately*!?! I said my goodbyes as quickly as I politely could.

In my car, I fluffed my curly brown hair and touched up my lipstick. As soon as the Bluetooth had engaged my phone, I called Michael and pulled away from the curb. "Should I bring Eric?" I asked. Eric, my assistant was in charge of computers, the internet and all things techy.

"No just you." Just me?!? Was that good or bad?

I rang off. At the first red light, I pulled the mirror down and looked at my face. I wished I'd applied make-up that morning. Just a little, not a lot, but at least some. There was a stirring inside my pelvis. Lee Brandt! Do *not* get ahead of yourself. Besides, Michael had told me that he had a new articling student who would be sitting in on all meetings. Part of the learning experience, he'd explained.

Inside the elevator to Michael's office, I looked at myself in mirror and smoothed down my vest and below-the-knee skirt, both navy blue wool-blend, my best business suit. The suit hugged my curves, especially my bosom. I smiled back at myself, a not unattractive package! Still, a little foundation would have brought out my blue eyes. I had thought about leaving my vest in the car, but had decided that my white semi-transparent blouse would be too suggestive. Now I compromised by undoing the vest's top two buttons.

Michael's articling student led me to a small boardroom. He was tall, skinny. His suit and tie made him look distinguished beyond his years. And eager, oh so eager.

Michael, tall and resplendent in his custom-tailored three-piece suit, came in a moment later and the three of us were about to settle into our chairs when Michael turned to his student. "Just Ms. Brandt."

Disappointment flashed momentarily across the student's face, in spite of his best effort to hide it.

But Michael had caught the disappointment. "You can work on the Gillies cross-examination," the lawyer consoled him.

When the door clicked shut behind the skinny student, Michael opened his laptop and entered his password. "The Cyber Culprit has made a new posting."

A few keystrokes later and Michael, virile and in charge, turned the laptop to me. I had expected to see the new internet posting, but instead there were two photos of me. I had no idea when or where the one in jeans and a T-shirt had been taken. The other photo—me in a short skirt and bosom-hugging blouse had been taken at Hendricks, moments before I'd picked up Mark. I'd been on the job, searching for the Cyber Culprit, at the time.

"I thought you were going to show me a new posting by the Cyber Culprit?" I queried.

"This *is* from the Cyber Culprit," he told me.

I did a double-take. The photos were innocuous, but still…

Michael turned his laptop back towards him and entered a few keystrokes. When he turned the screen back to me, it was displaying a video of me at Hendricks when I'd picked up Mark. The video showed Mark taking out his billfold and then the two of us leaving together.

"He didn't pay me," I protested.

Michael raised an eyebrow. "Video doesn't lie."

"Video can be cut. And cut video can give the wrong impression. I just wanted to see him work his billfold with his magical fingers."

Michael smiled. Was he teasing me? He inserted a small flash-drive into his computer, entered another password and then turned the screen towards me. This time the full video played, showing Mark returning his billfold to his pocket without paying me and my honor was restored.

Michael reached for the laptop but I lightly slapped his hand. "Beast!" I told him.

He reached for the computer but I pulled it towards me. "I want to finish watching the video," I told him. And make you pay for teasing me!

The video started up again and I was voluptuous, teasing, charming. Since then, I'd lost a little more weight (thanks to the MMA exercise routine Eric had put me on) and I was back to my optimal one-hundred and forty pounds.

The video ended with Mark and I exiting the bar. I turned the laptop back towards Michael. "And he posted this?!?" I exclaimed.

Michael shook his head. "Only the shorter version."

"But why?"

"To show that he can."

"We already know he can. Why me?"

"To show us that he knows we're watching him."

"And to tell us he knows we're after him."

Michael nodded. "Why did you want to seek how Mark played with his money?" he asked.

"I wanted him to touch me the same way he touched his money."

I watched Michael cue up the shorter version of the video. He turned the laptop so that we could both watch. His fingers fiddled with the laptop as the video played. I wondered how his touch would compare with Mark's.

Michael hit the spacebar where the video had been edited to make it look like I'd accepted money from Mark. "Our tech guys confirm that there'd been an edit, something taken out and two parts spliced together. The source is directly from the bar's own security camera."

"Where else would it be from?"

He pressed the spacebar and the video showed my hips swaying as I left the bar. "It could have come from the firm's servers."

"Your law firm's servers?"

He nodded, "We have a copy of everything on our own servers."

"How can you be sure that the Cyber Culprit didn't hack into your servers?"

"First, topflight security. Second, we replace the metadata on everything that goes onto our servers. The posting still had the metadata from Hendricks on it."

The video started to play again. I hit the spacebar to stop it. "Such a sad place," I mused. "So many people unhappily married."

"You've never married, have you Lee?"

I shook my head, trying to hide my reaction to this wonderfully intimate question. "No, not unless you count Peter. Have you?"

He shook his head.

"Why not? You're young, virile, healthy, successful."

He cocked his head to one side. "I guess I've never found the right woman."

I moved my hand towards his, just an inch. He moved his hand towards mine, just an inch.

Then he jerked his hand back. "There's something else I have to show you." An emotion flickered across his face. Sadness?

I watched his laptop as he entered a second level password. The opening frame of my sexual frolic with Jack Harding, Judy Bell's rival back when they'd both been politicians, both had hopes of becoming Prime Minister.

"Have you watched this?" he asked.

I shook my head. "I was there. You?"

He shook his head. I moved next to him. We weren't touching, but our thighs were within an inch of each other's. I could be making it easier for us to watch the video, or my moving closer could be an invitation. Before Michael had a chance to process the possibilities, I pressed the spacebar and the video started to play.

The computer screen showed me stripping down to a sheer pink bra, sheer pink panties, and sheer pink stockings held up by a garter belt. I took a sip of champagne, sat on Harding's lap and titillated his nipples. There was some talking on the video, but Eric hadn't recorded audio, so Michael and I couldn't hear what was being said. I turned to Michael who was watching the video with rapt attention.

"Is this turning you on?" I asked.

He nodded vaguely as the video showed me standing in full profile. "It's nice to see you losing weight," he mused.

He *is* keeping track! It was such a sweet comment that I automatically moved closer and we were touching, ever so lightly, along our arms and thighs.

On the laptop screen, my pelvis was inches from Harding's face, my buttocks clenching and unclenching.

"How would you feel if the Cyber Culprit ever got ahold of this?" Michael asked.

"I don't know."

He took out a portable hard drive, moving his arm away. Then he cued the video on the screen to delete and our arms were touching again. "These are the only copies," he said.

I reached over and move the cursor to cancel. The video started to play again.

Michael took a deep breath. "Certainly an Academy Award level performance." On the screen, I was pressing Harding's fingers into my crotch. Michael looked at his own fingers. "But I guess that lets me out of the running."

"Why?"

"There's no way I could ever keep up with you."

I shook my head. "You have so much more to offer than Harding ever could."

"Lee—"

"I never want to see Harding ever again. Mark was only one night. You…"

Our eyes were fixed on the laptop screen. Harding was beginning to lick my pussy. Michael's little finger touched mine. I moved my little finger, pressing against his. He pressed back sending tingles up my spine. We watched in silence, not daring to breathe, not daring to move our fingers, enjoying the touching, not willing to risk anything further, not wanting to endanger the intimacy we'd obtained. On the screen, Harding and I moved to the bed and I sucked his cock into my mouth. Michael rubbed up and down my finger. In a moment we'd be holding hands!

Michael's phone rang and he moved his hand away to answer. Our hands were no longer touching. Our arms were no longer touching. He shut the laptop screen and our legs were no longer touching. The phone rang again. Michael laid his phone on top of the laptop. The incoming call was from Eric and the phone rang again.

Michael pressed to answer in speakerphone mode. "Hi, Eric."

"Hello, Mr. Rayburn."

"Eric, I'm here with Lee," Michael advised. "What can we do for you?"

"I have a report on the Judith Bell posting."

"Okay."

There was a pause and in my mind's eye I could see Eric taking a deep breath. "The photos were hacked from Ms. Bell's cloud server account. The hacker had her cloud account password— her old one, she changed it after the hack. The password she gave Ms. Brandt was her new password. But the hacker hid his trail; I couldn't trace him. The next time the photos showed up was on the server CC uploaded them to."

"CC?" Michael wanted to know.

"The Cyber Culprit."

"What about the video of Bell having rough sex with the black guy?"

"The metadata on the video had been wiped clean. A professional grade wipe down. Maybe wiped before CC got ahold of it. So it was impossible to trace it."

"It was a larger file," I interjected. "Did that make it harder for the Cyber Culprit to post it?"

"It was larger, but CC had hijacked a server with large bandwidth. Posting didn't seem to present CC with any difficulties. And I didn't have any more luck tracing him through the video posting."

"Another dead end." The frustration in Michael's voice was clear to me and I hoped as clear to Eric.

But Eric's tone didn't change. "'Fraid so. But every time I put out a trace or watch what CC's done, I add to my profile of him."

Michael was silent for a moment. But when Eric didn't say anything further, Michael thanked him, terminated the call and turned to me.

"Have you had dinner?" he asked.

I looked at my watch. It was already eight o'clock. I shook my head, not daring to speak.

A quick stop in his office where he slid his laptop into to a small over-the-shoulder messenger bag and we were off. In the elevator, he proposed Italian. I nodded, not wanting to break the spell with words. I had resolved that this was a date and I didn't want words to contradict the dream. On the street Michael hailed a taxicab. I had been about to ask who was driving, but if he wasn't going to worry about his car, I decided not to worry about mine.

In the taxi, he told the driver, "Ignazio's, on Queen West."

His hand was on top of mine. If I turned my hand, we might be holding hands! Or it might startle him to lift his hand off mine. I kept my hand as still as I could.

Ignazio's had three levels. I'd only ever been to the first level before. The first level was small round tables with bright red-and-white checkered tablecloths. Take out and fast food. The second level had more subdued lighting. The tablecloths were white. It was filled with the loud conversation and laughter of diners enjoying good food, good wine, good company. At the entrance to the second level, Michael told the host, *"Privato, per favore."*

The host nodded and snaked her way through the throng of celebrants. The noise was almost deafening. Finally he ushered us into a smaller room at the back. There were four tables, larger than the ones in the second level and all separated by articulated room dividers with Italian scenery spread across the panels. My ears luxuriated in the silence.

Everything on the menu sounded fantastic. I had no idea what the Italian meant, but thankfully each item came with English translations underneath. There was every sort of pasta: simple tomato, seafood, Alfredo, chicken, soft, spicy. There were five flavors of Gnocchi. Almost everything you could think of was available in a ravioli. Chicken came Cacciatore, roasted in rosemary, Veneto, Milano, or Florentine. Mercifully veal was only available Piccata.

Our waiter hovered close by.

"What would you like?" Michael asked.

"You choose," I told him. If the man chooses, it's a date, right?

Michael ordered for the both of us, but didn't seem to put any emphasis on it. He ordered salad, Fettuccine Alfredo, and Pinot Grigio, which I vaguely identified as a white wine, to go with them. The main course was to be lamb chops with olive oil and garlic. For this he specified Amarone, a red wine. The word for love was in our wine! Was he sending me a signal?

I smiled as he handed the menus back to the waiter. "Sounds heavenly," I cooed. He smiled back at me.

The salad was crisp Romaine lettuce with cherry tomatoes. Every time I bit into a tomato, flavor gushed into my mouth.

After the salad, Michael pointed to the glass of white wine the waiter had poured. "Try the Pinot Grigio."

I took a sip. It was tart. I took a full mouthful and there was a wave of acid throughout my mouth, like dilute mouthwash. But it left behind a tangy fruit basket inside my mouth. Lemon, lime and green apples. Honeysuckle tickled up my nose.

Next was a dish of Fettuccini Alfredo done *al dente*. Al dente is a fancy word for undercooked and chewy. But it was a perfect match for the Pinot Grigio. I finished my glass and Michael refilled it. Then I noticed that Michael's glass was still half full and slowed down on the wine.

While waiting for the main course I kept my hands on the tablecloth. Michael could have reached over to hold hands, but it would have been a stretch. But the tablecloth was silk. So smooth under my fingertips. Was Michael being smooth too, or was I being presumptuous?

The lighting was subdued and soft. Thankfully, Michael was

under a light and I could feast my eyes on him. His suit hugged his body as if it had been painted on his lean physique. Wide at the shoulders, slimmer below. Light sparkled inside his blue eyes. His brown hair was straight, but the lighting gave it light fulsomeness and masked the grey at his temples. When he smiled, shadows appeared inside his wrinkles giving character to his handsomeness.

As far as I could tell, there was one other couple in the private room. Their conversation was muffled and I couldn't make out what they were talking about. I gestured around the room and over our table, finishing up pointing at his wine glass. "This is wonderful!"

"Glad you like it." He was about to say something more, but the waiter came to the table, removed our plates, and topped up Michael's wine glass. Light sparkled in the golden liquid. The waiter angled the bottle to my half-filled glass, but I shook my head.

"He's going to take the bottle away, Lee." Right, different course, different wine. I removed my hand and allowed the waiter to fill my wine glass. I was careful to match Michael's consumption.

"Lee, I appreciate the work you're doing on the Cyber Culprit case."

"Thanks." Work!?! Definitely not a date. I did my best to hide my disappointment.

"But I worry that it might be taking a toll on you."

I shook my head. "No, I'm fine." Why would you think that?

"All the men you have to deal with."

"I don't mind dealing with the men. It's just..." Michael, take the bait. Please!

But he didn't take the bait. He took a sip of wine instead. I cursed myself for trying to be subtle.

Michael was about to speak again, but the waiter appeared out of nowhere and removed our wine glasses and the bottle. He replaced the glasses with new ones and deposited a new bottle, dark and mysterious, on the table, it's cork still intact.

As soon as the waiter left, Michael pursed his full lips and enunciated carefully, "Lee, you said you didn't mind the men."

I nodded. He hadn't forgotten! "The men are fine. But it's just physical, just a fleeting moment."

"You want more." His words fluttered precisely through his lips.

I nodded and readied to open my mouth. But the waiter was back.

Our intrepid interrupter popped the cork off the Amarone and poured a mouthful of deep red liquid into Michael's glass. Michael picked up the glass and tipped the wine so that it touched his lips. Lips I longed to kiss! He opened his lips, ever so slightly and wine trickled into his mouth. He swished and swirled the wine inside his mouth, paused, then swallowed. He smiled—such a glorious smile!—then nodded.

The waiter filled both our glasses, then left. Michael didn't take another sip, so I left my wine untouched. I had made the last contribution to our conversation, so I waited for Michael. But he didn't say anything, so I was about to ask what he wanted in life when the waiter reappeared with our main course.

The lamb smelled strong and the garlic added to the pungent aroma. I cut off a small bite. There was just a thin inner layer of pink that dribbled a reddish watery liquid. Medium and just right! The meat tasted slightly gamy, but the Amarone cut through the gamy taste and left behind a symphony of fruity flavors dancing inside my mouth.

Michael's lips caressed each morsel of lamb before they drew it into his mouth to be carefully chewed by his bright white teeth. I watched his lips caress the lamb and kiss his wine into his mouth. Oh, how I longed for those lips to be kissing mine!

The waiter returned with a dessert menu. Michael pointed at it but I shook my head. Too many calories.

"Just coffee," he said.

The waiter left.

Damn! I still didn't know if this was just work colleagues having dinner or something more. I decided to take a different tack and pointed to the messenger bag holding his computer. "You take your laptop home?"

He nodded.

"Is that safe?" I followed up.

He nodded again. "All work files are only on the firm's server, so no harm if it's stolen. And I have a DSL link at home, no WiFi."

The coffee arrived. Without Michael getting the hint that I was interested in his apartment! He took a large gulp. Black. I usually had a large helping of cream and sugar in mine, but I followed suit. Protests inside my stomach made me immediately regret my choice. I was about to reach for the cream and sugar, but Michael's question stopped me.

"What about you? How's *your* IT security?"

I abandoned my coffee and was about to tell him that Eric had given it a thorough going over only last week. Instead, I answered, "Fine, I guess…"

"Maybe I should have a look."

"Sure." Was my answer nonchalant enough? I put cream and sugar in my coffee and gulped it down as quickly as I politely could. The waiter took forever to bring the bill. And another eternity to get Michael's credit card processed.

"Should I leave the tip?" I asked.

He shook his head and pointed to the credit card machine. Definitely a date!

Up in my apartment, I sat Michael down in front of my laptop and gave him my password.

He smiled. "I'll just check your security and see if our techs have any suggestions." Such a heavenly smile!

I scampered into my bedroom, removed my skirt and replaced it with a pair of jeans—tights really—and unbuttoned my vest. The vest was still hiding most of my bra, but the semi-transparent blouse clearly suggested what was underneath.

In the kitchen, I lifted Michael's jacket off, just to make him more comfortable, but I had no way of unbuttoning his vest without appearing too forward. Thankfully he unbuttoned it himself as he watched my laptop screen.

And then he loosened his tie as he turned towards me with his phone. "I didn't see anything untoward, but I sent a report to our IT department for them to give your security a once-over."

I nodded and took my phone out from my back pocket. "Thanks. But now it's time to turn these little beasties off." He hesitated but when I made a show of turning mine off, he followed suit. I took the phones and put them in the small alcove next to the fridge.

He stood and I reached to pull his tie the rest of the way off.

But Michael turned just enough to indicate that he didn't want me to touch his tie. "Lee, I…"

"Don't know whether this is a good idea?" I finished.

"Yes."

"Do you like me?"

He nodded.

"Do you want to touch me?"

"Very much so."

"Well, I want to touch you too." My nipples poked forward their agreement, my pussy warming her concurrence. "Do you promise to bring me joy?"

"Tonight, most certainly, but—"

"I promise to bring you joy too. As for tomorrow, let's talk over breakfast."

He gulped and nodded. So it had been a date. And soon it would be consummated! Weakness in my knees mirrored the discomfort in his throat. Now when I stepped forward, he let me remove his tie. He slid my vest off my shoulders and laid it carefully atop his suit jacket. I lifted my arms and removed his vest, then unbuttoned his shirt. He unbuttoned his sleeves and laid vest and shirt atop my vest. I quickly unbuttoned my blouse and when he turned back to me, I handed it to him.

There was a thin layer of flab over his torso, but clearly muscles underneath. I could smell him now, a vague odor of musk—not from a bottle—genuine and natural. There were only slight wisps of hair. His nipples were dark little buttons on his chest.

He stepped forward, bent down and we kissed.

His lips covered mine perfectly and he puckered and released, so slightly, so subtly than the movement would be invisible to anyone watching. But the movement let me feel the softness and power of his lips on every nerve ending on my own lips. I puckered back. The whole universe was our lips, then just where out lips touched. A glorious moment of eternity. Suddenly I needed to suck air into my lungs and his scent overpowered me. It was virile and sharp, yet soft and comforting all at the same time. I held on to him, my fingers luxuriating in the softness of his skin, of his thin layer of flab. His muscles rippled underneath my fingers stirring moist heat inside my pussy.

He kissed me again, this time his tongue sneaking through his lips to lightly moisten mine. The universe was in the tip of his tongue and I was aware of nothing except where it touched. My upper lip tingled, jolts of electricity sparked through the tip of my tongue and down my spine, the side of my tongue swooned as he caressed down her length. Then one hand was cupping my buttock while his other held me up by my waist.

I recovered control of my knees and led him to my bedroom, to the side of my bed. I turned and lightly ran my fingers up and down his zipper. He was protruding and hard. I carefully undid his zipper and lifted his pants and underwear up and over his erection. He was only average in the penis department, but I suspected that he'd know how to make the most of what he had and his pecker was certainly showing its enthusiasm!

I turned to lay his pants on my dresser and felt his hands caress my rump. I spread my legs and his hand ran slowly up my thigh, sending warmth and excitement ahead of its advance. I tried to concentrate on my breathing. And then he was caressing back and forth across my pussy. My toes curled.

I turned back to Michael and he hugged me into another kiss, this time full and passionate. Animal aggression and passion. He undid my bra and it fell away as he pushed, then gently lowered me onto the bed. Only my ankles dangled over the side. His fingers brushed against my nipples and he alternated sucking with his mouth and thrusting with his tongue. His oral onslaught was so strong that I could barely respond. Except down below where I could feel my whole sex hot, where I could feel droplets leaking down my nether lips.

Then he sucked my left nipple and I felt a twinge inside my pussy. My right nipple and there was almost a contraction. Then he lifted himself up and pulled my jeans over my hips, then slowly down my thighs as we locked eyes, his promising to ravish and control and cherish, mine to submit and worship.

Jeans off my feet, Michael bent to his knees and kissed back up my legs, starting at my outer calves, looping his tongue around the protrusions atop my knees. On my thighs, he started with a brushing kiss, then soft suction, then hard suction as he moved higher. Just below my sex, he gave a light nip.

Then he ran his tongue up and around my engorged outer ridge, up into my pubic hair and down the other side. At the very bottom, his tongue touched the point were my inner lips joined and pressed forward, almost as thin as a finger, into my vagina. His tongue flicked in and out, three times in quick succession. I tried to gasp air into my lungs, but I was paralyzed.

Then mercifully, he withdrew his tongue and I could breathe again. His tongue traced up my pussy lip, crossing up and over as he moved towards my clit. But instead of caressing my love knob, he pressed against my urethra, then down into the front of my vagina, then back up again, over and over again, torturing me each time by stopping a hair's breadth short of my swollen love button.

Just as I thought he was finally going to let his tongue caress my clit, he angled down my other pussy lip, rapidly down one side and just as rapidly up the other. His tongue was as precise as his pronunciation and I swooned under his control. But unlike his usual orations, Michael Rayburn was being obtusely slow in getting to the point!

He slipped his left hand under my back, almost at the bottom of my spine, and placed his right atop my pubic bone, pressing down, compressing my pubic hair. Then he pulled his upper hand back, arching my pelvis forward and sending a delicious caress into my clit.

His tongue pressed and circled just above my clit, my pubic hair allowing it to grip my skin and pull up on my clitoral hood. Passion *was* building inside but the pace was tortuously slow. I tried to tense my pelvis to hurry it along. But he licked up and down the outside of the hood covering my clit, rubbing her against its inner covering and now I relaxed into the uncontrollable tension increasing heartbeat by heartbeat inside my pussy.

He kissed my love knob and I almost came. I tightened my kegel muscles to prevent my orgasm, to prolong the pleasure. Then he sucked my clit inside his mouth, lapping her bottom ridge with his tongue and spasm after spasm of ecstasy wrenched all control from me. By the third spasm, I was completely lost. It rocketed up my spine, then softly rolled back down, spreading warmth and release. The fourth spasm was heat inside my cunt. The fifth spasm turned my legs into jelly.

Michael lifted himself up and caressed up my body with long firm strokes, becoming gentle only when he reached my breasts where little jolts swirled each time his fingers circled my nipples. When he was satisfied that my breathing had returned to normal, he kissed his way down my belly and back to my sex.

This time there was no subtle teasing. He flattened his tongue and lapped broadly up and down my sex. He licked up and over my clit. As soon as he heard me gasp, he inserted two fingers inside me and quickly found my sensitive spot. He curled his fingers to call me thither.

And thither I came! All over his fingers, all over his hands I spurted. He laughed a throaty joyous laugh and lapped at my spurts, trying to find each drop, savoring each the same way he'd savored the lamb and wine hours earlier. He licked the last drop off his lips and smiled laughter down at me.

I propped myself up on my shoulders and looked down at the large wet spot on the sheet between my legs. "Most men are put off by that," I observed.

"I guess I'm not most men."

I pushed him flat on his back. "Let's find out what type of man you are," I told him.

I spread his legs and crawled up between them. He had more hair on his legs than he did on his chest, but it was wispy and soft. I placed a hand on each end of his hips. His pubic hair was full and deep brown, darker than on his head. In the middle of the forest, one bare tree stood up proud.

I sucked his penis into my mouth. It was large enough that I could only go half way down comfortably. I sucked up and down rapidly until he was thoroughly lubricated. Then I brought my right hand over to slide up and down his shaft as I withdrew my mouth upwards. Every time I slid my mouth down, my right fingers caressed his balls. His musk assaulted my nostrils.

He'd stopped breathing so I lifted myself entirely off him. "Breathe!" I commanded.

I let him take half a breath before I sucked him back into my mouth, smiling to myself as I heard his breath cut off short once again. His cock was hard and hot, little purple ridges for his veins. I slid my right hand up and over each ridge as I sucked slowly upwards. On the downward stroke, I gave his balls a firm squeeze.

He started to gulp short little breaths and I knew he was about to come. His hands were balling my sheets. The first taste of salt on my tongue, I moved my right hand back to his hip and used my arms to pump my head up and down his shaft as quickly as I could.

My mouth filled with his semen, salty and sticky. I raised my head to the very tip of his cock and swallowed, his spunk cloying my mouth and throat tight. A firm grip on his cock with my hands up and down milked the last of the life force out of him. His eyes were locked shut. As his orgasm began to subside, I loosened my grip. He opened his eyes and smiled up at me.

He had come in a matter of minutes. Pleasuring me had brought him to the precipice as it should any attentive lover. I smiled back.

Later, in the kitchen, Michael turned his cellphone back on. "Fifty messages," he grumbled as I popped a tray of brownies into the oven. He looked totally silly in one of my old robes.

He was just checking his last text when I popped a brownie into his mouth. He took a bite, then swallowed it whole. "Damn!" he swore, anger clearly visible on his face.

I quickly tasted a brownie. It was okay. Not gourmet, but nothing—

He turned his phone to me. The Cyber Culprit had struck again. This time his postings showed photos of a well-known political-party fundraiser. It was said that his success in raising money had made the difference in the last election. The photos showed Irving Smith whooping it up at a local swinger's club. The fact that it wasn't his wife he was whooping it up with likely made it worse. He was dressed in leather, she, whoever she was, was wore lace.

I grabbed my own phone and quickly opened up the club's website. Tonight's theme was leather and lace. The Cyber Culprit had been broadcasting live! *In real time.* If I hadn't been fooling around with Michael, he would have got the message sooner... I would have— I dialed Eric, then ran to my closet.

When I came back into the room, Michael was on his phone, "Yes, sir... Right away sir... Yes, I know what this means. I'll be in the office right away."

Michael pushed away from the table, but I grabbed his robe. "Have another brownie. You're no good without a full stomach."

Michael wolfed down three brownies and I followed him to the bedroom where he dressed at lightning speed.

"Who was the guy in the posting?" I asked, then mimicked his voice, "*I know what this means.*"

He paused at the door to give me a perfunctory kiss. "The man in the posting. He's a client of the firm. A very *very* important client." And then Michael was gone.

He hadn't even noticed that I was wearing a shorter-than-short black leather mini-skirt, a black bikini string top, and a black collar. And nothing else.

I quickly pulled on a pair of panties, grabbed my purse and

shot out the door. Maybe there was still time to catch the Cyber Culprit swinging at the club.

Rum Balls , Lusty Lee Log #13

I was still breathing hard when I arrived at the swinger's club. The Cyber Culprit had posted a video from inside, likely just hours before. *And he might still be here!* It was chilly, especially given that I was clad only in a shorter-than-short black leather mini-skirt, a black bikini string top, a leather collar with one chrome ring in the center and a pair of black silk panties. So I moved into the lobby and sat down on the only bench located there.

The Culprit's posting had featured a well-known, and even better-connected, political fundraiser whooping it up at the club with a woman not his wife. Even more important, the fundraiser was an important—a *very* important—client of Michael Rayburn's law firm. And since Michael was hiring me and paying all my bills, said political fundraiser was now a very important, if not the most important man in *my* life.

I shook my head. No, the *only* man in my life was Michael Rayburn. I'd had sex with Michael just an hour before. First time sex. Not penis in vagina, but *everything* else. Floating and ecstasy and fireworks. Please let it have meant as much to him as it had meant to me! I bit my lip.

A new couple entered the lobby and I half listened to the receptionist explaining the rules of the club as I tried to slow my heartbeat. "'No' means 'no', if you don't like what's happening to you, just say so. Many of our members are swingers, but many couples come solely for the erotic atmosphere. If you are offended by nudity or public displays of affection..." I'd heard it many times before so I tuned it out and inspected myself in the mirror. Voluptuous bosom, wide sensuous hips, dark red lipstick enhancing an alluring smile and curly brown hair dancing about my head would signal just the right invitations tonight.

Eric burst in. My assistant was wearing a cute pair of leather shorts and a leather harness. He shivered and rubbed his bare arms. Red hair atop his lanky six-foot-three frame, white skin, and black leather was the perfect color combination.

Inside, the main area is composed of a bar, a large dance

floor surrounded by couches, stools and standing areas. Many of those in attendance are wearing leather, but many are not. Some are wearing leather masks. A few are wearing leather blindfolds and being led around by a leash. As usual the women are dressed more sexily than the men.

But one man is dressed even more outrageously than Eric: he's nude except for a blindfold and a cock ring fastened under his balls and over the top of his penis. His mate, a tall woman dressed in a leather corset, is stroking his balls with a peacock feather. Occasionally she offers the feather to anyone passing by. Her round rump is enhanced by loose-fitting leather panties and tight leggings that end just below her buttocks.

Our target, political party fundraiser Irving Smith and his lady are sitting on a couch, located up and away from the dance floor. He's wearing black leather pants, a white shirt with puffy sleeves and a black leather vest. His shirt is unbuttoned to his navel revealing light wisps of hair. She is wearing a black lace body suit with black leather panties on top and black patent leather stiletto-heeled shoes. Since she's wearing nothing else, her breasts jiggle when she moves and her nipples try to press through the body suit. Irving appeared oblivious to the fact that his night out on the town was already the subject of a social media posting. A social media posting which was starting to unleash a political shit-storm.

I move to a free table that gives me a view of Smith and not-Mrs. Smith, the dance floor, the bar, and the alcove of seats off to one side.

Eric joins me, but I nudge him away. "Get us two beers."

Irving's black leather pants and vest are keeping any paunch well contained. He appears fit, late forties, just over six-feet tall, dark hair with just a hint of grey. She's just slightly shorter than he, almost ten years his junior, short light brown hair with blonde streaks. Breasts and hips smaller than mine, but still pleasant handfuls. A power couple on the prowl for new adventures.

Eric comes back with two stubby-bottled Red Stripe beers. He'd obviously gotten a taste for it down at Hedonism. Me, I don't particularly care for beer and that will make it easier to sip slowly.

Up on the couch, Irving slides his hand under her leather panty. He caresses softly, but she wants more and bucks her hips up against his hand. Her left hand strokes lightly against his zipper. Eric and I scan the room, but no one seems to be watching the amorous couple. I finally locate the spot from which the videos which had been posted earlier in the evening had been taken.

I point the spot out to Eric. "Check for a camera."

Eric ambles over, doing his best to look nonchalant. On the couch, "Mrs." Smith adjusts her buttocks to allow Irving's fingers better access. By the time Eric returns to the table, she's shuddering in the early throes of an orgasm.

"Anything?" I ask.

He shakes his head.

Mrs. Smith completes her climax and turns her full attention to his zipper. But he has different ideas and pulls her to the dance floor. I cock my head towards them and Eric gets the hint.

"Dance?" he asks.

I take his hand and allow him to pull me to the dance floor. Irving is behind his mistress, his hands caressing her breasts. Her eyes are teasing in my assistant's direction.

I grab Eric's balls. "Don't look at her. If you look into her eyes, you'll be accepting her invitation to swing with them."

"But—"

I squeeze harder. "But what?"

He shrugs and I relax my grip into a gentle caress.

"Should we be doing this?" he wants to know. "You're my boss and—"

"—and we're undercover."

He shrugs and places a hand on each of my hips.

"Put your hand up my panties."

"Lee!?"

"Do you want to blow our cover? Do it! You're dancing like you're at a high school prom and the chaperone's watching."

He sighs and places his right hand between my legs, just below my panty.

I give his gonads another squeeze. "Like you mean it!"

Finally Eric's right hand relaxes into it's under cover—or rather its *up my skirt*—role. His long fingers allow him to stroke along my entire slit all at the same time, all the way from my perineum and up into my pubic hair. The strokes below my vagina relax my entire crotch, backwards and forward into enjoying his caresses. My vulva, and especially my inner lips and clit, engorge and his gentle upward pulls on my pubic mound spark jolts throughout my entire sex.

My left hand squeezing his butt keeps him close and I can feel his cock stiffen under his shorts with my right.

Mrs. Smith is stroking the front of Mr. Smith's pants where there's a bulge even more prominent than Eric's. Warm dampness envelopes my sex and I'm sure that Eric can feel it. Mrs. Smith has turned Irving sideways to make her strokes even more obvious, but so far Eric and I have been successful in avoiding eye contact. But my pussy—hot and wet—is urging me to revise my strategy and allow her to envelop Mr. Smith's prominence. Eric's cock has the same thought.

Finally not-Mrs.-Smith gives up on us and my moral dilemma is solved. Her next target couple is a chubby red-haired woman and a tall blonde man who's even skinnier than Eric. Is she rubbing in her point that Eric and I could have had them? In a moment, the two couples are in a swinger's sandwich, women in the middle, their mates behind them. The women bend slightly forward and rub their butts against their mate's crotches.

Since everyone's now watching the swingers sandwich, I relax my grip on my assistant's crotch and he immediately drops his hand to his side. I grab his butt to hold him close, his crotch pressing pleasantly against my lower belly. Eric follows suit and cups his fingers around my left buttock.

Mrs. Smith and the redhead pass an eye-signal and in a moment they rotate such that they've swapped husbands. The two women kiss and fondle each other's breasts. When masculine hands move to their breasts, the women fondle lower. The song ends and the women stand up. When the new song starts, the women turn to the men and the switch is complete. Hands excitedly explore new bodies. The two women smile at each other. I look around, but there's no indication that anyone's concentrating sufficiently on either pair to be filming them.

"Body shots!" reverberates the DJ's voice. "Get your body shots!" There's a rustling at the corner of the dance floor as one of the bar staff unfolds a large massage table. I know from past experience that someone, usually female, was meant to strip nude or mostly nude and lie on the table. Others would dribble alcohol onto her, then lick and suck it off her body. "And tonight, we have something special," the DJ continues. "Rum balls!"

I pull Eric over to the massage table and quickly strip down to my panties. My tummy is almost flat, thanks to the MMA exercise routine Eric has me on. My nipples engorge at the prospect of alcohol being sucked off them by strangers' lips and tongues. The bartender brings out two bowls of rum balls, one white, the other dark, and places it next to the massage table. "Get your body shots," the DJ repeats. "Straight up or rum balls!"

I pick up one of the rum balls. It's slightly moist. I bite off half. The outside is rum-soaked cookie crumble and nuts. Inside is a round chocolate mold which I bite into. Custard bursts out of the mold and dribbles out of my mouth, down my throat and between my breasts. The custard is cold at first, then warms and turns gooey. This is going to be *fun*! I mash the rest of the rum ball into Eric's mouth.

When my assistant has succeeded in swallowing part of the rum ball, I pull his right ear down to my mouth, "Watch to see if someone is trying to film me."

He nods uncertainly.

I pull his ear even closer to my lips. "Under *no* circumstances are you to intervene," I hiss.

He nods.

I climb onto the table, lie on my back and close my eyes. Several fingers trace up and down the sides of my torso and legs. Cologne wafts, then disappears. Then nothing. I open my eyes. A man in a black mask is staring down at me. Beside him is a thin white woman. She's wearing only a black leather collar and bikini bottom. A leash is attached

"Would you like to suck her breasts?" the masked man asks. His mask bulges around his eyes with thin black latex covering from the top of his face down to the tip of his nose and strapped below his chin. His entire torso is covered in the same black latex.

I nod and he pulls her down such that her right nipple is between my lips, her blonde hair falling around my face. I shut my eyes and suck. Her nipple, now the size of my pinky, thrusts out into my mouth. She smiles down at me as her left nipple is moved into position. As I suck, I feel a hand move up between my legs, touch the bottom of my panties. I relax for the sensations to come but the hand vanishes and the nipple pulls gently away.

I open my eyes to see Black Mask smiling down at me and gesturing towards his woman. "May she remove your panties?"

I nod and feel my panties being pulled down my legs, letting in a cool draft.

He begins to roll a rum ball under around and between my breasts in a figure-8 pattern. "Hard or soft?" he asks.

"Thorough." Something between his extremes seems safer.

He breaks open the rum ball and extracts the hard chocolate core. He momentarily holds it between his teeth, then masticates it while looking down at me with mastery and glee.

At my feet, I feel something being mashed onto my big toes. The custard from the rum balls dribbles down the soles of my feet, tingling and curling my toes. Lips envelop one of my big toes and suck. A tickle jolts up my spine. Fingers dance up and down the sole of my other foot snapping spasms up and down the other side of my body. I grip the sides of the table to stop the thrashings of my body from tossing me off the table.

Then there's a half a rum ball covering each of my nipples. The balls rotate slowly, the rum infused inside providing just enough lubrication to offset the friction from the rough cookie-crumble and nut mixture but still pin my back to the table with the force of the pleasure pushing down and into my breasts.

"Just you, just me," his soft voice whispers into my ear. "No WiFi, no phones, no Google, no FaceBook. Are you ready to be pleasured?"

I'm about to whisper back 'yes', but he twists the rum balls in the opposite direction and jolts of delight freeze the air inside my lungs.

A new voice from above asks, "May we cut in?"

The masked man mutters, "Sure."

I'm immediately covered by more fingers than I can count. Strong male hands squeeze my breasts and I open my eyes. The arms to my left are white and scrawny, the two on my left are thick and black. Below, something dribbles into my belly button and is then immediately sucked out with a mixture of tickle and arousal. Fingernails play with my pubic hair while softer fingers tease up my legs. Two shots of whiskey splash onto my breasts which are quickly licked clean. Below, a finger teases my pussy lips.

"Bye, sweetie," calls a female voice from below and I'm alone.

But almost immediately Black Mask returns. He holds a rum ball in front of my face as he pulls his submissive towards him with the leash. She smiles down at me. "What would you like to eat, this rum ball, or her?" He hugs his submissive close.

"Both."

He smiles and peels off the outer part of the rum ball, feeding it to me piece by piece. When he gets to the chocolate core, he holds it between thumb and forefinger before carefully placing it in my belly button.

Then he helps his submissive up onto the table, sliding her knees into my armpits and I stare up into her steely blue eyes. She edges closer and I see that her pubic hair is blonde as well. Her only scent is chocolate with a bit of rum. She slowly lowers her sex onto my mouth and I flick my tongue upwards. Finally there's a female smell, sharp and pungent. She's wet, not from my tongue, but from her own arousal. She tastes first chocolate, then salt, then vinegar. She moans and strokes the side of my head.

Her pussy lips are small and delicate, barely there. But her whole vulva has engorged with blood, making it hard and hot. Her little pleasure button is even harder. I lick and suck and she moans again, louder.

Below a rum ball rolls around my pubic mound, up and down my thighs. Then I bend my knees and it slides up and down my slit. The ball returns to the center of my pubic prominence, then stops. Slowly, but inexorably, the rum ball is pressed into my pubic mound until it begins to fall apart.

"How does this feel?" he wants to know.

I try to answer, but she's grinding her sex hard into my mouth.

Then the ball bursts and custard dribbles down between my legs.

"What does this feel like?" I want to tell him that it feels like heaven my pussy's gone to heaven.

The woman above me clenches her sex tight. Then convulsions begin to ripple inside and down into her thighs which are pressed against my cheeks. Her taste turns sweet and creamy and I realize that custard is dribbling out of her vagina. I lap it up. Cunt custard! There's little bits of chocolate in with the custard. Sex and chocolate and custard—all of my favorite things.

In a moment, her contractions subside and the masked man helps her off the table.

He holds another rum ball up for me to see, then places it atop my pubic prominence and pushes. "How does this feel?"

"Anticipation, potential."

"Savor the reality in the present tense." He grinds down, mashing the rum ball hard enough that it begins to disintegrate. "And this?"

"Hard and sexy."

"Good—reality in the present touch." He pushes all the way down and the ball falls apart, custard dribbling down into my sex. "And now?"

"Like heaven petting my pussy."

"Such a sexual woman you are. Tell me what you like."

"I like a man who takes me without asking questions."

"Shut your eyes."

I obey, glad that Eric's watching what needs to be watched. Pieces of rum ball fall onto my torso. Two halves are placed over my nipples and gently rotated. More pieces of rum ball fall onto my chest. The smell of rum bites into my sinuses. The balls atop my nipples are rotated again, grinding against the sides of my engorged nipples.

Below lips kiss my pubic hair, then down my inner thigh. When the lips come back up, they are centered right below my pussy. A faint groan escapes my lips as I feel warmth and moistness swell inside my sex. A tongue darts up and down my pussy and my wetness escapes outside to lubricate my pussy lips. A finger pokes inside and I have to grip the sides of the table to absorb the jolt up my spine.

Then something else is in my pussy. Warm and round. Then another, and another. Is she putting custard balls up my cunt? They feel warm and slippery and succulent. The creamy sweet smell of chocolate mingles with the rum's aromas of alcohol and molasses.

Her hands leave me and there are only his hands massaging rum and cookie crumble and custard up and down my torso, caressing the rough and smooth mixture over around and into my breasts. His power penetrates down to my sex and I spread my legs, dangling my calves and feet over the sides of the table. But he continues to concentrate on my breasts, ignoring the invitation below.

"Touch me," I breathe.

His hands move lower, press against the sides of my pubic bone and pull up. I suck all the air in the universe into my lungs knowing I'll never breathe again.

But he lets me breathe again, rubbing in round circles, slowly arousing the fires within my sex. His fingers are different than Michael's. Michael's had been precise, targeted. His are everywhere at once, sometimes soft, sometimes hard, pleasuring all over all at once.

One hand cups my entire vulva, squeezing my inner pussy lips and clit between my outer lips, as if they were meat inside a sandwich. The other hand presses my pubic bone. He contracts the hand embracing my vulva while pulling up against my pubic bone. The fires within my cunt *beg* to be let out!

Keening noises sound within my throat. "Please," I beg.

But his hands show no reaction, continuing with their rotations and squeezings. He relaxes the pressure on my vulva and pushes down on my pubic bone, stirring the torrid passions within. The hand on my vulva presses down while the hand on my pubic bone pulls up expanding and stoking my interior cauldron. He pulls up on my vulva forcing heat to contract while his other hand rotates, stirring the roiling contents inside my cunt.

Then he releases his grip on my vulva. Something warm and gooey oozes out of my pussy. The custard! His fingers massage it all over my sex, slipping and sliding with the excess lubrication. Little pieces of chocolate prick against my skin then melt away.

Slowly the custard is pressed aside or absorbed into my skin and I can feel the surface of his fingers again, every whorl against my skin, stroking my pussy lips, brushing up and down my clit, kneading my engorged outer lips.

Hands above cup my breasts, then stroke in circular motions, slowly at first, then accelerating as they move inexorably towards my nipples. Her fingers are delicate, soft, unlike the larger, more powerful fingers below. The sensations coalesce, my whole body hot.

Then everything stops. The tips of two fingers press just below my pussy. I'm aware of bits of rum ball and custard coating my body. But that fades away leaving only the two fingertips. My whole consciousness is sucked into these two points of pressure.

The two fingers move up, slowly, ever so slowly. They poke into the lower edge of my pussy. Up they slide. Then in, pushing my pussy wider for them to slip inside. My juices gush out to greet them. The first knuckles pause their process, then push wider and inside. The second knuckles slide in without pause, all the way in.

As slowly as the fingers had penetrated they withdraw until

just the tips are teasing against he bottoms of my pussy lips. They slide back in, faster this time and the hands return to my breasts, squeezing and caressing. Another hand reaches below and grabs a buttock, then slides up to my lower back, pulling my hips up and into the two fingers plunging in and out of my sex.

I'm dimly aware of other fingers, other hands and lips, of alcohol being spilled and sucked, of rum balls being mashed and spread. But only the two fingers inside my vagina hold any power over me.

The fingers inside join and intertwine into a spiral and rotate as they go in, rotate as they recede. All the air inside my lungs is sucked away. The universe collapses into the spiral fingers rotating in and out of me.

Then the fingers stroke my g-spot, just lightly enough to show they know it's there, to show that they have complete and total control of me. The fingers stop their thrusts, separate out of their spiral and circle around the outer edges of my pleasure spot. Like wolves circling their prey.

Someone is licking my belly button, someone else sucks a nipple into their mouth, someone else kneads my other breast with both hands. The wolves circle. Custard is drizzled into my pubic hair and massaged until it's sticky. The wolves circle. A tongue licks my pubic hair and sucks strands into his mouth. The wolves circle. Hands lightly caress my breasts. The wolves nuzzle. Liquid pours onto my belly and a hand pushes it into my pubic hair. The wolves breathe down my spine. Tongues lap at the alcohol-softened custard.

Then there is only fingers inside me. They move together, right on top of my g-spot, pressing lightly enough to inhale my lungs full of oxygen, pressing with just enough force to draw all sensation into their tips. Then they curl and stroke. The first stroke lights my cunt on fire. The second stroke lubricates the fire. The third stroke tightens every muscle in my body. The forth stroke collapses my cunt hard around the fingers inside. The forth stroke explodes contraction, wave after wave inside my cunt, up my spine, down to my toes.

"No!" I scream. "No!" This can't end. But a contraction in my neck chokes off my protest. Gradually the fury of the convulsions subside into gentle waves of warmth.

Then he kisses me, full on the lips. "Catching you with rum

balls was so much better than catching you with a Pokémon Go Ball."

I heard his voice through the fog of orgasm, comforting, deep, throaty. I was under warm water, held safe from all the cares of the world. But dimly I became aware that I'd heard his voice before. At Hendricks. Ranting against people hooking up through computers instead of face-to-face. My eyes shocked open. This wasn't just some random swinger! I tried to sit up. But the sub's leash was attached to my collar and my neck wrenched to one side.

Black Mask and his blonde sub were leaving. I tried to call to Eric, but the force on my collar choked off my words. I gestured violently towards my assistant. Then I saw Eric. The entire front of his shorts were filled with rum balls. Custard oozed out onto his thighs. He could barely walk.

I got the collar off and sprinted out to the lobby. Everyone was looking at me. I looked down. I was nude, dark chocolate and yellow custard spread all over me. Even if I'd had car keys, I was too messy to give chase.

Two hours later, Eric and I were back in my apartment, he looking silly in my terry cloth robe, me draped in towels: my hair wrapped in a smaller towel. But at least we were fresh as new after lengthy showers.

I'd decided to keep my suspicions about the identity of tonight's masked man to myself. I had only vague recollections and nothing to substantiate my suspicions. After all, if they'd really been the same man, why hadn't I recognized his voice as soon as he'd asked me how it felt when he had fondled me?

I turned to Eric and, not for the first time, suppressed a giggle at his appearance. "Did you see anything suspicious?" I asked.

"No. Nothing."

"Anyone filming?"

"No."

"Another dead end."

Eric shook his head. "Every dead end eliminates a possibility."

"How?"

"His postings have been random. A sportscaster. Swingers. An up-and-coming banker. A philanthropist. A businessman. An adulteress. An actor. A politician. A party fundraiser."

"You think that the previous attacks were to mask the fact

that he's after politicians? And their enablers?"

"That's one possibility. Or he's after something, not someone."

I looked at Eric. He might be right. Nevertheless, our progress was exceedingly slow. But at least his ideas didn't *sound* as silly as he *looked.*

Two nights later, I was alone in my apartment with Michael. As soon as he'd arrived, I'd made a show of turning my phone off. He'd gotten the hint and immediately turned his cellphone off as well. I poured us each two fingers of whisky.

"The other night was wonderful," he began, vaguely.

"For me too." Just as vague, but just as positive.

"I don't want to take advantage of you."

"*I* want you to take advantage of me."

"But it's unfair. Our firm employs you..."

"This, you, me *that,*" I said, allowing anger to flicker in my eyes, "has nothing to do with your firm *employing* me."

"How can you be sure?"

"Because I like you. And I like you more every time we're together."

Michael was about to reach for my hand when his phone rang. Insistent. His face reddened. "It must be my assistant. I installed the Open Call App for Lucy. But only for Lucy."

The Open Call App allowed a caller to turn your phone on. Even when you had it turned off.

I wanted to wring his neck. "Why would you let her—"

"It must be important," he apologized. He turned and cupped the phone. "Lucy?"

I could hear her voice, but just barely. "... Culprit threatening another post... serious."

"Has he posted anything yet?"

"No."

"Okay. Then there's nothing we can do at this point." He made a show of turning his phone off and turned to me. "Sorry."

"Where were we?" I asked.

"We were telling each other how much we enjoyed being together." He placed his hand atop mine.

"And worrying about your taking advantage of your power over me." I turned my hand over and gave his a gentle squeeze.

"And your wanting me to take advantage of you."

I pulled him up off his chair and led him to the bedroom. I opened the drawer in the little cabinet next to the bed, removed a condom and laid it on top. I didn't want Michael to have to ask for a condom. And I wanted to make it clear exactly what type of sex I was hoping for. He'd already pleasured me with his fingers and his tongue. Tonight I wanted to take our lovemaking to a higher level.

We quickly stripped nude and tossed our clothes into the corner. I had only a moment to register Michael's six-foot tall masculinity, muscles ready for action, handsome face, blue eyes and brown hair flecked with grey before his lips enveloped me with his passion. His body was already hot, his penis standing proudly erect below. Swiftly his desire spurred my passions to match his.

We hugged close but kept out hands still. All our attention was focused on our mouths. His tongue plunged its full length into my mouth and I pushed mine under his, rubbing the rough top of my tongue on the smooth underside of his. Then he clamped suction tight and our tongues were fastened tightly together. Our tongues could only rub a millimeter back and forth. It was hot, incredibly hot!

And in that moment, I became aware that my breasts were rubbing against his torso, millimeter by millimeter. And further below, my pubic bone was rubbing against his pelvis. My whole body was afire and I wanted him every way everywhere all at once. We were breathing hard through our noses. Every time he exhaled, I sucked his breath into my lungs.

Out of breath, we collapsed onto the bed. I climbed on top of him, knees on either side of his thighs, and kissed him ferociously. This time Michael thrust his tongue under mine, its roughness adding flame to the fire. Once again, he clamped suction tight locking our tongues together. I rubbed myself up and down his body—his *magnificent* body—and felt the heat in our mouths trickle down where his penis was hot against my thigh.

My pussy knew what she wanted. She wanted his phallus stroking her interior, his pubic bone caressing her insides. And she was luring his pointed shaft ever closer to her opening. Each frisson of passion—his and mine—edged her closer to her goal. Soon he would be inside. Soon—

But I had seen the look of appreciation on Michael's face when I'd taken the condom out. So I pushed myself up to my knees, reached behind and held the condom wrapper up for him to see.

Michael held out his hand, but I ripped the wrapper, lifted myself up and over his throbbing cock and slowly, tortuously slowly, unrolled the condom down over his cock. He was big and hard and hot. A gentle tug up to unwrap the last roll and his sheath was in place.

Michael gently lifted me up and placed me on my back. He was old-school. He felt he should do the work, perform the ceremony. And in that moment, I gave myself to him, my body, my heart, my soul, my eternity.

The tip of his penis brushed up and down my pussy. Oh how I wanted him! How I wanted him inside, taking me, possessing me. Please, Michael, please!

He pressed the tip of his penis right in the center of my pussy. He wasn't inside, but he was right at the doorway. He paused, as if asking permission.

"Yes, Michael, yes!"

He pushes in an inch. It feels so wonderful to be pushed open and I feel his heat through the condom. "Lee."

"Michael!"

He presses himself in all the way then holds himself still as if he can lengthen the moment into infinity.

But I'm too far gone to hold myself still. I rock my hips. I dig my nails into his torso. "Michael!" I want the same passion of our kisses down there, in our genitals. I need—

"Lee!" He pulls himself out and thrusts himself all the way back in. A flash of heat envelops my sex. Out then another hard thrust in. Yes!

But then he shudders to a stop. Is he going to come now?!? So soon!? No!! I need—

Michael takes a deep breath and his body becomes a wave, centered on his pelvis, pulling himself out, plunging himself back in, stroking all my pleasure parts. I feel him on my pussy lips. I feel him deep inside. I feel him in my lungs. I feel him behind my eyes. I feel my entire body move in sync with his undulating wave. I push myself up and we kiss, an animal kiss of tongues and slobber. We suck as much of each other's saliva as we can. I feel Michael's pubic bone pull at mine, caressing my clit. Inside, I feel him teasing my g-spot.

Above me he pulls his mouth away and gasps and gulps air into his lungs. I suddenly realize I'm out of breath and almost choke. Then air floods into my lungs and I breathe again, over and over.

Below I clench my cunt around his cock. I massage it, I milk it. He's going to give himself to me. I'm going to control him. I'm going to suck his being into mine, force him to give himself to me, the way I gave myself to him.

"Come, Michael, come!"

"Lee," he whispers, deep, throaty.

But his rhythm has shifted into a lower gear. It's the same wave up and down his body, anchored at his thrusts in and out of me, but now it's slower, more gentle.

I try to claw back to the precipice, to where I could push him over, to where we would abandon ourselves to each other. But his new rhythm is too soothing and all I can do is float.

And float we do. Forever and ever. Michael loves me and I love him. We will be entwined for all eternity. His body sends wave after wave of energy up the length of my body and I caress the energy, making it into a protective cocoon for us to live inside. Our beings are joined in one undulating wave. I shut my eyes and slip into Michael's warmth, sliding into bliss.

A gentle nudge at my g-spot rouses me and I stretch. Michael's rolling waves are still anchored at our genitals, but there's a slight shift in his frequency. His eyes are closed. His cock strokes my pleasure spot again arousing heat and tingling, bursting our cocoon. I angle my hips upward and his eyes flutter.

I rock my hips in opposition to his thrusts and his eyes open fully. I stare up into his eyes watching lust gather and consume his soul, the way it's consuming mine. We thrust at each other, wild animal ferocity. We thrust at each other, raging savagery.

Above he shudders. I rock harder. Then his thrusts intensify. No longer waves, but plunging his cock from his hips straight into me. His orgasm bursts my climax: Heat and convulsion from his cock into my hips, heat and convulsion burning up my spine, heat and convulsion frying my toes into a curled crisp. A pause, then heat and convulsion whipping the entire length of my body.

I open my eyes, we gasp breath, we smile at each other, the smile of lovers.

In the kitchen, I pressed the button on the coffee maker and Michael pressed the button on his phone. Without warning, a female voice shouted out from the phone: "Michael! Where are you?!?" I recognized the voice as belonging to Lucy, his assistant. "There's been another posting. All hell's breaking loose! Call me!"

He pressed a few buttons and held the phone to his ear. "Michael! Thank God!" Her voice was fainter now, but still clearly audible.

"Slow down," Michael entreated. There was concern in his voice, but also calm and control. "Take a breath and tell me what happened."

"Why didn't you pick up when I called? I opened the Open Call App?"

"I didn't hear it. Lucy! What's going on?"

"He's targeted a Judge. A sitting *Supreme Court* Judge! Video and audio. It shows her *paying* for sex!"

"Did you send me the link?"

"Yes. In my text of 11:45. Mr. Rayburn, someone's calling me."

"It's okay, Lucy, go. Call me when you can."

I set a mug in front of Michael and he took a sip of the hot coffee before turning his phone towards me so that I could see the link Lucy had sent him. I opened the link on my laptop. There were photos of a Supreme Court Justice. I recognized her from stories on the selection process. In the photos was driving. Then getting out of her car. Then entering a non-descript door; beside the door was a neon 'Massage' sign. Entering a room inside. Then exiting, looking much, much, *much* more relaxed. Definitely a happy ending. The video showed her nude in a massage room with an extremely large European woman. Olga or Ursula? I settled on 'Olga'.

The audio on the video was crystal clear. Surely the mic had to have been inside.

Justice: The usual.

Olga: Front or back?

Justice: Both.

Olga (making a circular motion in front of her pelvis): And?

Justice (nodding and making a circular motion over her breasts): Yes.

Olga (jutting her huge butt out): And?

Justice (nodding and smiling): And.

The Judge gave Olga several hundred-dollar bills. Olga smiled back.

The video then jumped forward to show Olga, now also

nude, massaging the Judge's breasts. Another jump cut and the large woman's fingers were fondling the Judge's most intimate parts. The video faded to black.

Michael pressed the button for the video to play again. He watched it, sipping his coffee. I drifted back to memories of our lovemaking, thankful that Michael's phone had not interrupted us. Whatever it was that had interfered with the Open Call App, I was grateful.

Massage , Lusty Lee Log #14

For a sitting Supreme Court Justice, Diana Willber's house was rather modest, certainly not in keeping with her position in society. I had expected more than a bungalow in a non-descript suburb of Ottawa, Canada's capital. Her career had been meteoric—appointed to the trial bench after the minimum ten years at the bar and elevated to the Court of Appeal a mere three years later. The fact that Justice Willber was fluently bilingual and rumored to be involved with the LGBT (Lesbian Gay Bisexual Transsexual) community made her a prime, and ultimately successful candidate to be elevated to Canada's highest court two years ago. One of the Court's upcoming cases will pass on the constitutionality of the new prostitution law.

Justice Willber's ascendency had hit a major bump in the road when the Cyber Culprit's latest posting had shown her negotiating for sex at a local massage parlor. The fact that the video had portrayed the actual sex—in rather high resolution—hadn't helped the salacious tongue wagging and waggling.

Diana Willber was shorter and thinner in person than she had looked in the photos I'd seen of her in the press. She had dark brown hair with a fleck of grey at the top. The strength of her grip as she shook my hand was matched by the steel in her grey eyes.

"Thank you for meeting with me." I said as I tried to protect my knuckles.

"Thank *you* for trying to get to the bottom of this."

She ushered me into a compact office just inside the door and sat down behind a small desk while indicating that I should sit opposite.

I put my laptop onto the desk between us. "Do I need to

review the video?"

She shook her head. "The first time I watched it, I was mortified, the second aroused and by the third time I was bored."

We smiled at each other. Even I had been aroused when I had watched the video of Justice Willber having sex with a big-bodied woman, both women nude, with the larger woman pleasuring the smaller.

"Where was the video taken?" I asked.

"Merry Mary's Massage Parlor."

"Is that in Ottawa?"

She shook her head. "Gatineau. Across the river."

An hour later, I crossed the river into Quebec, Canada's French-speaking province, and drove the short distance to the semi-rural region of Gatineau.

For a massage parlor, Merry Mary's had gone to great lengths to be discreet, locating itself at the end of a country lane. But even Merry Mary's could not resist having a blinking neon sign proclaiming "Massage" in the window.

There were several security cameras in the lobby. They were small and barely visible, but obvious enough if you knew what to look for. I spotted the one under the "Massage" sign. Two of the walls had floor to ceiling mirrors. No one was in the lobby. A sign behind a bell on the desk requested patrons to "Please ring for service".

I inspected myself in the mirrors. The blue skirt suit I'd selected was upscale but not too flashy. Nonetheless, the fact that it hugged my hips and ample bosom showed that I was connected with my body, showed that I was someone who could pay and would want to pay for the 'extras'. My curly brown hair and sparkling blue eyes would begin the negotiation but my red lips widening into a smile would seal the deal.

Behind the desk, on a large blackboard, someone had written a tariff of services in flowing script:

Shiatsu: $60 half hour; $90 full
Swedish: $50 half hour; $85 full
North American Therapeutic: $70 half hour; $100 full
Nuru: $160 half hour; $220 full
Aromatherapy: $10 extra per half hour
Foot massage: $30 (half hour)
Foot massage fetish: $100 half hour; $150 full

Extra time: negotiate with your Masseuse/Masseur

I rang the bell for service and a man came out. He was tall and strong and handsome and muscular and blonde. He smiled. I smiled back. He was wearing a tight Tshirt and even tighter white shorts. He looked me up and down, grinning with obvious enjoyment. I grinned back, enjoying his attention, enjoying the fact that he enjoyed being ogled by me.

"Hi, I'm Johan," he announced.

"Lee," I beamed back.

He touched my right hand and I realized I had left it on the desk by the bell.

With my left hand, I pointed at the tariff board. "Why is therapeutic more expensive than Swedish?"

"It's actually good for you."

"Then the foot fetish must be even more good for you?"

He smirked. "If that's your fetish, it's *very* good for you."

A big-bodied white woman came forward from the back and stood behind Johan, but half to his right. She was wearing nurse's scrubs, but these were of a stretchy material and tight to show off every curve and fold of her skin. I recognized her from the video with Justice Willber. I would have preferred to keep flirting with Johan, but since I was on the job, I turned my attention to the newcomer.

I removed my right hand from under Johan's and held it out to her. "Hi, I'm Lee."

"Ella," she smiled back. This was obviously a very *friendly* establishment. I had guessed her as being an 'Olga', but somehow in person, Ella was more fitting.

Thanks to the MMA exercise routine my assistant Eric had designed for me, I was down to my optimal weight—almost no belly fat and elsewhere just enough to preserve my full bosom, undulating hips and round bum. I estimated that Ella, six inches taller than me, big-boned and chubby to the max, weighed almost twice as much as I did. The power of her body radiated feral appetites.

I pointed to the board listing the parlor's available services. "What's Nuru?" I asked, moving so that I was closer to her than to Johan.

"Nuru massage uses a special gel for the massage. Some is done with my hands and elbows. Advance techniques involve bodies sliding against each other."

"Nude?"

"I wear a swimsuit." Her smile was less intense.

"Sounds sexy," I said, touching Ella's arm. Johan got the message and left the room.

"Would you like a massage?" she asked. She pulled out a form for me to sign which broke off my contact with her arm.

"Definitely."

"What kind?"

I wanted to try Nuru, but I was getting a tentative vibe from Ella. I pointed to the North American Therapeutic line on the posted tariff.

She relaxed. "How long?"

"Can we start with an hour?"

Ella smiled and led me to medium-sized room. There was a chair and a small table at the back. To the left was a massage table with sheets pulled back. On the other side of the room there was what looked like a small rectangular inflated swimming pool. On closer inspection, there were inflated tubes on the bottom, but no water.

Ella pointed to the massage table. "Please undress as much as you are comfortable and lie on your tummy."

Ella left the room and I quickly stripped down to my panties, laying my clothes on the chair. What I really wanted was for Ella to strip, for her to stand large, powerful and confident in front of me. I wanted all the ripples in her physique to be mobilized to wring out every last drop of tension, sexual and otherwise, from my body. Her bulk proclaimed her culinary appetites. The way she carried herself declared that she had other appetites as well.

I hesitated at my panties. They were black, thin, French cut. Would Ella be scared off if she came back to find me totally nude? Our plan was to allow her to "seduce" me by offering sex, pretend to be a cop, and pressure her to show the camera and audio feeds. I rocked back and forth on my feet trying to decide. I would need to communicate to Ella that I wanted a 'happy ending' but if I was too obvious about it, she might be scared into thinking that I was an undercover cop out to arrest her. I decided to play it safe and leave my panties on. I laid down face first on the massage table and adjusted my head in the cradle at the end of the table. It was nice and warm.

Ella returned and I felt her strong fingers start to knead the muscles in my shoulders. "Where do you want me to concentrate?" she asked.

"All over," I sighed.

"You have a lovely body."

"Thank you."

She pushed down my spine, loosening it, but moved around my hips to avoid my bum. "Such healthy skin, well-defined muscles."

"I just started a new workout."

She let her fingers slide between my thighs, not touching my genitals, but perking their interest nonetheless.

"What got you into the massage biz?" I asked.

"I enjoy helping people relax, get in touch with their bodies."

Ella began to pull and prod and rub all the muscles of my back. I shut my eyes and felt tension melt away. I floated in softness' midst.

"Lee, please turn onto your back." I must have dozed off because the words were loud and she was rocking my torso back and forth. I pushed myself up off the table and rubbed my eyes.

When I turned over, Ella was a changed woman. Gone were her nurse's scrubs. In their place was a skimpy black bikini. And her entire body, every roll of jiggling fat, was flushed, happy. She began to stroke up and down my body, her flab rippling sensuously. Every time she got near my panties or touched my breasts, I moaned appreciatively.

She began to rotate her palms softly over my tummy and I shut my eyes. Her hands touched the top of my panties. I let out a low "mmm" and spread my legs as far as they would go on the table. She started to knead my left calf, then slowly worked up my leg, past my knee, up my thigh until she was just below my crotch. The side of her hand touched my panty and sent a jolt up my spine. My moan was unmistakable in its intent.

But she crossed to the other side of the table and worked up my right leg. When she got to the top of my leg, I could feel the heat of her hand through my panty. But she was careful not to touch it. I opened my eyes, begging for her to touch my pussy.

Ella's every square inch radiated sexual power: her huge arms, her tree-trunk legs, her chunky ass, the rolls of fat on her belly. I watched her as she circled my body, lightly caressing one spot, kneading more vigorously as required. Her boobs were swollen over-ripe melons barely contained by her bikini top. Below, the folds of her skin practically swallowed her bikini bottom. And, as she circled, Ella was watching my reactions.

"How much more time did you want to spend?" she asked.

"All the time in the world."

"Another hour?"

I nodded. "Plus tip." When was she going to touch my pussy?!?

Ella moved to my left hip, occasionally pulling my panties taut across my sex. It wasn't much, but at least it was something. She looked down at me. "You were asking about Nuru?"

"Yes."

"Nuru is expensive."

"That's okay."

She moved to my right hip, letting her fingers brush across the top of my pubic bone. I gasped at the sensation shooting down into my pussy. There was a look of consternation on Ella's face. "Are you okay?"

I smiled. "More than okay."

She ran her fingers back over the top of my panties. I moaned.

"Did you like that?"

I nodded. "Very much."

"Nuru is intimate and erotic."

I smiled up at her. "Sounds fun. What's so special about Nuru?"

Ella reached behind her back, undid her bikini and released her massive breasts from their constraints. Her left breast, in all its ponderous glory hung in front of me. I wanted to reach up and hold it gently between my hands.

"Nuru is the gel we use for the bodyslide," she answered. "Right now I'm lubricating you with almond oil. But in a bodyslide, oil becomes too hot and greasy. Some people complained that it was smelly after a while. But the Nuru gel is cool, clean, smooth and incredibly sensual."

"Body slide?"

"Bodies rubbing together." She moved to massage down my right arm. Intermittently her nipples brushed against my skin. They were hard and hot.

"Mmm," I groaned.

"Are you a chubby chaser?" Ella wanted to know.

"Chubby chaser?" That was a new one on me.

"People who chase after plumpers because they think we're an easy lay or because they feel sorry for us and think that it's good karma to be nice to us."

"No."

"Then why didn't you stick with Johan? I could see that you liked him."

"Because I wanted something different."

"Nuru involves a lot of touching."

"I like your touch." Inviting but not too forward, I thought, pleased with myself.

"Is there anywhere in particular you'd like me to touch?"

"My breasts." Time to find out how far she would go.

She had been pulling out the tension from my left arm, but now moved to lightly caress both my breasts. Her hands were warm and firm and wonderful. Then she leaned in and we were breast to breast, her lips next to my right ear. "Anywhere else?"

"My pussy."

She pulled off my panties, trailing her nipples down my legs. Then she walked her fingers up my legs. This time they kept on going and fluffed my pubic hair. Her touch was *so* delicate!

"Is there any part of your body you don't want me to touch?"

I shook my head.

"Is there any part of my body you're uncomfortable with me touching you?"

I shook my head. "No."

"Would you like to touch my breasts?"

I nodded. She bent forward. Her breasts were so *soft*! My fingers sunk into the warm, welcoming flesh. She smiled down at me.

"Why don't we do another sixty minutes?" she asked.

I smiled up at her. "Plus tip."

Ella undid the strings on her bikini bottom and pulled it free from her body. But the folds of flat around her crotch prevented me from seeing her genitals. She extended her hands, helped me off the table led me towards the inflated swimming pool. Now that I was up close, I could see that it was a basic outdoor swimming pool, measuring about six by eight feet. Inside the pool was a plastic inflatable mattress. Earlier I had thought this was the pool bottom.

Inflated tubes ran down the length of the mattress which had a larger tube—one long pillow—at the head.

Ella laid me down on the mattress facing up. The mattress was cold and immediately grabbed ahold of my skin. She looked down at me, clearly in control. I was at once her prey and her beloved pet. She knelt down on the mattress beside me.

"If you're at any time uncomfortable," she whispered, "just say 'stop'. If there's anything you want me to do, just ask."

"Is it okay if I touch you?"

"By all means." She bent down and kissed me full on the mouth, answering my next and final question. Her tongue was large and strong as she licked around the inside of my lips. I shut my eyes and my mind joined my pussy which had long ago abandoned itself to what was about to occur. The mattress still held me tight in its grasp.

Ella reached over to a large bowl next to the pool and picked it up with her left hand. She reached the fingers of her right hand into the bowl and they came back with a stringy gelatin substance. Some of it dribbled back into the bowl, some onto the mattress. But the rest dripped onto my belly. It was cool—not cold. Cool, I needed because the whole experience was making me incredibly hot. The gel flowed down my belly, then off over the side of my torso.

Ella repeated the process several times, up and down my body until everything below my neck was completely covered in the gel. Little pools had formed on the mattress next to me. Ella moved the bowl over my pubic bone and tipped it, sending a large dollop of Nuru gel onto and into my genitals. By now I was too hot for it to cool me down.

"Are you ready to slide?" she asked.

I nodded which caused me to slither all over the mattress. The sliding motion was nice, but hardly worth two hundred dollars an hour. I was about to protest the obvious rip-off when Ella lay down next to me. She placed one of her legs up and over my thigh, pressing her pubic area against my leg. Then she rubbed her whole body up and down my entire left side.

Every time her leg came up and over my pubic bone, my whole pussy sizzled. But as soon as her leg moved onto my belly, the gel cooled pussy down. But when Ella's leg returned, pussy heated right back up! Every time she went up and over, I was hotter than the time before. Every time her leg slid off my sex, I cooled down. But the gel was gradually losing its ability to chill. And every time Ella's slid over my pubic bone, my pussy just got hotter and hotter.

She licked up and around my left ear, then down and around my right before her tongue slid away. Tongue upwards over ear, tongue downwards over ear. Leg stoking fire below. I would have lost control but I was so hot I had forgotten what control was.

This time she slid up and close by my ear, Ella whispered, "Come." An invitation, a command, permission, a single word.

Every drop of moisture inside my cunt *boiled* violently, burst up my spine. Her leg down over my pubic bone propelled the next spasm down my legs. I shuddered and slithered on the mattress below me. Her leg up and over and my butt clenched tight. Her leg down and over burst a spasm outward into toes, fingers up my neck—

"Yes!" I yelled.

"Louder," commanded Ella.

"Yes! *Yes*! Yes! Yes."

She lifted her leg off me and lay still beside me. "Did you come?" she asked.

"Yes," I gasped. 'Come'. That single word from her lips had been all my pussy had needed.

We lay together in silence.

After a heavenly eternity, she asked, "Are you ready for the next stage?"

My brain couldn't believe that there was more, but couldn't suppress its curiosity. "The next stage?"

"Your turn to slide on me."

She lay down beside me. I did my best to climb on top of her, but promptly slid off the other side. She burst out laughing and then I started laughing. Every part of her was jiggling in laughter and the mattress was bouncing up and down.

When we stopped laughing, I tried again. This time I managed to stay atop. It was like a rollercoaster, but much, much sexier. I straddled her right leg with my legs and rubbed my right led up and down her crotch. As long as I only rubbed up and down an inch or two, I was steady enough that I could make large circles around her humongous breasts. I played with her nipples whenever I could, but my fingers kept slipping off.

Then I lost my grip and I was sliding off, climbing back on, over-compensating and sliding off Ella's other side.

"Don't try so hard," she told me. "Just slide and enjoy."

She was right. I managed to slither up and down her body, sometimes sliding between her legs, sometimes straddling one of her legs as I slid down. Going up, I was always able to make contact with her breasts. And nipples! Once I managed to kiss her. We tried to hold onto each other to lengthen the kiss, but I squirted away.

Then I fell into a groove and had my right leg going up and down between her crotch. Her face flushed and she groaned with pleasure. I held her and stroked and stroked and stroked. After several minutes, I felt her orgasm. It was only a small climax, but still.

I extended myself upwards and we kissed again. This time Ella managed to hold onto me. Her mouth was hot, her tongue hotter. She thrust her tongue full into my mouth, pushing my own tongue back. She was ferocious and I had no choice but to submit. Except submitting meant that I relaxed and started to slide off. But Ella was ready this time and slid me under her, maintaining her kiss.

At first I was under Ella's full weight. I couldn't breathe, but I was kissing. And what a glorious kiss! She must have sensed me weakening because she turned us on our sides and softened the kiss. I thrust my tongue into her mouth as vigorously as she had thrust hers into mine. But in her mouth there was room to spare and her tongue pinned mine to the side of her mouth.

She broke off the kiss and lay on her back, panting air into her lungs. I scooted down between her legs and discovered that the sides of the swimming pool had a cloth covering against which I could gain a foothold. And given Ella's weight, I could exert pressure against her without significantly moving her body.

All of which meant that I had *two* hands with which to pleasure Ella's pussy. I began by exerting very firm pressure against the two folds of flab on top of her genitals. I knew that I would have to press hard for her to feel any pleasure. I was rewarded by a gasp from up above.

"Beg me to keep going," I demanded. "Tell me what this feels like."

"Don't stop, please." Her voice was plaintive.

"Tell me what this feels like."

"It feels like I'm being fucked by a sledgehammer. Don't

stop, please don't stop."

"Tell me you'll do anything."

"Anything, yes, anything!"

"Are you hot?"

"Yes!"

I continued sliding my hands up and down and around, alternating deeper and shallower pressure. Suddenly I felt her whole body start to tense.

"Are you ready to scream?"

"Yes!"

"Then come, and scream like your life depends on it!"

"Fuck!"

Just the one word and only subtle twinges against my fingers. I let her breathing return to normal and then gave her a few more moments relaxation.

"Are you ready to go again?"

There was a muffled "Yes" above my head.

This time I pressed between her folds of fat, pushing layer after layer aside. And then my fingers found heaven. Her inner pussy lips, hard little ridges. And above, her clit poked out, rigid and ready. I stroked up and down her lips and up and over the hood of skin covering the top of her clit.

"Jesus!" she yelped. "How did you—?!?"

I kept on stroking. "Persistence. Are you ready to be my slave?"

"No!" She pushed down and rolled me over on my back but in the transition I managed to reverse head to toe. Her legs were outside, straddling me, her crotch just above my belly button. Once again I managed to press between her layers of skin and fat to access her genitals. I stroked up and down her pussy lips. She groaned and shuddered.

"Are you ready to be my slave?" I demanded.

All she did was groan. I placed a finger on either side of her clit and stroked up and down.

"Are you ready to be my slave?" I repeated.

Another groan.

I pressed my fingers together in a gentle pinch. "Say it!" I demanded.

"Yes."

"Say that you're my slave!" With my other hand, I started to stroke two fingers inside her pussy. She was hot and wet, and not from the Nuru gel!

"I am your slave!" she shouted.

Now I had her, this giant, in my power. I released the pinch on her clit and stroked up and down her pussy lips. The folds of her skin pressed in against my hand, pressing all her genitals together. She gasped. I pushed my other two fingers inside and found her walnut. If I tapped twice on her g-spot she was sure to come, but I wanted to extend my mastery.

I formed my two fingers inside into a spiral and to began to fuck them slowly in and out of her pussy. Another gasp from above and every muscle in her body tensed tight.

"Tell me what you like, you big slut!" I encouraged.

"Fuck me!"

"Harder?"

"Faster!"

I slowed the thrusts of my spiraled fingers. "Beg me. Tell me I'm you're master, your mistress." My fingers were barely moving in and out and only an inch at at time "Beg!"

"Master, please," she whimpered, her body loosening. "Faster, please. Faster!"

I thrust my spiraled fingers in as far as they would go and held them for a moment as I used my other hand to slide up and down her pussy lips. Her love button jutted out and I stroked up and down its shaft. I slowly pulled my spiraled fingers back out.

"Faster, Master, please! Faster!" She tensed her whole body to add force to her plea.

I shoved my spiraled fingers in to their hilt, then out again. I made sure to tease the edges of her g-spot with every thrust. She began to whimper. I accelerated my thrusts. The muscles in her legs rhythmically clenched and relaxed. I unwrapped my fingers and raked their tips across her g-spot.

"Fuck!" she yelled.

I maintained my rapid pace, massaging her g-spot with every thrust.

"*Fuck*!" she screamed. "Fuc—"

Inside her cunt massive contractions squeezed all the air from her lungs. Rapid pulses clutched at my fingers. Every time there was a moment of release, I did my best to stroke in or out. She was hot!

Then the contractions stopped. Every muscle in her body went slack. She collapsed on top of me. Thankfully, I got my wrists out of the way just in time. But now this very satisfied behemoth was sliding up my tummy and starting to suffocate me. I tried to protest, but not even a wheeze emerged from my lips.

I tried to push up. Nothing. I lifted my knees but they didn't have any way to slide between Ella's tree-trunk thighs. I tried to push my head up, but all I got was the spongy flesh of her breasts. Just before I passed out, I pressed my legs right and my head left. A jiggle! I pressed harder and back and forth. Ella slid left just enough for me to scoot out from underneath.

I lay beside her, gasping air into my lungs. I shoved the side of her body in exasperation.

Ella's eyes flickered, then opened fully. An evil gleam began to form, then take hold, spreading across her entire face.

She pulled my head to hers and rolled half onto me, pinning my right leg beneath her massive thigh. She reached under my neck, grabbed my left wrist and extended it. "So, bitch, you think you're fit to be my mistress?"

I tried to wriggle free, but she had me too tight. "I made you come, slut," I challenged.

A quick slap to my right breast made it clear that that had been *exactly* the wrong thing to say.

"You're my bitch now. Spread your legs!" commanded Ella.

I had no choice but to comply. She turned slightly over me, angling her breast where, if I strained, I could just touch her nipple with the tip of my tongue. As soon as I had managed to flick my tongue around it, I felt her fingers rub my sex.

It wasn't a gentle rub. It was a master rubbing her slave. "Beg for mercy," Ella demanded.

"Mercy," I gasped.

"Do you promise to lie still, to not resist, no matter what I do?"

"Yes." What choice did I have?

She rubbed harder.

"Yes, mistress!" I shouted.

Ella's rubbing became slightly softer and I could tell that she'd scooped up some of the gel from the mattress. I felt heat building up all over my vulva and inside. She rubbed faster and faster with just the right pressure. I could feel all my strength being drawn into my genitals.

"Yes, mistress," I wailed.

She withdrew her hand, leaving me panting, bereft. "Mistress!" I wailed.

"Do you want to come?"

"Yes, mistress!"

"Can I do anything I want?"

"Yes mistress. Of course!"

"You'll do whatever I tell you to do?"

"Yes, Mistress!"

"Turn over on your tummy and spread your legs as far as they will go."

I complied and saw only grey, then darkness and then nothing. But I felt her straddle my left leg. "Spread your arms," she commanded.

I complied.

A gel-lubricated finger began to circle my anus. Her voice whispered in my ear, "I want you to tell me what you're feeling, what it felt like when you were playing with me, what it felt like and feels like when I'm playing with you. If you stop talking, your massage will be over. Do you understand?"

"Yes, mistress."

"And I want you to talk dirty, vulgar."

"Your finger on my ass feels hot, like it wants to fuck me."

Her finger pressed inside.

"Fuck me!" I screamed. Not a finger, a thumb! "I should have fucked your ass when I had the chance."

She laughed and inserted two fingers into my cunt.

"Not cunt and ass both," I protested.

"Do you want me to stop?"

"No, mistress." A thumb pressed above my clit and began to rotate. "It feels like I'm being fucked harder than I've ever been fucked. Open, helpless, immobile, sexy, hot."

"What did it feel like when you were fingering me?"

"Like I was in the center of a mountain, that I set off the dynamite. That the mountain came crashing down on me."

"And now?"

"It feels heavenly, like I'm floating."

Ella pulled the fingers inside my cunt half out and curled them. "Now?"

"That's my g-spot! Yes, please—give it a gentle push—*please*!"

"Tell me what it will feel like, my little *bitch*, if I do?"

"That you, the mountain, is inside me, that all the coal inside me is igniting, that my furnace is ready to explode."

She rotated the finger she had up my ass. "Tell me where to touch you."

"In my cunt, on my button!"

She pulled the finger she had in my cunt out so that it was just barely pressing on the opening. "Your ass. Tell me where to fuck your ass."

I did a quick calculation as to where my g-spot was in relation to her thumb and where the inner arms of my clit extended.

"Press down and rotate and fuck." She did. Sweet Jesus!

"What does it feel like, my little bitch?"

I kicked up and down with my feet. "Like you're fucking my insides out."

"Quiet now. When you're ready to come, yell 'Fuck' and I'll do your cunt as well."

I could feel her fingers fluttering along my pussy lips. I could feel the thumb up my ass rotating, brushing up against my g-spot, stroking my clit from inside. I could feel—then I was flying out over the edge, nothing below me. My ass clenched tight on her thumb.

A contraction clamped my cunt tight, but there was nothing there. "Fuck!" I yelled.

Her fingers slipped into my cunt as the contraction released. Then another spasm clamped down on her fingers and everything exploded into whiteness. Just white, no sound, no sensation, no movement. Then white became hot and exploded in my cunt, in my ass. I thrashed and the white became red heat jolting half up my spine. Another contraction thrashed me and this time the orgasm rocketed the rest of the way up my spine and into my head. I felt more pleasure in my sex that I'd ever felt before. The next spasm coursed down my legs. I lay helpless on the mattress, Ella's fingers still playing with me...

After a quick shower—thankfully Nuru gel cleans off faster than oil—I made a show of starting to get dressed. What I really did was to activate my phone and send out a pre-arranged text.

Eric burst into the lobby just as I was settling up with Ella.

As soon as she saw him, Ella scrunched the money into her fist and hid it behind the counter.

"You're cops!" she wailed.

I shook my head. "Private investigators. Not cops. We mean you no harm."

Half an hour of negotiating later, the massage parlor allowed Eric access to their security system and internet router in exchange for our promise that if we found anything we'd share the results with them.

The next morning, or rather the next afternoon because I didn't wake up until after one, I called Eric. "Have you had any luck with the massage parlor's video feeds?" I asked.

"Yes, and it's all bad. Turns out that a group of local teenage hackers managed to break the massage parlor's firewall two months ago. The little buggers have been jerking off to massage porn ever since. And they've been spending so much time jerking off, that they didn't notice when the Cyber Culprit snuck into their computers and helped himself to some of their footage. The police started to investigate the hackers two days ago. That finally woke them up and they erased everything. There's still enough for the police to charge them, but nowhere near enough for me to trace how the Cyber Culprit hacked in."

I swore underneath my breath and rang off.

The next call only increased the foulness of my mood.

"Ms. Brandt?" It was Michael Rayburn's assistant, a bad sign as he almost invariably called me directly.

"Yes, this is she."

"Mr. Rayburn asked me to inform you that the Cyber Culprit has struck again and has succeeded in blackmailing an internet service provider employee with the result that numerous passwords have been compromised."

"Okay. Does Mr. Rayburn want me to come in?"

"No. He has sent you an email."

I pulled up the email while she was still on the phone. As soon as I saw it, I swore. And this time not under my breath.

"Ms. Brandt?"

"Sorry, yes, I have the email. Was there anything else?"

There wasn't and she rang off. The email was worse on the second reading. Almost half a million passwords had been hacked. But that wasn't the worst part. All—and I do mean *all*—of the passwords used by Michael Rayburn's firm had been compromised. The passwords of the mail boy, the cleaning lady, each and every secretary, the articling students, the associates and even those of the partners had been accessed.

I turned on the news. Everyone across the city was scrambling to change their passwords. There were the usual people-in-the-street interviews, lots of wailing and panicking. I pressed the mute button. Then the story switched to a high-rise tower. I was about to change the station when I recognized the building. Michael's office was in that building! Lights were blinking on and off everywhere.

I turned up the volume to hear the announcer say, "...internet of things. At this building the hacked passwords have turned some offices into ovens, others into freezers. Lights are turning on and off in no apparent pattern. The elevators are out of control."

Shit! This was no random attack. It was directed specifically at us. Maybe even focused on Michael's law firm. I felt a momentary pang of guilt that I had not shared my suspicions that I had met the Cyber Culprit last week at the swinger's club. Eric and I had been undercover. I'd laid down on a table for other swingers to slurp up alcohol—body shots—from every imaginable part of me. A masked man had fondled me, breaking rum balls over me. But it was the memory of his voice that was making me feel guilty. I had heard it at Hendricks when I'd investigated CC's posts of an adulteress, I'd heard it last week but had said nothing. And now he was making a direct attack on us. I couldn't help but think that my budding relationship with Michael had provoked this attack, but that was nonsense.

I wanted to go down to Michael's office. To comfort him. To help. But I knew I'd only get in the way. A text came in from Eric. He confirmed that he was working on the latest breach. I smiled at the prophylactic text—it was clearly meant to foreclose inquiries from me.

Finally, hours and hours later, Michael called.

"Are you alright?" I asked.

"I'm deadbeat tired. I know we were supposed to get together tonight..."

"Don't worry, go home, I'll bring dinner."

"Okay."

He didn't even have the energy to protest. Poor baby!

I brought over a roast chicken with vegetables and potatoes in the same pot. Michael collapsed onto his favorite recliner, still in suit and tie as I popped diner into the oven. I found a beach towel, draped it on the couch, pulled Michael up standing, stripped him down to his underwear and laid him faced down on the towel. Compared to Ella, he was skinny and hairy. And unlike her softness, every muscle in Michael's back and arms was tensed rock solid.

Half an hour of kneading and he was human again. We ate in silence. The food seemed to give him some energy. He pointed to the towel on the couch. I smiled and stripped down to my bra and panties.

Michael shook his head. "Everything."

I complied and lay face down on the towel. His fingers were long and probing, more focused than Ella's had been. It was wonderful.

After he had worked his way up and down the length of my body, Michael turned me over. He, now nude as well, quickly kneaded any remaining knots out of my shoulders. Then it was time to play. On each breast, he spread his fingers out as far as they would go, carefully keeping his palm from touching my nipples. Then he drew his fingers upwards, closing them around my areolae in a twisting motion, slowing bringing each fingertip against my nipples and rotating. My nipples immediately engorged and sent approving pleasure up my spine.

Michael gently and repeatedly pressed and released my breasts with one hand as he traced his other down to my sex. He slipped fingers straight down my slit—dry tickle sparks—and one slid into my hot, and ever so wet pussy. Suitably lubricated, the finger slid back up my pussy lips to circle my clit. Now the sparks intensified, setting off thunder deep in my cunt. I felt a low moan escape from my throat.

Michael massaged my pussy in a circular motion. Ella's ministrations had been more therapeutic, less focused on moving straightaway to sexual congress. Then again, it wasn't Michael's first time with me, so seduction wasn't necessary. When Ella had touched my sex, she was direct and in control; it was an organic part of engaging my whole body. With Michael, each touch was a step towards the next stage.

"Time to bed," Michael told me, lifting me to my feet. Right on cue. His cock swayed, fully erect. Bed, Michael; what could be more delicious?! But his phone rang.

"Leave it," I told him.

He shook his head. "No rest for the wicked."

A moment later, he turned his phone towards me. It was connected to the internet, playing a video of the federal Minister of Communications leading an informal staff meeting.

"The Cyber Culprit's latest posting," said Michael, confirming my suspicions.

On the video, cabinet minister Seth Cooper was telling his subordinates that, "Every website deserves the same level of government support."

Off camera, a staffer asked, "does that include porn?"

"Of course," answered the Minister. His answer was as emphatic as it was politically damning. A Minister of the Crown mandating government support for pornography. The nuances of web neutrality would be lost on the electorate.

The Aide , Lusty Lee Log #15

Michael's influence had been necessary to secure me a meeting with Seth Cooper, the federal Minister of Communications. 'Lee Brandt' just didn't have the same clout as 'Michael Rayburn'. Last week, the Minister had been firm in his defence of internet neutrality—all users of the 'net should be treated equally. Such a mundane topic would usually not be the source of interest. But when Cooper had specifically included pornography as being included under the government's protection, it had become a source of uproar. It hadn't helped that Cooper's response had been contained in a now-viral video.

Thankfully, the Prime Minister had understood the importance of internet neutrality and Cooper had been able to keep his job.

"Do you know how the video was recorded?" I asked.

Cooper nodded. "It was done on a cellphone by one of my staff."

"Who?" Was it really going to be this easy?!?

He smiled at me sitting on the edge of my chair and shook his head. "She's been cleared. Her phone was hacked."

"May we examine her phone?"

He shook his head again, his smile broadening. "Your assistant has beat you to it. If you would follow me."

He held his hand out and in a moment we were standing at the door to a small meeting room. Several cellphones were lying on the table. Eric, my assistant, was moving briskly from phone to phone, his red hair bobbing up and down.

Eric reached across the table and turned a phone on the opposite side towards him. His arms were long, but still he needed his full six-foot-three lanky frame to reach across the table. He began to look up and down between the phone just in front of him and the one he had just turned towards him.

Eric straightened up, a broad smile spreading across his face. He pointed to the phone just in front of him.

Beside me, Minister Cooper's face was as aghast as Eric's was triumphant. "Jack Abernathy?" he asked, incredulous.

Eric nodded and pointed to the phone on the opposite side of the table. "That phone recorded the video. This phone," pointing to the one immediately in front of him, "hacked into the other phone and then uploaded the video to the internet."

"Jack Abernathy…" Cooper's voice now had ruefulness mixed in with his incredulity.

"Who's Jack Abernathy?" I asked.

Cooper shook his head. "He's my most senior aide, political and policy advisor. Been with me for years. Jack Abernathy raises oodles—and I do mean oodles—of money for the party."

Minister Cooper was obviously in shock, so as soon as we had acquired Abernathy's laptop, I ushered Eric out while muttering as many platitudes as I could.

Three hours later, Eric was standing beside a whiteboard in the largest of Michael's law firm's boardrooms. I was sitting right in front of him, contributing to the narrative where appropriate. Our tone was one of mutual admiration and praise. The whiteboard was full of circles and squares and lines connecting each. Jack Abernathy's name was in the center with lines connecting him to every square and circle.

I had attended at Abernathy's home with the police and secured his home computer. It, along with the aide's laptop and phone, was on the table to my right. But I wasn't looking at computers. I was looking at Michael Rayburn. I was looking at his light brown hair framed with flecks of grey. I was looking at his tall, powerful body. Not muscular, powerful. I was watching the sparkles flash within his blue eyes every time I made a point. I was watching his full lips spread into a smile as Eric recounted each stage in our investigation.

Eric finished his detailed presentation and began summing up, "Thus, as soon as we had a solid indication that Mr. Abernathy was the Cyber Culprit, was the one who had posted all the embarrassing photos and videos to the internet, we were able to utilize all the information we had painstakingly gathered during our investigation to document his true identity as the one behind the cyber attacks." Eric pointed to the circles identifying the swingers, the businessmen, the philanderer, the actor, the politician and the judge and to the squares—the corresponding internet nodes—that Abernathy had used to embarrass each one.

Later that night, there was a celebration in the main lobby of Michael Rayburn's law firm. Well-wishers were constantly pressing their hands into ours resulting in Michael, Eric, and I becoming separated. However, Michael did his best to swing his orbit back to me as often as he could and every time he did, he pointed out another of the firm's senior partners. Justice Willber was gracious and grateful, sportscaster Tom LeBlanc energetic and effusive, retail executive Sarah Grant beaming and beautiful. Actor Earl Brandis slipped in and out of various character roles depending on whom he was talking to. Several assorted politicians, including Seth Cooper, who'd been shuffled to another portfolio, circulated. Cooper was doing the best to hide his discomfiture.

I noticed Peter Henge, my former partner and lover in a corner. Peter's muscular chest looked good under suit and tie but his spiked black hair looked out of place. I leaned over to whisper into Michael's ear, "Why's he here?" I was mortified to hear the question come out as a hiss instead of a whisper.

Michael followed my line of sigh, turned to me, smiling, and whispered, "It's strictly *pro forma*. This client always demands an audit. Part of their Six Sigma protocol. Always looking to see if things could have been done better."

"The client's not happy?" This time I managed to whisper.

"The client is *very* happy," Michael said, his smile widening. "There should be a hefty bonus for you."

"Then why the audit?"

"It's for next time. Could we have done even better, caught the Cyber Culprit—Abernathy—even earlier. Strictly *pro forma*, I promise. No one expects to find anything and since they don't, they won't. It would actually be extremely inconvenient to the client if the audit finds the least thing wrong with your investigation."

"You're sure?"

"I'm sure, time to celebrate!"

I wasn't sure. But still this was too good an opportunity to pass up. An opportunity I did not intend to fritter away. Tonight was my chance to imprint myself into a strong memory in Michael's brain, a memory that would combine celebration, intimacy, triumph, professional recognition, and of course sex.

For the evening, I'd worn a skirt suit. Grey and loose so as not to overly emphasize my curves. My curly brown hair was tied in a bun at the back of my head and I'd worn understated makeup to accentuate my blue eyes. On the outside, I was demure. But underneath was a different story. Underneath was a sheer red bra which perfectly cupped my large round breasts and revealed the outline of my nipples. Below, I was wearing a red garter belt holding up black hose, and above these, even blacker silk panties.

Michael, resplendent in his blue pinstriped suit, drifted away once more and I saw the senior partners of his law firm shake Michael's hand. Their smiles and admiration made it clear that Michael was on the fast track to make partner himself. Maybe they'd even add the name 'Rayburn' to the firm's moniker.

On the theory that one should keep one's enemies even closer than one's friends, I drifted over towards Peter and soon we were alone in a corner. "I hear you're to audit us," I told him.

He nodded, "It's just *pro forma*."

I was beginning to hate that phrase. "Who knows where *pro forma* might lead…" I cursed myself for being too obvious. But Peter only shrugged. "What cases are you working on?" I tried again.

"A matrimonial. Two personal injuries." In other words boring stakeouts. For a moment—but only for a moment—I felt sorry for Peter.

"Do you have an assistant?" I asked, changing tack.

"Why, you looking for a job?" he leered, leaning over me. I had obviously underestimated the amount of alcohol he'd consumed. But at least he was showing the initiative.

"You hiring?" I teased.

At that moment, Michael's fingers on my elbow rescued me and led me towards the elevators. The party was breaking up.

"Send me your resumé," Peter called out after us. He looked sad to see me go. Hopefully not sad enough to render a negative report. *Pro forma* my ass.

But a moment later we were in the elevator and Michael's kiss erased the rest of the world. It wasn't the first time we'd kissed. We'd even had sex once or twice. But each kiss was new, a different revelation of his passion and sensuality. Michael was safety, honesty, excitement and adventure all in one. He was generous, encouraging, inventive. Every time we were apart, I felt an empty aching in my chest. Every time we were close, I felt an overwhelming desire to be with him forever and a craving to have him touch me. I reached up for another kiss, but the elevator doors were opening.

Michael's apartment had three rooms, not counting the bathroom: a large kitchen, a dining room and living room combination, a small den, and of course a lovely master bedroom.

As soon as we were in the door, Michael announced, "I have something to show you." He led me straight to the bedroom. A bit forward and presumptuous of him, but what the hell, it was his night.

He pointed to the bed. There were no covers, just a red blanket strapped to the mattress. "What do you think?" he asked.

"It's a blanket."

"Not just any blanket. I've been saving it for a special occasion. It's waterproof."

I reached out and touched it. It was soft, like any ordinary blanket. "Waterproof?"

He nodded. I shrugged. It was his blanket, his bed. I moved towards the bed, ready to test Michael's new toy, but he pulled me back. "First a snack to replenish our energies," he said, taking me by the hand and pulling me out of the room.

In the kitchen, Michael takes out a plate of strawberries from the fridge and lays it on the table in front of me. I take a bite out of one. It's ripe, but still firm. A rivulet of juice trickles down my chin. Michael puts a bottle of champagne into an ice bucket. On the stove, he brings a bowl of chocolate pudding to boil.

At the table, I feed him a bite of a strawberry. A drool of juice escapes his mouth. I try to scoop the juice with the rest of the strawberry, but that just adds to the juice running down his chin. We laugh at each other. I come around him, loosen and remove his tie.

"We don't want juice stains on your clothes," I tell him as I remove his shirt as well.

There's a ding on the stove and he turns around to the pudding. He stirs the pot and proclaims, "Perfect."

I go back to the other side of the table. Michael places a bowl of chocolate pudding in front of me. The aroma is intoxicating. A moment later, a bowl of chocolate ice cream joins the pudding. I look around the table. There's no spoon.

I look up and Michael's teasing me with the spoon. "Hot or cold?" he asks.

"Hot," I answer and he carefully places half a spoon of pudding on my tongue. It warms my whole mouth and down my throat.

Next he places an almost perfect ball of ice cream on my tongue. I swirl the wonderful cold inside my mouth. Even colder as I swallow.

Michael holds out another spoonful of pudding, but this time I take the spoon from his hand, circle the table, and deposit the pudding on his right nipple. Some dribbles below and I lick it back up his chest. At his nipple I suck, perking up his little bud. Somehow the pudding tastes twice as good.

"You like hot *and* cold?" he asks.

I nod.

A wide smile spreads on his face. "Good, then we have a treat for you."

He points towards the bedroom. I turn and trot towards the door. I don't need a second invitation.

"And take off anything you don't want stained," I hear behind my back.

I lift up my skirt so that he can see the top of my black hose, bare skin above and the garter belt strap holding up my hose as I sway my butt into the bedroom.

I'm barely out of my blouse and vest when he comes into the bedroom with a canister of whipping cream and the chocolate pudding. The pudding is in a plastic pitcher.

"Hot or cold?" he asks.

"Hot."

I'm rewarded with a dollop of pudding in the cleavage

between my breasts and his tongue licking it away.

On his second trip, he brings in the strawberries and champagne. I drop my skirt to the floor. "Hot or cold?" he asks.

"Cold."

He takes a strawberry and places it just under the top of my panties. Frigid as a knife stabbing up to my belly button.

"Lower," I tell him.

He pushes the strawberry halfway down my pubic hair and stops just above my clit. It's even colder.

"Lower," I repeat.

He slides the strawberry around my clit and lodges it between my pussy lips. I gasp at the cold. He moves the strawberry up and down until I've gotten used to the freezing fruit on my sex.

The next time Michael returns, I'm lying flat on the bed wearing only bra and panties. The strawberry makes a mound at the bottom of my panties. He's carrying two mugs and a small bowl. The smell of steaming coffee wafts from one mug. Ice cubes clink in the other. Michael sets the mugs down on a night table and strips nude. He bends over my panties and presses the strawberry into my sex. Then he reaches inside my panties, extracts the strawberry and thrusts it into his mouth. In a moment, it disappears down his throat.

"Blindfold?" he asks.

I shake my head.

"Promise to shut your eyes when I tell you?"

I nod.

"Shut your eyes."

I shut my eyes. The cork pops loudly out of the champagne and I smell a hint of white grapes, bursting bubbles and alcohol. Then there's cold all over my chest and I can feel the bubbles burst. I feel Michael's tongue lap up the champagne, paying special attention to the liquid that has seeped through my bra. His erect cock brushes up against my thigh.

Two more dribbles of champagne tingle my nipples. My eyes jerk open and I catch Michael's smile moving towards my breasts. In a moment, he's sucking the champagne from around my nipple. She's hard, warming my entire chest. The second nipple is even hotter and harder when he sucks her. His leg is between mine and I brush my sex upwards against it. I want him! I want him *inside* me!

He props himself up and looks into my eyes. We smile at

each other.

"Take me," I plead.

Michael shakes his head. "All in good time. He reaches over and lifts up the pitcher of pudding. I can smell it, so it must still be hot. He lifts up my panties and pours a small dollop inside. "Ready?" he asks.

I nod and shut my eyes. Moments later my pubic bone and sex are engulfed in the hot gooey liquid. I hear the pitcher being set down on the night table. Then Michael's hand presses against my panty, pressing the pudding into every nook and cranny. Up and down his fingers go, then rotate. The pressure of the pudding increases then recedes, sucking and pressing against every nerve in my sex.

But after a few moments, the pudding has been pressed out and I begin to feel silk rubbing up and down against my pussy. At first it's soft, then the friction builds as less and less of the pudding is lubricating Michael's strokes.

I open my eyes, pleading for more from my lover. But Michael's only reaction is to shake his head. "Shut your eyes," he demands.

I comply and there's a strawberry under my panties. I can tell that he's using it to scoop up some of the pudding. The roughness of the fruit stimulates my already aroused nerve endings even deeper. I open my eyes and watch him lick the chocolate off the strawberry before taking two quick bites and swallowing it. He motions for me to close my eyes and once again I'm in darkness.

This time the item under my panties is smooth. And hot! It's round and hard. I have no idea what it is.

"Michael!?"

"It's a ben-wa ball that I heated up. You like?"

"I love it."

He massages it up and down my pussy lips and all the tension in my body vanishes. I'm descending so deeply that I was only vaguely aware of the ball being taken away and then my panties being pulled down my thighs.

Michael's tongue licking away at the pudding along my pussy lips jolts my eyes open. Little frissons tickle up my spine. He had pulled me to the side of the bed and is kneeling between my legs which are dangling over the side of the bed.

I kick back against the side of the mattress. "Michael, please,

I need more." He lifts his head off my pussy. At last! He's going to take me like a man. But no! He's leaning back in towards my pussy. "Michael, I want—"

The freezing cold of his mouth against my pussy chokes my words off. My whole sex is numb. His tongue flicks inside my pussy. It's cold, but not as cold as on the outside. My body heat warms me back up but now the cold hits full force. "Michael! What have you done?!?"

He pulls his head back. "Would you rather have hot?" he asked, his voice full of innocence.

Before I can respond, I smell coffee. Then his mouth is back on my sex. This time hotter than hot and my pussy is rescued from the cold only to be thrown into the fire.

Michael repeats the hot and cold several times. Thankfully my body knows what to expect and the effects are less extreme. Besides the wonderful sensations of the hot and the cold, the heat wakes up different responses than the cold and each suppresses the arousal of the other. The overall effect is to keep me on a plateau of heightened arousal without allowing me to climax.

Then he puts both hands up under the top of my rump. His tongue presses deep inside my pussy. I would have preferred his cock, but there'll be time enough for that later. Michael's tongue is out, fluttering up the outside of my pussy lip, over the hood of my clit and down the other lip. My back tightens under his hands. He knows he has me and will show no mercy.

He lifts his tongue slowly, ever so slowly up the center of my pussy lips, waggling it back and forth. At the top, he flicks the underside of my clit. A jolt flies up my spine. He turns his tongue over and drags it down the entire length of my sex, then laps the flat and rough upper side of his tongue up my sex. Heat builds inside my cunt.

Up and down flicking specific targets to unlock my passion. The full flat of his tongue to raise my arousal higher and higher. I feel my legs go slack, my arms go slack, my lungs pump air into my lungs. At the center of my body all my muscles are taut, screaming for release!

Then Michael finds the perfect spot. The spot where her can achieve suction with his mouth while still being able to flick his tongue in and out, up and down, sideways, rotating. He slowly increases the suction, pulling more and more blood into my entire vulva.

He angles his head slightly and the suction is released. I grab a quick breath. But the suction comes back and he's found an even better spot, one which allows him to flick his tongue right on my clit! He folds his tongue almost in half and strokes his rough tip up and down the bottom of my shaft. The muscles on each side of my spine snap straight. Then he circles my entire clit with the soft underside of his tongue, round and round and round, softening my back muscles with each rotation.

I float softly on the clouds, warm, aroused, every nerve in my body full to the brim with delight. I'm dimly aware of his mouth sucking and releasing, propelling me forward, of his tongue circling my clit, lifting me higher off the ground.

But then I'm starting to fall out of the sky. Alarms are sounding in my pussy. Everything is being drawn towards my sex. His mouth is being sucked inside me. The alarms are stronger, more persistent, strident. My eyes jerk open. They're not alarms, they're—

Explosions! Cracking inside my cunt. Zipping into my feet. Roaring up my spine. Smashing my mouth open to suck air out of my lungs. Pinning the back of my neck to the mattress with too much pleasure to handle. White hot heat bursting out of my cunt, then sucking everything back into its absolute center.

Then the waves of energy recede and I become aware of Michael's mouth massaging the softer waves, tickling them up my spine, letting them wash over my sex. I gulp air into my lungs.

Finally my body was mine again. I pulled Michael forward by his hair. "You've been a bad boy," I told him.

His only reaction was a silly smile.

I pointed to everything which was hot. "Heat these up. And bring more ice."

He scooped up the hot, now barely warm, items, and scampered out of the bedroom. Thank goodness! Now I'd have a few moments rest.

When I heard his footsteps, I got off the bed and stood up. After he'd set everything down on the night table, I pointed to the bed. "On your back," I told him.

Michael did as he was told and there he was: a full six feet of handsome male virility. A smooth platter, except for his cock which throbbed, demanding attention.

I picked up the champagne bottle, placed my thumb firmly over its opening, and gave it a good shake. When I released my thumb, champagne sprays all over him.

"Hey!" he protests.

"Poor baby," I mock, holding the bottle over him, ready to pour.

He doesn't move, but his eyes beg me not to.

I dribble a small amount on his chest, then kneel on the mattress, ready to lick it up. He grabs for my breasts.

"No touching!" I say, pushing his hands away.

I pour a small amount onto his chest and watch it dribble down his sides, Then I lap the rest up, especially the droplets on his nipples. Michael moans.

I shake the bottle again and spray up and down his body. He shivers, but doesn't protest. I climb atop his torso, spreading my legs on either side, and try to slide up and down. There isn't really enough lubrication, but it feels great nonetheless. Especially when my sex touches the tip of his penis.

I spray whipping cream onto each of his nipples and onto mine as well. The cream isn't as cold as it had been, but it's still cold enough to elicit a gasp from Michael's lips.

"Shut your eyes," I tell him.

He shuts his eyes and I circle his right nipple with my tongue. As I move to his left nipple, I check to make sure that he's kept his eyes shut. His left nipple is a hard little button. I suck it forcefully into my mouth and give it a gentle nip.

"Ow!" he protests, but not like it hurt, like he enjoyed it.

I nip his right nipple, this time eliciting only a low moan. He opens his eyes, watching me.

I lift myself up and place my mouth over his cock, positioning my head so that he can't see my face. Without touching anything else, I open my mouth and position my teeth just below the head of his penis and administer a light nip.

"Yikes!" he yelps.

"Eyes shut," I remind him.

He whimpers until I spray his cock with whipping cream. "Are you okay?" I ask. I watch him carefully as I remove the champagne from the ice bucket and replace it with the whipping cream.

His only response is a low moan, an obvious sign that he's

fine. I lap away at the whipping cream, eliciting moans whenever my tongue contacts his cock. When there's just a little whipping cream left, I put my mouth atop the head of his penis and gently lick where I'd nipped him before. He moans.

Right in the middle of a moan, I plunge his cock all the way down my throat. He gasps his moan back into his lungs. I pull back, then plunge back down the length of his shaft. Up and down as fast as I can go. He's not breathing—he's mine totally! His cock is ramrod hard sliding through my lips, into my mouth, down my throat. Up, then down and I can feel his heat on the back of my neck.

I hear him breathe and I pull my mouth off his cock. Time for a snack. I bite off the top of two strawberries and position one over each of his nipples. "You can open your eyes," I tell him.

He watches as I slowly lower each of the strawberries. "They're very cold," I tell him.

He doesn't respond. Good boy! I lower the strawberries, touching the tips of his nipples. He shudders slightly, but does his best not to react. I press the fruit the rest of the way on. This time he can't suppress his reaction to the cold wetness. I rotate each berry slowly, grinding juice which dribbles down the sides of his his chest.

Michael reaches up towards my breasts, but I lift myself up. "No touching, Mr. Rayburn," I remind him.

I reach my own hands up to my breasts and play the strawberries across my nipples. "Do you want to watch, or do you want to feel?" I ask him.

He watches me eat the rest of the strawberries but shuts his eyes as I take two more berries out of the bowl. These I draw cruelly back and forth across his nipples, doing my best to draw a protest against their rough friction being raked across his tender buds. But he keeps his silence. I have a way to fix that!

His cock is still pointed upwards, straight and hard. Just like it should in the presence of my beauty! His balls are pulled tightly upwards, just below his cock. I dip my right hand into the ice water and my left into the coffee which is still hot. My coffee hand is first to caress his balls. They loosen in the heat and are soon dangling loosely below his cock. He moans. Ice-water hand jumps his balls back up under his cock.

"Lee!" he yelps.

My right hand, which had gone back into the coffee, quiets

his whimpers and his balls relax back down. Icy hand sends balls right back up, but this time Michael controls his reaction and the only thing which escapes his mouth is a non-verbal gasp. I take a gulp of coffee, swirling it around my mouth before I swallow. I lick his balls, then suck them into the heat still inside my mouth. They're rough, with a bit of hair. As they relax, they expand into two large eggs. I let one slip outside my mouth and tongue and suck the other. Above, a low moan escapes from Michael's lips. I pop the ball out and exchange it for its mate. Michael has to adjust his hips.

It's time to move on to the central figure in this drama, to give him his reward since he's been waiting so patiently up above. I swirl coffee in my mouth, then gently slide it down his cock. There's a low moan and I can feel every muscle in Michael's body, save the one in my mouth, go slack. I suck on his cock until I feel my mouth cool off. I repeat the swirl of coffee, sucking Michael's cock back into my mouth just as I swallow the coffee.

"Mmmm," moans Michael as he savors the sensation.

I quickly grab two ice cubes and begin to rub them up and down Michael's cock. I smile at the smile still lingering on his lips. His body has confused the icy cold for heat and I lengthen the confusion as I place my lips over the head of his cock while I continue to rub the ice cubes up and down his shaft. Then I feel Michael's belly jerk taut. His body has figured out that it's getting cold, not hot. But the penis is wonderful this way; even though when it's flaccid it shrinks when subjected to cold, this is not the case when it's erect. When it's erect, it remains as hard as ice.

Michael has opened his eyes and is watching my hands go up and down.

"It's cold," he protests.

"If you want warm, shut your eyes."

He reluctantly complies. I swing my leg over him and slowly lower my pussy onto his cock, sliding her slowly down his length. He gasps, confusing the warmth of my pussy for the cold of ice, but he keeps his eyes shut. In a moment, he's rewarded for his obedience as his cock registers the heat of my cunt enveloping it.

"What does it feel like?" I demand.

"Like the warmth of heaven."

I pump up and down and enjoy a mini-orgasm knowing that the cold treatment I've administered will delay Michael's own orgasm. Michael's eyes are shut as he floats in seventh heaven.

When the last contraction leaves my body, I lift myself off my lover.

Now it's time to confuse Michael's senses once more. First I place my knees against his thighs so that he can feel their warmth. Then, I reach over, take the whipping cream out of the ice bucket and spray generous dollops into my left hand. Hand on cock and he moans with the false sensation of warmth as I caress up and down his shaft. As soon as he recognizes cold and stops moaning, I take him full in my mouth, sliding warmth all the way down his shaft and his moans resume.

I lift myself up and over and slide my butt onto his chest, facing towards his cock. "Okay?" I ask.

"Sure."

This time, I place only a small amount of whipping cream on my hands so that my warmth will overpower the cold of the cream. I massage up and down his cock, carefully monitoring his breathing. When I sense that he's about to come, I release his cock, place my hands on his chest and angle my pussy towards his mouth. I can feel his eyes open as he smells my sex and soon his tongue is flicking up and down my pussy lips.

I keep my eyes on his cock. It's stopped throbbing. Three more flicks of Michael's tongue and I lift myself off his mouth and sit back down on top of his chest. More whipping cream on hands sliding up and down his cock. He's gone slightly soft, but a few strokes up and down his shaft and he's rock hard once more. Michael steadies my hips with his hands.

This time when Michael's breathing indicates he's about to come, I accelerate my strokes. But I don't grab on hard. With any luck, we'll be able to go another round after a short nap. Michael's palms on my thigh, on the other hand, are holding me really, *really* tightly. My hands whizz up and down and in a spiral. The lubrication of the whipping cream allows my hands to go up and over the sensitive head of his penis without difficulty. Michael's fingers are digging into my thighs. I reach below to caress his balls, then up and around and—spurting warmth, gooey warmth into my hands.

"Lee!" he screams.

"Michael!" I bump up and down on his chest, trying to loosen his grip on my thighs.

"Lee!"

He finishes spurting and finally loosens his grip on my

thighs. A few more jerks up and down and his hands fall to the mattress.

I slip beside him and we fall into a light sleep. Floating over infinite clouds…

I'm dimly aware of a buzzing in the distance.

Michael has lifted his right arm and made a languid move towards his phone. After what seemed like an eternity, he had it in his hand. After another eternity, he lifted it to his ear. Then he held the phone towards me. "It's for you."

"Lee!" It was Eric.

"Don't shout," I remonstrated. But it was too late. His voice had already burst the calm cocoon that had enveloped us.

"Lee. It's not Abernathy. We got the wrong guy."

"But you said—"

"I was wrong. It was all a hoax perpetrated by the Cyber Culprit."

"But—"

"He's posted again. Stuff from our computers, our investigations, all with the same signatures we thought were Abernathy's."

"Maybe that's because Abernathy posted those too."

"Not possible. All his computers have been confiscated. Besides he's been locked up with the cops."

"Could it have been a delayed release?"

"With a photograph of this morning's papers? No, it's not a delayed release."

"Shit!"

"What's wrong?" Michael wanted to know as he pulled me toward his kitchen.

"We got the wrong guy," I told him. "Abernathy's innocent."

We sat at opposite ends of the kitchen table. Michael didn't say anything. He just hung his head in his hands.

Eric was chirping in my ear again. "He really screwed us. He convinced us to publicly accuse someone in power. He's evaded our scrutiny, not to mention embarrassing Mr. Rayburn's firm."

Michael lifted his head. "We need to meet at the office. Now!"

He started to stand up, but I put a hand on his shoulder. "Shouldn't we wait until the morning? What good are we now, all bleary-eyed? We won't really be able to accomplish anything."

Michael nodded and trudged to his bedroom. I turned off all the lights and followed. In the bedroom he had removed the waterproof blanket and curled up in the center of the bed. I found a comforter and laid it over us. I cuddled against his back all night long.

The next morning, Michael, Eric and I met in the law firm's largest boardroom. The three of us were huddled together at one end of the table. Peter Henge—my former lover and erstwhile auditor—was meeting with two other lawyers at the other end of the table. Hushed tones all around.

Michael turned to Eric. "You're sure that we screwed up?"

Eric hung his head and nodded. I was grateful that Michael had not said "you screwed up". Certainly he would have had the right.

"What's in the new post?"

Eric raised his head and opened his laptop. "It's from Desire Pearl, south of Cancun, Mexico. It exposes one of our senior trade negotiators, Donald Reisman as a swinger. Negotiators from other countries are clamoring for his removal from Canada's negotiation team."

"Where is Reisman now?" Michael wanted to know.

Eric consulted his computer. "Apparently he's still at the resort."

"Desire Pearl?" I asked. It would be good, really good, to get away while this fiasco blew over. And I couldn't imagine a better place than a Mexican swingers resort. And with the new buff bod Eric's MMA exercise routine had favored me with, we'd have our choice of couples.

"What is his game? Why did he do this?" Michael muttered.

I wished that I'd voiced my suspicions that some of the Cyber Culprit's motives had become personal, especially towards me. But now it was too late and I'd have to keep that theory to myself. At least until there was new evidence to support it. If I piped up now, I'd never be able to explain my previous silence.

Eric sighed. "He obviously wants to maximize publicity, especially at the expense of anyone trying to catch him."

At that moment, Peter and the two lawyers who'd been meeting with him left the room.

I pointed to where they'd been. "Is the audit still going

forward?"

Michael nodded, forlorn. "And there may be a recommendation to take us off the case."

"What are we missing?" I wondered out loud.

"Maybe we should try to profile him," ventured Eric.

"You mean like a psychological profile?" Michael asked.

Eric nodded. I looked at Michael who thought for a moment, then nodded too.

"I'll start working on it," Eric promised.

"From Desire Pearl?"

Michael nodded again and my feet did a little dance under the table.

Negotiator , Lusty Lee Log #16

Upon arrival at Mexico's Desire Pearl, my assistant Eric and I were ushered to the front desk and favored with a cold wet towel followed by a glass of champagne.

The young woman behind the desk took our passports and entered them into her computer. "Congratulations *Señora*, *Señor*, on selecting one of our master suites!"

She then gave us a map of the resort. The restaurants were to the south, the pool and disco in the center and the rooms to the north. The ocean, blue and inviting, was to the east.

A nude couple walked in, made arrangements for an excursion at the tour desk, and then exited the lobby.

"Clothing optional?" whispered Eric.

I nodded. "Clothing optional."

Our exchange caught the attention of the receptionist. "*Si, Señor*, the resort is clothing optional. But clothes are required in the restaurants."

"What about in the Jacuzzi?" Eric pointed to a large red dot to the west of the pool.

"Of course not, *Señor*. That is one of the areas where sex is allowed."

"And the other?" I asked.

She pointed to an area attached to the disco. "In the playroom."

"Wow, not here three minutes and you're already asking about the playroom!" It was a female voice behind me. I turned around. The speaker was wearing a crocheted dress and I could see her nipples through its generously spaced holes. Regrettably a bikini bottom blocked the view below. A man stood behind her, clad only in a bright orange thong. He had a towel draped over one shoulder.

I smiled at her and she smiled back before favoring Eric with an even broader smile. "Maybe we'll run into you later?"

And then they were gone.

"Were they trying to pick us up?" Eric queried.

I nodded. "Welcome to paradise!"

We turned back to the receptionist who was scowling into her computer.

"Is there a problem?" I asked.

She nodded. "The passport of *Señor* Craigie has been flagged by the *Instituto Nacional de Migración.*

What the hell does Mexican Immigration want with my assistant?!

She scowled at her computer then looked up towards Eric. "Don't worry, Señor, we will work it out for you."

She returned my passport to me but kept Eric's. I did my best to think happy thoughts.

In our room, a large suite really, we quickly unpacked, grouping our clothing in order of the resort's nightly, not to mention lascivious, themes. "Does Desire have a foam party?" asked Eric.

"Yes, but here it's during the day and in the pool."

Eric finished unpacking first and cracked open his laptop.

"Where are we in the investigation?" I asked. The investigation was our search for the Cyber Culprit, the internet criminal who'd been hacking into websites and posting embarrassing photos, videos and other assorted information to the world wide web. Last week we thought we'd had him. But it turned out to be just another hoax perpetrated by CC to embarrass us.

Eric shook his head. "Realistically, we're back to square one."

I shrugged and looked at my watch. The manager wasn't due to arrive at the resort for a few hours. "At least we get to work on our tans." I squeezed into my skimpiest bikini and headed for the pool. Halfway through my tanning session I'd remove my bikini. Sunburn on one's back or tummy was one thing, but sunburn on...

Back in the lobby, my dress may have been white, but beneath it my skin now had a tinge of red. The manager was dressed in an elegant beige linen suit. He sat us down on the couch in the lobby, me beside him, Eric opposite. After a brief introduction, I angled my phone towards him and showed him the Cyber Culprit's latest posting.

"But that's *Señor* Reisman!" he blurted, aghast. *El señor y la señora Reisman*, they are still at Desire."

I nodded. "Do you know who took these pictures?"

He concentrated on my phone for several moments before shaking his head ruefully, "*Lo siento*--sorry, no. Our guests, they need their privacy. What should I tell them?"

I put my hand on his thigh. "Don't tell them anything. We're in hot pursuit. If you tell anyone, you'll just spook the culprit, the man responsible."

He nodded, grateful to have responsibility lifted from his shoulders and we all stood, indicating that the meeting was over.

Eric and I then did a tour of the resort to determine where the photos had been taken from. It was a worthwhile exercise, but it failed to yield any results.

Except that I spotted Mr. Reisman—senior trade negotiator Donald Reisman—sitting alone in the gazebo located at the end of a long dock. He appeared to be staring out to sea. I turned towards the dock and Eric strode ahead.

I stopped. "Eric."

He stopped and came back to me.

"I think I should speak to Mr. Reisman alone," I told him.

He looked back and forth between Reisman and me.

"You were going to work on the Cyber Culprit's psychological profile," I reminded him.

He nodded and turned towards our room.

My sitting down at the opposite end of the bench occupied by the trade negotiator did not seem to disturb his concentration on the ocean's waves. Donald Reisman was in his late forties. There was still some dark brown in his hair, but his well-trimmed goatee was entirely grey. He had the sleek body of a runner. I estimated his height to be just under six feet. He was wearing a bright Hawaiian shirt and pink shorts.

After three minutes, I'd had enough of quiet contemplation. "Isn't the ocean beautiful?" I asked him.

"Yes." Other than his lips, he hadn't moved.

This time I lasted only two minutes. "I have something else for you to look at."

He turned to me and slowly looked me up and down. His face was angular. Somehow I knew that his expression could vary between mean and threatening to friendly and charming. Now it was poker-face expressionless. I waited for him to ask 'and what might that be', but he started to turn back towards the ocean. I took out my phone and held it towards him. He watched himself dancing with his wife, then with another woman as her partner danced with his wife. Then the foursome danced together in the classic swingers' sandwich, everybody fondling everybody else. There were some still shots of Reisman in the playroom and at the Jacuzzi, nude and in sexual congress with several women. In one, his wife was in the background, similarly engaged.

"Where did you get these?" he asked, his face still expressionless.

"It's been posted to the internet."

A series of emotions, lasting only a fraction of a second,

flickered across his face. But the flicker was immediately replaced by his poker face. I thought I had seen anger, fear, concern, but the flicker had been too rapid for me to be sure.

I gestured with my phone. "We're chasing the person responsible for the posting. We're hoping you can help us."

"And why should I help you?"

"Don't you want to catch the guy who did this?" I tipped my phone back and forth.

"What good will his capture do me?"

"You don't seem very co-operative," I told him.

Reisman shrugged. "Why should I be? For me the damage has been done." He turned back to the ocean.

I stared at him, flabbergasted. When I finally found my voice, "Mr. Reisman—"

He turned back to me, a no-nonsense expression on his face. "I'll tell you what. If you want my cooperation, here are my terms. First, you won't tell my wife Sabrina anything about this posting."

I nodded.

"Second, my wife and I are leaving for an overnight trip to Campeche to visit the Mayan pyramids at Calakmul tomorrow morning. When we get back, you, your partner, Sabrina and I will pleasure each other in intimate fashion."

I nodded again. Had I just pimped Eric out to Sabrina!?!

"After that, we'll have a full sit-down meeting and I'll give you as much help as I can."

I nodded. He turned back to the ocean. The meeting was over.

Later in our room, I described my conversation with Reisman to Eric. "He's a bit of an S.O.B., but why would the Cyber Culprit target *him* of all people?" I wondered.

Eric looked at me aghast. "You're kidding, right? Trade deals are an end-around by the merchant elites to surreptitiously alter the constitutions of subject states for their benefit. National legislatures are emasculated to deal with capitalist abuse."

I nodded. My assistant was a revolutionary! I did a quick internet search. He was also right.

That night, we went to bed early, sleeping at opposite ends of the king-sized bed.

Eric and I spent the following day climbing the walls wishing we could interview the Reismans. After a late dinner, we went to the resort's nightclub show. The dress theme for the night was Glow Party. Eric and I were wearing white and bright orange striped shirts, he white pants, me a white mini-skirt.

The first act was a vampire. He started out with pants and a puffy-sleeved shirt, but quickly stripped down to the bare basics: red satin thong, cape red on the inside, black on the outside and vampire teeth. He recruited a woman from the audience to join him in his act and quickly wrapped her in his cape. A moment later, she emerged, somewhat disheveled, vaguely happy, and with a hickey on her neck.

The next performer was female: tall, blonde and buxom. She looked like she worked out. Her outfit was neon: lime green top, orange mini-skirt, chartreuse stockings. She raised her skirt to reveal that her stockings were held up by black garters. The lights inside her wedge high heels blinked a variety of colors. She smiled at Eric and raised her skirt all the way to reveal a bright yellow thong then dropped her skirt and strode over to stand right in front of us. She pointed her finger at Eric, then slowly crooked it, inviting him to become part of the show.

Eric didn't need any more encouragement and jumped to his feet. He was barely taller than her but his red hair and green eyes were much more striking. She ran her hands over his skinny body, not touching, but the effect was sensuous nonetheless. Eric had a silly smile on his face.

"What's your name?" she asked him.

"Eric."

"I'm Erica."

A chair suddenly appeared and she gently pushed him down sitting on it. She kicked off her high heels and did the splits in front of Eric. The crowd cheered. She then brought her legs together and stood back up. Then women gasped. The splits they understood, but the way Erica had stood back up without using her arms or hands was beyond them.

Next Erica stood right in front of Eric and flipped her skirt up. She immediately turned around, bent over and flipped the back of her skirt up. Her butt was so close to Eric that the rest of us couldn't really see much, but it was clear that he'd got an eyeful!

She stood, turned around and slowly lifted one foot, positioning it between Eric's legs. Her balance was so good that she was able to reach her foot forward and gently caress his crotch. Her toes encouraged him to swell underneath their attentions. Then she withdrew her foot and bent over, her ample breasts straining to escape the lime green fabric of her top. Eric reached for her breasts.

But she'd tricked him. Erica grabbed his hands and pulled him standing beside her. Without her high heels, she was almost a head shorter than Eric. She circled him, touching him as she went. But this time there was no tease; it was clear that her fingers were making contact with his torso, chest, butt and crotch.

When he tried to touch her, she stepped back and wagged her finger up at his face. When Eric lowered his arms, she pointed to her lime green top and at his shirt, then back to her top. She lifted her top half way, revealing the underside of a bright white bra. Eric was standing motionless, transfixed by what her hands were revealing.

Erica pulled her top back down and motioned at his shirt. "You first," she told him.

Eric quickly removed his shirt and she pulled her top over her head, flinging it into the audience. There were cheers for the roly-poly man who caught the lime green piece of heaven.

Eric removed his pants. She removed her skirt and twirled her Amazon curves. Eric was down to an orange thong. She pointed back and forth between her bright yellow thong and what was pressing against Eric's orange counterpart.

Eric removed his thong and his cock, released at last, stood proudly forth. Erica covered her mouth in mock surprise. She bent down as if to remove her thong but instead unsnapped the garters holding up her left stocking and slowly slid it off her leg. She twirled the stocking over her head as she pranced around to stand behind Eric. She held the stocking in front of Eric's cock, as if to shield it from prying eyes, then reached under and through his legs to grab the other end of her stocking. Her hands pulled the sheer material up and down the shaft of Eric's cock. He turned beet red and almost lost his footing.

Erica pulled him back towards her and laid him flat on the floor. She climbed on top, her crotch at his face, and stared down at him. She lowered her sex slowly down towards his lips, but when he opened his mouth to try to lick her thong, she scooted her hips down his body and brought her head to his. She held her lips inches from his, mocking him. When he gave up, she kissed him full on the lips.

Eric reached up to hug her close, but she was already moving down his body. When her head arrived above his cock, she made sure that her hair and hands were obscuring it from view. She bobbed her head up and down. Was Erica giving him oral sex? It was hard to tell. But whatever she was doing, Eric was *enjoying* it.

Erica raised her head and climbed back up his body. This time when she kissed him, she let him hug her close. She started to gently rub her crotch against his. Dry humping it might have been, but it was certainly humping! Eric tried to turn her on her back, but she squirted free, stood over him and bowed. The room erupted in rowdy cheers and male cries of 'Me!', 'Me next!'.

The next day, Eric was called to front desk to deal with his passport issue. There were several *agentes* of the *Instituto Nacional de Migración* waiting for us.

When the manager saw us approaching, he pulled me

aside. "It would be better if *Señor* dealt with this by himself."

I didn't like the Mexican macho foolishness, but this was likely not the time to make that point. Besides, Eric could take care of himself.

Back in our room, it was time to decide what to wear to the foam party, Desire's excuse to fondle and be fondled by strangers under visually impenetrable foam. I quickly stripped nude and inspected myself in the mirror. For twenty-nine, I was youthful. Eric's mixed-martial arts exercise program had allowed me to strip almost all the fat from my body. Thankfully it had left fatty tissue where it belonged — in my ample breasts and round bum. The face which my curly brown hair framed was only adequate. But I brought my nose close to the mirror and smiled. Lucky for me, few men could resist my lustrous blue eyes, especially when my smile put a special sparkle inside them.

I did a slow pirouette, admiring my curves. I had two bikinis to choose from. The first was dark blue, the second light pink. The pink bikini was slightly larger and would thus hold my tummy in while cupping my butt and accentuating my cleavage. The blue was a string bikini, softer and would go with the flow. My breasts would sag slightly and the curve of my butt would less pronounced. I decided on blue. After all, under the foam I'd be invisible unless someone was all but touching me.

I passed through the enclosure holding the large Jacuzzi pool on the way to the swimming pool. There was a cute redhead lounging on one of the beds. She had so many tattoos on her body, I couldn't tell whether she was clothed or whether she was completely nude.

At the pool, the foam machine has already started up. A large barrel is spraying a steady stream of foam over the surface of the pool. Half of the pool's surface is covered by a foot of foam. Closer to the barrel, the foam is three feet high.

I slowly lower myself into the pool. The water is about four feet deep. I walk towards the edge of the foam. A couple joins me walking towards the deeper foam and we gradually come closer and closer together. The couple splits and walks around me. When they're in front of me, they turn around and slow because they're walking backwards. I smile at her. She comes in front of me and we touch. I kiss her lightly and hold an arm out for her husband. The foam washes over us and all I can see is white. I'm in the middle of them and hands and fingers caress my bottom and breasts and pussy. Her pussy is hot and moist. Behind me, I grasp his erect cock. Other people bump into us and my couple leaves me. I'm all alone in the whiteness. I adjust my bikini and walk forward.

But I walk the wrong way and my head pops out of the whiteness into the open air. Erica, the stripper who'd had her way with my assistant last night, spots me and rushes towards me. Her husband is behind her, but I can't really see him.

"You're Eric's friend," she gushes. She's topless, her long blond hair in wet strands on her shoulders. She's wearing swimmer's goggles.

I nod.

And with that her lips are on my lips and her tongue is in my mouth. She hugs me close and I have no choice but to hug her back. I catch a glimpse of her husband. He's wearing swimmer's goggles as well, but his are opaque. Erica propels us back into the foam. Our breasts rub together as I backtrack as quickly as I can to avoid falling backwards. Thankfully, after a few steps she stops advancing. But her tongue is relentless, asserting her domination over me. I melt into her. She twists and turns, connecting our nipples and I feel heat start to build down below.

Then her husband is behind us. "Ready to party?" he asks.

I raise my hands above my head and wiggle my bum. "Never readier!" I proclaim.

I feel his cock hot against my thigh. He's obviously fully nude. His hand reaches around under my bikini and caresses my pubic hair. Is Erica as nude as her husband? One way to find out. I reach between her legs as she gently squeezes my breasts. My hand slides right between her pussy lips. She moans. Definitely nude!

"You are so beautiful," the male voice behind me soft, smooth. "You're the type of woman men admire from afar, despairing of ever being allowed to come close."

"And now you're close, what does that mean?" I spread my legs.

His hand accepts my invitation and moves lower. "It means that I have you for a moment, but when you leave the pool, you'll go back to your phone, your computer, and the moment will be broken."

"Phones and computers can be turned off."

His fingers are between my pussy lips moving up and down with compact circular patterns. I'm glad I can lean back on him to remain standing.

"Would you be willing to turn your phone off forever?"

"No." I've said it without thinking and my response sounds harsh. "Why would I do that?" I say to soften my answer.

"Because as long as you say 'no' so automatically, so vigorously, your phone owns you."

"In this moment, *you* own me."

"Let's see about that." He turns me around and kisses me. His kisses are soft and tender. His tongue flicks just inside my lips but does not venture further. "Lift her up," he tells Erica.

Behind me, her hands propel my thighs forward and he grabs ahold of them. Her hands drift back to my buttocks. Both of them lift me up and I'm almost above the foam. My pelvis is against his torso.

Then they lower me down right onto his cock. Inch by inch, I'm impaled, filled.

"*Now* I own you!" His voice is full of triumph. They've lowered me all the way down and are holding me motionless. The sexual sensations inside my pussy begin to dissipate. "What would your boyfriend think of this?" he probes. I'm so motionless I can't feel anything down there.

"He's not my boyfriend," I reply. "My boyfriend is up

north." An image pops into my head. It's Michael — Michael Rayburn, the lawyer who'd assigned us to pursue the Cyber Culprit, Michael, now my lover — and I feel a familiar tingling in my crotch.

"Does your boyfriend know what you're doing down here in Mexico?" He pronounced it in Spanish: *Méjico*.

"What happens at Desire, stays at Desire."

"Is he allowed to see other women while you're down here?"

I hesitated. Just what was our arrangement? Michael knew that this case required a certain promiscuity on my part. But we had never exactly discussed the parameters. I shook my head. "No, he's not. Just like I'm not allowed to see other men up north in Toronto."

He started to bounce me up and down on his cock and my pussy was filled and fulfilled!

I was down to the sense of touch alone. The whiteness had blanked out my vision and deadened all sound except for our breathing. The bubbles had deprived me of my sense of smell by forcing me to breathe carefully through my mouth. Breathing through my mouth meant I couldn't try to taste the man upon whose cock I was impaled. Whether it was this deprivation or being bounced in the water while two hands clenched my butt and another two caressed my breasts, whatever it was, I came quicker than I'd ever come before.

It wasn't a great orgasm, more slippery than explosive, but still…

I was lowered gently to the bottom of the pool. Something was fluttering around my ankles.

"You'll never catch him," he said.

I'd heard, but not heard. "What?" I opened my eyes, but all I could see was white.

"You'll never catch him," he repeated.

He was no longer touching me. I tried to walk in the direction of his voice, but my ankles were tied tight and I ended up face first in the water. By the time I got out of the pool, Erica and friend were nowhere to be seen.

Back in the room, my assistant was absorbed in his computer. Could Eric ever turn it off forever, I wondered.

"How'd you make out with the *Instituto Nacional de Migración*?" I asked.

He turned his computer towards me. "The Cyber Culprit was behind my passport problem. He somehow hijacked my passport number and used it to enter Mexico."

"Is he still here?"

Eric nodded.

"Do they know where CC is?" I persisted.

Eric shook his head.

"Were you able to make any progress in compiling your psychological profile of the Cyber Culprit?" I asked.

"He's extremely intelligent and technologically proficient. But there's an undercurrent of resentment towards the way in which tech is being used. He's arrogant to the point of taking risks. And he takes everything personally. So if he was to become aware of someone following or investigating him, he would follow and investigate them in return."

I thought back to my encounter in the pool. "What would he do if he found someone following him?"

"It's too early to say. He might—"

At that moment, my phone beeped. It was another post from CC. This time it showed Michael Rayburn—my Michael—with another woman. They appeared to be kissing, but it was hard to tell. But it certainly called for an explanation!

I was about to comment when there was a second beep, this time from Eric's computer. The *Instituto Nacional de Migración* had found Eric's passport in a garbage bin at the airport.

"Let's go!" I shouted. In less than a minute, we, me still in my bikini, were at the front desk. "El Taxi," I shouted, then lowered my voice, "*por favor.*"

But the receptionist behind the desk shook her head. "*Señor* Craigie is not allowed to leave the resort without his passport."

"But they've found his passport, at the airport," I told her.

She shook her head. "*El Instituto Nacional de Migración* was quite specific. No passport, not allowed to leave."

I stomped my feet, frustrated. I was about to tell Eric about my encounter at the pool. But if we couldn't go to the airport to search for Erica and friend, there was no point. I decided to keep my suspicions to myself until I had something more solid.

The next morning, Eric and I met the Reismans at breakfast. "How was your trip?" I asked.

"Great!" enthused Sabrina before biting off a large piece of her omelet. Her hair was light brown, cut short. She had the same runner's body as her husband, hardly any tits. I estimated her as half a head shorter than her husband. Her face was round, out of place on top of her thin body. Maybe she used to be heavier? She smiled at me as she swallowed. It was a friendly smile, without subterfuge.

Donald's account was more detailed. "The first day, the driver took us to a bed and breakfast hotel within a mile of the ruins at Calakmul. So we were able to get to the archeological site bright and early the next morning. We strolled around the grounds and climbed a pyramid. Coming back yesterday, we drove through the night."

"Show them the pictures," interjected Sabrina between bites of egg.

Donald angled his phone towards Eric and me. There was a large almost pyramid-like structure which seemed to emerge out of the jungle, then several shots which appeared to have been taken atop this structure. Donald rapidly scrolled through images of smaller buildings before turning to me, "So, are you and your partner still interested?"

I nodded, bracing for the promised (threatened?) negotiation.

Donald inclined his head towards his wife who was engrossed in finishing her breakfast, "Sabrina needs long and varied stimulation to climax."

"Like Tantric?" asked Eric.

Donald flattened his hand and extended it palm down. He tipped it back and forth. "Similar, but without the mumbo jumbo."

"What do you want?" I asked him.

"Orgasm delay." The Reismans smiled at each other. I suddenly understood the lack of subterfuge in her smile. Donald did all the negotiating; she didn't have a care in the world.

"We'll go our separate ways, each with a new partner, but we'll end up in our suite."

"It's easier for me that way," said Sabrina, smiling at Eric.

Back in our room, Eric changed into jogging gear. Sabrina's long and varied stimulation apparently started out with a run along the beach.

My long and varied stimulation required a languid sun tanning session.

I met up with Donald at lunch. "You said you need orgasm delay. Just what did you have in mind?"

"Anything and everything. Like I said, Sabrina takes a long time to climax. But for her to be turned on, I need to be turned on. Erect. Throughout. On a sustained basis. If my penis goes flaccid, she goes back to square one and we have to start over from scratch."

"So you want me to touch you, but just lightly, keep you on the edge without sending you over?"

He nodded. "That's part of it. But I want you to give me new techniques for when she touches me vigorously."

"To stop yourself from coming?"

He nodded and we ate in silence for a moment.

"Why are we meeting back in your room?" I asked. "Why don't you come to my room and leave yours to Eric and Sabrina?"

"She'll need a line of sight to me if she's going to climax."

This deal was proving to have as many sticky details as the Caribbean-Canada Trade Agreement. I wanted to shake my head in dismay but instead I smiled. After lunch, we strolled down the pier and sat together in the gazebo, obviously his favorite spot on the resort.

Donald and I arrived at the ocean-side door to Reisman's ultra-luxurious suite just as Eric and Sabrina returned from their run. Donald had explained that the run would be Sabrina's first level of stimulation but that stimulation of the more intimate variety would begin when she and Eric shared a shower.

Donald took me on a tour of the suite while the runners washed the sweat off their bodies. The bedroom had a king-sized bed with bench at its foot. The sliding door, through which we had entered, opened out to a terrace from which there was a spectacular view of the ocean. The terrace also had a double chaise lounge and an intimately small plunge pool.

Donald got me to help him move the wide lounge chair into the bedroom. "Two couples, line of sight," he explained.

Next was the large and luxurious bathroom located between the bedroom and main living areas. Donald opened the door to show me but the room was steamed up from the shower Eric and Sabrina were enjoying.

The main living area was spacious and included a soft couch, two chairs and an enormous flat screen television. Donald lifted the remote to turn the TV on, but I shook my head and cocked my ear towards the bathroom. We could hear Eric and Sabrina finishing their shower.

Donald moved to kiss me, but I held up my hand.

"Orgasm delay requires you to give her a head start. Do your best to get her worked up before you even start."

"But—"

"You said she likes to run and that turns her on."

He nodded.

"What about the shower? Does that turn her on?"

He nodded again.

"Good. Let her have her shower alone."

He nodded.

"What about romance?" I continued.

"Yes, that turns her on."

"So when she comes out of the shower, read her poetry, serve her strawberries and whipped cream, light a candle. Anything which turns her on, without arousing you, is a good idea."

Eric and Sabrina came into the living room. Both nude. She had fluffed her hair and looked beautiful—certainly none the worse for wear after a long run. Eric looked a little winded, but game. His penis was half way to being aroused.

Donald started to quickly strip out of his clothes. I put my hand on his before he could remove his briefs. "Keep your clothes on. Let her get aroused first."

Donald shook his head. "Unless I'm nude, she can't get turned on." I removed my hand. Donald's negotiating skills obviously stopped at the bedroom door.

I stripped too and in a moment we were all nude. I looked over at Donald. He was looking Sabrina up and down, consumed by her beauty. He was also fully erect.

Sabrina flitted among us, kissing and fondling. Her touch on my breasts instantly filled my nipples hard. Between my legs, her fingers concentrated all feeling into my sex. Her breasts were small and hard and hot. I brushed up and down her pussy, eliciting a low moan. When she stroked Donald's cock, just for a moment and barely touching, I swear he almost climaxed.

Then Sabrina took Eric by the hand and led him into the bedroom.

Donald turned to follow, but I held him back. "Learn to attend to her partially," I told him. Even when you're kissing, touching."

"But—"

"Just enough to keep you erect, not so much that you want to come right away."

He nodded and we moved into the bedroom.

Sabrina was lying on the side of the bed, her knees dangling over. Eric's head was between her thighs. She was pulling his head forward, as hard as she could and moaning every time Eric managed to move his head. I wished I could see what his tongue was doing.

Donald and I positioned ourselves on the wide lounge chair, making sure that he could see Sabrina.

"She turns you on?" I asked.

"Yes."

"What about me?"

"Yes." But his tone was less definite.

I caressed his cock. It was hard, but he did not react to my touch. "But even though I'm here, next to you, my nipples pressing into you, my hand on your cock, I don't turn you on as much as your wife?"

He looked down at me and shook his head.

Sabrina was kneeling on the bed and Eric was taking her from the rear, doggy style. Obviously her need for a wide variety of stimulation meant that oral sex would only take her so far.

"Does she have to see you watching her?"

He shook his head. "Just the security of knowing I'm close by."

I turned his head back towards me. "Then don't watch her. Concentrate on me."

He turned towards me and we kissed. His kisses were gentle, sensuous. My hand on his cock told me that he enjoyed kissing me but that the enjoyment was less than that generated by looking at his wife.

"Now caress my breasts," I told him.

His fingers traced a circle around the bottoms of my breasts, then spiraled ever upwards, teasing my nipples with the attention they were about to receive. And receive they did. Donald's fingers continued their spirals slowly — even tortuously — up my nipples, squeezing and releasing as the ascended their peaks. Sabrina had taught him well! When he reached the tips of my nipples, he spread his fingers down my breast until the full surface of his palms were touching me.

"Imagine you're touching Sabrina's breasts," I told him.

There was an immediate pulse through the entire length of his cock.

"Lift up your palms. Just use your fingers. Fingers stimulate her; when you touch with your palms, both of us are stimulated." He obeyed and the throbbing in his cock subsided, but only ever so slightly. Three quick jerks and I'd have Donald spurting all over me.

"Now touch my pussy," I told him.

He did and once again I enjoyed the benefit of Sabrina's tutelage. His cock calmed down; apparently he was not imagining that my pussy was Sabrina's. I shut my eyes to concentrate on his fingers flitting up and down the entire length of my sex. Donald touched every part of me. He obviously had a system, but he kept it so well hidden that I couldn't guess his method. Then he squeezed my outer lips together, compressing my entire vulva. Squeezing and releasing, pulling up, then down, rotating, he used my outer sex to massage deep inside without any direct friction being applied.

"Faster," I encouraged.

He sped up and in a moment I felt my cunt tighten.

"Yes, Donald," I enthused, breathing hard. His cock remained interested, but there was no indication that he was about to join in my impending orgasm. "Faster!" I urged.

He sped up as fast as he could go, mashing my pussy lips together and stroking up and down my clit. I was barely holding on. Then he rotated his cock ever so slightly and my climax exploded deep inside. It reverberated around my sex but stayed inside my pelvis as if his fingers compressing my vulva tight had imprisoned all sensation within.

When my breathing subsided, I asked, "What's Sabrina doing?"

There was an immediate jolt within his cock. "She's sitting on his face, rocking back and forth." His cock was throbbing. I held my hand as still as I could, but still I feared that he was about to come.

"Look at her foot, only her foot," I directed. The furies inside Donald's cock subsided. "Good. You must train yourself to see only as much of her as you can without losing control."

I waited a moment. "Now what's she doing?"

"She's lowering herself onto his cock! She's going to fuck him!" His voice trailed off into a high-pitched wail. Not so his cock. It vibrated so hard I had to let go for fear he'd come.

"Look at me!"

He didn't move.

"Look at me!" This time I slapped him across the face and he finally wrenched his attention away from his wife. But his cock was still throbbing and I didn't dare touch it. "Shut your eyes and think about the ocean."

He shut his eyes and his cock stopped throbbing. His breathing became slow and relaxed. "Now look at her foot," I told him. His cock stiffened. "Her foot, nothing else!" He took a deep breath but his cock remained stiff. "Now, even though you're looking at her foot, imagine the ocean. Imagine you're looking out to sea. See the ocean, nothing else. Not her foot, only the ocean."

His cock relaxed and I positioned myself on the chaise so that Donald would be able to penetrate me while still watching his wife. My therapy was working—he was even beginning to lose his erection. I massaged briefly up and down his shaft and he was hard again.

I helped him move into position while still keeping his eyes on the ocean inside his wife's foot. Then his cock was inside me. He wasn't looking at me, but muscle memory had kicked in and he fucked my cunt as expertly as he'd fingered my vulva earlier. His cock stroked my entire sheath, his pelvic bone rotated mine at the end of every thrust, stirring arousal deep down into my clit. At the end of each stroke, he angled upwards, teasing passion into my g-spot.

I could feel myself tighten around his cock. When he

pulled out, he pulled the suction with him. And when he pushed back in, my tightness allowed his cock to stimulate every part of me. My orgasm was building, but I pushed it back down, intent on letting gather its power.

Donald arched his back, jerking himself even deeper inside. I was being fucked by a master! I clenched my cunt even tighter and waited for his next thrust. But he shuddered and stopped! I tried to push myself up towards him, but I was pinned between his torso and the sloped back of the chair.

"She's fucking him," wailed Donald. "Her ass muscles! She's *fucking* him!"

Warm gooey stickiness began to ooze down my thighs. The bastard had come without me! I try to rock my hips, but I was being held too tight.

"She's fucking him," Donald kept blubbering, "She's fucking him."

At last I understood the full depth of Sabrina's frustrations.

After Donald made sure that Sabrina was comfortable and drifting off to sleep, he came out to the main living area wearing a robe. "That was great!" He enthused. "Now what can I do for you?"

I turned my phone towards him and played the video of he and his wife in the swingers' sandwich. "What can you tell us about that?"

He shrugged. "It happened. I didn't know it was being recorded. I have no information as to how it was recorded."

"That's it?!?" I blurted.

He nodded. "That's it."

The bastard had played us. He had nothing. Eric had given the performance of a lifetime and I'd sacrificed my own pleasure! I raised my hand to slap him across his deceitful face. But Eric grabbed my wrist.

"What happens to you now?" Eric wanted to know.

Reisman shrugged. "When we get back to Toronto, I'll have to resign from the civil service and look for a new line of work."

At that moment, I had a sliver of pity for Reisman. But I still wanted to slap his face.

Back in our room, I turned on Eric, "You should've let me slap that bastard silly!" I yelled.

"Have you ever seen the inside of a Mexican jail?"

He had a point, but still. I tried to come up with an argument which would convince my assistant to let me march back to the Reisman's suite to enact our revenge.

My efforts were interrupted by a beep from my phone announcing a new text message. I touched the screen. It was from Michael Rayburn. The Cyber Culprit had made a new posting. This time the victim was Chuck Gaines, the famous National Football League player. The video showed Gaines and another man. They had a woman between them and it was obvious that they'd both penetrated her and were having sex with her. The venue looked familiar, but it was too indistinct for me to place it.

Linebacker, Lusty Lee Log #17

I spotted Chuck Gaines three blocks from his gym. The former National League Football linebacker was walking at a fast pace at the head of a small group, his head leaning into his phone. Chuck was a lot smaller in person, especially without his shoulder pads. Still, trying to dodge around him would be the last thing I'd want to have to attempt. Suddenly he stopped, tapped on his phone, then made an upward swipe. He turned around, a smile on his face. The group around him veered across the street at high speed. It suddenly dawned on me that he was playing Pokémon Go.

Gaines was the latest victim of the Cyber Culprit and I had attended outside his gym in the hopes of interviewing him. He was a local Toronto boy, but had made fame and fortune south of the border in the NFL. His publicist/agent had tried to ward me off so I'd been left to my own devices.

But I wouldn't be a very good private investigator if I couldn't discover the daily routines of a mid-level celebrity!

Chuck Gaines, and his thousand-watt smile, had several lucrative endorsement deals, including with an upstart cellphone company. The Cyber Culprit's post of images of Chuck and another man having sex with a woman at the same time put those endorsement deals in jeopardy. The fact that the images made it clear that both men had penetrated the woman, even though exactly how or where, had made matters worse. The background in the images looked vaguely familiar and I wanted to ask Mr. Gaines where the images had been recorded.

Chuck turned towards his gym, continuing to seek Pokémons. I knew better than to interrupt this endeavor in mid-quest if I wanted his full attention focused on answering my questions. He was wearing a skin-tight workout suit. It was light blue which accentuated rather than covered his thick chest, thick arm muscles and even thicker legs. Around his neck, he was wearing a thin silver chain with a small pendant at the end. His waist was slim; obviously he'd continued to work out after his playing days were over. His black head was shaved and glinted in the sunlight, almost as brightly as his teeth. Today he was scowling into his phone, so his face was hard to describe. But the photos I had seen of him showed symmetry and well-defined cheekbones. Without a doubt, Chuck Gaines was the type of man any healthy female, me especially, would want to have in her bed.

The former football player and present-day Poké-hunter twirled his finger on top of his phone, then swiped upward. He stared at his phone for a moment, a look of triumph spreading across his face and I stepped forward, holding out my hand. "Mr. Gaines?"

Chuck looked me up and down, took my proffered hand and continued to look me up and down as he shook it. I was glad that I'd taken the time to research his preferred type. He was still into cheerleaders, so I'd worn running shoes, short bobby socks, an even shorter mini-skirt around my round hips and even rounder butt, and a Tshirt to accentuate my bounteous breasts. Best of all, the Tshirt was short enough to allow Chuck a glimpse of my belly button. At last his eyes stopped at my face, taking in my curly brown hair and red-lipped smile before concentrating on the sparkles inside my blue eyes.

"Miss?" he queried.

"Brandt. But friends call me 'Lee'."

"Lee it is then," he said, flashing me a broad smile.

"Mr. Gaines, I'm—"

"Call me 'Chuck'."

"Chuck." We exchanged smiles. He was still holding my hand and somehow we had drifted closer. I could feel his heat and his animal magnetism deep in my chest. "Chuck, I'm investigating the person or persons who recently exposed your private business all over the internet."

He stopped shaking my hand and took half a step back and I got a good look at the pendant at the bottom of the chain around his neck. It was the symbol of the invitation-only swingers club I'd seen on a documentary and been itching to be invited to ever since. But I joined Chuck in taking a step back. The photos of Michael Rayburn—boss and now lover—with another woman had made me promise myself that I would engage in sex with other men only when absolutely necessary, undercover investigation or no.

I could feel hot desire for Chuck brewing within my loins. But I clenched my jaw. A promise was a promise.

"Exposed my private business is right," said Chuck, shaking his head. "My very *private* business." He looked rueful as he held the door open for me. I did my best not to sway my hips as I entered in front of him. A wave of hot air hit me.

He moved behind the reception desk. I looked around the fitness center. There was a running track around the edge of the gym, exercise equipment in the middle. We were the only ones in the room. I pointed to the pendant around his neck. "That's for Club Rati, isn't it?"

Chuck nodded. "Named for the Hindu goddess of love and lust."

There was a pause. Did he want me to ask for an invitation? Was he thinking of inviting me? Heat between my legs hoped he was! Was my face betraying me?

But I regained my composure, "Do you have any idea how the photos of you ended up on the internet?"

"No."

"Was it on your computer?"

He nodded.

"Could we please see your computer?"

"We?"

"I have an assistant who specializes in information technology."

Chuck shrugged and moved to sit on a weight training machine and pulled down on the bar above his head. The muscles in his arms and neck bulged as he lifted the metal plates behind them. If they were labeled correctly, he had just lifted the equivalent of my entire weight.

He continued to lift and softly release the weights in a fluid motion. "You want to see my computer." There was no hint of strain in his voice — the man was fit!

I nodded. "If we can find the person who posted the photos of you, he will go to prison for a long, long time."

Chuck shrugged and moved to a stationary bicycle. His legs pumped with such ferocity that I thought that the spinning wheel might fly off. He was starting to sweat. On him, it looked good. "That won't put the genie back in the bottle, though, will it?" he asked. Again, there was no hint of how much oxygen his legs were sucking out of his lungs.

"Genie back in the bottle?" My mother said that men are attracted to dumb women.

"Even if you catch this guy, you can't change the fact that the universe has seen me in the act of having group sex. And with a white woman to boot."

I slowly shook my head.

Chuck got off the bike, went to the front door, locked it,

turned the 'Open' sign to 'Closed' and watched me watch him return back behind the reception desk. It was all I could do not to shift weight from one foot to the other. He unlocked a drawer at the bottom and lifted out a laptop computer which he placed on top of the reception desk.

Chuck pointed to the laptop, "The photos which were posted to the internet, and their connection to other photos, how they're stored, how and when they were accessed, all of that's important to your investigation?"

"Yes sir," I nodded. "It's all important."

"You want me to be open with you, show you *all* my photos, tell you the names of the people in the photos, all that?"

I nodded.

"Then don't you think that you have to be open with me?"

I took my phone out. "You want to see my photos?"

He chuckled, then pointed a circle around me with his finger. "I want to see you, *all* of you."

"Sex?" I asked. My heart was beating, hoping, begging that that was what Chuck was demanding. If I had no choice, my conscience would be clear.

For a moment I wonder about the woman who'd been with Michael. But Chuck's gleaming smile and nodding head erases everything but the present moment.

He makes a circle with his fingers to take in my shirt and skirt. "Let's see your routine."

I smile back at him, put my hands on my hips and take a deep breath. My skirt is black, everything else white, the colors of the now-defunct Macon Marauders football team. "M," I shout as I begin to rotate my hips, "A" as my hips extend in the other direction. When I get to the next "A," I thrust my hips forward.

"The Macon Marauders?"

My answer is to quickly finish spelling out the team's name, making sure that Chuck's eyes remain transfixed on my skirt. Then I shout, "Macon!" and kick my right leg up as far as I can. "Macon!" I propel my left leg off the floor—

He holds up his hand. "Stop!"

I bring my leg down and stumble. What's the—?! A drop of sweat trickles down my spine.

Chuck points at my skirt. "Red is not a Marauders color."

I suddenly remember that the first stitch of clothing I'd put on that morning was a red thong. I smile, reach under my skirt, walk out of my thong and fling it at his face. But it lands short of its target. We both look down at the thong, then raise our heads until we're looking into each other's eyes.

"That uniform violation will cost you ten pushups."

I drop to the floor and proceed to start with the pushups. Full-body pushups, not the 'girl' version. At five, he walks beside me. At six, he lifts my skirt up and my bum is suddenly cold. At seven he starts to caress up my legs. His hands reach my bum as I complete my punishment.

I roll over and smooth my skirt down, looking up at him, determined not to take the initiative.

He helps me up and leads me to a set of pull up bars. I step up, lay my forearms flat and begin to raise my legs extended straight forward in his direction, forcing him to step back.

"Spread your legs," he commands, spreading his arms to emphasize his point.

I spread my legs and feel a breeze up and down my sex as I continue to lift my legs up and down. It's harder with my legs spread, but I resolve not to complain.

Chuck steps between my legs as they're halfway up, slides two hands under my skirt, cupping my butt and lifts my sex to the level of his nose. I relax my knees, resting my heels on his back. He holds me there for a moment, reveling in his mastery of me. I shut my eyes and melt into his control.

His tongue touches first, just the tip. One cell on his body, one cell on mine. The tip of his tongue on the center of my left pussy lip. Then he lifts me up and the single cell of his tongue tickles jolts down my left pussy lip, engorging it to double the size of its mate.

When he reaches the bottom of my pussy lips, he holds me still a moment.

"Don't stop!" I beg.

He flicks his tongue back and forth, sending tingles up my heretofore pure right pussy lip.

"More!" I plead.

He pulls me forward until his entire tongue is pressed against the bottom of my pussy. Then he slowly lowers me so that his tongue licks up the length of my pussy. Up and down he lifts me. I'm so hot I can feel my juices dribble onto his tongue. He lifts me as if I'm a barbell and he's doing reps. Every muscle in my body starts to go slack. Except inside where I'm tighter and tighter each time he slides me up and down his tongue.

I'm on the verge of climax when he lowers me down to the floor. I mash myself against him, against his swollen cock underneath the thin material of his exercise outfit, desperate for enough sensation to finish what he's started. But he pushes me away, holds my hands above my head with one hand and turns me around away from him with the other. A sharp thwack envelopes my bottom with sharp hot pain.

Chuck turns me back facing him. "Now you're going to run. If you don't run fast enough, you'll feel more of my hand hard on your ass. If you run well, you'll reap the rewards of your exertion."

He turns me towards the track and I'm off and running before he can aim another blow at my bottom. It's not that I wouldn't have enjoyed a good spanking, but that wasn't the game we we're playing.

The gym is hot and I'm sweating profusely as I round the second corner. He passes me on the straightaway. He'd stripped down to his jock strap and his butt jiggles invitingly above the two white straps separating his ebony bum from his thighs. I speed up and manage to touch his butt. For a moment, I can feel his hard power pumping him forward. Then he accelerates away and I'm touching only air.

Suddenly he turns and I crash into him and we fall to the track. But he's anticipated and breaks our fall gently. His hands quickly strip off my shirt and bra, the perfect mixture of accomplished dexterity and animal savagery. The part of me that's already nude is the hottest, wet with anticipation of the ferocious fucking she's about to receive!

He turns me around to unclasp my skirt and I feel it slide down my legs as I turn around towards him. Thwack! Hard and hot on my bottom. I complete my turn, but gingerly, to avoid the spot he's just spanked.

He's standing over me, his cock expanding his jock strap as far as it will go. "I'm going to run and you'd better follow. Fast. If I catch you again, your ass'll be getting more than one light little swat!"

He's around he first corner before I scramble to my feet. He isn't running fast, but he'd already established that he can easily outrun me. And that was before my bouncing boobs were slowing me down.

Then I saw it. A bottle of water! By the side of the track. I grab it up. Chuck is gaining on me. I hold the water to my boobs and pump my legs as fast as I can. Chuck is only a few paces behind. The part of the track which goes through a series of padded mats is just ahead. I can almost feel Chuck hand swatting my butt. I reach the edge of the padded mats, get the water open and spray the track.

Chuck slips, slides and careens onto the mats to the right of the running track. He lies there, not moving. Have I hurt him?!? I race over to check—

As soon as I touch him, Chuck grabs both my wrists and pulls me under him. He straddles my torso and pins both wrists to the mat. "So, little Lee's a trickster, is she?" he sneers down at me.

"It wasn't fair. You knew I couldn't outrun you."

"And so you think you can out-wrestle me?"

"No, I, but..."

He sits back, relieving some of the pressure on my wrists. I try to struggle, but all that accomplishes is to jiggle my boobs.

Suddenly, I'm on my tummy. I have no clue as to how he's accomplished this, but one hand is holding both my wrists tight, his legs have trapped my left leg, his free hand is caressing my butt and he's whispering into my ear, "You may not be able to out-wrestle me, but you'd better try!"

With that, he administers a sharp thwack to my butt and shoves me away. His sweat has made him slippery and the force of his shove pushed him onto his back. I seize my chance and climb on top of him, right angles across his chest.

Ordinarily, he'd be able to push me off with ease, but now all his efforts accomplish is to slip and slide our flesh against each other. My nipples harden and trace little patterns all over his chest. I get the hang of it and manage to counter each of his moves. His cock below is still in his jock strap, but I manage to lift the top of his underwear up and over and he springs free. He's at least twelve inches of wide hard heaven, twice as black as the rest of his skin.

But I've shifted out of position and he slides me off him. I grab for something but all my fingers grasp is his jock strap which slips off his feet. Now I'm on my stomach and he's pressing down on my back, his cock between my legs.

"Maybe it's not a spanking your ass needs," he whispers. "Maybe it's a good fucking."

"You're too big," I tell him.

"Spread your legs." His tone leaves no room for anything other than instant obedience.

I spread my legs, dreading the imminent assault on my back door. But he's shifted out of position! I turn onto my back, slide down his body, and take his cock between my lips. For added security, I grab onto his balls and hold on tight. I lick his sweaty cock. He tries to lift himself up. I squeeze his balls and he holds himself completely motionless. I lick until there's no more salty sweat left, but it's an awkward position, so I slide out from underneath, being careful to maintain my grip on his balls.

"On your back," I tell him and he complies. I suck up

and down his cock until he moans. All and well for him, but I'm not getting any, so I rotate around his cock, lift one leg up and over his head an press my pussy against his mouth.

I realize my mistake just as I was settling in. I'd released his balls. In an instant I'm on my back. Chuck has two fingers in my cunt and is holding my arms above my head with his other hand. I try to wriggle free, but once again, his legs have captured my left leg and I'm powerless to escape. He fucks me vigorously with his fingers. It feels good, actually *really* good, but what I want is his cock, not his fingers, inside me.

I use all my force to try to wrench myself free, but he's holding me too tight. "Too bad," I tell him.

"I'm not the one on my back having her cunt violated."

"Maybe I like having my cunt *vio la ted*." And I did. An orgasm begins to swirl around his fingers.

He picks up the tempo with his fingers. "You're the one who can't escape."

I was almost on the edge. "If you can't spank me, I don't need to escape." I had decided that it would be best not to taunt him with his other threat. Maybe then he'd leave my back door alone.

He withdraws his fingers from my cunt, lets go of my arms, puts one hand under my shoulders, the other under my hips and starts to turn me over. I resist by spreading my legs except he just pulls harder. But that is all I needed. I go with the flow and end up on my back again. But he's out of position, falling forward. I slide down and grab his cock with one hand and his balls with the other as he puts his arms out to break his fall.

"Surrender," I demand. "Complete, final and unconditional!"

He tries to wriggle free, but my squeeze terminates his efforts.

"I surrender," he wheezes.

"You promise not to escape?"

He nods, his head hanging.

"On your back," I tell him.

He flops over on his back and I climb on top of him. I straddle his cock, positioning it between my pussy lips. He's hard but dry. I rock my hips, ever so slightly and feel the head of his cock caress my pussy lips. His cock is now wet and slippery and I introduce it inside me. He's too thick for me to slide myself quickly down his shaft, but the discomfort of accommodating his girth is delicious.

Halfway down Chuck's cock, the discomfort turns to joy and I slide myself the rest of the way down his magnificent phallus. Up and down, his cock pushing and caressing all of my pleasure spots together, then sucking them back out along with his cock. Up and down his shaft I slide, savoring each sensation. I bring my knees off the floor and lie flat along the entire length of his body, our sweat providing enough lubrication for me to slide up and down.

Chuck bucks up from below, encouraging me to go faster, but I ignore the hint, intent on relishing every sensation of the magnificent maleness inside me.

"Faster," he pleads.

"That's as fast as I can go."

"Faster."

"I want it slow. You surrendered, remember?"

"Faster!" All trace of request has vanished from his voice. If he had surrendered before, now he's on the verge of revolt.

I try to speed up.

"Faster!" He bucks up against me and I almost fall off. I spread my legs and return my knees to the floor. This allows me to increase the length and speed of my ascents and descents.

But it's not enough for Chuck's taste. Seemingly without any effort on his part, he lifts me up, then pulls me down and under him as he performs the complimentary motion. I beat my fists against his chest. He ignores me, spreads my leg and slams himself into me. His revolt is complete. I try to hit him again, but when he withdraws his cock, he sucks all my life force out with it.

Three more thrusts and I join the revolution. Chuck's cock twists my cunt, caressing my clit deep inside. I want to come, to give myself to the powerful plungings of his cock, but it's so powerful that it corrals my climax and refuses to let her go. Each thrust stokes my fires hotter and higher inside their glorious prison.

Then he shudders and stops. His spunk spurts inside. My climax is released and I feel wave after wave undulate along his entire shaft. My climax does not escape my pelvis, but expends its full force inside my cunt. Its wrenching contractions are just short of painful. I cannot move a muscle.

Chuck collapses on top of me, then slowly slides off. After an eternity, we begin to breathe again.

The next afternoon, my assistant Eric and I were at my dining room table reviewing the contents of Chuck's laptop. Eric had his larger laptop hooked up to Chuck's to perform a plethora of diagnostics in the background.

There were a wide variety of photos on Chuck's computer. Some were innocent, including from his NFL days. If you could call brain-jarring hits innocent. There was a road trip through Louisiana ending in the Fat Tuesday parade. A set of costume—cosplay—shots included women dressed as Cinderella and Sailor Moon kissing Chuck. He was dressed as Blade, biceps and deltoids bulging under his breastplate, and looked even better than Wesley Snipes. There were numerous solo shots of Chuck, some nude, occasionally showing him erect. I made a mental note to save one for my private collection. Then there were the sex photos, most clearly heterosexual, but some equivocal. There were women of all shapes, sizes, ages and races. Most, but not all of the photos included Chuck.

Eric toggled the screen to monitor the diagnostics he was running and I shifted to my own computer. I was running a background check on Michael Rayburn, the lawyer who'd given me the Cyber Culprit case, my first and only case. Back then, my former partner had just dumped me and all I had were bills. As the case had picked up steam, I had hired Eric to provide assistance. Michael and I had recently become lovers but the picture of him with another woman had made me concerned that I might have misjudged him.

Initial checks had disclosed that the other woman, the elegant and skinny blonde woman Michael had been seen kissing, was Gretchen Hughes, the successful manager of an A-list hotel. To make matters worse, she was Michael's former girlfriend.

Eric had made some generic suggestions to get me started on my background searches, but as soon as I had entered them, a remote 'bot had appeared on my computer screen and had given me even better suggestions. The 'bot appeared to be able to access any and all databases, including police, commercial and proprietary databases at will.

I searched high and low, driven to find out anything and everything I could about Michael and Gretchen. I pursued each new avenue that opened up. But I prayed that I wouldn't find anything bad about Michael, especially anything that might cause us to lose our one and only case.

Michael had never told me about Gretchen. And he had certainly never told me that he had been *engaged* to her! I took another look at the photo which had been posted to the internet. Michael and Gretchen certainly had their heads very close together. And they certainly appeared to be kissing!

But that was it. There was nothing in my background check to indicate that Michael was other than the squeaky clean and successful lawyer he appeared to be. And there was nothing to indicate that Gretchen had ever done anything wrong.

The 'bot which had been helping me do background searches on Michael and Gretchen vanished from my screen and I brought up the image of Michael and Gretchen kissing. I stared at their lips and zoomed on to where they appeared to be touching. There was certainly nothing to indicate that he was being forced to kiss her. Not like with Chuck. Sex with Chuck had been *necessary* for the investigation.

I sighed. No point in torturing myself. I got up and stood behind Eric. I couldn't make head nor tail of the boxes and streaming words and numbers on his screen. "Progress?" I asked.

"Too early to tell." None of his red/orange hairs had moved. His thin shoulders remained motionless. "It could take several hours before I have even a hint of anything."

I looked at my watch. It was almost six-thirty. Michael should be at his apartment. And he should be *alone*. Time for an unannounced visit.

Michael was alone when I entered his apartment and he seemed genuinely pleased to see me. Still, I decided that a direct interrogation was in order. I pulled out my phone, called up the image of him kissing Gretchen, and turned the screen towards him. "Who's this?" I asked.

He gave me an odd look and ushered me to a chair at the kitchen table where we sat down opposite each other.

"Her name is Gretchen Hughes. She's a friend. She needed my help."

I turned my phone back towards him. "And that help required kissing?!"

"No." He was being excessively patient. "It required whispering."

"What kind of help?"

"Lee, that's solicitor-client privileged."

"Is it *solicitor-client privileged* that she's your former girlfriend?"

"No." He let his answer hang.

"Michael."

"Lee, what is this about? How did you get this photo?"

"What it's about, you tell me. The photo was emailed to me anonymously."

"There's nothing going on between me and Gretchen." He took a deep breath. "I swear."

I looked into his eyes. I didn't think he was lying. I let the tension drain from my shoulders.

A smile flashed across his lips. "You're jealous!"

I shook my head, but he had already begun a sing-song chant of, "Lee is jealous, Lee is jealous, Lee is jealous. Lee is *jealous*!"

"I am not jealous!"

He has stood up, I've stood up, and we're facing each other, me shouting, he sing-song mocking, "Lee is jealous."

"Am not."

"You are to!"

"I am not."

"Are to."

"Am not!"

"Are to!"

"Am—" But he's begun to tickle me under my ribs and I can't get another word in.

"Are *to*."

"I am not jealou—" Now he's moved his fingers up to my armpits, where I'm really ticklish and I can barely breathe. Worse, my thrashing is brushing his hands against my breasts and the whole effect is turning me on big time!

I step back and try to wriggle free, to hold onto my anger at his philandering with Gretchen, but he steps forward and pins me against the wall.

"Jealous," he mocks me. His leg moves between my legs. His fingers tickle my armpits without mercy.

"Not!" But my wiggling is brushing my breasts against his hands and against his chest, my nipples begging to be released from my bra.

Then he kisses me, just lightly on the lips, but firmly enough to ignite the fire of past kisses. He pulls back. "Are you jealous?"

I teeter on the edge between jealous rage and unbearable desire, my mind demanding answers, my body demanding something else entirely.

He kisses me again. I struggle mightily but lust overwhelms intellect and I press my crotch against his leg uniting the fires sparking along my lips with those simmering inside my sex. I shut my eyes to savor the heat building over every inch of my skin.

I feel his fingers unbuttoning my blouse. I resolve that his punishment for Gretchen will be to force him to do the work in undressing, undressing both of us. My blouse drops to the floor. And when we're nude, when his punishment's complete, when Gretchen's banished into distant memory, all will be forgiven. My bra is unbuttoned and it too slides to the floor. Warm lips kiss my nipples. Warm wet mouth sucks them inside turning my knees to jelly, pressing our bodies together.

I feel myself being led, and I follow willingly, opening my eyes just a crack. In the bedroom, he pulls down on my stretch pants and panties all at once as he lays me on the bed. I shut my eyes and feel him caress my feet as he removes my shoes, little jolts going up my legs and into the bottom of my spine.

His touch has vanished. I open my eyes and watch him carefully, but quickly, remove his clothes and lay them on a chair. His body is lean and tall, his muscles understated but sexy. There is lust in his blue eyes and his full, well-formed lips are smiling in anticipation. At the top of his legs, his prominent phallus makes it clear just what he's anticipating!

Michael climbs on top of the bed and lightly runs his hands up the length of my body. His touch is devotion as opposed to Chuck's exertion of mastery. And his devotion includes pleasuring my pussy as he ascends, unlike Chuck who made me beg and scream for his touch. I surrender to his eyes watching me as his eyes surrender to mine.

His fingers dance up to my tummy and onto my breasts where they squeeze and knead, fanning the flames lapping against my body and bringing the passions inside my pussy to their boiling point. In a moment, his fingers have fluttered back down to my pubic hair where they fluff and gently pull up on my delicate curls. I feel the wetness inside me even before his penetrating fingers confirm my readiness. His cock sways as he adjusts his position and I arch my hips, ready for it to plunge inside.

But his fingers want more—the greedy little buggers! The two already there stay inside my pussy and begin to search for my g-spot. The fingers from his other hand pull up on my pussy hair, then slide lower to caress the sides of my clit and up and down my pussy lips. I feel everything tighten inside.

Michael's been here before, he knows what to do. His fingers find the key to my pleasure, tap on it three times and the tightness releases in three sharp and two gentle pulses.

I take a deep breath. This is just the first stage. This is just Michael ensuring my pleasure so that he can concentrate on his own. After a few strokes without additional pulsations, Michael withdraws his fingers and wipes them on his leg. He re-inserts them and again wipes them on his leg. Once more and he's satisfied that there'll be enough friction.

He lies down on top of me and slides himself inside. Not a quick ramming, not a slow tease, just right: just enough that I have time to feel him fill me, just enough force that I feel him against my pussy lips, just enough penetration that I feel our pubic bones touch, just enough to ensure the first gentle upward pull 'round my clit. And he's got the lubrication just right—enough friction that I can feel him, but enough lubrication that I'm protected from even a twinge of discomfort.

Michael's thrusts are designed to maximize his pleasure: out so that his penis head remains inside me and in just until our pubic bones touch. I relax into being fucked and concentrate on accumulating just enough sensation that I'll have gathered more than enough for an explosive orgasm when the time comes.

Michael continues to thrust in and withdraw out in steady rhythm. He's not breathing hard, there's only a hint on a flush on his chest. Delight is in his eyes, enjoyment on his lips. Intermittently, he bends to kiss me and I use these moments to rock my pelvis upwards to force his pubic bone to steal pleasure into my clit.

One moment, he's slow and steady. The next, Michael

is pumping as fast as he can, gasping air into his lungs. His face and chest are flushed. Is he coming too soon, have I had enough time? I press myself upwards and grind our pelvic bones together. His thrusts are erratic and he lacks the control to hold us apart. Pleasure is swirling through the top of my clit into my pussy, roiling and contracting.

Just one more minute, one more minute and I'll have enough. Michael's cock is hot! Heat is being rubbed into the length of my cunt, contract— Then he shudders and stops. I press up, I squeeze, for him, for me. Then he's pumping again, releasing his spunk into me.

I trip the switch to my own orgasm, I'm not quite ready, but it's now or never. In a moment he'll be spent, flopped beside me, heaving air into his lungs. It's not the explosive orgasm, I strive for. But it's different, nice. Warm waves flow outward from my pussy. The waves envelope both of us, connect us, seal our love.

It was hours—days?—later before Michael turned his phone back on. Well, this was certainly progress! I had been his sole focus of attention. But then his phone beeped wildly. He tried to scroll through what seemed to be a large number of texts as new texts flooded in.

I turned my own phone on and Eric was immediately on the line. "There's been a layered attack. On a hospital! This is serious!" He paused to suck air into his lungs— apparently he hadn't had much there before he'd started the conversation.

"Eric! Slow down. Start from the beginning. What's a layered attack?"

"It's a multi-staged attack." Eric had slowed down, but at least he was breathing normally. "This one started off, as many do, as a phishing scheme designed to get staff to turn over their passwords or to click on a malware link. This provoked the usual cautioning emails from IT warning staff about how to spot phishing schemes and what to do if they suspected an attempt at hacking."

"That's pretty standard, isn't it?"

"Yes. But here, the second stage took place while the hospital's IT center was distracted by the phishing attack. The hackers mapped the hospital's entire network."

"And a map is a big deal because?"

"It can be used to plan another, deeper hack into the hospital. The hospital can be forced to pay a ransom to get the plan back. Or the hacker can sell the network map on the dark web."

"The dark web?"

"The part of the internet where the bad buys hang out, the part not mapped by Google."

"Okay, so a hospital got hacked. Why is this our concern?"

"It was hacked by the Cyber Culprit."

"How do you know that?"

"Because he made a post bragging how he did it. As usual, he posted a photo of someone engaged in embarrassing behavior."

Eric texted me a link. The Cyber Culprit's personal target was a doctor. I recognized him; he was the anesthesiologist who had botched my aunt's operation three years ago. There were two photos: in the first, Doctor Serturner was checking a text on his phone in the middle of an operation, in the other he was dressed as a Superman knock-off at a Cosplay Ball. The same Cosplay Ball Chuck Gaines had attended as Blade.

Cosplay, Lusty Lee Log #18

Our trip to the hospital was like slamming into a stone wall. The Cyber Culprit had hit the hospital with a serious and multi-staged attack. The hack had resulted in the hospital's databases being breached with the result that its financial, operational and disciplinary records had been compromised. Worse, there was evidence that the hacker had accessed patients' medical records.

Eric and I had attended the IT department first. They took my red-haired assistant and I into a small room. I sat and watched as tech after tech came in and spewed jargon at Eric. After an hour, there was a pause and I turned to Eric, "Anything useful?" I asked.

He shook his head. "Nothing. They're blowing hot air. They won't disclose the vulnerability which CC exploited. Every question leads to a vague description of the steps they've taken to ensure that there will never be another attack."

"It sounded pretty specific to me."

"In theory, I suppose. But in terms of information which might actually be useful, no."

Our next stop was an attempt to meet with the anesthesiologist who'd been featured in CC's latest hack. The unflattering photo had showed him dressed as a comic book superhero at a cosplay ball. Doctor Serturner had botched my aunt's operation three years ago, so we had agreed that Eric would do the talking. Safer for Serturner, not to mention hospital property, that way.

At the Department of Anesthesiology, Eric bent over the desk and smiled at the receptionist. "We'd like to see Doctor Serturner, please," he asked.

"Do you have an appointment?"

"You mean like phoning ahead?"

She nodded her head, sending the purple ribbon she had tied in it flapping. She was also a redhead and appeared to be enjoying the chance to flirt with Eric.

"What, and lose the chance to meet you?"

She blushed and lowered her head. But her smile was unmistakable. She pretended to be looking in a date book to give herself a chance to recover. When she looked up she had managed to regain partial control of her smile. "I'm Megan," she told him.

"Eric."

They stared into each other's eyes for what seemed to be an eternity. I was about to clear my throat when she glanced back down at her date book.

"Doctor Serturner is not here now," whispered Megan.

Eric bent closer, "When will he be in?" he whispered back.

"Not until next week. He never comes in before the ball."

"The ball?"

"The Kosu Panplay ball."

At that moment a white-coated doctor rushed up and we had to cede our position in front of Megan's desk. But Eric had seen the look on my face. "What's so special about this cosplay?" he asked.

"How do you know it's a costume play party?" I temporized.

"'Kosu' is Japanese for costume."

"My nerd-in-chief knows Japanese but hasn't heard of the *Kosu Panplay*?"

"No."

Eric's admission was so complete and unaffected that I had no choice but to tell him. "The Kosu Panplay is an underground, actually *the* underground, costume play party. Very upscale. Advertising is by word of mouth only and you need someone to vouch for you to get an invitation."

"And the 'Pan'? Why Pan instead of Cos?"

"It means that the play is pan-sexual, open for all genders and sexual orientations."

A few phone calls secured invitations to the cosplay for Eric and I. It was located at a gated resort outside of the city that had been taken over for the event. So there was a large ballroom with several smaller rooms available for private rental. Guests could also book a room to stay overnight.

I was dressed as Harley Quinn, a character for whom my five-foot five buxom and curvaceous body was perfectly suited. My blue eyes and curly brown hair conveyed Harley's mischievous sexuality and unpredictable personality perfectly. My top, was a red and black latex bustier with clasps starting just above my belly button and ending between my breasts. Around my hips was a shorter than short latex miniskirt, red black and white, pleated so that it would float up as I pranced around from man to man. My left legging was mostly black with red and white diamonds around the top; the right legging was mostly red with white and black diamonds on the top.

Eric was aptly cast as Jimmy Olsen, Clark Kent's nerdy and bumbling cub reporter side-kick. His lanky six-foot three frame was encased in a tight-fitting shirt the sleeves of which ended well above his wrists. His sports jacket was even smaller. The red bowtie suited him perfectly; I'd have to buy him a green one for Christmas.

Some cosplayers were masked, some not. A Japanese couple, dressed as clowns, made a raucous entrance. He was roly-poly, she thin. They were both wearing bright orange tights with blue polka dots and equally tight-fitting tops, red with the same blue polka dots. Each sported a bight green acrylic wig that wobbled when they walked.

Chuck Gaines, the buff former linebacker who'd tipped me off to this party, strolled in with a cheerleader on his arm and I waved him over. I pointed to Eric and the two men shook hands, "Chuck, this is my assistant, Eric." Chuck didn't introduce us to his cheerleader who was busy flirting with all and sundry but he did promise to keep his eyes open and to tell us if he saw anything.

I spotted Doctor Serturner on the far side of the room. He was dressed as Superman. This time he'd sprung for a real Superman costume. I estimated him to be just under six feet tall, black hair, oiled and combed back. He looked fit under the thin spandex of the costume which didn't appear to have any padding. His face was contorted into a glare, directed at his arch nemesis, Lex Luthor.

Lex Luthor, being a mere mortal, was wearing a warsuit which, in the comics, would provide him with protection and a set of weapons. Tonight, the warsuit consisted of a purple body-suit with a green thong and green gloves. Over this was a hard multi-layered breastplate with numerous metal rings which extended into a backpack. His head was covered by a semi-soft mesh hood which masked his face but allowed his shaved skull to shine through. Lex oozed danger, power, and an evil sensuality.

Lex was accompanied by a dark-haired Amazonian woman dressed in black pleather leggings and a revealing red latex top. She had firm round breasts. We were drifting in their direction.

I nudged Eric, pointed to the woman and asked, "Who's that with Lex Luthor?"

Eric took out his reporter's notebook and pretended to read. "Mr. Luthor took DNA from Lois Lane and layered it over a robot. Loisbot. Then—"

"Wasn't Lois Lane Superman's girlfriend?"

"That was before." He returned his notebook to his jacket pocket.

"If she's a robot with DNA, doesn't that make her an android?"

Eric ignored my question. "Luthor gave her a conscience in an effort to balance his psychopathy." He stepped away from me and held his hand out for Superman to shake.

Serturner took Eric's hands and shook it vigorously. "Hi, Jimmy," he beamed. They don't notice Lex and his Loisbot edging closer.

"Golly! Superman!" Eric took his notebook out and held a pen over the open page. "May I ask you a few questions?"

Serturner nodded. "Anything for the press."

"What's it like protecting Metropolis?"

"Well, Jimmy, it's—"

At that moment Loisbot took Eric by the ear and pulled him down to her face. "Superman has more important things to do than to answer stupid questions."

The Kosu Panplay obviously involved active role-play in addition to the usual prancing around in costumes. This would be fun!

I grabbed both of Loisbot's ears and pulled. "Let him go!"

But before I could do anything more, I felt two strong hands take my wrists and pull them up and back. I was about to wrench my right wrist free when I heard a 'click' and felt it restrained by cold steel. A moment later, the same thing happened to my left wrist.

All I could see was purple leggings behind and below me. I presumed that I had been captured by Lex Luthor's warsuit. Loisbot turned around, grabbed both my ears, and kissed me full on my lips. Her tongue darts inside, warm and wet and hungry.

Eric pulls her off me. "Hey, that's not nice!" he protests.

Loisbot aims a hard uppercut in Eric's direction, but she misses and makes it obvious that she intended to miss.

Eric, playing Jimmy Olsen's lack of co-ordination perfectly, reels from the 'punch' and stumbles back into Superman Serturner's arms. Serturner holds Eric carefully, almost lovingly. The two men look into each other's eyes.

Serturner's gay! I quickly calculate ways to turn this to our advantage. The two men kiss.

Loisbot returns in front of me and grabs my breasts. Even through the latex, her hands are hot. Eric spots her and pulls back on her shoulder.

"Careful!" warns Serturner. "She has the strength of six men!"

Loisbot gets Eric to the floor where they wrestle. A group of onlookers gather.

"Is your friend gay?" Lex Luthor asks from behind me.
"Bisexual."
"Then he's about to have the time of his life."

Jimmy and the Loisbot wrestle vigorously on the floor. I quickly realize that they're not trying to hurt each other. And their efforts to gain the upper hand over each other are diluted by their efforts to feel each other up. Eric loses his jacket and Loisbot rips the buttons off the front of his shirt with her talons. But she's out of position and Eric pulls her top far enough up her arms that the only way she can wriggle free is to let him pull it the rest of the way over her head.

There's padding in the front of her top and Loisbot's real breasts are small, vaguely male. There are wisps of hair in the center of her chest. For the first time I notice the hint of an Adam's apple on Loisbot's throat.

"Loisbot is a guy?!?" I blurt out.

Behind me Lex chuckles. "Transsexual, actually. He's moving from male to female, but hasn't had any surgery yet."

"Surely those aren't the boobs he was born with?"

"Hormones can do wonders."

Loisbot has Eric by his hair with one hand and with the other she — he — pulls down Eric's pants and releases his fully erect cock. Loisbot slides his leggings down brings Eric's head to his own cock and it slowly disappears down Eric's throat. Both men moan. The crowd cheers. Pan — pansexual — play for real! More and more partygoers crowd around and I lose sight of the two men.

I rub my bum against Lex's crotch and smile when I feel something hardening. "Do you think I'm beautiful?" I ask.

"Do *you* think you're beautiful?" responds Lex.

"What does it matter what *I* think?"

"If you want to be truly beautiful, you have to let yourself shine though."

"Seriously, do you think I'm beautiful?"

"It matters more what *you* think."

Lex puts his hands on my hips and begins to move us forward through the crowd. Superman pulls Loisbot's hand away from Eric's hair. Even though he's been released, Eric continues giving Loisbot a blowjob until Superman administers a fake uppercut to Loisbot which staggers the android backwards. Before Loisbot can recover, Superman places him in a full nelson. Eric fits Loisbot with a cock ring.

Lex marches us forward until I'm so close to the combatants that I can smell them. If my hands were free, I'd pinch one of Loisbot's nipples. Lex fishes something out of a pocket. It's a small rock emitting a golden glow.

"Gold kryptonite," gasps Eric.

"Gold kryptonite!" exults Loisbot as he wrests himself free of Superman's grip.

"No superpowers for half an hour," gloats Lex.

Loisbot strides over to me, glorying in his triumph and my helplessness. He's completely nude. Except for his nascent breasts, his body is hard gristle and muscle. He presses against me and I feel his cock slip under my skirt. Once again he kisses me full on the mouth. I extend my tongue forward, but his voracious counterpart mashes it back inside my mouth. His hands work at the clasps of my top and in a moment my breasts are almost entirely free, restrained only slightly by the one remaining clasp atop my belly button.

His kisses are so intense I'm barely aware that hands are on my butt, under my skirt and caressing my breasts. Somehow my panties have been removed. I'm hot all over but the power of his kiss is concentrating feeling inside my mouth leaving my pussy in only the initial stages of arousal.

Suddenly my mouth is free and Loisbot clasps one of my breasts between her hands. Only now am I aware that his mouth has tasted of hot ginger tea. I gasp air into my lungs. But before I can exhale, his lips have clamped onto the nipple of the breast he's holding. He sucks in and roughly rakes the coarse topside of his tongue across my nipple.

Now the jolt goes down to my pussy and I feel other fingers gently fondling up and down my pussy lips. The first hints of wetness join the heat inside.

Loisbot releases my nipple, then my breast. His hands clasp my other breast. The longest of the fingers down below presses gently but firmly against the center of my pussy.

Again Loisbot clamps his mouth over both nipple and areola and sucks. This time he uses the soft underside of his tongue and the sensation is warm wetness instead of hard electricity. I shut my eyes. Below the finger moves a millimeter inside. Coarse raking roughness across my nipples jolts my eyes open as a flash of searing heat shoots through my breast. He rakes his tongue against my nipple again sending a series of jolts into my pussy. Below the finger slides an inch inside her.

"Want to get fucked?" asks Lex from behind.

"Isn't that what we're all here for?" I respond, rubbing my butt against his protuberance.

Loisbot steps back, leering at me. He flicks his long hair behind each shoulder and caresses his mini-breasts. He finds a condom, from where I can't see, quickly rolls it down over his cock and then steps forward, pressing his body into mine. The smell of his sweat is laced with ginger which softens it but also adds a piquant edge. He's hard and firm, except for his baby breasts. He takes a deep breath that sounds loud in the moment.

Loisbot dips his legs, I spread mine and he slides effortlessly inside. His body is hot, as if some inner fire is burning him alive. His thrusts are equally ferocious and I have to angle my hips to prevent him from hurting me.

I'm about to ask him about his upcoming surgery, trying to figure out how to ask in a way that doesn't come across as 'why would you want to cut off such an impressive cock' when his thrusts shudder to a stop. But the pause is only momentarily. He jabs inside with even more force, fast and hard, accelerating. Five more thrusts and he shudders again, then stops. In pulling himself out, he almost collapses to the floor, but recovers. The tip of his condom is filled with whitish spunk.

"Give me a hand," demands Lex.

It's obvious that Lex is talking to Loisbot as my hands are still chained to Lex's chest. Loisbot goes behind Lex. Removing items from Lex's backpack? There's a series of metal sliding into other metal and snapping into place. Something curved slides behind each of my thighs. Below, there's a strut support angling forward and away from Lex down to the floor.

"Lift her up," commands Lex.

Loisbot lifts my left leg off the floor and onto the curved support which is soft but firm. He follows suit with the other leg and I'm completely in sitting position, my thighs resting on the curved supports. Loisbot steps back as Lex ratchets me first up and then back down.

Loisbot is about to nod when two pairs of hands grab his arms. One pair is Eric's, the other Superman's. Lube emerges from one direction, condoms from the other. From somewhere else a padded sawhorse appears. Jimmy bends Loisbot face-first over the sawhorse and kicks his legs apart. Superman applies copious amounts of lube on and into Loisbot's ass.

I feel glee in the pit of my stomach. Let's see how Loisbot does on the receiving end!

Eric and Superman do rock-paper-scissors. Eric ends up with a closed fist, Superman with two fingers spread in a flat 'V'. Rock beats scissors.

"Ever seen your friend fuck someone before?" Lex asks from behind.

"A woman. Once."

"Does the thought of seeing him fuck someone who's just fucked you turn you on?"

The question brings a sudden flush to my body. I nod.

Lex's hands are gently caressing my arms and into my armpits. Our sweat is mixing together, pungent. His touch is gentle and firm. It's clear he knows when and how to touch me for maximum effect. "You're beautiful," he tells me, his voice soft and deep.

Eric sidles up behind Loisbot, quickly rolls a condom over his cock, and positions his cock at the opening of Loisbot's anus. "Beg!" he demands.

Loisbot says something, but it's barely a whisper.

"Louder!" demands Eric.

"Fuck me!" This time Loisbot's compliance is unmistakable.

Eric presses gently at first, and slowly but surely his cock slides into Loisbot's ass.

"Fuck!" yells Loisbot, hanging his head.

Eric withdraws himself back out. His right hand is on Loisbot's back. Eric pulls on Loisbot's hair with his left forcing Loisbot to lift his head. Eric grunts and there's a cheer from the crowd.

Eric begins to methodically pound away at Loisbot's ass and Lex's fingers stray to my breasts. His hands are warm as he cups their undersides, slowly lifting and squeezing. Then his fingers separate and he circles around the outer edges, gradually moving closer and closer to the center. In front of us, sweat is beginning to run down Eric's back. Loisbot's hands are gripping the sawhorse, his knuckles white.

Lex reaches the outer edges of my areolae and he uses just the right amount of pressure to circle his fingers around their outer edges. As he moves towards my nipple, he alternates the amount of pressure. Every time he presses a bit harder I feel a jolt inside my pussy. It's as if Eric is fucking *my* pussy, not Loisbot's.

Lex reaches my nipples just as Eric picks up the pace. He squeezes and gently rotates, applying just enough pressure to avoid pinching and twisting. My pussy and nipples are as firmly in his control as are my wrists.

"Fuck!" cries Loisbot.

"Beg!" wheezes Eric, half bent over Loisbot.

"Fuck me!" responds Loisbot.

Eric pounds him savagely. I feel him pounding me. Eric stands straight up, ramrod still.

"Arragh!" yell each man in unison.

Eric pounds away again.

"Fuck!" they both yell.

"Fuck!" the crowd roars back.

Eric withdraws his penis from Loisbot's anus. Loisbot stands. Someone gives him a bottle of water which he quickly drains. Superman has removed his red bikini. There's a hole in his blue spandex bodysuit. He's facing Loisbot. Both men are fully erect. They play rock-paper-scissors, best two of three. Loisbot crushes Superman's scissors with his rock. Then Superman smothers Loisbot's rock with his paper. Third and deciding is a repeat of Superman smothering his opponent's rock.

Loisbot bends over the sawhorse. Superman applies a red condom to his cock. Thankfully for Loisbot, Superman's cock is slightly smaller than Eric's.

As Superman sidles next to Loisbot's ass, I feel myself being lowered. As Superman's red cock nestles up to Loisbot's anus, I feel Lex's cock touch my pussy lips. As Supercock's head presses inside Loisbot, Lex's cock edges inside me. As Supercock slowly but inexorably pegs Loisbot, my pussy is as slowly and surely impaled atop Lex's cock.

If penis size is the determinant, Lex would trounce Superman. My pussy is filled and warmed all at the same time. Lex and I have a limited range of motion, but if I rock forward while Lex rocks back, the sensations are marvelous. I'm thoroughly aroused and the first stirrings towards orgasm dance inside my pussy.

We sync up our movements to Supercock's thrusts. Watching Superman pegging Loisbot is the hottest mind fuck I've ever experienced. The fact that the fuckee had just fucked me makes it sizzle. The fact that I am being fucked at the same time makes it even hotter. Mind-fuck and fuck-fuck all at the same time!

Now that we have our rhythm established, Lex begins to fondle me with his hands. First he rakes his fingernails up and down the inside of my arms. Then he grabs my breasts and gives them gentle tugs and squeezes in time to our pelvic rockings. He twists my nipples, just to the point where I gasp. I try to wriggle free to touch his chest, to squeeze his nipples, to kiss his lips but no matter how hard I try, I can't break free. "Let me go!" I cry.

But all Lex does is laugh and tease my nipples all the more mercilessly. Below, he places his hands atop of my thighs, then presses down with one at the same time as he pulls up with the other, caressing my pussy lips against his shaft. Gradually, inch by inch, Lex is pushing me towards the edge and there's nothing I can do to resist.

Superman is pumping harder. There's a streak of sweat down the back of his tights. I tense my butt muscles to lift myself up and manage to increase our strokes by an inch. Lex does something and the length of our strokes increases another inch. He begins to rotate beneath me. Each rotation pushes me right to the edge, then claws me back again. But each rotation pushes me further away from safety. It's so hot — what I'm seeing, what I'm feeling — that I hold onto the moment as tightly as I can.

Superman shuddering to his orgasm breaks my grip. The first contraction rockets up my spine and out my temples. The second ricochets off the sides of my cunt, refusing to escape, bounces my butt up and down against Lex's pelvis, then dribbles into my thighs.

Behind me, Lex is thrusting as hard as he can into me. His arms are wrapped tightly around me. Inside my cunt, waves after waves squeeze up and down the shaft of the cock inside me. Gradually I breathe again and luxuriate in the warmth wrapped around my body.

The show in front of us is starting to break up. I hope that Eric had been in a better position than I to learn something about Serturner and why the Cyber Culprit was interested in him than I had been.

"Did you come?" whispers Lex.

"Yes," I whisper back. "It was wonderful." I take a languid breath, then remember my manners. "Did you come?"

"Not yet."

Lex adjusts something below us and we begin to wheel away, towards the wall. He's still inside me, still rock hard. Every step he takes tickles my pussy back to life. I redouble my efforts to wriggle free, to touch him, but my wrists are held fast.

At the wall, Lex puts straps around my thighs and cinches them tight. He lowers me until my feet touch the floor. Then he releases the portion of his warsuit contraption which had been attached to the thigh supports and I'm standing flat on the floor, about two feet from the wall. He undoes my wrist clamps and pushes me forward. His cock slides out. I have no choice but to grab the wall to prevent myself from falling.

Lex grabs my hips and smashes his cock so hard and so fast inside me that it lifts me to my tiptoes. Sitting down had been soft and gentle. This was anything but! Each thrust stokes heat from friction, heat from pain, heat from joy into my cunt.

Then he stops. I can tell he's on the edge of orgasm. I try to stand on my toes to lift my cunt up his cock, to push him into climax, but he presses me against the wall and I can't move.

"No, my pretty, not yet. There's one more thing I want to show you."

He lets go of me then and steps back, pulling himself out of me. I turn and kiss him. I'm free! I pinch his nipples. Now *he* can't escape. Now he's mine. Now *I* will push *him* over the edge, when and how I want.

I reach for his cock and he hugs me close. He's hot and throbbing. One firm stroke and —

Lex reattaches the thigh supports to his contraption. Now they're bent on the middle via some sort of a hinge and formed into a seat. The seat is on rollers and I slide back and onto it. I grab onto the thigh supports beneath me to prevent myself from falling backwards and to the floor.

Lex grabs my wrists to steady me. Two quick clicks and my wrists are clamped back to the same place they'd been clamped to earlier! I try to wriggle free, but all I manage to do is to hurt my left shoulder.

"You bastard!" I hiss.

His only response is to smile, then to let his smile turn into a leer. He raises the thigh supports, then slowly pulls the seat towards him. His cock, his heavenly cock, slides back inside me.

I can't touch him. But I can move in several directions, all of which I slowly and gently attempt as he rocks himself back and forth. I pull close to him, then push away. I rock my thighs sideways, back and forth. I rock my pelvis up and down.

"Are you ready to come?" I ask as sweetly as I can.

"Only when you are, my sweet." He smiles, a smile so full of affection that I almost abandon my plan. But smile or no smile, he's still got my wrists clamped tight!

I rock my hips back and forth, unsteadying him and his contraption, his warsuit, his *fucksuit*. He reaches out to stabilize us. That's all I need! I push myself towards him, plunging his cock all the way into my cunt. Then I pull back until just his tip is inside me. I get in five long strokes before he has his fucksuit stabilized enough to allow him to attempt to restrain me. But he's flushed. At the edge. I rock my pelvis back and forth and watch his eyes surrender control to me. He shudders and rocks his cock as deep inside me as it will go. Hot sticky wetness dribbles down my thighs.

Loisbot, once again fully dressed, comes over and releases me from Lex Luthor's warsuit. I hug Lex as he and I enjoy our afterglow. Loisbot disassembles the warsuit around us and when Lex kisses me, it's fully disassembled into the backpack which Loisbot hoists over his shoulder.

Lex gives me another light kiss. "It was nice to get to know you on dry land." Then he, and Loisbot, turned into the crowd.

I was still mellow, so they were swallowed up into crowd before I even thought of taking a step to follow. I was stiff from previous exertions and from being clamped into Lex's contraption and had to pause to stretch. Then it hit me. That voice! Lex was the same person who had fondled me in Mexico. At the foam party. I tried to race to follow but Lex and Loisbot were nowhere to be seen. At the front door, a car was driving off. I pointed at it. The parking valet shrugged.

As I turned around I realized I couldn't tell Eric about my suspicions. I was already too far down the rabbit hole. I wouldn't be able to explain my inaction. Besides, these strange occurrences might have nothing to do with the Cyber Culprit. Coincidences were called coincidences for a reason.

As I reentered the ballroom, Eric was waiting for me. "Did you see anything?" I asked.

He shook his head. "No one filming, or even taking special interest in us."

We waited until the party began to break up and cornered Doctor Serturner, who was now dressed disturbingly like Clark Kent. I glared at him, ready to play bad cop if necessary.

Eric shook his hand. "We're investigating the recent cyber attack on the hospital," he told the anesthesiologist.

Serturner looked back and forth between Eric and I and decided it was better to concentrate on Eric. "How can I help?"

"You were the only one who had an image of yourself posted to the internet. Do you have any idea as to why you might have been singled out for special attention?"

Serturner considered for a moment. I wanted to mash my fist into his face for not giving as much attention to the treatment of my aunt three years ago. Then the anesthesiologist shook his head. "No. Sorry."

"It showed you dressed up at last year's PanPlay. Were cameras allowed last year?"

Serturner shook his head.

Eric showed Serturner the photo of himself dressed in a wannabe Superman costume. "Then how was this taken?"

Serturner shrugged. "Your guess is as good as mine."

When Serturner saw Eric's disappointment, he put his arm around my assistant's shoulders. "Don't worry, the hospital's beefed up our firewalls. It won't happen again."

The next night, Eric worked out of my office trying to track down the Cyber Culprit through the ransom the hospital had paid CC to regain control of its network while I spent some quiet time with Michael Rayburn at his apartment.

Michael was the lawyer who had given us the

assignment to track down the Cyber Culprit. Partway through, he and I had ended up in a romantic relationship. I had sworn off sex with anyone else—unless it was necessary for the investigation. Michael had likewise pledged monogamy but I'd seen a recent photo of him with an old flame which had called his vow into question. Michael had claimed that it was nothing and I had decided to believe him.

Michael was wearing a dress shirt and casual pants. For Michael, this was relaxed. But throw on a tie and a sports jacket and he'd be ready to meet a client at the office. I had gone fully casual—Tshirt and jeans.

I snuggled myself into his slender six-foot frame and watched his face in the reflection in the television. His face, framed by brown hair with just a hint of grey, was masculine and handsome. We were watching a romantic action-adventure, the best of both worlds. Michael's blue eyes were fixed on the heroine as she talked her way out of danger. In a moment, she had the villain tied up and helpless. Which gave me an idea.

The couch on which we were seated had two little spherical pedestals at the top of each corner. I had seen some string in a drawer in the kitchen. When the next action sequence started up, I carefully moved away and returned with the string. Michael was so engrossed in the movie that was unaware of my tying his wrists to the couch. But as the action sequence was ending, he tried to hug me and it was game on.

"Hey!" he protested.

But the bulge in his pants told me he wasn't serious about his protest. I quickly unzipped his pants and pulled them, and his briefs, down his legs and off his ankles.

"You won't get away with this!" he warned, tugging at his restraints.

Since sucking his hard dick was what I wanted and since he was already fully erect, I was pretty sure I wasn't going to have *any* problem getting away with it.

I knelt beside him, caressed his balls and nipped his

ear. "Shush," I told him. "Don't do anything stupid and no one will get hurt."

He had stopped tugging at his restraints but he'd managed to twist his right wrist around to where his fingers could start to work away at the knots I'd tied. I estimated that I had a five-minute window at most, so it was time to claim my prize!

A faint whiff of musk and sweat wafted up from his pubic hair. His cock was subtly salty on my tongue. He rocked his hips, trying to pull his cock away.

I lifted my head and nipped his nipple. "You want me to bite him?" I threatened.

He stopped rocking his hips. The only movement was the throbbing of his cock. I bent down and sucked his circumcised head into my mouth and ran my tongue around it. Above there was a gasp.

"You'll never get away with this!" he said, but his voice lacked conviction.

I sucked half his cock into my mouth, swirling my tongue around his shaft. The fingers of my right hand caressed his balls. My left hand was behind his back, massaging the bottom of his spine. I raised my head until he was almost out and flicked my tongue into the hole atop his penis. He moaned as I descended his shaft once more.

My technique was perfect and he tasted so good — warm and hot! He would spurt his life-force into my mouth in five minutes unless he managed to free his wrist before then. My pussy was almost as hot as his cock but all she wanted was to watch Michael's undoing.

His balls pulled tight up into his crotch. He moaned. Behind, my gentle massage was making him rock his hips back and forth in time with my motions up and down his cock.

This time when I went down, I paused at the bottom, sucking hard, then releasing, sucking hard, then releasing. Above he stopped breathing. Then I sucked hard again, but this time, I slowly brought my head up while maintaining suction. As my lips touched his pleasure ridge, I brought my hand up to grasp his shaft, sliding it with the lubrication my mouth had provided. I popped my head off him and looked into his face. He had had his eyes closed, but now they popped open as he sucked air into his lungs. He had stopped trying to escape.

I gently massaged his cock up and down with my hand until his arousal receded a notch and his fingers resumed their struggle with the knots I had tied on his right wrist. He was still breathing heavily. I let him see an evil smile on my lips before I returned them to my prize.

Below, I held him steady with my hand and sucked the head of his penis into my mouth. I pumped my head vigorously up and down. He gasped and stopped breathing. I alternated between sliding my hand up and down his shaft while holding my head motionless, with pumping my head up and down the top of his steadied shaft. I began to rotate my hand. I could feel him almost—

Two firm hands lifted my head up and off my prize, drawing my eyes up his heaving chest and into his steel-blue eyes.

"I told you that you wouldn't get away with this," he reminded me. He slid his hands under my Tshirt, unclasped my bra and slid both halfway up my arms. As I pulled them the rest of the way off, he wrapped one of the strings I'd used to bind his wrists around my arms and tied them in a loose knot.

While I struggled to free myself, he unzipped my jeans and pulled them down, along with my panties. He lifted my bum gently onto the couch. I was concentrating on trying to free my arms and was only dimly aware of him kneeling on the couch above my head. While I was still distracted by trying to free my arms, he lifted one of my legs up and over the back of the couch. He bent his body down over mine and hot lips, hot mouth enveloped my sex. Hot tongue! Hot tongue flicked inside me where my own roiling juices were even hotter.

His chest was tight against my chest, keeping his cock safe.

Michael teased my clit with the tip of his tongue as two fingers slipped inside and began to beckon my pleasure spot. The bastard was going to make me come, to make me scream while preserving his own composure and chastity!

I finally managed to free my hands and began to administer a sharp spanking to his butt. He raised himself up to escape my swats and I had my prize once more! A gentle caress to his cock and balls drew his belly tight. Strokes up and down his shaft brought him rapidly back to the edge.

Two more swift strokes and I felt the first contraction at the base of his cock. The first surrender of his life force. But there was only one contraction. Something was holding — it was me! He was holding himself until he made me lose control! We'd see about that! I stroked my fingers up and down. I had him; he would not escape! But a familiar gathering, a familiar compression told me that *neither* of us would escape. Deep in my cunt, the compression pulled its edges against each other then snapped them violently apart. We both shuddered out our life forces. His hot spunk spurted down to the bottom of my chest. My contractions sent slipperiness onto his fingers. Spurt after spurt pumped onto my breasts. Electricity whipped up my spine, down into my clit, hard hot pain pleasure. Smacking my hips apart, curling my toes. Spreading warmth and light through my consciousness. Fading into blackness. So warm, so wonderful.

I was vaguely aware of Michael helping me into his bed, of snuggling next to him. So warm, so wonderful. He kissed my forehead and sleep welcomed me into its arms.

Somewhere, deep in the jungle, a beast of prey called out. Fear shot through me as I roused myself. The fire was a mere flicker. Michael was moving to tend to the fire. The beast called out again. But it wasn't a beast, it was a ringtone. Michael reached the fire and pressed it to the side of his head.

Over coffee, Michael explained the call. The Cyber

Culprit was up to his old tricks. This time he'd posted a video of the daughter of a prominent client at her fetish wrestling establishment. The client had wanted his daughter to be a gymnast. A foray into competitive gymnastics would have been excellent exposure for her, especially if she made it to the Olympics. Furthermore, he'd touted gymnastics as an excellent foundation for later careers in business or politics (or both!). But at fifteen, daddy's pride and joy had rebelled and become a wrestler. Sarah Boulton hadn't made it to the Olympics but had wrestled at the college level before fading from the public view. Until now. Now the public was feasting on a video of her in a bikini wrestling an overweight middle-aged male pinning her to the mat and celebrating by gleefully rubbing her crotch.

Wrestling , Lusty Lee Log #19

The Cyber Culprit's latest posting had shown Sarah Boulton engaged in fetish wrestling. Sarah was the daughter of an important client of Michael Rayburn's law firm. Actually a *very* important client with family ties stretching back to Confederation. Sarah had broken Daddy's heart by rejecting gymnastics in favor of wrestling. CC's posting had included several photos of her wrestling. But the kicker had been a video showing her being pinned by an overweight middle-aged male who had then gleefully rubbed her crotch.

Sarah's website, SB Wrestling Club, was pretty bare-bones. Other than Sarah herself, there were no photos of wrestlers. Wrestling fantasies could be acted out in a ring, on mats or in a mocked-up apartment. There was no explicit mention of sexual touching. The only contact provided was via leaving a message.

Last night, I'd spent an hour at the gym with Eric learning basic grappling techniques. The plan was to gain Sarah Boulton's trust and then ask her everything she knew about CC's latest posting.

Sarah had responded to my message and I met her the next morning. In person, she was a friendly and attractive blonde, a few inches taller than me and a few years younger. I estimated 5 foot eight inches tall and 26 years old. She was skinny with defined muscles, but no boobs or butt. Today she was wearing a light blue one-piece exercise top over grey yoga pants. All in all, she was pretty and effervescent, even with her thin-lipped smile.

SB Wrestling's premises were clean, but smelled faintly of sweat. There was a front office with a small desk and a flat screen television. As soon as I arrived, Sarah took me on a tour. The square ring was slightly smaller than standard size, but with the usual canvas mat and three ropes surrounding the wrestling surface. There was a room with mats on the floor, corner to corner, and three feet up the walls. The kicker was the mock apartment with real furniture. Almost everything was padded and there were no sharp corners, but it was done unobtrusively so you'd feel that it was a real apartment room. At the back were change rooms, each with a shower and each with a rack of clothes.

Back at the front desk, Sarah explained the club's rules. "There are two levels, casual and members. Casual wrestlers pay by the hour, must remain clothed and are strictly restricted with respect to the type of touching which is allowed. Of course, everything must be consensual."

"And members?" I asked.

She smiled. "Members have more leeway. What did you have in mind?"

"I heard you have bikini wrestling?"

She nodded and activated the television. "This is the basic bikini wrestle." Two bikini-clad women were in the ring circling each other. Then the one in the white bikini took her opponent to the mat. Sarah, dressed in referee's stripes, watched in the background. "Some of our patrons prefer to go topless, even nude. Usually there's an agreement as to how much force each wrestler is permitted to apply." On the television, there was a scramble and white bikini ended up on the bottom.

"Do you wrestle?"

Sarah nodded. "Quite often, it depends what the customers want."

"And casual customers?"

"Casual customers must use soft force only. Pinning is allowed, but no submission holds, no striking, and no sexual touching."

At that moment, the outside door opened and a petite Asian woman came in. "Miss Boulton?" she asked.

Sarah stepped forward and extended her hand, "MayLin?"

MayLin smiled, "Yes. We spoke yesterday. Bikini wrestling." She held up a small athletic bag.

"I can be ready in a few minutes. I was just finishing up with Ms. Brandt."

"Lee," I corrected.

MayLin looked back and forth between us. "Maybe I should wrestle with Lee."

Sarah looked first at MayLin, then at me. "It would let you get first hand experience of our facility."

I started to nod. "But I don't have a bikini," I remembered.

Sarah smiled, "We have extras. I can lend you."

By the time I exited from the dressing room, MayLin was already in the ring. She was wearing a tiny string bikini. On her butt, it was more thong than bikini. The material was thin and shiny and black.

MayLin held the ropes open to help me climb into the ring. One of the ropes pulled back on her bikini top and I caught a clear view of a hard dark nipple. When I looked up, she was smiling at me. The ropes were a smooth nylon weave, pleasant to the touch and held taut by the turnbuckles at each corner.

Once in the ring, MayLin indicated that I should pirouette to allow her to inspect me and what I was wearing. Sarah had outfitted me in a sleek metallic gold bikini. It was also a string bikini, but, unlike MayLin's, it fully covered my glutes. The mat beneath my feet was canvas, though smoothed from much use, and well padded.

MayLin and I circled each other in the ring, sizing each other up. But Sarah stepped in between us. She had replaced her light blue top with one having white and black vertical stripes. Where the blue top had separated her buttocks, this one cupped them.

"Remember the rules," Sarah reminded us. "No slapping, choking, submission holds or removing or touching under bikinis." She reached behind my head and grabbed the ponytail into which I'd bound my curly brown hair. "And no hair pulling."

"And the winner?" MayLin wanted to know.

Sarah looked back and forth between us. "You have agreed that the winner gets to feel up the loser on the outside of her bikini."

We each nodded.

Sarah stepped back and we began to circle each other again. MayLin was lean, lithe and quick. My advantages were height and weight.

As soon as Sarah circled around behind me. MayLin made her move. She feinted right and before I could recover my position, she had circled around my back. Her hands were immediately all over the front of my bikini. Before I could shout out the flagrant rule violation, I discovered that her touch was soft and sensuous. MayLin made a show of trying to wrestle me to the mat, but when I defended the attempt and tried to grab her arm, she pulled back.

I was breathing hard, both from the exertion and from the pleasure of her touch, but MayLin was still fresh. She continued to circle me. I turned to keep her in front of me, but my steps were small, conserving energy. As soon as she had maneuvered Sarah behind me again, she reached up to her bikini top and flashed her tits at me. She may have had small breasts, but her nipples were puckered and hard.

Before I could recover, MayLin shot in again. Both hands squeezed my breasts, found my nipples and gave a gentle twist. That was all it took to disorient me and she managed to trip me down to the mat.

MayLin landed on top of me and immediately grabbed both of my wrists in an effort to pin me. This was a bad move as this spread her weight too thinly. I pulled my arms up which unbalanced her and easily rolled her over onto her back.

I was about to pin her when MayLin's leg rubbing up and down my crotch finally clued me into her real game. She wasn't trying to pin me. Her game was to cop as many feels as she could before she either lost the bout or Sarah disqualified her.

"You little bitch," I whispered.

"*You* like it," she teased back, matching my whisper.

I pulled myself up and grabbed both of her legs. She tried to wrench her legs free, but my grip was firm. I dragged her around the ring until the shiny material of her bikini had formed a pronounced cameltoe around and into her sex. Nice!

I moved forward to pin her but I was too slow and she scooted up and around. MayLin kicked out my lead leg and I fell onto my back. She flopped across my chest, rubbing back and forth across my breasts. That and the effects of pulling her around the ring had loosened her bikini top. When I bucked my hips up, she fell across my face and I sucked one of her hard nipples into my mouth.

Sarah pounded the mat. "Wardrobe malfunction!" she shouted. "Fighters to their corners."

MayLin locked her eyes on mine as she fumbled with tying her top tight, making sure I was getting a good look. She adjusted her bikini bottom, almost caressing herself.

Sarah looked back and forth between us. MayLin and I smiled at her. Sarah shrugged, motioned us to the center of the ring and shouted, "Fight!"

MayLin shot in straightaway. But she stumbled and I pinned her against one of the turnbuckles. I placed a leg in between hers and rubbed up and down the front of her crotch. She was hot—really hot!—against my leg. Her hands were all over my breasts, pinching and twisting my nipples.

I pulled the small Asian forward, threw her onto the mat and jumped on top. Her right arm ended up pinned between our bodies. I pressed her shoulder to the mat. Sarah hit the canvas once, but MayLin pushed up, escaping defeat for the moment.

Between our bodies MayLin's right hand took the initiative, her fingers working themselves under my bikini and into my pussy hair! I pinned her shoulders again and Sarah pounded the canvas. If I could keep Sarah preoccupied, MayLin's fingers would be free to do their work unhindered! Sarah hit the canvas again while MayLin's delicate fingers caressed my pussy.

I lifted my weight slightly, and MayLin managed to buck her shoulders off the mat. Her fingers spread my juices all over my pussy lips and slipped inside so quickly that my legs turned to jelly. Sarah hit the mat twice and MayLin just managed to buck her shoulders up in time.

Below, she wiggled her fingers inside and rotated my clit with her thumb. Bang! Bang! Bang! thundered Sarah's hand on the canvas. MayLin's fingers had felt so good, I'd forgotten to lift myself up. Sarah had to help me off MayLin. Otherwise the diminutive Asian woman might have been squished flat!

Sarah held my right hand above my head. "Winner by pin, the lovely Lee Brandt!"

MayLin was still sucking air into her lungs when I led her to the middle of one of the sides of the ring. I wrapped her arms and wrists around the top rope, then stepped back to admire my prey. Sarah stood to my left, watching with rapt attention.

"You wouldn't dare," hissed MayLin.

"You little bitch," I hissed back. "I would *so* dare!"

MayLin turned to Sarah. "Miss Boulton, you can't let her—"

"You both agreed," Sarah reminded her.

I extended my arms in front of me as far as they would go and wiggled my fingers. I took a step forward and my fingers were an inch from MayLin's bikini top. A bikini top through which her nipples strained to burst through. She could easily unwrap her arms but she made no move to do so.

"You wouldn't dare!" she repeated. "If you—"

I gripped each nipple and gave the hard little buttons firm twist.

"Ow!" gasped MayLin.

"No pain allowed," remonstrated Sarah. But she made no move to interfere.

I let go of MayLin's nipples and danced my fingers down her belly. She tensed and writhed with the tickle.

When my fingers touched the top of her bikini, MayLin made a show of pulling back. "Don't you dare," she pleaded.

With my hands, I indicated that she should spread her legs.

"Don't," she begged.

I motioned again with my hands and this time she spread her legs.

I rubbed lightly over the surface of her bikini. Even through the material, I could feel the heat underneath. Her knees buckled momentarily and her left arm came loose from the rope around which I had wrapped it. I helped MayLin wrap her arm back around the rope then pressed my hand between her legs, stroking my fingers back and forth as they rose up her thighs. When I reached the bottom of her bikini, I pressed a finger into the middle of the thin material and felt it slide between her pussy lips. MayLin moaned, then bit her lip as my finger moved up and down the soft material. She shut her eyes and moaned again when my finger continued its caresses.

I glanced over at Sarah. Her face was flushed, her eyes were locked on the finger stroking up and down the front of MayLin's bikini and the smile on her lips advertised obvious enjoyment.

There was dampness on my finger. I stepped sideways to block Sarah's view of my hand and slipped my fingers under the top of MayLin's bikini and whispered, "Now it's time for some sushi."

"No," moaned MayLin as my fingers danced over her hairless pubic area and down her delicate soft pussy lips.

Out of the corner of my eye, I saw Sarah move around in

front of MayLin. I withdrew my hand from inside and resumed stroking the front of the Asian woman's bikini.

"MayLin, are you alright?" asked Sarah.

MayLin nodded but her eyes remained shut.

The phone at the front desk rang and Sarah left to answer it.

I slipped my hand under the shiny black bikini and spread my fingers, two down each side of MayLin's vulva and one in the middle lifting her bikini away from her sex. At the bottom of her vulva, I pressed my middle finger just inside her vaginal opening. Then I softly dragged my freshly lubricated finger up her pussy lips, lightly grazing her clit before I withdrew it out the top of her bikini.

MayLin's eyes rocketed open. "You can't stop now!" she complained.

"You begged me to stop." I made a show of smelling her sushi scent, then licked it off my finger. "Now beg me to finish you."

"Yes, please!" she nodded. "Hurry, before she comes back!"

I could feel the triumphant smile on my lips connect with the lips engorging under my golden bikini. I stepped into MayLin, inserting my right leg between her legs. As I rubbed up and down the front of her crotch, I could feel MayLin's right leg angle towards my sex. We tribbed together, pussy to pussy, adding each other's heat to the other. Her hands gripped the rope tightly. I unloosened the strings holding her top and slid my hands underneath, caressing her breasts. A deep moan sounded from within MayLin's throat.

"Fuck me," she begged.

I stepped back and thrust my hand down the front of her bikini. She was soaking, so I withdrew my hand and pressed her bikini into her sex to absorb her excess moisture. Then my hand was back inside. I caressed up and down her pussy lips, more firmly now, and her breathing became sporadic. Two fingers inside her cunt made her breathing stop altogether.

"Breathe!" I commanded, holding my fingers still.

When she drew a deep breath, I curled the fingers inside her cunt until I found her sweet spot. Then I used my other hand to pull up on her pussy lips and gently caress her clit. She was taking short shallow breaths punctuated by moans.

I heard Sarah finishing up her call and concentrated on MayLin's g-spot, curling and uncurling my fingers for maximum contact. Sarah's handset clicked into the cradle. MayLin's cunt contracted in pulsing waves.

"Fuck!" she shouted.

"Softer," I whispered.

"Fuck!" she whispered back, barely louder than the screams from inside her pussy.

Sarah was approaching, but from behind MayLin. The Asian's orgasm finished just as Sarah climbed into the ring. I withdrew my hand and stepped back.

Sarah stopped short, looking back and forth between the thoroughly disheveled MayLin and my flushed body. The expression on her face was somewhere between rebuke and congratulation.

Just as MayLin left for the showers, a large white male entered through the front door. He was wearing a well-tailored business suit that accentuated his broad shoulders and minimized his belly. When he extended his hand a gold bracelet jangled and a large diamond ring flashed.

"Hi, Bret," greeted Sarah, shaking his hand. What're you looking for today?"

"Full contact on the mat." His smile was warm, sensual. He was balding, but there were only flecks of grey mixed in with his black hair.

"Okay, I can be ready in ten minutes," she responded.

Bret angled his head towards me, "What about her?"

They both looked up and down my flushed skin and gold bikini. Sarah raised her eyebrows. I nodded back towards both of them.

Sarah shrugged. "Very well, Lee Brandt, I hereby make you an honorary member of the SB Wrestling Club."

Bret entered one change rooms and Sarah and I the other. MayLin was just coming out of the shower. Her nude body was a jewel. When she saw us looking at her, she did a slow pirouette. A jewel from every angle.

At the back, Sarah selected a white spandex exercise outfit. "This is his favorite," advised Sarah. It was the same construction as a one-piece bathing suit, though the only thing that would 'cover' my butt would be a thin strand of material between my round glutes. If the outfit had been any lighter, it would have floated on air.

I quickly stripped out of my bikini and pulled on the white exercise outfit. The spandex hugged my curves. Sarah inspected me up and down, pausing at my engorged nipples and the wisps of my pubic hair that were clearly visible through the almost diaphanous fabric.

"Bret is okay," she said. "If he is hurting you, just say 'Ow!' and he'll back off. Let him know what you like and he'll oblige. If you want to throw him or reverse position or put him in a hold, just make it obvious what you're trying to do and he'll almost always make it easy for you."

"What does he like?"

"He likes to feel me up, and for me to resist."

"Are there any rules?"

"If he wins, he gets to fuck you."

"Doesn't he usually win?"

Sarah shook her head. "He only beat me once. Depending on my mood, I jerk him off or make him jerk me off."

"Or both?"

She smiled. Or both."

"How do I win?"

"Get him in a hold and demand that he 'give'. If he says "give", you've won."

Back in the reception area, Bret had stripped down to his underwear. A bulge advertised the availability of his manhood under the stretchy green material. We smiled at each other. Michael Rayburn, my lover and boss, knew that my current assignment required all sorts of sexual shenanigans, but the deal I'd made was that I'd keep any sex, especially with men, to the bare minimum. Since wrestling Brett was necessary to gain Sarah's trust, I was free to have all the fun I wanted!

As we moved to the mats, I heard MayLin ask, "How much is a membership?"

As soon as we got onto the mats, Bret grabbed me in a bear hug. He was *strong*! I tried to wriggle free, but all that accomplished was to rub my nipples against his chest. After a few moments, he gently laid me onto the mat.

I took the opening to grab his cock and gently stroked it through his briefs. Bret was going to go down! But Bret had other ideas. Beefy hands grabbed each of my wrists and held them over my head. Quickly he transferred both wrists to his left hand and used his right to fondle my breasts sending tingles all the way down to my toes. Then he put his hand atop my sex. I crossed my legs and all he could touch was my pubic bone. He tried to pry my legs apart but I held them tight together. Somehow I managed to get my wrists free, but all I could do was push ineffectively against his arm.

Then Bret lifted one of his legs and placed it between mine. He pressed down between my legs gradually forcing them to part.

And then his beefy hand and beefy fingers had full access to every part of my sex. I could feel his heat through the sheer spandex. Every muscle in my body relaxed. If he wanted me, I was his! My legs flopped apart and he climbed on top of me, dry humping his hard cock against my sex. I was warm and wet, hungering to have him inside!

Bret lifted himself up to push his briefs down. And then I remembered Michael. I tried to pull away. By rights I shouldn't have succeeded. But Sarah had been right; if I wanted to do something, he'd let me. I was on my side facing him.

I grabbed his cock. The fabric on his briefs was modal—the best fabric ever invented, soft as silk, but stretchy and just a little slippery. He played with my tits and I stroked him. He was hot, just about to come.

But he scooted down and put his head between my legs. His tongue pressed against the spandex and he slurped my juices through the thin fabric. He held us close, side by side. Now *I* was the one ready to come!

It took every ounce of my control to turn on my back and scoot away. He was on his back but I ended up on all fours facing his knees. I scampered up and over his torso and sat on his face. He tried to lick my pussy, but his tongue wasn't quite in the right position.

"Give!" I demanded. I couldn't see behind me, but all he'd have to do was to rock his hips back and forth and I'd go flying.

But he shook his head, rubbing his nose against my sex. Pleasure shot into my pussy and up my spine. I stifled a moan, moved slightly forward and clamped my legs tighter against his cheeks. "Give!" I repeated.

He shook his head again. Thankfully this time his nose wasn't pressed against my pussy. And he was having trouble breathing. "Give!" I commanded, mashing myself into his face.

This time he nodded. *That* I felt on my pussy!

I lifted myself up slightly. "Give!"

"Give," he conceded.

I swept around to face down his torso and planted my sex once more over his face. Everything was smooth except the bulge beneath his briefs. I bent forward and stroked his cock with both hands, letting his mouth and tongue pleasure my pussy—not so much that I'd lose control but enough to turn him on.

My hands wrapped around his cock through the fabric of his briefs, his worship of my pussy, our exertions were all too much for Bret and with a few short strokes he spurted inside his briefs. I used his come as lubricant and continued stroking his cock until it began to soften.

I was sweaty after my double bouts, so I had a shower before I dressed back into my red pleated skirt, white blouse and the red jacket that matched the skirt. The jacket and skirt were linen, light to the touch.

Sarah was back at the front desk.

"Thank you for making me an honorary member," I told her.

"Thank *you* for helping out with Bret. I hope you'll let me know if there's ever anything I can do for you."

"Funny you should mention that."

She looked at me quizzically and I quickly explained our search for the Cyber Culprit, then asked about the recent postings involving her and her wrestling club.

"You got an expense account?" asked the blonde.

I nodded. "Two hundred dollars sound right?"

"I wouldn't feel right taking it unless you got something in return."

"Your information will be enough."

Sarah shook her head. "Not after all your help with my clients. Especially since *they* got *all* the pleasure! You've been in the ring and on the mats. Care to check out the apartment?"

At this point, all I needed was whatever help she could provide in our quest for the Cyber Culprit. But it was clear that she felt in my debt and that if I let her repay it by showing me her mock apartment she'd be more forthcoming.

I shrugged. "Sure."

And with that, Sarah took me by the hand and led me to the mock apartment. There was a couch, loveseat and chair, all of them black. Every surface was padded, but the design was artistic; so I wouldn't have noticed the extra padding if I hadn't been planning wrestling moves. The floor was wall-to-wall carpet, beige with extra padding. In two of the corners, there were beanbag chairs. Against the walls in the other two corners were racks made of rope attached to the ceiling and hanging loose about a foot off the floor. Attached to the racks were pieces of rope, Velcro ties and a variety of other soft and soft-edged bondage gear. Three feet up from the floor was also padded, but this was made to look like wood paneling.

Sarah went to the door on the other side of the room and opened it. On the inside of the door was a list of choices ranging from 'soft' to 'no-holds barred'. I chose 'full-contact/no injuries'. Sarah had the advantage of height and youth and even though she was skinny, her muscles looked powerful enough. And I had already had two bouts that afternoon.

"Clothes ripping?" asked Sarah.

"Sure, why not? I started back towards the change room where I'd remembered seeing a rack of clothes.

But Sarah grabbed my arm. "It's hotter if we rip what each other happens to be wearing. If yours are damaged beyond repair, you can wear one of the one-size-fits-all dresses in the change room." I didn't relish the thought of damage to my favorite white blouse. The red skirt and jacket would be covered by Michael's expense account. Not to mention that my white bra and panties were new. But Sarah had changed back into her blue exercise top and it would be fun to pull its bottom up into her butt crack. Not to mention ripping her grey yoga pants asunder.

I shrugged. In for a penny, in for a pound.

Sarah pulled out a drawer. Inside was a range of fetish gear ranging from feathers and strap-on dildos. "Pick your penalty," she demanded.

"If I lose?"

"For whomever loses."

I checked out the dildos. One was acrylic, hard in every way. The other two had ribbed soft-silicone surfaces. One of these was rigid, the other flexible. I held up the flexible one. It had a strap with a dildo in the middle, poking out each side. Sarah took it, shut the drawer and hung the dildo on one of the rope racks.

My practice bouts with six-foot-three Eric had taught me that taller opponents were vulnerable to being taken down by ducking under their guard. When Sarah turned around, I stood up to my full height and held my arms out loosely, as if preparing to grapple. When Sarah adopted the complimentary stance, I shot in, grabbed her around the waist and threw her onto the couch.

She landed face-first and I climbed onto her back. Her left arm was pinned underneath her. I grabbed her right arm with my left and pulled it around under her throat. With my weight on her, Sarah was unable to move. "Give?" I asked.

There was a muffled "No" from underneath, so I reached my right hand under her chest, found her nipple and pinched it.

"Give?" I repeated. When there was no response, I twisted the nipple. "Give?"

Sarah managed to lift her head far enough up to shout "No!" and began to thrash around, but she was unable to dislodge me. I let go of her nipple and slid my hand down to her crotch. But this shifted my weight and when she thrashed, she moved me half off her, half over the edge of the couch. We struggled there for a moment, rubbing up and down against each other's bodies, but Sarah had gained the upper hand and I fell to the floor, with her on top.

Before I could counter, Sarah had pulled my jacket down over my arms. In the instant when I was deciding whether to try to pull my jacket back up or slough it off my arms, Sarah had ripped open my blouse and attacked my tits. She pinched each of my nipples through the sheer fabric of my bra and gave them a hard twist. I bucked up and she went flying up and over my head.

I had got halfway up the front of the couch when Sarah was on me. But I dodged to one side and she ended up face first on the couch. She twisted onto her back and I seized the top of her exercise top with my left hand and pulled down between her breasts. With my other hand, I reached around behind her, grabbed the bottom of the pale blue one-piece just above her buttocks and pulled it tight up into her crotch.

"Bitch!" she screamed.

"Give?" I mocked.

She thrashed again. I smiled. The position we were in meant that her only escape was to slip out of her exercise top. She must have had the same thought because she shifted her shoulders and scooted upwards.

We each scrambled to our feet, facing each other, breathing hard. Her little breasts were tight against her chest, but her nipples stood out, full sized, engorged, hard. I could feel my own nipples, equally hard, pressing against the sheer fabric of my bra. Sarah wasn't wearing panties and I could see the outline of her sex under her tights. I took a deep breath, faked high and shot low.

But this time Sarah was wise to my trick and I ended up face first into one of the beanbag chairs. I felt and heard the back of my blouse rip open and her fingers unclasp my bra. Her hands gripped my panties and pulled them up into my crotch.

"Whore!" I screamed but all this accomplished was to make her pull up harder.

I managed to turn to my side but this allowed her to pull my panties down and off. I spun to my back to let her have a good look at my tits hanging out of my bra between wisps of my blouse and my skirt hiked up over my hips displaying my ready and available pussy. I shut my eyes as I heaved air into my lungs and let my arms dangle over the side of the beanbag.

She took the bait. Her lips were full on mine, her tongue darting inside. One hand caressed my nipple, the other feather-touched my sex. I moaned. She put a finger between my pussy lips and pressed just far enough to feel my moisture. I moaned again.

When she inserted her finger inside my pussy, I hugged her lightly. She shifted her weight atop me and rubbed her thigh up and down my crotch.

"Ready to get fucked?" she breathed.

My answer was to slide my hands down to her yoga pants, squeeze a handful into each fist and pull up and apart. Sarah screamed as the flexible fabric went right up into her pussy. She pushed herself up to escape pressure, but I pulled sideways, ripping her pants right down the seam. I kept ahold of her tights as I whirled to stand ripping her yoga tights to tatters.

She pulled the remains of her yoga pants off, her eyes daring me to remove the remains of my own outfit. I did and we circled, each nude. Her blonde pubic hair was trimmed in the shape of a heart.

She charged at me and I ended up with my back in a corner, pressed against one of the rope racks. She dropped to her feet and before I knew it, she had attached my ankles to a spreader. I tried to break free, but my legs were held firmly apart.

Sarah stood and pressed her right hand against my crotch. "Ready to get fucked?"

I tried to wrench free, but she was pressing me tight into the corner.

She inserted two fingers into my pussy. "Beg for it," she

demanded.

But I managed to back and twist and now it was Sarah in the corner. I spotted two Velcro straps, pulled them off the rope racks, and secured them around her arms. Now it was my hand on her crotch, my fingers inside her pussy.

"Beg for it," I mocked.

"Please," she begged. Her sex was engorged, inflamed. I caressed up and down her pussy, stroking her clit with each stroke. She gulped little breaths. Her body was flushed, ready to come!

With my leg between hers, her right leg entangled in the spreader she'd attached between my legs and her arms firmly bound to the ropes, Sarah had no escape. I inserted two fingers inside and moved them back and forth, searching for her g-spot.

"Beg for it, or I'll stop," I told her.

She moaned and I tasted victory for the third time that day. MayLin had been small and easy—in fact that was her game, to be easy! Bret had been a big beefy handful, but no match for my charms. Sarah was—

Two hands pulling down on my hair cut my celebration short.

"Never trust someone else's bindings to secure her," Sarah hissed as she spun me around. One of the bindings which had been around her arms was suddenly around my wrist. Sarah loped the other binding between my bound arms and the spreader between my legs effectively hog-tying me as she lowered me to the couch.

She kneeled down and held her left breast next to my mouth. "Lick," she commanded.

I sucked her hard hot nipple into my mouth.

But Sarah immediately pulled back and slapped my face. "Lick! If I want you to suck, I'll tell you!"

This time I licked and her hand was between my legs, two fingers slowly being inserted into my pussy.

"Give!" she demanded.

I shook my head, being careful to keep licking her nipple.

Two thumbs and two forefingers pinched my nipples. Sarah looked deep into my eyes. "Give!" she repeated.

I shook my head and pulled at my bindings.

She twisted my nipples sending hot sharp jolts of exquisitely pleasured pain into my chest. "Give!"

I shook my head again. She undid the binding which had

pulled my wrists down to the leg spreader and threw it on the couch. She took my head, entwining her fingers into my curly hair, dragged me to the wall and pressed my back against it. Her right hand rubbed roughly up and down my crotch.

"Give!"

I shook my head defiant. Every inch of my body was flushed hot.

She slapped lightly against my crotch. I'd never been slapped there before. Her eyes were evil, sucking all the air out of my lungs. My pussy didn't know what to make of the new sensations flooding across her surface. I shook my head.

Sarah slapped my pussy again, harder this time. It hurt.

"Give!" she demanded.

I couldn't decide whether my pussy was enjoying the abuse being inflicted on it but I decided that I'd had enough. "Give," I gasped.

She lightly massaged the front of my pussy reestablishing pleasant sensations. "You okay?"

I nodded.

Sarah reached to her left and pulled the dildo from the rope rack. In a moment, she had it strapped around her hips, one end of the soft-silicone dildo inside her pussy. "You ready for this?" she asked. She pulled the dildo in and out, obviously turned on.

"Yes," I breathed, watching the dildo wag back and forth.

Sarah grabbed me by the arm and led me, waddling, to the couch. She undid my wrists and used the binding to tie my right arm up and over my head to the back of the couch. She pulled the other binding out from under me and tied my other wrist down to the front leg of the couch.

She pulled up the spreader with her left hand and inspected my pussy while jerking off with the dildo, obviously enjoying the sensations inside her own pussy. I'd never felt so exposed in all my life!

"You want to be fucked?" she asked.

I nodded.

Sarah pulled up on the spreader, lifting my back off the couch, then down again, then up, all the while playing with the dildo between her legs.

"Beg," she commanded.

"Fuck me."

"Louder!"

"Fuck me!"

She ducked under the spreader and used her right hand to place the dildo at my pussy opening. The fingernails of her left hand dug into my buttocks. "Beg!" She demanded.

"Fuck—"

The dildo slammed into my pussy. Three hard strokes and Sarah was floating. Three more strokes and she started to keen little cries of joy. Three more strokes and I could feel the pulses of her orgasm through the dildo. The pulses went on and on and she kept stroking with spasmodic little thrusts. The thrusts had hit my sensitive spot and each one pushed me kicking and screaming towards the edge. Sarah's pulses kept coming through the dildo as if she was in the throes of a perpetual orgasm. Each pulse raised my temperature. Each thrust squeezed my impending orgasm tighter and tighter.

Sarah stopped all movement. Her pussy was still pulsing, but her hips had stilled. She looked down at me, an evil glint in her eye. "Beg me, or I'll stop."

I bucked my hips up. I was so close! I let myself back down savoring the glorious sensations of the dildo raking across my pleasure spot.

I flexed to lift my hips up again, but Sarah put a hand on my left hip, holding me still. "Beg!" she demanded.

"Fuck! Fuck me. Fuck me hard!"

She thrust the dildo in, slammed me over the edge, rocketed lightning up my spine, exploded heat inside my cunt, tickled electricity down my legs until my toes curled into little balls. Her pulses were still coming through the dildo and wave after wave of pleasure undulated up my spine in harmony with her pulses. Wave after wave floated up and down my body picking up strength each time they touched the vibrating dildo holding sway over my sex, over my body, over my soul.

After we'd showered, I met Sarah back at the front reception. The generic stretchy dress she'd given me hugged my curves nicely but I'd have to change before meeting Michael. Sarah was back in yoga tights and exercise top, but this time they were red over black.

"So what can you tell me about the video?" I asked.

"At first I was mortified, even thought of closing the club down. But then there was a sharp uptake in new inquiries and bookings. Memberships shot up. Now that my secret's out, maybe I should rethink my emphasis on downplaying what goes on at the club."

I smiled. At least the postings hadn't had the same effect on her that they'd apparently had on her father. "Do you have any idea who recorded the videos?"

She shook her head.

Another dead-end, as usual. "What about who took the photos?" None of the victims ever knew, but I had to ask.

She nodded. My whole body perked up. "It was an old client. We were fooling around. He had a camera on remote control." She pointed to a small black fob in his hand in one of the photos.

"Who had the images?"

"He did. After they were posted I gave him an angry phone call. He apologized. Said they'd been on an old computer that was hacked. After the hack, he destroyed the computer and, in his words, 'any incriminating images'"

"Is it alright if I have my assistant interview him?"

"Sure."

She gave me her old client's contact information, I gave her a friendly kiss on the cheek and then I left for my apartment for a well-deserved nap.

When I woke up, there was a text from Eric on my phone. Sarah's old client had been a bust. But the hack on his computer had been two years ago. This pushed our timeline on the Cyber Culprit way back in time. This wasn't exactly a break in the case, but it was certainly something new. I couldn't wait to tell Michael!

I pulled Michael Rayburn up on my contacts and a photo of him—lean, dark and handsome, resplendent in a three-piece suit— filled my screen. I was about to press dial when an alert for a new posting by CC rang out. I switched over to it.

The new post was a video from a laser-tag emporium. There was a group of eight players, all in bikinis and thongs, fooling around. One woman pulled down her bikini and a man fired his laser right at her nipple. His reward was a chance to fire at her other nipple. But he missed and had to pull down his thong. She fired at the tip of his penis and scored a direct hit. Her mouth immediately moved in front of her target but then the screen went black.

I switched back to calling Michael and made a mental note to replace his photo with one of him in a swimsuit. I would of course have to persuade him to let me take one of him in a thong. Persuading him would be half the fun!

But before I could dial there was another Cyber Culprit alert. It was probably just a duplicate of the laser tag alert. I almost decided to ignore it and check it out after I'd spoken to Michael. It would be so good to hear the lawyer's dulcet tones in my ear!

But maybe it was a new post and Michael was sure to ask me about it. I sighed and opened the alert. The video came on. It was Michael! And he was kissing another woman. I recognized her as Gretchen Hughes, Michael's former girlfriend. Michael's chest was nude. She was wearing a sheer white bra.

Michael had assured me that his relationship with Gretchen was in the past. Maybe this was just an old video. After all, Michael had been adamant and I'd decided to believe him about his recent meeting with Gretchen 'being nothing'. Still, watching his hand caressing her breast made my blood boil.

Michael removed her bra and the camera opened to show them on a bed. I recognized the room as being in the hotel she managed. Michael was nude and very, very much aroused. He pulled Gretchen's panties down her leg and they were both nude. They kissed, a long and *lingering* kiss. Then he climbed on top of her and their body motions made it clear exactly what they were doing together. Michael was doing to Gretchen what I had stopped Bret from doing to me!

The camera widened further and I could see out the window. There was a ticker tape in the background. I recognized it as one that showed the day's news headlines, the weather and current stock quotes. I relaxed. The ticker tape would show that the video was old, that it was from before I'd met Michael.

I watched the ticker tape for a story I recognized. Michael continued to pump himself into Gretchen but I did my best to ignore them. There was a news story. It looked recent. Then the date flashed on the tickertape. It was *yesterday*!?!

20 Anger, Lusty Lee Log #20

I had decided to follow up the Cyber Culprit's laser-tag posting first. I was too angry about the video of Michael Rayburn, my ostensible lover, in bed with Gretchen to deal with him. There were laws against homicide!

CC had posted a video from Cosmic Laser Tag showing a group of eight players fooling around. They were all dressed in bikinis and thongs. One woman had pulled down her bikini and a man had fired his laser right at her nipple. His reward had been a chance to fire at her other nipple. But she bounced her boob and he missed and had to pull down his thong whereupon she'd fired at the tip of his penis, scoring a direct hit. Her mouth immediately moved in front of her target but then the screen had gone black.

However, when I arrived at the address I had for Cosmic Laser Tag, it was a used clothing store. The proprietress laughed when I mentioned laser tag, telling me that it had gone out of business two years ago.

I was mulling over possible reasons why CC would have gone to the trouble of posting a two-year old video when I received a text from Michael Rayburn requesting that I meet him in his office. I looked at my watch; it was already six o'clock. We'd have a meeting, he'd invite me to dinner, we'd end up at his place or mine, then...—not tonight we wouldn't!

In the elevator going up to Michael's law firm, I fiddled with a well-engineered piece of technology. It was in the shape of a ring, two-and-a-half inches in diameter with knobs and screws designed to loosen or tighten it. My fiddling slid one part inside the other and the ring tightened to less than half-an-inch in diameter. Underneath my windbreaker, I was wearing jeans and a plain white Tshirt. Meeting Michael was no longer worth getting dressed up for. The ring I was fiddling with was in the pocket of my windbreaker.

In my other hand I was carrying a manila envelope containing our report to date. We—my assistant Eric and I—had spent the last day and a half compiling all available data on the Cyber Culprit. We had analyzed all his attacks and made predictions of his possible future attacks.

Michael met me at the elevators. One look at his slender muscular body encased in a light grey suit, at his full masculine lips, at his penetrating blue eyes and I lost my resolve. I let go of the ring in my pocket and reached up to his cheek. We kissed and I immediately knew his lips had kissed Gretchen. I dropped my hand and resumed opening the ring in my pocket as wide as it would go, then closing it shut.

None of the other lawyers seemed to be working late. Michael ushered me into his office but let me enter the room after him. And that was the only opening I needed. I turned around as soon as as he'd cleared the door and pressed him against it. Just as it clicked shut, I slid the lock in place and rubbed myself against his crotch.

"Lee," he protested. "The client will be here in an hour."

But now was not the time for words. I grabbed his crotch and gave a gentle squeeze. At least some part of his body still remembered me.

"Lee," he objected, but this time with less conviction. He was already half erect.

I quickly unzipped his pants and slid his almost-erect penis out. I bent down and sucked him into my mouth.

"Lee!" No conviction whatsoever in the protest. I had him!

He leaned back against the door as I sucked and stroked his phallus. His knees buckled and he slid down a few inches. I reached a hand up to caress his balls. From above, he moaned. I pulled his pants and briefs to the floor. He thrust his cock forward into my mouth and moaned again.

I removed the ring from my pocket and slid it down the shaft of his engorged and fully-erect penis. He didn't even notice! I tightened a set of screws, then flicked a lever. The cock-ring locked into place.

"Lee?" He'd become aware that something was different.

I stood and swiftly removed my windbreaker, Tshirt, jeans, and panties.

He pulled at the cock-ring. "Lee! What is this?"

"It's a cock ring. As long as it's on, you'll remain fully erect."

"Take it off! The client will be here any minute!"

"Oh, I'll take it off alright. But not before you pleasure me in every which way possible."

"Lee!"

"You had enough energy to satisfy Gretchen two nights ago. You'd better pray to God that you have enough left over for tonight. For *me*!"

"Lee!" he cried, continuing to fidget with the cock ring. "What is this thing?!?"

I pointed to his crotch. "I wouldn't fiddle with that. You

might make it tighter."

"Lee, what kind of game—"

"If it's a game, this is the kind of game it is. You're going to fuck me and I'm going to fuck you until we're both exhausted. Then, and only then, I'm going to remove the cock ring."

Michael eyed at me with a dumbfounded look on his face. Since simple English was obviously beyond his legal mind, it was time for a demonstration. I grabbed his cock and led him over to the small couch in the far back corner of his office and pushed him down into it. He landed perfectly, his butt just barely on the edge and his legs together.

I walked myself up the outside of his thighs, positioned myself over his erection and slid it into my cunt. Since I was barely aroused, my cunt was tight around his cock and it didn't move fully in and out as I raised and lowered myself. What it did was to massage my pussy lips up against his cock as I lifted myself up and to press them against the rest of my vulva as I lowered myself down onto him. The lack of friction intensified the sensation, almost to the point of pain, but not so painful as to erase the pleasure of my mastery over Michael.

Michael's face was at first shock, then discomfort with the friction, then amazement. He tried to use his arms to push me off but he was out of position and I easily slapped his hands back down to the couch.

"Lee!" he protested.

"You're going to fuck me, Michael Rayburn. No ifs, no ands, no buts."

"Lee."

But his protest was muted by the fact that I had become lubricated and was now starting to bounce vigorously and rapidly up and down his cock. I altered my angle so that he was missing the best parts but still relentlessly stimulating the juices and building up the heat inside my cunt.

Michael was lying back, defeated, but beginning to get turned on. Good—He'd receive his punishment for that in due course. Meanwhile the heat inside me had enveloped my entire pelvic region and was starting to rise up into my spine. That and the fact that my legs were beginning to tire meant that it was time to claim my first orgasm.

I altered my angle of attack and immediately felt Michael's

cock brush against my g-spot. Another slight modification and we were stroking her right in the center. I slowed my cycles down to feel every ridge of his cock glide up and down the center of my pleasure. Every ridge of his cock tightened my cunt and sent flutters up my spine.

Suddenly my cunt clenched every muscle in my body in her whip hand. The only muscles I could move were deep inside my pelvis and I pumped them around Michael's cock, trying to stimulate my g-spot.

Then my cunt unclenched and I seized the opportunity by lifting myself up and dropping myself back down Michael's cock as quickly as I could. He gasped. I didn't know—I didn't care— whether he gasped from pain or amazement or pleasure. I only cared that he was in my control. I pumped up and down, faster and faster.

And then the pumping took control. Michael gasped in the distance. I shut my eyes and surrendered to the heat inside me. Michael had ceased to exist, my head vanished, my torso was no more. My legs were mere appendages of my cunt, pumping up and down at her command.

Contraction wrenched control from cunt's whip hand, sucking everything into its vortex, then exploding all her little pieces into the universe. I regained consciousness to waves of energy pulling up my spine, lifting my head up, then slithering back down between each of my vertebrae. The energy swirled into a tight little ball that split in two before thundering into my legs. Once inside my legs the tight balls of energy whipped my muscles up and down sliding my cunt up and down Michael's cock pushing wave after wave of joy and delight up my spine, up my neck, into the back of my head.

Gradually the waves subsided into gentle alterations of heat and warmth up and down my body and I opened my eyes. Below, Michael's eyes were shut. He was heaving air into his lungs. I slapped his face and his eyes flickered opened.

I stood up and his cock popped out, swaying beneath me. It was still rock hard. His erection would not be released until I released the cock ring. I looked around for his briefs, found them, and used them to wipe the excess lubrication from my pussy.

I pointed down at Michael. "Your turn to do the work," I told him.

He looked at me quizzically. I pulled him up by his ear.

"Lee!" he protested. But he pushed himself up by the arm of the small couch.

I led him over to his desk, his cock swaying with each step. I smiled at how gingerly Michael was holding himself.

I jumped up onto the desk, laid down on my back, and lifted my feet to the ceiling. "Fuck me," I told him.

"Lee, the client will be here—"

"—any minute," I finished. "Then you better get to it."

He positioned himself between my legs and penetrated my pussy. His thrusts were slow, almost lazy and he let my legs lie loose against his chest.

"Hold my legs together."

He grabbed my ankles with his right hand and moved them to his right shoulder.

I let him hold me here for a few thrusts. "Left hand, left shoulder," I commanded.

He complied and immediately his thrusts became harder, not to mention better angled towards my clit. Now that I had come once, I could bring myself to the brink of orgasm almost on demand. But tonight, Michael was going to have to *work* for it!

I relaxed onto the hard and polished wood of the desk, feeling the leather desk mat draw a line across my shoulders. Michael pumped himself dutifully and regularly inside me. Long full strokes. Sometimes I felt his cock ring press into my skin.

"Faster!" I demanded. The bastard needed to *work*!

Michael obediently picked up the pace, using his right hand to grip my hip to accelerate his thrusts, and I leaned back on his desk. I was starting to feel pleasantly warm, but nowhere near to climax. For a high-priced lawyer, he had a rather ordinary ceiling— smooth white with a fluorescent fixture in the center.

When I felt my back start to sweat, I pushed myself up by my arms so that I was half sitting and allowed my legs to flop down. This forced Michael to bend his knees and put his right hand onto the desk to steady himself. Our pubic bones were now brushing against each other and ordinarily I'd rotate my pussy around his cock to heighten our mutual pleasure. But tonight was all about *me* and *my* pleasure and making Michael *work*.

Michael took a deep breath and slowed his pace. I lifted my right hand, slapped his thigh, then returned it to the desk to stop myself from falling backwards. "Faster!" I demanded.

I lifted my legs up and onto his shoulders and he moved his left hand to lift the small of my back upwards. With my legs on either side of his head, I could rub them back and forth on his ears, just hard enough to be unpleasant, just hard enough to spur him to greater effort.

Michael sped up again, but he was clearly flagging. I rotated my cunt around his cock, grinding our pubic bones together. I felt the heat in my cunt start to spread up into my lower back. But even better, I felt heat radiating off Michael. The bastard was about to come! I smiled and shut my eyes.

Heat had now traversed my torso and was swirling inside my breasts, making my nipples feel like miniature volcanoes. It was like noonday sun at the beach. I basked in the flush on my skin, skating along the edge of orgasm.

Above, Michael's breaths started to come in staccato gulps. His thrusts slowed, paused. I felt him pull back for one last run up the hill. He slammed himself in, his passion mixed with fury at what I was doing to him. Abruptly his body ceased all movement.

"Ow!" he cried. Loud pain. I smiled.

He pulled himself out and looked down at his cock.

"And that's what's going to happen every time you try to come." I opened my eyes to enjoy his discomfiture. "So if you don't want to feel that again, you'd better concentrate on pleasing *me*!" I rubbed my calves back and forth on his ears to make sure he'd gotten the message.

He put himself back in and began careful thrusts in and out. "What have you done?" he wailed.

I smiled an innocent smile. "The cock ring is specially designed to prevent premature ejaculation."

"I do not suffer from premature ejaculation." My allegation had wounded his pride and he picked up the pace of his thrusts.

"If you come before *I'm* ready, it's premature," I reminded him.

He glared down at me. I smiled up at him and began to rotate my pubic bone around his cock. The pause in the action had allowed me to fade away from the edge and it was time to get back. Slowly the heat inside my cunt started to come to a boil, slowly it spread into my pelvis, slowly it started to move up my belly.

Michael's hands were on my breasts. I knew what he was trying to do. He knew how sensitive my breasts were. He knew if he could stimulate them, and especially my nipples, that my orgasm would be hastened. Ordinarily I'd be saluting his prowess. Today he was just being lazy. And instead of holding my hips steady, my back was sliding and scraping on his desk.

I was about to spread my legs and slap them back on either side of his head when his cock flopped out of my cunt.

I flipped my legs around to his right and slid to his left. He hadn't had time to react so he was in the perfect position and I landed my cupped hand directly against the underside of his balls.

"Shit!" he wailed. His knees buckled and he almost hit his cock on the top of his desk.

I readied my hand for another blow but he cringed and turned away. "Don't you dare let yourself pop out again!" I swatted him hard on his rump and lay down on his carpet. I spread my legs and propped myself up on my elbows. "You're not finished yet," I reminded him.

"Lee…" he pleaded.

"Fuck me Michael. Fuck me hard. Fuck me so that I'll forget *Gretchen*."

"Lee—"

"Fuck me so hard that *you'll* forget Gretchen."

He took a big breath and had the grace to hide his sigh. He dropped to the carpet and rammed himself inside me. I tried to keep my legs spread wide, but he knew that I'd come faster if my legs were pressed tightly together, my cunt wrapped around his cock. He was too strong for me to resist his legs moving outside mine and pressing my hips together.

He fucked me now, fucked me with all his power and rage and might. He fucked me *hard*! No love, no tenderness. Just pure animal aggression. It was hot in every meaning of the word: hot with sweat, hot with sex, hot with our anger. He put one hand under my buttocks and squeezed my tits with the other. And he pumped hard and fast and furious.

"Come!" he yelled.

"Make me, you bastard," I shot back.

He dug his fingers into my buttock. "Come!"

"Fuck you!"

He squeezed my breast harder than it had ever been squeezed before. "Come!"

"Make me!"

He twisted my breast. "Come!"

"No!"

He pulled himself out and I reached to slap at his balls, but he straddled me, his face over my crotch and pinned both my arms with his legs. In a moment his mouth was covering my pussy and his tongue was slithering and sliding all over her sensitive parts. Two fingers from one hand slid into my cunt, immediately located my pleasure spot and began to stroke her inexorably towards oblivion. One of the fingers from his other hand slid into my anus and he positioned it to compliment the fingers inside my cunt.

I tried to resist what he was doing to me. I tried with all my might! But he was touching and caressing all he right spots with just the right pressure and just the right technique that he dragged me, inch by inch, kicking and screaming to the precipice.

"You bastard!" I yelled. I tried to wrench my arms free but he had them pinned too securely. "You bastard, you bastard, you *bastard*!" My body jerked once and my climax mixed with my tears. My chest heaved over and over again. After an eternity, everything subsided.

I relaxed and he released my arms. We ended up kneeling together. I fiddled with his cock ring and I guess he thought I was going to let him go. Instead I quickly sucked him into my mouth. He reached up to steady himself on the desk. A few quick sucks and he was on the verge. I undid the cock ring, lifted my mouth and he ejaculated all over his desk, all over the carpet. The perfect ending!

Michael shuffled around to the back of his desk and waddled back with of box of wet-wipes and a box of tissues. He bent down to the carpet and did his best to clean up his ejaculate.

The phone rang. Michael was still wiping away at his mess so I moved behind his desk, sat in his chair and picked up the handset as his head popped up to favor me with a warning glance. "Mr. Rayburn's office, "I answered demurely.

"This is security downstairs," said the voice in my ear. "Please tell Mr. Rayburn that his client has arrived."

"Thank you, please send him up."

When I came around the desk, Michael was bent over, wiping frantically.

"Our client is here," I told him.

Michael rocketed to his feet and cleaned himself off with last remaining wet-wipe and threw on his shirt. He turned to me, "Lee, my client is dissatisfied with the lack of progress in your investigation."

"These things take time." If he'd been more friendly, or fair even, I would have opened the manila envelope in my hand and shared the report Eric and I had compiled. *'My'* client?!?' Where did he get off assuming full ownership of the client?!? And before, it had always been *our* investigation. And why did he have both wet-wipes and tissues in his bottom drawer? I pulled on my jeans.

Michael was buttoning his shirt. "My client isn't going to give you any more time. All you've done is document what the Cyber Culprit has done after the fact. All the client sees is expense accounts from Jamaican sex resorts. My client is demanding that we take the initiative before the Cyber Culprit's postings do even more harm to him and to his friends."

"*Your* client!?! *Our* client is and his precious friends are incidental damage. The Cyber Culprit isn't after them. He has grander targets."

"Grander targets?" He put on his pants and pulled up his zipper.

"Yes, Michael, grander targets. Targets like dishonesty."

"The client isn't interested in philosophy or even ethics. All he wants is this guy, this *criminal*, caught."

I finished dressing first and unlocked the door.

"Lee." His voice was soft enough that I couldn't object to it, but just loud enough that I couldn't pretend not to have heard. And since I had my back to him, his speaking my name had just enough command to force me to turn around.

I turned around. "Michael?" My tone was formal but devoid of sarcasm. As such, it carried a rebuke, but the rebuke wasn't harsh enough to allow him to take offence.

"Lee. Please stay in my office. You're not dressed for seeing clients. When the meeting is over, I'll come back and we can discuss it."

I decided not to give him the satisfaction of asking what 'it' was. Instead, I flopped down on his couch, clutching the manila envelope containing our report in my hand.

Michael returned to his office an hour later and strode to his desk, not looking at me. He threw the writing pad down onto his desk and began to read from it: "Why aren't there any results? Why the high expense accounts, especially the week-long stays in the

Caribbean? Why just question the victims after the fact? Why not
initiate searches before the so-called Cyber Culprit strikes again?"

"Are those the questions the client asked?" I got up and
stood in front of his desk.

He looked up at me, anger and defeat visible under the
bleariness of his eyes, and nodded. "He also wanted to know what
the Cyber Culprit's next target is."

"Pity I wasn't in the meeting to answer his questions," I said,
tapping the manila envelope containing our report on the desk in
front of him. But the client had been right about CC always having
the initiative and our need to take the fight to our opponent.

I waited until Michael started to extend his hand toward the
envelope, then pulled it back. "CC seems to have backed away from
politicians; more a war on technology," I opined.

"Technology is technology," he said, infusing the phrase with
profundity. Empty and baseless profundity, but still.

"Technology is ruining our lives and relationships."

"Relationships are people."

"People like *Gretchen*?" I sneered.

"At least I don't jump into the sack with anything on two
legs!"

"You know it's for the case!"

"If it was for the case, you would have caught the Cyber
Culprit by now!"

"Sex on the job isn't cheating. Gretchen is a different story.
Lying about *Gretchen* is a different story!"

"I didn't—"

I pulled out my phone.

"Is this part of the *technology* that's ruining our
relationship?" he asked.

I ignored Michael until I found the video of he and Gretchen
Hughes, his former girlfriend, kissing and then fucking on one of the
beds in the hotel she managed. I turned the video towards him and
watched the expressions on his face cycle through curiosity, guilt
then interest. When his expression turned to lust, I pulled the camera
back and threw the envelope containing our report into his face.

As I turned and stomped out the door, I heard his voice
behind me. "Lee! Where did you get that? Lee!"

In the elevator, I couldn't help myself. I watched the end of
the video of Michael on top of Gretchen, pumping himself into her,

of the camera widening further out so that current news stories were flashing on the tickertape outside the hotel window. A tear landed on the screen. I wiped off the tear and thrust the phone back into my pocket.

The elevator was half way down to the ground. I pressed the button to the main floor over and over again. I just wanted to get home! I needed safety and solitude! I needed to curl up into a little ball!

The elevator door opened and there was Peter Henge. Peter, Peter, Pumpkin-Eater was my former lover and business partner. He had left me because he had felt 'unfulfilled'. It had hurt—deeply— at the time. The pain he'd caused me now felt like it was in the distant past, but in actuality, it was not that long ago. As usual he was wearing a black leather jacket with dress-casual underneath. But he was still six-feet plus of manly masterly muscle. His brown eyes were immediately wary as soon as he caught sight of me.

"Here to pick up the spoils?" I lashed out at him bitterly. He had left me high and dry with only bills. The Cyber Culprit case had been all that had kept me from the poor-house. Now Peter was here to take that away from me too.

"Lee—"

I stared back at him with such ferocity that his voice was paralyzed for a moment.

I stepped around him and walked past.

But he recovered his voice before I could escape. "Lee—can we talk?"

I turned my fury back on him, but he looked like he was trying to be genuinely friendly. "About what?" I'd dialed my hostility back by half, but the question was still penetratingly sharp.

His shoulders drooped. "Us, work, life…?" He looked vulnerable.

I put my hand on his jacket sleeve. "Thanks, Peter. That's the friendliest thing anyone has said to me all day. But this case is giving me conniption fits. No rest for the wicked."

And with that, I was gone. Should I have given him more time? I didn't know, and I didn't have the time to find out. I just wanted to get home, to the comfort and security of my apartment, to a hot bath relaxing warmth into every one of my pores, perchance with water jets between my legs. More than anything else in the world, I just wanted to lie on my bed and curl up under the covers.

But if I wanted to keep this case—my only case and sole source of income—I'd better hustle over to Eric and get some more answers for Michael, notwithstanding the shyster that he was.

I had resolved to be professional in front of Eric, but as soon as my assistant opened his door, I marched straight to his dining room, sat down and had a good cry. In between tears, I brought him up to speed about what Michael had told me at our meeting. I told him that we'd argued, but left out the details.

"Never fear, Eric's here," he said, pushing his fingers into his red hair and smoothing it back on his head. "I tracked down the laser tag video through social media. Still images concealing the identity of the participants from the video were posted through anonymous websites two years ago, shortly after the video was recorded. But the video itself was never posted until the Cyber Culprit put it up a week ago. The owner's computer was hacked two years ago. And here's the kicker: the person who hacked the owner's computer is the same person who posted the video last week."

"The Cyber Culprit has been planning this campaign for *two years*?"

Eric nodded, turning his laptop towards me. The laser tag video was starting. I moved behind Eric so that we could both watch the video together. The lasertagger hit her nipple, then took aim at the other. A group in the background watched. Everyone's swimsuits were covered with sweat. They were all laughing and smiling.

Eric re-cued the video back to to the point where he missed her second nipple and had to pull down his thong. She took careful aim with her laser gun and hit his cock dead center. "This much we've already seen," he noted. On the video, her mouth moved towards her partner and her head momentarily blocked the camera.

But instead of the screen going black, the video continued. The other couples, likewise in various states of undress, commenced firing their lasers at each other but the camera was locked on the couple who'd just exchanged bursts of light directed at nipples and penis respectively. She was a petite blonde; he was a short but stocky brunette. His penis emerged from her mouth, then was swallowed again. She pulled her breasts back inside the top of her bikini and used them to rotate around his glistening cock as she drew her head upwards. When she reached the apex, she slowly sucked her mouth back down his length.

When Blondie lifted her head up to the top of his cock, his powerful hands lifted it the rest of the way. Muscles turned her around, pulled down her bikini bottom and moved his cock towards her crotch. She leaned over a counter and spread her legs. His cock was short, but more than made up for it's lack of length with its girth. She knew what was coming and took a deep breath.

Muscles was very gentle, but as soon as he was most of the way in, Blondie pushed back against him and his thighs slapped against her buttocks. After that, there was no pretense of anything except animal lust. He tore into her. She rocked forward just enough to take full advantage of his girth while not putting him in danger of falling out of her. Every time their thighs slapped together, her breasts started to slip out of her bikini. Her nipples poked out every time he slammed into her. Then her breasts were free and in a moment, she shuddered and screamed. He kept pumping, but was now careful to match what she seemed to want.

When she was still, he pulled himself out of her. She knelt down a few feet from him and he began to stroke his cock. He moaned. She opened her mouth, watched for a moment, then closed her eyes, opening her mouth as wide as it would go. His first spurt hit her eyes which she scrunched shut. But his second and third spurts landed squarely in her mouth. The rest of his spunk dribbled over his knuckles.

The video stopped. Eric selected its icon and brought up the video's metadata. There it was, a two-year-old creation date.

"Two years?!? Are you sure?"

He nodded again.

"Doesn't this open up whole new lines of investigation?"

He nodded and spoke while opening another file, bring up a bullet-point list on the screen, "This is what I'm suggesting going forward:"

* Deploy a 'bot to track him online
* Compile character profile to determine where to strike next
* Post a video survey
* Track credit card he used

"Why haven't we done this before, especially the credit card?" I asked.

"We didn't have enough information to program the 'bot with, nor enough for a character profile. Until I learned that CC has had this in the works for years, there didn't seem to be enough scope for a survey."

"What will the survey do?"

"First it will give us information from anyone CC has run into or had a run-in with. Second it will spook him into making a mistake."

"But why haven't you been tracking his credit card before?"

"This last posting, from the laser tag place, is the first time he used the same credit card twice."

I felt a broad smile spreading across my face. "Put all this into a supplementary report and courier it to Mr. Rayburn."

"Don't you want to deliver it yourself?"

"No." I was too tired to explain.

Ten minutes later I was standing in front of my apartment door fiddling with my key. Home! Peace. Quiet. I would open the door and hang my jacket on the peg next to my other outerwear. A few steps in and the kitchen table would be empty, just the way I'd left it this morning. In the fridge already-cut vegetables would be waiting along with a fresh container of the new diet dip—the perfect light meal ahead of my bath. To the right would be my leather couch. Further in was the bathroom and it's deep tub with water-jets. If dinner gave me energy, I might even try out my new waterproof vibrator.

I opened the door and was half way to my kitchen before I stopped dead in my tracks. The door to fridge was open and all its contents had been scattered over the table and onto the floor. The seat pillows on my couch had all been removed. The padding on the back of the couch had been slit open. Other possessions and papers were scattered about.

I slumped against the wall, pulled out my phone, and dialed 911. A disembodied voice came on the line, "What is your emergency?"

"Someone has broken into my apartment." I slowly slid down to the floor.

Cops, Lusty Lee Log #21

One minute I was ringing off from my 911 call and sliding inch by inch down the wall of my apartment entrance until I was sitting slumped on the floor in my ransacked apartment. The next, Rambo is jumping from corner to corner, his gun drawn.

Rambo is a uniformed police officer. Physically fit and oozing testosterone from every pore. He's checking to make sure that the person 'or persons' who'd broken into my apartment have left. I push myself to standing and inspect the contents of my fridge which are scattered over the kitchen table and floor. In the living room, the back of my couch has been slit open, as have its seat cushions and pillows. My CDs and personal papers were strewn about the floor.

Rambo reentered the living room. "Are you okay?" he asked.

I nodded. Sex with Rambo would be hot. But I'd just had angry sex with Michael—Michael Rayburn, the lover I'd caught cheating on me, and the lawyer who'd given me my one and only case—and I wasn't sure that another round of savage sex would be good for my karma. So I decided that if anything was going to happen, Rambo would have to take the initiative.

Rambo started taking down my account of what had happened. When he asked for my contact information, my heart skipped a beat, but I realized that this was merely *pro forma*, for his report. Still, when he asked whether there was any other way to reach me, I could tell that his interest in me went beyond my break and enter.

"Do you have any enemies?" he asked.

I shook my head and watched him enter the answer in his notebook with his strong and powerful hands.

"Should we check out your bedroom?" he asked.

I favored Rambo with a broad and inviting smile. Embarrassment fluttered across his face as he realized what he'd just asked me. Then the enthusiasm of my smile registered and he smiled back.

He was glancing into my bedroom when Eric arrived.

Eric was disheveled, only half of the buttons on his shirt were done up and one of its front flaps hung outside his jeans. At least my assistant was wearing a Tshirt. The red hair atop his head was unkempt. Worse, he looked like he hadn't shaved for days. But Rambo, his shaved dome half a head shorter than Eric's six-foot-three, his uniform perfectly maintained, seemed to find him adorable. Rambo was wide-shouldered and muscular, Eric thin and lanky.

"Is she okay?" Eric asked Rambo, his tone flirtatious.

Rambo shook his head and smiled up at Eric. "No, she's fine." He pointed back and forth between Eric and me. "Are you..."

Eric shook his head—dearie me no—and I swore he almost put his hand in front of his mouth. "She's my boss."

Rambo and Eric smiled at each other. Rambo flexed his arm as he poised his pen over his notebook. "Where can I contact you?" I cleared my throat. Rambo looked at me. "In case I need it for the investigation."

Eric placed a finger atop the notebook and, when Rambo turned back towards him, began to dictate his address and phone number.

"No, I don't have any enemies," I told Rambo, intent on refocusing attention where it belonged.

Rambo made the appropriate entry in his notebook.

"What's missing?" Eric asked.

Rambo looked back at Eric.

"Nothing from the kitchen or the living room," I advised, determined to have both their attention on me.

"What about the bedroom?" asked Eric.

I look at Rambo, "Was it..."

Rambo nodded slowly, trying to look sympathetic.

I sighed and started towards my bedroom. Eric and Rambo took half a step closer to each other but neither made a move to follow after me.

I was about to make a loud 'harrumph' when a Crime Scene Tech shuffled in. He was thin to the point of being scrawny. He had a sallow complexion into which large, dark-brown eyes had been inserted. His eyes scanned my apartment and leered at me but the polite expression on his face balanced the intrusion of his eyes. He was wearing a white shirt, black pants and a black polyester jacket with CSI in large white letters on the back.

Rambo waved at the tech, "Hi, Marty."

Somehow I knew that Marty hadn't been laid in months but that I'd still have to be subtle if I wanted to seduce him. Just what my unbalanced karma needed!

Rambo gestured towards me, "Marty, this is Ms. Brandt. It's her apartment."

Marty turned towards me and gave half a nod, his expression formal, "Ms. Brandt."

"You can call me Lee," I told him.

Marty nodded but didn't say anything. He made a beeline towards my emptied fridge.

"Marty, do you need me?" Rambo asked.

Marty, now staring intently into my fridge, shook his head.

"Okay, I'll shut the door behind me," Rambo responded. Out of the corner of my eye, I saw Rambo and Eric traipse off together.

I removed a half-squished cup of yogurt from the seat of one of the chairs in the kitchen and watched Marty slowly and methodically scan the remaining contents of my fridge. At last, his eyes poked around the edge of the fridge door.

"Ms. Brandt, this may take some time." His voice was soft, soothing.

"Please call me 'Lee'. I have time."

He shrugged and moved to the cabinets above the counter next to my fridge.

Nothing had apparently been disturbed in the upper cabinets, so he transferred his attention to the cabinets below the counter.

"Is it okay if I call you Marty?" I asked.

"CSI Cormack would be more respectful, not to mention more accurate."

"Very well, CSI Cormack, what are you looking for?"

"I'll know it when I see it."

"What about fingerprints?"

He shook his head. "They wore gloves."

I looked around the shambles of what was left of my apartment. "How do you know they wore gloves?"

"There was latex trace on your lock from when they picked it."

I had forgotten that Marty—CSI Cormack—hadn't needed to knock when he'd arrived.

Marty pointed to a CD on the kitchen table. "What's this?"

"It's from the living room," I said, moving to pick it up.

But Marty's hand—latex gloved hand—blocked mine. "Don't touch."

"It's just a—"

"It's just the only CD the burglars brought into the kitchen."

I looked around. Marty was right. It was the only one they'd removed from the living room. It was a compilation of Barry White's love songs.

Marty pulled a thin knife from his pocket and pried open the CD cover. Inside was the Barry White CD. He carefully removed the CD, then replaced it, grunted and moved into the living room.

"What are these papers?" Marty pointed to a fan-shaped pile of letter-sized pages to the left of my coffee table.

"Case reports." He looked at me, obviously dissatisfied with my response. "I'm a private investigator," I expanded.

"Are they all from one case?"

I nodded. I only had the one case.

Marty pointed to the coffee table. "They photographed them there, then tossed them aside." He pointed to the fan-shaped pile of papers.

He moved towards my bedroom while I looked back and forth between the papers and my coffee table. He was right!

Marty was standing in the door to my bedroom when I caught up. "Ms. Brandt. You might not want to see this."

"It's *my* bedroom why—"

"Did you leave your lingerie on your bed when you left?"

"No. It was in the dresser. Why do you ask such a question?"

"Ms. Brandt, you—"

But I had already managed to peer around him. Up one side of my bed, arranged as if they were for sale at a high-end store, were all my panties. Down the other side were my brassieres. In the center was my favorite fetish outfit: black leather mini-skirt, a black bikini string top, a leather collar with one chrome ring in the center. The crotch of a pair of red silk panties poked out the bottom of the miniskirt. Below the miniskirt, as if they were a pair of legs, was a pair of stockings.

"—not want to see this," he finished.

Where my head would have been was a book. Between the stockings was my favorite vibrator.

Marty turned to face me and did his best to block my view inside the bedroom. "Ms. Brandt—"

"'Ms. Brandt', seems to be a bit formal for someone who's seen so much of me, don't you think, CSI Cormack." I pointed at his chest with my finger, making it plain that I intended to imminently poke him with it.

"Lee," he conceded.

"Marty."

He nodded. "Marty."

"Now that we're on first-name basis, what the f— heck is up in my bedroom?!?"

He stepped to one side and we both peered in.

"When you left this morning…"

"Everything was in the dresser drawer."

"Do you have a stalker?"

"No. Do you have a fetish freak?"

Marty shook his head. "No, we don't have any other cases like this."

We stood looking at what was on the bed, each in our own thoughts. I suddenly became aware that we were standing very close to each other and that my right foot was in front of his left. I tried to step away but stumbled and he had to catch me.

"Sorry," I apologized, taking two backward steps into the bedroom.

He didn't comment and once again we were in silence. Then Marty took a step into the room and pointed over my shoulder at the book. "Is that the one where the hero ties the woman, a buxom brunette, to his wall with leather bindings? Her hands are high above her head and her legs are spread apart. She is nude. When he wants he fondles her and sucks her nipples. She's just the right height so that he can penetrate her at will. When he's not in the mood, he ignores her."

He turned to me, his face expressionless.

I shook my head, "No, it's the one where the heroine leads the man by the leash. He's a thin studious type. She drags him wherever she goes with only his leash and harness on. When he has been bad, she spanks his bare bum without mercy. When he had been good, she slides her hand lower..."

"I haven't read that one, but it sounds interesting." There was the hint of a smile on his lips. "Is it anything like the one where he pursues her for weeks and months and the final scene has her quivering on the bed, her hips propped up with a pillow, her tight pinkness liberally lubricated ready for his merciless thrusts?" I couldn't tell for sure, but there seemed to be delight under his poker face.

I favored him with a broad smile and shook my head in my

best coquette fashion. "It's more like the one where she teases him without pity and when he has become uncontrollably hot, she rubs him all over with ice, slides an ice cube up his ass and then gives him head with a milkshake dribbling out of her mouth."

"I may have read that one. And by then he's so horny that his erection stays hard despite the cold milkshake and he takes her with passion just short of violence?" I nodded and Marty continued, "But what about the one where they paint each other into one grand mural for all eternity?"

Now he too was smiling from ear to ear. He stepped around me, fully into the room and waved his hand over the bed, "What is your choice pretty lady?"

I reached for a red bra, but his hand blocked me. "Please don't; it's still a crime scene." He looked back and forth between me and my bed full of lingerie. "I have to process all this. And I won't be able to concentrate with you here."

"When will I be allowed back in?"

"In a day or two."

"So, I have to stay in a hotel tonight?"

"'Fraid so." He did look genuinely sorry.

"Maybe we could meet later for drinks?"

That brought the smile back to his face and he nodded. "In a day or two, once I've finished my initial investigation."

Two days later, he was already at the hotel's bar when I arrived. He was still wearing his white shirt and black pants but now he'd substituted a suit jacket for his CSI polyester. "Do you want anything to drink?" he asked.

I shook, my head "No." and he took my hand and led me out of the bar. I was wearing a Maple Leafs hockey jersey which stretched down past my knees.

In the elevator Marty turned to me, "Do you have anything on underneath that sweater?"

I shook my head. He gave me a gentle kiss on my cheek. The elevator mirror reflected an odd looking couple—me jiggling breasts under the jersey, its blue bringing out the color of mischief within my eyes, his formal jacket, the somber dark brown eyes. He was half a foot taller than me, his short dark hair another contrast to my lighter curls.

Moving out of the elevator, he placed an arm around my elbow, then slid his hand down and we held hands all the way to my room. It was so *sweet*! I fumbled one-handed with the key card; I didn't want to let go of his hand.

In the room, he stopped just inside and amazingly we were still holding hands. I turned to stand just in front of him. He bent down and kissed me gently on the lips. I kissed him back being careful to keep my tongue back behind my teeth. He pulled away and I smiled up at him. He kissed me again, this time placing his left hand lightly on my hip. I kissed back and squeezed his right hand.

We kissed like that for several moments, like teenagers, not sure how to move onto the next stage. I took half a step back and he followed, then another and another and the wall was pressing against my butt. But Marty didn't get the hint. He was still kissing with just his lips. He was a good kisser, varying pressure, altering the areas of contact—but I wanted more. And I wanted more than hand-holding and a hand resting on my hip.

I pushed forward from the wall and our legs touched. My breasts were pressed against his suit jacket. I let go of his hand and pushed his suit jacket open so that my breasts were now pressing against his shirt. At last I could feel heat! He groaned, so softly I could barely hear, but a groan nonetheless.

I began to caress his torso and around his back. My finger on Marty's spine seemed to throw a switch and he moved one of his hands under my jersey, up my thigh, just below my buttock. His tongue touched my lower lip and at last it was safe to release my tongue towards his lips. I went for his upper lip, then moved right along the top surface, just where moisture started. He moved his tongue left and we met at the right side of my mouth. Then we slid back to the center, poking forward into each other's mouth as we went.

His other hand gave my other buttock a gentle squeeze through my jersey and I pressed forward against him. Marty groaned again, loud into my mouth. He pulled back aghast.

"Lee, I'm sorry—"

I reached up, pulled his lips back to mine, and darted my tongue inside his mouth. He could groan as loudly and as often as he liked! Reaching up had the effect of moving both his hands under my sports jersey and atop my buttocks which I wiggled to show my delight. I'd never had such a gentle lover, never anyone who made me feel this soft and safe.

I let my hands slide down his spine. Each vertebra elicited a different moan from within Marty's throat. I was starting to map out how his spine could be played as a musical instrument when he moved one of his hands to my spine. A jolt shot up and out my eyeballs.

Marty had pulled back and was looking at me with a concerned look. We were no longer touching. "Are you okay?" he asked, removing his jacket and preparing to place it over my shoulders.

"Never better." I pushed his jacket aside so that it ended up on the doorknob and pulled his head back to my lips. As soon as our lips touched, I shut my eyes. Once again our tongues were dancing in each other's mouths.

Marty's hand moved up to the next vertebra and this time the jolt zapped down my legs. My knees gave way and I had to grab hold tight on his shirt. I could tell that he wanted to pull back to check up on me again, but I held on tight and in a moment, he relaxed back into our kiss.

The next vertebra he touched didn't send a jolt. Rather it radiated heat directly into my sex. And then the heat in my pussy was flowing up and into his fingertips. I moved my fingers to the corresponding vertebra on his back and could feel heat flowing into my own fingers, hands, and wrists.

I moaned and held on tight to Marty, swaying against his hard pole of a body. And there was something new pressing out below his pelvis. I tried to reach around to unbutton his shirt, but he was pressed too tightly against me. I backed up against the wall and managed to get two buttons undone before he pinned me firmly against the hard surface.

His right leg slipped between my legs, the coarse material of his pants rasping against my sex.

"Ow!" I protested.

Marty took a full two steps back.

"Lee, I'm sorry, I—" He had picked up his jacket with one hand and was reaching for the doorknob with the other.

"Stop!"

Marty froze, his hand half an inch from the doorknob.

"Look at me," I told him.

He turned around but was careful to maintain distance between us.

"Marty, I like you kissing me. I like you *touching* me. You won't break me. You don't have to pull back every time I make a sound."

"But you—"

"It wasn't you. It was your pants. They're rough."

I pulled my jersey over my head and tossed it aside. I let him look up and down my body and back up to my eyes. I motioned that he should remove his clothes.

Marty hesitated for a moment. I motioned again. He replaced his jacket on the doorknob and undid a button on his shirt. I nodded. He swiftly undid every button and all but ripped the shirt off his back before placing it over his jacket.

I motioned towards his pants. He looked down, unclasped his belt buckle, then looked up at me. "My underwear isn't really…"

I rocked my hips side to side. "Your underwear will shortly be on the floor."

I had never seen anyone remove pants so fast. And when he stepped out of them, he slid his socks and shoes off as well with the same movement.

Marty stepped forward to touch me, but I scampered the rest of the way into the room and around to the other side of the bed, turning on the lights as I went.

But when I turned around, Marty hadn't moved.

"Marty?"

"You find me ugly."

I stepped down the foot of the bed so that I could see him. He *was* scrawny, his joints round circular globes between the bones on his arms and legs. It didn't help that his expression which was sad and forlorn. His cock was the only thing which wasn't thin and knobbly; it stood high and strong, unashamed of its desire.

"Marty, I do not find you ugly. Not in the least. Do you find *me* ugly?"

He slowly shook his head and took a step forward. I moved to the top of the bed and pulled the comforter and sheets off the bottom of the mattress. Marty had taken another tentative step forward. I jumped onto the bed, hoping that my girlish abandon and jiggling breasts would encourage him.

But he stopped at the side of the bed. "Shouldn't we turn the lights off?" he asked.

I fluffed my hair and shook my head. "I want to see you." I

pointed up and down his body, circling his pelvis where his cock continued to stand ready. "I want to see your eyes enjoying looking at me." I caressed my breasts, then turned slowly towards him, lifting my left leg to better display my pubic bush.

He gulped and nodded but did his best to hide his bashful smile.

I turned onto my tummy. "Look at my backside. Enjoy looking. There's nothing for a man to be ashamed about if he enjoys looking at a woman."

There was only silence behind me. I wiggled my bum.

"Even a beautiful woman?" he asked.

I turned over onto my back. "Especially a beautiful woman," I responded. We smiled at each other. I motioned for him to come to the bed and he slipped in next to me but was careful to prevent contact between our bodies.

I lifted my left leg and turned slightly towards him, careful not to be the first to initiate contact on the bed. "Touch me," I told him.

He turned towards me and in so doing his chest grazed my breast. He froze.

"Touch me," I repeated.

Marty gingerly reached over and touched the bottom of my other breast.

"Touch me, Marty," I urged.

At last he brought his hand up my breast and brushed his fingers across my nipple. Little sparks of electricity tickled across my breast.

"Kiss her," I told him.

His kiss on my nipple was as tentative as had been his kisses on my mouth, but this only heightened the pleasure as it allowed me to experience each stage of the kiss fully. His dry lips on the tip of my nipple, his dry lips sliding down the shaft of my nipple, then wet at the top. Wetness tenderly enveloped my nipple. Then suction, slowly, softly building until my nipple started to be sucked into his mouth. His dry lips advancing over my areola until it too was lubricated by the wetness of his mouth. He held my entire areola and nipple in his mouth for a delightful moment, then pressed his tongue against one side of them. This he also held for a delightful moment. Then he began to circle his tongue round and round, tightening a string that pulled my hips forward against his leg.

Side by side, our bodies were so *warm* against each other!

I reached down between us and lightly caressed his cock and balls. He moaned. His cock was hot in my fingers. He released my breast from his mouth and lightly caressed her with his hand. He lapped his tongue around the nipple of my other breast duplicating the little sparks of electricity across her entire surface.

I stroked up and down his cock. "Do you like it when I touch you?" I asked.

"Yes." It was half moan, half syllable.

"I'm sure I'll like it when you touch me."

He continued to tongue the breast closest to him, but his right hand left my other breast and his fingers walked down my torso. At my pelvis, he explored back and forth, as if this was virgin territory for him. But when he found the edge of my pubic hair, he pulled his fingers through my curls as if luxuriating in the finest fur.

His fingers worked their way though my bush like a band of explorers marching through a forest. When they reached my pubic prominence, they stopped. My clit cried out for their caress, but Marty's attention was in his mouth. He had sucked my nipple into his mouth and was licking his tongue around its areola. Each time he circled, he sucked a little more of her in. As soon as he reached her outer limit, he stopped.

I turned onto my back and my nipple popped free. At the same moment, I let go of his cock and spread my legs.

"Touch me," I begged.

Marty pulled up on my pubic hair. Pent-up jolts roiled up and down my clit. Waves of heat coursed through my pussy lips. Juices bubbled inside. My entire pelvic region squeezed together in the most enjoyable fashion imaginable. He relaxed his fingers, then pulled up again.

"Marty!"

His fingers froze in place. "Lee?"

"Don't stop, Marty. Whatever you do, don't stop!"

He relaxed his fingers, but more slowly this time, then tentatively began to pull up again.

I bucked my hips upwards. "Touch me lower."

He ran his fingers across my sex. I readied to buck again. I tried to tell him how good his fingers felt. The moan in my throat could not escape. Everything was held motionless, everything was in the thrall of his fingers which were lightly brushing up and down my sex.

Then finally I could breathe again. His fingers were at the bottom of my pussy, one between my pussy lips, two on the outer edge of each lip. One finger trailed out to the side making tiny jerking movements and accentuating the pleasures of the fingers next to it. When his fingers were most of the way up, Marty pressed his thumb just above my clit and gently rotated. His rotations warmed my clit and when his fingers touched her, she melted, my pussy melted, my pelvis turned to jelly, then my hips.

"Am I wet?" I asked him.

He lifted his fingers, all except the middle one which he pressed downwards. I felt him slide easily inside.

"Very wet," he responded.

"Then it's time." I reached into the drawer in my nightstand, fished out a condom, ripped open the packet and unrolled it down the shaft of his cock which throbbed its approval. A gentle tug to seat the ring at the bottom of his penis and we were good to go. I leaned back and spread my legs.

At last, we'd reached the point at which Marty no longer required encouragement or confirmation. He lifted himself up and over my leg, carefully centered himself over me, and slowly advanced his cock towards my sex. When the tip of his cock pressed against my vulva, I reached down and guided him to the opening of my vagina.

Marty pushed himself gently inside, watching my face for any traces of discomfiture. But I'm sure he saw only a smile on my lips and sparkles in my eyes. His slow advance let me feel each minute adjustment my vagina was making to accommodate his penis, each relaxation and tightening of muscle. His deliberate approach let me sense when his pubic bone approached mine, let me feel its heat before its touch.

And then he was all the way in, our pubic bones pressed together. He gradually lowered the rest of his body down to me, inch by inch our tummies uniting. His skin released a burst of energy from my nipples to my pussy. As he brought our heads together, there was a most pleasant tickling against my pussy lips caused by his penis sliding out a couple of inches.

Marty bent down to kiss me, but his lips were at my forehead. He arched his back to bring our lips together and his penis tickled back into my pussy. His tongue darted into my mouth, then quickly retreated. But he wasn't going to get away! I thrust my tongue inside his mouth, found his tongue and teased the soft underside of his with the rougher upper tip of mine.

Our tongues danced around each other and Marty seemed content to remain here, his penis inside me, his arms supporting his body sufficiently that our skin touched but only lightly, content to confine the thrusts and parries of our lovemaking to our tongues.

But I wanted more! I bucked my hips upward, lifting him, then rocked my hips back, drawing his cock halfway out of my pussy. He moaned inside my mouth. I rocked my hips forward again and felt him slide all the way back inside me. He wasn't breathing. I accelerated the rocking of my hips, stroking joy, stoking heat.

Marty pulled his mouth off mine and gulped air into his lungs.

I grabbed for his buttocks. "Hips, not lips," I told him.

He smiled and nodded as once again oxygen flowed in his blood. Now it was Marty's hips, not mine, that were rocking his cock in and out. And since he didn't have to bend towards me, he was able to achieve longer strokes, strokes that caressed my pussy lips, strokes which sucked my cunt out, strokes which filled her up.

Sometimes it was nice to master, sometimes it was nice to be mastered, but today the mutuality of our lovemaking was exactly what I needed.

I reached up and fondled his throat, encouraged his arms, squeezed his nipples between thumb and forefinger until he moaned again. Marty's breathing was quickening and each breath was shallower than the last. He was on the plateau, but moving towards the edge. Pleasant as was his cock stroking in and out of my cunt, I was still only in the center of the plateau.

"Touch my breasts," I urged. He needed something to distract him from the sensations he was generating inside his cock.

Marty shifted his weight to his left arm, which altered his angle of attack down below in *most* pleasant fashion, and placed his right palm on my breast. I could feel the heat from his hand penetrate all the way into my lungs. He squeezed gently and there was a jolt down below. Through his cock, through our pubic bones, I felt a shudder at the bottom of his spine.

"Touch my nipples, use your fingers," I pleaded. Fingers would pleasure my breast as much as would his palms. But their focused touch would arouse Marty less than his full palm on my skin. Marty began to brush his fingertips across my nipples, circling them then pinching them gently, ever so gently.

I shut my eyes to concentrate below. Marty's cock thrust rhythmically in and out. I altered the orientation of my hips to concentrate sensation into my clit. Each thrust raised the temperature in my cunt, each thrust sped me towards the edge, each thrust accumulated energy within. Each thrust caught me up with Marty, but he was still ahead.

I opened my eyes. Marty's eyes were closed. Happiness and joy had returned color to his cheeks. I could feel him stepping out over the edge. I drove my fingernails into his chest. His eyes shot open and his hips wobbled to a stop. A plaintive 'why?' formed on his lips.

I pushed my hips up against him and rotated our pubic bones together. "Together. Let's come together." I concentrated on stirring my passions to boiling as my clit pointed to the hours of the clock-head.

He nodded and rotated his pelvic bone counter-clockwise. I caught up to him and we stood together at the edge of the precipice.

"Breathe," I told him, sucking a full breath into my own lungs.

He gasped and thrust his cock in as far as it would go.

"Now!" I shouted, rocking my hips away from him.

"Now!" he shouted back. He collapsed down onto me, grabbed my buttocks and fastened our mouths together. Tongues danced. Cock rammed in and out. Pussy whimpered.

A wrenching twist inside my cunt shocked my eyes open. Marty's head was above me, every feature on his face scrunched up. The end of the twist inside me whipped white-hot electricity up my spine, stopping just short of my head. I started to relax as the jolt slithered warmth back down my spine but my cunt was being twisted again and jolts, almost as hot as the first, were rocketing down my legs.

Marty was pumping away, making little keening sounds of pleasure. The electricity collapsed into my cunt, then another contraction sent it back out in all directions. Marty shuddered to a stop. I rocked my hips up and down as fast and as far as I could. He opened his eyes and we shared the final pulses of our orgasms. An eternity came, an eternity reigned, an eternity faded into nothingness.

Hours later, after we'd showered and finished our room-service snack, Marty motioned me over to the bed. He'd made it up and now had a variety of reports spread out on top of it in an organized grid. He pointed to each report in turn, "There were no fingerprints, no chemical trace, no indication of anything taken, no link to any other break and enter."

"In other words, nothing."

He shook his head. "There was one thing." He turned over one of the reports. There was a baggie attached. It contained several flecks of paint.

"I thought you said there was no chemical trace."

"Technically—officially—there wasn't. We weren't able to connect this to anything. But I recognized it."

"You recognized it?"

He nodded. "It's from a paintball club I used to attend."

"Shouldn't that be in your report?"

He shook his head. "The club is run by my former girlfriend. She said that if she ever saw my head, if she ever heard from me, that she'd file a report that I'd used my police status to extort free paintball games."

"Is that true?"

He shook his head. "I didn't extort anything."

"But you never paid?"

He looked down at the floor and nodded.

So she'd be able to make out an initially plausible case. "What's the address?"

He gave me a small piece of paper on which he'd written 'Patty's Paintball' and the address.

Marty took me back to my apartment and walked through the mess to make sure we were alone. "Do you want me to stay to help clean up?" he asked.

I thanked him but I just wanted to be alone.

An hour later and I had everything mostly cleaned up and the remains of my couch piled on what was left of it.

There was a knock at the door. Eric's face smiled at me through the peephole. As soon as I opened the door, Eric strutted in, followed by Rambo. Eric fluttered over to my kitchen table, took my laptop out from his messenger bag and booted it up, making no pretense of not knowing my password. "There was no effort to break into your laptop," he announced, looking pleased with himself.

"So we don't know whether your firewalls worked or not?" I pointed out.

I was pleased to see that my query had punctured his balloon somewhat and turned to Rambo. "Has there been any progress in the investigation?" I asked.

Rambo shook his head. I was about to ask a follow-up question when my phone rang. It was Michael Rayburn, wanting to come up to discuss the revised report Eric and I had submitted. I managed to quickly scoot the two lovers out of my apartment and still have time for two deep breaths before Michael arrived.

Michael Rayburn, the lawyer who'd retained me to track down the elusive Cyber Culprit, Michael Rayburn, my cheating lover, stepped tentatively into the room. He held out the report. "There are some good ideas in here," he ventured.

"Thank you." Since he had made the first move towards peace, I ushered him to the kitchen table. He stared at the remains of my couch without comment.

We sat across the table from each other. Once again, I waited for him to speak first.

He opened the report. "The client likes the idea of pursuing the Cyber Culprit, instead of just tracking him after the fact. He especially liked the idea of assembling a psychological profile because there's no telling what the Cyber Culprit will do once you're hot on his tail."

"There will be expenses," I told him.

He reached into his jacket pocket and withdrew a cheque. A very *generous* cheque!

"Thank you," I told him, secreting the cheque.

Again I waited for him to speak first. Again, I was rewarded. "Lee, I know that you were angry with me, and I guess I deserved what you did to me in my office. I hurt for days afterward." He paused, but I kept my silence. "Still, it was hot."

"No more Gretchen."

He nodded, "No more Gretchen." Gretchen was the former girlfriend I'd caught him sleeping with.

Paintball, Lusty Lee Log #22

"Hi, I'm Patty," she said, indicating her business card.

I told her that my name was Lee and we shook hands. Patty — her card said Patricia — was a petite, and very attractive, Korean woman. We were in the front room of Patty's Paintball Palace. It had a long glass-topped counter displaying various-colored ammunition underneath and a cash register at one end.

Patty moved behind the counter and stood expectantly in front of a list of prices on the wall. Beside the list was a rack holding a wide variety of paintball guns, a door separating the high-end from the low-end weapons. The other walls held a selection of masks, goggles, vests and gloves. Patty herself was wearing a form-fitting vest that pulled in at her waist accentuating her feminine curves. Her long black hair was wound in bun and held in place by the straps of the mask perched on her forehead.

Patty pointed at the list of prices on the wall. "What'll it be?" she asked. She looked me up and down and pointed to my jeans and the T-shirt struggling to contain my breasts. "You'll need some protective gear." Her smile was full, a welcome counterpoint to her delicate features. We even had the same lipstick.

"Actually, I'm not here to play," I told her. I pulled out the baggie containing the paintball chips which CSI Marty Cormack had recovered from the break-in of my apartment and laid it on the counter separating us. "I'm trying to tack down who might have used these."

Almost as soon as I'd shown her the baggie, I realized that the direct approach had been a mistake. Patty's smile vanished. She turned, grabbed a gun and ran through the door behind the counter. She was pulling her mask down over her face as the door shut behind her.

I grabbed a mask, jumped over the counter and pushed through the door. Patty was nowhere to be seen. The room was much larger than I'd expected. It had a small sand-bag fort to my left, then there was a large open area. Overhead were large industrial-style lights casting an orangey hue over the entire area.

A paintball whizzed by my right ear and I ducked behind one of the tubular barriers, wishing that I'd taken a gun with me when I'd charged into the paint-war area. I heard two paintballs smack into the other side of the barrier.

The lights snapped off and I decided that I was '3' for '3' in the mistake department today. In the distance, Patty's voice announced, "Fresh meat, boys!" Narrow beam laser lights of a variety of colors shot out of the darkness and began a search pattern.

One of the lasers hit my leg but I jerked it back and the paintball hit the barrier instead of me. More lasers started to move towards me, so I ran as fast as I could. But I smashed headlong into another tubular barrier, knocking it down and landing on top of it. Another laser beam found my belly. I whirled and ran, but there was a sudden *stinging* on my buttocks. I was hit!

Lasers followed me as I zigzagged around barriers. My eyes had adjusted to the dark and the ambient light and the light from the lasers let me see the rough outline of the paintball zone. It appeared to be a large open area filled with barriers, some of the soft tubular variety covered in vinyl, some made of wood. In the distance, there was what appeared to be a mock-up of a house but only partially constructed — room-to-room combat?

I headed for what appeared to be a twenty-foot wall made of wood. But just before I was safely behind it, the lasers converged on me and I was hit on my thigh. Damn, it hurt!

I came out the other side of the wall but was immediately hit by at least ten laser beams. As I ducked back, *splat* after *splat* hit on the wall and the area I'd just vacated. I tore back the way I'd come and ran smack into one of the paintball warriors. He was a skinny little guy and I sent him flying, ending up with his weapon in my hands.

At the edge of the barrier, I saw — actually more sensed than saw — something move and I fired.

"Ow!" my victim protested.

But I didn't have time to gloat. I ran away from the barrier at right angles to the it. Laser lights flickered behind me, probably distracted by the skinny little guy and the other guy I'd shot.

I got behind a tubular barrier and turned around to see the laser beams tracking in a disorganized search pattern. I fired off shots in the direction of the base of the lasers. A few splats and another "Ow!"

A new *sting* on my thigh. I turned in the direction the shot had come from and fired off a shot, but all I heard was *splat* on wood. I was hit on my ribs, just below my bra. Damn! Then a hit on my belly. Fuck that *hurt*!

I moved to the other side of the barrier away from the sniper who obviously had me in his sights, but now the combined lasers found me. I turned to run, but was hit repeatedly on my legs and I stumbled to the floor. I tried to get up, but couldn't. I was hit again in the ribs. Shit! All I could do was to try to cover my chest and head.

"Cease fire!" a male voice called out and the lights came on.

"So *how* is Marty?" said Patty somewhere behind me.

"Who said anything about Marty?" I retorted.

"Any other CSI would have had the balls to come himself."

"Marty's fine."

"Fuck Marty." This was the male voice, full of force and command. "Why don't you just tell us why you came here?"

I took a breath—it had to be shallow because my ribs hurt like hell, "My apartment was broken into. Marty—CSI Cormack—found trace evidence of a paintball. He said the paintball was special order, manufactured here."

"She's right," Patty chimed in. "It was one of mine."

"Who did you make it for?" I wheezed.

"Marty's *bitch*." Patty paused to allow all and sundry to absorb the particular derision with which she was describing me, "wants to turn me into her *snitch*."

There was some rustling off to my right and I heard a male voice behind me whisper, "Who'd you make it for?"

Patty whispered something back, but I couldn't make out what she said.

The male voice, even more obviously in control now came from off to my right, "If she can pass the test—"

"But—" protested Patty.

"—we'll tell her what we know." His voice had the finality of an order.

There was a disjointed chorus of "Yes."

"You want to know who Patty made the balls for?" It was the male commander, obviously talking to me.

"Yes." Since this is just one word, I managed to put more force behind it.

"Then stand up."

I stood up, wobbly. Three men helped me out of my paint-splattered T-shirt and jeans. They dabbed alcohol onto my wounds. It stung for a moment, then I felt better. Patty, Commander, and the rest of the group moved off in the direction of the mocked-up house.

After I'd been cleaned up and allowed to put my T and jeans back on, the three men picked up their weapons and indicated that I should march towards the house. It was framed-in, with chipboard nailed to the outer walls. There was a doorway, but no door.

Inside the house was one large room. The floor had interlocking rubber mats, the kind favored by gyms and daycares. The walls were unfinished drywall, unfinished that is except for paintball splatters so numerous that they virtually covered the entire surface. The ceiling was open, joists every two feet.

There were twelve candles in a circle in the center of the floor. Dangling from the ceiling, in the center of the ring of candles, were two ropes. Each of the ropes had a handle on its end dangling a couple of feet off the floor. I took a closer look at the candles. Each was set in small dish of water. They were of various heights but none was more an inch above the water.

Patty, now wearing a leather bikini, and the Commander were standing on the other side of the circle. He was in leather pants and a white spandex shirt. I estimated that he was six feet tall and muscular. Swarthy. He had a scar on his right cheek.

"Put her in the circle," Commander ordered.

The trio behind me motioned me forward with their guns. When I was in the center of the circle, they joined their mates who were sitting cross-legged on the floor against the walls.

The lights shining through the ceiling started to dim and I watched Patty begin to light the candles. But Commander snapped his fingers indicating that he was in charge and that I should attend only to him. In spite of myself, I felt a tingling in my crotch.

He pointed to the ropes dangling from the ceiling joists. "You will hold onto the handles." I reached for the handles and held on, my hands dangling by my sides.

He smiled and continued, "If you let go before the candles are re-lit, the lights will be turned on and you will have failed." Patty lit the last candle and we were in darkness except for the twelve flickering flames. The only sound was Commander's voice, "You may speak or scream. We may or may not pay attention." He grabbed my hair with both hands and pulled back, then let go. His fingers traced down my arm until he reached my hands where he wrapped his fingers around mine. Our bodies touched with each breath. "But if you let go, it will be over and you will leave. Do you understand?"

Relief mixed with my fear. He had given me a way out. But what was going to happen while I managed to hold onto the handles long enough to get the information I'd come for?

I took as deep a breath as I could manage. "Yes. I understand." Another mistake?

"Good." His lips were so close his voice sounded as if it was coming from the center of my head. "Hold tight."

He let go of my hands and pulled on something and my hands were drawn up level with my ears. One of the candles winked out, the water in its bowl making a soft hiss as it extinguished the flame.

Male voices on the periphery whispered. "Big boobs." "Bigger hips." "Curly brown hair." "Lips ripe for kissing." "Young and ready." "Nice round ass." "Long legs." "Legs spread wide." "I bet she likes it."

"Quiet!" thundered Commander.

Patty's voice from behind me began to read from an Edgar Allan Poe story describing the villain preparing to dismember a corpse. Another candle went out. There was the sound of a knife being sharpened and a third candle fizzled out. Patty described each body part being severed, each body part being carefully placed into a freezer.

Each time a body part was placed into the freezer, a candle went out. By the time the villain shut the freezer, there were only four candles burning. The villain cemented the freezer into the wall. Two more candles went out. I felt a cold draft.

The freezer began to make knocking noises. Another candle succumbed to the water surrounding it. As the dismembered corpse arose in the dead of the night to claim its revenge the last candle went out and I screamed. A clammy hand touched my belly. I *screamed* blue bloody murder!

Hands began to grab at my clothes. Somewhere the knife was being sharpened again. Hands reached up my shirt, grabbed my tits. Someone breathed on my neck. Hands grabbed every corner of my T-shirt and slowly ripped it away. A knife's cold steel pressed against my belly, then upward. I stopped breathing and kept absolutely still. The knife kept moving upward. It twisted, then pulled away. My bra gave way releasing my breasts.

A hand reached down the front of my jeans. Other hands unbuttoned and unzipped my pants. The first hand continued downwards and stroked lightly against my panties. Other hands pulled my jeans down and away.

Hands lifted my panties, pulling them up into the center of my sex, first softly, then tightly, then painfully. The knife came back and I heard it slice through my panties and the rest of my bra. There were fur and tongues and mouths all over my body. A strange tongue on my knee. A wide tongue up my pussy. A wet cold nose slid up my butt crack. Gross and sexy all at the same time.

The buzz of a stereo turning on morphed into the pounding rhythms of Wagner's *Ride of the Valkyries* and began to play in the background, softly, then louder. There were the sounds of saws and hammers, worse than the sound of the helicopters from *Apocalypse Now*. Water sloshed back and forth. There was evil laughter, evil laughter gleefully assembling implements of torture. I held onto the handles as hard as I could and concentrated on my breathing. I wanted to run and run and *run*!

Patty was reading again, now a poem of frozen dark death.

Cold, wet. Large chunks of ice were sliding up the back of my legs to my buttocks. *Freezing*!

"Frozen dark death," intoned Patty's voice.

The ice came around, sliding across the top of my pubic hair, up my belly and frigid onto my breasts. My nipples retreated inward to escape the cold. Then the glacier moved lower, stopping halfway into my pubic mound. It began to melt, dribbling ice water into my sex, sending shivers up my spine.

"Frozen dark death," repeated Patty.

There were mournful, painful wails all around me. I *screamed* louder than I'd ever screamed before.

Then laughter. I stopped screaming. My belly heaved air into my lungs.

The *Ride of the Valkyries* began to shriek to the clang of metal beating on metal. Demons ready to tear me apart.

Fingers began to probe my sex massaging her warm and wet. The fingers were experienced and I had a new need to hold tight onto the handles at the end of the ropes.

"The dark gets inside you," Patty's voice softly soothed "It burrows inside every orifice. Its worms eat inside you until there's no light anywhere. Until you are darkness' worm. And the worm's going inside is pleasurable, oh so pleasurable."

The fingers began to probe inside my pussy. I was wet and hot. The fingers slid upwards and I loosened my knees to lower myself onto them. Tightness and tingling were rippling inside my sex. Other hands caressed my taut nipples. Another finger began to explore my ass, pressing at the opening of my anus. A mouth kissed my lips full force and its tongue slithered inside.

The music stopped abruptly and Patty's voice was suddenly harsh and loud, "But you must not let the darkness inside."

I tried to clench my cunt to prevent the invading darkness but the fingers inside were rotating and brushing against my sensitive spot. On the outside, they were gently stroking my clit. The invaders had overwhelmed all resistance and I was floating blissfully in their captivity, oblivious to my impending doom. I shut my eyes, surrendering.

"The worms like the warmth of your ass where they can slide inside to burrow upwards."

The finger behind inserted itself up my ass and began to move upward, wiggling, just like a worm. My eyes shot open, but I was still in the grasp of darkness. The worm wriggled upwards.

"Upwards, ever upwards." Patty's voice was at the back of my neck. "Other worms, other openings."

The tongue tickled the inside of my ear. I bit my lip to stifle the scream.

Then all the fingers and all the tongues left me. I floated alone. I shivered in the sudden coldness. Without warning, without a sound, there was something large between my legs. Hard and *warm*.

"Mmm." Patty's lips sounded next to my ear. "But the

biggest worms especially love your cunt where they can hide inside..."

The tip of the cock pressed against the opening of my sex. My cunt wanted to be fucked, oh how she wanted to be *fucked*! I was aroused in every which way and now, without sensation, frustration seized and constricted my entire insides. But I didn't want to give into the worms. I didn't want them slithering inside me. I—

"If you want, you can let go of the handles." It was the Commander's voice, hard and throaty. His body pressed against mine, his chest hair brushing against my nipples.

"The worms," said Patty. She paused to lick up the back of my neck, sending shivers up and down my spine. "Come out at night to crawl inside your eyes."

A squeal escaped my lips. I felt her tongue slither down my spine. Then her teeth began to nip my butt.

"If you want, you can let go of the handles," the Commander repeated.

"Fuck you!" I whispered so that only he could hear.

His cock slid slowly into me, delicious inch by delicious inch. His fingers grabbed my buttocks, his thumbs on the front of my hips. He rocked himself in and out, the entire length of his cock, filling me, then leaving a painful void behind. He angled his cock at just the right spots. I tried to resist, but every time Commander's cock was fully inside, he ground our pubic bones together and my clit sent out signals of surrender.

The ropes were being pulled higher with every thrust, lifting my heels from the floor. Commander dragged me forward completing his control over me. I felt heat in my breasts, then in my cunt and she gripped and clasped herself around his girth, squeezing and releasing uncontrollably. I felt my wetness dribble down. It had all been too much and I was spurting with each contraction.

He pulled out before my orgasm was complete. The *bastard*!

"She's come," he announced triumphantly.

Small fingers massaged my ejaculate all over my pussy. Up and down my pussy lips, round and round my clit.

"She *is* a special one." It was Patty's voice, tinged with awe. She pressed her fingers inside and milked my g-spot, spurting even more salty goo into her hands. When I stopped spurting, she scooped up the liquid and spread it over my breasts. Her tongue lapped it up, her lips sucked at my nipples. I felt the quivers of the half-spent orgasm tickle up and down my spine.

Patty pulled away and the Commander was back, his cock pressed against my pussy opening. "That was soft. Now it's time for hard." There was an edge in his voice. What did he want? My hands were sweaty on the handles, his hands held me firmly by butt and hips. Was this another test? Was—

"If you want, you can let go of the handles." His voice was loud, for all to hear. Even in the darkness, I could hear the sneer in his voice.

"Fuck you!" I shouted back.

His cock slammed inside wrenching a yelp from my lips. His cock pulled back, sucking my insides along with it. Before I had time to breathe, his cock slammed back inside and his pubic bone mashed violently against mine. He sucked my internal organs back out then smashed back inside before my organs could brace themselves for his unremitting onslaught.

In and out, his cock maintained its relentless assault. Struggle as I might, I began to move with its thrusts, to submit to its girth, to yield to his mastery, to pledge allegiance to his glorious cock! My entire consciousness floated down into my sex, lighter than air.

He pulled back out. "Breathe," he mocked.

And that was his downfall. I raised myself up by the handles and moderated his next thrust just enough to let me gasp my lungs full of air. When he pulled back out, I let myself down, throwing him off his rhythm. He plunged himself back in, attempting to regain the upper hand, but I lifted myself up and down in quick little lunges and he was lost. His hands let go of my hips and instead moved up to my waist.

I bounced up and down his cock. He gasped. He hugged my torso, holding us together. But his grip was no longer the grip of mastery but the grip of desperation. He was holding us together; I could lift my pussy up and down his cock. He was standing flatfooted, held motionless by my sexual power.

I lifted myself further up this time, until he was almost out, then lowered myself slowly, clenching and unclenching my pussy as I went. The Commander gasped and swayed slightly before regaining his footing. This time I went faster up and even faster down. He almost lost his grip on me, but recovered in time. Up and down I went, as quickly as I could.

"Breathe," I mocked. And breathe he did! Every breath brought him further and further into my thrall. He altered his stance to force his cock to worship my pussy with even more rapt devotion. After two deep breaths, his breathing became shallow. He was ready to come! I rubbed my clit against him; this time he would not escape before giving me a *full* climax!

"Grab my ass!" I demanded. "Fuck me like a man."

And he did. Of course he did. He was no longer commander. He was my slave! His cock plunged deep into my cunt, over and over again. His cock was *my* cock. And my cock rubbed against my g-spot with every stroke, caressed my lips. And his pubic mound pulled up on my clit, teasing my cunt every tighter, ever closer to the point of no return.

He dug his fingers into my ass and I twisted back and forth rubbing my nipples along the hard hair of his chest. Tingles in my breasts flickered down to my pussy and they purred together. I smiled, swooning, ready to come, ready to —

But in that moment of bliss, I had lost control. An animal growl rumbled in Commander's throat and he gripped my ass with feral fury. He smashed himself into me, no longer caressing my clit, no longer stroking my pleasure spot.

And then growl became roar as Commander shuddered his spunk into me. Hot and hard he shot his life force into me. And in that moment, he demanded my climax. And in that moment, my cunt was once again in servitude to his cock, my cunt exploded heat upwards, then as it sunk back, she sent jolts down my legs, turning them into jelly. Somehow I didn't fall. Behind my pubic bone, jolts of electric pleasure bounced around my sex, jerking my clit inside, then out again.

The animal growl in Commander's throat was louder, as if he was sucking my essence into his chest.

I sucked air into my lungs. "Fuck!" I wheezed.

"Fuck," he growled back. I tried to speak, but all I could do was breathe. We were standing together, spent, motionless.

Dimly, as if in the distance, I heard a male voice say, "It's okay, she's had enough now."

I felt Patty's finger's on my fingers, prying them off the handles. As I let go of the handles, I opened my eyes. All twelve candles had been relit. Commander was standing in front of me, nude. I noticed a welt on his lower leg and smiled. I'm sure that some of the welts on my own body were from his gun. At least I'd given as good as I'd got. All the other males were gone.

Patty wiped him off with a towel, careful to avoid his welt. Next Patty wiped the sweat off my body. The towel was moist and hot. The Commander left as she gently dabbed each of my welts.

"What happened between you and Marty?" I asked.

"It was hot and heavy. We moved in together. I thought he was the one. Then he started tracking what I was eating and drinking and measuring it against my urine chemistry."

"That's weird."

"Claimed it was for science."

"Still."

"When he mentioned that 'measuring blood was more accurate', I'd had enough."

I nodded. "Which brings us back to the break-in at my apartment."

"You remember the guy you ran into?"

"The guy who's gun I got?"

Patty nodded. "His name's Gorgon Fifty-five. He got shot by the guy I mixed the balls for. The remains of the paintballs must have fallen out when he came to your apartment."

"Why the special batch?"

"He likes to know who he hits."

I shrugged. "I'm presuming that Gorgon Fifty-five is not the name his mother gave him."

"No."

"Why did he agree to your giving up his name?"

"First of all, it wasn't me. And besides, he didn't agree, you had to pass the test first."

"But why take the risk?"

"He got overruled by the leader of his troop. And Gorgon likes to watch. He has low light and infrared cameras set-up in the framed-in house. He can combine the videos into full high-definition color. He's probably jerking off to it now."

I digested that happy thought for a moment, then it was back to the task at hand: "How did Marty realize that you'd mixed up a special batch?"

"Marty liked to play with color."

"Marty is a man with many layers."

She nodded. "It's just that some of the layers are decidedly disgusting."

Half an hour later, I put the piece of paper with Gorgon55's real name and address on my kitchen table, stripped down to my hastily repaired panties—what had happened to my bra I never did find out—and flopped down on my bed.

I woke up to a painful stinging on my lower leg. As the

fog of sleep cleared, I realized that Eric was applying alcohol to my paintball wounds. He moved to the one on my belly and it *really* stung.

"Ow!" I protested. "What the hell are you doing?!?" I slapped his hand away.

Eric, my six-foot three and skinny-as-a-fence-post assistant, shook his head. "You have to take care of your wounds. Otherwise they'll get infected." He gently, but firmly pushed my hand away and reapplied the cloth to the welt on my belly. At least now that I was expecting it, it didn't hurt quite so much.

"Ow!" I protested again, more for effect than actual pain. I took the cloth from him and made a show of dabbing the welt under my panties. "I can handle this. There's a note on the kitchen table. I need you to find that guy."

He smiled, took the cloth from me and dipped it into the bottle of alcohol he'd brought bedside. "You mean Gorgon Fifty-five?"

"Yes. But I got his real name." I took the cloth from his hand.

He nodded. "You mean Alfred Goldstein?"

I nodded, doing my best not to wince as the alcohol found open skin.

"Goldstein is an alias. Alfred Bartholomew Poindexter is a twenty-something self-employed computer geek and graphic novelist."

"So he fits the profile for the Cyber Culprit!" The Cyber Culprit was the computer genius whom Eric and I had been pursuing for several months.

"Not to mention that he broke into your apartment."

"Not to mention."

I shooed Eric out of my bedroom and quickly pulled on a pair of sweat pants — old, loose, comfortable — and the matching top. In the kitchen, Eric was staring into his laptop and tapping a finger at the edge of his keyboard.

"What's wrong?" I asked.

"The psychological profile showed that the Cyber

Culprit was a leader, not a follower. Patty said that Gorgon Fifty-five or Alfred or whoever he is was definitely in the follower category."

"Let's not report that to Michael just yet." Michael Rayburn, my erstwhile lover, was the lawyer who'd employed us to track down the Cyber Culprit, our one and only assignment. I had caught Michael cheating on me — and punished him for it. He had indicated a desire to reconcile, but the next move in the romance department was still his. Unlike in the Cyber Culprit department where Eric and I owed him a report.

I sat down opposite Eric, opened my own laptop and navigated to my locked folder. "What about the other tactics you deployed to find CC?"

"The online 'bot tracker I deployed has so far come up empty and there's no trace of him using a credit card."

"Any response to the video survey?"

"I'll check."

I opened up my locked folder and reviewed the notes I had compiled. We might be tracking the Cyber Culprit, but he was almost certainly tracking us, me in particular. When I had attended at a local pick-up bar in search of his trail, he had posted images and video of my attendance. But the kicker was a private video that had somehow been emailed to me yesterday. It showed me being fucked by a man I was pretty sure was the Cyber Culprit. He'd been dressed up as Superman-nemisis Lex Luthor at a cosplay ball. The video camera had obviously been part of Luthor's costume, a bulky warsuit which used robotics to enhance Luthor's strength. If my intuition was correct, it hadn't been the first time the Cyber Culprit had touched me. Nor the first time he'd looked out for my wellbeing.

I pressed replay and watched the video again. Luthor's robotic warsuit was holding me as we had sex standing up. This freed Luthor's fingers to fondle me. First he raked his fingernails up and down the inside of my arms. Then he grabbed my breasts and tugged and twisted them in time with our pelvic oscillations. Twists of my nipples making me gasp. I tried to wriggle free to touch his chest, to squeeze *his* nipples, to kiss his lips but no matter how hard I tried, I couldn't break free. Luthor smiled at my frustration.

The video stopped and I stared into space. Should I show the video to Michael? No, that would be the end of any chance at romance with him. And he'd likely fire us to boot. Maybe if I shared a vague suspicion with Eric. But that would lead to... questions. But I needed to do *something*.

I became aware of Eric looking at me quizzically and quickly returned my locked folder to its hiding place on my hard drive. "Any luck," I asked?

He shook his head. I took a deep breath, picked up my phone, and dialed Michael Rayburn's office.

"Michael Rayburn," he answered. But there was traffic noise in the background. He wasn't in his office.

"Michael, I was calling to make an appointment to come in to give you an update." Eric was staring at me, trying to read my face. His continued employment rested on Michael's reactions.

"No need for an appointment. I'll meet you at your apartment."

"At my apartment?" I did my best to keep the surprise, not to mention the discomfiture out of my voice. "When will you be here?"

"Five minutes."

"Okay. See you then." There was an odd crackle on my phone as we rang off.

Eric's eyes asked the obvious question. "Five minutes," I told him. "You need to leave!"

Eric helped me tidy up the apartment and he was out of the door in three minutes. I did the new meditation exercise he had taught me to help me move my energy up my chakras. It felt so good that I'd forgotten that I was dressed in an old pair of sweats until I saw the smart-alecky look on Michael's face when I opened the door.

He entered the apartment, then turned around as I shut

the door, making a show of looking me up and down. "Taking me for granted, are we?" he asked.

I fought back the flush on my face. "No, it's just that we, that we weren't expecting…"

"We?"

"Eric was here when you called. We think we've found the Cyber Culprit."

His face brightened, but only momentarily. "Think?"

"We won't be sure until we check him out, but it's not like last time."

"How can you be sure?"

"This time the suspect is a nobody. And he fits the profile." Last time we'd accused a prominent political aide, only to have the evidence prove us wrong.

Michael cocked his head to one side, digesting the information. He pointed up and down my sweats. "I'd figured that a beautiful woman like you would be more of the yoga pants set." As usual, Michael was wearing a suit and tie. As if he needed to dress up his six feet of muscular sexiness. His brown hair with flecks of grey conveyed just the right mix of experience and virility — in whatever room he was in: court *or* bed. But right now, it was his sparkling blue eyes that were holding me in his thrall.

I lifted up the left leg of my sweat pants and showed him one of the angry welts I'd received yesterday.

Michael's attitude immediately changed to concern. "How did you — who did this to you?"

"It's nothing."

He looked up and down my sweats. "There's more, aren't there?"

When I didn't answer, he gently grabbed the loose material on each leg of my pants and slowly lifted them up until he'd revealed three more welts. Without a word, he took me to the bedroom, pulled back the sheets, laid me gently on the bed, rooted through the medicine cabinet and came back with the same alcohol that Eric had used an hour earlier. But instead of the cloth, he brought a box of tissues.

Michael tenderly removed my top and pants. Notwithstanding that I was now nude except for a pair of skimpy panties, he had eyes only for my wounds. His face darkened as he saw each one. I rolled over on my tummy so that he could see the ones on my back, then rolled back to see his reaction.

"Those need to be taken care of, young lady."

"But—"

He shook his head. There would be no 'ifs', 'ands' nor 'buts'. I sighed and let him dab each welt with alcohol-soaked tissue.

"Ow!" I protested on the third welt. It didn't hurt, but I wanted to play up the sympathy angle.

"Shhh. It only hurts a bit. They'll hurt more if you don't take care of them."

I was pleased to see something extra in the front of his pants when he finished tending to the last of my visible welts. He set the bottle of alcohol and box of tissues on my night table.

"You missed one," I told him.

He looked me up and down but didn't see any he'd missed. I smiled my most teasing smile and slowly turned onto my belly. Even more slowly, I pulled my panties up so that he could see the outer edge of the welt on my butt.

He reached for the alcohol and tissues.

But I shook my head. "You can't see under *my* panties until I can see under *yours*." I wagged my finger in the area of his crotch which was pleasantly expanding.

We looked into each other's eyes. The moment of truth. It was all up to Michael. He knew that I didn't want a relationship where he was free to play around on the side. He knew that I wasn't going to have sex with anyone else, unless it was for the job his law firm had hired me for. If he undressed, if we had sex, it would mean that he was accepting my terms. I lay motionless, hardly breathing. The moment stretched forever.

Somehow his hands were in a different position. Like a

glacier moving so slowly you couldn't see movement unless you looked away and then when you looked back you compared its current position with your memory of where it had been before. Finally, his fingers were at his tie, unloosening it, pulling it around his collar and laying it on the chair by my bed. His hands picked up speed as he unbuttoned his shirt and removed it and his jacket in one movement.

His fingers were flying as he unzipped his pants and placed them atop his other clothes. I carefully slid my panties down my legs and he matched me with his briefs. By the time we were both nude, he was fully erect. By the time were both nude, I was wet and tingly.

I turned over on my tummy and felt him gently dab alcohol on the butt welt. Then he lay beside me, turned me towards him and we kissed. He tenderly lifted my leg up and entered me. It was the first time in ages I'd made love in the sideways position. Usually there wouldn't be enough friction to make it a satisfying experience. But today it seemed fitting as Michael gently moved in and out of me.

Our bodies undulated in sync, steadily warming with the exertion. Bit by bit our chests and groins became hotter than the rest of our bodies. Gradually our movements accelerated. Michael's quickened and he broke sync. I tried to match his rhythm, but sideways there was nothing to gain purchase on. He shuddered to a stop and I felt a new warmth between my legs. Now that he was still, I had better control of my angles and, with a few short sharp thrusts, I managed to achieve my own climax. It was soft waves of warmth spreading up to my belly. Not exciting, but very, very nice. I shut my eyes and floated, vaguely aware of Michael shouting his climax, of his semen dribbling...

Later, much later, I sensed Michael leave the bed and begin to dress. I reached over and turned my phone on. Something was different, as if the icons on the front screen had been rearranged. I shrugged, probably just a new update.

Interrogation, Lusty Lee Log #23

I didn't think that Poindexter would recognize me from our previous encounter, but, just to be safe, a disguise was in order. I straightened my curly brown hair and colored it black. Contacts turned my blue eyes brown. A few judicious applications of make-up made my face more angular. A corset tucked my tummy in. And instead of blue jeans and a T, I was dressed to the nines: stiletto high-heels, red mini-skirt, black silk blouse and gold chains on my right ankle, left wrist and neck. And all of this on a five-foot five, buxom and curvaceous bod would have all of Poindexter's attention rooted in the present, not trying to place me in memories of a past encounter.

Alfred Bartholomew Poindexter was a twenty-something self-employed computer geek, graphic novelist and paintballer. My one and only previous encounter with Alfie had been when I had run over him at Patty's Paintball Palace. I'd ended up with the skinny little paintball warrior's weapon before being molested and fucked in semi-darkness. Patty had told me that Poindexter—Gorgon-55 to his friends—had probably videotaped me being molested and...

But the previous encounter wasn't why I was pissed off with Alfie.

I was pissed off with Alfie because he'd hacked into my phone. It was the *worst* possible invasion of my privacy.

First there'd been a crackle while I was in the middle of a conversation. Then the icons on my screen had been rearranged. But when the dates on my private photos had suddenly been changed to today's date, I'd known for sure. Someone had nosed around in all my private photos, nosed around in my investigation logs. But the cruelest violation had been when the invader had read my journal, my most private thoughts about my lovers, past, present, and hoped-for.

I'd given my phone to Eric, my computer nerd of an

assistant, with clear instructions to find out who'd hacked my phone, with equally clear instructions not to poke around in my private files.

Two hours later Eric had jumped up and pumped his fists in the air. A lanky and slim six-foot-three with carrot-top hair jumping and pumping was a sight to see!

After Eric's glee at nailing Alfie subsided, we hatched our plan. We'd have to move quickly — Alfie was not only suspected of being the twerp who'd hacked my phone, we now suspected that he was the Cyber Culprit himself.

And that was why, two hours later, I'd transformed my appearance and sat myself down on a bar stool at Alfie's favorite watering hole, Sidekicks. For a bar, Sidekicks was brightly lit. Its theme was superheros and movie characters, but second fiddle. Think Robin instead of Batman, Tonto in place of the Lone Ranger, Jimmy Olsen, not Superman. The male wait-staff were dressed as Bucky; the females as Harley Quinn.

Eric was nearby for backup.

Half an hour after I'd arrived, a steady trickle of patrons started to fill up the bar. Some of them were dressed as their favorite sidekick. Alfie, like most, couldn't be bothered. He was dress-casual, with a tie. Probably hadn't changed after work. As soon as I spotted him, I flashed a smile, then looked away.

As I suspected, it'd been awhile since a woman had favored Alfie with a smile and he couldn't figure out what to do with the invitation. Or whether his eyes had deceived him. He sat down close to me, but left an unoccupied stool between us.

I half-turned towards Alfie. "It's nice to see someone dressing like a real man and not some comic-book goof," I told him.

"Nice to see a real woman," was the best he could muster as a comeback. However he was only half a putz and slid onto the open stool that had previously separated us.

But then Alfie lapsed into silence.

"I'm drinking Crown Royal," I told him, holding up my glass which by now had only a slim layer of the whisky at the bottom of its ice cubes.

"Me too," he advised and ordered two, mine on the rocks, his neat.

He made a show of downing his in one gulp, but then had to sit still for a moment to recover.

"Whisky's made for sipping," I told him and signaled the bartender to refill Alfie's glass.

Alfie reached for his wallet, but this time I paid. "Nowadays women make almost as much as men," I told him. "Why should the guy always have to foot the bill?"

He nodded and took a tentative sip. "I haven't seen you here before."

"First time," I admitted. "This your regular spot?"

He nodded and took another sip.

"What kind of establishment is this?"

"It's called Sidekicks, so its theme is the second banana, the supporting actor."

I waved my hand around the bar. "That much is obvious. What I meant was is this a drinking bar or a pick-up place?"

Half of Alfie's whiskey disappeared in one gulp. "Both?" he ventured.

I set my almost-empty glass next to his. "And what about for you? What about tonight?"

"My place is around the corner?" he offered.

I stood and picked up my purse. He stood as well. Once again Crown Royal had worked its magic; the last vestiges of Alfie's shyness had been banished.

Alfie's place was a modest-sized one-bedroom apartment located about halfway up a tall tower. The view out the window was mostly blocked by two adjacent buildings, but the sparkling lights of downtown were visible through the unobstructed sliver in the middle. Inside, it was, in a word, cluttered. Dishes half-filled the sink. Pillows and remote controllers were strewn about the couch which faced a flat-screen TV. The coffee table was littered with comics, books about paintball, and DVDs. On the far wall were several computers with wires linking them. I counted at least five monitors. There was a gaming console. The carpet was in need of vacuuming.

His bedroom couldn't be worse, so I grabbed his tie and gently led him out of the living room.

But his bedroom *was* worse. The bed was small. The bottom sheet was pulled off the lower left corner. The upper sheet and a comforter, if you could call it that, and two pillows were thrown to the floor on the other side of the bed. It was an old bed, the kind with tubular steel for the headboard, but nothing at the foot.

The only redeeming parts of the scenario were that the bottom sheet appeared clean and that the bulge in the front of Alfie's pants meant that I wouldn't have to use the sex toys in my purse. At least not yet. I pushed Alfie onto the bed and lowered my purse to the floor. While I was bent over, I surreptitiously pulled his bottom sheet over the corner of his mattress. No need to embarrass the boy.

I took out my phone and made a show of turning it off. But what I was really doing was sending Eric a pre-arranged text. Unless he heard from me in half an hour, he was to come bursting in through the door.

"Lie still," I told him. I removed his shoes—boring and scuffed lace-ups— along with his socks, and then signaled for him to undo his pants. He moaned relief as his erection claimed a modicum of freedom. I pulled his pants off and threw them atop his sheet, comforter and pillow. He was wearing white cotton briefs: vanilla topping on vanilla ice cream.

I took off one of my stiletto high-heels and kissed the toe. I slowly lowered it and touched the spot where I'd kissed to the heel of his left foot. As I brought my shoe up his sole, his toes curled to meet it and he gasped. I kicked off my other shoe; his right foot would have to die frustrated.

I straddled his legs and hiked my red mini-skirt high

enough to let Alfie see that I was wearing garters but not high enough for him to see the color of my panties. I undid the garters holding up my right stocking. Moving around, parts of my body touched parts of his body. His erection transmitted its urgency to my thighs.

As I shuffled up his body, Alfie's hands reached towards my black blouse, but I brushed them away. "No touching," I told him.

He reluctantly lowered his hands as I succeeded in removing the stocking from my right leg. I reached over and tied his left hand to one of the tubes on the headboard. Alfie's lips kissed through my blouse, through my corset, through to my nipples.

I shuffled back down his body, sat just above his knees and stroked my fingers up and down the mound pressing against his briefs. "Remove your tie," I told him.

As he fumbled to do this with only one hand, I tickled his balls, sending his cock into a tizzy under his briefs. Finally his tie came loose and I stood to his right and used his tie to bind his right hand to the headboard. I undid the top button on his shirt.

"Please," he begged.

"Take off your briefs," I responded.

Alfie thrashed and thrashed, but his briefs were held tightly in place by his erection. He collapsed in defeat.

I undid another button on his shirt.

"Please," he begged.

I ignored him and slowly, ever so slowly, undid the remaining buttons on his shirt. My fingers tickled down, lifted the top of his briefs up and pulled them down his legs. His erection sprang free. It was darker than the rest of his skin, slightly purplish, and larger than I'd expected given the diminutive proportions of the rest of his body. He was uncircumcised, but his foreskin was pulled way back, exposing the tender head of his penis.

I pulled my miniskirt up so that he could see my black silk panties.

"Please," he begged.

But all I did was to remove my miniskirt. "Would you like me to remove my blouse?" I asked.

Alfie nodded.

Starting at the bottom, my fingers undid the buttons on my blouse as slowly as they had undone the buttons on his shirt. When I reached my breasts, I gave a gentle squeeze. Alfie inhaled sharply. I smiled down at him, undid the last button and pulled my blouse off. I touched the bottom of the blouse on his chest, between this sides of his shirt and then lowered it inch by inch as I dragged it down his belly. His penis throbbed as the silk touched it. He gasped as the silk caressed his cock.

"Please," he begged.

"You'll do anything?"

"Yes. Anything! Please, yes, please."

"*Anything*?"

"Anything."

I placed my hand atop my panties, then slid my middle finger down my slit. "Wouldn't you love to be able to touch your cock, the way I'm touching myself?" I asked. My finger stroked up and down and it was my turn to gasp. Silk is so, so wonderful stroking between my pussy lips and cuddling my clit.

"Yes, *please*!" Alfie moved his hips from side to side.

"Promise to lie still?"

He nodded and bit his lip.

I leaned down over him and pulled his shirt open across his chest. I leaned in further and raked the rough material of my corset across his nipples.

"Aiee!" he yelped.

I stood upright. "Do you want me to stop?"

He shook his head vigorously from side to side.

I bent back over and pressed my corset against his chest, my ample breasts molding themselves over his skinny chest. Then I moved up and down and twisted. It felt wonderful on my nipples, as wonderful to me as it had to be painful to Alfie. But he kept his silence as little jolts of pleasure danced from one of my nipples to the other.

I raised myself up and sat on his right side. My right hand stroked up and down the center of my panties. I stroked Alfie's cock with my left hand; it was *hot* — ready to boil over.

I shut my eyes and concentrated on the middle finger of my right hand, concentrated on the silk rubbing up and down my pussy lips, on the hard button of my clit being tapped inch by inch towards ecstasy, concentrated on the juices frolicking inside my cunt. I was transported into the Sultan's palace where the captain of the guard was making feeble keening noises next to me. I was all-powerful. A few quick strokes of my left hand and the captain would spurt out his life force. Suddenly the Sultan was there, towering over us, fury flashing in his eyes.

The unpleasant end to the fantasy jerked my eyes open. Alfie's eyes were shut. His lips were smiling, his cheeks flushed. His cock was ramrod stiff.

I unclasped the gold chains from my right ankle and left wrist, wrapped them around Alfie's cock and clasped them tight.

"What are you doing?" he wanted to know.

"Do you want me to stop?"

"No." But there was a hint of uncertainty in his voice.

I unclasped the chain around my neck and drew it tight just below his right nipple. I dragged it back and forth across his nipple and he wheezed with pleasure. "That's what I'm doing," I told him.

He smiled up at me as I reached into my purse, came out with a condom and carefully rolled it down cock. It pressed the gold chain into his skin. It didn't hurt now, but it would be tighter when I was fucking him. And afterwards, it would hurt like hell. I smiled at the thought; the little nerd would think twice before hacking into someone's phone again.

I pulled my panties to the floor and stood close enough to his face that he could smell my sex. "Ready to get fucked?"

I asked, trying to make my voice sound as innocent as I could.

"Yes. Yes, oh *yes!*"

I climbed atop, straddled his midsection and grasped his cock in my hand, making sure not to press the gold chains against his skin. From the look in his eyes, I could tell that the sensation of my pussy sliding down his cock was a major improvement over one finger sliding up and down the outside. The ridges of the gold chains wrapped around his phallus added an extra frisson of pleasure. Thankfully, the condom was providing a measure of protection — at least for me.

Not so for Alfie. His face was a mix of bliss, pain and consternation.

I dug my fingernails into his chest.

"Ow!" he protested.

I dug my fingernails deeper. I wanted his mind to locate any pain in his chest, and not to associate it with what was happening below. There would be plenty of time later for pain below. Alfie stifled his protests. Good boy!

I let go of his chest and lifted myself up. Then I dug my nails back into his breasts, just outside his nipples at the same instant as I dropped back down his shaft.

"Fuck!" he screamed.

I bounced little bounces, but mostly I rotated and ground our pubic bones together. Alfie shut his eyes. I channeled all my anger at his violation of my secret thoughts into my sexual arousal, giving it a harsh bite. My cunt had teeth and was chewing into him. My cunt had teeth and was roaring anger up my spine. My cunt had teeth and was tightening sharp pleasure up into my belly.

I took a deep breath and pulled myself up and down his cock, rubbing us urgently together, rubbing two sticks to make a fire, rubbing off any remaining layer of control. Alfie's eyes fluttered open, then shut. The edge was approaching in the distance. Ordinarily, I'd pause to be sure that he had also sighted the edge. But today, I didn't care. Today I wanted to fly off the edge as quickly as I could.

I shut my eyes. It wasn't Alfie inside me. It was all my lovers rolled into one. I wasn't in some dingy unkempt apartment, I was in a luxury aircraft soaring above all the cares of the world.

But most of all, I was inside my sex, feeling her being stroked and stoked and cuddled and caressed. She was warm and hot and slippery. She was being filled and emptied, bursting at the seams, sucked hollow, then sucked out some more. And every lunge up and down was propelling her closer to the edge, was contracting the horizons tighter, was building storm clouds all around.

Then I was there, teetering at the edge. I didn't want to go over. I wanted to pump myself tighter. I wanted the storm clouds to build into hurricanes and tornados. I wanted the flames inside me to consume the universe. I held myself at the edge, each pump up and down gathering the forces of the cosmos into my cunt. I—

No! I had promised Michael that there'd be no unnecessary sex. And he'd promised to be faithful to me. Michael—ever so sexy lawyer Michael Rayburn—knew that there'd be sex on the job. After all, he was the one who'd given me this assignment. Yes, I'd needed to fuck Alfie, so I was in the clear. But there was no need to climax. It was time to stop pumping up and down. I—

—snapped right in the middle. My cunt was totally engulfed in flame, in explosion. Fire turned my legs to ash then brought them back again, ever nerve begging to escape. The inferno rocketed up my spine and warmed my head with more pleasure than it could withstand. The force of the orgasm sent little pieces of me flying off in every direction. It was the only way I could stand the intensity.

Then I was one piece again, rolling waves heaving up and down my body. My whole being was sexual pleasure. My whole body gloried in its revenge on Alfie. I pulled myself off and finished my orgasm with my finger.

Alfie's eyes snapped open. "No!" he cried.

My finger touched all the right spots, sending swirls of

pleasure to be savored in each nook and cranny of my body.

"No?" I asked.

"I didn't come," he pleaded.

"You didn't?" There was as much innocence in my voice as I could muster. My orgasm was undulations of warmth and pleasure. Fading and not as powerful, but deeper somehow.

"Please, let me…," he beseeched. We both looked at his cock. It was hard, but somehow forlorn. As if it too was beseeching for release.

"Remember, you said you'd do anything?"

He nodded, a smile renewed on his face.

I picked my purse and pulled out my phone. Eric's countdown still had three minutes left on it. "Tell me everything about the hack on my phone," I told him, holding the phone for him to see.

"First finish me off!" Demanding, desperate.

I slowly shook my head. "First, *Alfie*, or would you prefer Cyber Culprit? Anyways, first you're going to tell me how and why you hacked my phone, what you found out and what you downloaded."

"You're crazy!" he shot back. He tugged at his restraints but they held fast.

"*Second*, you're going to tell me about all the computers you hacked," I continued, without losing a beat, "all the lives you ruined, and just why you went on your little rampage."

"Crazy bitch!" screamed Alfie. He tugged at his arms and the bed shook so strongly I thought it was going to collapse. Instead, his left arm ripped free from my stocking. We both stood transfixed by the sight of his freed arm. He moved first and swiftly freed his right wrist as well.

"*Bitch*!" he screeched, lunging at me. My head barely managed to dodge his fist. I reached into my purse and pulled out a small canister of pepper spray. He swung at me again and I sprayed him full in the face.

"Bitch!" he yelled. "That's stuff's *illegal*!" His arms flailed the air, but since he couldn't see me, it was easy to elude his fists.

There was a bang outside the room and a moment later Eric burst into the bedroom.

The pepper I'd sprayed into Alfie's face must have worn off because he landed a solid right on Eric's jaw. Eric was stunned but managed to sidestep Alfie's next right hook. The two men circled each other. Alfie tried a bull rush, a mistake. Eric easily parried the attempt, pushed Alfie to the ground and twisted his arms behind him.

"Who the hell are you guys?" demanded Alfie, his voice muffled by the floor.

"My name is Lee Brandt. I'm an investigator," I told him. "Eric, the man you assaulted, is my assistant."

"He broke into my apartment and assaulted me!"

I ignored that technicality and continued, "We've been hired by Michael Rayburn. He's a prominent lawyer, but you know that. Mr. Rayburn's clients — including Judges and other prominent citizens — have had their privacy rights trampled on by you in your guise as the Cyber Culprit. Now that we've caught you, we're going to put an end to that."

"I want a lawyer," demanded Alfie. Eric was still kneeling on Alfie and had his arms extended upwards and twisted.

I put my right foot, the bare one, lightly against Alfie's head. "You're not getting a lawyer and you're going to tell us everything."

"Fuck you! I'm not saying another *word* until my lawyer gets here."

"You hacked my phone without *my* lawyer being present," I reminded him. I signaled Eric to lift him up.

Eric dragged Alfie to the living room and held him as I tied one of his hands to a doorknob and the other to a sturdy light fixture embedded in the wall. Alfie did his best to pull free, but his bonds held tight and he stood motionless in the middle of the room.

I returned to the bedroom to retrieve my purse. When I returned, Eric had finished setting up a video camera up on top of a tripod. He flipped the LED screen to verify that he was recording the entirety of Alfie's nude body. Actually not quite nude. The condom was still on his flaccid penis. Along with my gold chains. Eric pressed record and the little red light on the camera blinked on.

Eric retreated to Alfie's computers as I circled our captive. There was a succession of beeps.

I bumped myself against Alfie and swayed my hips. "What's the password?" I asked politely angling my head towards Eric's carrot top.

He smiled. "You'll never—"

I slapped him across his face. "Password."

"Why would I give you my password?"

I walked around behind him and held his head directly towards Eric, my hands forming blinders on the outside of his eyes. "Because that's the computer you used to make your web postings."

When Alfie remained silent, I moved around in front of him, took each of his nipples between thumb and forefinger and twisted hard. "Password!"

Alfie spat in my eyes. The bastard! I wiped his spittle from my face and grabbed his cock. A light fondling was all it took to manipulate it erect. Eric's keystrokes clattered noisily in the background, but his only reward was a succession of beeps. I continued my hand job and Alfie gasped, ready to come.

"Tell me," I demanded.

"Tell you what?" Alfie sneered back.

I pinched him hard and squeezed off his ejaculation.

"Bitch!" he screamed.

Eric turned towards us and shook his head. Alfie's password had eluded him.

Alfie's cock was still erect in my hand. "My, you're an easy one," I mocked. "I'll do it again and again until you tell."

"Never." Alfie looked down at his penis which was becoming flaccid and smiled, "It looks like your magic has left you. But don't worry, I'll get hard again once I'm alone with your photos, your journal… Alone with the video of the commander shagging you at Patty's Paintball."

I exchanged a look with Eric and he nodded. Alfie has just crossed the line. I remove Alfie's condom and begin to give him a blowjob. He is instantly erect. I pop him out of my mouth and tickle his balls with my fingers. Eric joins us, kisses Alfie and fondles his chest.

"Get away from me, you faggot," Alfie screams.

"Afraid to walk on the wild side?" coos Eric.

"I'm not a homo!" proclaims Alfie.

Eric kisses him again. Alfie tries to turn his head, but Eric holds him still, his hands on Alfie's ears. I resume my blowjob. The gold chains on his cock take some getting used to, but they're not a major impediment. In short order, Alfie is once more at the edge of climax. But instead of letting him come, I pinch him.

"OWWW!" protests Alfie finally managing to escape Eric's grip.

I stand up and place my lips almost touching Alfie's ear. "Tell us," I demand.

"Never!"

Eric and I press our bodies against each of Alfie's flanks. I grab his cock and Eric places his hand over mine. Behind, our hands meet at Alfie's ass, holding him in place. His erection returns full force.

Alfie breathes hard through his mouth, once again betrayed by his body. "Don't please. Stop!. Enough."

"Password," demands Eric.

"No." Alfie's voice is smug.

I begin to fondle his cock. Eric's hands fall away. Alfie shuts his eyes, enjoying the sensations.

When Alfie's starting to swoon, I place my lips next to his ear. "Where's the video of me at Patty's paintball?"

"It's on your phone." All his attention is in his cock and his voice is slurred.

"Why on *my* phone?"

"He was going to wipe it off my computer."

"He?"

"Ja—. The guy you call the Cyber Culprit."

"And the video, it's still there?"

He nods, his eyes still shut, his consciousness still swooning. I reach into my purse and pull out my phone. Light pressure on the gold chains circling his cock jolt Alfie's eyes open. I hold the phone an inch from his nose. "Where?" I demand.

"In the deleted videos folder."

Navigating to the folder takes my attention away from the gold chains and Alfie's eyes shut. By the time I find the video, his lips have formed into a wide smile. I start the video and hold it in front of his face. My other hand finds the chains and I press them into the tenderest of his tender skin and rake them up and down his cock.

"Oww!" screams Alfie. "What the fuck!?!" His eyes jerk open as, on my phone, the Commander's cock starts to penetrate my pussy.

"Ever heard of aversive therapy?" I asked. He shakes his head and bites his lip as I jerk his chain. Literally.

"Aversive therapy associates pain with deviant sexuality. It cures people from jerking off to illegal videos."

Alfie gasps as I rake the chains up and down his cock. But he can't take his eyes off my phone.

I shut the video off. He's enjoying it too much. "What's your password?"

"You'll never guess and I'll never tell."

"Yes you will," I hiss. I give the chains a brutal twist. "Yes you will," I repeat.

Alfie smiles smugly back at me. Obviously we'll get nothing more from his cock. I carefully remove the gold chains and drop them into my purse. They will require a very, *very*, thorough sterilization.

I remove my hand from my purse and hold a large penis-shaped vibrator and a jar of lube up to Alfie's face.

"Do your worst, sweetheart," he smirks.

I move behind Alfie, press the vibrator against his ass

and make a thrusting motion forward. The force of my thrusts pushes Alfie's crotch forward but he doesn't say anything. Eric adjusts the video camera to focus on the center of Alfie's body. I turn the vibrator on, press it against Alfie's anus and make small in and out motions. He groans, but I can't tell whether it's from pain or pleasure.

I press in further. "The password."

"Fuck you."

I walk around in front of him and hold the vibrator under his nose. "That's no way to talk to a lady," I remonstrate. "Last chance to give me the password."

Alfie sneers and shakes his head. I hold the vibrator out to one side. Eric steps forward and takes the vibrator from my hand.

Alfie's eyes bug out. "No! Please!"

I step behind the video camera and adjust it to follow Eric. He steps behind Alfie and holds the vibrator beside Alfie's head. Eric dips fingers from his other hand into the jar of lube and places a generous dollop on the head of the vibrator. Eric pulls the vibrator behind Alfie. I keep the camera focused on Alfie's eyes but my eyes are watching what's going on below his waist. Alfie's cock is flaccid, shrunken.

The buzz of the vibrator turns on. Alfie does his best to clench his buttocks but Eric's cuff across his ears distracts him. Alfie's hips lurch forward. Eric's arm makes small back and forth motions. Alfie's eyes wince.

"How does it feel to be fucked?" I ask.

"Fuck you!"

Alfie's naughty language earns a hard thrust from behind and his eyes bug out in horror. "No!!" he screams.

"Tell us the password and he'll stop."

"No."

Another hard thrust and Alfie screams in agony.

"Tell us!"

"No."

Eric thrusts again and Alfie's scream is even louder.

"Tell us!"

"No!" He stamps his feet like a little child.

Three more thrusts from Eric. Three more screams of agony from Alfie.

"Tell us," I demand. Alfie's only response is to shake his head. I adjust the video camera to take in Alfie's entire body and move in front of him. I gently take his cock in my hand. It remains limp but starts to expand. "If you come when you're being fucked by a man, you'll be a faggot for life." It's a lie and homophobic but the terror on Alfie's face shows that my remark has hit home. "The password," I repeat.

"There's nothing on my computer."

That's interesting, disheartening, but interesting. "We'll see for ourselves," I tell him. My continued fondling has restored Alfie's erection. "He likes it," I tell Eric.

"No, please," pleads Alfie.

"No, please," I mock back.

The rhythm of my strokes up and down Alfie's cock are now synced up with Eric's thrusts up his ass. Alfie is being fucked for real.

"How's he doing?" asks Eric.

"He's almost there," I respond.

"Another one for the club!" gloats Eric.

"No, please," begs Alfie.

"The password." My voice is as soft as a rose petal. His cock begins to shudder in my hand.

"Stop!" screams Alfie. "I'll tell."

I hold my hand still while Eric continues to pump from behind. My grip tightens. "The password." My voice is steel.

"Fuck Lee."

I resume my handjob in sync with Eric's thrusts. "No, fuck Alfie," I tell him.

"No!" screams Alfie. "That's the password. FuckLee. Fuck underscore Lee. All one word. Capital 'F', capital 'L'. Fuck_Lee."

Eric removes the vibrator and plops it into the lube.

Shit! That was a new jar. Men are such *pigs*! I keep ahold of
Alfie's cock, my hand as still as a statue. Behind me I hear
Eric's keystrokes. No beep.

"We're in!" exclaimed Eric.

A familiar voice intoned from all the speakers in the
room, "Congratulations on capturing my assistant. Tune into
YourOwnTube channel YYZ5 for my latest post."

I let go of Alfie and joined Eric in front of the
computers.

"Bitch!" screamed Alfie. "Aren't you ever going to
finish me?"

At the main computer, Eric has brought up the video.
It's a muscular man. His face is round, puffy. He moves
swiftly through a calisthenics routine with the ease of a
professional athlete. He's vaguely familiar. He pauses, sits on
a bench and pulls out a needle which he injects into his arm.
He pulls the needle out and plunges it into a glass vial. Again
he injects his arm. The camera moves to the vials. One is a
well-known steroid, the other contains human growth
hormone. Both banned in professional sport.

The camera returns to the athlete. It's Chuck Gaines.
The Linebacker. He was more muscular when last I saw him.
But his thousand-watt smile has disappeared.

The video ended and Eric's fingers danced across the
keyboard. Gaines vanished and the monitor was filled with
text. Eric leaned back. "The Cyber Culprit uploaded this
while we were with Poindexter."

"Alfie's not the Cyber Culprit." Shit!

"I told you bitch," Alfie's voice spat from behind us.
"Now let me go!"

"What else is on the computer?" I asked Eric, making a
show of ignoring Alfie.

"Nothing. It's been wiped clean."

"Just like I said," screamed Alfie.

"Can we trace the Cyber Culprit?" I asked Eric.

Eric shook his head.

"Let's see what Alfie knows."

Eric and I walked back to Alfie. I waved Eric towards the jar of lube in which the vibrator was resting precariously. Alfie watched Eric pick up the vibrator and walk behind him.

I put my finger on the side of Alfie's nose and turned his attention back to me. "Who is the Cyber Culprit?"

"I've told you everything I know."

"You started to call him by his name. Ja—. James. Jacob. Jared. Jasper."

"Jason," joined in Eric as he jerked his arm forward.

"Jack, it's Jack!" screamed Alfie.

"Jack…" I prompted.

"Jack. That's all I know. I promise!"

Alfie slumped forward, only the ropes on his arms holding him up.

Eric and I shared a glance. Eric shrugged. I nodded. We weren't going to get anything more out of Alfie.

I dressed while Eric tidied up and uploaded information from Alfie's computer into his USB memory key. At the sound of Eric opening the door to the apartment, Alfie perked up and pulled against the ropes holding him nude in the middle of the room, "What about me?" he wailed.

Over my shoulder I promised to send someone.

In the elevator, I slumped against the well. "Back to square one," I lamented.

Eric shook his head. "Not exactly."

"How so? This guy's not the Cyber Culprit. We've got squat."

"First, our profile of CC is correct. We were right, he's a leader, not a follower. And we were right about CC being a self-centered narcissist, he let Alfie swing in the wind."

"But he's still one step ahead of us."

Eric shook his head and held up his memory key. "Half a step."

I pushed myself up from the wall just before the elevator doors opened. There was hope in the world. "I'm going to report to Michael."

I had met Michael—Michael Rayburn—when the

lawyer had hired me to pursue the Cyber Culprit and to bring him to justice for the internet posts CC had used to destroy the careers of several of his firm's clients. Our professional relationship had turned friendly, then romantic and finally sexual. He had cheated on me, but we had reconciled. We had reaffirmed that our relationship was monogamous, the only exception being for me, and then only when I was pursuing CC.

Michael was tall and muscular and sexy. His light brown hair, with only flecks of grey, framed a handsome face. And the sparkles in his blue eyes never failed to melt my heart.

Our last encounter had been at my apartment when he'd dabbed alcohol in the wounds I'd sustained at Patty's Paintball Emporium. Which had led to Michael providing *other* comforts to my body! So this time it was my turn to surprise him at *his* apartment.

Inside Michael's apartment — I'd have to tell him that I'd made myself a copy of his key — his television was on. It was a video of us making love! His butt was pumping himself into me. Vigorous power propelling every stroke! We'd definitely have to get a mirror on the ceiling. I wasn't aware of Michael having taped us. It must be part of his new smart house system. He'd bragged that the cameras were so sensitive that they could tell who was entering a room and adjust the lighting and temperature accordingly. Turns out he had something else worth bragging about!

The sound was perfect, the slight creaking of the bed, our bodies slapping against each other. But as I approached the TV, I realized that there was no sound coming from it. The sound was coming from the bedroom. Michael must be watching on his laptop. Sure enough, the sound got getting progressively louder as I approached the bedroom.

I turned into the bedroom, excited by the prospect of sitting next to him as we watched ourselves. I stopped as violently as if I'd slammed into a glass door. Michael wasn't watching. Michael was doing. Michael was *doing* another woman!

His ass which had looked so magnificent when it was pumping himself into me, now looked positively horrid. I padded into the kitchen, filled a pot with cold water, padded back into the bedroom. They were on the cusp of climax. I threw the cold water on both of them, smiling as the water splashed against their genitals.

Their howls of horror sounded music to my ears as I tossed the pot into the front closet and snuck out of the apartment.

An hour later Eric and I were drowning my sorrows in expensive whisky. "Men are shit," I told him.

He nodded. "Men are shit, but we can't do without them."

"Why does this happen to me?" I was shocked at how weak and mournful my voice sounded.

"Maybe you need to meditate, move your consciousness up your chakras."

"Chakras?"

"The levels of consciousness in your spine."

"And what level is *your* consciousness at?" I asked, badly slurring the s's.

"At the consciousness that I need to get a new job."

"Why? Michael didn't see me, so it's business as usual."

"But he has to know it was you."

I shook my head. "If the bastard's cheating on me, no telling how many other girlfriends he has that he's cheating on."

"So I'm off to see the linebacker?"

"So you're off to see the linebacker."

And with that, Eric and I toasted the silver lining of the storm clouds hovering over my life.

The Athlete, Lusty Lee Log #24

There are many ways to exact revenge on a lover who has cheated on you. The possibilities expand if the cheater doesn't know that you know what you know. This was the position I was in with Michael Rayburn.

Michael had given me the lucrative assignment of tracking down the Cyber Culprit, an internet ne'er-do-well who had been hacking into various computer networks and posting photos and videos embarrassing to Michael's law firm's clients. The good news was that my assistant and I had captured CC's accomplice and verified a key-component of the psychological profile that we'd compiled of the Cyber Culprit.

Michael was my lover. We'd had steamy, very *steamy* sex. Our relationship had had its ups and downs. Michael had pledged to be monogamous and I had thought our relationship had been placed on an even keel. That was until I had let myself into Michael's apartment with the key I'd surreptitiously made. That was until I, hot, horny and about to give Michael the best Valentine's Day surprise of his life, had caught him bonking another woman. I'd thrown cold water on them before dashing out. I was pretty sure that neither of them knew who had doused their passion.

I had spent an enjoyable hour planning my revenge as I had dressed for my meeting with Michael. First were sheer black stockings. Red was sexier, but too obvious for a law office. The stockings were held up with a black garter belt. For some reason men find retro lingerie incredibly sexy and Michael was no exception. Over the garters went red silk panties so sheer you could see the outline of my sex through them. My bra was red and just as sheer. Looking in the mirror, I couldn't tell who was more turned on—me or my nipples!

I applied light make-up—understated sexy for the law-office crowd—and did a slow pirouette for the mirror. All in all, a perfect package for the morning's caper: five-foot five, buxom and curvaceous curly brown hair prancing as I twirled. I smiled which set my blue eyes sparkling with the full, mature sensuality of my twenty-nine years.

Over this went my light blue skirt suit. I'd lost enough weight that it was slightly loose on me which was good for this morning's outing because I wanted to be able to easily slide my skirt up over my hips. I selected a light linen blouse which was short enough that it didn't need to be tucked into my skirt. Over this, I wore a vest. As I did up the four buttons on the vest, I was glad that I hadn't lost any weight on my bosom; the vest fit perfectly.

The feeling of pressing the button to Michael's office was electric. I felt it tingle into my core. I was ready!

Outside his office, I told his assistant that Michael was expecting me and she nodded that I could let myself in. Michael, ever the lawyer in his blue tie and even bluer pin-stripped suit, looked up from his desk as I made a show of shutting, and locking, his door behind me.

He smiled as I entered. He was older than me but the flecks of grey in his light brown hair made him all the more handsome. He was just over six-feet tall, slim but muscular. His blue eyes radiated masculinity. A wide, full-lipped mouth was tailor-made for precise pronunciation and even more precise kissing.

I leaned against the side of the desk and smiled down at him. "I have news," I told him, undoing the top button of my vest.

"What kind of news?" he asked, standing.

I took a step back. "Eric and I found the Cyber Culprit's accomplice." Eric was my assistant.

"That's great!" he exclaimed, taking a step towards me.

I let him kiss me, only a light kiss, before I took another step back. "But we couldn't identify the Cyber Culprit." I pretended to lightly brush up against the client chairs in front of Michael's desk, just enough to lift my skirt sufficiently for him to catch sight of the top of my stocking and the garter holding it up.

"What do we have here?" he asked, with obvious interest.

"Be serious," I told him, "Eric analyzed the contents of the accomplice's computer. It had been wiped clean. Nothing there. So we have no way to connect the accomplice with CC."

"So it's just another dead end."

I was stepping back, Michael stepping forward, as I undid two more buttons, revealing the soft white, almost translucent linen blouse, and the red outline of my bra beneath. "Not quite," I told him.

That brought him another step forward. Our bodies weren't touching, but I could feel his heat. "Not quite?"

"CC's name is Jack."

"Lots of guys are named Jack." Michael's shoulders slumped. "And, it can be short for John, not to mention Jacob or Jake."

I took another step back. I was now two steps from the couch at the back of Michael's office, three steps from the wall. I put my hands on my hips, lifting my skirt enough to give him a good view of my naked thighs and the garter straps holding my stockings up. "I thought you'd be more excited."

He pointed to the spot between the top of my stockings and the bottom of my skirt. "*That* I'm excited about. 'Jack' not so much."

I waited for him to move. Depending on Michael's approach, I'd either end up pressed against the wall or sprawled on his couch. "There's more," I told him.

"More?" he queried, stepping forward and placing his right hand on my thigh. His legs pressed against my legs, his chest sent tingles into my breasts. He had angled me towards the wall. My back wasn't touching it, but I could sense its proximity.

"Our psychological profile has been confirmed as being spot on." That was an exaggeration but I didn't care. I pressed myself against the wall and Michael pressed himself against me.

His only verbal response was a low moan. I felt his right hand glide across my thigh, over to my sex. His left undid the last button on my vest and floated up to my breast. My nipple screamed to be released from my bra. A finger sliding up and down between my pussy lips buckled my knees. I was hot and wet!

But today was not about me. Today was about Michael. I grabbed his crotch with my right hand and was rewarded with something hot and hard. He moaned and kissed me. Using the leverage in my right hand, I slowly squeezed out from between Michael and the wall and maneuvered him so that now it was *his* back against the wall.

I reached my left hand up to his face to concentrate his attention on our kiss, then let it drift to his chest so that his nipples could join in the fun his tongue and penis were having. Then both of my hands were on his crotch and I broke my lips off his mouth to let them kiss his neck, his chest, his other nipple, his ribs, his belly, and finally his crotch.

I pulled Michael's zipper down, but left his belt in place. I pulled, and prodded and pressed and pulled again. Finally Michael's penis, his long and broad and ever so fully erect penis sprang forth.

Quick as a bunny, I had the tip of his penis in my mouth. I circled my tongue around its tip as if I was playing with an ice cream cone. But instead of cold, my mouth was filled with heat. Above me, Michael groaned his appreciation.

My hands were now free to play with his zipper and I pulled gently up on it, pressing the opening against Michael's penis. I pressed some of the loose skin into the place where the zipper's teeth came together and pulled upwards.

"Shit!" he screamed.

I had managed to get a generous fold of skin caught in the zipper, Michael's attention having been otherwise engaged. Michael was screaming blue blood murder, but his words were unintelligible.

"Michael, I'm sorry," I lied.

He delicately pushed me away.

"What should I do?" I asked.

Wordlessly, his face as red as a beet, he manipulated his zipper. His first effort to extricate himself failed and his face contorted in agony. His second effort succeeded in releasing the skin of his penis from his zipper, although, judging from the expression on his face, only at the expense of greatly *increasing* his agony.

"What can I do?" I asked, pleased with the wail I'd injected into my voice.

But his only reaction was to limp back behind his desk and wave me towards the door. I popped my head out and asked his assistant for some ice. A moment later, she came back with a glass full of several large ice cubes. I shut the door, took out three of the ice cubes, came around Michael's desk and moved them towards his crotch. One of the ice cubes just happened to drop down his underwear, another down his pants. I pressed the last one against the wound on his penis. Michael made a weak smile of gratitude.

I gave him a kiss on his forehead.

Michael's assistant watched as I exited and gingerly closed the door behind me. When I was halfway to the elevators, I waved in the direction of Michael's door. "Mr. Rayburn needs to see you," I told her. Michael might have got his zipper back up, but the ice cube I'd dropped down his pants should have left a very visible circle of wetness…

As soon as I came out of the elevator, I dialed my assistant.

"Eric here," he answered.

"I told Michael about capturing the Cyber Culprit's sidekick."

"Did the name Jack mean anything to him?"

"No. But he was pleased that the psychological profile seems to be panning out."

"Did you resolve the other stuff?"

"His penis got caught in his zipper."

"Just by accident." His tone was a mixture of query and accusation.

"I put ice on the boo-boo," I said in my defence.

"Lee." Accusation and reproach.

I let silence be my answer.

"Lee, if you keep accumulating negative karma, your consciousness will remain mired in the lower chakras."

"*He* was the one who cheated on *me*."

"Karma is about your acts and reactions, not about the sins of others."

"*Karma schrarma.*"

"Enough negative karma and we'll lose this gig and CC — Jack — will get away."

"Relax. Michael thought it was an accident. Besides, he wouldn't risk having to explain our firing to his partners."

Eric's sigh inside my phone was loud and clear. "Okay, I'll go see Chuck Gaines," he concluded. CC had posted a video of Gaines, the former linebacker, injecting steroids into his arms.

Peter Henge's face popped up on my phone as my assistant rang off. How had my former, and now much-despised, lover's face just *happen* to pop up on my phone?!? Peter's brown eyes smiled up at me, inviting me to a raucous round of meaningless sex. Meaningless, but highly enjoyable! Peter, Peter pumpkin eater! I shut my eyes and conjured up a vision of Peter. Six-feet-two inches of hard wiry muscle. Ten inches of wide and full manhood, tattoo of a Roman soldier pulling his sword from his sheath. When Peter flexed the muscles on his chest, the sword became an oversized cock. Why not, I thought to myself, I may as well get all the revenge out of my body. Besides, it wasn't like I was in a relationship any more.

The last thought brought a tear out of my eye, but I wiped it away as I pressed the photo of Peter's face on my phone.

"Peter," I said as we connected.

"Lee?"

"Your photo popped up on my phone and I thought..." There were a thousand possibilities in what I left unsaid.

"Kismet?"

"Karma." My voice was definite. I was offering myself.

"Lee, I've missed you. I —"

"Action, not words."

"Show, don't tell."

"Yes, but fewer words."

An hour later we were in a hotel room located midway between our apartments. Better someplace neutral. We'd broken up at my apartment and it was too soon for his apartment. Once in the room, we had slowly and gently removed each other's clothes. We had kissed lips and touched the tips of our tongues. Our fingers had traced the familiar pathways of each other's body, mine ending up on the scar under the tattoo on his chest. I was backed up against the wall, his erection teasing my belly.

"Ready?" he asked. He wanted to know if I was sufficiently aroused for the rigorous physical activity which characterized our sexual encounters.

I shut my eyes. Every inch of my skin tingled. My nipples strained to touch him. Between my hips I was hot through and through. And wet.

"Yes," I whispered, my eyes flashing open in challenge.

Peter cupped my buttocks in his hands and slowly raised me up. I tussled his gel-spiked black hair as he held me quivering over his cock. Then he slowly lowered me down. The tip of his penis tickled my pussy lips. It pressed against my vagina, pressing her open millimeter by millimeter. At any moment he would drop me down his shaft. My anticipation was his wicked torture.

The head of his cock had pushed itself inside my pussy. I rocked my hips back and forth for us to purr together. Peter dropped his hands away and I plunged — But he caught me after only an inch and slowly lifted me back up until his cock was barely inside me.

"Bastard!" I accused, trying to pull his hair.

"Slut," he responded. And I *was* his slut, his glorious

and wanton and sexy slut. All I wanted, all I wanted in the world, was to kiss his cock with my cunt. And he was holding me up, malevolently frustrating my arousal.

"Bastard!" I repeated.

He twirled around slowly, planting his feet carefully so as not to break off genital contact, holding me firmly so that I couldn't slide down his cock. He held me over and slowly lowered me to the bed, only then breaking off sexual contact. I scooted to the top of the bed and spread my legs. He climbed on top and reinserted the head — but only the head — of his penis into my pussy. He didn't notice my legs spreading apart under him.

He'd want me to beg him to fuck me. But not today! I angled my hips, pressed my pelvis up, and pushed myself down the bed. My cunt swallowed his cock full! She caressed and kissed all the way down his shaft. I rocked my pelvis up, sliding him half out, then rocked back down, sucking him back inside. I pinched and twisted his nipples.

Today I had his body. Today I had him inside. Today he was fucking me with savage fury. Today, *he* would beg *me* to let him stop! Peter's cock plunged in an out, bereft of control. His cock was fucking my cunt but I was the one in control, *my* mind *fucking* his. He slammed in, compressing everything together, then wrenched himself out sucking me along with him. I lay still, making him work, savoring each sensation of his cock plunging into me, each sensation of him pressing against my pussy lips on the way out, each sensation shooting through my clit as he mashed our pubic bones together. He was moving so fast, so ferociously that I couldn't help joining in his passionate pulsations. I shut my eyes to concentrate on the pleasures gyrating at my core. Then I was pushing up and pulling down and we were in rhythm together, surrendering into each other.

He popped out. I opened my eyes to help guide him back in. But he was kneeling above me, a triumphant smile on his lips, his palm up, his fingers moving towards my pussy.

"Fuck me!" I demanded.

"When you're ready," he retorted.

I reached for his wrist to pull him down to me, but he brushed my hand aside and inserted his fingers into my pussy.

I thrashed and beat my feet against the bed, like a two-year old having a temper tantrum. I wanted his cock, not his fingers!

"Fuck me," I cried. "Please! I need to be *fucked!*"

And then his fingers found my pleasure place. I gasped and collapsed on the bed where the sheets held me motionless. He stroked his fingers forward, beckoning. I couldn't talk, I couldn't move. All I could do was to lock eyes with him, my needs silently pleading. *His* eyes leering back, his evil power exultant.

"Please," I begged.

"When you're ready." And then he chuckled. The bastard *chuckled.*

I raised my arms to scratch out his eyes but a familiar feeling in my cunt dropped my arms back to the bed. I need to hold on to something solid, anything solid. I felt the sheets scrunch up in my palms, my eyes scrunch as tightly shut.

His fingers left me and I felt control coming slowly back to me. In a moment Peter would get what he *deserves.* Then his belly was pressing against me. My fingers readied to scratch up his back. His cock was inside. His cock was just barely inside, touching my g-spot, teasing it, sucking my control out of me. I held hard onto the sheets.

He rammed himself into me, now barely brushing up against my g-spot. In and out he slammed himself, fucking me. He didn't care for my pleasure, just his. He lay his full weight on me. I couldn't move. He rocked himself in and out of me. I tried to breathe.

"Fuck!" he yelled. His body shuddered. His thrusts stopped, then recommenced, but slower now, and slipperier.

He rolled me over, holding my buttocks close. Once I was on top, he released his grip, slapped my butt and squeezed my breasts. I rocked my hips to pull him out of me, then rocked him back in. But he was too slippery for good friction. I rocked faster and faster and it felt good, but not good enough. Then he pulled me up and the tip of his penis touched my g-spot. He held me in place as I stroked and stroked. It was hard work, the position he was holding me in. But every stroke clenched me tighter and tighter, hotter and hotter. I held my breath, concentrating on the commotion building inside.

I floated for an instant, then searing heat exploded inside my cunt, up my spine. Peter whirled me beneath him and fucked me even harder than before. My orgasm shot down my legs. Then all the contractions were inside my cunt and I felt spurt after spurt shouting glory to the heavens.

Peter finished panting first. "That was great!" he exclaimed.

I nodded. It *had* been great. Just what I needed to get Michael out of my system.

"Are you seeing anyone?" he asked.

I hesitated, then shook my head.

"Me neither. I'd like to see you again."

I nodded. This was a bit forward, but what the hell.

"Next week?"

I nodded, suddenly aware of how warm and fuzzy and happy I was. I propped myself up and kissed him.

But then it was back to work. I rolled over and turned my phone on. It rang instantly.

"Lee! Where are you?!" It was Michael Rayburn, terror in his voice.

"Michael! What's happening?"

"It's the Cyber Culprit. He's intermittently jamming cellphone towers across the city. Eric's here. We've set up a command center in the main boardroom."

"I'm on my way."

The main boardroom at Michael Rayburn's law office was out-of-control pandemonium. Eric was at one end of the large table, Michael at the other. In the middle of the table, several techs from Michael's firm were huddled with a representative of the phone company. A senior partner came in and whispered in Michael's ear. Michael shook his head and the other man left. Michael's face was ashen.

I sidled up to Eric. "What's happening?" I whispered.

"Randomly, cellphone towers are cutting out." He pointed to the map of the city on his laptop. Red dots were flickering on and off. "The red dots are cellphone towers. When it disappears, the cellphone tower is off line. And we," he gestured towards the other techs, "can't put up a new firewall until the attacks stop."

I watched the map. There was no apparent pattern. "Can you call up a list, alphabetical, numerical?"

Eric nodded, entered a few keystrokes and there were two lists side by side. "The left favors alphabetical, the right numerical." He made a few more keystrokes and the towers began to be greyed out when they went offline. Again, there was no apparent pattern, at least not that I could see, but Eric was staring intently at the screen.

He entered a few more keystrokes and another list popped up between the other two. "This one is a combination of alphanumeric factors."

This time, there was an obvious pattern going up and down the list. Five towers were offline at any given time, just enough to disrupt cellphone traffic. As the first came back online, another, at the bottom of the rolling five, went offline.

I pointed at Eric's screen. "Can you use the pattern to track him?"

Eric nodded and began to type furiously on his keyboard. One of the other techs had heard my question and soon they were all clustered behind my assistant. Michael looked up, a glimmer of hope and gratitude in his eyes.

"Got him!" shouted Eric. The greyed out bars had all disappeared. The other techs raced to the middle of the table. Eric continued typing furiously. Michael drifted down to us, his eyes pleading for a report.

"Eric stopped the attacks on the cellphone towers. The other techs are putting up an improved firewall."

Eric nodded confirmation of my report.

"What about the Cyber Culprit?" asked Michael.

"Maybe," was all that Eric said, random lines of text scrolling up and down his computer screen.

I looked over at Michael. I'd never seen him look so forlorn.

Eric slumped back, defeated. "Jack escaped," he confirmed.

Michael sat down beside Eric and waved me to sit on his other side. "There's another problem. Someone has put our phone number up all across the city. Our receptionists are being flooded with calls looking for apartments, escorts, taxis, you name it."

Eric heaved a deep breath of air into his lungs, sat up, and began typing. "I'll look into it," was all he could promise.

The techs in the middle of the room started to celebrate. Michael excused himself and walked towards them.

My phone rang. But it wasn't an incoming call. It was a video. A man was in an elevator. As the doors opened, he stepped forward and I could see that it was Peter Henge. The video went black for a second, then it picked Peter up walking down the hall. He turned in front of an apartment, pulled out a key from his pocket and inserted it in the lock. The camera was directly above the apartment door and I could see the hairs on the back of Peter's neck. He entered the apartment. I stared at the door. It wasn't Peter's apartment. What was he doing there? The video went black.

Eric was typing away. "Any luck?" I asked.

He nodded. "The phone numbers from Mr. Rayburn's firm ended up on a bulletin board and then got copied onto other boards. I installed a 'bot to correct the phone numbers."

"Aren't you just foisting Michael's problem onto someone else?"

He shook his head. "One number for a taxi company, another for an actual apartment service and a third for pizza."

"What about the escort service?"

He nodded, "I'm spreading the calls among several

agencies."

My phone rang again. It was another video and appeared to pick up where the previous one had left off. A woman walked up to the door, inserted a key into the lock and entered the apartment. The screen went black.

I sent Eric off to interview Chuck Gaines, the former linebacker, while I went downtown to report to Michael.

Michael was with the senior partner when I entered his office. "We've solved the telephone problem," I told him.

Michael thanked me and both men smiled. In the elevator going down, I heaved a sign of relief into my lungs. I'd broken up with Michael, but kept my job. My phone rang. Video of the same apartment door. A pizza deliveryman knocked on the door. Peter and the woman I'd seen earlier came to the door. Somewhat disheveled, somewhat undressed, very lovey-dovey. Peter gave the pizza-guy his credit card. When pizza-guy handed the terminal back to Peter, I could see the date and time. It was today! The video was streaming live!

My fists slammed against the elevator door as my voice yelled, "Men are shit!"

When I returned to my apartment, I curled up in my bed, cellphone off, alarm clock off. It had been a long and unhappy day. I would let my body sleep as long as it wanted to.

The next morning when I stretched myself awake, it was almost noon, eleven-fifty-nine to be exact. Eric's report of his interview with Chuck Gaines was already in my inbox so I gave it a quick read. There was nothing there to help us find the Cyber Culprit, but there *was* plenty of kinky sex to get my engines roaring.

I arranged my favorite vibrator — rabbit ears and pearls — on the left side of my bed along with a couple of bottles of lube and skin creams. I set my computer to read the salacious parts of Eric's report out loud and to cycle through his photos in my slideshow app. Then I arranged my pillows to let me sit up to view the laptop screen comfortably and to have easy access to my vibrator, cream and lube. Clothes off. I made the final adjustments to my laptop and pressed [Enter]. The computer would repeat on a loop; I'd have my hands completely free for more important tasks!

I rubbed my favorite skin cream up and down my body. Not only was it good for my skin, but it had the effect of heating up my breasts — especially my nipples — not to mention my vulva and pussy lips. Time for a threesome — but without the male egos or the male sweat!

A ping sounded on my computer and I stared at the selfie Eric had taken of himself hugging Chuck downwards to get them both in the frame. My nipples perked forward and my pussy lips engorged. Eric's red hair made his smiling green eyes pop. He was half a foot taller than Chuck and next to the linebacker, really, really skinny. Chuck's black head was still shaved and looked like onyx next to Eric's pale chin.

The computer version of Eric's voice came on behind the selfie. "Gaines is on steroids and human growth hormones to prepare for an upcoming mixed martial arts bout. Apparently the organizers have a lax drug policy and, according to Chuck, everyone is doing it. It's made his skin slightly puffy. Emotionally he reports being aggressive, which may not be a bad thing given the size, skill and speed of his opponent."

Chuck seemed to have aged since our last encounter and there was sadness in his smile. But his teeth still gleamed between his black lips. His chest was even thicker than before and the rippling muscles in his arms and legs could crack Eric like a matchstick. Chuck radiated feral sexuality.

A video of the two men inside the octagon took over the screen as Eric's voiceover continued, "Chuck also appeared paranoid, so to gain his trust, I offered to help him with his grappling."

The two men circled each other, nude except for their training shorts. These were tight and skimpy, almost translucent. It was obvious that neither was wearing a cup. I lightly stroked my hands over my sex.

Eric hit Chuck's body rapid-fire. But the only visible effect was to jiggle the linebacker's gonads and he laughed off the blows. Eric spun around his opponent and Chuck followed. Eric pinned the shorter man to the side of the eight-sided ring, his leg rubbing against Chuck's genitals. But it was Eric who appeared most aroused. I slipped a finger between my pussy lips and a shiver of delight shot into the bottom of my spine.

Chuck spun Eric's back to the fence but Eric used the force of the spin to trip his opponent to the canvas. Before Chuck could recover his bearings, Eric had used his height and flexibility advantage to pin one of Chuck's arms behind his back. Using both his own arms, Eric joined Chuck's hands together, undid the Velcro on the linebacker's gloves and Velcroed his hands together. Pinned behind his back, it took only one of Eric's hands to hold Chuck's arms in place.

Eric stroked the larger man's gonads with his free hand and Chuck's cock expanded in response. In fact, all of Chuck's muscles were expanding as he strained to escape. I stroked my fingers up and down in time with Eric's strokes, slipping them inside my pussy as far as they would go, yearning for Chuck's cock instead of my little fingers.

Chuck wrenched his hands free and turned towards Eric. The linebacker was fully erect and the gleam in his eyes made it clear what he intended to do with his erection. Eric circled, a broad smile on his lips.

The slide show started. Chuck had Eric pinned against the fence, one hand pinching a nipple, his teeth biting the other one. Pain and joy competed for control of Eric's face. My left fingers pinched my left nipple, then twisted it until I almost yelled out. Below, my fingers lightly rubbing up and down the shaft of my clit joined the joy in Eric's face. Fingers twisted my other nipple until I bit my lip.

The next image was Chuck's hands pressing Eric's head down, his fingers wrapped in red hair, Eric's mouth just above his cock. I wished I was there, kissing that massive rod, licking up and down the linebacker's phallus. I could feel my throat yearn to have it inside. I swallowed at the thought and my buttocks tightened in response to the needs deep inside my pussy.

Eric had swallowed half of Chuck's cock. Chuck's fingers were holding Eric's head in place. Eric looked like he wanted to swallow the rest. I grabbed my vibrator and inserted it halfway into my pussy. I stroked it an inch in, then an inch out, shutting my eyes to imagine Chuck's cock in my mouth, to imagine it stroking in and out of my pussy. Chuck pulled himself out and used the head of his penis to stroke up and down my pussy lips. Then he pushed back inside to search for my g-spot.

The ping of the slide show app opened my eyes to Chuck holding Eric's head to make him spit into his hand. I needed no such external lubrication and slid my vibrator all the way into my pussy, the rabbit ears tickling my clit as its shaft filled my sex. Out and suck, in and fill and tickle. Eric's drool into Chuck's fingers. Out and suck, in and fill and tickle. Warmer and warmer and warmer.

Eric kneeling, butt up, Chuck's foot on his hair holding him in place, his fingers sliding into Eric's ass, Eric enjoying it. I pulled the vibrator out, put some cream on my fingers and played with my own ass. Chuck's fingers invaded my back door, slithering around in triumphant conquest, searching for targets to ravage. The cream was hot in my ass, just like in Eric's. The heat spread upwards, roiling and boiling my pussy juices.

Chuck held Eric from behind his back, half-sitting sideways, his left hand around Eric's neck, his right grasping Eric's cock to hold him in position for his own cock which was starting to press against Eric's ass. I pulled my fingers out of my rear, grabbed my vibrator and held it against my pussy lips. The moment of anticipation, the moment where everything is yet to come, the moment I was powerless against the future.

Another ping and the men were fully sideways, Chuck still holding Eric's back but now his cock had slid inside Eric.

Eric's face had the same mix of pleasure and pain, but now pleasure was very much ascendant. I plunged my vibrator all the way inside, gasping at the invasion. In and out, fast and furious, until my face had the same look as Eric's, until my cunt quivered the same way his ass and his cock were quivering.

Eric was lying flat, Chuck's cock fully penetrating my assistant's ass. Eric's cock was just as fully erect. I'd had Eric's cock, I'd had Chuck's cock, but never together at the same time. I wish I'd had another vibrator to stick up my own ass, but if I got up from the bed, I'd have to start all over again. To compensate, I turned my vibrator on high and felt pulsations overpower my pussy and jiggle all the way down into my ass. Everything melted, liquefied. My core turned molten and the warm softness of the melt spread up my spine and down my legs.

Chuck had reached his hand around to stroke Eric's cock. I reached down with my left hand, pulling up on my pubic hair, touching the shaft of my vibrator sliding in and out, holding my clit at just the right angle against the wiggling rabbit ears. I slid my fingers around, pressed another button and the pearls inside the shaft of my vibrator began to rotate. Rotate against my pussy lips going in, rotate against my g-spot, rotate against the contraction building deep inside.

Both men's cocks inside me overpowered my will and I shut my eyes to hold onto my identity, my individuality. But they were too strong and I became two cocks, one pushing up and into my cunt and the other pulling out of my ass. One entering as the other exited, never leaving me alone, each vying to push me into the ocean below the cliff, each vying to burst the red-hot lava churning inside my cunt.

A ping revealed that Chuck's hand around Eric's cock had had the expected result and white slippery cum was leaking through his fingers. Similar liquid was leaking out Eric's ass. *Now* it was my turn and I flipped on my vibrator's in and out function and the vibrator did the bulk of the work, fucking my cunt the same way Chuck's cock had fucked Eric's ass. It tickled mercilessly on my clit, it rotated the pearls relentlessly over my pleasure place, it pushed in and out inside my cunt to possess me, it fluttered insistently along my pussy lips. It sucked all the powers of the universe inside and pushed me teetering at the edge.

I bit my lip to forestall the explosion but forestall was not to be. Chuck and Eric swirled and sucked my entire being into a tight little ball inside my cunt, pure evil glimmering in their eyes. Smaller and smaller the ball became. Then it snapped like a rubber band up my spine erupting heat into my belly, my neck, my head. The lava was a whirlpool, sucking everything back and down and inside but the whirlpool exploded wave after wave of pure pleasure up my spine and down my legs. My feet were free, my buttocks squeezed, my back stretched. I gasped and gasped for air as the rest of the heat spread. Only when I was about to pass out did the heat begin to dissipate.

I kissed my vibrator and held it to the mirror. It had never let me down. Men are shit, but *you* are a girl's best friend.

As I set my vibrator down, I heard something else vibrating. On my phone, there was a video exposing a serial online scammer. The scammer's M.O. was to set herself up on a dating app, seduce a gullible male, then take him for everything he had. There was an interview with her latest victim describing the damage she'd done to his bank account and more importantly to his ability to trust.

By now I'd learned a thing or two from Eric and managed to trace this video back to the same sources as the ones exposing Peter's supposedly nonexistent relationship. I hoped he got food poisoning from the pizza. Maybe I needed to take up Voodoo.

I called Eric over and an hour later showed him the video exposing the online dating scammer. "Can you trace it?" I asked.

He worked on it for half an hour while I rustled up dinner but the video was a dead end.

Just as we were finishing desert, a new video came over my phone. It looked like it was coming over the same channel. I watched it while Eric tried to track the feed.

The video featured a launch party for a new online dating site. It was critical of the site, and dating sites in general but stopped short of alleging anything illegal. A chef famous for his food-for-sex-creations, was being honored at the party. Sploshing Sal was cheered as he rolled out a tall cake topped off with an even taller pyramid of whipped cream. All around the cake were bowls made of chocolate and filled with custard. Several bikini-clad women pranced out. One presented her bum to Chef Sal who pulled her bottom forward and poured custard down her bum. She wiggled.

The video ended and I turned to Eric. "Were you able to trace it?" I asked.

He shook his head.

"Well, tomorrow, you and I are going to meet Sploshing Sal."

Splosh, Lusty Lee Log #25

The only way I'd been able to set up a meet with Sploshing Sal, the chef who'd been outed by the Cyber Culprit at the grand opening of a web-based dating service, had been to obtain a media pass for his latest event. The invitation strongly suggested that I come ready to be sploshed. Sploshing seemed to involve the application of a variety of foods to one's body, custard being the most prominent, and copious amounts of fondling. There were showers on site but I'd been told to bring a plastic bag—preferably water-tight—containing a second set of clothes.

The splosh party wasn't until the next day, so I decided it was time to tidy up my apartment. Two hours in, I stumbled across my old diary. The timing of the discovery was perfect as it rescued me from another hour of the drudgery of tidying up.

I cracked open the diary and began to read. It appeared that before I'd met Peter—Peter Henge my former lover and business partner, the man who'd introduced me to the life of a private investigator—I had been naïve, awkward and desperate. I hadn't had a date in four months, talking to men left me in a tongue-tied mess, and, to cap things off, I'd been out of work.

Then, after a short and torrid affair, I had invited Peter to move in with me. Life was a blast: I had a wonderful lover, employment, and someone to help with the bills. Now, having been my own boss for several months, I had a better idea of cash flow. I took out a pen and did a few calculations. Son-of-a-bitch! Peter might have cured my awkwardness and desperation, but not my naiveté! He had set me up to cover his expenses and then some. I shook my head. No telling what he'd done with the extra cash.

Then the entries got shorter, less analytical, steamier. Love, job, sex: I had it all. Each entry focused on one or the other. The time Peter took me into the woods and we sat for hours watching the squirrels play. Catching a philandering husband on video after a thirteen-hour stakeout. Holding onto the bannister for dear life while Peter lifted me up by the hips and took me from the rear—faster, slower, faster—making it last forever.

I turned to a blank page and started writing. *Was I moving my career forward? Or just marking time? Did I want another relationship? Was a relationship even possible without trust? Should I be concerned with spiritual development?* I reread what I'd written. Too many questions. And I had no idea how to answer them. I decided to write a quick summary of life after Peter. *After Peter broke up with me,* [A tear falling onto the page told me that I hadn't completely gotten over him, or maybe it was his latest lie about being single?] *I was lucky to be retained by Michael Rayburn's law firm to chase the Cyber Culprit. Michael and I had become lovers. But then he too had cheated on me. At least twice. We seemed to be getting closer to the Cyber Culprit, but CC was always just out of our grasp. Was CC toying with us—I certainly had that feeling, the feeling that he'd gotten close enough to me to speak, to touch.*

And tomorrow, I'll attend a food-sex party hosted by Chef Sploshing Sal in our latest attempt to gather intelligence about the Cyber Culprit. We know that CC's first name is Jack but we have no surname, so we're still using 'Cyber Culprit'. Eric, my assistant was in bed with a cold, so I'd be alone at the party.

The videos I'd downloaded of past sploshing parties showed that those wearing elegant clothes which would turn translucent—or even better transparent—with the application of liquid were the life of the party. So, I'd selected an almost sheer white blouse and white linen pants. My red satin underwear would hold almost any pudding known to man before letting it slowly seep out.

I was one of the first to arrive, so I marched straight up to Sploshing Sal. He was a rotund man whose middle jiggled as he turned this way and that shouting orders to a trio of waiters dressed in white latex from head to toe. Sal was only five-foot-ten, shorter than the two male waiters but the same height as the female. A white beret perched precariously atop his bald head.

After the last of his minions had finally scooted away, I held out my hand to the chef, "Hi, I'm Lee Brandt, media. I wonder if I could ask you a few questions?"

He looked me up and down, smiling at the thin fabric hugging my legs, round bottom and curvaceous hips. His smile widened as his eyes caressed my ample breasts and widened even further at my curly brown hair. Apparently I was everything a splosher could desire! But when his gaze reached the blue of my eyes he shook his head. "Those who participate in the party get the best interviews." He paused and looked towards the door. I followed his gaze. Guests were starting to filter in and a group of four couples was heading our way. "Would you like to be part of my first creation?" he asked, his eyes focused over my right shoulder.

I looked in the direction of his gaze and his three latex-clad minions were wheeling in an odd-looking contraption. At the bottom was a large aluminum canister, about the size of a beer keg. A metal pole extended up from the canister, about seven feet off the floor. At the top of the pole, five sets of three tubes radiated out to a ring, then pointed downwards, a nozzle on each of the fifteen tips.

I shrugged. Why not?

Two of the four couples were also game and the waiters positioned them under the sets of three nozzles, alternating men and women. Sploshing Sal positioned me under the remaining set of nozzles and handed me a small control box attached to the canister by a black electrical cord. The only control was a red button. He motioned me to press the button. When I did, a trail of LED lights on the top of the canister flashed on and off, creating a circular pattern. Then the lights climbed up one of the tubes, ending at the three nozzles pointing down at one of the women.

Chocolate custard squirted down on top of her blond hair. Then yellow custard dribbled down her face and under her pink silk blouse, revealing the outline of her breasts. The yellow custard was followed by a steady stream of whipping cream which covered the front of her blouse. The man to her right stepped over to her, kissed her lightly and then scooped some of the custard onto his finger which he inserted into her mouth. She joyfully sucked his finger. The woman to her left came up from behind, licked whipped cream from her hair, then reached around to fondle the blonde's breasts. Chocolate custard oozed out between her fingers.

When all three resumed their places under the nozzles, Sal motioned to me again. I pressed the red button. This time Sal's Russian roulette sploshing machine deposited a large dollop of whipping cream atop the man to my right. He was swarthy and muscular, dressed in a tux, but without a shirt. The woman beside him unbuttoned his jacket, scooped two finger-fulls of whipped cream from his head and deposited them on his nipples. She took great glee in licking and sucking the whipped cream off and in a moment his chest was clean again. She scooped again, deposited whipped cream on his other nipple and motioned for me to do the honors. The whipping cream was cold and sweet, his nipple hot and hard. He groaned as I twirled the last of the whipping cream into my mouth.

A crowd had gathered around Sal's machine, so I surrendered the control button to a pretty Asian woman dressed in a light blue silk gown and drifted towards the wall.

There was a queen-sized bed in the middle, completely covered by one of the new waterproof blankets from nomorewetspot.com. Against the far wall were three single beds with white plastic coverings. To my left was a shallow blow-up swimming pool, the type parents deploy for young children in the summer. To my right was an X-shaped St. Andrew's Cross. Two bikini-clad women pulled a chubby man onto the queen-sized bed, stripped him to his waist and began to tease his nipples with strawberries.

The rest of Sal's waiters, two men and three women, all dressed in turquoise body-hugging latex from neck to ankle, circled the room. Each was carrying a tray of puddings, fruits and rum balls. Each tray also had a sex toy at the back end. Two men in janitor uniforms stood by the entrance. Each had a wet vac, presumably to keep the floors safe from slippery substances.

The pretty Asian woman to whom I'd surrendered the red button control, pressed it. She was immediately drenched in yellow custard. Her light-weight gown clung to her skin revealing a total lack of underwear. Nipples pointed prominently. She was set upon by two men and a woman who began to slurp and lick the custard. I caught a brief glimpse of her shutting her eyes and swooning as the men sucked at her nipples.

Behind Sal's Russian roulette contraption were two more small swimming pools. Sal's mainstays were clearly puddings, whipped creams and fruits but these two areas were a nod to guests whose tastes ran to the savory. A woman, dressed in what had at one time been a white one-piece bathing suit, was allowing men to pull her top out and away from her breasts and to then pour in a mixture of tomato paste and small round pasta shapes. When her swimsuit was full, she pressed against it causing the tomato and pasta to ooze out the bottom edges until the swimsuit clung salaciously to her vulva, butt cheeks, breasts and nipples.

A man was lying on his back in the other pool. He was wearing only a loose-fitting white brief. Two women, one blonde, one redhead, were laying sushi—rolls and finely-cut pieces of raw fish—up his legs and down his arms. The blonde deposited several shelled oysters onto his belly, laughing as each gooey glob landed with a splat and jiggled. Then they poured olive oil and soy sauce onto his brief, revealing the clear outline of one very, *very* erect cock. The redhead carefully balanced a piece of pink salmon on top of his cock.

Just as the blonde was readying to suck the salmon into her mouth, a voice drew my attention to my left. "This is the first time you've been to one of Sal's extravaganzas, isn't it?"

The voice belonged to a man only a few inches taller than I was. Brown hair, brown eyes, long skinny fingers. I nodded.

He was wearing a cream-coloured shirt which billowed out from his body exposing a slit cut down almost to his navel. His pants were loose folds of a similar fabric held around his waist by a white linen rope. His only other salient attribute was his ramrod straight confidence.

He smiled at my inspection and did a pirouette.

"That's some outfit," I said, smiling to hide a guffaw.

He cocked his head to one side. "I'm glad *somebody* likes

my harem pants."

"I didn't say I didn't *like* them." The speech seemed to come from the man, but it was clearly female. Just then, she stepped out from behind the harem master. "I said that they were out of place." She was a gorgeous ebony woman, half a head shorter than he. Her hair was a thin layer atop her head. In fact everything about her was thin. She was wearing a pink blouse and matching skirt both made of a loose and light material I'd never seen before. Her lipstick was the same color as her clothes. And she was right about his harem pants being out of place; every other male was wearing dress pants, either tuxedo or something similar.

He held his hand to his chest. "I'm Seamus, and this," he said turning his hand to the ebony goddess, "is Lilly."

"Lee," I said, pressing my hand to my left breast.

"Lilly has expressed an interest in the St. Andrew's Cross. Would you like to help me show her its potentials?"

I nodded and we strapped her in with the leather belts attached to the cross, one arm up either side of the upper X, her ankles to the lower arms. The little sticks of her body were spread, completely vulnerable. Lilly tried to pull free but the bonds held her tight. She pretended to glare at Seamus.

Seamus held out the sides of his harem pants and did a half curtsey. "We'll let you go if you want," he told her. "But if you stay on the cross, you're agreeing that we can touch you in whatever manner we see fit."

She remained silent. He unbuttoned her blouse. She wasn't wearing a bra. One of her nipples was pierced and the pin sparkled in the light. Seamus waved a waiter over and selected one of the bowls of yellow custard. He handed the bowl to me. It was so cold I had to hold it by the edges. The waiter gave Seamus a spoon.

Seamus scooped a spoonful of the custard out and held it just above Lilly's unpierced nipple. "Last chance," he told her.

Lilly shook her head.

Seamus lowered the spoon to beneath Lilly's nipple, rotated the custard upwards towards it, then held the custard and the spoon against her nipple.

"Shit!" she screamed. She tried to stamp her feet but couldn't. "You bastard! It's *cold*!"

I waved a waiter over and selected a bowl of very warm chocolate pudding. Lilly tensed as I held the spoon above her pierced nipple but she relaxed as I drizzled a few drops onto her hard little bud. The pudding was barely darker than Lilly. I emptied the spoon, then bent forward and sucked the chocolate-covered nipple into my mouth. My tongue had fun playing with the pin, pulling it up, down and sideways. Lilly moaned.

As I straightened, Seamus was holding a spoonful above Lilly's bellybutton.

"Don't you dare," she hissed.

He touched the spoon to her belly.

"No!" Her voice wasn't a scream, but it was emphatic.

He shrugged, dipped his fingers into the custard and moved around behind Lilly, caressing her breasts. She relaxed against the cross, relaxed into his caresses, but her eyes were on me.

I stepped forward into her and placed a hand on each of her thighs, just below her skirt. When I bent my lips to hers, she brought her head forward. As soon as our lips touched, her tongue darted inside my mouth. I brought my hands up her skirt to just below her tiny firm buttocks. She leaned back, breaking off the kiss. Her eyes, deep dark dark brown and black, locked into mine as I brought my hands across the front of her hips and touched the edge of her panties.

"Are you ready?" I asked.

She nodded and smiled. I caressed her panties, glorying the damp heat pressing through into my fingers. She shut her eyes. I found her slit and pressed. She was so wet that I almost penetrated inside. She moaned, her teeth biting her lower lip. I pushed the panty aside and slid my finger into her. Her whole body shuddered.

Seamus looked around to see what I was doing and motioned me to hand him the bowl of chocolate pudding which I was still holding in my other hand. He took the bowl in his left hand, pulled the top of Lilly's skirt and panty backward and poured the pudding directly under the top of her panty. It was warm and gooey as it dribbled into the bottom of her sex, warm and gooey as I massaged it into her pussy lips.

"Jesus!" enthused Lilly as she swayed.

"Want to taste?" Seamus whispered down to me.

I nodded and knelt down in front of Lilly. Seamus gathered her skirt up and I saw that her panties had clasps at the top. I undid the clasps and Lilly's pussy was completely exposed. It was wonderfully pink inside, her pussy lips light chocolate, her outer lips dark black. And all around, it was framed with tight curls of shiny black hair.

I licked up and down her sex. The first taste was all chocolate pudding. Then sharp salt mixed in. As I licked the last of the pudding, the taste became pungent, demanding. Up and down her lips elicited a moan from above. A flick of my tongue inside, a soft "Jesus", a light nuzzle of her clit, a loud "Jeezus!" But when I sucked her clit into my mouth and licked all around its shaft, she screamed "Shit!" and tried to wrench herself free.

I pulled my head back. "Are you okay," I asked, oozing innocence.

"Please! Don't stop, she pleaded. "Please!"

I returned my head below, licked all the way up her slit and flicked the tip of my tongue up the underside of her clit. Every time I flicked my tongue up, she rocked her pelvis down towards me. She wasn't aware of doing it; she was a slave to my tongue.

Pudding started to run down the top of my nose onto Lilly, into my mouth. The taste was now sweet and I used my lips to massage it all over her sex, then sucked it off with my mouth. Above, Lilly moaned and I could feel her legs turning into jelly.

The pudding stopped flowing and the tastes in my mouth turned from sweet to salty to pungent. Ferociously demanding pungent. I felt warm wetness begin between my own legs in response. I licked harder, faster and Lilly moaned louder.

Then there was a hand coming in from below. Two of Seamus's long fingers pushed gently into Lilly's pussy and began stroking in rhythm with my tongue. He apparently knew just where to touch because there was a sharp intake of breath above and Lilly's legs tightened into long straight poles against my cheeks. Her pelvis moved in sync with us, then suddenly stopped.

"Shit!" Lilly screamed, then her whole body shuddered. The shudders were strongest in her sex and I felt vibrations through my tongue and into my mouth. Then the shudders were only in her sex. The rest of her body went completely stiff. Then she bent backwards and shuddered all the way into my neck, wave after wave.

A breath heaved into her lungs. "Shit," she moaned.

We caressed her softly until Lilly's breathing returned to normal. Then Seamus undid her wrists whilst I freed her ankles. She stepped away from the St. Andrews Cross and pulled me up.

"Your turn," she announced.

I looked back and forth between Seamus and Lilly who both nodded. I shrugged. Why not?

Lilly began to fondle my crotch. "Last chance to say no," Seamus reminded me.

They tied my wrists, but left my ankles free. Seamus brought the bowl of yellow custard up to my chest and held it above my breasts. He poured down, exposing the outline of my red bra through the now translucent fabric of my blouse. It was *cold*, even through the fabric. At least the custard made it difficult for Lilly as she unbuttoned my blouse. The black goddess pulled my satin bra forward and Seamus readied to pour, lengthening the torture of anticipation. My only hope was that the custard had warmed up while we were pleasuring Lilly.

Shit—it was still *freezing* cold! I bit my lip to stop from crying out. They each massaged the custard into one of my breasts and gradually feeling returned as the custard leaked and oozed out. Then I was warm and my nipples hot as they used the friction of my bra to tease my breasts through the custard-drenched fabric.

A small crowd had gathered in front and smiles were exchanged. But all eyes were on my boobs now, boobs almost completely exposed through the now translucent fabric of my bra.

Lilly pulled my bra forward and Seamus poured more of the custard inside. "Aiee!" I yelled, as much for the benefit of the crowd as in reaction to the cold goo freezing my skin. This time they both sucked a nipple. The heat in my nipple while my breasts remained cold was *delicious* pain-pleasure.

Then they pulled back and I readied my breasts for more, but they had other ideas. Lilly pulled forward on my pants. I tried to wrestle free.

"Do you want us to let you go?" teased Seamus.

He had me. I stood still and shook my head. Lilly held my pants forward. Seamus positioned the custard over the opening. "Shut your eyes," he told me.

I really *didn't* want to shut my eyes. I wanted at least some warning before cold custard assaulted my most delicate of delicate parts. I really *didn't* want to shut my eyes. I shut my eyes. I felt Lilly's fingers reach inside to pull my panties forward. There was to be no mercy for the condemned!

The *cold* shocked, then I didn't feel anything. Then it was really, *really* cold as Lilly's fingers rotated around the front of my pants, pressing the freezing goo into every nook and cranny. Then cold and *hot* as my horniness heated up the custard.

I felt my pants being undone, my zipper being drawn down. I opened my eyes. Lilly was pulling down on my pants. I lifted my right, then my left leg to help her out. In a moment, I wished I hadn't been so co-operative. Seamus stopped a waiter and handed a bowl of warm chocolate pudding to Lilly. For himself, he took a fresh bowl of freezing yellow custard. The sides of his bowl were completely covered in frost.

Seamus stood behind me, Lilly in front. They passed their bowls back and forth between them. "Shut your eyes," cooed Lilly.

I shut my eyes. What choice did I have? I could feel the bowls being passed back and forth, or were they faking? I had no idea where the warm bowl was or where the cold one was. The top of my panties were pulled away from my skin, both at the back and at the front.

The first thing I felt was goo. Then wonderful warmth all over joining the heat inside my sex. Then *cold* behind. Right down my butt crack. I clenched my ass to prevent it going you-know-where! But a stinging slap on my butt put a stop to the clenching and Seamus poured a river right onto my ass. Then he pushed it in! A shiver shot up my spine. A really, really *cold* shiver.

"You bastard!" I shouted as I stamped my feet to attempt to restore sensation. All *Seamus* did was chuckle.

Then there was more warm goo in the front and Lilly began to caress my sex with serious intent. I felt her reach around behind me. Seamus pulled my panties back and I readied for another frigid assault. But this time there was warmth on my butt as well. Fingers outside my panties pressed the pudding in but gradually almost all of the wonderfully warm goo oozed out.

They each pulled down on my panties and I opened my eyes. Almost all those in attendance, me included, were now watching to see what would happen next. Lilly dropped down out of sight. Her lips kissed my pubic hair, then all over my sex. Intermittently her tongue flicked its hot little tip out to tease my skin. Then she reached the bottom of my pussy lips and dragged her tongue right up between my pussy lips. I almost came!

She pressed my legs apart and placed her thumbs on my pussy lips to open my sex. As her tongue descended my lips, she wagged it back and forth. Then there was something pressing against my sex from below and behind. Seamus's fingers? No, too wide. And too hot!

His cock! He was pressing his cock into my cunt. He was going to *fuck* me. In public. For all to see. Well the bastard had better do a good job. Otherwise everyone—

My eyes popped out of my head. He had shot to the top of my cunt. His *entire* cock. And Lilly was flicking her tongue up and down my clit. And everyone was watching. And it was so fucking hot! Seamus began to shudder behind me. And—

I was over the edge! Massive convulsions jerking and twisting up my spine. Contractions pulling everything into my cunt then exploding out. Wave after wave of pure pleasure undulating up and down my body. I felt myself spurt into Lilly's mouth. Seamus pulled himself out and she sucked and lapped every last drop of both our orgasms. If my wrists hadn't been secured above, I would collapsed onto the floor. I breathed and breathed and breathed.

Lilly and Seamus stood beside me and kissed me until I returned to earth. Then they released my wrists. I had thought I was okay, but I stumbled into the arms of one of the onlookers. I looked up and he smiled down at me.

The man who held me in his arms, and judging by the ease with which he held me, they were *muscular* arms, had a round, almost beatific face. He was South Asian dark brown, likely Sri Lankan. His broad shoulders flanked a firm chest. My feet glided across the floor as he half carried me to the central queen-sized bed where the waiters were replacing the waterproof blanket cover. His gaze directed my eyes to the bed. When I nodded, he gently set me in the middle of the mattress. "Hi, I'm Kasun," he told me.

"Lee."

When Kasun undid his tuxedo top, the outline of his semi-erect cock was clearly visible under his light grey tights. He waved another man over, "This is Ravindu".

Ravindu was also Srik Lankan. Ravindu was shorter and skinnier and where Kasun had a confident bearing, Ravindu was awkward. But I could see that physical flexibility accompanied his awkwardness. Even better, once the fires of passion were lit, awkward also often meant uninhibited. He was nude from the waist up and wore the same grey tights below.

Kasun joined me on the bed. "We'd like to share you," he

advised, pointing to Ravindu. "Every time the music changes, we'll change places."

For the first time that night, I became aware that music was playing in the background. Right now, it was a country music ballad. I smiled and nodded, "Two for the price of one." Ravindu smiled shyly down at me. Kasun handed him his jacket.

I pushed Kasun onto his back, waved a nearby waiter over, and selected a bowl of cold custard. I dipped my finger inside the bowl and held it for Kasun to lick the custard off it. "Nice and cold?" I asked.

He nodded and smiled. I poured a dollop on his right nipple. He gasped. I held the bowl over his lift nipple. "Breathe," I commanded. As soon as he started to inhale, I poured an even larger dollop onto his left nipple. His gasp choked off the rest of his breath.

By the time I had licked and sucked the custard off his nipples, Kasun was breathing regularly again. I held the bowl over his cock which was now fully erect, straining against the thin lycra of his tights. He sucked little gulps of air into his lungs.

But Kasun's cock was reprieved by the music changing to a rock-and-roll standard and Ravindu quickly moved to exchange places with his friend. I removed my blouse and skirt and handed them to Kasun.

When Ravindu was lying still on his back, I let him lick custard from my finger.

"Cold," he noted.

"Cold," I agreed as I poured two large dollops of cold custard onto his nipples. Ravindu gasped, but continued breathing. "Touch me," I directed. I had been right about his physical flexibility and his fingers stroked lightly on my panties and bra as I sucked the custard from his nipples. He moaned as I licked the last drop off.

Below, I could see every ridge and vein on Ravindu's long and skinny cock as it pressed against his tights. I rubbed the bowl of custard up and down its length. It quivered but Ravindu kept breathing steadily. His fingers softly pinched my nipple and stroked the length of my pussy, warming her up. I tipped the bowl, spilling custard down the entire length of his phallus. It stopped quivering and Ravindu stopped breathing. His fingers were similarly paralyzed.

I set the bowl down and slowly caressed the freezing goo up

and down his shaft. When Ravindu began to breathe again, I lifted his tights up and over his cock, poured a mouthful of the custard into my mouth and enveloped his cock with my lips. Cold custard dribbled down his cock and onto his balls. His breathing was short sharp gasps. On my breasts, his fingers were steady but below they were jerking spasmodically. I lifted the bowl of custard to my lips, but before I could pour it into my mouth, the music changed to R & B.

Kasun was swiftly in Ravindu's place. Without any preliminaries, I lifted up the front of his tights, poured the rest of the frigid custard inside and dropped the tights back to hold the custard, and its immobilizing cold, in place. I squished the custard down to his balls, choking off Kasun's first attempt to breathe.

As he lay helpless, I waved a waiter over and selected a bowl of warm chocolate pudding. Kasun still wasn't breathing, but his eyes were locked onto the bowl of pudding and remained locked on it as I poured a generous amount down my panties. Kasun's eyes left the bowl and watched the pudding begin to trickle out the sides of my panties and to ooze out through their thin fabric.

"Breathe," I directed.

He gasped a breath, then exhaled. He inhaled again, this time slower and deeper. I positioned my crotch over his face and let him lap pudding with his tongue as he took another breath. Then I lowered myself onto his face. His nose mashed pudding into my pussy. As more pudding oozed out, his lips kissed her, sending a shiver up my spine. Then he sucked the rest of the pudding through the satin and used his tongue up and down my slit to spread softening warmth through my body. I shut my eyes and became one with the tongue circling my clit.

But it was time to let Kasun breathe again. I climbed off, grabbed handfuls of his tights on either side of his balls and pulled sideways. The thin lycra fabric let loose with a gratifying rip and Kasun's cock jumped up. I sucked his grateful girth into the warmth of my mouth and he sucked in a deep moan.

I lifted my head up to adjust my positioning and looked directly into Ravindu's eyes. "Take me from behind," I told him.

As my lips kissed and my tongue licked slowly down Kasun's cock, I felt Ravindu's thighs against my buttocks and his cock poke all the way up my cunt. His fingers unclasped my bra, then caressed my breasts before squeezing my nipples. Heat and ecstasy filled my body, connecting both cocks and sending little jolts of pleasure sizzling from the soles of my feet up to the top of my neck.

Ravindu's hands left my breasts which swayed loosely and I concentrated on Kasun's cock. It was wide and gnarly and hot. I peeled back his foreskin and rotated my tongue around his tip. My lips sealed tight and I slid down his shaft, circling my tongue as I went. At the bottom, I sucked hard and maintained suction as I slowly drew my mouth upwards.

Behind, a pudding bowl rested on my rump then tipped backwards, pouring warmth down my butt and into my pussy. Ravindu slid one hand back to my breasts and the other down above his cock to stroke his fingers along my pussy lips and around my clit. Nothing beats physical flexibility! I felt myself swooning into the zone where all sensation merges into one all-encompassing pleasure.

I felt warmth, then goo, then hot as I came out of my swoon—and the hot wasn't pudding!—inside my mouth, inside my cunt I separated out the sensations. Ravindu was slapping himself vigorously against my thighs. Kasun's cock was quivering inside my mouth. Their orgasms tripped mine and we exploded our consciousnesses into the universe together before rolling into a ball and collapsing onto the bed. I was vaguely aware of applause in the distance.

The shower was heavenly, but it made me want to curl up and fall asleep. A jolt of ice-cold water banished that thought. Back in the main room, I concentrated on trying to spy someone recording the festivities, but I didn't see any indication of this.

At long last the party started to break up and I was finally able to corner Sploshing Sal in the doorway to the kitchen. "Do you have any idea why Jack—the Cyber Culprit—would target you?" I asked.

"Jack and I had a falling out over my support of the online dating service. Since his fiancée died last year, he's had a hate-on for anything cyber. Your moniker—Cyber Culprit—sums it up pretty good."

"Why was he against the dating service?"

"He claimed the site was nothing more than a platform for rip-off artists. I disagreed. We had words."

"Do you know where I could find Jack?

Sal shrugged. "Jack moves around a lot. But you met him

here tonight."

"Tonight!?! Where?!?" I jerked my head around madly, then back to Sal.

Sal was looking around, then he shrugged and returned his attention to me. "On the cross. He was with Lilly."

"Seamus?!?"

Sal nodded. "Seamus is the Irish version of Jack."

"I thought you said the two of you had a fight?"

Sal shrugged, but this time with just one shoulder. "It was more of a difference of opinion than a fight. Listen, Jack's a fan. He used to be a really good fan. Now he comes out only when it's convenient for him."

I cursed myself for not being more vigilant. Not to mention inquisitive! But there was no point in crying over spilt milk. Spilt custard. And maybe there was more Sal could tell me. "You said his fiancée died last year?"

Sal nodded. "That's when Jack started hacking and exposing. She was just walking across the street. The driver who killed her was texting his secretary. And it didn't help that Jack got fired for shutting his phone off in violation of the company's 24/7 availability policy."

The next day, I brought Eric chicken soup for lunch. My assistant was in bed, looking miserable. His nose was as red as his hair. Tissues littered the opposite side of his bed. But the chicken soup and my description of the sploshing party perked him up.

"Don't tell Michael," I told him. "But I think that the Cyber Culprit is after me."

"We have to tell Mr. Rayburn that the Cyber Culprit was at the party."

I shook my head vehemently. "No!"

"But he's the client."

"If I tell him now, he'll fire us. Or worse, hire Peter and use me for bait."

Eric pushed himself up on the bed. "That's a great idea! Then we'd have CC cornered."

"What we'd have is Peter drooling while watching me making out."

"Lee—"

"We can't tell Michael. I need more time—"

Our debate was interrupted by an insistent ring on my

cellphone. It was Michael Rayburn. He was talking rapid-fire so I put him on speaker, "...firm is under attack by internet trolls. There's wave after wave of negative comment on social media, Twitter, Facebook, Yelp—everything! And unpleasant photos on Flickr, Tumblr and SnapChat. There are multiple complaints to the Law Society and to the Better Business Bureau. Exposés on consumer television programs, newspaper columns, blogs—you name it! Negative, negative everywhere."

"I'll be right in," I told him. Now was not the time to remind him that all publicity is good publicity.

By the time I arrived at Michael's law office, things had calmed down, at least a touch. Three of the firm's top litigators had been dispatched to seek interim injunctions to shut down the firestorm of negative publicity and the firm's publicist had launched a broad-based counter-attack.

Michael was in his office shouting instructions into his phone, a glass of whisky in his left hand. His face was flushed. He slammed down his phone as I scooted into he chair across his desk. He took another sip of whiskey, set the glass down, and stared into it. I made a mental note that he did not offer me any whisky.

"We found out why the Cyber Culprit is so pissed at the internet, smart phones in particular," I told him.

This piqued Michael's interest and he looked up at me for the first time since I'd entered his office. He was exhausted, his eyes bleary, bloodshot.

"His fiancée was killed by a distracted driver texting on his phone", I continued.

All the color drained out of Michael's face. He tried to speak, but couldn't.

And then I knew. "The distracted driver—"

"Lee—"

"The distracted driver—he was CC's first victim, wasn't he?"

"Lee..."

"He was, wasn't he?"

Michael slowly nodded.

"Show me the post," I demanded.

"Lee—"

"Show me!"

Michael entered several keystrokes on his laptop, then turned it to me. A video was playing. It was amateurish, with lurid texts accusing "Murderer!" flashing across the screen. In the background was surveillance camera footage. A man driving a car, texting into his phone. Something slammed across his hood, over his windshield and out of the view of the camera.

"That was him, hitting Jack's fiancée?"

Michael nodded.

The driver looked vaguely familiar, but I couldn't place him. "Who is he?"

Michael turned his laptop back towards him. When he turned it back to me, the screen was filled with a business story detailing the prospects of a major corporation and the financial exploits, past and present of its CEO, Alexander M. J. Lippert. The photo of the CEO matched the face of the distracted driver in the video.

Michael reached around and hit another key. Now I was reading a story about criminal cases being thrown out on technicalities. One paragraph was circled: "Among the cases dismissed yesterday was that of a driver who'd killed a woman while texting his secretary. His lawyer, Michael Rayburn stated, 'My client just wants to get on with his life.'"

Back in my apartment, I opened my diary and began to write: *Yes, I have much to be thankful for. My employment might be precarious, but I'm my own boss and not burdened with any major debts.*

Men find me attractive—witness the steady stream of lovers. Maybe not lovers, since relationships seem to elude me, but sexual partners certainly. The muscular and dominating Peter. Michael the romantic. Kasun and Ravindu, one for each end. Ella with her soft folds of never ending. The women more imaginative, the men more exciting. And of course Lilly, and the Cyber Culprit. Seamus, Jacob, Jack.

Would I ever find a lover, someone to love? Someone who would love me?. Someone who would be truthful, faithful*. But I seemed to be attracted to an endless stream of new experiences. Maybe I was the problem.*

Michael and Peter just wanted me for a side dish. Their real attentions were elsewhere. The only one who was pursuing me relentlessly was the Cyber Culprit. At least Jack had the grace to bring a different woman to each of our encounters... What the hell does he want with me*?!?*

I set my pen down. Everything was a mish mash. I shook my head. Not everything. One thing was clear, clear enough to be committed to writing: *Tomorrow, I would have to tell Michael. Tomorrow, I would have to tell him* everything*!*

Choosing, Lusty Lee Log #26

I *have* to tell Michael. Even though his client deserved what had happened to him, richly *deserved* to have had his personal affairs aired far and wide across the internet. I'd woken up in a sweat. I couldn't remember the dream, but I knew that it meant that I had to tell Michael that we had found the Cyber Culprit. I racked my brain for an alternative.

But there was no escaping that Michael Rayburn had paid me to track the Cyber Culprit down and, just because CC had a reason, didn't give him the *right* to destroy careers and lives, didn't give him the right to violate privacy, to show people in their secret sexual moments. Except maybe the distracted driver who'd killed the innocent woman because he *just* had to send one last text. Except him. *He* deserved.

And I could understand CC's rage intensifying after Michael had got the distracted driver off on a technicality. The driver might have escaped prison but CC had imposed a different punishment.

However, and here was the tragedy, CC in his righteous anger had cast his net of punishment too wide. Innocent parties had been harmed. Parties who'd had no blame in the death of his fiancée. And now I would have to turn him over to Michael. And now Michael would impose his own punishment on CC.

But the Cyber Culprit—Jacob, Jacob Donaldson, was a person too. Not to mention a rather spectacular and *creative* lover. My nipples still tingled from where he'd mashed rum balls into them. No swimming pool would be the same after he and Erica had sandwiched me between them under the foam. Now, when I went to a cosplay, I would search the room for the warsuit on which he had impaled me. And custard—hot or cold—would always taste like heaven after the splosh party.

Jacob. It hurt to have to turn him in. But after Sal had confirmed Jacob's identity, it had been a quick step to learn his last name. And now, I had a full dossier on the Cyber Culprit. A dossier which belonged to Michael Rayburn.

I took a deep breath as I turned into the underground parking lot to Michael's law office. *Eric!* I pulled the ticket from the machine and kissed it. My assistant! My devoted side-kick deserved to share in the glory, deserved to be present to see the look of gratitude on Michael's face. I entered the parking lot, then turned my car around.

At the exit, the attendant wanted to know why I'd only spent three minutes in the parking lot. I told him it wasn't any of his business. He shrugged and said I'd have to pay the $5.25 for the half hour anyways. The S.O.B! I told him to go jump in the lake. He pointed to the barrier blocking my exit, then held out his hand for payment. I told him where he could shove his $5.25.

He shrugged and slumped back into his chair.

"Fuck you," I told him.

"Fuck or not, you still have to pay."

I slumped back into my own seat, mimicking his posture. I had all day. I smiled to myself; I literally had all day. And while I was sitting here, I wasn't turning CC in. I texted Eric to tell him that I'd be coming to his apartment. His only response was that I should let myself in. Strange—he was usually hyper security-conscious. I began to drift to my happy place, floating in the ocean, feeling the waves gently caress between my legs—

A honking horn behind me jerked me back to Toronto's cold concrete. There was a black Mercedes behind me. A very *large* black Mercedes.

I smiled sweetly at the parking attendant. He scowled back at me, but waved me through as he turned his scowl to a smile for the driver of the Mercedes.

Eric was still in bed with a cold. His nose was as red as his hair. That's why he had told me to let myself in. His voice—all two syllables worth—was raspy. So I made chicken soup for him. From scratch. Home made, especially from scratch, preserves the nutrients best. Besides from scratch meant two more hours before I'd have to turn CC in.

First I popped three chicken thighs into boiling water. After the chicken was half-cooked, I separated it from the bones and cut it into little pieces. Michael had given me the Cyber Culprit case when I had nothing else. The professional loyalty I owed Michael was obvious; the personal was ambiguous—he'd been a good, but unfaithful lover. I returned the bones—for strength—back into the broth along with the chicken pieces. Then I cut up the carrots, celery, radish, and whole onions. Jacob had no right to target innocents—a Supreme Court Justice for god's sake! But to lose your fiancée to a jerk on a cellphone—I couldn't begin to imagine the pain. Last to go in were frozen peas and green onions. Maybe Eric would be able to see a way out of the conundrum. As the concoction boiled, I added copious amounts of salt to soothe Eric's throat.

I waited until Eric was sipping his soup before I sprang it on him. "I know who the Cyber Culprit is."

"What?!?" he rasped. It was going to be a one-way conversation; even a monosyllable would be a strain on my fallen comrade.

I smiled as I continued. "I know who he is. His name is Jacob Donaldson. I know where he lives." I turned my phone to Eric to show him a photo of our soon-to-be-former nemesis.

Eric raised an eyebrow and I took my phone back.

I nodded. "I know he's not much to look at." I swiped my phone to a different photo. Jacob was thirty-five: a few years older than me. And he was barely taller: five-foot eleven. His eyes and hair were brown, the latter with a few streaks of grey. He was clean-shaven which accentuated his round and non-descript face. Although he was only reasonably fit, he held himself with a relaxed confidence that projected strength. "But he's warm and articulate. You wouldn't know it to look at him, but he has the sexual appetite and prowess of a tiger. And he knows just what to do with his long skinny dexterous fingers."

Eric held up his own fingers, extending and retracting them as if playing a piano. We both watched his fingers until Eric put them better use—sipping my soup.

"Have you told Mr. Rayburn?" Eric asked, proof that my chicken soup was perking him up.

I shook my head.

"But don't we have—"

"It's complicated."

Eric shook his head. He was a computer nerd. Zeros and ones; black and white. "Lee, just because he's a good guy..." A rasp cut off the rest of his thought.

"It's not just that he's a good guy. The guy Michael's trying to protect killed a woman because he was texting instead of paying attention to where he was driving."

Eric shook his head and locked eyes with me. There was pain on his face. I couldn't tell from where. But the message deep inside his green orbs was crystal clear—if I didn't turn Jacob in, he would have to.

"You're right," I conceded. "Are you up to coming in with me?"

He tried to lift himself, but his arms gave out and he flopped back onto the mattress.

"Maybe I should stay here to take care of you?"

"Lee."

"Right. Michael. Law Office. Report."

"A full report."

I nodded.

As I turned into the underground parking lot below Michael's law office, I still hadn't come up with an excuse for not turning the full Cyber Culprit dossier over to him. And if I didn't turn the Cyber Culprit in, Eric had made it plain that he would have to. And if it was Eric making the report, instead of me, he would, in effect, be turning *me* in as well.

The law firm corridors were a beehive of panicked activity which intensified the closer I got to Michael's office. I joined the line of assistants, paralegals and junior lawyers outside his office. One by one, each approached the lawyer's desk, received terse instructions, and scooted off to obey. It was clear that Michael was still dealing with the fallout from the troll attack on his firm.

Michael held up an envelope to the paralegal in front of me. "Get this to Flickr," he barked.

"You mean Yahoo?"

"And Verizon. Everyone!"

Michael's face brightened momentarily as he saw me. "Lee, I'm sorry, I can't."

I vaguely indicated the folder containing our dossier on Jacob Donaldson. "Should I come back later?"

Michael nodded and waved the junior lawyer behind me forward to his desk.

As I left, Michael's secretary poked her head into his office. "It's the Law Society," she told him. Michael picked up the phone, but I was too far away to hear what he said.

In the elevator, my glee at the postponement of my moment of truth was tempered by concern for Michael. Would this troll attack be blamed on him? Would he be demoted, even fired? I clutched the Jacob Donaldson's dossier to my chest.

The elevator doors opened. I paid my $5.25 to the parking attendant. The only thing to do was to go to Jacob's apartment and verify the contents of our dossier. Maybe find more evidence?

Jacob's apartment was in a newly-gentrified area of the city. I raised my hand to knock and all but fell into Jacob's apartment when the door suddenly opened.

And there was Jacob! Smiling as I stumbled into his arms.

"Lee Brandt," he enthused. "It is indeed an honor."

"Jacob Donaldson."

"Call me Jack."

Jack was wearing a tuxedo and looked absolutely grand.

"You know I've been hired to find you."

He nodded. "And Michael certainly has gotten his money's worth. But today is about you. We both know what Michael wants. But what is it that *you* want?"

"I—" What the hell *did* I want?

Jack smiled at my discomfiture, as if he had expected it, as if it was okay. "Perhaps we should discuss it over lunch?"

He ushered me into his apartment. It was open concept. Several pots were on the stove. Further in, I caught sign of an elegantly appointed dining room table. There was a large bowl of salad and two large plates with empty salad bowls in the middle. In the center, a flame flickered atop a tall red candle.

Jack stood by the far chair and pulled it out for me. He was absolutely resplendent in his silk-blend black jacket, bright white shirt and black bow tie. A red cummerbund restrained his waist. I suddenly felt under-dressed in my white Tshirt and blue jeans. But Jack didn't seem to have noticed. I slipped into the chair and Jack nudged it forward before sitting down opposite me.

"So, *Lee*, what do *you* want?" he repeated as he spooned salad into the small bowl in the middle of my plate. There was spinach and fennel and cherry tomatoes and red onions, and parsley and radishes and grilled eggplant and cucumber and romaine lettuce and orange peppers.

"I want to eat my salad."

His smile told me that my response was the height of humor, but he didn't laugh and I didn't know what *that* meant. The rainbow flavors of the vegetables burst inside my mouth.

"Have you turned me in?" he asked.

I shook my head. "But he knows we're getting close."

"But not that you've found me?"

"He knows that it's about the death of your fiancée."

"But not that you've found me."

"No." I took another bite of salad.

"You don't want to turn me in, do you?"

"No."

"But you haven't figured out why."

I shook my head. He was right, I hadn't. I liked him, I liked being with him, and I understood why he'd been so angry. But that wasn't all of it. The number of innocent victims he'd targeted weighed heavily in favor of turning him in. So there had to be something more.

I finished my salad before him and watched him scoop the last two forkfuls into his mouth. I was aware of my heart beating and the need to take a deep breath to calm down. There were so many jerks walking free. Why did this magnificent man have to go to jail?

Jack moved over to the kitchen and I could only see his back. When he returned, he was holding two bowls of steaming soup. The interwoven fragrances of coconut, curry, lemongrass and ginger proclaimed that my taste buds were about to revel in the epitome of Thai cuisine.

The coconut milk smoothed the way for the tart sweetness of the ginger and the bite of the curry allowing the citrus flavor of the lemongrass to come through. I had half of my second spoonful down when Jack popped the question.

"You're in love with me, aren't you?"

I almost sprayed his tuxedo with the rest of my mouthful, but managed to choke the reaction back. "Are you *crazy*?" I sputtered.

"My mental status is a different matter. You didn't answer my question."

I gave him a sharp look out of the side of my eyes. We finished our soup in silence.

The main course was spaghetti Bolognese. The strong flavors wafted up from the plate as Jack ground first pepper, then parmesan cheese over it. I twirled a mouthful around my fork and chewed until butter and olive oil and carrot, onion, celery, garlic and minced steak each in turn caressed my mouth. Then there was wine, thyme and oregano.

Jack was right. I *was* in love with him. It made no sense. None at all. Then again it made no sense that all the varied ingredients inside my mouth should taste so good. I started to chew another mouthful and smiled at Jack.

He smiled back. I had answered his question. The universe enveloped me in warmth, in the sensation that all was right in the world.

It wasn't until Jack set a small ball of ice cream—Tartufo—in front of me, that I realized that I was in trouble. I was in love with Jack, just as I was in love with the desert in front of me. I was in love with the sweet chocolate outside. I was in love with the tart red strawberry at the center of the ball. But—

"I have to turn you in," I told him.

Jack chuckled. As if that was the funniest thing I could have possibly said. "I suppose you do," he granted. "But not today. Today is for lovers to enjoy."

He got up, took me by the hand, and led me to his living room. Suddenly there was music, a Viennese waltz and I was in his arms, my head on his shoulder, cuddling against his tuxedo. As he twirled me, I was suddenly wearing a fancy dress gown. I was safe in his arms, protected from any harm the universe might contain.

As the music ended, we ended up close to a wall beside a large wing-backed chair. Jack maneuvered me gently against the wall and undid the button to my jeans and I was immediately on fire for him. He didn't touch my zipper or let his hands stray to my breasts. He didn't push himself against me. But that one action of undoing my button unloosed *all* my pent-up passions. My breasts craved for his fingers to caress them. My nipples thirsted to be twisted. My pussy's pleas to be petted were even more insistent. She was hot and moist, her desire contorting my insides. Any resistance had melted away. My senses were consumed in the moment. I felt my hands removing Jack's jacket and laying it on the chair.

Now Jack's back was against the wall. Where his hands had been reserved, mine were unrestrained. I touched and fondled and squeezed every inch of his shirt. It was soft silk, so smooth, so sensuous. It was so thin that I could feel his chest hairs. I ran my fingers across his nipples and felt them harden. As they perked up, I grasped them between thumb and forefinger and gave them a gentle twist. Jack moaned. A deep guttural moan. And now we were *both* hot!

Undoing the cummerbund on his waist was a simple matter of undoing the buckle behind his back. But his black bowtie resisted all my attempts to unloosen it. He laughed, gently removed my hands from his throat and kissed my forehead. I shut my eyes. His fingers danced over my body. My skin was suddenly cool. I opened my eyes. Somehow he'd removed my jeans and Tshirt and laid them, properly folded, on the chair next to us.

Jack tried to turn my back to the wall, but I dropped to my knees, out of his grasp. Two hands on his crotch found a shaft jutting upwards and now outwards between my fingers, proof positive that Jack was as aroused as I was. Snap, unzip, pull and Jack was down to his briefs. Another swift pull and his phallus was out. Caress, stroke, lick, shudder.

I tried to put Jack into my mouth, but he used my change in position to pull me up and to turn my back to the wall. He had untied his bow tie and held the long piece of satin stretched between his hands. In a splendid chorography—five movements, ten?—Jack had the bow tie tied around my neck. It had been custom-made, without hook, slider or adjuster, so it hung loosely around my neck. Still, it was the height of fashion.

He bent to kiss me. First his lips brushed against mine. Then our lips were fully engaged. The suction began subtly, just the point where I closed my eyes. I vanished inside him. It was warm and wonderful and lustrous. I had ceased to be. I was a droplet of water in the universal ocean. I was the universal ocean. I was nothing and everything all at once. The tip of his tongue touching the tip of mine restored my consciousness of being Lee without disrupting my connection to the whole.

But Jack's tongue didn't stop at the tip of mine. He slid his tongue all the way to the base of my tongue. Then he sucked, rapidly withdrawing his tongue at the same time, jerking me back into my separate being, thrusting me into my churning horniness. Somehow he'd removed my bra and undone the bow tie. He had stretched the bow tie's satin band across the bottom of my breasts and was slowly drawing it upwards. When he reached the bottom of my areolae, he pulled it back and forth sideways. And every time the satin band slid sideways, it also edged upwards.

My knees gave way and I melted into him. His leg was between my legs; he was pressing me against the wall, holding me up. Every time the satin band moved right, it sent tingles to my nipples. Every time it moved left, the tingles swirled deep into my breasts. Then his bow tie rubbed against the bottom of my nipples and I felt the tingles open up my pussy. I just wanted him inside me. I tried to stamp my feet, but he was holding me too tight. I just wanted—

The satin bow tie was right across my nipples. Motionless. Holding *me* motionless. The moment stretched to an eternity. Then the satin strip moved. And I moved with it, twirling round and round with the heat being rubbed through my nipples into every cell of my body.

Suddenly I had Jack against the wall. The bow tie had disappeared. I gently squeezed his balls and concentrated on breathing. When I had regained a trace of control, I pulled his shirt up and over his shoulders and to the floor. I grabbed his cock in my hands. Now I had *full* control. His cock was hot and hard against my fingers. It quivered every time I stroked downwards. Jack gasped every time I stroked upwards.

His whole body was slack, in my thrall. Only his arms moved. And they moved down from my chest, paying tribute to my waist, echoing devotion as his fingers traced the curves around my hips. I would stroke him softly, keep him erect, keep him subject to my dominion, keep him forever. His arms dropped to his sides. His whole body was slack, enslaved to the sensations moving up and down his cock.

But his arms were moving, his fingers tugging my panties, sending little frissons of joy into my pussy. More importantly, his arms were escaping my dominion over them. I grabbed his cock firmly and accelerated my strokes. Jack groaned. I had him in full control once more. Soon his arms would go slack and I could slow my strokes, soften my strokes, keep him imprisoned in pleasure forever. Soon—

There was something in my panties. In my slit! Satin. Smooth. Stroking ever so slowly. I tried to move my hands faster but they had lurched to a standstill. The satin caressed my pussy lips, pressed lightly against my clit. My knees buckled and I started to collapse to the floor.

Jack caught me and I was his slave once more. He was holding me by my upper arms; I was completely in his mercy, but Jack had other ideas.

"Stand," he commanded.

I stumbled, but managed to stand. I looked below to where he had the satin strand of his tie inserted under my panties. He pulled downward to loosen it, pulling my panties down as well.

Then he pulled upwards with his front hand sliding the satin once again up my slit. The effect was electricity dancing down my legs and into my toes. Then he pulled both hands up, lodging his bow tie firmly into the depths of my slit. His front hand moved right, tickling my pussy lips, but missing my clit. Back and forth he pulled, arousing, tingling my pussy lips, drawing blood into them. But the satin was still missing my clit and I began to plot my revolt.

Jack's fingers began to walk down the satin strand. I reached for his cock, but his hands were blocking my access. But one more inch lower and his hands would no longer be affording him protection and I could regain my supremacy. I reached up to give his nipples a gentle twist to conceal my intent. His fingers moved down the satin. I slid my hands lower and touched his shaft with the tips of my fingers.

Satin on clit paralyzed me. He had found my weak spot and was now brushing his satin bow tie across it, caressing back and forth. Each tweak sent a jolt into my cunt, a jolt of electricity, and moisture and power. I stumbled. He caught me, pressed me against the wall. Now his finger had pushed the satin aside and was pressing and stroking my insistent little knob.

"Come." It was a whisper, a gasp, but it was the whisper of a man in control.

"No." The revolution may have failed. But I would not give in. "No," I repeated. The word was defiant but the quaver in my voice said otherwise.

"Come," he breathed.

My knees buckled. I held on to him. He pulled up on the satin band between my buttocks and stroked up and down my slit with the fingers of his other hand.

"Come," he invited.

"No." But I knew the heat and moisture on his finger was sending a different signal.

He vibrated his fingers rapidly back and forth, tightening the screws inside my cunt, tightening them to the snapping point. I tried to resist the coming surrender, but that just accelerated the quivering constrictions building inside.

"Come!" he commanded.

And the dam burst! The shock down to my feet made me jump in the air. A coil wound quickly up my spine sparking out jolts as it went. The contraction inside my cunt sucked everything in, pulling my hips and my knees forward and around. Then it burst out, sending everything in the opposite direction, mashing my pubic bone and my clit into his hand. In, out uncontrollably, painfully, so much pain it was pleasure, so much pleasure it was pain. White, then black, then white. Then red. The red was heat, but the pulsations had slowed, become less intense and I could taste each sensation without being overwhelmed by them. I floated on the waves of my climax, time without end. Floating, floating...

I opened my eyes. I really *was* floating. Bouncing. Being carried into a different room. Sinking into soft clouds. Gradually my mind emerged from the clouds. I was in a bedroom. Sinking into a memory foam mattress. And I was right in the mattress, no sheets. So while the foam was soft, it gripped my skin and I couldn't move.

Jack climbed on top of me, his cock at the opening of my pussy, his lips on mine. And he kissed me, the same way he had earlier that evening, shutting my eyes and drawing me into another reality. Carefree bliss. I felt his caresses on every inch of my body. All worldly cares were massaged from my brain.

Something below penetrated inside me. A large ripe succulent fruit, dripping juice and rapture. Warmth infusing joy up my spine. Ecstasy suffusing everywhere.

"Lee." A voice. Soft and in the distance.

"Lee." Closer now.

"Lee." Insistent. As if calling me to the surface.

"Lee."

I gasped air into my lungs. My eyes shot open. Jack's eyes were smiling down at me.

"Are you ready?" he asked.

I think I groaned.

"Lee?"

"Ready for what?"

"Ready to be taken again?" The pressure of his hips was rocking up and down my pelvis. His cock was sliding in and out of my pussy.

"Aren't you already taking me?"

"I'm having sex with you. Are you ready to be *taken*?"

"Taken where?" Maybe smartass would throw him off his game.

"Taken inside your fondest dreams."

All I could do was moan. There were no words. I shut my eyes and tiptoed to the edge of the dream world.

My head and neck could move, but just a bit. My back and legs were held fast by the foam. My tits, soft and languid, jiggled in rhythm with Jack's relentless thrusts below. My pussy was warm and wet and aroused. She was embracing Jack's cock, but it felt like he was embracing her.

I could feel the long strokes of Jack's cock tickling my pussy lips, rotating pleasure into my clit, intensifying the passion deep inside my cunt. I could feel the beginnings of my climax starting to swell inside, starting to surround my being. But somehow this was different. I couldn't tell whether it was the impending climax which would be different, or the way it was building up inside me, or something else. But *something* was different.

And then I knew. This climax wasn't going to be physical. This climax was going to be something more profound. This time I wasn't going to be consumed by the orgasm. This time I wasn't going to be the orgasm. Jack's smile told me that he was feeling the same thing. I hadn't opened my eyes, but I could see his smile. I could *feel* his smile. And I knew that he could feel my smile. We had become each other's smile.

I floated above the bed, above Jack's back which was patiently, resolutely pumping his seed into my body, muscles contracting down his spine, muscles squeezing his butt. Above the bed we held hands and watched each other's body explode in orgasm. Above the bed we felt the joy of orgasm without the nuisance of the physical spasms.

The next morning, I watched Jack snore. He had a soft snore. As if he didn't have a care in the world, as if he was caressing every molecule of air passing through his throat. He wasn't nearly as strong as Peter, as sensuous as Ella the masseuse, as creative as Michael, as exciting as Sarah the wrestler or as sweet as Crime

Scene Investigator Marty. But he was more tender than any of them. And he was more *present*—nothing else mattered but me, nothing else mattered but the moment.

"What did Michael say?" Eric wanted to know.

I had popped by my assistant's apartment on the way home. Jack had still been asleep when I'd left. But I wanted to see how Eric was managing with his cold. His door had still been ajar, but in his bedroom, there was evidence that he'd risen from his sickbed long enough to fix himself breakfast. And since he was sitting up in bed and typing into his laptop, long enough to retrieve his computer.

"Michael doesn't know," I admitted.

"Lee?!?"

"He was busy. I couldn't tell him."

"Lee, Lee." His tone moved from flabbergasted to sorrowful.

"But I did go to Jacob Donaldson's apartment. So his residential information is confirmed."

"Lee?" Questioning and accusing all at once.

"Yes. I did meet with the Cyber Culprit. He knows that the jig is up."

"Is it?"

I looked at him quizzically. Just what was he implying?

Eric sighed. "I really should report all this to Mr. Rayburn. But all that would do is get you in trouble. And you *have* been good to me."

"Don't worry. I'll tell Michael."

"Will you?" He sighed again. "Lee, if you don't, I have to tell him."

Then there was an incoming mail beep on his computer. He opened the message. A smile started small, then widened on his lips.

"No matter," he proclaimed. "As of this moment, I'm no longer your employee. I have a new job. It's a tech start-up."

"So, if you're no longer my employee, you don't have to report me to Michael."

"Lee—"

"Do you? If you're no longer part of the business, the decision is mine, not yours, as to how to report to the client."

"I guess so."

I bent to the bed and kissed him on the cheek. Pity he happened to be sick. Pity that his hard and flexible body, and pity that his ever so creative fingers were stuck in a sick bed. Now that he was no longer my employee...

I made an appointment with Michael's secretary to see him the next morning. I went to sleep fully intending to keep the appointment and to tell Michael everything I knew about the Cyber Culprit. Maybe he wouldn't need to know how good Jack looked in a tux or what mischief we had gotten up to the day before. Everything else I'd have to tell him.

But I woke up with a stuffed nose and pounding headache. Every other breath was a cough. Every time I breathed, it felt like my throat was on fire. I fished out my phone and texted Eric, "Caught your cold. In need of emergency chicken soup."

Half an hour later, Eric arrived with take-out chicken soup. I reached for the elixir, but he insisted on inserting a thermometer between my lips first.

"This isn't just an excuse to postpone your meeting with Mr. Rayburn, is it?"

I looked up at him, pleading in my eyes. How could he even *think* such a thing?

Bondage, Lusty Lee Log #27

I was curled up in a little ball in the middle of my bed, clutching my covers as close as I could to my body. I was trying to curse Eric for having given me his cold, but my throat was too sore. And it was getting sorer by the minute because my nose was too stuffed to allow me to use *it* to breathe. If I kept my head still, I could control the pounding inside my temples.

I sensed something move beside my bed and opened one eye. It was Jack, the erstwhile Cyber Culprit. Friend or foe—my brain was too foggy with over-the-counter cold remedies for me to be sure. Light was coming in through the door but not through the window. My two functioning brain cells concluded that it was nighttime.

Jack was fiddling with a small disc-shaped object. It looked like a space ship for pint-sized aliens. He made an adjustment and the cone on top lit up turquoise. Smoke started to come out of the cone. I moaned my disapproval.

"Relax," he told me. "It's aromatherapy."

I did my best to scowl. If this cold didn't kill me, his new-age BS would. I suddenly felt very hot and pushed the top layer of blankets off my body.

Jack turned his face sideways and inspected me. "You look like hell," he observed.

I mouthed "fuck off" back at him and closed my eyes.

"Rest in bed. Plenty of fluids. The aromatherapy will cycle automatically; don't touch it."

I kept my eyes shut and ignored him.

"And no email, cellphones or gadgets for the next twenty-four hours."

I thought about mouthing FU again, but decided it wasn't worth the effort.

I felt him kiss my forehead. The pounding in my temples abated. "No email, cellphones or gadgets," he repeated.

I nodded, then slipped into sleep.

I woke up to a beam of sunlight stabbing into my brain. With a great deal of effort, I managed to turn away from the window. I really should file a report with Michael Rayburn, lawyer, employer, lover. I didn't want to. It would mean turning Jack in. But it was my duty. I started to rouse myself. Then I remembered the promise I'd made to Jack. No email. Damn. I flopped back onto the bed.

I was shivering. It was dark. I was being wrapped. Wrapped inside a huge pancake, heavenly and warm. I opened my eyes but it was dark, so I shut them again. The smell of the pancake was stronger. I opened my eyes again. Dawn's early light through the window.

Somebody was cooking pancakes in the kitchen. That would be Eric, my assistant, making amends for having foisted his cold on me.

I tried to sit up. No, I *did* sit up. My fever was gone. My headache was gone. I took a deep breath. Through my *nose*! I tried to call out to Eric, however the best I could manage was a whisper. But at least the effort hadn't burned pain down my throat. Jack's spaceship belched a puff of white smoke.

I threw on a robe and shuffled to the bathroom. A bleary-eyed monster stared back from the mirror. I splashed water onto my face. It would have to do.

In the kitchen, it wasn't Eric's carrot top hunched over my stove. It was Jack's much more conservative grey-streaked brown hair. "Hi, gorgeous," he greeted without turning around.

I grunted and moved towards the table.

He flipped the pancake. It was golden brown, almost ready. Jack reached into the fridge and poured me a glass of orange juice as I sat down.

"Hi, gorgeous," he repeated.

"You need your eyes checked," I told him.

He chuckled and watched me down the OJ in one gulp. Jack returned to the stove, flipped the pancake, put it on a plate and slid the plate in front of me. He squirted a line of syrup back-and-forth onto the pancake until I nodded my head.

He watched me cut a piece of pancake and insert it into my mouth. "You didn't even try to use your phone," he said.

I looked at the clock. "Twenty-four hours aren't up yet."

"You weren't even tempted?"

"Once." I swallowed and folded another piece of pancake into my mouth.

"What did you do?"

I made him wait while I took another bite. And another. And another. "Went back to sleep."

He pointed to the clock. "Actually, your twenty-fours *are* up. Are you ready for your reward?"

The last bite of hot syrup-covered heaven swirling around my mouth was reward enough, but I nodded. Two rewards had to be better than one.

"You like BDSM, don't you?"

I nodded. "But I don't have any bondage equipment here."

"BDSM isn't whips or tools or bindings. It's a state of mind."

"The 'B' is for bondage. By definition that includes bindings."

He shook his head. "The hands and ankles of slaves picking cotton in the field weren't bound. But there's no dispute they were in bondage."

"But—"

"No buts. You are hereby in bondage. And your first task will be to go into your room, clean your face and dress in something nice."

I looked at him as I prepared my response. His round face, slightly older than mine, made him look wise. Like a Tibetan monk. His white dress shirt and black dress-pants fit him well, projecting physical power. His full lips hinted at a mocking smirk but his brown eyes demanded obedience. I shrugged and padded into my bedroom.

Since I was in bondage, I busied myself in cleaning my face. The puffiness was mostly gone, but there were still patches of red. So I applied a light layer of make-up. Make-up can go on either fast, or slow. I decided on slow. Bondage or no, I was going to test Jack's limits.

My first choice was leather. The leather miniskirt smelled intoxicating and felt even better. But I decided against it. Jack's theory was that bondage was not about the physical accessories. Why not make him prove his theory from square one?

So, leather off. Basic cotton panty over my full hips and ample bottom, smooth beige bra to cup my burgeoning bosom, a black skirt of uncertain material and a pink poly/cotton/spandex top, only one step above a T-shirt.

Jack was lounging on the couch when I slid into the room on my white bobby socks. I did a pirouette for him, allowing the centrifugal force to pull my skirt up, but just slightly.

When I returned to face him, his eyes were still demanding obedience. "Remove your bra," he told me.

Most men think you have to remove your shirt to remove your bra. Even if they've seen it done with the shirt remaining on, they still think it. I reached behind me, unclasped my bra, slid the right shoulder strap under my sleeve and off my wrist, then pulled the bra down the left sleeve of my top. I dangled it in front of Jack while wiggling my breasts. My nipples liked the feel of the poly/cotton/spandex.

Jack raised himself slowly off the couch without using his hands or arms. "Stand still," he told me before floating into the kitchen.

When he came back out, he was holding two dinner plates with teacups in the middle of each. "Hold your arms out," he commanded, motioning for me to hold my arms out to the side at shoulder height. He placed one plate on each palm. "Whatever happens, don't drop them."

His remonstrance was unnecessary. They were my only clean plates. He took a blindfold from his pocket and fitted it over my head. Everything turned black as he made the final adjustments.

I felt him leave and return. He held something beneath my

nose. Fresh roast coffee!

"May I?" I pleaded.

He held a straw to my lips and I sucked the warm liquid into my throat and into my belly. I took a deep breath, then another draw from the straw. Warmth filled my entire chest.

Then there was gurgling and the plates got heavier. The bastard was filling the teacups with coffee! Now if I dropped the plates, not only would they crack and break, but my carpet would be *stained* dark brown. The straw came back to my lips and I took another deep gulp of coffee.

Fingers on my ribs. Fingers moving, searching. I wished I could see Jack, see what he was doing. Tickle! He had found the edge of my ticklish spot. But I'd managed to suppress my reaction and the fingers on the right side of my torso moved away.

"Would you rather be tied up?" he whispered.

I decided not to answer. If I was tied up, maybe he could compel me to answer, but not now.

His hands left my ribs and moved to my breasts, gently caressing them. "Would your breasts rather be tied up?"

His voice was louder this time, leaving no doubt that I would have had to have heard. So this time my silence was a more obvious answer. He kept up his light caressing drawing heat and arousal into my nipples, rubbing my hardening buds against the poly/cotton/spandex.

He grabbed my nipples between his fingers with just enough force that I knew they were being pressed on both sides, but not so forcefully that I felt any discomfort. "Would your nipples like to be tied up?"

I kept my silence. He squeezed my nipples. I felt a gasp in the center of my lungs, but managed to take a deep breath instead.

"What say your nipples?" he demanded.

I managed to begin a slow and gradual exhalation.

Jack twisted my nipples. Hard! "Ow!" I gasped. The teacups rattled.

He untwisted my nipples, but still held them firmly. "Do your nipples need to be tied up?" He began to slowly twist them.

I held out as long as I could, until my nipples could take no more cruelty. "No," I whimpered.

"No, what?"

"No, Master."

He untwisted my nipples, but when he got back to the starting point, he kept twisting in the opposite direction. "Tell me about your investigation."

"Investigation?" The sensations at the center of my breasts were still pleasant, just starting to release endorphins throughout my body. But his fingers kept twisting and I bit my lip to suppress a gasp.

"Into the Cyber Culprit," he clarified.

"It's finished."

His fingers released my nipples and apologized by gently kneading my breasts. "And what did you find out?" his voice gently prodded.

"That the Cyber Culprit hacked numerous accounts and published private information on the internet."

"Whose accounts?" His hands moved up the sides of my right leg, stopping to fondle my knee.

"A judge, a politician, an actor, a doctor."

"And just who is this Cyber Culprit?"

"That's confidential."

His fingers fiddled with my skirt and I felt it slide down my legs to my ankles. Thwack! Sharp pain on my buttocks. Clattering teacups. "Who am *I*?" he demanded.

"You're my Master."

"And the Cyber Culprit, who is he?"

"That's confidential, Master." I tensed for another swat on my buttocks, but none came. I could feel the muscles in my arms. I adjusted my fingers under the plates.

"You dare keep secrets from your Master?" He was whispering, but his lips were right next to my ear.

"Yes, Master, sorry, Master, but I must."

"And this Cyber Culprit, what will happen to him?" His tongue touched the bottom of my earlobe, then gently traced upwards.

I shivered. The teacups rattled. "That will be for others to decide."

"You are going to report this Cyber Culprit?"

"Yes, Master. I must."

"What if I told you not to?"

"Master, please…" What *would* I do?!?

"Spread your legs." He had stepped back. His voice was no

longer a whisper; not loud, but no longer soft, no longer intimate. "Spread your legs," he repeated, his voice full of firm authority.

I started to spread my legs, then pressed them tightly together. "I have to pee," I told him.

"Spread them."

"But—"

Thwack. "Spread them!"

I spread my legs and clenched my pelvic floor muscles as tightly as I could. His fingers moved up my legs and traced the bottom edge of my panties. Then his fingertips lifted away from my skin, returning to touch my belly.

"What will you tell them about the Cyber Culprit?" His fingers had returned to my ribs and his voice was coming from behind.

"I—"

His fingers had found my tickle spots sending spasms up to my armpits. The teacups rattled. He was holding his fingers motionless, but my arms were heavy.

"I have to pee!" I yelped, scrunching my pelvic floor as hard as I could.

"You have to *answer* my questions."

His fingers moved. The teacups clattered. My bladder popped a drop. "Please," I pleaded.

"What will you tell them about the Cyber Culprit?" he repeated.

His fingers stroked my tickle spot, sending jolts up and down my spine, choking off my breathing. I barely managed to hold onto the plates. My legs snapped together and my hips twisted to squeeze off my urine.

Thwack! "Spread your legs."

I slowly inched them apart, but only an inch.

Thwack! "All the way."

Another few inches were all I could manage. His fingers returned to my ribs, just below my tickle points.

"I know who the Cyber Culprit is. You know who the Cyber Culprit is. And I know that you know." His fingers stroked back and forth. Another centimeter higher and I'd be in uncontrollable paroxysms. "You need to tell me."

"Yes, Master," I gasped. "It's you, you're the Cyber Culprit."

"Are you sure you have to tell?" His fingers continued to stroke back and forth. I took a deep breath. Maybe I could hold on.

"Tell?" Stupid!—he knows you know.

He moved his fingers up. One stroke back and the spasm shot up to my neck. One stroke forward and the spasm tickled my toes. Stroking back peed my panties. Forward and I stumbled, dropping the plates. I managed to grab one before it hit the carpet but the other teacup clattered noisily.

Two steps forward and I'd regained my balance enough to hold the plate with one hand. I ripped the blindfold off my head and whirled, ready to lay into Jack for ruining my carpet.

But there he was, holding the other plate, smiling from ear to ear. I looked down at the plate in my hand. There was only water in the teacup. Even if I'd dropped it, the carpet would have been fine.

"You tricked me!" I accused.

He nodded. "Bondage is all in your head."

I looked down where my soiled skirt should have been. Instead, there was a bowl filled with yellow liquid sitting on the carpet.

"You tricked me!" I scolded.

"That I did." He laughed as I tried to figure out whether to be angry at him for ruining my carpet, not ruining my carpet, making me piss my panties or being grateful that the only damage done had been to my dignity.

"You bastard," I told him.

He chuckled, padded to the kitchen, and came back with another bowl and a couple of towels. He pulled off my panties, put them in the urine-filled bowl. The new bowl had warm water in which he dipped the towel, then patted it all over my crotch. When I was completely clean, he bent over again, and patted me dry with the other towel. Somehow during all of this my shirt was removed and I was completely nude.

"I still have to turn you in," I told him as he straightened up.

"Do you?" he asked. He was no longer my Master. He was my equal, someone with whom I'd shared the chase, shared bodily fluids, shared emotions.

"Do you?" he repeated. And in that question was the definition of our relationship. Were we more than hunter and quarry? I remembered how it felt to be with him—the reckless abandon, the rock-your-socks sex. I remembered his solicitude for my pleasure, for my well-being. I remembered him revenging my betrayals.

I looked into the depths of his deep brown eyes where the question was wordlessly repeated. And this time the question was between duty and love. My whole body cried for me to choose love. My womb cried for love. My lungs cried for love. Every inch of my skin cried for love.

But duty cried loud and shrill deep inside my brain. I shut my eyes to shut her up, but that just made her voice sound louder and clearer. I wanted Jack, he made me feel *so* good. At *every* level. But it would be wrong to let him escape. The voice inside my head was right. I had to turn Jack in.

I opened my eyes to give Jack the bad news and was immediately sucked deep into the black circles in the center of his eyes. Everything went dark. Then warm. Then wonderful. I was floating, and flying and dancing. I was kissing and being kissed and sucking and being sucked inside.

Strong hands on my shoulders pushed me back and I gasped air into my lungs. Jack was smiling at me.

How could I even *think* of turning him in? How could I even think of harming him, even for a moment?!?

Jack didn't have any clothes on. I couldn't remember what he had been wearing. I couldn't remember him taking his clothes off. But he was nude. He took me in his arms and we glided over to the couch where he tenderly laid me down.

"Shut your eyes," he told me.

I did. His musk was pungent and sweet all at the same time. The world turned warm and red. He gently touched the skin on my temples, just beside my eyes. My whole face relaxed, removing any need for effort to keep my eyes closed. Red faded to grey, then black. Deep dark black. No sound, no taste, no smell, no touch, no light.

His fingers pressed the sides of my neck. Nothing else existed except the skin and muscle and bones and nerves under his fingers. His fingers moved to the base of my neck and trailing wisps of light swirled within void. Then the fingers departed, returning the ebony darkness.

Touch atop each nipple pulled them higher, wider, tighter, hotter. Touch receding as my nipples poked higher. Circling fingers led the heat out and down my mammary mounds. The fingers vanished. My body vanished.

Warm wetness in my navel radiated sensation outward and my body gradually returned, alive and vibrant at my navel, awareness diffusing in the distance. Jack's tongue circled, drilling all the way down to my spine. When it reached the bony center, his pulsing wet snake sent music up my spine, sent warmth down my legs.

Lips tickled around my navel as Jack withdrew his tongue. I felt him breathe in, sucking my belly subtly upwards. Then he held his breath and time stopped.

Vibrations, *slobbery* vibrations, throbbed laughter into my belly and curled my toes. As I recovered, I was aware of his lips trailing down to the top of my pubic hair. He kissed all around the border of my forest, awakening the edges of my sex. I could feel the ridge atop my pussy lips, the tip of my clit, moisture at the opening of my pussy.

Then fingers replaced lips and tugged up on the tufts of my pussy hair. My full sex came alive: tingling down from the tops of my pussy lips, hard desire throbbing in my clit, heat all the way up my cunt.

"Touch me," I whispered. I felt my eyelids flutter. Red was at the edges, but the center remained black.

His fingers danced over my thighs—on the outside, on the inside, above my knees, below my knees, just below my sex.

"Touch me," I begged, my voice soft, barely above a whisper.

His hands pressed atop my vulva, then pushed apart, prying my sex open. The air was cool but that only inflamed my passion.

"Touch me!" My voice was loud, insistent, just like the red cravings in my eyeballs.

Without releasing my vulva, two fingers—thumbs?—began to play up and down my sex. The cool air had evaporated all the moisture from my pussy lips and clit, but his touch was so delicate that frissons of joy tickled over my sex, hinting pleasure up my spine and down to my toes.

"More!" I pleaded and the force of my voice snapped my eyes open. But all I could see were the edges of his face.

His lips on mine, barely touching, even more delicate than his fingers below. His lips full on mine, locking, sucking our mouths into mutual vacuum. His tongue flicked forward and I felt mine move to meet it, sealing the wedding of our mouths. Below, his hands released my vulva and a finger dipped itself into my pussy. Now moistened, the finger played with my clit, its movements starting to match the movements of his tongue. My tongue and my clit synchronized with his movements; my mouth became my sex.

His tongue and his finger stroked my clit and my tongue *was* my clit. Everything was dark. All I could feel was my sex being stroked. Mouth, spine, cunt. Two hot glowing balls of sex connected by a pole. Mouth becomes cunt, tongue becomes clit, pussy lips kiss his mouth. Climax tingling everywhere. Tingling! *Tingling* everywhere. Tingling! Not stopping! My eyes jerk open, glimpse of Jack, then shut into darkness, open shut, tingling! The climax is never-ending tingling up and down the taut pole. Orgasm—"the little death"—

Jack's fingers are gone. Jack's tongue is gone. I open my eyes into his smile.

"Breathe," he says.

I gasp and air floods into my chest shocking my eyes shut. My lungs explode into exhalation forcing my eyes open again.

"She's alive!" Gratitude and glee swirl around his every syllable.

I take another deep breath.

"Ready for more?" he asks. His cock is huge, hard.

I'm about to shake my head. But somehow my body *is* ready and I nod.

Jack carefully places his penis at the opening of my vagina. Just inside. I'm too exhausted to move a muscle so I just lie there. Jack is exerting just enough forward pressure to lubricate my pussy, just enough to move forward. But it's like molasses, if you watch it, it doesn't feel like it's actually flowing.

I look up into his face. It's roundness and his unabashed smile would make him look like a cherub if he wasn't too old to be an angel-in-training.

"Fuck me," I tell him.

"Make me." His voice is pure glee. He knows I'm exhausted beyond exhaustion.

I shut my eyes and concentrate down below. He's about two inches in, still moving slowly. But his pace has picked up, now I can feel his girth enlarging my pussy, stroking her lips.

"Fuck me," I plead.

He pushes harder and I can feel his whole cock sliding in. I shut my eyes to enjoy every sensation. But he holds himself short, just before our pubic bones should be touching.

"Please," I beg.

"Open your eyes."

It takes all my energy, but my eyes flicker open. He presses our pubic bones together and rotates. Our bones are hard against each other, my skin being pulled up from down below rubbing pussy lips against my clit together, stroking in upward circular motions. I can feel the root of every hair being pulled, then released. I shut my eyes and luxuriate in being gently, but firmly, fucked.

His rhythm rocks me, like a baby in a cradle, and I drift deeper into my couch, deeper into the wonderful warm blackness, deeper into the paradise of love without demand, deeper into eternal bliss. The light above shrinks into a pinpoint, then winks out and I'm in complete blackness. I slide deeper into pleasure so complete it doesn't require the release of orgasm.

There's a light up above. High, higher in the night sky. One lonely star. And the wind must have picked up. The hammock is swaying back and forth. The star is brighter and I squint against its light. I almost fall out of the hammock, so I grab on and open my eyes.

But I'm not on a hammock! My hand is squeezing the pillow on my couch. And it's not wind causing the swaying. It's Jack's cock *slamming* into me. I'm holding on for dear life. His smile leers down at me.

"Isn't this what you wanted?" he taunts.

It isn't and the bastard knows it. But he's made a fatal miscalculation. I'm no longer exhausted. My trip into the underworld has rejuvenated me.

"Please. Gentle," I beg.

He pulls himself almost all the way out, hesitates, then slams himself all the way in. Fast, hard strokes, banging from every direction.

"Mercy," I plead with all the plaintiveness I can muster. But that just makes him rock more violently from side to side as he plunges himself in and out. And that is all I need.

On his next upstroke, I pull myself upwards and use the hand holding onto the side of the couch to pull me off the couch. He lands on his side as I stumble to standing beside him.

"Please. Gentle," I mock.

He tries to get up, but now *he's* the one who's energy is spent and I easily push him back down.

"Want to get fucked?" I tease.

He nods. It's a tentative nod, but it's enough.

"Lie on the floor. On your back. Put your hands behind your head. Intertwine your fingers. And don't move until I tell you."

As soon as he's in position, I turn away from his head and straddle him. I slowly lower my pussy to his cock. I'm well stretched, *and* well lubricated, so I slide easily down his shaft. I feel him relax and am tempted to bounce up and down hard. But my revenge, warranted though it is, would only delay his orgasm. And since I'm on top, doing all the work, any such revenge would cost me more than him.

This position—the reverse cowgirl—has several disadvantages. First, there's me doing the work, second, I will have exert myself to lean just right for me to get his cock to rub my g-spot, and third, all I get to look at are his ugly feet. But I will be totally in control and if he tries to move, he'll slide right out. Even more importantly, I will be able to touch my little love knob exactly like she needs and so richly deserves.

I lean forward, my hands on his thighs and thrust against his cock. This is easy and mildly pleasurable to me. More importantly, it'll bring him swiftly to his plateau. When I'm sitting secure enough to raise one hand, I begin to tease my clit with feather strokes. A gentle moan from behind confirms that Jack has reached stage one.

Now I lean back so that his cock will rub, at least a little bit against my g-spot. Left hand to hold steady, right hand on clit. I rub up and down the sides of my clit, then press her against his sliding shaft. A tightening deep in my cunt tell me that I have reached my own plateau and another groan from below tells me that he'd felt it on his cock.

Now I can really do the cowgirl and I start to bounce up and down. He's too far aroused to be hurt. I rock my angle back and forth, first to favor me, then to favor him, keeping us both on the plateau. Finger on clit at exactly the speed, pressure, angle and time she calls for. When she's satisfied, my nipples receive their own titillations!

But my legs and arms are beginning to tire. It's time to bring this pony home! I angle forward and thrust fast and hard. He gasps, then goes silent. I lean back and stroke my clit until I feel contractions start inside my cunt. Then forward.

"Fuck!" he yells from behind. He doesn't move, but sticky stuff starts to ooze out the side of my pussy and onto my hands. I use Jack's cum to lubricate my clit which allows firmer pressure. Three sharp strokes and my own contractions squeeze around his cock. The first one wrenches to my tummy. The second all the way up my spine. The rest swirl heat and pleasure all around my pelvis. As the waves recede, little jolts spark up and down my cunt.

Somehow I manage to lift myself up, off Jack, and onto the couch where I stroke the last thrills of self-indulgence from my clit. From above, a blanket floats down over me.

Someone was in my kitchen, cooking. I opened my eyes but immediately squinted them mostly shut against the sunlight beaming in through my window. I was on my couch, nude, and suddenly cool. As my brain unfogged, I remembered Jack torturing me, then making love. I breathed deeply. Garlic chicken!

In the kitchen, Jack was wearing a white dress shirt and black pants—a wool and polyester blend. I made a mental note of this, relieved that my powers of observation were still intact. He was stirring the garlic chicken in a skillet. When he turned around, I saw that he had a large bath towel tucked into the front of his pants.

He served me at the table, garlic chicken over steamed rice. Sex *and* food. I had found what most girls can only dream of.

He finished first. "What are you doing next week?" he asked.

I shrugged and took a quick swallow. "Nothing, I guess." The case of the Cyber Culprit, my *only* case, was now over, one way or the other. I was effectively unemployed. And since I hadn't turned Jack in, I was likely to remain that way.

"I want you to come down to Hedonism with me."

I swallowed as quickly as I could. "Okay. Sounds good." I didn't need to be asked twice to sojourn at Jamaica's notorious sex resort. "But, ah, I, ah, don't have any money."

"Get Michael Rayburn to pay for the trip."

"Why would *he* pay for me to go to Jamaica?"

"Tell him you have a new lead."

I ate in silence for a moment. I had already crossed one moral threshold by deciding not to turn Jack in. Now he was asking me to cross another—to actively tell an untruth. I swallowed. "I don't want to lie," I said and laid my fork down.

"The way he lied to get that driver off?"

He had a point. His first victim had been the distracted driver whose texting had directly led to the death of an innocent woman. An innocent woman who'd just happened to be Jack's fiancée.

"It's Tantric week," he said.

Tantric was long drawn out Kama Sutra sex with a dollop of meditation thrown in. There would be no better way to spend next week. Especially since the alternative had every indication of me sitting alone in my apartment watching the paint peel. Still, lying to Michael, lying to *anyone* for that matter, didn't sit well with me.

"You have to decide which side you're on."

"I have decided."

"Great!" he smiled back. "I'll make the arrangements."

Riding up the elevator to Michael's office, I continued to have second thoughts. Being on Jack's side was okay. The little guy fighting for justice against the machine and all that. But how far was I willing to go?

In the corridor outside Michael's office, I could see that he was in a meeting. His assistant spotted me. "Hi, Lee. Mr. Rayburn's in a meeting. Is there anything I can do?"

"I need authority to go down to Jamaica."

"No problem, Mahn," she said in her best imitation of Jamaican patois.

She pulled out the requisition form, entered the name and file number for the Cyber Culprit case and gave it to me. "Just take this to accounting and send them the invoice as soon as possible."

Accounting was on a different floor. I found a quiet corner and texted Jack: "I need you to send me an invoice for next week. One person. For me only."

Two minutes later, Jack texted back, "Ok."

Ten minutes after that, I had the invoice on my phone. Half an hour later, I had a cheque. I hadn't actually *told* a lie. Did that make a difference, I wondered…

I had dinner with Eric that night. While we waited for dinner, I unfolded the law firm cheque and showed it to Eric.

"That's all they're paying you?!?" he blurted. "That doesn't even cover my salary."

I shook my head. "It's for expenses. Jamaica."

"Hedonism?"

I nodded.

"But why?"

"I'm going down with Jack."

"Why would Rayburns' firm—you didn't tell him!"

I shook my head. "No."

"Lee…"

"It's Tantric week," I said, folding the cheque back into my pocket.

"It doesn't matter if it's Kund—. Just make sure to stay away from Kundalini. Your karma's screwed up enough already."

"What's Kundalini?"

"Lee—"

"How can I avoid it if I don't know what it is?"

He gave me a 'yeah right' look, then took a deep breath. "Kundalini is yoga science for releasing the full energy of the soul. But if you're not ready, the energy will overwhelm you. Really screw you up."

"But Tantric is okay?"

He nodded. "It's just sex and meditation. Everything in moderation."

Eric's phone buzzed and he had to dash off mumbling an excuse about 'work'.

I ate my desert slowly, all the while staring at his on the other side of the table. I pushed my plate away, amazed at my willpower. I was actually leaving food—New York cheesecake to boot—on the table.

I unfolded the cheque. It had not been wrong to take the cheque from Michael's client. That scum of the earth had no right to anything after walking scot free from the death of the innocent woman. So no guilt there. Michael's firm? No, they're still making plenty off this whole mess. Besides, the Cyber Culprit—Jack—was on the right side of justice. He was right to punish the distracted driver. He'd been right to strike back at the machines—huge and gadget-sized—that were consuming our lives.

Michael! Michael Rayburn was the only one who might be harmed because I'd taken a cheque when it had not been necessary for the investigation. Michael had befriended me, entrusted me with the investigation. He had been an economic life-line—literally! If there was an audit into the investigation and they looked too closely… But Michael had also betrayed my love, cheated on me. What did I really owe him? Michael… Michael… I jumped up; I had somewhere to go, something to do.

Four hours later, I entered my own apartment, checked to make sure that no one else was there, slid in the deadbolt and fixed the security chain securely in place. Tomorrow, I would sleep in Jamaica. And the day after I'd be doing full-tilt yoga to get my karma back in balance. I slid between the covers, ready for a good night's sleep.

But the last four hours? What had *they* done to my karmic balance? My eyes jerked open. I shut them again, but any chance at sleep had fled.

The last four hours? I'd swung by Michael's office. Invited him to go dancing with me. Played footsies with his cock under the table.

"Does this mean that you've forgiven me?" he'd asked. He was smiling, the way that self-important entitled men smile.

I had shaken my head and been pleased to see the smile fade from his face. "It means that I want to have sex with you. No relationship, no strings."

Michael had smiled again, but more tentatively this time.

On the dance floor, I'd rubbed his cock hard. If we'd been alone, he'd have come. But on the dance floor, pressed in with all the other bodies, there'd been too many distractions, too many inhibitions.

But outside, in his car, there had been just me, just me and my mouth. The steering wheel and middle console had meant that he couldn't touch me, but I'd already been touched enough for one day.

I'd licked the head of his penis. I'd stroked up and down his shaft. And soon I'd gathered in all his pent-up energies from the day's frustrations, from my footsies, from the dance floor. And soon all of that had come spurting into my mouth.

Tantra, Lusty Lee Log #28

I was being really, really nice to everybody. On the flight down, I all but jumped out of my seat to help the cabin crew clean up. Since we were going down to Jamaica for a Tantric Yoga retreat, I needed to put as many karmic credits into the celestial good-deeds bank as I could. At the airport in Montego Bay, I let the porter take my bag—usually I insist on carrying my own luggage—so that I could tip him generously.

On the bus ride to Negril, Jack shut his eyes. "Meditation," was the only explanation he'd offered.

I shut my eyes and tried to join him in blissing out, but every thought in the universe cried out for my attention: how stupid it was to come to a tropical paradise, then shut my eyes to its beauty; what if I missed something; had I turned off the stove; had I tipped the porter sufficiently, or not enough; did the resort's prohibition on tipping apply to the driver, it was hot, the seat was uncomfortable, what level of sunscreen did I need—

My eyes snapped open and I started to swear under my breath about how moronic meditation was but stopped mid-expletive; swearing had to be bad karma.

Outside the window was a thin patch of green, then blue-green ocean waves then deep blue sky with just a hint of cloud in the distance. The scenery was mesmerizing. For about five minutes! Then blue green blue became almost as boring as meditation. Beside me, Jack's face was as content with himself as he was with the universe.

I wished I had my phone! I could play a game. I could check email. I could draw. I could do a report. I smiled at that thought—if I filed a report, I'd be whisked back to cold and dreary Toronto instead of staying down at Hedonism II, Jamaica's premier sex resort. So maybe it had been a good thing that Jack had made me promise to leave all my gadgets at home and to disconnect myself from the cyber universe. If I'd had the means to send a report, I'd be accumulating bad karma every time I failed to do so...

Halfway to Negril, Jack opened his eyes. "Having fun?" he asked.

I nodded. He shut his eyes and went back to contemplating the mysteries of existence. Or non-existence for all I knew.

Jack was the reason I was coming to Negril, where Hedo II was located. Or rather the ostensible reason. Michael Rayburn had hired me to find Jack when all we'd known about him was that he was a Cyber Culprit making embarrassing postings to the internet. And then I'd identified Jack as our nemesis. But I hadn't reported him to Michael. Instead, I'd found out that Jack had good reasons for doing what he had done. Michael wouldn't think that Jack's reasons were adequate excuse. *I*, on the other hand, did think that they were an adequate excuse.

The problem was that, excuse or no, it wasn't my call to make. I shouldn't be in Jamaica. I should be in Toronto turning Jack in. Hence my karmic deficit.

As soon as we arrived at the resort's reception desk in front of its art-deco blue-polkadot wall, we were whisked through to chairs just beyond and plied with a passable champagne.

"Are you here for Tantra Week?" the receptionist asked.

Jack pressed his palms together and bowed slightly. I thought for sure he was going to say 'Namaste' but he contented himself with a simple, "Yes."

"Excellent," she gushed. She was a thin Jamaican woman, red tunic, black pants, deep red lips, white teeth, happy smile. Then she whizzed back to the front desk, returning moments later with our key entry cards and the resort schedule for the week. Apparently there were lessons each afternoon, the first being in two hours.

As the receptionist turned back to the desk, a porter came up with our bags and led us to our room. Jack had booked us a garden view room. I would have preferred the action of a room facing the nude beach. But Jack had said that Tantra required peace and serenity. Just how much peace and serenity he'd have in a room with a full-sized mirror above its luxurious queen-sized bed would remain to be seen.

I quickly stripped nude, jumped on the bed and motioned for him to follow me. I stared up at the mirror while the bed stopped jiggling. Just short of thirty, buxom and curvaceous. Curly brown hair framing sparkling blue eyes and a full-lipped smile. I was, in a word, voluptuous. Jack, being more careful with his clothes, took a moment to arrive beside me.

I turned on my side and looked over at Jack. He was just shy of six feet, half a foot taller than me. His brown hair was darker than mine, straight, with flecks of grey. His face was round, which made a half-day's stubble stand out. His body was also roundish, fleshy, but he was fit enough when it counted. I ran my hand over my breasts, down my torso up and over my hip, projecting my voluptuous at him.

But Jack made no move towards me. Not even a kiss! And

he was flaccid. Well, this entirely unsatisfactory state of affairs would need to be changed, and fast! I reached for his crotch, but he gently but firmly grabbed my hand. The overall effect was romantic. However, after a four-hour plane ride followed by two more on the bus, I wanted the hard stuff. Romance could wait until after dinner. I moved to rub myself against him.

He shook his head. "Lee." So much meaning in the monosyllable of my name. "We need to hold ourselves for the sessions."

I slumped back onto my back. This *tantric* stuff had better be worth it!

The first tantra session was in the courtyard which was part of the spa. At night, the courtyard was used for something else, and hopefully Jack would stop being high and mighty long enough for us to enjoy its other pleasures. But today we were on yoga mats on the floor facing the two small pools.

Between the pools was the couple who would be guiding us into Tantra. They were both slim and tall and flexible. Tim was wearing loose-fitting linen, Bri was in a bikini.

"Tantra is an ancient philosophy which anyone can practice. It doesn't replace your religion," Tim began after welcoming us.

"But it works for atheists as well," Bri chimed in.

Her comment seemed to provoke titters in the audience. There were six other couples. The two white couples were a study in contrasts: one was a pair of scrawny grey-haired hippies. The other, much younger, featured two red heads: he was short and stocky, she tall, shapely and busty. The two black couples were in their late thirties, one skinny, the other roly-poly obese. These eight were all in swimsuits, black except for the tall redhead—she was wearing a shimmering silver bikini. The light-skinned Asian couple was wearing loose-fitting linen robes down below their knees. The darker south-east Asian couple were the epitome of upper-class Brahmin and looked as if they could be running the workshop. She was wearing an elegant Sari with hints of gold at the edges, while he sported a diaphanous white Kurta and even whiter loose-fitting thin cotton pants. They looked ageless.

"The first thing you must learn in your Tantric practice," Tim continued, "is to relax. Is everyone comfortable with nudity?"

We all nodded. He and Bri quickly shed their clothes and indicated we should all do the same. When we were all in our birthday suits, Tim formed us in a circle, standing facing each other, hands on each other's shoulders. Tim and Bri stood back-to-back, their arms stretched behind, entwining each other's fingers. Without letting go, they raised their arms up and over their heads. How did they get to be so flexible?!?

"Breathe," he told us.

"Inhale," she echoed, demonstrating, pulling her breasts frontward and taut, her nipples straining forward like loyal soldiers.

"Hold your breath," exhorted Tim. "Feel the power of creation inside your lungs."

After an eternity during which I felt only burning desperation, Bri gave permission to exhale. There were several gasps of gratitude around the circle.

Tim took a deep breath in.

Bri told us to, "Feel the power of your breath in your heart, in your yoni, in your lingam."

"Yoni?" someone whispered to my right.

"Female sex organs," someone whispered back.

I breathed in, as deeply as I could manage. I felt the oxygen in my lungs. I felt its power swirl in my heart. My breasts lifted out and forward. But try as I might, I couldn't feel anything below the waist. I looked at Tim's phallus—it was nice and round and long. But it was flaccid, so what was the point?

Three more breaths, then they asked us to sit down.

Tim crossed his legs in full lotus fashion. Bri stood behind him. No one else attempted a full lotus. He waited until everyone had turned to face him then smiled. "We'll meet here every day at this time. You're all on vacation, so we'll call them playshops, not workshops. Each day we will explore different aspects of yoga and Tantra and sexuality. Our goal will be to tantalize your imagination, explore your sensory reactions and use pleasure to connect your minds, bodies and souls."

Bri placed her hands atop her partner's head. "We will stoke your passions," she began, "while guiding you in their control and maximization," he finished.

She mussed his hair. "There's more to Tantra than denial and control. We'll show you sensual massage, erotic dancing, and most importantly, we will show our Goddesses how to harness the power of their G-spots. Towards the end of the workshop, I will demonstrate snake charming." Her whole body swayed and I thought for a moment I saw a snake slither up her spine.

There were several questions to which Bri and Tim gave succinct and to-the-point answers.

After we'd settled down again, Tim told us that, "If you want to delve deeper, please speak to Bri or I about private Tantra sessions. Most workshops—"

"*Play*shops," someone corrected to a chorus of sniggers.

Tim smiled, "Most playshops will end with a simple meditation. Please shut your eyes and join me in the chant." I shut my eyes and he continued, "AaaUuuMmm."

He inhaled again and repeated, "AaaUuuMmm." This time one or two others joined in.

"AaaUuuMmm." This time everyone, including me, joined in. I felt a weird vibration from the bottom of my lungs and up to my neck as I exhaled the chant.

We continued to chant 'AaaUuuMmm' as Bri began to softly whisper in the background, "This chant connects us with the divine energy of the universe."

AaaUuuMmm. "Its vibrations relax the body and lead us into meditation." The only thing I felt was ticklish—all the way from the top of my head down to my butt.

AaaUuuMmm. "It centers us in the now, ready to experience our bodies in new and profound ways."

AaaUuuMmm. "It readies us experience sex as prayer." Making out in church?!?

"AaaUuuMmm," Tim raised his voice. Then in the middle of our inhalations, "And open."

We all opened our eyes and smiled at each other. Tim rose and the group began to break up.

"Hold on," remonstrated Bri. "You need your homework for tonight." We all quieted and turned to her. "Don't worry, it's easy. Your homework is to make love to each other, slow, languid and romantic. And you'll want to make it last because it will be the last physical sex you'll have until the last day of the workshop."

That night, Jack rolled out the whole nine yards of romance. At Pastafari, the Italian restaurant, we had a special bottle of Pinot Grigio with dinner. Afterwards, we wandered the beach, holding hands and admiring the sunset. Back in the room he read poetry: everything from Elizabeth Barrett Browning's *How Do I Love Thee?* to Leigh Hunt's *Jenny Kiss'd Me*. After each poem, I had to remove an item of clothing. It was romantic, it was erotic, it was *loving*.

After poetry, Jack laid me face-first on the bed, my head cupped by pillows, and used his long dexterous fingers to massage tension out of my muscles, replacing it with excitement and anticipation.

Just before I turned into a bowl of jelly, Jack removed his fingers from my back and touched along my right side summoning me to roll over. And there he was, nude as the day he popped out of his mother's womb. Not quite as pudgy as then, certainly hairier and more muscular, certainly a *man*.

He lay down beside me and we hugged. Our lips brushed against each other, barely kissing. Then full, deep suction. The tips of our tongues touched. They traced around each other's tip, then moved lower down each other's shaft. But our tongues weren't hungry, weren't urging passion. It was a friendly kiss, a kiss of warmth, of comfort, of camaraderie, not a kiss of lust or longing. His body was warm against me, especially in his midpoint against my thighs, but even here in the center of his lust he was flaccid and friendly, not demanding or impatient.

Somehow, without the moment being forced, we both drifted into the next level. But it was mutual adoration, not carnal desire. Yes, I was horny and aroused, yearning for climax, but that was the effect of our mutual adulation, not something separate or distinct. The physical was resonating with the spiritual, each elevating the other. I floated onto my back, my head propped up on pillows.

Jack kneeled beside me. His fingertips walked up and down my body, a mixture of platonic touch and sexual foreplay. I touched his thigh in loving appreciation. What I *really* wanted to touch was just out of reach. His lingam stood erect out from the base of his legs, as if in prayer position. I looked up in the mirror, at his lingam straining towards heaven. He caressed my knee and I relaxed into the moment, detaching from the end point, centering in the here and now. Jack's lingam would be mine to touch when it would be mine to touch. And if that was never, that would be never.

Jack's fingers moved to my belly, his soft touch pulling my energies into my center. My breasts and my sex willingly gave up their claims to be the focus of my lover's attention but I felt their power grow through the sacrifice.

Jack lifted his right knee up and straddled me. His balls momentarily touched my pubic prominence sending a jolt through my pussy. Then his fingers were on the outside rim of my areolae tracing round and round, reestablishing the softness of his touch. The energies in my navel swirled up into my breasts, then back down again. I reached for Jack's lingam, but it was still beyond my grasp so I ran my fingers up and down his forefingers feeling our energies meeting at my breasts.

As soon as Jack's fingers touched my nipples, the energies which had been swirling in my belly were sucked lower and seized by my sex. There they went from pleasantly warm to burning and boiling. I rocked my hips to escape the scorching heat. Jack placed his palm on my vulva. It was just a light touch, but was enough to trigger orgasm. The waves radiated outward from my sex, dissipating the searing pain and transforming it into a cozy blanket which enveloped the room and wrapped us closer together.

Jack mounted me then, the smiles in our eyes joining with the consummation of lingam into yoni. I felt him sliding in, each inch sparking a new climax. Our pubic bones touched igniting a wrenching clenching orgasm that held us both powerless in its grasp until I gushed all over him. When he pulled back out, the orgasm faded. And when he thrust back in, there was only pleasant comfort and somehow I knew that I was done for the night and needed to concentrate my energies on him the way his fingers had concentrated his on me.

I watched his butt in the mirror above me and quickly synced the rocking of my hips with the depths of his thrusts. The power of my cunt tightened around his cock, squeezing and caressing. My fingers twisted his nipples, connecting his energies up and down his spine.

"Kiss me," I whispered.

He bent down to give me a gentle kiss, but I grabbed his head and plunged my tongue into his mouth. He gasped, but his tongue did not hesitate to slide down the length of mine, did not hesitate to wring passion from the universe.

His body pressed against me, all desire to postpone collapsing. His cock lunged harder and I tensed myself in futile resistance to his attack. All pretense had gone, replaced by carnal craving. I had him. He was *mine*! He had yet to climax, but I had brought him to the point of no return. His body was tethered to mine, able only to push in and outward, but powerless to withdraw entirely. Soon he would quiver, soon he would shudder his life force into me.

I felt him stop, felt a little ball of heat inside me. I rocked my hips, pooling his heat in my core, coating the heat up and down his shaft, coating it up and down my sheath. Lingam and yoni combined into one. Above Jack groaned loudly; below he pumped even as his hips froze motionless.

As we lay beside each other looking up into the mirror, I had pang of regret. I shouldn't have tried to possess him. But he was smiling from ear to ear in the mirror and I smiled back.

Day 2 of the workshop/playshop was Yoga. Bri started us out with some simple standing poses. The Mountain Pose was easy; all you had to do was stand up straight. All the women tried to stand as tall as the red-headed beauty, but none of us could match her height. She must have been six-feet tall for chrissakes!

Then Bri had us bend over backwards in the Upward Salute. Next was sitting in the Chair—but without the chair. That woke up some muscles! When Bri saw that some of the men were trying to show off by dipping too deeply into the non-existent seat, she remonstrated: "It's not an Olympic sport. Just do what you're comfortable with." All the men except Muscles stood up.

Bri then had us lay on our backs for the Corpse pose. After we'd settled, she told us: "This pose, Savasana, is the most important of the yoga poses. It lets you control the amount of tension you allow to invade your body. It lets you feel each spot of strain, worry, rigidity or stress. Go from your head to your toe. If you feel tightness, tighten the muscle, then let it go." Lying flat on my back—this was my kind of yoga!

After another reminder to just take it easy, Bri led us into downward facing dog, the cobra pose and too many twists for me to name.

Meditation was the focus of Day 3. Tim assumed the full lotus pose in front of the group, but immediately popped his legs out into a simple cross-legged position when he saw several of the males and at least one female try to imitate the spaghetti bending of his legs. "You must be comfortable. Don't strain your bodies," he rebuked.

We had moved into the disco, where apparently the remainder of the workshops would take place. Bri put a candle in front of each of us, then lit it with a barbeque lighter.

"Concentrate on the flame of the candle. Banish all other

thoughts from your mind. When a thought intervenes, gently push it away."

As soon as I shut my eyes, Michael Rayburn appeared out of the darkness, nude and delectable. I pushed him away and the candle's flickering flame reappeared. I enjoyed thirty seconds of bliss but then Michael was back. He refused to go away. Jack came and grabbed Michael's hands, like wrestlers. They circled, each trying for an advantage. I would have to choose. I would have to turn Jack in, tell Michael that Jack was the Cyber Culprit, the villain he'd hired me to capture. Then I pushed them slowly away. They were part of the physical, the inconsequential world. The candle came back, wrapping me in its warmth.

Walking back to our room, I saw a man furiously texting into his phone. He was hunched over, oblivious to the blue sky, sandy beach and ocean waves. I suddenly realized how good it felt to not be connected, to being in control, to being able to let go. My mind was suddenly clear, an addict freed from her drug. The man continued to text. He looked up momentarily and I smiled at him. Even though I was resplendent in a bright blue bikini, it was as if he didn't see me.

Back in our room, Jack uncharacteristically fired up his laptop.

"I thought the rule was no gadgets?" I teased.

"Just a few minutes. I heard Tim and the old hippies talking about Kundalini. It sounded interesting."

I shrugged and laid down for a nap.

Day 4 began with a sort of musical chairs. We were encouraged to exchange partners and to attend fully to each person we were with in turn.

"Exchange unconditional positive regard," Tim urged.

"Say nice things," Bri explained. "And please feel free to shed your clothes." Amid a chatter of compliments everyone's garments were removed. Except for the older hippies; I noticed them standing at the edge of the group, still in their tie-died swimsuits. "Praise each other's bodies, share your admiration for each other's sexiest parts."

After everyone had exchanged adoration with everyone else at least once, Tim called us back together. "The next stage involves you sitting across from each other, holding hands, sharing. We will be guiding you into an orgiastic orgy in your minds. You may arrange yourselves in any way you wish."

We ended up in a circle, one inner, one outer. Everyone except the hippies who seemed to have vanished. We were all sitting opposite our partners, the women in the center facing outward, our knees touching our inward-facing partners. Bri and Tim sat in the center of the circle, opposite each other. Like the rest of us, they were holding hands.

"AaaUuuMmm," chanted Tim and we joined in.

But on the third breath, Bri told us to breathe silently. "Let Tim's chants lift you up, floating above the circle. Hug each other in spirit. Kiss each other. Wordlessly remind everyone how good they look. Imagine touching each other, especially their sexiest parts."

I floated up on the wisps of Tim's chants. I had a body, I didn't have a body. I felt the Brahmins pass through me, tingling me everywhere. Muscles took me from behind, doggy style. I felt his wife—in my mind I'd nicknamed her 'Skyscraper'—lick my pussy, then I was licking her pussy. Her hair below her navel was as red as that atop her head. She tasted as salty as the ocean. Skyscraper floated away and her husband's cock was in my throat. He was long and wide, but I accommodated him easily, all the way down between my breasts. The roly-poly black couple touched me all over and I touched them. Jack floated by, making love with the Asian woman. The skinny black couple sandwiched in with the muscle-bound white couple. We were all joined together, sometimes shimmering body to body, sometimes purely in spirit. Which connection was most important, most intense—corporeal or incorporeal—seemed to vary moment to moment. The Brahmin couple floated around and through us, completing the unity.

Bri's voice came from far away, more thought than speech, "Now touch each other, without touching, mind to mind, everyone bring each other to omnipotent orgasm."

A phallus slid smoothly into my ass, another into my pussy, another down my throat. Hands adored my breasts. Somehow I was aware that the penises penetrating me were penetrating other women at the same time. Gradually, I had only one cock in me, deep inside my cunt. It was Jack and he was kissing me. Then he moved through me, thrusting me from behind and I tasted pussies: sushi, curry, oyster, fried chicken, gumbo one after the other and all at once.

My sex organs grew and grew until they were huge and there

was nothing else. Then they receded and I was back inside my whole body. Pulsations squeezed my vulva into my pelvis, then twisted it, as if wringing a face cloth. Wringing/loosening pulsations clenched me into more and more intense sexual arousal. Everything was wringing/loosening lust, passion and desire. Then desire faded, then lust. Passion pulsations.

"Now!" shouted Bri in the distance.

Contractions collapsed the pulsations. Everything was a loose wave up and down my spine, up my feet, through my legs, anchored in my sex, up my spine, into my neck, swirling in my mind, then back down. When it reached my feet, my body evaporated into the ocean where the orgiastic waves circled the globe, warm and powerful and wondrous.

Day 5 was designed to forge connections with our partners. Each couple kneeled facing each other, each in a corner of the disco so that we couldn't hear what other couples were saying.

"Hold hands," Bri encouraged. "Speak your innermost thoughts and fears. Speak love, speak anger. Hold nothing back."

This was pretty deep, scary. "Hi, Jack," I ventured. Maybe we should start off slow.

Jack had no such qualms. "Has any man ever been faithful to you?" he asked.

I shook my head. Not Peter, not Michael. Even Jack, exciting as he was, was a work-in-progress.

"Have I been unfaithful?"

"We haven't established the parameters of our relationship."

"So nothing to be unfaithful to?"

I nodded.

"Has anyone actually been present when he's made love to you?"

"You were. Three days ago."

"Never anyone before?"

"Yes, but not as much as you were."

"And now?"

"I love you, Jack." Shit! Where had that come from? All I had needed to say was 'yes' or 'no' or—

"Even if I might be unfaithful?"

"You're not—"

"How do you know? We haven't established any parameters."

"No other lovers."

"When I'm with you, I'm with you exclusively."

"Do you love me?" I asked. Bri had said to face our fears.

"I love you, Lee."

"Forever?"

"Forever."

"Forsaking all others?"

"You demanded that of Peter. You demanded that of Michael. How did that work out?" When I didn't answer, he continued, "Would you rather have monogamy or honesty?"

"You'll answer any question? Truthfully?"

"I will."

"Are you in love with me?"

He nodded.

"But not me exclusively?"

Jack shook his head. "I'm not promising monogamy, only honesty. What about you, Lee? What are you promising?"

"The same."

"Total and complete honesty?"

I nodded.

"What do you think of our vows?"

"At some point, I want monogamy."

He smiled. "We have love and honesty. Who knows what the future will bring?"

I smiled and squeezed his hand.

Day 6 dawned with a deep blue sky. This was to be the last day of the workshop, the day on which Bri had promised we could resume physical sex, *real* sex! When we arrived at the disco, a projector had been set up. On the screen were images of Tim and Bri as well as their contact information. When we were all present, Bri pressed a button and a video of an attractive Indian woman began to play. She was wearing a sexy Sari, her belly exposed. The music was simple, vaguely Eastern. Gradually her clothes disappeared and she began to wrap a large snake around her nude body.

"As promised, today we will show you how to charm the snake. But no reptiles will be harmed in the process, I promise."

The last comment provoked a scattering of titters and one guffaw. Bri waved Tim in front of the screen and swayed her hands and body around him. Even though she wasn't touching him, his clothes fell off. She swayed in front of his lingam which began to engorge.

Bri turned to us, stepping in front of Tim. Several of the females, me included, exhaled in disappointment. "The charming of the male snake is the most obvious. But we women have a snake as well. It properly resides in the genitals and, if properly stroked, moves up the spine and assists in enlightenment."

"And play?" the rotund black man wanted to know.

Bri smiled. "And play." She stepped aside. Tim's lingam had gone flaccid. She began to sway around it and once more it began to engorge and perk up. "Charming the snake is all about intention, whether it's your lover's snake or your own. Your intention must be strong and pure."

We all got to practice charming each other's snake. Jack's reaction was obvious. And when he swayed his hand over my sex, even though his fingers never came closer than six inches from my skin, I felt her become warm and wet.

Once we were aroused, Bri and Tim led us in a series of breathing exercises meant to allow us to postpone orgasm. The males were shown how to orgasm, to shed sexual tension, without physically ejaculating. Homework was to try it out in the privacy of our own rooms.

"Have a full lunch—You'll need your energy," Bri enjoined all of us. "Then after dinner, we'll meet back here to share notes."

Up in our room, Jack and I stripped wordlessly out of our clothes. We stood back to back, our bums and shoulders touching, eyes shut, feeling our own breath, feeling each other's breathing. The deeper we breathed, the more powerful we became, our awareness expanding, our bodies expanding. Becoming giants.

We turned facing each other. Words were unnecessary. Our consciousness was one. Our lovemaking was organic, flowing as needed, unbidden, unforced, natural. Our hands and fingers fluttered over each other's body, not touching, at least not touching physically. But I could feel Jack feeling my energy and smiling up and down his spine. I could feel his lingam chanting joy into my yoni, warming her with bliss. I could feel my nipples singing to his fingers.

Our fingers touched each other. By the sides of each other's chest, exactly opposite our nipples. Our nipples joined their energies but there was no spark or force, just union. Our fingers walked slowly down the sides of our bodies. At our navels, there was another joining, our intuitions joining, multiplying their insights. Fingers now held fast against each other's skin, to the outsides of our hips, then to the front of our legs.

The vibrations inside our genitals were palpable. Though my fingers were touching only his pelvic bone, I could feel his lingam engorge and rise towards me, almost touching my skin. I could feel him sense the readiness inside my yoni.

Slowly we drifted to the bed, kissing once along the way. Our lips barely touched. But my eyes flashed open. Jack was bathed in white light, as if he were an angel. And the same light pulsed out of my heart. My knees gave way.

He lay me down on my back. His palms were spread flat at my ankles. As he brought them up my calves, I felt my knees rise without any will on my part. When his hands moved up my thighs, my knees relaxed into the bed. But he was drawing my pelvis up off the bed. I tried to resist this force, but my pelvis rose towards his hands, touching my pubic hairs to his palm. Electricity ran down my pubic hairs into my yoni uniting me with the center of the universe. The effect began to overwhelm my consciousness.

Then he raised his hands, mercifully, diminishing the force of our connection. He climbed over me and placed his lingam directly against the gates of my yoni centering my consciousness on her. And now, with his intention directed into his lingam, our consciousnesses were woven together, supporting each other within the power of our connection.

I welcomed him through my gates, I welcomed him into the courtyard of my yoni. We were one below, our navels were one navel, our nipples danced, not caring who was who. And our minds swirled into each other, each of our synapses bonding with the corresponding synapses of our lover.

Wave after wave in the center of our bodies pulled us back into the corporeal, into physical sensations. Lust demanded that he plow his seed into me. I rubbed my nipples against his body calling forth fire the same way our ancestors had at the dawn of time. I gloried in my pussy lips rubbing up and down his shaft. I strained to pull him deeper and deeper into my sex.

I was being fucked. I was fucking. Meditation had surrendered to sensation. Sweat was pouring out of my body. Up in the mirror, Jack's buttocks were clenching his cock into me, then pulling it out. Faster and faster. Hotter and hotter! We were racing towards the explosive conclusion. We—

Breathe! A faint whisper.

Our bodies writhed in carnal passion. Our eyes were shut, all our consciousness focused in our genitals.

Breathe! A command far away in the distance.

Jack pulled himself up, ready to ram himself to conclusion.

"Breathe!" I shouted.

His eyes shocked open and we looked deeply inside each other. And through our eyes, we heard the command and we breathed into our lungs. We held the air, mastered it, let it master our genitals. Gradually, bit by bit, our mindfulness regained control of our genitals. And when we had control, we let a gentle orgasm radiate out from our groins, we let our sexual tension dissipate.

Jack began to move his lingam in and out in time with our breathing. Meditation once again subjected lust to a higher level of awareness. My yoni was the servant of my consciousness, not the mistress of my reality.

We inhaled in unison, sucking in energy—prana—from the universe. Our undulating bodies—one wave, one stroke of lingam into yoni—matched our inhalations. A wave in the opposite direction, lingam being withdrawn, accompanied our exhalations. Each cycle gave us more and more control over our sexual vitalities. Each cycle rendered our sexual vitalities more and more powerful, but we ruled the power, it did not rule us.

Organically we knew that we had built up our sexual arousal to the limits of what we could handle. And without the need to concentrate or to exercise will, we floated into a gentle orgasm which enveloped our whole bodies, our entire beings. It was bliss and pleasure and release all at the same time and it went on for an eternity.

Then the clouds broke and we were back in our bodies. Jack looked down into my eyes and I up into his. We knew that we had been to heaven. But now it was time to come back to earth. He pumped rapidly into me. No longer was it lingam sliding into yoni, it was cock ramming into cunt. And when Jack shuddered his semen into me, I could feel it smash into the bottom of my spine. And when my climax thundered out from my cunt, every nerve in my body protested, every nerve in my body cried for joy!

After dinner, we all met back at the disco. Apparently

everyone had had mind-blowing sex all afternoon, the old hippies—Paul and Marg—especially.

Afterwards, people began to drift away. Jack didn't want to leave.

"But you haven't come without ejaculating yet," I reminded him, visions of continuing the afternoon's festivities dancing in my head. Tim and Bri were having a deep conversation with the hippies and it looked like it might drag on forever.

"I want to ask them about Kundalini."

Tim's sentence stopped halfway through. Paul pushed his grey hair back and shook his head. Both looked sharply at Jack. "Stay away from Kundalini," Paul warned.

"Why?" Jack wanted to know.

"You're not ready for it yet."

"I'm more ready than you, you silly hippy."

"You don't know—"

"Then I'll find out." Jack spun on his heel and marched away. The hippies pulled Tim into a corner and whispered worriedly.

"What's Kundalini?" I asked Bri.

"It's the power of the serpent." She pointed towards the bottom of her spine.

Tim, Paul and Marg joined us. "Why did you say that Jack wasn't ready?" I asked Paul.

"Kundalini amplifies. Jack has too much anger. Kundalini will turn that anger into rage. Kundalini will overwhelm Jack, he won't be able to handle its power."

"What can I do?" I asked.

Marg laid a hand on my arm. "Don't worry, sweetie, you'll be fine. You're much more ready to ride the serpent than Jack is. Just stay close to him and try to help him when the time comes."

Kundalini, Lusty Lee Log #29

Warning: Kundalini is powerful and can be misused. Please do careful research before you delve into Kundalini.

Back in Toronto, Jack hailed a cab and whisked us to his apartment without so much as a 'by your leave'. I was resenting his presumptiveness in assuming that I would want to stay with him until I saw his condo: a large penthouse with floor to ceiling glass windows overlooking the lake. It was mega-cool looking down at planes landing at the island airport.

The next morning, I did a pit stop at my apartment to do laundry and pick up a few things.

When I returned to Jack's condo, he had a stack of books on the dining room table. Most were about Kundalini but there were a few about yoga and spiritual development in general. Jack was reading like a madman and muttering about people hiding the truth for their own gain.

After an hour of prancing back and forth from kitchen to dining room in a vain effort to gain Jack's attention, I picked up one of the books, *Kundalini, Awakening of Inner Energy* and flipped a few pages. "You're serious about this Kundalini, stuff?" I asked him.

He nodded vigorously, happy that I was taking an interest, oblivious to the skepticism in my voice. "You remember Tantra from last week? How my lingam stimulated inside your yoni? Well, Kundalini is ten times more powerful. And not just sex."

Lingam and yoni might just be other ways of saying penis and vagina, but last week had taught me that there was more to the *Kama Sutra* than gymnastic sexual positions. "Just how does Kundalini work?" I asked.

"It releases energies in the lower chakras."

"Whoa, tiger — in English, simple English, please."

He smiled and leaned back, "In the Hindu-Yogic spiritual system, chakras are nodes or centers of spiritual energy. Some deal with our sense of identity. Others deal with love, our ability to relate to others, or intelligence. In most people, these chakras are not well developed."

"The more developed a person's chakras are, the more powerful he is?"

"A simplification, but yes."

"So if my love chakra is well developed, I'd be a loving

person?"

"You would be able to love where appropriate, you'd be able to love very deeply, you'd be able to use love to accomplish positive goals."

"Would I be able to disrupt the attempts of a rival to seduce my beloved?"

"Yes, or you could welcome her into your relationship with your beloved."

I thought about cuffing him sharply about the ears, but he had returned to his book and his last comment didn't appear to be directed at anything specific.

"And what about kundalini? Which chakra does it reside in?" I asked.

"The lower one." He gestured towards his groin without looking up from his book.

"Men always did think with their penises."

He shot me a sharp look. "Not in the penis, at the base of the spine. For men and women both."

I did my best to look contrite. "And how does one develop this kundalini chakra?"

"Kundalini isn't a chakra, it's a coil of energy."

"And how does one uncoil it?"

"Most of the writings talk about developing higher order aspects of one's being—good deeds and enlightenment, but I think that it's possible to develop kundalini directly as both a physical and psychic force. The propaganda about good deeds and enlightenment is designed to restrict kundalini to the upper classes—the Brahmins—and out of the hands of ordinary folks who have to deal with all the crap of day-to-day life."

"Speaking of all the crap of day-to-day life, Michael Rayburn is going to expect a report on what I found down in Jamaica last week."

"Michael, your lawyer friend?" he asked.

"Michael, the lawyer who paid my way last week. Michael, the lawyer who hired me to track you down."

"Are you going to turn me in?"

Wow! No beating around the bush as to what might be in my report, whether I'd be hinting at, or even revealing Jack's identity outright. No query about diluting what I had found out with obfuscation or nuance. No, Jack wanted to go straight to the bottom line. My duty to Michael Rayburn was clear; I had to tell him that Jack was the Cyber Culprit who'd been destroying lives, lives of various degrees of innocence, with illicit internet postings. But I had fallen in love with Jack. Head over heels in love! Every fiber of my being wanted to be with him, to be with him every moment of every day, to support him, to have sex with him, to cook for him, to care for him, to know his every thought, to—

"Are you going to turn me in?" he prodded.

"No."

"Honesty."

"Honesty, total and complete."

"Honesty and truthfulness." It was the vow we'd made to each other, last week in Jamaica. It was the foundation of our relationship. Jack didn't seem to care that I wasn't being honest with Michael.

He set down his book, rose, and gave me a kiss. It was just a light peck on the cheek, but his lips lingered there, just for a moment. But that moment was all I needed. I turned, moved my lips to his, kissed him full-on, then with suction. When he moved his tongue to the edge of my lips, I pulled my head back, daring him to re-initiate contact. My eyes made it clear that if he kissed me again, he would not be returning to his books anytime soon.

But Jack chose neither me nor his books and instead trotted out of the room. I was watching him carefully for any sign of ill-effects stemming from his investigation into Kundalini. Several people had told me that Jack wasn't ready, that the power of Kundalini would overwhelm him. But so far, he seemed to be fine.

Jack returned a moment later with a file which he handed to me. "Would you be able to help with this?"

He returned to his book as I opened the file. It

contained some initial surveillance and background information on Sarah Grant, the retail management executive whom I had met when she'd been featured in one of the Cyber Culprit's earlier internet postings. The video had showed her picking up a one-night-stand in a bar.

"Why are you interested in her?" I asked.

"I'm investigating her for kickbacks. That's why I was shaking her tree."

"You mean the Cyber Culprit posting?"

He nodded, not looking up from his book.

"Why do you care if she's taking kickbacks?"

"It's a side venture to help with paying the bills. You could help. I'll do the cyber, you can do the on-the-ground investigating."

I looked at him, trying to will him to look up from his book. When that didn't work, I coughed. When that didn't work, I moved beside him and bent over holding my cleavage just above his book. He glanced at my breasts, then returned to his book.

I moved next to his ear and whispered seductively, "You know that my undercover work often involves me having sex."

"That's fine," he responded, his attention still focused on his book.

I watched him in silence. I could see my relationship with Jack unraveling the same way my relationship with Michael had ended. Jack the alley cat.

At length, he looked up at me. "But you don't want me to have sex with anyone else?" he asked.

It wasn't fair, but he was right. I shook my head.

He shrugged. "Then I won't."

"Honesty and truthfulness."

"Honesty and truthfulness," he repeated, going back to his book.

My thoughts raced back to Sarah Grant, her apartment, her hot tub, the dark-haired beauty and I *together* in her hot tub. Nude. Most of all I thought back to how Sarah had begun to seduce me. Hopefully this time her cell phone wouldn't interrupt her efforts.

When I awoke the next morning, Jack was already up, but still in his loose-fitting pyjamas. He was doing some sort of freeform dance, a combination of tai chi, ballet and yoga. When he saw me, he came to a standstill on one foot, his other leg forming a triangle with his foot on his knee. "I've figured out how to release the serpent," he announced.

I quickly climbed atop a chair. "You have snakes?!?" I squealed.

He shook his head, smiled and took my hand to help me down. "Kundalini is often referred to as the serpent because its energy is coiled at the bottom of the spine, like a snake."

I allowed him to mollify me with croissants and coffee as he explained. "The books try to hide the process, but if you read between the lines and discard the irrelevant highfalutin' garbage, it's pretty clear."

He placed a large bottle of distilled water in front of me. "The first step is purification—not the renunciation of physical wealth, that's propaganda—but purification with pure water. Drink up."

He reached for his own bottle, already half empty, and rapidly consumed the remainder. Then he pulled out a nasal irrigator, one of the units now being extensively advertised on TV. He demonstrated its gentle but powered suction on his own nostrils, then handed it to me.

As I placed the nozzle against the opening of my left nostril, Jack explained, "Clear nasal passages are essential for the breathing exercises to have their full effect."

It felt strange, but I was able to breathe easier. I repeated the irrigation through my right nostril.

When Jack was satisfied with the state of my nasal passages, he led me in a bending exercise, starting by standing straight up, arms extended forward at right angles, then knees bending until our bums almost touched the floor. "This is the Crow Posture," he explained. "It will activate the root chakra, where the power of the serpent resides."

The Crow Posture was followed by meditation and breathing exercises. Jack explained that it was necessary to draw kundalini upwards into the lungs through breathing and visualization.

We ended the exercises with the freeform dancing Jack had been performing earlier in the morning. He explained that we should just go where our bodies wanted to take us, that this would free us up for the release of kundalini from the bottom of our spines where it was currently locked away.

As Jack twirled and dipped and glided into jumps and landings, I tried to compare him to how he was before we'd gone down for Tantra week in Jamaica. He seemed more supple, yet stronger, leaner. And his mind appeared sharper; whether this was from kundalini or merely the effect of a new obsession, I couldn't tell.

Later, over lunch, it was time to return to the physical world. Kundalini or no, there were bills to be paid.

Jack made me summarize the Sarah Grant file to be sure I had all the pertinent details down pat. Then he showed me a USB memory key. "I need you to insert this into her computer."

"Why would she let me do that?"

"Because you're going to show her a video of her typing into said computer while badmouthing her boss."

"If you can already hack into her computer, why do you need me to insert that memory key?" I asked, pleased with my insight into the obvious.

"Because the evidence of the kickbacks isn't on her computer, it's on her phone. The memory key will turn her computer into a data dump."

"Can't you do that remotely?"

"Theoretically, yes. But it would leave traces, both during the data dump and after. It's too risky."

I pointed at the memory key. "Won't that leave traces?"

He nodded. "But only while it's working. You'll have

to distract her." He lifted a bottle of Sauvignon Blanc. "Perfect for sipping in a hot tub," he noted, winking.

Riding up the elevator to Sarah Grant's upscale condo, I inspected myself in the mirror: twenty-nine years old, five-foot five, buxom and curvaceous. Unless Sarah Grant had changed since our last meeting, she would like the package. I smiled and was pleased to see sparkle in my blue eyes. I fluffed my curly brown hair. I was wearing a form-fitting dark pink pantsuit. Since Sara was shorter than me, I had chosen flats over high heels. The only other gear I needed for the mission was the red bikini in my purse.

Sarah was wearing the same long white wrap buttoned at her left shoulder and waist she'd worn for our first meeting, her long dark hair draped over her left shoulder. She was as ravishing as before, the sparkle in her eyes hinting at her fulsome libido. When she turned to usher me in, her left thigh teased out from under the wrap, just as it had the first time. Her condo was as I had remembered it: large, luxurious, a breathtaking view of the lake and of the hot tub on the balcony.

She took the bottle of wine with a smile of gratitude and put it on ice.

I flipped open my laptop and showed her the video of her typing into her computer and describing her boss with a series of creative expletives. "This is the Cyber Culprit's latest posting. But it hasn't gone viral yet. We've managed to suppress it, but to keep it suppressed, we need to find out how the Cyber Culprit hacked into your computer."

She nodded, brought her computer into the dining room and logged on. I inserted Jack's USB memory key. "This could take a while," I told her.

"Hot tub?" she asked, smiling.

I nodded, pulling the red bikini from my purse.

Sarah took a few steps towards the balcony, turned around and undid the clasps on her wrap letting it fall to the floor. Her breasts were smaller than mine, but just right for her thinner figure, a small handful, but certainly enough to caress and squeeze. And her nipples were perky dark buttons. She was clean-shaven down below revealing a flying dragon tattoo on her pubic bone. Her legs were strong and firm, matching the wiry muscle elsewhere on her body. By the time my eyes had returned to hers, her eyelids were flapping flirtatiously as she whipped her hair behind her shoulder.

I dropped my bikini back into my purse and watched Sarah watch me strip out of my clothes. Her smile widened just before she turned around and headed for the hot tub, her hips swaying suggestively, squeezing and releasing her delectable glutes each time she took a step.

The hot tub was circular with molded seats on three sides and a bench on the other. Jets were churning the water, turning it white with bubbles. Sarah had already slid under the water and all I could see of her body was the top of her breasts.

Before I could slip into the warm water myself, Sarah raised a hand-held showerhead out of the water and sprayed me.

"Hey!" I protested. But the water was warm and salty, nice in the cool air. It felt heavenly as it tickled up my legs.

Sarah made a show of putting the showerhead between her legs and angling her head towards a second showerhead. I settled onto the bench, grabbed the showerhead, shut my eyes and floated in the bubbles. The jets from the showerhead tickled between my pussy lips and the rest of the universe faded away.

The water jets around me shut off. Then the showerhead lost its power as well. Presumably they had been on a timer. Street sounds came up from below. Then there was the sound of spray on top of the water. The sound got closer and I felt a few drops. Then the sound disappeared and I relaxed into a deep breath. Dimly, there was a jet of water at the bottom of my legs. The jet got stronger as it moved up my legs. Stronger yet stronger, then tickling my pussy lips.

Stronger yes! And full on warm right inside my pussy.

And there was something else. I opened my eyes to Sarah's smiling face. She brought the showerhead up to caress my breasts and we kissed.

I knew from our previous encounter that Sara was an accomplished kisser. Her mouth was small, so she couldn't initiate suction without help. But she coaxed my lips to pucker. Then once we were in suction, she darted her tongue inside my mouth, flicking just inside, scurrying away whenever I approached with my own tongue.

The water jets between my legs faded away and Sarah began to knead my breasts with both her hands. I reached for her breasts but she pulled away.

"Just lean back and enjoy," she remonstrated.

I shook my head. She picked up the showerhead, readying to spray me into submission.

"Rock, paper, scissors," I compromised.

Sarah reluctantly nodded and positioned her right fist over her outstretched left palm. I did the same and we hit our fists on our palms three times. She held her fist against her palm.

I had both palms flat against each other. "Paper smothers rock," I gloated.

She slumped down into the water and I positioned her sitting on the bench, my body between her legs. This time when I kissed her, it was completely different; she was passive, but engaged, reacting only when I took the lead. She let her smaller mouth be engulfed by my full lips. When I slipped my tongue through her lips, she willingly let her tongue be coaxed forward.

When I touched her breasts, she brought her hands forward to touch mine, but I pressed her arms back against the side of the hot tub and extended them out from her body at right angles. She submitted, with just a hint of reluctance. "You do know that I get a turn after you're finished with me?" she claimed.

"I wouldn't have it any other way."

She smiled up at me, watching my reactions as I

caressed her hard breasts and even harder nipples. I let my expression slack into a poker face as I gently caressed her breasts and ran my fingers across her nipples. Then when her protuberances were between my thumbs and forefingers, I gave them a sharp twist. She gasped and I let a smile return to my lips.

I ran my right hand down her belly and she shut her eyes. I could feel her consciousness through my fingertips. Her public bone was smooth, her hair having been permanently removed. Her pussy was warm, even hotter than the water.

"What shall I do to your ass?" I asked her, lightly flicking up and down her pussy lips.

"You wouldn't *dare*," she challenged. But her pussy lips fluttered, engorging at the prospect.

"Should I fondle it, penetrate it, *lick* it?" A definite reaction on 'lick' and her eyes opened.

"It's not clean," she noted, a smug look on her face.

"Lick it is."

"No!"

"Up and down, sideways, all around—"

"No!"

"Hard little tongue poking inside?"

"It's not clean." Her clit had engorged, even harder than the lips below. Her voice might be protesting, but it was clear that she would thoroughly enjoy having her ass reamed.

"Stand up." When she complied, I turned her around and gently pushed her forward. "Turn around, hands on the deck."

"But it's cold," she protested. She was right, it was cold.

I grabbed both of the showerheads, turned them on, and gave her a full spray. "That better?" I asked.

She nodded.

"Spread your legs."

She spread them a bit.

"Further," I demanded.

She spread them as far as she could. I dropped one of the showerheads, grabbed her left buttock and directed the showerhead at her pussy. She moaned with delight. I raised the spray so that it was divided between her pussy and her ass.

"Lower was better," she complained.

I gave the top of the showerhead a twist and now the spray was concentrated and focused directly on her ass.

"Hey!" she protested.

I pinched her left buttock. "Next time, clean her *before* I come over."

She whimpered.

"Now, I want to hear you loud and clear. All your naughty words. All your dirty *filthy* words. Is that clear?"

"Yes." It was barely a whisper.

I let go of the showerhead and lightly swatted her right buttock. "Louder!"

"Yes!"

I thrust a finger into her cunt. "Fuck!" she protested.

I withdrew the finger and pressed two against the opening to her vagina. "Is that the best you can do?"

"You fucking bitch! When I get ahold of you—"

I slid the fingers inside. "You'll what?" I taunted.

She moaned as I thrust in and out. "I'll fuck you silly!" But it was more of a groan than a threat. I formed my fingers into a spiral. Sara groaned again and moved back and forth against my fingers to increase the sensations provoked by the spiral thrusting and wiggling inside her.

I lowered my face to her ass, kissing first left then right. When I came to the center and licked around, but just above her ass, she stopped stark still. "Bitch!" she screamed. "I'll fuck your ass *and* your cunt. So hard you won't be able to tell which is which!"

I touched the center of her ass with my tongue, then swiftly withdrew it. "Whore!" she wailed.

I licked up her entire ass crack with the flat of my tongue. "No!" she wailed. Her cunt was clenched hard around my fingers and I could barely move them in and out. I licked up and down, pressing saliva into every ridge and crevice. "Bitch!" she sobbed.

I pressed the tip of my tongue into the center of her ass and wiggled. She screamed. *Screamed* blue bloody murder. But it wasn't words. It was defeat and pleasure and ecstasy. Her cunt squeezed pulses against my fingers. Waves rippled up and down her body. She beat her fist against the deck.

It took several minutes for her pussy to go slack. Only then did I lift my face from between her buttocks and pull my fingers out.

She turned around, an evil glare in her eyes. "You won't be able to stand upright when I finish with you," she cackled.

I smirked back.

She reached over, pressed a spot on the deck and a small door opened. She reached in and pulled out three dildos. One was a simple butt plug, narrow at the tip, then gradually wider before flaring at its base. The next was clear acrylic in the shape of a phallus. The third was purple silicone vibrator, long and thin, with a small bulb at the end. She held them out to me. "Choose one. For your *ass*." She hissed.

I pointed to the long purple one.

She reached into the cavity from which she had lifted the dildos, came back with a jar of lube, covered the long purple dildo with the clear gel and handed it to me. "Put it in your ass," she instructed. "As far as it will go."

I put one foot on the bench and inserted the vibrator up my ass. Thankfully it was thin and well lubed!

"Now, reach behind your head, hold onto the deck and float on your back."

With her purple rod up my ass, that was easier said than done, but I managed. She held me up with one hand under the small of my back and began to lick up and down my pussy lips. I marveled at her strength; even with me half floating, the position could not have been comfortable for her. After a few moments, my ass had relaxed and I began to enjoy her tongue licking first up the one side of each pussy lip and then down the other. She was remarkably adept and managed to entice a mini-orgasm out of me with only a few moments work.

I relaxed completely as her tongue began to perform figure-eights up and down my pussy. Just when I had become used to this pattern, her tongue started to move rapidly side-to-side, as if it was a sewing machine laying down stitches. I was halfway to another climax when the purple rod began to vibrate and I remembered her threats. The vibration was not unpleasant and I knew that my next orgasm would be much more powerful than the first.

But Sarah wasn't through with her bag of tricks. She withdrew her hand from my back and my legs began to drift slowly downwards. "Hold on tight," she commanded.

Her left hand, which had formerly been holding me up, now grabbed ahold of the purple rod and began to slowly pull it out. "Tell me when you feel vibrations on something interesting," she directed.

I did my best to concentrate on the wand up my ass. The vibrations seemed to be centered in the rounded bulb at the tip of the rod. But the vibrations now had competition for my attention. Sarah had inserted two fingers into my pussy and was drawing them back and forth. Her thumb which was pressed against my pubic bone, just above my clit, was stimulating my little pleasure knob. The overall effect of Sarah's efforts would, without much delay, be to engorge my g-spot, the spot towards which her fingers were inexorably approaching.

The vibrations from behind hit *just* the right spot to maximize the pleasure building inside my cunt. "Shit!" I exclaimed.

The evil glint in Sarah's eyes told me that I should have held my tongue. But it was too late. The vibrations inside me rose to maximum, Sarah's hand slid up the rod and lifted my butt upwards, her fingers inside my cunt found and mercilessly fondled my g-spot while her lips sucked up and down my clit each time it rose out of the water.

"Let it loose," she teased. "*All* your dirty words."

I don't know what I'd yelled, but it must have been good, judging from the look on Sarah's face. All I knew was that my pussy pulsed a rhapsody to the tune being stroked out of her by Sarah's fingers. All I knew was that the orchestra gathered its power inside my sex and then roared a relentless beat up my spine. All I knew was that my entire body was reduced to a quivering mass of rapture atop the purple popsicle stick. All I knew was that each wave of ecstasy wrung out the last of my energy, then wrung out some more. At last I melted into the salty bubbles.

When I returned to Jack's apartment, he kissed me, said Grant's phone had all the evidence her employer would need to implicate her in the scheme, and then immediately turned the subject back to arousing our Kundalini serpents. He was wearing only a black speedo, so I put on the red bikini that was still dry from not having been used at Sarah's.

First was purification: a full bottle of water down my throat and almost as much flushed through my sinus cavities. Second was breathing and visualization. Then it was on to the Crow Pose. As we did our arms-out squats, I watched Jack carefully. He seemed younger than his thirty-five years, even the streaks of grey in his dark brown hair had receded. He had lost his belly paunch. His muscles were leaner, stronger, but he wasn't muscle-bound, in fact he'd become supple, flexible. He seemed to have grown an inch or two. His eyes and his mind appeared sharper.

Jack then led us in the Frog Pose which started with us standing with our feet slightly apart but heels angled inwards. We squatted down, pressing our outstretched fingers to the ground between the fronts of our feet. That opened up *lots* of stuff! Then we straightened our knees to push our butts up in the air while keeping our fingers on the ground. Jack said that the Frog Posture would open up our sacral chakras.

Next was sitting and directed breathing. Second time around, it was easier to envision a snake being drawn upwards by the force of my breath. Jack then added chanting: *OM AIM Haram Hareem Kul Kundalini dahi dahi SWAHA*. I tried to follow as best I could. After twenty minutes, I started to feel comfortable with the sequence of words. I managed to sync them up to my breathing and a vibration started at the bottom of my spine, strengthened and began to move up one vertebra every time I repeated the chant.

One moment I was floating, relaxed, the next a bolt of lightning thundered up my spine and smashed into my head. The lightning surged out ever orifice—eyes, ears, mouth, nose. It surged over and over and over, so many times that I lost count. My whole body tensed rigid. I couldn't breathe. I must have lost consciousness because I started to be able to see again, but blurry. And the "I" was inaccurate; I had no sense of who I was or where I was or what had happened before.

The man opposite me was writhing on the floor, having a seizure of some sort. I wanted to help him, but I couldn't move. Then somehow I knew he would be fine and I stopped worrying about him. I shut my eyes and sucked deep rhythmic breaths of universal life-force into my lungs.

After an eternity, I remembered who I was, where I was, and that I had been trying to tap into my kundalini. I opened my eyes to help Jack but he was kneeling in front of me, a palm beside each side of my head, a smile spread across his face from ear to ear.

"Did you feel it?" he asked.

I nodded, at first uncertainly, then with growing conviction.

Jack removed his speedo. His lingam was fully erect, and larger than I'd remembered him being. I removed my red bikini. We stood nude, several feet apart. I could feel heat coming off his body despite the distance between us. And heat being stimulated inside my own body.

We each took a step forward and kissed.

Wonderful warmth spread upwards from the tip of my spine into my yoni. It was as if we started at the point of orgasm and then went higher and deeper from there. Whereas each sexual experience I'd previously had ended with orgasm, this one *began* with orgasm. As soon as Jack's lingam touched my lower belly, I felt a small ball of energy inside my yoni begin to radiate heat and power. It pulsed up my spine and trickled down my legs and into the soles of my feet. If Jack hadn't been hugging me, I would have floated up to the ceiling.

The pulsing up my spine stimulated all my senses, tipping them over the edge, joining them into the ecstasy swirling in my lower loins. The sky outside Jack's window deepened into cobalt blue then darkened into midnight black. An airplane soared out of the darkness, circled us, then flew away, returning the sky to shimmering cobalt. The breeze became a roar, then a symphony of joy.

Jack's kiss tasted of blueberries and chocolate and cinnamon. He smelled of jasmine and oysters, somehow the most powerful and pleasant aroma I'd ever experienced. His skin felt like velvet and silk and steel.

Jack's penis started to enter my pussy. I wasn't sure if I was still standing. My feet were no longer on the floor, but neither had they left it. My consciousness was centered in my yoni where Jack's lingam was penetrating. But my orgasm continued to undulate up and down my body and even though I was focused on my bottom chakra, this orgasm was like none I'd ever experienced. I was not riveted in the moment, but remembered the past and was aware of the future. I was not imprisoned within the orgiastic sensations, they were merely the center from which my awareness radiated out into the universe.

As I absorbed the last inch of Jack's lingam within me, I became aware of how intensely his body was quivering. He didn't move, he didn't thrust in and out. We didn't need physical sensation to have sex. Being together was enough. Feeling each other's ecstatic peak was enough. Our orgasms combined. Jack's male energy coursed up and down my vertebrae, roiling the fevered energies at the bottom of my spine, whipping them up my back to boil inside my mind.

Then our orgiastic energies receded from the peak of their climax. I could still feel electricity undulating up and down my spine, but other sensations and events and conditions combined into my consciousness. I was a ball of white light pulsing into the universe, and the universe was pulsing into me, through me. Jack's ball of light shimmered all the colors of the rainbow as it rotated around us.

I had a vision of three deities, august in their powers. The first had four heads and was smiling as he created the universe. The second god had a bluish face and was smiling as he followed the creator, maintaining and preserving his works. The third spirit had a beard and multiple arms, one of which held a sharp trident atop a spear. He was using the trident to destroy the excesses of creation which was then renewed by the other two deities. I felt all three move through my spine creating strength, pruning over-growth and combining and strengthening the powers throbbing inside me.

Jack's multi-colored light became the three divinities, the bearded trident-bearer battling with the four-headed god. But the contending divinities were calmed and harmonized by the smile of their blue-faced brother.

The feelings of orgasm were becoming more powerful, their intensity increasing. But instead of undulating pulses, everything in my body was vibration. This new feeling was the electricity which had heretofore shocked bolts of lightning uncontrollably up my spine, the electricity which had clenched me within its powers, the electricity which had wrung defeat and screams from my being.

But now the vibrating electricity was my friend and we danced together throughout all space and time and eternity. I held the vibrations close to feel their full power, spun them away to soften their effects, then hugged them into me to absorb their full intensity into my being.

Then the power of the electricity faded, became tingling in the background. My whole body, my whole mind, my spirit were harmonized into unity with the universe. Jack and

I jumped up and down around each other, smiling and blissful. But our bodies remained motionless. We were love and loving kindness now, forever, through all continuities.

"Are you ready?" Jack asked.

Somewhere in the distance, but close by and all around at the same time, I heard myself say, "Yes."

He started to rock his hips, his scepter of light moving within my sheath of wonder. Every time he thrust in, everything became illuminated by cool white light, every time he withdrew from within me, I was bathed in warm darkness. Jack radiated might and majesty into me; I welcomed his glow with accelerating excitement, the electricity of orgasm building once more.

I began to feel a familiar contracting within my cunt and I opened my eyes. We were standing. Jack had me backed up against the wall, his body sliding with his sweat, his lips at the side of my head. He was boiling. My skin was just beginning to warm, to flush. His hips were thrusting his cock into me with animal intensity. He grunted moist and wet by my ear with ever thrust and sucked air every time he pulled out. I bit his shoulder, matching his ferocity.

Jack's body went rigid, shuddered, but somehow his thrusts maintained their rhythm. I was mashed against the wall, unable to move. His cum ran down my thighs like a river. He kept thrusting and grunting and thrusting. I had to match his inhalations to survive.

There was so much lubrication in my vagina that his penis slipped out. Only then did he stop thrusting. We both gulped a deep breath.

The tightening inside my sex diminished without the spasmodic contractions that usually characterized my climax. The electricity within me faded and then was gone. It had been the best sex I'd ever had. We fell asleep under warm clouds.

Jack had still been asleep, breathing contentedly in his bed, when I'd awakened. He'd been disoriented after our lovemaking, but I'd managed to walk him to his bed and clean him off. Then I'd collapsed nude on his chest.

I slowly extricated myself and changed back into the pink pantsuit I'd worn to Sarah's. I padded around the condo. Sarah Grant's file was on the desk in the den. I sat down in the overstuffed chair behind the desk and flipped through it. The evidence seemed clear that her lavish condo had been paid through kickbacks at the expense of her employer. Pity — I liked Sarah.

There was a framed picture in a corner, barely visible in the shadows. I bent close to look at it. It was a head and shoulders portrait of a woman. It wasn't me, but there was a resemblance. I opened the cabinet under the photograph. There was a file with surveillance of Alexander M. J. Lippert, the distracted driver who'd killed a woman because he had just *had* to send out one last text. There was a newspaper article describing how Michael Rayburn had got the driver off. In the column next to the article was a picture of the woman in the photograph.

I left Jack a note, that I'd be back with food for supper.

While I was out, I met up with my former assistant, Eric Craigie.

His first question, right out of the box was, "Have you turned Jack in?" Eric had left my employ almost right in the middle of our argument as to whether I should make a full report to Michael.

I shook my head. He looked forlorn. "How's the new job?" I asked.

"Great! Full benefits. *Interesting* work. What's up with you? Other than not reporting to Mr. Rayburn?"

"Jack and I did Kundalini."

Eric's face went ashen. "I thought I warned you that Kundalini was dangerous."

I nodded. "You did, but Jack researched *everything*. Very, very carefully."

"Lee — "

"Alright, so you say there are dangers. Can you be more specific?"

"The seizures can lead to heart attacks."

I raised my arms then pointed at my chest. "We're fine."

"There can be spiritual damage."

"*Living* in the twenty-first century can cause spiritual damage."

He sighed. "There have been reports of psychiatric disorders."

"Such as?"

"Raging paranoia."

"I'll keep my eyes open."

"Lee." The rebuke in his voice was obvious.

"I'll keep my eyes open." This time I said it without sarcasm.

"You have my number on speed-dial?"

I nodded.

"What about the cop who investigated the break-in at your apartment?"

"Rambo?" Rambo had been big and strong, oozing testosterone. Eric had whisked him away before I could seduce him.

Eric shook his head. "The other one. The Crime Scene Investigator."

I smiled at the memory. Marty had been a peach—in and out of bed. I shook my head. "Nope, haven't seen him."

"You should give him a call. He might be able to help if there's a problem with Jack."

I gave my former assistant and playful jab on his shoulder. "Stop worrying! Everything'll be fine."

Back at the condo, Jack wolfed down his dinner. Seconds—he might have actually tasted the pasta marinara—were consumed at normal pace. He savored his third portion.

"I hope you're ready for tomorrow," he noted over dessert.

"Tomorrow?"

"We need to have Kundalini sex again."

"Again?!?"

He nodded and smiled.

"Don't you think we had enough this afternoon to last us a week? Better yet, a month?"

He shook his head. "Sex is integral to maintaining the awakening."

Warning to Readers: Please remember that this is a work of fiction. There is just enough of actual Kundalini practice in the above to allow the story to flow properly. It is certainly insufficient for any actual Kundalini awakening. Poetic licence *has* been taken. Jack's avoidance of advance spiritual preparation and his lack of a learned guide is likely highly dangerous. The literature is replete with both positive and negative outcomes associated with experiencing a Kundalini awakening. So please be forewarned of the dangers. Do not attempt an awakening without the assistance of an experienced guide. And of course, read the next Lusty Lee Log!

Confronting, Lusty Lee Log #30

When I woke up, Jack was already preparing breakfast and I lurched, bleary-eyed into the kitchen. After dinner, I'd gone back to my apartment to pick up a few things. When I'd returned to Jack's condo, I'd stumbled into a life-sized statue of Shiva the Destroyer in Jack's living room. Shiva had freaked me out and it had taken hours for me to fall asleep. This morning, the Hindu deity was still there, mocking me with his beard and teasing me with his trident. Overall, the statue's effect was intimidating, as if my time alive was soon destined to end.

Jack watched me eat the large plate of bacon and eggs he'd prepared for me. He was nude, as was I, but he was watching *me*, not my body. All in all, very affirming. When I was halfway through the hearty meal, he asked, "Are you ready?"

Jack's reference to my readiness, or lack of it, was a reminder that we needed to have Kundalini sex again on the basis of his assertion that, "Sex is integral to maintaining the awakening."

Yesterday had been exhausting and I wanted to beg off, but Shiva's baleful stare was a clear indication that I'd better get my act together. "Maybe we should do a few exercises first," I temporized.

Jack enthusiastically led me in the Crow Posture. I'd since learned that there was a more-involved version of the crow pose, but I was pleased to go along with Jack's less strenuous version. As we squatted, arms out front, I marveled at the changes Jack was undergoing. His dark brown hair was no longer streaked with grey. He still fit into his clothes, so I knew he was still just under six feet, but he seemed taller. He was muscular, powerful and all trace of fat seemed to have vanished.

While we were doing the frog pose, I caught sight of myself in the mirror. Like Jack's, my body had lost a layer of fat, but I was still half a foot shorter than him and didn't feel any taller. I was still buxom and curvaceous, but I looked younger. Even though I looked tighter everywhere, I was actually more flexible than I'd been last month. My brown curly hair was shinier and the blue in my eyes was a deeper shade.

When Jack was satisfied with our imitations of frogs, he demonstrated a stretch pose. We laid on our backs, then lifted our heads and feet six inches off the ground and stared at our feet. It might sound simple, but it required a lot of abdominal exertion.

"Now do the breath of fire," he instructed.

"Breath of fire?" I lowered my feet and head and rolled towards him.

"Short shallow breaths, inhalation and exhalation exactly balanced, centered on your navel."

He demonstrated and I followed suit.

"That's right," he told me. "Now do it in the stretch pose."

Of course in the stretch pose, the breath of fire was ten times more difficult!

Then we sat cross-legged to meditate, our breathing designed to pull energies upward from the base of our spines. And yes, the same crazy chant as yesterday.

At the end of the chant, Jack announced, "now Mula Bandha."

"Bandi what?"

"Mula Bandha. Bandha means lock. If you can lock your muscles, you will gain power. The Mula Bandha uses the same muscles you use to prevent your bladder from flowing." This one was easy since I'd been doing the same thing for years. I restrained myself from telling Jack that what he was describing was very Western — Kegel exercises. But I shut my eyes to concentrate on the little muscles around my urethra.

When I opened my eyes, Jack was standing flat footed, bouncing his fully-erect lingam up and down. He'd obviously found a new set of muscles!

"Are you ready for full-power sex?" he asked.

I had no idea what 'full-power' sex might be, but the wild gleam in Jack's eyes and his wide smile made it easy for me to nod my head.

He led me to his leather couch, lifted me up as if I was a bouquet of flowers and gently laid me down. I spread my legs and felt his lingam press against the opening of my yoni. Even though he wasn't inside me, I could feel his power pulsing through my sex and all the way up into my belly. And I could feel my warmth enveloping the entire shaft of his lingam even though it was only its tip touching me.

Then he was inside, filling my yoni completely. His shaft, now enlarged as part of the Kundalini awakening, should have hurt as it pressed me open, as it forced my sheath to accommodate his length and girth, but instead its strength empowered me and made the accommodation joy, not burden.

We weren't moving but the arousal of desire, the passion of pure love, and the power of sexual congress was building nonetheless. Pulses of energy built and swirled around where lingam and yoni met, the excess tickling down to the base of my spine and coursing up my back and into my lungs.

The swirling inside my yoni accelerated and less and less energy was leaking out. The energy intensified. *Accumulating* instead of dissipating. Jack touched his forehead against mine. I begged him to release the tension rising inside me. But instead he shook his head, rocking his forehead back and forth against mine.

I was hot. The heat was spreading down into my buttocks. I had never been this horny or aroused or tight inside before. Before, I had always climaxed well before this point. It was scary and *exciting* all at the same time. I could feel my sweat against the leather. I squirmed —

Connected clit to pubic bone to cock to cunt as if closing an electric circuit and detonating infinite explosives! My cunt contracted cold, then fire, then cold then burst fire over and over and over. The bottom of my spine vibrated with the concentrated pleasure of every orgasm I'd ever experienced. Each of my vertebrae exploded. My lungs filled with air and I flew throughout all creation.

Before I could recover, or even think about bringing Jack to climax, he had lifted me up off the couch, backed me against the wall and gently set my feet on the floor. Our bodies united themselves once more without the typical effort required to coordinate penetration standing up and once again my yoni was filled with Jack's lingam. This time the pulses of energy didn't swirl, instead they rushed right up our spines and connected through our lips and tongues. Jack's tongue warmed mine, warmed my entire head.

My eyes could still see, but my entire attention was on our tongues dancing and sliding and slithering. Slithering like snakes mating and hatching because the power of Kundalini had now risen to our heads. I felt the power of every man I'd ever made love to, even if both of us had been oblivious to it at the time. My eyes were open but I could not see outside my mind.

This time I came inside my head. No wrenching or clenching or explosions. Just bliss. Lightness darkness fluctuating over a warm breeze. Everyone I'd ever pleasured or given joy to drifted by to kiss me. And when I kissed them back, their spirits smiled. I felt Jack withdraw himself and I slowly settled back to earth.

Jack picked me up and carried me into the bedroom where he laid me on a waterproof blanket, just like Michael's special blanket. It was soft and smooth against my skin. I floated between wakefulness, sleep, and eternal knowledge.

A dollop of cold on my navel brought me back to the present on wings of infinite love. Jack was there, kneeling beside me, spooning whipped cream atop my belly. My body didn't need food, in fact it had no needs at all. But there was love and sustenance in the food. There was Jack's devotion, both to me and to creation in general. Today, food was part of our universal communion.

Jack had brought three bowls: whipping cream, strawberries and chocolate. There were cups of milk and orange juice. We knelt and kissed, then smeared chocolate all over each other's bodies and licked it off. Warm chocolate on Jack's even warmer lingam was delectable, and twice as delectable when followed by cold whipped cream. We traced the strawberries around each other's nipples, then fed them to each other.

We were suddenly thirsty and gulped down the orange juice. But the milk spilt and pooled in the center of the blanket. The fact that the blanket was waterproof was suddenly hilarious; divine laughter filled our bellies and elevated our awareness to a higher plane.

Jack laid me down, my yoni just above the pool of milk. He used the spoon to dribble milk into my navel where it trickled down through my pubic hairs and along the edges of my pussy lips. He bent to use his tongue to lap up the milk from my belly button. The power of his consciousness drew my entire perception into my belly. I knew complete contentment for the first time in my life. Infinite contentment meant that I didn't have to climax, that I was already in ecstasy before and after and forever. Laughter and enlightenment. The milk on the bed was jiggling and splashing. Jack smiled down at it, at me, at everything.

We continued to laugh as Jack lifted me up and cleaned me off with a face cloth. Then he led me back to the kitchen where he sat on a chair and beckoned for me to lower myself onto his still-erect lingam. This time, I had to adjust the angle of my descent to accommodate his full girth. He slid inside easily enough, but I was filled, really full, from the front of my pubic bone back to my spine, from hip to hip and up into my belly. I breathed in Jack's power, sucking it into my lungs and up my spine where it tickled the back of my neck.

Jack started to move from side to side, vibrating his lingam inside me. Then I became aware that his legs hadn't moved. The vibration was from his *lingam*, directly inside me! The vibrations touched every cell in my body. I felt all the little hairs on the back of my neck stand up and vibrate at exactly the same frequency.

Jack started to chant, *OM AIM Haram Hareem Kul Kundalini dahi dahi SWAHA*, his breathing full and deep and regular and melodious. The waves of his voice pulled my spine back and forth to match the cadence of his chant. The frequency of his chant gradually synced up with the frequency of our genital vibration until they hit resonance.

And as soon as the vibrations within my yoni and the waves undulating up and down my spine resonated at the same frequency, their power grew exponentially. First they contracted at the bottom of my spine, then my whole yoni was wrenched tight around Jack's lingam. Then each chakra in turn was locked tight, the same way that my kegel exercises had locked around my bladder. At the top of my neck, my orgasm exploded like a bullwhip being cracked. The first *crack* was painful. The second was a chiropractic adjustment, but along my entire spine all at once. The third crack was pleasure too intense to be enjoyable. But the fourth and fifth and sixth sent me into heaven. After that my body was a wave on the ocean and I lost count.

Jack gave me a hug and I suddenly became aware that I had had orgasm after orgasm, that I had given myself to him over and over, but that he had never once given himself to me. It was time to change *that*!

I lifted myself off and swayed my hips to realign my internal organs. I reached my hand out to Jack and he must have thought I was going to help him off the chair because he took my hand. But that was not my intent and I used his moment of inattention to push him to the floor. I sucked his cock. I gave him the best hand-job. And the best hand-job *ever*. But all he did was smile up at me.

I scooted my hips over his cock and slid down over its girth until the entire length of his shaft was inside me. This time it was my turn to chant and I was pleased to hear that I was getting it just right: *OM AIM Haram Hareem Kul Kundalini dahi dahi SWAHA*. My yoni began to vibrate around his lingam. I bounced up and down in sync with my vibrations. I could feel pulsations all the way up into my nipples. Jack's breaths became shallower and he was breathing faster than I was chanting. A red flush started to spread up his chest, a centimeter every time I finished the chant.

I accelerated my bouncing to match his breathing.

"Aiee!" he yelled. It was just once, but it was a yelp of surrender! He stopped breathing. His body shuddered. His lingam pulsed all along the length of my yoni. He arched his hips upward, impaling me atop his cock. I had him! I'd made him *come*. I kept bouncing until the pulsing stopped and he lay still.

But when I lifted myself off him, there was no semen. Nothing dribbled down. There was no foam on his cock. I reached a finger to my pussy. The only juices were mine. The bastard had held himself in. He still hadn't ejaculated!

I glared at him angrily. "What the—"

The feral gleam in Jack's eyes choked off my protest. In my moment of hesitation, he reached up, flipped me onto my back and mounted me. His cock had slammed into my pussy so quickly, I hadn't even felt it. But now she burned with friction and he pumped his cock ferociously out, and even more ferociously in.

"I'll come when *I* want to!" he roared.

I finally got lubricated and began to enjoy being fucked. There was nothing ephemeral or spiritual about this. *This* was an old fashioned fucking. He was splaying my pussy, impaling my cunt, mashing my ass to the floor. His thrusts were so strong and fast that I couldn't push up against them. All I could do was lie there and take the full force of his rage.

Rage!?! It *was* rage. His eyes were bugging out. There was no affection. Unless you can call animal lust affection. It was pure aggression of the strong against the weak. His hands were gripping my shoulders and it hurt.

"Jack?"

"Bitch!" He flopped his full weight onto me, almost smothering me. But at least he'd let go of my shoulders. "Shut your mouth!" he screamed.

Thankfully, before I could figure out what the hell was going on, he shuddered to a stop and I felt the warm wetness of his semen dribble down between my legs.

When he pushed himself up and off me, he smiled. The old Jack had returned. He cleaned us off, helped me into my pajamas and gave me a tender kiss. We lay together on the bed, tenderly holding hands.

Jack's last words before our contented exhaustion welcomed us to sleep were, "Sleep tight for tomorrow."

I didn't have to ask. Tomorrow would be another round Kundalini sex. After all, sex was 'integral to maintaining the awakening'. I slipped into a contented sleep, fantasizing about the 'morrow.

The next morning, Jack was sitting in the living room typing on his computer. I made lots of noise fixing my coffee, but he didn't come into the kitchen. So I fixed myself a bowl of yogurt and blueberries, each berry a cobalt pearl in the snow. I was nude under my robe and was looking forward to giving Jack a quick flash. I poked my head around the corner. Jack was still sitting on the couch, his head halfway into his laptop, oblivious to the rest of the universe.

I strode into the living room, my gait combining the embodiment of Marilyn Munroe, Sophia Loren, Elizabeth Taylor and Madonna. Jack didn't look up. I put my hands on my hips, trying to decide whether to let my robe slowly fall open or to rip it apart.

I looked up into the mirror over the couch and decided that the more dramatic the reveal, the better. I ripped the robe apart and was pleased to see just the right amount of jiggle in my boobs. Hips right, hips left, then pubic hair thrust forward. It was a performance for the ages. I should have had a band—hell, an orchestra!

He didn't lift his head, but at least he spoke, even if it was only a monosyllabic, "Yes?"

"Jack?"

He glanced up at me. His face was blank and immediately retreated behind his laptop.

"Jack?"

Jack slowly raised his head. He made a show of affecting patience, like adults do when being forced to attend to a prattling child. "Yes?" he repeated.

"Aren't we going to…?"

He stared at me as if he had no idea what I was talking about.

"Sex is integral to maintaining the awakening," I blurted.

He slowly shook his head, projecting patience, making me feel not just like a child, but like a *dimwitted* child. "Once you've awakened, Kundalani no longer requires sex." He returned his attention to his computer.

All I could do was look at him. I couldn't move a muscle, formulate a thought. Jack had been friendly ever since I'd known him. Not to mention horny. Not to mention *very* horny. And even hornier the past few days. Now, when I'd practically thrown myself at him, he had shown no interest, *no interest at all.*

Jack's head jerked up and he shot me an angry glare. "Get dressed. We have work to do."

I scampered into the bedroom. Between Jack's foul mood and Shiva's ill-omened portents, defiance seemed risky.

When I came back out dressed in my pink pantsuit, there were two pistols, a rifle, a knife and what looked like a grenade on the kitchen table. Jack was pacing back and forth in front of the window, gesturing as if he was making a speech to a cheering crowd.

"The criminals must be *eliminated!*" he shouted.

"Jack?" I whispered. But he ignored me.

"Time is running out. Time is running out for everyone who has plotted against me. They will be *punished!*"

"Jack?"

"Those who are addicted to their screens will have them *wrenched* from their clenching hands!"

"Jack?"

"Those who have done the addicting, those who have exploited the weak with their *gacha* schemes, will be sent into the depths of *hell!*"

Jack continued to pace, muttering to himself. For some reason, I suddenly became aware of what he was wearing—a black turtleneck shirt and black pants. It was the first time I remembered ever seeing him dressed entirely in black.

He whirled, strode to the right side of the living room, and smashed his fist into the wall. He put a *hole* into the wall! Jack raised his fist, oblivious to the blood on it, "Death to the enemy!" he shouted, standing there quivering.

I carefully slid in front of him and lightly slapped his face. "Jack?"

He looked back at me without comprehension.

"Jack! Who is the enemy?"

"Everyone who has ever stood against me." His voice was flat, his face blank.

I needed to restore a connection. "Jack, did you break into my apartment?"

"Of course I broke into your apartment; you were the enemy." There was a glimmer of recognition in his eyes. Maybe I could get him back.

"What about my phone?" I persisted.

"Of course I broke into your apartment *and* your phone; you were the enemy."

"Why was I the enemy?" Maybe higher-level communication would bring him out of his funk.

"Because the enemy hired you."

"Michael Rayburn?" Michael Rayburn, my former lover, was the lawyer who had hired me to track Jack down for a variety of cyber misdeeds. I still owed him a report.

Jack glared at me. I couldn't tell if that was a good thing or not. But I had no choice except to proceed. "Michael Rayburn is the enemy?"

"Rayburn is a *tool*." The derision in Jack's voice was palpable. But at least I was beginning to connect.

"Who is he a tool of?" I persisted.

"Alexander M. J. Lippert."

"Why are you angry at Alexander M. J. Lippert?"

"Because he killed you!" Jack continued to pace.

"If he killed me—." I suddenly remembered the photograph in Jack's den. The one of the woman who looked like me. I popped into the den, retrieved the framed photo, and held it towards Jack. "Is this your fiancée?"

He nodded, then roared. His voice was raging wild. He ran right at me, his bloodied right hand raised above his head. I managed to dodge him and he slammed into a wall. I slid the photo of his fiancée behind the couch. He came at me again. I ran into the bedroom and put the bed between us. He tried to climb over the bed, but it was too soft and he got tangled in the sheets. By the time he'd crossed the bed, I'd managed to get back to the doorway.

Jack went into the ensuite bathroom and came back with my toiletries. He flung my toothbrush at me. "Get out!" Toothpaste. "Get out!" Shampoo. "Get out!" Face wash. "Get out!" Deodorant. "Get out!"

Then he moved to the armoire and started flinging clothing at me. Bikini. "Get out!" Bra. "Get out!" Panties. "Get out!" Then the closet: skirt. "Get out!" Blouse. "Get out!"

As I bent to pick up my blouse, he bull-rushed me again. His fist hit my left shoulder—*hard*! But thankfully he hit his head on the wall and this stunned him. I managed to escape out the door.

In the hallway, I dropped most of my stuff on the floor. This proved to be a very good idea as Jack slipped on my skirt and I managed to get out into the foyer without him hitting me again. My left shoulder stung.

I made it to the elevator and pressed the down button as he emerged from his condo. He was halfway to the elevator when the chime sounded. The doors opened and I pressed the down button before I was even fully inside. I caught a glimpse of Jack as the door closed. I sucked in so much air I almost choked.

Downstairs, I hailed a cab, made him turn this way and that. I had him stop in the middle of a busy shopping district and paid cash. I crossed the street, hailed another cab and gave him Eric Craigie's address. Eric, my six-foot three tall former assistant, was into martial arts and computers. He'd know what to do.

Eric was in his pajamas but welcomed me into his apartment without hesitation.

"Thank goodness you're still home," I blubbered.

"It's Saturday," he explained.

I decided not to dwell on the fact that I had been unaware of the day of the week. "I need your help."

He touched my left shoulder. I yelped and looked down. There was a rip in my pink jacket. I looked up into his questioning eyes. "It's a long story."

He ushered me to his kitchen table. "Spill."

"I went down to Hedo for Tantra week with Jack."

He nodded. This much he knew already.

"When we came back, Jack wanted to get into

Kundalini—"

"I warned you about that."

"You did," I nodded. "Anyways, we did some exercises, had sex—mind-blowing sex—and I do mean *mind-blowing*."

"And now his mind is blown?"

I nodded. "Really blown. He was ranting and raving and—"

Eric pointed to my shoulder. "And he attacked you."

I nodded and felt a tear trickle down my cheek.

Eric touched my cheek and brushed the tear away. For a moment, I felt completely secure, at peace.

A screech sounded on the street below Eric's window. We ran to look down. Jack slammed the door to his car shut and raced to the front door of the building. Eric walked calmly to the door of his apartment and checked to make sure that his deadbolt was in place.

A moment later, there was a knock at the door. I could feel Jack's presence. Eric held a finger to his lips to indicate I should keep quiet. The knocks became louder. Jack's presence entered the apartment.

"I know you're in there!" Jack shouted. He slammed his palms against the door and I covered my ears. "You'd better come out!" He banged his fists against the door, rattling it on its hinges.

"Go away!" yelled Eric. "Or I'll call the cops."

"Too chicken to fight me?" Jack's voice was derisive.

"Too smart," was Eric's response.

"Lee, this is your last chance," Jack's voice boomed, almost hypnotic. Eric shot me a concerned look.

I took out my phone and called 911. "I'm calling the police," I announced, loudly enough for Jack to hear. Eric looked relieved.

"You'd better," boomed Jack. Threatening had replaced mesmerizing. "You've made your choice, and I'll leave and leave you alone." His voice was emotionless, stony.

"Leave!" shouted Eric.

Jacks fist rattled the door to its hinges, but the door held. Then a moment of silence followed by the cold steel of Jack's voice, "But if I catch you outside this apartment, or trying to interfere with what needs to be done, you will wish you'd never been born."

And then Jack was gone. I felt him go, even before I heard his feet stomp off.

Eric retrieved his phone. "Did you really call the police?" he asked.

I shook my head.

He dialed. "I'm calling Marty."

I nodded. Marty was the CSI who had investigated the break-in at my apartment. We had become friends. With benefits.

Marty came right away. He smiled at me and shook hands with Eric. The two men were both skinny to the point of scrawny. But scrawny or not, I knew that their muscles packed power. Marty was a bit shorter and had brown hair and eyes while Eric's were red and green respectively.

I smiled back at Marty. But Eric reminded us that we had a crisis to deal with, "The man who broke into Lee's apartment came here and threatened her. He's armed."

"And dangerous," I added.

Eric nodded and continued, "A rifle, pistols, knife. Maybe a grenade. He's going after Alexander M. J. Lippert."

"The distracted driver?" asked Marty.

"Lippert killed his fiancée," I explained.

Marty took out his phone. "We should call the Emergency Task Force."

"How long will it take for SWAT to deploy?" Eric wanted to know.

Marty put his phone away. "Too long."

Jack's car was already there when we pulled up in front of Lippert's house, a large mansion in the city's west end. The house was situated in the gully at the bottom of a tree-covered hill.

We spotted Jack on the hill setting up his rifle. He was

sufficiently absorbed in his task that we managed to sneak up on him from the rear.

Marty took out his service weapon, pointed it at Jack and yelled, "Freeze!"

Jack whirled around with his rifle. Marty shot his pistol. Jack was hit, but didn't drop his rifle. Eric tackled Jack and his rifle flew sideways, striking me around the knees. Marty tossed me his weapon. What the hell was I supposed to do with a gun? And where the hell was the safety?!?

The three men wrestled on the ground in the center of the clearing. Marty and Eric were trying to pin Jack's arms behind him, but Jack was holding them off. Marty ended up on the bottom with Eric on top and Jack between them. Eric tried to twist Jack's right arm, but Jack tossed him aside. Jack got Marty in some sort of an arm lock and the CSI's face contorted in pain.

Eric propelled himself at Jack and landed a fist on his head. Jack let go of Marty, stood up and traded blows with Eric. A hard right against Eric's head stunned him. Jack kicked Marty, sending him flying. Eric and Marty advanced on Jack, but before they could close, Jack grabbed his rifle and fled down the hill.

Marty carefully pried his gun from my hands and tore after Jack. Eric tried to go with him, but he was still woozy from Jack's blow and only managed a single step before sitting his butt down on a large tree stump.

Eric rubbed his head. "He's a madman."

"Marty?" I asked.

"Him too. I hope he calls for backup. But I was talking about Jack."

"Is that the effect of the Kundalini?"

"Probably."

"What about his super-human strength?" Eric was a mixed martial-arts fighter and Marty a trained policeman. Yet Jack had got the better of both of them.

Eric nodded and rubbed his head.

"I thought Kundalini was just spiritual and mental," I

said.

"It's many things. And most of all, it's a power not to be trifled with."

"What about me? I felt the awakening as well."

Eric shrugged. "I guess you were more ready for it."

"I won't turn into Jack?"

"Apparently not. But you will need to confront the issues in your life, to work through them."

I helped Eric back to his apartment where we had lunch and played chess. I wanted to keep him awake to rule out a head injury. But I also wanted to make sure I didn't end up like Jack. The first step was to confront the issues in my life. Since Eric didn't like talking while he played chess, I'd have solitude even though I was sitting right across from him.

The first issue in my life was also the most urgent. Why hadn't I turned Jack in to Michael Rayburn, the lawyer who'd given me the case, as soon as I'd discovered that Jack was the Cyber Culprit? At first it was because I wasn't really sure that Jack was the CC. And then it was too late; I'd have to have made awkward explanations. And by then my obligation to report had become entangled with the disintegration of my relationship with Michael, his cheating with Gretchen. Then lust took over—Jack was really, really sexy. Falling in love with Jack had made it even harder to turn him in. I shook my head. I had let my selfish needs interfere with my clear duty to report to Michael.

"How's Michael?" Eric asked, as if reading my mind.

"Fine," I answered. But Michael wasn't *fine*. He'd cheated on me and that was part of the reason I hadn't been forthcoming about Jack. Or was I merely rationalizing for my lapse in duty? I took a deep breath. I was human and I'd screwed up. The only thing to do was to try to fix things and to do better tomorrow. What was it the legendary Blue Jay's pitcher Dave Steib had said, "tomorrow I'll perfect"?

I took another deep breath and dialed Michael. "We've identified the Cyber Culprit," I told him.

"Lee! That's great," Michael's voice boomed over the

phone. I could see the sparkle in his blue eyes and a wide smile forming on his full lips. The tone of his voice told me that all was forgiven — but would his forgiveness last if he suspected my transgressions?

Michael rang off to spread the good news while I wrestled with how fulsome my report should be.

Eric made a foolish move and I checkmated him. I shone a light into his eyes and made him smile — he managed wide and symmetrical — and his speech was fine. His hands were steady as he reset the board. So maybe his blunder had been a fluke. Still, I would have to continue to watch him like a hawk.

The second issue was men — and even the occasional woman. Anything on two legs turned me on and I enjoyed pleasuring all of them. Most objective observers would call me a slut. And they wouldn't be completely wrong. I took a deep breath. Maybe that was just me. I had to confront who I was, I had to accept who I was. As long as I didn't tell lies. As long as I didn't hurt anyone. I was not built for monogamous relationships and I shouldn't expect them from my lovers. I resolved to stop trying to put my square peg into round holes.

This time Eric checkmated me, a good sign.

"Time for a nap," he yawned.

"No way Mister, I demand a tiebreaker." Head injury — no sleeping!

Halfway through the third game, my phone buzzed. It was Marty. "Got him!" he announced. Partway through Marty's rapid-fire recounting there was a knock at the door. Grand central station! The knock at the door was a work colleague for Eric, so I left them to talk geek and left to hook up with Marty.

Marty was just finishing up with his post-arrest paperwork when I arrived at the police station, so I called Michael Rayburn. "The Cyber Culprit is in police custody," I told him.

"Lee, that's great!"

"I'm just at the police station." Marty was coming out.

"Can I call you once I finish up here?"

"Sure. Looking forward to it." I rang off just before Marty smothered me with a bear hug.

"My apartment's just around the corner," Marty informed me.

I kissed him full on the mouth. "Let's go!" It was time to celebrate.

The first time I'd had sex with Marty — the only time I'd had sex with him — he'd been tentative and unsure of himself, unsure of my desire for him. This time he was assured and methodical. The first time, I'd had to encourage him every step of the way. This time was by-the-book, hitting all the right spots, sounding all the right notes. He ejaculated — none of Jack's tantric-kundalini withholding bullshit — and he quivered as we smiled into each other's eyes.

"That was nice," I told him afterwards. "But I have to go meet up with Michael Rayburn."

Marty nodded. He was a cop. He understood duty. "Will I see you again?" he wanted to know.

I gave him a big wet kiss. "Fate has brought us together twice already. I'm sure she's not finished."

It was an oblique, non-committal answer. But it was enough to leave Marty smiling ear-to-ear as I dashed off.

It was dark by the time I arrived at Michael's apartment. I had fomented an elaborate excuse for my delay in reporting what I'd discovered about Jack. But he took one look at the rips in my pink pantsuit and ushered me into the kitchen where he took out a first-aid kit. He pointed to my left shoulder and knees. "We need to tend to those."

The obvious implication was that I should remove my clothes. I wasn't sure that that was a good idea but I had no logical reason to refuse. I temporized by removing only my jacket and blouse. Michael inspected the small cut which was surrounded by a large bruise. He cleaned the cut with alcohol which *stung*.

"Ow!" I protested.

"Sorry." But since it wasn't his fault, there was no

emotion in his apology. He bandaged the cut.

He looked at my knees. Since he hadn't tried to cop a feel of my breast, or even ogle them, I removed my pants. My lingerie was beige. I suddenly wished I was wearing something sexier. This time the alcohol didn't sting and he quickly bandaged the three cuts on my knees.

"Have you eaten?" he asked.

I shook my head, suddenly realizing how famished I was.

"I have some Chinese I could warm up."

The Singapore Fried Rice was scrumptious beyond words.

"You're looking good," he told me as I wolfed down the last bite. Whether he was referring to my svelte body or to the deeper blue in my eyes, I couldn't tell. The grey in Michael's light brown hair stood out now that Jack's had vanished. But he was still tall, fit and handsome and the grey in his hair made him look wise, not old. His blue eyes sparkled as he watched me, his wide mouth and full lips subtly and unconsciously mimicking the movements of my own lips.

"Are you still seeing Gretchen?" I asked then winced at the sharpness of my response. Kundalini may have honed my perceptions, but I'd have to learn to process them fully before imposing my insights on others.

But Michael hadn't taken offence. He nodded, not smiling, but not scowling either. "Are you still looking for an exclusive relationship?"

I shook my head. "I've realized that that's not me."

"And what *is* you?"

I wasn't sure how to answer. I took a deep breath. And then, as oxygen filled the final few alveoli in my lungs, I finally confronted my essential nature. "I like to touch. I like to be touched. And every time I touch, I hope I leave those I've touched better off, both physically and emotionally."

"That's a tall order."

I nodded. "Sometimes."

He reached out and hugged my head to his shoulder, just like the first time we'd touched so long ago. I raised my head, our lips close and he kissed me. The first time our lips had met, I had all but swooned. Now it was nice, but not overwhelming. Which was fine; we had had good times, but also angry sex. When he had betrayed me, I had cinched a cock-ring around his erection and tortured him mercilessly. Now it was time to repair that physical and emotional damage.

As we kissed, I remembered the intimacies we had shared, the intimacies that had nurtured our souls. As we kissed, I returned Michael to those intimacies, so that together we could use them to heal ourselves. We were transported back to the kisses that had made the universe vanish in a glorious moment of eternity. Back to the pleasures of his tongue on my pussy paralyzing my body. Back to my lips on his cock sucking the breath from his lungs. Back to the first time he'd entered me, filled me, our bodies rubbing their entire lengths together, climaxing together and looking down at creation from its apex.

Jack had caught Michael cheating and Michael had lied, turning the heat of my jealousy into hot rage, then hot sex. But tonight I was turning deception into forgiveness. I used the energy of past conflicts to deepen our present reconciliation. We pulled our heads apart and looked into the depths of each other's eyes.

"Ready for dessert?" he asked, bringing us back to the present. He pulled out a box with a woman with her face propped up by her hand smiling at us, removed a brand new "play" blanket and threw it over his shoulder.

"Champagne?" I asked.

"And strawberries."

"And pudding?"

He nodded.

I pulled the light blanket off his shoulder and sashayed my hips into the bedroom where I laid it, beige side up, atop his bed and climbed on. It was nice and soft.

A moment later, Michael came in with a bottle of champagne and two bowls. He was nude except for a pair of briefs as white as my underwear was beige. He popped the cork off the bottle, put his thumb over the opening, shook it vigorously and sprayed me mercilessly until my lingerie started to melt into my skin.

He set the bottle down and reached for one of the bowls. I grabbed the champagne, shook it and sprayed it directly on his briefs, revealing the outline of his very, *very* erect cock. He reached around my back and undid my bra. I sprayed down his back revealing the outline of two round buttocks.

Now it was my turn to be punished as he reached into one of the bowls and pressed two *freezing* cold strawberries against my nipples. I sucked the champagne from his brief, then sucked the real dessert deep down my throat.

Michael readied to mount me and I leaned back. But instead he poured warm chocolate pudding from the other bowl down my panties. It felt heavenly, and even better as he pressed the outside of my panties and massaged the pudding into my pussy. Drops leaked out, making a funky pattern of dark spots on the beige blanket.

But Michael was out of position and I smeared pudding up and down his cock. Then champagne to cool him down. Hot and cold. All he could do was grab onto the headboard. My hands slid the warm goo up and down his phallus until he sprayed milky white atop the chocolate, completing our healing. Milky white making art — abstract art — of the highest order.

The next morning as we sipped coffee, he slid a file folder across the table. "Ready for your next case?" he asked.

The end of the Lusty Lee Logs! ☹

Warning *to Readers*: Please remember that the Lusty Lee Logs are works of fiction. Attempting to recreate them at home will likely result in injury, both physical and psychic.

For example, there is just enough of actual Kundalini practice in them to allow the story to flow properly. It is certainly insufficient for any actual Kundalini awakening. Poetic license *has* been taken. Jack's avoidance of advance spiritual preparation and his lack of a learned guide is likely highly dangerous. The literature is replete with both positive and negative outcomes being experienced as the result of a Kundalini awakening. So please be forewarned of the dangers. Do not attempt an awakening without the assistance of an experienced guide. Further, many of Lee's actions will result in broken bones, even death...

Backnotes

Thank you for reading this story. If you enjoyed it, **please** take a moment to **post a review**.

For my **most recent publications**, please see my author profile

My Most Recent Stories
Tickle Test
Pay Back
Panty Play
Webcam Spank
Tiebreaker (A SleeperKidsWorld.com story)
Couples: Adventures at Hedonism II
Gunge Girl
Squished
The Prize
Ava's WAM
Sex Wrestler
WAM Mix (a wet and messy story)
Truth be Dared
Spank Me—if you Dare!

Stories featuring Mistress Megan:
Pro Dom Her First Client
Pro Dom 2 Hugo
Pro Dom 3 Cross Dresser
Pro Dom 4 Hugo & Sheila
Pro Dom 5 Cold
Pro Dom 6 Lucas Comes Again
Pro Dom 7 Walk-in
Pro Dom 8 Womyn
Pro Dom 9 Priest

Please also consider reading other titles that I have authored as follows:

I **Alien Vacation**, a novelette

II Connie's Crop, a novel
   Wherein mild-mannered Marsha pursuit of the magical whip pairs her with sexy Sheila and connects her with the darker side of sexuality.

III **The Christopher Carter Series—already published**

Carter's Chance II
Private Party His
Private Party Hers
Private Party Box Set
Ryan's Reprieve
Cashmere Congress
Melissa's Moxie
Molly Madness
Melissa's Memories
Blackmail Bounce
Assisting Audrey
Splosh Scoundrel (my most popular splosh story)

Jody's Journal
Busted Bonds
Solicitor's Slip
Stakeout Story
Aural Artifact
Mayan Magic
Party Photos
Buying Before
Cardiac Caress
Credit Card Con
Formatting Foam
Clinic Caper
Cosplay Clue
Witch's Wrath
Carter's Climax Box Set: All 25 stories

And please check out my author profiles at
http://www.amazon.com/Jason-Pinaster/e/B00YSLUDNG/ref=sr_tc_2_0?qid=143490818 8&sr=1-2-ent   and at
https://www.smashwords.com/profile/view/JasonPinaster

For more adventurous versions of the covers, follow me on **Pinterest**: https://www.pinterest.com/jasonpinaster/